Heaven't You Heard?

GEANNA CULBERTSON

BQB

North Carolina

Published in the United States by BQB Publishing
(an imprint of Boutique of Quality Books Publishing Company, Inc.)
www.bqbpublishing.com

978-1-952782-46-6 (p)
978-1-952782-47-3 (e)

Library of Congress Control Number: 2022930520

Book design by Robin Krauss, www.bookformatters.com
Cover concept by Geanna Culbertson
Cover design by Ellis Dixon, www.ellisdixon.com

First editor: Pearlie Tan
Second editor: Olivia Swenson

EXPLORE THE FANTASTICAL BOOKS IN THE CRISANTA KNIGHT SERIES

Looking for more magical shenanigans, epic adventure, and heartwarming heroic journeys?

Visit: www.GeannaCulbertson.com

DEDICATION

This book, like everything I shall ever accomplish, is dedicated to my mom and dad. You are my heroes, my coaches, and my best friends. I am thankful for you every day for more reasons than there are words in this book.

Special Thanks

Terri Leidich & BQB Publishing
The greatest publisher in the history of the universe.

Gallien Culbertson
The person I can always count on for support and guidance.

Veronica Reynosa
The friend who I didn't know I needed and I could not be more grateful to have found.

Pearlie Tan, Olivia Swenson, & Ellis Dixon
The women who make me better, and who I couldn't do this without.

I also want to thank Julie Bromley, Ian Culbertson, The Fine Family, Alexa Carter, Claire Bretzke, // TECHYSCOUTS, the Girl Scouts organization, and all the other wonderful people who have supported this series so actively, and my many fans who I hope to continue to amaze, enthrall, and surprise in the future.

Dear Reader,

I am so excited to welcome you on this new journey. The *Heaven't You Heard?* guardian angels series will be filled with incredible world building, magical shenanigans, fantasy action, sassy dialogue, morally rich themes, and endearing, honorable characters that you can love, laugh, and grow with.

Just a note out the gate—though the subject matter has to do with guardian angels and the afterlife, please know that this is NOT a book about religion. The settings, premises, and so forth of this story are pure works of imagination intended to delight and inspire smiles and wonder. They are not intended to promote any finite view about the universe and spirituality, negate anyone's beliefs, or make presumptions about what is and isn't out there. Faith is entitled to exist uniquely in each of our hearts, and my only goal here is to bring a little extra joy to the hearts of my readers with creative and compelling fiction.

Now, without further ado, on to your next adventure!

MY PURPOSE

" **I**'m sorry to have to tell you this, but you're dead."

The light was blinding at first. I blinked as my surroundings came into focus. A woman's face partially obscured the disorientating glow of a powerful sun relaxed in the sky. Its rays illuminated her angelically. For a second, I thought I saw a ring of light above her head, and the faintest outline of giant wings behind her back. When I blinked again both were gone.

The late twenties woman looking down at me was unusually beautiful. My first guess was that she was Filipino, though the haircut made it harder to tell. She had a shaved head like a monk, which she totally pulled off. Her eyes were warm and shimmery like cola watered down by ice. And she wore a sleeveless top that showed off toned arms, just one aspect of a physique that was lithe and strong like an acrobat or a superhero.

She reached out a hand. In autopilot, I took it and in one smooth pull she helped me sit up.

As far as I could see, rolling hills of waving grasses and wildflowers created a lush, surreal landscape—the kind of beauty even postcards only hoped to emulate. Banana yellow chrysanthemums and vibrant purple lavender dotted my periphery. Magnolia trees boasted white blossoms the size of honeydew melons and branches full of flittering canaries. Their peaceful chirping accompanied the tranquil trickle of a nearby river.

While far to my left a crest of cerulean mountains reached for the cloudless roof of the world, miles to my right, white skyscrapers, golden bridges, and tall towers of glass glimmered. The city looked as if the architects of New York, Dubai, Moscow, San

Francisco, and Singapore had joined forces with King Midas and the inventor of glitter.

The stunning, strong woman knelt beside me. Her top and cargo pants—like my simple fitted t-shirt and jeans—were white.

"The First City is a lot to absorb," she said gently, tilting her chin toward the metropolis. "We'll take this slow." She offered me her hand again, this time to shake. "I'm Akari."

Still in a stupor, I accepted the gesture, but as I did the hairs on my neck rose and my heart quickened—my subconscious trying to alert me to something.

"I'm sorry," I said, scrunching my eyes as my brain fizzled. "Ma'am, what did you say?"

"It takes a while to adjust," Akari responded.

"No. A minute ago. Before that . . ." My eyes darted around more warily.

"Oh, right. First, hold this."

From behind her back, Akari produced a baby Labrador the color of coffee creamer. It had simply appeared like magic. She handed me the soft creature without acknowledging my bewildered expression. The puppy tried to lick my face. He felt as warm as fresh laundry and smelled like sweet dreams. It was distracting, but I tried my best to regain focus and reconnected my gaze with Akari's.

"You're dead," she said.

I blinked. Then—

"WHAT?!"

My heart took possession of me with such fervor that its desire to leap out of my chest was single-handedly responsible for yanking me to my feet. Akari stood too. The puppy tried to chew on my hair, so I tossed the locks behind my shoulders. The shimmering sunlight brought out the dark red and gold strands in my otherwise dark brown layers. It would have been an optimal time for a selfie if I wasn't having a complete freak out.

Panic pulsed through my veins and constricted my lungs. "Here. Take this." I held the dog toward Akari.

She accepted the puppy and let it lick her cheek. "Hm. I thought you were a dog person?"

My hands were on my knees as I tried to breathe. I gave her a dismayed look. "I *am* a dog person. But how is this a time when that matters?"

"Well, in Heaven, it's customary to give someone a puppy to hold whenever extending really bad news. It softens the blow."

An ivory watch on her wrist flashed and the puppy vanished. It was not the weirdest thing my brain was trying to grasp.

"*Heaven?*"

I spun around and took in the city with fresh eyes.

My feet moved forward though my mind remained in a state of still grace. It seemed like time slowed and reality amplified. For a brief moment I felt everything—the spark of neurons connecting understanding in my brain, the breeze teasing goosebumps on my skin, the individual scent of each flower, the vibration of all the birds' wings beating in the sky. It was like every part of me was uploading information faster and sharper than it ever had in order to make sense of the biggest, most important, most *complex* truth I'd ever confronted.

"I'm dead . . ."

My body felt heavy and rigid as I stopped and stared into the distance. A gentle wind hit my face and I sensed its crispness against the sole sad droplet that escaped down my cheek.

Surprisingly, the rest of my tears restrained themselves at the corners of my eyes. As if my body knew that to let them out would only let fear in. Now was not the time to cry. I had to float above that or surely I would drown under the circumstance.

Akari came to stand beside me. The wind kicked up glittery golden pollen from the flowers and it swirled around us like magic dust.

"Do you remember how it happened?" she asked.

I closed my eyes and searched my memory. I saw nothing at first. Then explosions of color danced into existence like I was walking through a cosmic storm. I remembered seeing these . . . *beings*, silhouetted like shadows but made of pure light. They surrounded me, mixing with the colors to form a tunnel.

Their presence made me feel warm, loved, and safe; however . . . I was being pulled away from them. I began to move backward in my memory in slow motion like someone was rewinding a movie. The feelings and beauty drifted farther away. Suddenly, a single monarch butterfly flew past me and headed toward the tunnel. The splendor of light and color was almost gone now—a speck in the distance with blackness everywhere else, swallowing me. I reached my hand toward the butterfly; its orange-and-black wings and a dot of white light were all I could see in the void. Then, with a flash, both were gone. Pure nothingness again until I heard a voice.

"You and I are going to have a serious talk when we get home, Grace," my mother said.

I turned my head and took in her stern, tired face. I sat in the passenger seat of our car while she drove. It was dark out, but my mother's wavy orange hair illuminated every few seconds from the streetlamps we rode past.

"How is that any different than the lecture you've been giving me the last ten minutes?" I crossed my arms and sunk in my seat, feeling small. "Haven't I had enough beratement for one night?" I muttered.

"That is not a word, and I am not berating you, dear," my mother replied. "I am trying to help you. I am *always* trying to help you. I just . . ." Her fingers tightened on the wheel. "I don't know what it is going to take. Why can't you follow my example, or your sister's? Why do you always have to do things that are so beneath the person I raised you to be?"

I straightened a bit as my own fingers clenched with aggravation. "Mom, *I'm trying*. Honestly. I realize I disappointed you tonight, and I'm sorry. But do you understand that you disappointed me too? That's the reason we're even in this situation."

My mom took her eyes off the road for a moment. "I beg your pardon?"

"You should have been there."

She sighed. "Grace, I realize you veer toward a self-centered and impulsive world view, despite my standard, but take a breather from your hot-tempered tendencies to think of someone other than yourself. It's hardly a small responsibility to manage a national charitable foundation. I had a meeting with donors that took precedence over a silly recital."

My face heated with indignation and my fists clenched. "The recital wasn't *silly*, and I am not self-centered or hot tempered."

She shot me another quick glance. "Tell that to your face, dear. Your aggression is like a neon sign, clear and defining even in the darkness."

A smoothie of shame, anger, and unhappiness churned inside me. It egged me to heighten my reaction, but I opted against that. Instead I forced restraint and a tempered, but earnest tone.

"Mom . . ." I sighed, pained. "I know that I shouldn't be this way. I wish I could be a daughter that didn't constantly let you down. But it's not ideal for me to have a mother constantly letting me down either. I understand that you work hard, but it feels like there is always something you'd rather do than spend time with me."

My mother huffed. "You're being ridiculous, Grace."

"Am I?" I leaned toward her. The glare of streetlamps dared me to blink but I refused to. "Tell me that you don't prefer keeping me at a distance because you get tired of me failing your expectations."

The lights flashed in my mother's eyes. She didn't answer.

I shook my head dejectedly. "Mom, just once I wish you'd try and see that I'm—"

A pair of headlights abruptly threw her face into harsh contrast. Fear and instinct barely had time to reach my brain.

"LOOK OUT!"

Those bright, glowing beams consuming my mother were the last clear image I had of this memory. My world became screeching brakes and metal, jarring images of a black truck and red lights. Then—

I gasped and my eyes burst open in real time. I whirled to Akari. "Where's my mom? Is she also . . ."

Akari nodded, eyes full of sympathy. "She died in the car crash with you, Grace. I'm sorry."

I gulped and drew away, pacing a bit to put a few feet between us before facing her again. "Where is she?"

"Somewhere else."

A beat passed. I wasn't a super religious person, but afterlife basics usually accounted for a good place like Heaven and a not so good place . . . downstairs. I glanced at the ground a moment, then shook my head adamantly. "That's not right. My mother wasn't a bad person. I wouldn't say she was a particularly great one either, but—"

"Don't worry, Grace. The afterlife is not that simple. Just as things in life are not always black and white, neither is eternity. Come on, I'll explain more at our offices." Akari reached for my hand, but I took a step out of her reach.

"Offices?"

"Yes. In The First City." She pointed at the sparkling utopia. At my blank look, she elaborated further. "When we enter Heaven, we land somewhere that fills us with calm. You know how yoga teachers or life coaches tell you to picture your happy place? This is quite literally yours. The universe created this from the elements that inherently bring you peace." She gestured at the majestic landscape surrounding us. "Normally, we would have more time to relax here, but our boss is eager for me to get you back to the GAs as soon as possible, given the outlier we're dealing with."

I shook my head and raised my hands. "You're saying a lot of words that I don't understand. Boss? GAs? Outlier?"

Akari held up three fingers and counted off her answers. "Boss meaning God. GAs meaning Guardian Angels. And outlier," she pointed at me, "meaning you."

Her form glowed and I realized I hadn't been imagining things. A perfect golden halo appeared above Akari's head and a second later, glorious wings emerged from her back. The feathers shimmered. I held up my hand to shield my eyes; it was like staring at a wishing fountain full of coins when the sunlight hit them.

"Holy—" I cut myself off and looked at Akari. "Do I get re-located to down below if I curse in Heaven?"

"Cursing is fine as long as it is used tastefully, has comedic value, or is an endearing part of a person's character. Like Deadpool or

Jason Statham. That being said, if you use it around children or people who don't like that sort of thing, Heaven will intervene."

"How?"

"Is that really the most pressing question on your mind?"

"No. *Definitely not.*"

Shock was giving way to my natural curiosity—or blunt inquisitiveness, as my mother liked to call it. It was in the top three qualities she disliked about me, and right now it overpowered my sea of emotion and came gushing out in a rapid train of thought.

"Questions off the top of my head—What's the deal with Stonehenge? Are the Easter Island Heads stone aliens ready to come to life and defend Earth when humanity needs them most? How many US presidents ended up in Heaven? How many of the *Boston Celtics* ended up in Heaven? Is the legend about all dogs going to Heaven really true? Are giraffes—"

"Whoa, whoa." Now it was Akari's turn to raise her hands as I assailed her with inquiries. "There will be plenty of time for random questions later, Grace. Like I said, we need to get going." She reached for my hand again, but once more I backed up. Anxiety twisted within me.

Akari sighed. "Grace," she said steadily. "I wasn't sent here to greet you by chance. I have been specifically chosen as your mentor, your guide. It is . . ." she took a moment and carefully selected her words, "an *honor*." She sighed again. "And I promise to help you get through this and all that comes next. But there can't be a next unless you take a leap of faith and trust me."

She held out her hand. I studied it guardedly before looking into her eyes. It was so overwhelming to feel such wonder and curiosity at the same time as I tried to repress mourning and regret. My heart felt stuck as I tried to articulate the tangled emotions inside of me—resisting like a wad of hair clogged in a shower drain that someone was trying to pull free.

Eventually I managed to get the right words out in a small voice.

"I wasn't ready to die . . ."

A moment passed and Akari's face turned sympathetic. "I know, Grace. Hardly anyone is. However, humanity is a roll-with-the-punches deal. We work with what we've got. And I promise you, just because one part of your existence is over doesn't mean *you* are over. In fact, this is only your beginning. So take my advice and try to focus on the here and now."

I glanced at the city then closed my eyes a second. Following a deep breath, I accepted the advice and Akari's hand. When I did, her whole body glowed with the same soft radiance as her halo, spreading over me too. Her wings flapped mightily. Once, twice, then—

"*WHOOOAAAA!*"

We shot straight up spaceship style. Although Akari held my hand, it didn't feel as though she was carrying me. I felt almost weightless, like a balloon Akari held by a string and pulled along with no effort at all.

With the speed and grace of an eager falcon, we soared toward the beautiful city. As we flew, I acknowledged three things with absolute certainty:

1) When someone asks you whether you'd like to have the power of invisibility or flight, always pick the latter.

2) I don't think angels can be afraid of heights.

3) Maybe even the cloud of death could have a silver lining.

I meant that last part figuratively, but as we drew closer to the city, I noticed that many buildings had literal silver lining edges. The fluffy clouds we passed, meanwhile, fluxed with a rainbow of colors. It reminded me of when my sister Gaby and I would put multicolored lights inside our pillowcases when we camped in our backyard. An image of us laughing as our dad came out with a bowl of popcorn filled my mind.

Gaby . . .

Dad . . .

I cleared my throat and searched the skies for anything to distract me from the sudden heartache. Thankfully, there was plenty to work with.

"Hi, Akari!" a winged boy called as he whizzed above us.

My guide waved back and then zigzagged neatly through giant inbound floating lanterns. The *Tangled*-esque things decorated many parts of the sky, bopping tranquilly in the breeze.

Suddenly Akari adjusted course, zeroing in on the tallest building in the center of the city, a cross between the Seattle Space Needle and the Oriental Pearl TV Tower in Shanghai. The massive vertical construct was interspersed with large spherical offices and flat, disc-like expansions at various floors.

Coolest. Office building. Ever.

The top of the tower held the biggest sphere, but I was only able to take in its glimmering color for a second before averting my gaze. A weird, involuntary instinct made my eyes dart away. I tried to look again, but felt the same sting in my corneas. On my third attempt, my head panged with pain and I cringed. "*Ow.*"

Akari glanced at me. "If you're trying to look at the top office, don't," she said. "You can't. It's a reverence thing."

"Sorry?"

"That's God's office. This building is Angel Tower, where the most important departments of Heaven are kept. *There* is where we're going." She pointed at one of bulbous extensions in the middle of the tower; a glass balcony rimmed it. Akari's wings pulled in and we descended fast, then they stretched, slowing us, and we alighted there. She released my hand and her wings, halo, and our glow vanished.

Akari lifted the face of her wristwatch to a scanner on the glass door. Both shone then a neon yellow light lit up over the entry, indicating it was unlocked. She held the door open for me. My eyes widened as I took a step into a command center like no other.

In the middle stood an amazing Southern live oak tree, so large and beautifully branched that it appropriately reminded me of the famed "Angel Oak" in Charleston. Though there was one very specific difference. This fifty-foot-tall tree featured flat screen TVs of all sizes stemming from its mighty branches and decorating its trunk. The screens showed constantly changing images and videos of people and places and maps.

Desks encircled the base of the tree and expanded outward in larger and larger rings like ripples in water. Each desk came equipped with floating hologram screens and gold-and-silver computer monitors. It was as if Iron Man and Louis XIV of France made a Pinterest board together. Add in a touch of Wall Street, à la the screens that rimmed the rounded walls displaying numbers and symbols, and you had a perfect snapshot of the place we'd arrived in.

Hundreds of employees in white suits or dresses filled the room, busy but not frantically so. For a moment they all blurred together. It was a lot to take in. My senses of wonder, curiosity, and nausea only multiplied when I saw *my* face and the notation **98%** flash across one of the tree's larger screens. My two thoughts in reaction were:

1) When was that picture taken? It certainly beats my high school ID photo.

2) What is the deal with that number next to my picture?

"Hey, it's Ninety-Eight!" called out one of the desk jockeys. He stood and pointed at me. All working stopped. Every face in the room pivoted to look at me.

Good God, I feel uncomfortable.

I wondered if it was inappropriate to think that since God was right upstairs.

"Okay, okay, nothing to see here," Akari said. She grabbed my wrist with one hand and waved off the gawkers with the other. "Back to work."

A few continued to stare as Akari led me around the perimeter of the room. One girl even dared to poke me in the arm, as if to make sure I was real.

Opposite where we'd entered the command center, we stepped into a corridor with a crystal floor. The wall on the right was one long waterfall. On the left stood a row of doors to different offices. Akari and I made our way down the hall until we stopped at an office with the following nameplate mounted to the door:

AKARI BROWN
Senior Guardian Angel
Long-Term Assignments
12:1

"What do the numbers mean?" I asked as she opened the

door. I kept my gaze on her, trying not to be distracted by the gorgeous view of the city offered by the glass wall on the other side of her office.

Akari paused. There was a slight shift in her expression. She waved me inside and shut the door behind us. "That's not the number you most want to understand, *is it*?"

She was right.

"Ninety-Eight," I said. "That's the number that guy called me out there, and it was by my picture when it flashed on one of the tree screens. What does it mean?"

"Sit down, Grace."

Akari gestured to a hot pink velvet armchair in front of her desk, a replica of the larger one that she settled in. Her watch glowed and a file appeared in her hands, which she splayed open on her desk and read over for a moment.

I made my way to my assigned chair, pausing when I noticed the cat tower made of bamboo in the corner. Instead of a cat, a baby panda was playing on the structure. It somersaulted down a slide, then—*BAM*—tiny silver wings spouted from its back and the creature flapped back to the top of the tower.

"That's a panda," I stated. "A baby panda. With wings."

"What?" Akari looked up. "Oh, that's Chaz. My pet angel panda. Don't pay him any attention."

"Right. Don't pay any mind to the baby panda *with wings*," I said with an air of sarcasm.

I sat down and wrung my hands with nervous energy. I would say this had been the weirdest, most overwhelming day of my life, but my life had already ended so I didn't know how I would describe this exactly.

I took a deep breath and focused on the woman in front of me. "Ma'am, if I could ask a few more questions—"

"Grace," Akari cut me off. "You saw my name on the door. It's just Akari. And before we get to the questions you have for me, I have one for you." She folded her hands over the open file and looked at me sternly. "What do you think are the most important qualities a human being can have?"

The query was surprising, but I'd had my share of college interviews in recent months; I could think on my feet. I certainly was not about to look like a dumb-dumb in front of an angel.

"Empathy, perhaps? Understanding? The ability to drive without being distracted?"

That last one came out as a nervous joke. I did that sometimes to lighten the mood. My mother didn't care for the tendency. Thankfully, Akari smiled a little.

"The first two are definitely high on the list, and guesses most angels make. The truth is there are several key characteristics to living up to humanity's potential, Grace. But one quality most people overlook is purpose. True, fulfilling, individual purpose. Without purpose we drift, we wander, and we feel incomplete, like our lives don't have meaning because, well, they don't. Purpose to the soul is butter on bread—a complement so intrinsic that existence with them separated wouldn't seem right. Purpose is the reason people get up in the morning. Purpose is the thing that pushes people to evolve into something greater. And purpose is what keeps you from feeling empty, being useless, and becoming a burden to humanity—a person that doesn't give, only takes from the world. As such, purpose can prevent people from falling into the clutches of the folks down there." She pointed a finger firmly at the floor.

"The lobby?" I jested.

Akari raised an eyebrow. "This is no joking matter."

"Sorry." I fidgeted in my chair.

Akari walked over to the window and beckoned for me to follow. I joined her as she stared out at the cityscape.

"Heaven is paradise, Grace. It is everything people would like it to be and more. It just may look different to our residents, and be experienced differently. Depending on personal beliefs and religion, what each mind processes here changes. After all, if you earn a place on this side of the afterlife tracks, it is meant to be your nirvana. But it can hardly be that if what you see conflicts with what you've spent your life believing. So this world looks like what your innermost heart and faith hoped it would, and aims to meet and exceed those expectations. Individual experiences

are tailored further from there. This city is only one trillionth
of Heaven's real estate. People spend their afterlife in the areas
designed to make them happiest. For example, we're hardly going
to place a saintly farmer in a bustling city, or an angelic Eskimo on
a tropical beach. And there are areas for all eras in Earth's history
to suit souls who don't wish to move forward with the times. In
sum, in Heaven we give people what they want. Make sense?"

"Uh-huh," I said, my eyes wandering to Chaz. The baby panda
was now turning somersaults around the ceiling—floating on his
own it seemed, and just using his wings to change directions.

"That being said, all versions of Heaven share a few
commonalities," Akari continued. "The first is embracing purpose. People love paradise—no stress, no mortgages, no future
to worry about. Here in Heaven, you can cuddle with a litter
of puppies while eating calorie-free cake for breakfast, ride a
unicorn, go ziplining with Benjamin Franklin, then change into
a ballgown for a pizza party at Walt Disney's house. The thing
about paradise, though, is that it can get old. Even people who
have awesome vacations on Earth want to return home after a
while because, as human beings, we have a deep need in our soul
to *do* something. If we don't—if we just partied in perpetuity—
we'd all end up like those loser kids of celebrities who live off their
parents' coattails and never accomplish anything for themselves.
So in Heaven, there are jobs."

I gave her a severe look. "*Jobs?*"

"Don't say it like that."

"How am I supposed to say it?" Emotion bubbled inside me
like bursts of magma in a volcano, causing my voice to heighten.
"I'm seventeen. I'm a kid. I had years before I had to pick a career
on Earth; now you're telling me that five minutes after dying I am
getting a job in Heaven?"

I tried to swallow through my constricting throat. Now was also
not the time to cry. Too many questions needed to be answered,
and I could hardly ask them with a face full of tissues and vocal
chords clogged by sorrow.

"I can understand your disinclination," Akari said carefully.
"But these aren't nine-to-five, Monday-through-Friday occupa-

tions. There are no HR departments, no taxes, none of that boring stuff. When people get to Heaven, they are usually given five years to do absolutely nothing and simply relax. Then they get to pick a job of their choice from our extremely long list of amazing options."

Her watch glowed and an enormous book the size of three Oxford dictionaries appeared a meter above her desk, then dropped with a thud. Akari motioned me over.

"Jobs can be pretty basic," she said as we resumed our seats. "For example, if you were a chef on Earth, you could open a restaurant here. The difference is, in Heaven it's all for pure enjoyment. You would have your restaurant without ever having to deal with inventory, affording rent, or anything else annoying. It's the same with all straightforward career paths in Heaven; you get your dream job without any of the traditional worries that accompany the role on Earth. Plus, you can change jobs at any time. There are millions of possibilities in here." She patted the book. "Conventional, unconventional, and community service."

I tilted my head slightly, fascinated by the concept. "Volunteer work? In Heaven?"

"Technically it's volunteer work on Earth." With some effort Akari opened to the middle of the hefty text. "Here's an example." She planted a finger on a paragraph. "You know how penguins huddle together to keep warm in the middle of a frigid tundra? Maybe you'd like to be a part of the team of angels that redirects some of the frosty winds to make the creatures more comfortable." Her finger drifted. "And you know how sea turtles hatch on the beach and have to crawl all the way to the ocean on their own? You could assist the angels who flip upside down baby turtles right side up."

Akari continued turning the pages, stopping periodically to reference an entry. "You could use angelic magic to make flowers sprout through the concrete of sidewalks, be a part of the sunset and sunrise painting teams, help pandas find each other in the jungle so they can mate." She paused and glanced at me earnestly. "You know, those silly creatures usually live on their own in the vast jungle, but the females only ovulate for a few days a year. So when it's time to mate, the female pandas and male pandas have to traverse the jungle to find each other with an absurdly limited timeframe!"

I blinked, startled by her passion.

Akari paused, then she sat back. She'd been so collected since our introduction; this was the first sign of impromptu emotion she'd shown. It surprised us both. And I don't think she felt very happy about it.

"Sorry. I promised myself I would be professional. I just get a bit passionate with animals. That's inappropriate though."

"Passion is inappropriate?"

"More like ill-advised. Not in general—it's just how I have decided to approach my role as your mentor. I'll be more effective at the job with a reserved disposition. Getting back to jobs . . ." She gestured at the book tactfully as she redirected the subject. "The summation is that in Heaven they're all wonderful. They come with zero worries and you can essentially do whatever you want. Universally it's a win-win. Jobs here have nothing but positive side effects in Heaven and on Earth. And having a fun role gives you purpose and thus prevents you from going what we call 'paradise crazy'."

"That does sound . . . good," I ventured. I tilted my chin toward the book. "So is that why you brought me to this office? To help me find something that interests me?"

"Actually, no." Akari shut the text and it vanished. "The book was just to help illustrate the concept. Your case is more interesting and unusual. You see, most people can pick any job they want, but there are some people who have a higher calling. One of the most important jobs that a person can hold in the afterlife is Guardian Angel. That job isn't listed as an option in the book because it is only available to certain people." She drummed her fingers on the desk as if she was figuring out how to proceed. Then she sighed and leaned back in her chair.

"Human beings are measured in terms of good and evil, Grace; their percentages determine where they end up in the afterlife. Because the actions of Guardian Angels affect the whole of humanity, only the purest souls qualify—people with goodness at the helm of their hearts and a moral compass that always points true. As a result, we only accept those who are 90% good and up. That, Grace, is where you come in."

Akari glanced at the open file on her desk and picked it up, reading aloud. "Grace Cariño Reyes Cardiff. Sassy but not mean-spirited. Overdeveloped sense of justice. Genuine ability to understand human behavior. Always looking to help others. Loyal. Protective. High sense of honor. Fierce in her commitments. Always gets back up when knocked down. And unquestionably good."

I gulped. I didn't see myself that way. A *lot* of people didn't see me that way. Was I supposed to tell Akari that? Maybe she had the wrong file?

"That's a heck of a self-esteem boost," I said with nervous jest. "I think I need a towel after being showered with so many compliments."

Akari crooked her head. "You don't already know this about yourself?"

Chaz the panda abruptly rolled through the airspace between us, blocking my view of Akari. After he passed, I found her still looking at me expectantly. My nerve shrunk. I'd never felt so on the spot in my whole life. I didn't want to disappoint Akari, but I didn't want to lie either. I sighed and put my fears in their holster. I needed to be honest here, even if it was frightening and embarrassing.

"At the risk of creating an Eleanor Shellstrop situation . . ." I rubbed my hands against my pant legs. "I think you misunderstand what kind of person I am. There are plenty of people on Earth who wouldn't think of me that way, Akari. Myself included."

My angelic mentor closed the file with a minor shrug. "People are frequently unfair to each other on Earth because their own biases or flaws warp how they perceive the actions and intentions of others."

"But—"

"*Grace.*" Akari looked at me with a serious gaze. "This isn't a mistake. This is *you*. And you are more powerful than you realize. The average Guardian Angel is 93% good. That's what I am. The highest ranked Guardian Angel to ever work here was 97% good. You are 98% good. That's what the number you saw on that screen means. You are the purest soul to ever walk through these offices and as such, we are going to ask a lot of you. Guardian Angels don't typically get the five-year vacation period I mentioned; our services are too valuable and our numbers aren't as high as we'd like. Usually we start training after one month of adjustment and then get an assignment within weeks after that. Unfortunately, with you we don't even have that time. There's a serious Guardian Angel case emerging on Earth, and God wants you assigned to the task immediately. What do you say?"

I stared at Akari, my eyes wide as taco tortillas. Shock was too mild a word to describe my reaction. Terror was too tame. And the dozen or so other feelings inside of me may not have even had a name.

Chaz the panda passed between us again, chewing on his own foot as he floated by. When he moved out of our eye line, I guess I had the afterlife equivalent of a stroke because all that escaped my lips was one giant "HA!"

2

THE BIG QUESTIONS

I anxiously twirled my spoon on the table—index finger pressed on top of the handle as I swiveled my wrist, pretending the spoon was a ballerina.

The ice cream shop we sat in had plenty of happy people enjoying treats. The teal walls and ceiling were a pretty contrast against the checkered red and white tiles. My eyes wandered to the menu board. The eatery's name was printed in sparkling silver letters at the top: Your Perfect Ratio (Downtown Dessert Bar).

"Here you are," said a slender waitress as she placed a towering sundae in front of me and another in front of Akari. The dessert would've made Willy Wonka tip his hat.

"Thanks, Edith," Akari said. "And may I say, your smile is electric and your ponytail looks particularly perfect today."

"Aren't you sweet." Edith fanned her face and blushed before stepping away.

"In Heaven, we don't use money," Akari explained as she picked up her spoon. "We pay for everything in compliments. You can't lie here, so everything we say is sincere. That makes all compliments mean something."

"Sweet," I said. "The concept and the dessert." I took a big bite and felt some of the apprehension I'd been carrying melt away as the ice cream dissolved in my mouth. I couldn't help but smile. "This is . . ."

"Perfect?" Akari guessed.

"Yes. Yes, exactly! Normally sundaes skimp on the fudge; I always have to ask for extra. And there are usually too many nuts, and some weird maraschino cherry that almost nobody eats."

"Your Perfect Ratio is the most popular chain restaurant in

Heaven," Akari explained. "You know when you eat or drink something and you wish for a slight adjustment—a pinch more salt, less onions, extra sauce? Whatever you order at these restaurants always has the exact ratio of flavors and ingredients to make you fully content. This is a dessert location, but there's one of these restaurants for every kind of food—Mexican, Italian, and so on. Speaking of which, are you sure this is all you want for lunch? I have to cram about a week's worth of orientation into one day for you. If you thought this morning was a lot, I'm afraid there is still a ton more to go over."

I took another spoonful of ice cream and my insides melted again. I'd have said the dessert was sinfully good, but that adjective seemed oxymoronic here.

"Apologies if it sounds a bit crass, but unless you want to see a girl upchuck, this is about all I can handle right now, Akari."

"Good to know. Though it's worth pointing out that angels can't actually throw up in the traditional sense. Fun fact."

"Sorry? Angel?"

"That's what you are, Grace. An angel. It's not just a job title. Guardian Angels have powers that normal people who live up here don't. However, anyone fully assigned to Heaven in the after-life is classified as an angel."

Angel . . .

I mulled the label over. It didn't feel right. It didn't feel earned.

"That's neither here nor there," I said, changing the subject quickly. "At the core, I'm a teenager and a Capricorn. You just told me I have the purest soul you've ever seen and I have to use that to guard some person I've never met on Earth." I swallowed more ice cream to calm me. "That's a lot to digest without adding salsa or spaghetti to the mix."

"I can understand that," Akari said.

"And then there's processing the whole 'I'm dead' thing," I added. I took a breath and averted my eyes as another wave of loss washed over me.

"I *definitely* understand that . . ." Akari nodded. She folded her hands on the table between us as the sparkle in her eyes faded. "I died a week before my twenty-eighth birthday," she said with a sigh. "I'd recently married. We had so many plans. *I* had so many plans. It took months for me to come to peace with losing that life I'd envisioned. The thing that helped me the most though was being a Guardian Angel. There is no better medicine for the soul than helping someone else and spreading goodness."

"I believe you," I said. "I mean that."

"I know you do. We can't lie here, remember?"

"Oh, right." I realized that I was already halfway through my sundae. I ate quickly when I was stressed. I self-consciously put the spoon down. Then I paused. "Wait. You said *nothing* has calories here?"

"Correct."

I huffed. "That's going to take some time to wrap my mind around too." I picked up my spoon and scraped some fudge from the side of the glass. "I've always had a slow metabolism and have had to adjust accordingly. My mother has been packing salads in my lunchbox since I was six. I've never tried Alfredo sauce because of the fat content. In my house we only have muffins on the last day of—"

I stopped as embarrassment flooded me. Welcome to my mother's second least favorite thing about me. When I was overwhelmed, I had a tendency to vocalize my stream of consciousness a.k.a. babble. That was *before* Heaven's magical honesty filter. With that in play, I really had to watch myself.

I cleared my throat. "When am I going to get answers to all of my *other* questions? The list in my mind keeps growing, you know."

"One thing at a time, Grace. Like you said, you already feel nauseous from everything I've thrown at you. It's policy to ease new arrivals into the afterlife. I don't want to break your brain, even with the time crunch we're under to get you started on the new job."

"Tell me about the things that matter most then. Start with my mother. I've been patient enough, Akari. If she's not here and not . . . down below, what's the deal?"

"I think it's better if I show you." She stood from the table. "You done?"

"I guess so." I got up and we exited the shop. Though we were in the middle of a city, there were no traffic lights or cars. The walking area had the feel of a small town—one giant strip of sidewalk people could mosey down without fear of being run over. It was abundant with cherry blossom trees, flower gardens, cute fountains, and grass beds that swirled over the ground in beautiful shapes.

Everyone seemed so happy. Each person I made eye contact with gave me a smile. A man was making balloon animals for children. A woman with a cart of red roses offered them to couples holding hands. Hummingbirds stopped to snack on honeysuckle flowers that spilled off balconies.

"Not everyone is wearing white," I commented.

"Heaven doesn't have a dress code, Grace. This isn't private school. When you arrive here, you appear in a white outfit that suits your personality. You can wear whatever you want after that, although some jobs may involve uniforms when you're on duty. Guardian Angels do have a tradition of wearing white to work, as you may have noticed at the office."

I nodded thoughtfully, my eyes taking in the sights. Some of the towers stretched pretty high and I saw a couple angels soaring above, their wings catching the light.

"Why does anyone bother walking when they can fly?" I asked, watching as an angel disappeared around a skyscraper.

"Because not everyone *can* fly. There are plenty of magical experience centers around here that give people amazing abilities temporarily. Like that one over there." Akari pointed to a hotel-sized building with a sign out front that read Superhero Experience Center. "Want to temporarily fly through the air? Have telekinetic powers? Super speed? Places like that offer ways for us to enjoy those abilities for a short amount of time so we can live out superhero fantasies. But the way you and I flew earlier is not something most angels can do. The majority of people in Heaven travel by teleportation. Angels with certain jobs can borrow loaner wings, but only fully realized Guardian Angels earn permanent wings."

"So when do I get mine?"

Akari raised an eyebrow. "No clue. Do you feel fully realized?"

"No."

"Then I guess today is not that day."

Suddenly the entire city experienced what I would describe as a magical hiccup. A radiant, soft light started at ground level before spreading upward through every tree, lamppost, and building—travelling skyward so quickly that in less than three seconds it had passed the top of Angel Tower and vanished with a twinkle like a winking star.

Everyone had paused when the hiccup started. They held still a moment longer after it'd gone, staring up with wonder. Then the people of The First City resumed their normal activities.

"Akari, what was—" I glanced around and saw that she'd continued walking. I jogged a few steps to catch up with her. The second I did, she came to a stop and gestured ahead.

"Here we are."

We stood in front of two buildings. The marble one on the left looked like an embassy. Enormous pillars à la the Lincoln Memorial held up the roof. Three flags flew over the crystal double doors—one with a golden H over a background of blue sky and fluffy white clouds, another with a black H over a background of orange and yellow flames, and a third between them with a sparkling silver M over a plain tan background.

"The flags represent Heaven, Hell, and Middleground," Akari explained. "These are the three planes of the afterlife. This marble building is the Afterlife Assignments Bureau. We're going next door."

The building she directed us to was the same tan color as that center flag and made of adobe. It was over thirty stories tall with a plethora of windows and cube-shaped offices sticking out. The metal sign at the front read: Middleground Viewing Center.

"In the afterlife, every person is assigned a caseworker based on the plane of existence where they'll spend most of their time," Akari enlightened as we climbed the entry steps. "Like how sororities match new members with older members who can show them the ropes. Typically afterlife caseworkers only stay with their assigned souls for a short while, helping them adjust to the new surroundings, occasionally doing check-ins. Since you are a Guardian Angel, your caseworker—*me*—will serve as an ongoing fixed mentor in your life providing guidance, hands-on training, and support."

We pushed through the main door into a busy foyer where Creeping Charlie ivy climbed the walls. We approached a desk where a pleasant man with a crew cut greeted us.

"Good afternoon, ladies. Who would you like to check on today?"

"Darla Cardiff, please," Akari responded. "She just arrived. This is Grace Cardiff, her daughter. ID number 21722CA781HA. Can you put Grace in the system as a regular visitor so she can check-in online next time?"

"Of course." He typed something into his computer then nodded to a lady across the room wearing shorts and a ruffled blouse. She neared us with a smile, clipboard in hand.

"Howdy. I'm Angelica from the Middleground Management Team. Room Twelve is available. Would you like me to show you the way?"

"No thank you, I've got it," Akari replied. She beckoned for me to follow. My mentor moved fast. Did Heaven have a gym? Her toned calves and speed certainly suggested so.

"Hey, Akari?" I said, catching up. I glanced around, hands in my pockets. "Not that I can't appreciate the suspense of a slow-burn reveal, but I've had an intense day. Pardon the directness, but can you cut to the chase? What is this place?"

"Remember how I told you that people are measured in terms of their good and bad percentages based on their time on Earth, and that tells us where to put them in the afterlife?"

I nodded.

"Well, the fact is that most people aren't overwhelmingly good or bad. Most people spend their lives struggling between the two. We can't look down on them for that. Life is hard. Often, people don't even realize they're doing the wrong thing. However, just as it wouldn't be fair to put your average person who recycled in the same group as someone who built prosthetic limbs for three-legged dogs, we can't have a person who regularly cut others off in traffic spend eternity with serial killers. That wouldn't be reasonable. So the afterlife has a timeshare system."

I frowned. "My friend Bitsy spent two weeks every spring in Cancun because her parents had a timeshare there. Are you saying one plane of the afterlife is like Mexico?"

Akari paused. "Not exactly. Why don't we sit for a minute?" She gestured to a cushioned wooden bench. As soon as we sat, a pair of robins carrying lollipops flew over and landed on the bench between us. The bird next to Akari held an orange lollipop in its beak; the bird closer to me carried a red one.

"Thank you," Akari said, taking the orange sucker.

I blinked in surprise but accepted the red candy. "Um, thanks. Cherry is my favorite."

The birds tweeted and took off.

"Only people who are more than 76% good are admitted to Heaven full-time," Akari explained, pocketing her candy. "Only people who are less than 25% good earn a permanent place in Hell. Depending on their ratio, everyone else splits their time between here, there, and what we call Middleground—a third realm where everything is pretty mediocre. Your mother was 62% good. I checked out her file and she is going to be spending four days a week in Middleground, two days a week in Heaven, and one day a week in Hell."

My lips parted to ask a trillion questions and express a zillion emotions, but nothing came out. My mouth was as dry as the Sahara.

"Eat the lollipop," Akari suggested, alluding to the candy clenched in my fist. "It's not cherry flavored. May I?" I loosened my hand slightly and she plucked the sucker then read the label. "This has the flavor of '*the first award you ever won*.' That's a good one. It'll help."

She offered me the sweet. I was reluctant at first, but then unwrapped it, pocketed the foil, and popped the lollipop in my mouth. When I did, I instantly felt a deep sense of contentment and relief.

"We don't want anyone we love to suffer," Akari said, leaning forward as the candy somewhat pacified me, "but the afterlife *is* fair this way. Spending time in Heaven is a reward for doing good. Time spent in Hell is punishment for doing bad. Middleground is an earned average existence because that's what most people are—average. All timeshare people have jobs too. Either here, there, or down below, depending on what they're eligible for. And if people prove themselves over time, they can alter their afterlife sentences; their timeshare plans can be rewritten. For example, your mother could someday earn more days in Heaven and maybe even eliminate Hell from her schedule entirely."

I drew the lollipop from my mouth with a moderately loud *SMACK*. "Is there anything I can do to help with that?"

"I'm sorry, Grace. Nothing specific comes to mind. But I urge you not to dwell on your mother's fate too much. She is her own person, just as you are. You have to focus on being a Guardian Angel and embrace the afterlife that *your* soul earned."

"Kind of a paradoxical thing telling someone who is apparently now an angel not to care about someone who may be suffering," I said, pointing my lollipop at her.

"I suppose, but I didn't write the welcome manual or the rules of the universe."

"I didn't write the rules of the universe either, but I did write a lot of well-received English papers in school and no offense, as a guide who is supposed to offer me support, I think your word choice could be better. This is *my mother* we're talking about, Akari. You read my file—loyal, protective, and so on. Those are your words, not mine. The relationship between my mother and me may have been . . . less than ideal. But she matters to me. I don't want her to be miserable."

Even if she has a tendency to make me miserable.

Akari scratched the back of her head and fidgeted a moment, then nodded. "Noted." She paused briefly before releasing a breath of vexation. "Look, I'm sorry if I am not being as delicate as I should. To be completely honest, it's been a while since I mentored someone. I am getting my sea legs back."

"Aren't you some big shot Senior Guardian Angel? That's what the plaque on your office door said."

"You could look at it that way."

"You don't?"

Her expression grew exasperated. "You ask a *lot* of questions, Grace."

"Yes, I do. And if we're stuck together, you should know that's never going to change."

"Fantastic." Akari rolled her eyes and stood. "Let's keep going." She continued up the hall so I followed, sticking the lollipop back in my mouth.

Mmmm. I can taste the praise and satisfaction. This is my new favorite flavor for sure.

We arrived at Room Twelve and Akari held open the door for me. The place was set up like a living room with a navy couch, indoor plants, white beanbag chairs, a coffee table, and a giant TV. Akari went over to the number and letter pad beside the screen.

"You can come to the Middleground Viewing Center any time to see what your mother is up to or chat with her. This is a special experience that anyone in Heaven can use so long as the person in Middleground they're contacting has at least one day of Heaven on their timeshare plan. Your mom's ID number is 21722CA780TW," she said as she punched the corresponding buttons. "Use that code when you come back here."

The screen powered on and there she was. My mother.

She was sitting at a kitchen table in a small, unfamiliar house with an open floor plan—stirring her teacup with a spoon. Some of our family photos hung on the wall above a beat-up wooden piano in the corner. A couch with one of the cushions missing resided next to a fish tank with various goldfish. I noticed the ceiling was a tad low for her taste. Our house on Earth had grandiosely tall ceilings, which made her feel dainty despite her 5'11 height.

"Can she see me?" I asked.

"No. You're looking at her by magic means. If you want to engage with her, press this green button." Akari pointed to it. "A holographic screen will appear wherever she is. Do you want to talk to her now?"

I took a deep breath. Our last moment together had been filled with conflict and disappointment. Most of our times together were characterized that way, actually. But that didn't deter my instinct.

"Yes," I decided.

"I'll be outside," Akari said. "Press the red button on the pad when you're done." Once the door clicked shut, I stowed the lollipop in the wrapper and shoved it my back pocket. Then I pressed the green button.

"Mom?"

My mother was so startled that she almost dropped her teacup. A slosh of liquid did spill on her hand though, and she winced as she put the cup down and dried the angry red mark with a napkin.

"Grace?" She blinked at the screen in amazement.

"Hi . . . Sorry to scare you."

My mother got up from the table and made her way front and center. "My caseworker said there was no way for me to contact you. People on Middleground can only accept calls; we cannot make them."

"Oh." I glanced at the floor for a second. "So, um, you already know the whole deal about what's happening?"

She sighed sadly. "I'm afraid so."

A lull hung between us. My mother tried a couple times to say something, but each time held back. I didn't blame her for being unsure how to proceed. We'd just been in a car together hashing out deep wounds in our relationship. Now literally *everything* was different. Except her and me unfortunately. We'd never been able to understand each other or connect openly on Earth; woefully the afterlife appeared to be no exception.

Eventually she did speak. "Are you handling it, dear? Are you doing okay?" Her words reflected caring though her tone was brusque.

"As well as can be expected," I ventured, going for a more reserved response to mirror hers, lest all my feelings spill onto the floor.

I hated that. I wished we had the kind of mother-daughter relationship where we could just speak our truths without her holding back and me feeling like I'd be judged.

I rubbed my arm sheepishly. "How's it going with you? What's it like in Middleground?"

"It is . . . moderately acceptable," my mother replied. "But I suppose that is the point. It reminds me of that time we stayed at the Best Western when our flight home from Florida was delayed." She nodded at her teacup. "They don't have Splenda here. Just Equal."

"Tragic," I said.

We stood in silence—our gazes shifting from each other to the floor to absentmindedly looking around. My mother and I always had difficulty maintaining eye contact—like a bull with a bullfighter, it seemed to increase the likelihood of conflict, so we shied away from it.

Feeling awkward and weighed down by the emotions I struggled to keep at bay, I sat on the edge of my couch. My mother did the same on hers.

I sighed as heaviness deflated my heart. My mother was not a hugger, but I could sure use that kind of affection at the moment. Never underestimate the power of a parental embrace. Of all the miracles Heaven had to offer, it seemed cruel that the thing I needed most wasn't possible. I'd gladly settle for one of her annoyingly withdrawn side hugs right now, but the woman wasn't even on the same plane of existence.

"When do you get up here?" I asked.

"Normally I'll be in Heaven on the weekends, but they are having me stay in Middleground this weekend. I will start my regular rotation on Monday and remain here until Thursday. On Friday, I go . . ." Her face tensed.

"Down below," I tried. I gulped and fidgeted. "Are you scared?"

My mother gave me one of her classic, tight-knit frowns. "That is a foolish question, Grace. Shame on you."

"*I don't know a better one to ask,*" I protested, my voice tweaking to a higher octave.

"Then don't ask one. You don't always need to fill the silence."

But I do . . .

I crossed my arms. "Can we not fight, please? I'm sad, Mom. We *died*. We left Dad and Gaby, and our friends, and our lives." I felt my previously restrained tears welling up and my emotion start to snap open. "This sucks! We had so much left to—"

"Grace," my mother interrupted, severing my feelings before they could reach fruition. "I know, dear. And right now, I can't talk about Gaby or your fath—" She cut herself off and I saw her eyes turn glassy.

My mother took a deep breath. "You need to be strong. You can't complain either because you're in Heaven. You should be grateful, and in terms of moving forward I want you to be brave and carry on. Best face forward. It's what Cardiffs do."

"Mom, I—" My voice cracked.

"My caseworker tells me you were chosen for a special job?" she inquired.

I swallowed roughly and nodded. "I'm a Guardian Angel."

"Sounds like a lot of responsibility. Focus on that."

I took a deep breath and re-centered. "Yes, ma'am."

A beat passed. I tapped my shoe against the floor. "At least we can see each other in person when you visit next weekend." I said decidedly, thinking out loud. "Given everything that's happened, our latest argument hardly matters now, don't you think? Maybe we can let all that go and spend some time together and *really* talk. Like you and Gaby do sometimes."

She sighed. "We'll see what happens when I get there."

It took me a second to process the surprising statement. I'd really tried to make myself vulnerable for a moment—extend the olive branch even though in that car ride I'd been just as angry at her as she had been at me.

"Sorry?"

"Grace . . ." My mother's tone was crestfallen but her eyes were stern. "Considering how we ended up here, it's challenging for me to talk with you right now. I love you, dear, but to use your rather crass turn of phrase, this does in fact 'suck' and I need to be alone for a while to compose myself and accept our situation. The circumstances of us dying together in that car accident . . .

It's a terrible thing. Blame and regret are difficult for a mother to digest."

My arms crossed tightly around my diaphragm so that I was hugging myself. "Yes, Mom. I understand."

And despite my initial shock to her response, it was partly true. I hadn't thought about how blame would be affecting her. She must be racked with guilt over the accident. I still thought it would be better for us to address it directly, but what I thought didn't matter. I had never been able to force my mother to think outside her perspective and see things from mine, and I doubt that was going to change.

"So . . . does that mean you'd prefer I didn't call you for the rest of the week?" I said sadly. "Not even to speak casually?"

I already had a pretty good idea of the answer. What would we even talk about casually? My mother and I had nothing in common but shared frustration with one another.

"I believe that would be good for both of us as we find a way to deal with what has happened," she responded.

"Okay, Mom. Whatever you say." My fists clenched, instincts fighting against the decorum my mother favored. Emotion built up too much for me to stop it. "Can I just say one more time though that I don't think—"

"Grace. Take a moment. Take a deep breath. This is no time to lose control."

Fierce emotion flared inside of me even deeper, despite my mother's wishes and example. "I disagree, Mom. I disagree strongly." My body tightened. Suddenly I wasn't just sad about being dead, I was angry that my mother even made my feelings about *that* seem unwarranted and extreme.

"But you know what, fine." I slapped my hands against my legs. "I couldn't make you talk about your feelings or hear me out on Earth, so I'm not going to try and make you do it here. I just thought we could try for a fresh start and be real with one another. Sorry if it goes against the dignified, reserved airs you'd prefer that I put on. Forget I even said anything."

My mother shook her head. "*Oh Grace . . .*"

The disappointment in her tone doused all my inner fire. It was amazing and tragic. With just two words my mother could make me regret my instincts and reexamine my character. It was too bad that I had to let her if I wanted us to even have a semblance of a relationship.

We remained in silence for a slow, uncomfortable pause— me sitting in my own embrace while my mother fiddled with the napkin in her hands. Finally, I rubbed my hands against my pant legs and stood up. I couldn't take the quiet condemnation any longer. "I should probably get back to my mentor."

"Very well. Good luck, dear." My mother rose and went to reclaim her tea. When she picked up the cup, she nodded at me solemnly. "Be safe, Grace. I love you."

"Uh-huh," I said absentmindedly. "Bye, Mom." With a heavy heart, I pressed the red button and the TV clicked off. I stayed still for a bit, then went out to the hall in a zombie daze.

Akari was studying a little holographic screen projecting from her watch but powered it down when she saw me. "You look terrible," she said with dismay.

"Maybe death doesn't suit me."

She bit her lip. "Talking with family usually helps the recently deceased."

I stared at my white sneakers. "My mother and I have always had a complicated relationship. Add to that, it seems she blames herself for our car crash and is having some trouble speaking to me because of the guilt. She could barely look at me."

Akari's face filled with sympathy. "That's sad but understandable. Perhaps I should have prepared you for this. When family members or friends die together, one of them usually holds themselves responsible, and that guilt can be crushing. For a parent to be culpable for the untimely death of their child—"

"Let's not talk about it." I held up a hand. "I am going to take my mother's advice and stay strong by focusing on something else. I'm ready to hear more about my job."

Akari studied me a moment. Sympathy sparked in her expression. "You know what? Forget about that. We can discuss your Guardian Angel duties tomorrow. For now, I have the best thing to cheer you up."

I raised an eyebrow. "What is it?

"An answer to one of your initial questions *and* a reconnection you'll love."

"It's real," I marveled in awe.

Akari and I stood on the edge of a cumulonimbus cloud, the texture of the footing something like a stale marshmallow. A huge rainbow bridge sprouted from the far edge of the cloud and extended up to vanishing in the sky—glittering mist obscuring the far end and floating along the sides.

My mentor and I had been waiting in line with other recently deceased angels and their guides for twenty minutes. I knew it would be well worth it. Anticipation rose inside of me like an inflatable mattress being pumped full of air.

The next man in line, just ahead of us, moved to where the bridge met the cloud. He waited anxiously for a few seconds and then threw his hands up with joy when he saw a creature galloping down the rainbow bridge. It was a horse-sized Great Dane with dove-sized wings.

"Barney!" the man shouted. He raced forward as the dog leapt off the bridge to embrace him. They toppled over and Barney licked his owner's face. Everyone in the crowd melted like gelato on a South Carolina summer sidewalk.

"I can't believe the stories are true," I said to Akari in delight. "Our pets really are waiting for us in Heaven."

Akari nodded. "Pets have their own version of Heaven. When they die, they cross their first mystical Rainbow Bridge to reach a peaceful realm with wide-open fields, oceans, lakes, food galore, and plenty of warm places to sleep and nap. Animals that died sick or old are restored to their prime years and imbued with perfect health. They all play and frolic until their owner on Earth dies too. When that happens, the pet senses that a human they have been missing is close. The pet grows wings and knows to approach this second Rainbow Bridge to be reunited." She nodded toward the bridge as the man moved off, dog at his side. "It's your turn now, Grace."

I moved to the foot of the Rainbow Bridge. Just seconds after I raised my gaze, a silhouette came into view through the fog atop the rainbow. The form started to move down the bridge with an excited, playful gait. The white and brown basset hound that approached had enormous, uncontrollable ears and moderate-sized, shimmery blue wings that flapped incessantly, allowing the creature to only touch the ground every few steps.

"Droopy!" I raced forward with arms wide and fell to my knees as my dog bounded into my embrace. This creature had been my best friend all through childhood. He'd died three years ago, and it had taken my heart a long time to heal. Feeling how full it felt now, I wasn't sure if it ever truly had.

The drool that had built up in Droopy's jowls got all over me but I didn't care. I rubbed his loose-skinned face and hugged him tightly before scooping him up like a package. He wasn't light, but the weight felt right in my arms. He clung to me, his deep brown eyes full of trust, affection, and warmth.

"Are you happy?" Akari asked me.

"If you'd asked me that question earlier today, I would've told you I didn't think it was possible to ever be happy again. Now . . ." I kissed my dog's head. "Love has a funny way of destroying sadness."

"God wouldn't let pain exist without giving us a chance to counteract it," Akari said as we walked toward the brim of the cloud.

The sky was fading into sunset. Pinks, purples, and humpback whale blue tickled the edge of the afterlife. The luminescent paper lanterns and dazzling clouds above The First City were becoming more pronounced. Everything felt radiant, calm, and hopeful.

"Flying with the dog could be tricky," Akari said. "Let's travel by magic teleport instead." She took me by the elbow and her wristwatch flashed. A moment later, we stood in the middle of a suburban street lined with innumerable quaint houses. The city's skyscrapers glowed brilliantly in the distance.

"Welcome to your new home," Akari said. She gestured at an adorable cottage in front of us. It was powder blue with a triangular roof. A cute little chimney fashioned like a spire branched from the left side. An orange tree grew on the front lawn next to a swing set with two seats. And a simple brick path led to the red door.

I set a wriggling Droopy down and he clomped off to smell the lawn, ears dragging on the grass. He sniffed for a second, let out a big "*AAWWWHOO!*" howl, then went back to sniffing. I stared at the house—processing—before pivoting to Akari.

"Your file says you enjoy the excitement of city life, but love of your suburban childhood home is stronger," Akari explained. "You once told your sister your dream was to live in a cottage within short distance of the city. So, here you go."

I approached the house, turned the knob on my front door, and pushed inward.

The interior was fully furnished to my exact taste. *Seriously.* Things I hadn't even realized I favored or cared about, like the blonde wood floors and the stone fireplace with flickering candles on the mantle, set the cozy mood that I loved. Stepping into the living room, I was impressed by the flatscreen TV, gawked at the exposed wooden beams along the ceiling, and ran a finger along the blue-gray walls. Even those LED hanging light fixtures that I'd coveted on Etsy for a couple years had made their way here. They looked like storm clouds and were lit from within as if pulsing with thunder.

The most incredible decorations in the space, however, were silver-framed photographs of me with my family, friends, and Droopy. The real copies were on Earth in my former home, or on my phone, or scrapbooks I'd made. Seeing them here struck a vibration of emotion through my body like the deepest chord on a piano.

Entranced, I walked up to a particularly large frame on the wall featuring the four of us—my mother, father, older sister Gaby, and me. It was a vacation photo from last year. Gaby wore sunglasses; my mother, a floppy hat. I remembered that moment, all of us alive and together. Seeing it felt . . .

In reflex I reached for my chest. My fingernails clawed at my shirt over where my heart resided.

How could a person hold such fear, anger, and sorrow in the face of so much wonder, opportunity, and goodness? How was it possible to have your old life feel so close but know you could never go back? How was anyone able to make someplace paradise if loss couldn't be unwritten and would forever be a part of your soul?

I took a breath and steadied. Still not the time to cry.

Droopy clip-clopped inside and immediately nestled in a plush, crème colored dog bed near the fireplace. That's when I noticed a gift basket set upon the coffee table across from my puffy white couch. I approached it with Akari shadowing my footsteps.

"Your Welcome Kit," she announced as she watched me unwrap it. Once I had, she reached in and pulled out an ivory watch identical to hers.

"We don't have cell phones in Heaven—I feel like the reasons for that are self-explanatory—but we do have what people on Earth may compare to a smart watch. We call it a Soul Pulse. It works as a phone in terms of calls and texts, and it grants you admission to different parts of Heaven. Yours allows access to Angel Tower and the Guardian Angel floor for instance. Above all, it is the keeper of Heaven's magical fringe benefits. Let me see your wrist."

I extended my arm and she latched on the watch. The second it clicked secure, I felt a tiny zap like I'd gotten shocked by static electricity. The charge visibly traveled up my arm, through my chest, and out my other arm. It made my organs feel tingly.

Akari held up my wrist and placed her palm over the watch face. Five icons appeared: a halo around a globe, a conch shell, a gold coin, a folder, and a glowing W.

"This is our version of the Internet, only without the dark side," Akari explained, pointing to the halo globe. "It can tell you about anything happening on Earth, Heaven, Middleground, or Hell that's public knowledge. The conch is your communication icon. The coin will keep track of your miracle balance. The folder is for your job-related files. The last icon is our version of an app store."

She pressed the W on my watch screen and then a sparkly W the size of a grapefruit floated six inches above my wrist. "Welcome to Wonder," announced an automated female voice. "Currently available for download: 8,347 apps."

A menu of icons representing different types of apps popped up. My eyebrows raised. I could spend a solid month scrolling through that.

"This is where Heaven gets even more enjoyable," Akari said with a reserved smile.

It seemed I could attach the word reserved to almost every way she spoke and behaved. There'd been a few cracks in that during the day—moments of sympathy, moderate grins at my jokes, her passion about animals—but overall she was taking her role as a professional seriously. I wondered if she was putting on that face for my sake or hers though. Personally, I could've used a bit more emotion from my guide during this *incredibly emotional* time.

Akari began clicking icons for me. "To start with, you'll want Dang, That Sounds Good, which makes any food or beverage you desire; Fam&Friend Flix, which allows you to view what the people you care about are doing in real time on Earth; and Traffic is 4 Suckers." The trio of icons she'd pressed immediately started downloading. She powered down my watch by placing her palm over it again.

"You'll note how my watch was flashing throughout the day. Soul Pulses are uniquely connected to our souls; hence the energy link you saw and felt a moment ago when I latched yours on. Any downloaded app on here is tuned into you. All you have to do is think what you want, and *feel* what you want—and it will be so. That's as best as I can explain it. It'll make more sense when you try."

I blinked, totally stunned, staring at my new Soul Pulse. It wasn't *comparable* to a smart watch; it kicked the smart watch in the keister. I wondered if Steve Jobs was in Heaven and had a say in its design. If so, I bet he was out there somewhere wearing a white turtleneck.

Akari reached into my gift basket again. There were two other items in there: a dainty fern in a small pink planter shaped like a long-neck dinosaur, and a remote. She grabbed the control and turned on the TV. "Heaven has a bunch of its own channels, which you can browse on the guide. We also have a pair of video libraries synced to Earth and your tastes." She gestured at two icons on the screen. I read their names aloud.

"*Your Favorite Shows* and *Stuff You Haven't Seen, But Will Love.* Hm . . . neat."

"Lastly, we have Memory Prime." Akari gestured to the other option on screen. "This will let you rewatch moments from your life. Everything is on-demand and controlled with this remote."

"Like streaming services," I commented.

"Sort of." Akari huffed, minor amusement seeping through. "Actually, there's an ongoing debate in the Afterlife Assignments Bureau about whether or not the creators of streaming services should go up or down when they die. They have a live council meeting about it every Thursday morning on Heaven's local access channel. You should check it out some time if you want a giggle."

She powered off the TV.

I picked up the dinosaur planter, turning it over in my hands. "Let me guess, this is some sort of magical plant that will provide the freshest air I've ever inhaled?"

Akari scrunched her nose. "That's just a fern. It's polite to gift a person a plant when they move into a new home."

My brain fizzled. "Oh. Thank you."

I stared blankly at the planter for a long moment.

"I know this has been *a big* day, Grace," Akari said. "You're feeling overwhelmed, I'm sure, so let's regroup tomorrow."

"I still have so many questions."

"Another time. We have a solid chunk of eternity ahead of us, after all."

"Right . . ."

"Meet me in my office at Angel Tower at nine o'clock tomorrow morning." She turned toward the door.

"But I don't have wings," I replied, setting the planter down and pursuing her. "How am I supposed to get there?"

"That third app I downloaded for you," she replied, pivoting. "Remember how I said that all versions of Heaven share a few commonalities? One thing that all humans hate, which no part of Heaven will ever have, is street traffic. We don't use vehicles to get around. It's either magical teleportation or wings."

Akari tilted her chin at my watch. "With that app, you can think of any place in Heaven you know the location of and you'll be there. Instantly. Any place you don't know you can look up first with a search app."

"This really is Heaven. I'm never going to be late again."

My mentor opened the door, letting the night in. We stood silently for a few seconds. In that lull, I felt heaviness in my soul again. Deep and consuming like the dark sky.

Akari must've sensed it because she wavered from her professionalism enough to show real warmth for the first time, putting her hand on my shoulder. "Everything will be okay, Grace. Just take a deep breath."

For a moment, I really believed her.

She smiled at me softly and then drew the gesture back as quickly as she'd extended it. I stayed in the doorway and watched Akari walk down the brick path. The evening was coming in strong. So many stars gleamed in the sky.

Had God added more since the last time I saw the night?

When Akari reached the sidewalk, her form glowed. Her glorious wings and shimmering halo appeared. They shone so much brighter post twilight. Before taking off, she turned back to me. "By the way, *everything* about that cottage is designed to make it your perfect place. So if you want some of your 'special private time,' press the button under your fireplace mantle. Don't worry. It's programmed to leave you and Droopy alone."

"What?"

She winked and launched into the air.

I jogged over the brick path to the street, staring up at the sky as Akari's wings reached the heavens above Heaven. I spun around slowly, admiring the beauty. The sky was so clear, crisp, and electrifying—only enhanced in enchantment by the luminescent clouds and romantic lanterns floating over The First City, twinkling in the distance.

Suddenly, that magical hiccup occurred again. Everything shone with soft golden light, beginning from the ground and quickly rising through every non-human thing it could touch. I watched the light move past Angel Tower, ending with a spark as bright as the stars.

I'd have to ask Akari what that was when I wasn't distracted by a million other pressing questions.

I returned inside and closed the door then paused, noticing an idiosyncrasy.

"No lock," I thought aloud.

I supposed it made sense. Heaven wouldn't need locks. Everyone up here was good. No crime. No bad guys. No worries. That would also take a minute to get used to.

I meandered back into my perfect living room.

How many times had I thought, heard, and used the adjective *perfect* today? Probably too high a number to guess at.

Droopy snored on his fluffy bed. I smiled fondly at him and went to the fireplace mantle. Running my hand along the bottom with curiosity, I found a small button and pressed it. Flickering light lit up my peripherals and I turned to see a swirling portal—like a white black hole—appear in the center of my living room floor. It started to suck away my furniture as the lights dimmed.

My smile reemerged.

DYING DOESN'T GET YOU
OUT OF GYM CLASS

"Ninety-Eight is late."
An angel directly to my left caught me coming through the GA balcony doors. Like everyone in the bustling command center, he wore a smart white ensemble. This guy was as tall as a college basketball player, with thin hair and pale blue eyes. His comment had been loud enough that a number of angels pivoted at their desks to look my way.

I felt my cheeks turn hot with embarrassment and was about to offer some lame excuse when he put an arm around my shoulder and ushered me forward. "Don't worry about it. Even Heaven has an adjustment period. Let's get you to Akari."

He strode away, motioning for me to come with him. I struggled to keep up with his lengthy gait; my stomach swirled with nerves. I hadn't been this on edge since my first day of high school. Fresh starts were great, but difficult when you weren't sure where or *how* to start.

"I'm Gentry, by the way. Gentry Stein," said my guiding angel, extending his hand in greeting as we walked. "I'm a Senior Officer of the Guardian Angel IDS."

I shook his hand. "What's the IDS?"

"Immediate Deployment Squad. There are several divisions within the Guardian Angel department. You'll get the lowdown on your tour with the rest of your class."

"I'm in a class?"

Akari emerged from her office, raising her wrist to check her watch but stopping when she saw me coming. "I thought you were never going to be late again?"

"The alarm clock in my room was . . . jarring," I responded.

Gentry laughed and elbowed Akari like it was an inside joke between old friends. My mentor only mildly quirked a lip.

"Thanks for getting her to me, Gentry," she said.

"No problem." Gentry rubbed the back of his nicek. "Hey, maybe later we can meet for lunch or something? It's been such a long time and I'm really glad you're back on duty."

"Perhaps when things calm down, Gentry." Akari gave me an awkward glance before returning his gaze. "We have to run now." She grabbed my elbow and started leading me away.

"Good luck, Ninety-Eight," Gentry called.

"Thank you!" I waved back.

My mentor escorted me to a bank of cylindrical glass elevators. "Have you been taking some time off?" I asked as we stepped into a lift. The panel inside easily had three times the numbered buttons as the elevators at the Empire State Building. Akari selected a floor and we started descending through Angel Tower.

"I requested a leave of absence a while back," she replied brusquely.

"Why?"

The elevator dinged and we stepped into a small lobby. Akari strode to a set of silver double doors and pushed them open without answering. Perhaps she knew that the setting beyond would call my attention away from following up on my question.

It was a gym. Not the worn high school kind that smelled of sweaty shorts and melting makeup. This place was sleek and spotless with air as crisp as freshly fallen snow.

Obstacle course materials, mats, and shimmering gymnast equipment were scattered throughout. The angels utilizing the area were harnessing their halos and wings in various forms of advanced combat and skills training. Several flicked their halos like discuses at hanging targets—cutting the ropes they dangled from as if the halos were razor-sharp blades. Others created portals and fired beams of energy at objectives. One angel flew through a series of large hoops hanging from the far away ceiling, body lithe as he adjusted to soar through their centers. Above him, the tiled ceiling was all white except for a message set in gold:

THE ASSIGNMENT COMES FIRST

"This is our training center," Akari said. My eyes drifted back to our level and she glanced sideways, indicating for me to look. "Now I'd like you to meet your training class."

Akari motioned at four people walking toward us—three boys and a small girl. "There are several sectors of the Guardian Angel department," she explained as they drew near. "You and your two GA classmates are new recruits for Long-Term Assignments. That means each of you will protect and focus your energy on one person on Earth at a time."

The group joined us and Akari proceeded with introductions. "Everyone, this is Grace Cariño Reyes Cardiff. For the two of you who are new, I am her mentor Akari Brown. Grace, this is Leo Wells and his mentor Anahita Ayad."

Leo touched a spot on the bridge of his nose with his index finger then stuck out his hand, which I shook. He was roughly my height with a bashful smile and cobalt eyes pronounced by dark eyebrows and fair skin. Most notably, he seemed a few years younger than me. That was . . . tragic. Here I was, feeling cheated for tapping out on life at seventeen. Did this kid even have wisdom teeth?

His mentor Anahita was even younger. Maybe ten, eleven?

"Pleasure to meet you," she said. "Call me Ana." The young girl looked of Middle Eastern descent. She was cute with long eyelashes, deep dimples, and tousled chocolate hair. Her face was heart-shaped, like the gold locket around her neck. Overall, she seemed sweet and spunky, yet there was a mystifying seriousness to her dark eyes that made her look much older and wiser.

"And this is Monkonjae Seoul and his mentor Deckland Cruz," Akari continued. I pivoted and got goldfish eyes—big and astounded.

Monkonjae extended his hand. He was in the neighborhood of my age—perhaps a year or two older. His dark skin seemed to glow with warmth, and the brown of his eyes smoldered, drawing me in like freshly brewed coffee. My mind went mystifyingly blank. I looked up to meet the gaze of the 6'1" angel.

"Oh my God, you're attractive."

Everyone stared at me as a silent beat ensued. I blinked in a stupor; then self-awareness electrified my brain and my eyes widened even further. "Did I just say that out loud?"

Monkonjae nodded.

My face got hot and I felt like shrinking into my own skin. I pivoted toward Akari with a gulp. "Well, Heaven is ruined for me. You can go ahead and send me downstairs now."

"It's fine," Monkonjae said quickly, graciously. "You actually made this introduction easier for me. I was nervous about meeting the great Ninety-Eight that everyone's been talking about. I figured whatever words I chose first would probably make me look like a dope. Now—"

"Now I look like a dope," I finished.

"You know what, I think it's awesome," Deckland said, trying to add an upbeat tone to the terribly awkward atmosphere. He was in Akari's late-twenties age group with elaborate tattoos on his muscular arms—visible thanks to his white sleeveless shirt.

He patted me on the shoulder. "You're leaning into Heaven's honesty filter out the gate. Most people are reluctant about that. The file did say you were special."

"That's me. Special . . ." I said uneasily. I flicked my gaze to Akari. "Just so we're clear, does everyone know about everyone in Heaven, or is it just me people are super aware of?"

Akari grimaced slightly. "In the sense you're asking about, it's just you. I let Ana and Deckland have a glimpse at your file because we'll be training together and I could use their input. But your Ninety-Eight status is big news in general, so I would try to get used to the attention. A *lot* of people know you're here."

"Actually, *everyone* knows you're here," Deckland corrected.

"Fantastic," I muttered.

"Well then," Ana chimed in. "Now that introductions are out of the way, we better get started with basic training. There's a ton to learn before lunch. Especially considering that Ninety-Eight here has to leave tomorrow."

"What's that?" I perked up.

Akari rubbed a hand over her eyes. "I hadn't broken the news to her yet, Ana."

"Oh, sorry," she replied with a grimace.

I frowned at the two of them. "Will someone tell me something please."

"We usually like to train our guardians for at least a solid month before they return to Earth," Deckland explained. "But since your assignment is a kid in high school, and his new semester starts tomorrow, the boss thinks it would be best if you begin classes with him. Less conspicuous that way."

I spun on Akari. "You're sending me back to Earth *tomorrow*? Why didn't you tell me this sooner?"

"I was trying to ease you in."

"Like a lobster into a pot of water yet to boil," I retorted.

"You'll just be on Earth during the day for now," Akari said, trying to calm me. "You'll come back here at night and on weekends to continue training with Monkonjae and Leo."

I huffed. Now I knew why Akari said being a Guardian Angel helped her move on in the afterlife. When you were being thrown into the fray with a cosmically important new job and practically no time to prepare, there wasn't much opportunity to mope. Sadness always rode in back when panic and self-preservation entered the mix.

With a deep breath I did the only thing I could do: I nodded and forced myself to deal with the situation. "Okay."

"Okay?" Akari clarified.

"Okay!" Ana declared, pumping her fist in the air. "Back to basic training then—recruits, follow me." She led us to the back of the gym where the wall was taken up by a large mirror. I met Monkonjae's eyes in the reflection. He smiled at me and I darted my gaze down, swaying awkwardly on my feet.

Nope. Nothing to see here. Just a girl minding her own business and not staring at the impeccably hot guy five feet away.

"The halo is the most important tool in your Guardian Angel arsenal," Ana said, pacing in front of us like a general. "It has defensive and offensive functions for protecting you and your assignment. Your first lesson is conjuring the halo. Like the Soul Pulses on your wrists, bringing forth your halo and activating its abilities is about thinking and more importantly *feeling* the action with your soul. Focus on what you want with all of yourself. You can do this vocally or telepathically. Observe."

Ana paused in front of us. "Halo."

A marvelous glowing ring of gold formed a few inches over her head. The task looked easy enough.

"Now you try," she said.

I glanced at Akari. She gave me the thumbs up, and I redirected my gaze to the mirror. Leo had his eyes closed—thinking hard. After a few flickers, his halo came into view. Monkonjae stared at himself in the mirror with a stern expression then—*SHMING!*—the gold ring shone over his head too.

Deep breath, Grace.

"Halo."

Nothing happened.

"You need to *feel* the angelic power," Akari suggested.

"And for those of us who didn't have 'angelic power' on any vocab tests in school, what does that mean exactly?" I asked.

"Focus on that which makes you feel most alive," Deckland replied.

"But I'm dead."

"Your soul isn't. Souls never die; they just change forms or move on to other planes of existence. So think, Grace. What makes your soul feel alive?"

I took a moment then refocused on myself in the mirror. I locked eyes with that reflection as my heart filled with vitality. *Halo.*

"Yipes!" Ana exclaimed.

My halo flared into existence above my head so brightly that it would've shamed a lighthouse beacon. My classmates and mentors had to shield their eyes.

After the initial effect, the halo normalized, radiating the same gleam as the others.

Leo turned to me. "Geez, what were you thinking about?"

I gave him a smile. "I'll tell you when I know you better."

"Well, Grace, good show," Ana said. "I guess I know who is going to be top of the class. Come on, kiddies, let's move on. Who's ready for a crazy-awesome training montage?"

———————

So here's the thing. I wasn't the kind of kid who was acing eight honors classes and spent her weekends studying nonstop with nary a movie on the to-do list. But I *was* smart. Whereas I shied away in other areas of life, I was used to feeling confident in a class setting, impressing teachers, and assisting other kids who needed help to keep up.

After my halo performance, I had hoped I could utilize these skills to shine at Guardian Angel training and get the others to forget about my slip with Monkonjae. Between the halo trick and the Ninety-Eight reputation preceding me, everyone already expected me to be amazing and I planned to fulfill that expectation.

Sadly, I proved them all wrong.

"Grace, just throw it like a frisbee."

"Grace, you have to concentrate on the consequence of the action, not only the action."

"Grace, it's a small movement; you're not meant to dislocate a shoulder."

My crazy-awesome training montage ended up being a medley of epic flops, frustrations, and frisbee fails.

I released an aggravated breath and tried again, making my halo reappear over my head. We'd been working on one task— treating the halo like a magically sharp discus. I simply had to grab the thing from my head, aim, and throw. Simple.

Or so it seemed.

Across the room, Monkonjae gripped his halo and flung it with a purposeful flick of his wrist. As it left his hand, the ring changed into a solid glowing discus that jettisoned across the space and sliced through a metal chain holding up one of the punching bags. The bag fell. The halo boomeranged back to Monkonjae's waiting hand.

My hotter-than-Hell classmate placed the halo back over his

head. Deckland patted Monkonjae on the back proudly and his watch glowed. Magic shimmered around the punching bag and it returned to its initial position.

I took another breath and gave myself a small pep talk.

Come on, Grace. If Sailor Moon can do this, you can do this.

I took the halo in hand and flicked my wrist to release it. It transformed into a solid disc, but the aim went nuts the moment it departed my fingers. Despite starting off as a straight shot, my halo veered left and then abruptly careened right.

"Hit the deck!" Ana yanked Leo to the ground by the collar. My halo sped by mere inches above them before swerving off and colliding with a punching bag—not cutting or slicing it; just anticlimactically getting stuck.

I clenched my fists and focused, which made the halo vanish and reappear over my head.

Great. So far, the only part of being a Guardian Angel I am good at is making a magic accessory appear.

I started to reach for it again, but Akari touched my arm. "I think that's enough for now. Why don't we break for lunch?"

"You just don't want me to embarrass myself any further."

"It's your first day, Grace. There's no need to be embarrassed."

"All these people expect me to be some epic angel of pure goodness." I crossed my arms over my chest. "I got this high ranking and I look like a fool."

"This isn't *The Hunger Games*, Grace. No one around here is going to come at you because you have a high ranking or make you prove that you deserve it. On this turf, we're all good people. In Angel Tower we are the *best* people. You are safe here. As long as you're in this building, there is literally no chance of anyone judging you, making fun of you, or making you feel bad about yourself."

I studied Akari. "That's so . . ."

"Wonderful?" Akari suggested.

"Different," I replied. "I am not sure there is a single place on Earth where that's true one hundred percent of the time. People kind of have a way of making the world Hell for other people."

"Ain't that the truth," Deckland said as he and the others joined us. "Ana, Akari, and I have a meeting to attend," he continued. "We'll drop you guys off at the Angel Tower cafeteria and then come back to get you in an hour for your tour of the department. Then more training, individual meetings with us, and a surprise dinner planned for each of you."

"It's not much of a surprise if you're telling us about it," Leo pointed out.

"Or is it more of a surprise because you already see it coming?" Ana countered, her eyes sparkling mysteriously. "Let's go." She turned and our mentors began to follow her out of the gym.

Leo pressed that same spot on the bridge of his nose and frowned. "I don't think that makes sense."

I leaned closer to him. "Does any of this make sense?"

We shared an elevator down forty floors to Angel Tower's bustling cafeteria. It was an impressive dining hall featuring a grand domed ceiling and a school-bus-sized chandelier adorned with glittering strands of peridots. All the round tables in the room were made of a shimmery, moss green marble whereas the chairs were basic, unassuming white wood. Or so it first appeared.

When our mentors motioned for us to sit, each of our chairs transformed. Leo's became a black desk chair with wheels and a navy cushion. Monkonjae's changed into a comfy seat that one might see in a magazine editor's office. Mine morphed into a straight-backed armchair woven from natural fiber—identical to the chairs I had in my backyard on Earth.

"Whatever seat you choose in the Angel Tower cafeteria is always your preferred seat," Akari enlightened as I nestled in. "You can use your Soul Pulse powers to get food, or if you don't have anything specific in mind for lunch, the Infi-Buffet is that way. I think today's featured cuisine is Japanese."

"Yep. That's where I'm going." Leo got up quickly, causing his seat to revert back. "I've had *bupkis* to eat all day, and I smell tempura and sukiyaki. Be back shortly." He hustled off, scratching the back of his head as he went.

"Leo watched a lot of TV cooking competitions on Earth and

got really into all kinds of cuisine," Ana explained. "He didn't have a lot of opportunity to act on that interest, but he has the soul of a super foodie."

Something he and I can bond over, I suppose.

"Anyway, see you guys in a bit," Deckland said enthusiastically. "Be good."

"Like we have a choice," I jested.

He laughed and our mentors departed. Monkonjae and I sat in silence for a moment. When I glanced at him anew, his eyes were closed. Then a flash lit up the table in front of him and a steaming plate of shrimp étouffée and a glass of ice water appeared. He gave the meal a once-over.

"Amazing. It looks exactly like my favorite dish back home." He picked up a fork that'd also appeared, and took a bite of his food. "Tastes like it too." He pivoted to me. "Do you have the Dang, That Sounds Good app downloaded?"

I nodded. "Yes, but I haven't tried it yet." I glanced at the accessory on my wrist. Then I closed my eyes and concentrated. I sensed a bright flash and opened my eyes. A big bowl of lobster macaroni and cheese with a glass of nonfat milk had materialized.

"Sweet."

We exchanged a smile, but inevitably my natural awkwardness got the better of me. Monkonjae and I ate quietly for a minute. I stole a couple of quick glances at him when he was distracted by his delectable stew dish.

Say something to him, my subconscious urged.

I can't.

You can.

"So, um, Monkonjae," I tried. "Where are you from?"

He lowered his fork. "Well, I was born in Liberia, but when I was six my parents immigrated to France. We lived there for about five years then when I turned twelve, we moved to America—New Orleans. What about you?"

"Well, I was born in Greenville, South Carolina. When I was ten, we moved to *Spartanburg*, South Carolina. Then when I turned twelve, my family moved to a slightly nicer street in Spartanburg, South Carolina. So you and I are basically the same person."

I gave him a smirk and he laughed good-naturedly.

Monkonjae swallowed another bite of his food then alluded to the whole of the place. "So how are you adjusting to all this?"

My mouth twitched and suddenly I felt queasy, like my macaroni had morphed into trout pudding. "I died less than two days ago and was just told I have to go and save some random person on Earth starting tomorrow. So things aren't great . . ."

I stabbed a noodle, emotion tensing my hand. "When Akari told me yesterday about the general role of a Guardian Angel, I was already wary. Add in the hastiness of beginning the job so quickly, and I guess you could say I am adjusting as best I can. Heaven is a lot to handle." I took a bite of my food and swallowed roughly, deciding to change the subject to a more upbeat trajectory. "I did get my dog back, so at least there's that. Do you have a pet up here?"

"Yes and no. I had a cat that died a couple years ago, but we haven't reconnected yet."

"Let me guess—most cats are in the bad place?"

"No, there's a cat Heaven. But apparently most cats don't care if their owners live or die, so they don't meet you at a Rainbow Bridge for some grand reunion. They show up if they feel like it."

"That checks out." I took a sip of milk.

After another lull, curiosity outflanked my restraint.

"If you don't mind me asking . . . how did you die, Monkonjae?"

His expression turned sad. "Saving someone, actually. It was in the middle of my first year at university, and I was walking home after a late class. I saw some guys following a girl and I followed them. They tried to attack her in an alley. I went to help her. She got away, but one of the guys got me with a knife and . . ."

A terrible pause passed.

"I'm sorry I asked," I said eventually.

"Don't be. You're the first person who has. Despite the shared reason we're all here, most people in Heaven don't like to talk about death. It dampens the mood, I guess." He gave me an understanding look. "Do you want to tell me how you died?"

"Car accident," I replied. "Nothing quite so noble." I glanced around the room, taking in the demographics. "I wonder how many people here died because of accidents or murd—" I glanced at him. "Having their lives taken from them," I corrected. "Most people in our department seem pretty young."

"Deckland told me it's because goodness is harder to hold onto the more you age. Cynicism, pain, and the general harshness of life tend to whittle away at souls. It's rare for adults to be over 90% good. The likelihood decreases with every birthday."

"I suppose that makes sense. Though it's sad."

"What's sad?" Leo asked as he sat down with a tray loaded with tempura and enough sushi to fuel a Japanese swim team.

"Life," I said.

He shrugged. "Only if you let it. Life is like a plate at a buffet." He nodded to his platter as he picked up his chopsticks. "It's as full as you want it to be."

I stared at him a moment then nodded. "I like you, Leo."

"Now I know I'm in Heaven," he joked. "That's the first time a cute girl has ever told me that."

I blinked. "Sorry?"

"You're a looker, Grace Cardiff. I mean just take a gander at that round *punim*." He gestured toward my face. "Adorable. Like if a Disney princess had a healthy appetite."

He put a big slice of raw salmon in his mouth, and it took him several chews before he noticed my mouth ajar in stupor.

"*What?*" he said through his mouthful. "I can't be super awkwardly honest too?"

"Welcome to the Immediate Deployment Squad, kids," Gentry said as he guided our group around the outermost ring of the room. "Watch the magic for yourselves. Shouldn't be more than a half minute before the next call to action."

I wasn't sure what he was talking about, but I did know that "magical" was only one of the many magnificent adjectives I would use to describe this place. The latest stop on our GA tour had me second-guessing if we were still in Angel Tower or had somehow been transported to a really strange secret intelligence agency.

The entire level of Angel Tower dedicated to the IDS was

contained within one gigantic room. Its centerpiece was an epic series of eight tubes that began from a common base then splayed up in different directions toward the ceiling like human-sized hamster cage tubing. Rings of desks filled the rest of the room, each equipped with five screens that angels in suits monitored vigilantly. Beside each desk sat a stool for a second angel dressed in athletic attire—white zip-up jackets, running shorts, tracksuits, etc. All angels wore a headset.

I was about to ask Gentry several questions when a blaring red light like a police car signal went off at a desk across the room.

The moment the siren sounded, the desk's second angel leapt from her stool and raced for a tube that lit up. As she moved, her halo appeared. A panel in the tube's side slid open. When she bounded in, a pair of silvery wings shimmered into existence behind her, straps attaching the feathers to her shoulders like a backpack.

The tube snapped shut and a magic force sucked her up. I thought for a second she was going to smash into the top of the room, but a glowing light formed where the tube connected to the ceiling and she phased out of sight. Her counterpart angel—still seated at the desk—typed speedily while he spoke into his headset.

Not five seconds later the process repeated with a pair of angels seated right in front of us. This runner angel went for a different tube. I rose on my tiptoes to peer at the desk angel's monitors as his partner bolted. I heard him say something about miles per hour, and street intersections, and wind velocity. Maps, targeting systems, and street views lit up his screens. A countdown clock was ticking away in neon numbers on his upper right monitor.

Then I saw it. On the top left monitor, a semi-truck ran a red light. The screen below showed a view of a navy sedan driving along a forest-lined road. My eyes darted between the various vantage points and I realized what was about to happen.

"Watch out!" I blurted. It was pointless, as the inbound victim couldn't hear me, but my chest was too seized with panic to accept that reasoning.

The truck was seconds from T-boning the sedan when suddenly a blinding light appeared between them. The angel that'd just left had sandwiched herself where the vehicles would have impacted and projected an energy shield that acted as a buffer. As a result, instead of getting demolished, the sedan spun out into the street—a bit dented, but the driver was okay. Fascinatingly, though I watched this happen on one monitor, the screen beside it showed the exact same scene minus the angelic being. On there it looked like the truck had simply bumped the car into the intersection without destroying it by pure luck.

"You okay?" Akari whispered to me.

I nodded, though I wasn't sure.

Gentry pivoted toward us. "In your GA sector, half your staff is in the field with one Guardian Angel protecting a single important individual for years, while the rest of the workforce monitors the world around those selected humans—keeping track of things that could influence them, scrutinizing choices, exploring ripple effects. You guys are all about the long game. In this sector, we operate on pins and needles. We monitor *everyone*. Everywhere and all the time. The IDS scans the globe and the zillions of things happening each millisecond in search of imminent danger that one of our angels can prevent."

"That's incredible," Leo marveled.

"It's also stressful," Ana replied. "The IDS is the most demanding job in the afterlife. Our work in Long-Term GA Assignments has higher stakes because the humans we look after can make a significant impact on the world, but all lives matter, and in this department, angels have the chance to save any number of them."

"The problem is that there are over seven billion people in the world across seven continents," Gentry explained. He gestured at the grand scale of the operation. "We can't save everyone because there is just too much to keep track of."

Our guide sighed. It was strange to see such melancholy in the eyes of an angel, especially one who—until now—seemed to have it so together.

Maybe no matter how in control or naturally high-spirited you were, you couldn't completely escape the darkness.

"When bad things happen, people of faith wonder why they happened—how God could *let* them happen," our host continued. "The fact is, God and the angels do everything we can to prevent bad things, but we don't always find you in time, or know they're about to occur. At the end of the day, it's timing and luck; we get to some people while others slip through the cracks. Our GAs in this department go through years of extensive psychological prep before they can serve so they can learn to deal with the losses. Because believe me, we're at risk to take them as hard as the people on Earth do. The key thing to remember is that while we can't save everyone, we can save *some* people. That alone is plenty of reason to keep trying. Saving even *one* person is enough motivation."

A *DING!* went off in a side extension of the room with a glass wall overlooking the command center. The angel who had just prevented the fatal accident reappeared. She used the connecting door to reenter our space. Upon doing so she removed her strapped-on wings, hanging them on a hook next to the door. A moment later they sparkled to vanishing and the angel resumed her seat beside her partner.

"Those are the loaner wings I was telling you about," Akari whispered to me.

Three more sirens went off.

"Thanks for having us, Gentry," Akari said. "We'll get out of your hair now. Looks like a busy day. Come on, everyone."

The six of us exited the high-tension room and continued with our tour, which spanned several more floors.

"And here we have our Theoreticals Department," Deckland said as we journeyed through a corridor with glass windows that looked into various rooms. "Angels in this sector hash out potential scenarios based on upcoming decisions in our assignments' lives."

One room had two angels writing complex equations on chalkboards. In another, angels in silvery hazmat suits went in and out of pulsing portals. A third housed angels working over foaming cauldrons like they were witches in a classic Halloween movie.

Our group loaded into another glass elevator. Though hundreds of numbered buttons populated the inner panel, only a few had actual floor titles.

Ana pushed the up arrow and a rectangular button near the bottom labeled *TOUR MODE*. The lift began to rise at a slow rate—the names of the floors illuminating at the top of the elevator as we passed them. Ana narrated while we ascended.

"This is our GA Records Department, where you'll find info on every GA case ever taken on. Then comes the Review Board," we went by a new level, "for GAs in the field to discuss progress and plans for our assignments. Next is the Impending Interference floor." Another department went by. "When GAs foresee high impact events coming and need help, they can assemble a team to take coordinated action. After that there's the Counterthreat Department; we'll come back to that later." The floor flew by. "Then our GA private library where you can research tactics for guiding assignments, synergy options with different angels in Heaven, and so on. Lastly we have our museum."

Ana hit the stop button. The elevator door slid open.

I stepped out first. The floor was solid amber and branched into three paths. The left led to an arched entryway with a plaque that read *Fully Realized*, the middle archway was labeled *Gone Too Soon*, and the final hall was simply titled *Lost*. Each entrance was concealed by silky mustard curtains with tangerine tassels, and featured a podium out front with a glowing white orb mounted on top like an enchanted volleyball.

Deckland motioned us to the left and we stopped in front of the *Fully Realized* podium.

"These halls stretch on for a *really* long time, but if you just want to see one specific exhibit, all you have to do is speak the name of the person you're looking for, or the angel who protected them. There is also a shuffle function if you don't have a preference and want to learn about someone random. Watch." He put his hand on the white sphere. "Podium: Show me one of Akari Brown's assignments."

"Deckland, I don't think—" My mentor's protest came too late.

"Akari Brown has twelve fully realized GA cases," said an automated voice, the sphere blinking in sync with every syllable.

"Podium: Shuffle Mode of those cases," Deckland responded.

A shimmery flash went off behind the curtains. Deckland pulled back the drapes and waved for us to proceed. The room beyond had dark red carpet, regal white columns, and gold molding. It held all sorts of historical memorabilia—statues, paintings, documents in glass cases. At the entrance was a large marble bust. I didn't need to read the nameplate to recognize the man it depicted. His face was in plenty of history books.

"Winston Churchill," I said in awe. I spun around to Akari, who looked uncomfortable. "You were Winston Churchill's Guardian Angel?"

She gulped before responding. "He was my longest and most difficult assignment."

"Difficult?" Monkonjae repeated.

Akari rubbed her arm, reluctant to share.

"Yup," Deckland replied on her behalf. "This guy was one of the most important people to live in the twentieth century and he helped shape and save the course of humanity when Hitler tried to decimate it, but he was *SO* hard to keep alive. Go on, tell them, Akari." He nudged her encouragingly.

My mentor hesitated again, but finally acquiesced and sighed. "When Winston was in his twenties, he got captured during the Boer War. I had to help him escape a prisoner-of-war camp. Years later, he got hit by a car on a lecture tour in New York and almost died. He had a taste for cigars, fine alcohol, and fatty meats that should've ruined at least three major organs in his body and yet . . ."

"Yet somehow Akari kept calm and carried on, as the Brits say," Ana finished. "She was able to keep that wily fellow alive through adulthood and multiple terms as prime minister. He did everything his soul had the potential to do and that is why he is in the Fully Realized section of the museum."

Monkonjae and Leo wandered around the space with their mentors pointing out the historical significance of different objects. I stayed at Akari's side. My mentor's hands were on her hips as she absentmindedly glanced over the exhibit.

I tilted my head at her. "You were reluctant to answer Monkonjae. Are you not in the mood for questions?"

Akari flicked her gaze to me. "No. I just don't like talking about my past assignments." Her face darkened as she took in the exhibit again. Then she crossed her arms and addressed me in her normal professional manner. "I'm your mentor, Grace. One of my main jobs is to help you understand the afterlife. If you have questions about the GAs, Heaven, and so forth, fire away."

I shrugged. "All right then." I tipped my chin at Winston's bust. "How many years were you assigned to him?"

"Over five decades. We actually became really great friends and still meet every Tuesday for breakfast."

"Are all assignments that long?" I asked, stunned.

She shook her head. "The individuals we're assigned to are all different. Souls are stable things, so from birth a lot of people are on our initial radar—individuals of interest, you might say. However, *people* are not stable, so a soul's ability to impact the world changes."

"Aren't souls and people the same thing?"

"Not at all. The soul is your core—your inherent personality, skills, intelligence, and strength. How those things develop is dependent on outer influences—family, friends, media, teachers, enemies, environment, even chance. You've heard of the nature vs. nurture argument? Well, the truth is that both matter. Think of your soul or nature as a ball of clay. The nurture is the hands that shape you. So while nature may put you on the GA radar, we monitor the nurture until we can tell whether or not your final shape will be someone with the potential to achieve greatness and have positive impact on Earth on a grand scale. If you're recognized as such, our department assigns a Guardian Angel to protect you in a hands-on way until you can reach your peak—until your potential is fully realized. That could be in your twenties, forties, even your sixties. Again, each assignment is different. Most of my cases have lasted five to ten years, but some have been very short. Winston was my longest by far because his value became apparent to the GAs early on in his life and he had a lot to accomplish throughout it."

I bit my lip in thought.

Akari gave me a sideways glance. "You're quiet. Don't tell me you're out of questions."

"Actually, I have so many I'm having trouble deciding which to ask next."

"Of course you are." She rubbed her temple. "You know what, on second thought do me a favor. While I am committed to being there for you, Grace, my lunch meeting today was a bit draining. So if you could just pick two more questions for now and give me some time to regroup before your next batch, that would be great."

I nodded, then took a moment to decide what thoughts were pressing most heavily on my brain. "Okay, number one: We didn't pass any kind of assignments department on our tour. Where are the angels who decide which people are on your radar and who is deemed worthy of a Guardian Angel?"

"The department for that isn't on our tour because the information is so delicate," Akari explained. "We're talking fabric of the universe. The angels who work in that sector deal directly with God and are located on what you might call a hidden floor. I've only been there twice."

That spurred at least a dozen new questions, but I restrained myself and stayed the course. "Second question. The sphere out front said you had twelve cases that'd been fully realized. Your office door had the numbers 12:1. What's the one?"

Akari's expression soured *significantly*, also emanating hints of sadness and surprise. Maybe some resentment at me for having broached the subject . . .

"What did you say to Leo earlier? I'll tell you when I know you better."

"But—"

"Let's go, team!" Akari called to the rest of our group. She turned to exit the room and pushed past the silk curtains.

When the five of us followed her out, we found my mentor standing by the elevator. She addressed Deckland and Ana. "You two mind finishing the tour without me? I have some paperwork to complete in my office." She slumped slightly. "And I just—"

"Yeah, we understand," Deckland interceded, a depth of caring and empathy in his tone I didn't understand. "Meet us in the training center later."

Akari nodded. The elevator arrived and she stepped on without looking at me. I'd clearly touched a nerve. A glob of guilt squirmed inside me as I watched her fall below the floor line as the lift sunk out of sight.

Typical, Grace. This woman is an angel and you literally caused her to flee. How are you 98% good?

Deckland headed back toward the archways, calling our attention to the one marked *Gone Too Soon*.

"Eyes over here, you three. This part of the museum pays tribute to great souls who accomplished many amazing things in their lives but died before they could do everything they had the potential to." He put his hand to the sphere. "Podium: Shuffle Mode. Show me someone who impacted culture."

A flash occurred behind the curtains, and we proceeded through to discover an exhibit dedicated to Freddie Mercury.

"I love Queen," Monkonjae said.

"Same," I seconded, delighted to have something in common with him.

"Freddie and the band produced amazing work that impacted a generation and will continue to influence people for the rest of time," Deckland explained. "He's one of the greatest artists in the history of rock music. Sadly, he died of AIDS in his midforties. With his talent—*his soul*—our department predicts that he could've released another six amazing albums. But he didn't get the chance."

We bowed our heads in silence for a moment—out of respect and also remorse. I hoped Mr. Mercury was out there rocking with the angels right now.

"The world is lesser for having been denied the full scope of what he, and the others honored in this part of the museum, had the potential to do," Ana said. "Vincent Van Gogh, Marie Curie, Abraham Lincoln—they achieved such amazing things.

Humanity is left to wonder what else such exceptional people could've accomplished with a little more time. We pay tribute to them here, for what they *did* do and who they were."

Our group spent a while longer in the exhibit before Deckland and Ana escorted us out to the final curtained corridor, the one entitled *Lost*. Leo's mentor placed her hand on the sphere.

"Podium: Wide View Mode."

After the familiar flash, we ducked around the curtains to enter a long hallway. The walls on both sides were decorated with one framed headshot after another. There were so many of them and they seemed to stretch on for infinity. I stepped closer. I didn't recognize any of the faces or the names engraved on plates beneath their frames.

"Who are they?" Leo asked, moving beside me and scratching his head.

"People who never got a chance to be," Ana said sadly.

"I don't understand," I replied.

Ana joined us and pointed at the portrait of the young Asian girl we stood in front of. "This is Ariel Woo," she said. "My friend Ronnie was her Guardian Angel. Ariel had the potential to cure cancer, but she died in a train crash last year."

The small angel shook her head dejectedly. "She was the nineteenth soul born with the ability to cure that disease. Right now, we have seven souls on Earth with the same potential—five on the GA's initial radar and two with active Guardian Angels already assigned. But they keep dying before they're able to achieve their breakthrough."

"By accident?" I asked, astounded.

"You *could* say that." Deckland huffed with vague annoyance, crossing his arms. Ana eyed him, then noticed the distress in Leo's expression as he stared at Ariel's picture. She put a kindly hand on her mentee's arm for an extended moment.

I wandered off to give them some space. Monkonjae accompanied me in the exploration. The enormity of what the hallway of portraits represented sunk in deeper with every step and every pair of eyes I locked with in those photos.

Deckland and Ana eventually migrated off to the side to discuss something in whispers. When I noticed Leo hadn't moved from Ariel's picture, I went over to him. "Hey, are you okay?"

"I'm *verklempt.*"

"Pardon?"

"Never mind." He shook his head.

"So all these people . . ." Monkonjae got his mentor's attention as he approached the front. "They were all supposed to do something as important as cure cancer but got killed before they could?"

His face was a marvel of shock and furrowed with pain. While you never wanted to see a handsome person in this much distress, it was nice to be reassured I was not the only one feeling overwhelmed.

"That's the gist of it," Deckland said with a sorrowful sigh. "Invent a clean form of energy, raise the consciousness of a nation, create art that inspires countless people, and so many other important acts of science, writing, revolution, government, music, and so on. All these people's lives mattered, of course, but had they reached their full potential they could've mattered on a grand scale by impacting humanity in really meaningful ways."

"There's so many of them," Leo said. The kid looked positively shook. "How many have there been? Lost souls, I mean."

"That answer won't help you, so I'm not going to give it," Ana replied frankly. "We don't want to scare you, but all mentors bring their new recruits here at the start of their GA journeys. Let this museum be a reminder of how important your jobs are, and how greatly your work can affect the world. You are the difference between a breakthrough in humanity and another picture on this wall . . ."

I gazed around as the expectations, the stakes, and the huge responsibility crushed my shoulders. Monkonjae and Leo did the same. We were a trio of kids who'd just been tasked with the fate of humanity. It was a lot.

"Now then," Ana said, clapping her hands together with an abrupt enthusiastic turn. "Who's ready for more halo training?"

Ugh, kill me.

Again.

4

FAMILY REUNION

"If it makes you feel any better, halos can't hurt mortals," Ana said reassuringly, patting me on the arm.

I harrumphed as I extinguished my magic headpiece. Thank God there were only a few people around at this late hour in the training center—less angels to witness my ineptitude. I had not improved since the morning, whereas Monkonjae's and Leo's skills had progressed rapidly. They made Sailor Moon and her throwing tiara look amateurish.

Why can't I do this?!

"How often does a Guardian Angel even need to magically slice a chain anyway?" I asked. "Is my assignment a butcher who needs to get sides of beef down from meat hooks?"

"Your halo powers will make more sense later. As for your assignment, that's something you will need to discuss with—hey, Akari!"

I looked up as my mentor entered the training center.

"You doing okay?" Ana asked as she joined us.

"Fine. Sorry I took a while. Any improvement?"

"Do the burn marks in the walls and missing chunks of bleachers answer your question?" I replied, indicating my halo damage.

Akari unsuccessfully tried to hide a wince. "Don't worry. I'm sure you'll get the hang of it. Training is over for the day though. Right now, I have to discuss assignments with you individually."

Ana nodded and whistled like a super fan on the sidelines of a basketball game. "That's it for today, Leo. With me."

The kid trotted over. "Good night, Grace. Monkonjae." He offered us both high fives on his way out with Ana.

"Night, Leo," Monkonjae said. Then he looked at me. "See you tomorrow."

"And every day for eternity after that," I replied, giving him an awkward wink-smile and two thumbs up.

He blinked.

I laughed uncomfortably and rubbed the back of my head. "Sorry. That sounded less creepy in my head."

Monkonjae laughed amiably then left with Deckland. Once they'd exited, I turned and found Akari shaking her head and poorly concealing a grin.

"Oh, Grace."

"*What?* How would you talk to a hot guy?" I put my hands on my hips.

"Not like that!" she exclaimed. A genuine smile, the first I'd seen from her, overtook her whole face.

I huffed. "Well, this is literally my first time encountering one in the wild. I died as a teenager, remember? I've never even had a crush if you don't count that guy in the *Maze Runner* movies. I'm new at this. Maybe you could hook me up with Marilyn Monroe or Evita Perón for flirting lessons. Are either of them up here?"

"Yes, sometimes, but how about we concentrate on your job first. You have an eternity to learn to talk to cute boys. Though that may not be long enough . . ."

"Shut up," I replied with a pout. Then I stiffened. I'd said it playfully, but perhaps it wasn't an appropriate comment to make to someone I'd just met, much less my superior.

"I'm sorry, Akari. That was rude. I didn't mean to be so informal, or hostile."

Akari tilted her head like Droopy did when I said something he didn't understand. Which was often. "What? Grace, it's fine. Now come on. Let's go—first to my office to talk about your assignment, then to your surprise dinner."

Akari's watch glowed and all the halo damage I'd caused in the training center repaired itself. I'd have to ask what app was responsible for that. I had a bad feeling that I'd be using it a lot in the days to come.

We journeyed back to the main GA floor and I settled into the hot pink armchair across from Akari. Chaz the angel panda slept in the corner, his fluffy tummy going up and down with his wings with each breath. Outside, the miracle of sundown had begun. Seeing it from the suburbs was different than witnessing it from the height of Angel Tower in the center of the city. The sky was being crushed by shades of pink.

"It's time to brief you on your first assignment," Akari said, calling for my attention as she opened a folder on her desk. She plucked out a photo and slid it across the desk. "His name is Henry Sun. He's your age, loves surfing and food, has a twin sister and an eight-year-old sister, and he's gifted with science—particularly chemistry and biology."

I studied the face of my assignment. The kid was fairly tan, had loosely spiked blackish-brown hair, and friendly brown eyes—not deep and dark like Monkonjae's; Henry's were akin to the powdery cocoa on top of tiramisu. The best part of him was his smile. It was endearing, free of ego, and stretched wide to create deep dimples.

It made me want to smile too.

"He seems nice," I commented. "And he has a cool look. Where's he from?"

"Well, he's half Japanese and half Taiwanese."

"Wait." I sat forward and put the picture down. "Are you sending me to high school in Asia? The only other language I speak is Spanish, and my grammar with that isn't even perfect. I certainly can't speak Japanese or Mandarin."

"Technically, you can speak every language," Akari said. "When you enter Heaven, your brain becomes hardwired for all languages so that everyone can understand everyone. Deckland has actually been speaking Spanish to us this whole time. It translates in our minds, and when we speak it translates to Spanish for him."

"Like people who travel in Doctor Who's TARDIS?" I mused.

"Yes, exactly. There was actually a panel discussion about that at last year's Angel Con. That's Heaven's version of Comic Con."

I blinked. "Heaven has a Comic Con?"

"Of course it does. Only unlike Earth's version, tickets are easily available, everyone looks hot in their costumes, and nothing is inappropriate. We're getting off topic though." Akari cleared her throat and gestured back to the file. "Henry's father is Taiwanese and his mother is Japanese. They met when Henry's father traveled to Japan for a doctors' exchange program a couple of decades ago. Though Henry and his siblings were born in Japan, their family moved to Southern California when the twins were ten. *That's* where you're going."

"Sure. Why not?" I shrugged. "I'll just fake enroll in high school tomorrow to protect this science nerd surfer kid in California and try to keep him alive so he can cure cancer or achieve world peace or something as an adult. Anything else?"

I knew I wasn't supposed to get short or snippy with my superiors—goodness knows I'd been disciplined for that plenty over the years—but I couldn't help it. Panic was contorting inside me. At least my mother wasn't around to witness it.

Akari looked at me thoughtfully. "Grace, I know you're new here. I know telling anyone that they're responsible for another human life is an immense charge. But the point of seeing the museum on Day One of training is that you comprehend the seriousness of the matter."

I massaged my temple a moment.

Deep breaths, Grace.

"I do understand, Akari. I'm sorry if the sarcasm makes it seem like I don't realize how important this is. When I make light of something it's usually to keep the enormity of it from crushing me. And in regards to Henry . . ." I sighed. "It occurs to me that if he is so critical, then it really isn't a good idea to leave this responsibility on my shoulders. I'm not a half-baked Guardian Angel, Akari; I'm *barely* baked. I've only been in training for *a day*. I'm hardly holding my own emotional baggage together, we've only learned one halo trick that I can't even do, and I don't care what your goodness meter says—there's no way I'm the person you think I am. I'm not. That was established on Earth quite plainly."

Akari studied me for a long pause. The pink haze spilling in from sunset had darkened—shadows of bubblegum had never looked so severe.

"You really believe that." Akari spoke it not as a question, but as a fascinated observation.

"If you knew me, you would agree. I know you have some fancy file about my life, but how much of my past are you really aware of?"

"*All of it, Grace*." She leaned forward, hands folded, eyes intense. "GA mentors learn everything important about our mentees' souls because understanding them is vital. To everyone else here, you may be a number—Ninety-Eight, the girl with the practically pure soul. To me, you are Grace Cardiff, and the whole sum of everything noteworthy she's seen, done, and said."

"Oh."

Well, that's uncomfortable.

I once lost my marbles when my older sister Gaby read my diary. Was there even a proper way to describe how vulnerable you felt when told that someone had read your *soul*?

"Perspective is an elusive, wily thing," Akari considered aloud after a moment. "A big reason that so many people don't end up in the best slice of the afterlife is that they didn't have enough of it. Possession of perspective is as helpful as lack of it is harmful. My advice is that you try to find some greater perspective on yourself. It may allow you to see your past through new lenses. You should spend a little time watching Memory Prime, when you're ready, but with a more open and kinder mind."

I leaned back in my chair and crossed my arms with an aggravated sigh. "Maybe I'll have a marathon this weekend."

"I'm not sure if that was sarcasm or not, but I would take it slow. Life wasn't meant to be binged; TV shouldn't be either."

The sun was gone. In response, Akari's office illuminated on its own in the *coolest possible way*. Four dozen free-floating candlesticks appeared in the air like something out of Hogwarts. Their bright glow was calming, and they smelled like these sour cream cupcakes I used to bake, only more satisfying. I'd even say the smell was . . . fulfilling.

"Grace?" Akari called my attention from the luminescence.

I took a deep breath. The scent helped me re-center.

"I understand, Akari. I'll . . . I'll be okay."

I had to be after all—for me and for Henry.

In terms of my own second coming, both my mentor and my mother had advised focusing on this job to get over the distress of death. Perhaps they were right. And perhaps taking on this role was another chance to define myself—an opportunity to give my self-esteem reprieve from the many reasons I had for tearing it down on Earth. I mean, I may not have agreed with the angelic light Akari and the others cast me in, but Heaven was as much of a fresh start as I was ever going to get. I should try my best to handle my misgivings internally and put forth a face of maturity. Other than Akari, none of these angels knew me, so I could be anyone to them. I could strive to live up to that great Ninety-Eight mantle they had set me on.

Did I believe I could do it?

It seemed unlikely. I didn't think my nature was cut out for it. Then again, the same could be said of me meeting the ladylike expectations my mother had for me, and I'd spent a lifetime trying to live up to *them* anyway. Why not attempt another persona that seemed out of my depth? At least here I had a safety net. If I couldn't manage the role I'd been given, there was Akari. My mentor had once guarded the great Winston Churchill. When the day came that she realized this job was beyond my capability, she could take over.

In the meantime . . . knowing that was not an excuse for me to slack off, I had to try. That *was* in my nature. Though I'm sure my mother wished she could surgically remove the self-destructive quality, I never backed down from a fight.

Worrying that I would drown was not enough of a reason to keep me from throwing myself in the deep end and swimming like my life depended on it. Mine didn't, but someone else's did.

Henry.

If he was as important as these angels believed, he deserved someone better than me to protect him. Still, as long as I was being forced to fill the role, I would devote myself to his well-being. He could make a difference in the world. I would try to make a difference to him.

I sat up straight in my chair. "So how long am I going to be Henry's GA?"

Akari gave me a concerned look, no doubt wondering what was going on inside my head. "We don't get an exact end date when we start new cases," she said. "The angels in charge of GA assignments currently estimate it could take anywhere between two to six years for you to get Henry where he needs to be. But that can change depending on how life fluxes around him. They'll keep us posted."

"So theoretically he's going to do something important in his early twenties?"

"That's the notion."

"What is it?"

"I'm afraid that I can't tell you."

"Hilarious."

"I'm not joking, Grace."

"What, why not?!"

Well, there go my attempts at maturity.

Calm down, crazy.

I released a breath and adjusted my tone. "What do you mean?"

"I'm sorry, Grace. God and his most trusted advisors do not deem it wise for GAs to know every detail of what our charges are meant to accomplish. For one, it's like plausible deniability in a good way. You can't mess with the future if you don't know the future. Two, it keeps yours assignment from being influenced as well. Angels cannot reveal their identities to humans in general. However we don't have a policy about concealing our identities from the assignments we protect; we just strongly recommend keeping your identity a secret for as long as possible because revealing yourself complicates things . . ."

Akari drifted off a moment. Then she cleared her throat. "That being said, sometimes—particularly with assignments that last many years—it may become necessary to tell your charge the truth. When that happens, not knowing what the future holds means you can't accidentally divulge anything that will make your charge act in a way that alters his or her choices and life."

I processed this information then nodded. "That actually makes sense. I've read enough time-travel books to get it. I apologize for the overreaction before. It was pretty dramatic."

"So is life, which is fine as long as we factor in some zen now and then." Akari closed her folder and slid it to me. "For you to brush up on some background regarding Henry, your new cover identity, and school tomorrow."

I accepted the folder and clutched it tightly.

Studying. Finally something I was good at.

"We'll dig into more specifics as your training develops," Akari continued. "But in order to keep you from getting overwhelmed, focus on the basics of the job for now. Insert yourself into Henry's life, get to know him and the people around him, and keep him out of danger."

I frowned. "Are we talking *all* physical danger—like keep him from tripping, breaking a bone, getting a wicked paper cut? Or just intervene if he might die? Also, what about emotional danger? I need more specifics."

"He's a teenager, Grace. No one can protect them from emotional danger. Preventing him from *serious* injury and death should be the focus."

"So I just need to make sure Henry doesn't get hit by a bus or struck by lightning or trampled by wild goats then?"

"Yes, and any other events or people that could truly harm him."

I pensively drummed my fingers against my file. "But what about when I'm not with him? Who watches him in the non-school hours like all the time he's at home? Furthermore, what kind of people would even want to hurt—"

"*Grace*," Akari interrupted. "You're getting ahead of yourself. Trust me; I'll tell you more as it becomes relevant. For now, just look out for Henry when he's at school and remember the most important rule for a Guardian Angel."

My head was still trying to absorb what I'd already learned

while my natural curiosity fluttered with frustration that Akari hadn't answered my questions. Unsure, I replied with a joke and a shrug. "Don't spill any food on your white clothes?"

"The assignment comes first," she said firmly, not amused this time in the least. "Now then, that's everything for tonight." She raised an eyebrow. "Unless you have more questions?"

I opened my mouth, but Akari cut me off. "About the *immediate* future."

I sighed. "I'll save them for tomorrow."

"Wonderful."

We stood and Akari went to scoop a sleeping Chaz into her arms. I followed them toward the door, then stopped abruptly. "Actually, I do have one question that can't wait."

Akari sighed. "What is it?"

"What scent are these candles?"

Her mouth crooked up to smiling. "That's the smell of a job well done. I find it makes for a good work environment." She waved her hand. Her watch glowed and all the candles extinguished at once.

"SURPRISE!!!"

The lights of the darkened restaurant awakened suddenly— revealing balloons, streamers, and a bunch of people I didn't recognize. They sure seemed to recognize me though. Half a dozen bodies rushed at me. I got three hugs, five hand squeezes, and two kisses on the cheek before I managed to back away.

"Who are all of you?" I asked, totally bewildered, grabbing Akari's wrist in reflex.

"Grace." Akari delicately pried my fingers off. "This is your family. Your deceased family. That's your Nana Robin and Grandpa Jim from your mom's side." She gestured at an athletic couple in their twenties wearing matching tracksuits. They waved with giant grins on their faces. "Your Abuela Lupe and Abuelo Rolando from your dad's side." Akari pointed to a short couple in their early thirties who smiled warmly. "And your assorted uncles, aunts, cousins, great grandparents, great-great grandparents, great-great-great grandparents . . . you get the gist." The people around me beamed and waved.

"Uh, hi." I waved awkwardly then leaned over to whisper to Akari. "Yeah, I don't know who these jokers are, but that ain't my nana." I threw a thumb at the woman in the tracksuit. "She died at seventy-six. All these people are hot young adults."

"Dear—" my Not Nana started.

"Hold on a second, ma'am." I raised a finger then addressed the crowd. "Hi, everyone, there's been some sort of mistake. I'm—"

My Not Nana stepped forward and took both my hands. "Nugget . . ." She held my gaze and then I saw her change. The fullness of her face thinned and wrinkled. Age spots appeared. Her hair grayed. Her shoulders curved forward. The feeling of her fingers around mine became sharper as the skin over her hands loosened and I could better feel the bones beneath.

"Oh my God. *Nana Robin?*"

My beloved grandmother who'd died when I was eight now stood before me. She let go of my hands and stepped back. All around me the people of the room transformed in age—some more than others—but only for a few seconds before morphing back to their younger states.

Now returned to her youthful form, Nana Robin refocused on me. Her blue eyes were full and wrinkle-free, and her shoulder-length, bright red hair was fluffy as a Southern belle's.

"In Heaven, we take the form of our most powerful self-image," Akari said, stepping next to Nana Robin. "You look whatever age you felt your best *and* you look the most polished version of that age. On Earth, people are always picking themselves apart—if only I was five pounds lighter, if only those pimples would clear up, if only I was an inch taller. Here, when you look in the mirror, you will always be the version of yourself you always wanted to be. Nothing too drastic—you will always be you, because *you* are enough. You're just optimal you. It's like your dog Droopy. The magic of Heaven isn't going to turn a basset hound into a Dalmatian, but it can make him the best, healthiest version of a basset hound he can be. And like your pet, people are also restored to full health—no sicknesses, no weak knees, no blurry vision."

"I can run a mile in under six minutes!" Grandpa Jim said, slapping his knee enthusiastically. "Arthritis may as well be Big Foot because it ain't real around here."

"Well said, Jim." Nana Robin winked at him.

Akari looked at me again. "In Heaven, you can also change your appearance to different ages if you wish. As you saw, people sometimes do that when reuniting with family members who may not recognize them otherwise."

Emotion rippled through me. I gulped. "I genuinely am at a loss for words."

A phrase my mother no doubt had been waiting to hear my whole life.

Another gulp. "But I'm happy to see you. And I guess meet a lot of you too."

Feelings of love and warmth overcame me, eyes blurring as I looked at my family, my ancestors. In that daze, something happened. I wasn't sure if I was imagining it, but a bright, glowing light formed over my collection of relatives. It reminded me of—

"We were sad your time on Earth ended so soon, Nugget," Nana Robin said, wiping my cheek. I hadn't even noticed the tear that'd escaped. I took a breath to keep any others back.

"But we all came as soon as it happened to ensure you felt safe when you crossed over," she continued.

"The beings of light in the tunnel of color . . ." I remembered in awe. My eyes darted around, understanding. "That was all of you, wasn't it?"

"Whenever someone headed for Heaven crosses into the afterlife, all their loved ones on this plane of existence are instantly notified," Akari said. "They are there to help guide you through. Love is like a compass; the more there is, the easier it is for your soul to find its way home. To find its way here."

Nana Robin took my hand. "This is your welcome party, Nugget. All the angels in Heaven get one within their first few days of the afterlife. Now let's hustle that tustle." She pulled me toward the smiling faces. "We have many introductions to make and plenty of fun to have, but we have to wrap this up by ten o'clock. Your mentor insists."

"Why ten o'clock?" I asked, glancing over my shoulder.

"It's a school night," Akari replied. "Just because you died doesn't mean you can be tardy to your first day of the semester. After this morning we're not taking any chances."

My mouth gaped as I found myself at a loss for words again. Nana Robin closed it with a finger. "You're not a carp, Nugget. Best foot forward now. First, I want you to meet my mother." She yanked me deeper into the crowd of waiting family, and I was swallowed by hugs and a blend of smiling Southerners and Hispanics.

The restaurant that Akari had booked for my surprise welcome party was called Do You Remember That Time . . . All foods served were delicious things you'd once eaten a long time ago—on vacation, at a friend's house, a random bat mitzvah, a Superbowl party, and so on.

I wished I could've eaten more, but the meet-and-greet absorbed most of my time. I didn't know a person could be so exhausted from socializing. I met, hugged, and chatted with at least thirty relatives, two-thirds of whom had died before I'd even been born.

Around nine while my grandparents were reloading on food, I managed to pull away for a breather and sat out back on the patio, leaning my elbows against a dark green iron table. It was my first time being alone in hours. My first time being alone all day actually.

Mason jars containing flickering candles decorated the tables. Strings of turquoise lanterns crisscrossed above. To my right, ivy and jasmine blossoms covered the wall. The quiet roar of my relatives in the main room behind me was soothing.

"Ah, here we go," Nana Robin said. She and Grandpa Jim stepped through the door to the patio carrying plates and beverages. "One virgin strawberry daiquiri from your family's vacation to Jamaica in 2013 and a stack of Baker's Sweets pancakes from your trip to Sumter, South Carolina last spring."

Nana Robin set my drink down; her other hand was occupied by a *very* large piña colada. Meanwhile Grandpa Jim, who was toting his own piña colada, placed a plate loaded with hotcakes in the center of the table.

"Aw, the classic twelve-stack," I mused, picking up my fork.

"Because a six-stack is for suckers," said Nana Robin, clinking forks with me.

"Wait, can't forget the finishing touch," Grandpa Jim said. He removed a tiny flask from his tracksuit pocket and poured maple syrup all over the pancakes.

"I remember that flask," I commented. "I used to see you take it out of your jacket at the movies and pour it into your soda cup. Did it have syrup in it the whole time?"

"Nope. Now let's eat!" Grandpa Jim said, clinking forks with me too.

I smiled as I stabbed some pancake. I loved Grandpa Jim. He was technically my step-grandfather. Nana Robin divorced my Grandpa Thorston when my mother was just a kid, then married Jim a couple decades later. Throw-caution-to-the-wind Jim could not have been more different from Grandpa Thorston, who was so uptight and traditional he made my mother seem loosy goosy. I couldn't believe he and Nana Robin had ever been a couple.

Syrup delighted my taste buds as I mused on this. Sadly, my pancake peace lasted about seven seconds. After swallowing a bite, Nana Robin dabbed the corners of her mouth with a napkin. "So, Nugget, I hear you are practically perfect in every way."

My own bite got lodged in my throat. Following a rough swallow, I kept my eyes down and fiddled with my fork as I responded.

"That's Mary Poppins, actually."

"Tish tosh. You know what I mean. You are 98% pure good, aren't you? That is why you have been drafted into immediate service with the Guardian Angels."

"Akari told you?"

"She didn't need to," Grandpa Jim responded. "It's been the top story on our afterlife news channel all day." He raised his wrist and his Soul Pulse projected a small hologram-type screen. A man in a white suit with a silver tie sat behind a desk beside a woman in a sparkling white blouse. Between the two of them was a sign that displayed the name of the show.

"Thanks for joining us for the evening edition of *Heaven't You Heard?* Your place for top stories on our plane of the afterlife," the man said. His presence was reassuring, his voice full of gravitas. "I'm Walter Cronkite—"

I glanced at my grandpa. "Seriously?"

He nodded.

"In case you haven't heard," continued Walter, "the top stories for today are the addition of a new app on Soul Pulse called Kitten in a Laundry Basket, Julia Child has opened her latest restaurant in Little Paris, and most excitingly, Heaven welcomed the purest soul to ever *grace* us—Grace Cariño Reyes Cardiff of South Carolina. Join us at the turn of the hour for all the details we know so far about this young angel."

I put down my fork as Grandpa Jim powered off his Soul Pulse. Then I clutched my stomach with one hand.

"Do either of you know if it's against the rules to upchuck in public in Heaven?" I glanced left. "Because those rose bushes look like a fine spot for it."

"Don't be silly, Grace. We're proud of you," Nana Robin said, squeezing my arm. "My granddaughter—the purest angel ever. I've been bragging about you all afternoon. Not that I need to; I doubt there's anyone in the afterlife who doesn't know about you by now."

The pancake felt like it was trying to leap back up my throat.

"Nana, I—" Suddenly I bent over, losing control. Shockingly, instead of vomit, a large cloud of glitter spewed out of my mouth. When it landed on the cobblestones, several yellow daisies grew out of the cracks.

"Nugget, what's wrong?" Nana Robin put her hand on my shoulder.

"*Nothing* is wrong," I replied, sitting up and wiping stray glitter from the corners of my mouth. "At least that's what people seem to think about me, Miss Ninety-Eight. Everyone at the GA office already has me on their radar, and now this news story? I was warned people would know about me, but I didn't think it would be so . . . in their faces."

I shook my head and stared up at the star-lit sky. It wasn't just the Guardian Angels who had expectations for me; *all* of Heaven did. God, I didn't want to let them down. I'd spent my life letting people down.

I looked back at my grandparents with a touch of desperation. "Do you believe it? That I'm as good as they say?"

"We're not in charge of the mystical math, Grace," said my grandpa. "If God says you're 98% good then that's what you are."

"I'm not asking God. I'm asking *you*," I urged. "No one can lie here. Akari thinks I'm being too hard on myself and she believes in me, but I don't think I am worthy of the title they've bestowed; I've spent too much of my life getting negative feedback for my behavior. I know that people in Heaven can watch what their loved ones are doing on Earth through TV. From what you've seen of my life—of me—would you give me that number?"

My grandparents exchanged a look before my grandmother sighed.

"Nugget, you're a lot like me. I love that about you." She touched my chin briefly. "Even though your mother has tried to break you like a wild horse, when push comes to shove, you are still prone to being audacious. I have seen you struggle on Earth because of that. And even though I don't view it as a bad thing, I still ended up with a timeshare, not as a full-time Heaven angel, which means God didn't totally condone my boldness any more than the stuffier people of our world did. Given how similar we are, I *am* surprised that the divine powers that be didn't view you the same way. Goodness knows you have as much of a penchant for fieriness as I do."

"I try to rein it in," I protested sadly. "I've always tried to stay out of trouble and live up to Mom's expectations. Sometimes . . . the actions just get away from the good intentions."

"The road to Hell is paved with those," Nana Robin responded.

I stared at the pancakes.

"Look, Nugget. Honestly, none of that matters now—not what your mother thinks, or the people on Earth, or either of us." Nana Robin put her hand on my shoulder assertively. "We are not the creators or overseers of humankind. And neither are you. So maybe instead of making a list of all the reasons why you're not good enough, try and make a list of all the reasons that you are—*and* have a little faith. In yourself, and also in the idea that maybe people are more than they appear."

I sighed and leaned back in my chair, staring up at the stars again. Were they the same ones people on Earth could see? Or were these stars just for us?

"No need to get up, Droopy," I said sarcastically. My pet barely lifted his head as I came through the door. I wasn't insulted though; his laziness was endearing.

I grabbed the TV remote from the couch and sat down on the wooden floor beside the dog bed, massaging one of Droopy's ears with one hand while the other powered on the TV.

At first, I surfed through the local Heaven channels. I stopped when I landed on the *Heaven't You Heard?* show.

"According to our sources at Angel Tower," said a woman in a white pantsuit, "Grace Cardiff retained a solid 4.0 GPA throughout her high school career. We can expect no less as she enrolls in high school as part of her Guardian Angel cover tomorrow."

I groaned and flipped through the channels, eventually selecting the Memory Prime icon. There were several options to choose from for segmenting the content after that: By Year | By Theme | By Feeling.

I clicked on the By Theme option and a blank search screen came up. An automated voice pulsed through the room. "Voice command activated. What kinds of memories do you want to explore?"

I held the remote to my mouth. "Search memories regarding . . ." I sighed. "Why am I here? Why did they choose me as a Guardian Angel?"

The screen fluxed with color.

I was stunned. Was that actually going to work?

"There are eighty-six related videos. Engage shuffle mode?" the voice suggested.

"Um . . . sure."

The TV presented a loading symbol and I wondered what I was getting myself into. Suddenly the screen filled with an image of a school playground. A class of young kids, five or six years old, climbed and ran and frolicked around jungle gym equipment, a few teachers watching nearby. Other children ate snacks by an outdoor cubby full of backpacks. That's when I saw her. That's when I saw me.

Five-year-old me wore a navy, polka-dot dress and a red bow in her hair. She was making her way over to a fat tree in the corner of the playground, out of the view of the teachers. She held a lunch box in her hand. I stopped rubbing Droopy's ear and felt my chest tighten.

The angle of the scene changed. Little me was behind the tree now, meeting with two other young girls.

"Did you bring the ones we told you to?" asked one girl with a ponytail. I remembered her name—Katcha. More tension in my chest.

Little me opened her lunchbox and moved aside the food, revealing two small stuffed animals—a purple hippo and a green bunny. The other two girls grabbed them.

"Did your mom or dad see?" asked the second girl, a brunette with bangs—Victoria.

Little me shook her head. "I hid Bubbles and Floppy so they wouldn't see. Now will you please leave me alone?"

"Maybe," Victoria responded. "These stuffed animals are great for our collection. We'll let you know if we want any more of yours."

"But I don't want—"

Victoria pushed little me to the ground. The tiny bully bent over and pointed a finger at her nose. "Katcha and I want these animals more than you, Grace. Be nice to us and we'll be nice to you. If you're not, we'll be way meaner."

I almost cracked the remote in my hand.

Anger boiled like lava in my blood. Katcha and Victoria had been the first girls to try and push me around. I hated that I had *let them*. It was more than a decade ago and I still wished I could travel back in time and tell tiny me to smack them. Then again, that was the kind of aggressive behavior that had gotten me into trouble so many times later in life.

Sigh.

It was all very conflicting.

Regret curdled inside of me like spoiled milk. The little girl on screen just didn't feel like me. And I could tell looking in her young eyes that she was realizing it too. Realizing that the agreeable, unassuming creature her mother encouraged her to be didn't sync with her character.

I turned off the TV in frustration and stood up. I didn't know what this memory had to do with me being a Guardian Angel, but it was one of the moments I was least proud of. Only one thing could cleanse me of the fire burning within.

I tossed the remote on the couch, grabbed a hair tie off the end table, and made my way to the fireplace mantle. I pressed the hidden button beneath it, then pulled my hair into a ponytail as magic transformed the room.

The main lights dimmed, my storm cloud light fixtures crackled with LED lightning, and multi-colored backlighting that rimmed the room switched on. Meanwhile, a sparkling wormhole formed in the floor and sucked in every item in the living room except for me, Droopy, and his bed. I was left with a perfectly clear, smooth wooden floor.

Speakers sprouted from the four corners of the ceiling. A holographic playlist appeared on the mantle and I started scrolling through the options. I clicked on a song and kicked off my shoes as the music began to play. My socks glided over the wood while a melancholy melody full of soul flowed through the speakers. The lights of the room pulsed in sync with the tune.

My foot traced a long, slow circle, toes pointed. A ballerina would call this a rond de jambe. As the beat picked up, so did my heart.

Leo had asked me what I'd thought about when conjuring my halo—what made me feel so alive. This was it.

Dancing.

I'd taken some private lessons over the years, but doing so had always involved a grin-and-bear-it attitude. Despite my namesake, I was not inherently graceful and I had zero natural talent for dance. *But I loved it.* I loved it so much that—unbeknownst to my parents and sister—I had rented a room at the local dance studio for the last two years so that after school I could twirl and leap and spin for no one else but me. It had been one of the best decisions I had ever made. My special private time.

While I had no qualms about being confident in challenging areas where I was naturally skilled, such as academia, I felt nervous exposing myself in settings where I was vulnerable to failing and had to express myself so . . . openly.

When I was alone, I didn't have to worry about trying out different moves I knew I would be bad at. There was no pressure or expectations. No self-doubt. Alone, dance could be a pure expression of soul in as raw a form as possible.

I pirouetted and thrust myself back, spinning to the ground. The storm cloud lights pulsed overhead. I threw myself up and chaîné turned across the room five times before leaping sideways. My heartrate rose.

Besides getting Droopy back, of all the things Heaven had to offer, and of all the things Akari had done for me, this was truly my favorite. It was familiar. It was therapeutic. And in my changing world where fate and responsibility and a mantle of greatness had been thrust upon me, it was absolute freedom.

The angels could have Heaven for their paradise. This was my own happy plane of existence.

5

"PEARLIE" GATES

"Behold, the entrance to Heaven," Akari said. "What it looks like on this side, anyway. We call it the Pearly Gates."

"It has actual pearls on it," I marveled. "How appropriate."

Monday morning had begun early and didn't show any signs of slowing. Not exactly how I wanted to spend the hours before I assumed a new identity for a new high school, but so far my slice of Heaven didn't seem to be big on downtime.

The day started with a final orientation session for my assignment. Akari quizzed me on facts about Henry, the school I'd be attending, and my fake cover that had been in the file she gave me last night. Like most quizzes I'd ever taken, I aced it.

Then there was some general GA rules overview. Mainly my mentor re-stressed a half dozen times that the assignment comes first, and as such she advised me not to get too distracted by the mystification I'd no doubt feel upon returning to Earth. It was imperative I didn't take my eye off the metaphorical ball.

Now at quarter past seven, I stood on a cloud with Akari—Buckingham Palace-esque golden gates studded with pearls looming in front of us. Most of the gems were normal sized, but giant pearls the size of soccer balls crowned the tips of the ornate fence.

The gate hovered just past the edge of the massive cloud and spanned infinitely in both directions. Through the bars, I spied a distant trio of tall, glimmering structures on another cloud. They reminded me of lighthouses. One shimmered black, the second looked clear as crystal, and the third shone hazy pink.

On our cloud, a pure obsidian orb the size of a townhouse stood to my left. There was no signage and no windows, but the front of the orb had an arched entryway blocked by a mini pearly gate.

To my right resided a cube-shaped compound made of rose quartz. It had three rectangular entrances, also with identical mini pearly gates. A pair of winged angels stood outside both buildings. They were buff and intimidating, yet somehow still pleasant-looking.

While no one neared the obsidian orb, the rose quartz compound had a lot of foot traffic. People continuously approached the first gate, scanned their Soul Pulses, magically passed through the bars, and vanished. Every few seconds someone would appear behind the second gate then simply phase past the bars onto our side before teleporting away. The third entrance was a two-person situation. When it was their turn, angels in line would move up to the designated gate and hold up their Soul Pulses. Immediately after, a person would appear behind the bars of the entrance, phase through, take the angel's hand, and the pair would disappear via teleport together.

"Heaven has three main entrances," Akari explained. "The Pearly Gates are where souls from Earth enter our plane of the afterlife, and angels use this area to return to Earth as well. The rose quartz building on the right connects to Middleground. Door One is for souls returning there after completing their allowed Heavenly stay. Door Two is for souls arriving for their designated time here. And Door Three is for first timers—souls who are coming to Heaven for their initial visit. That is where your mother will enter this weekend. Every new arrival is brought up by a sponsor in Heaven, as arranged with Middleground caseworkers. Sometimes it's a neutral angel. Other times a family member fills in. I can connect you with your mother's caseworker if you want to be her guide. But since you are also new here, I wouldn't recommend it."

"Hard pass, please," I said immediately.

Akari raised an eyebrow.

"Because I'm new," I added quickly. "Like you said."

And because my mother undermined me when I tried to show authority and explain the rules of something as simple as a board game. Trying to explain the rules of Heaven to her would not go smoothly.

I pointed at the nightmarish orb to our left. "So, does that thing lead to Hell? Or am I being presumptive and that actually leads to a Metallica concert?"

"No, you're right."

"Then follow up question—I guess being good doesn't necessarily mean being prudent? There's seriously a direct gateway between Heaven and Hell? That's like building a subway station between Rikers Island prison and The Plaza in New York."

"It's not as though we are issuing free passes, Grace. Every soul in the afterlife, regardless of where they are, has a device like this." She tapped the accessory on her wrist. "Soul Pulses have different functions depending on where you land after you die. The devices make sure only people who are allowed into Heaven can gain access at the appropriate times. In the same way, they only let permitted individuals travel to Middleground and Hell. Those places have three entry points, just like we do, connecting to Earth and the other two levels of the afterlife."

"That's . . . organized," I replied.

What else could I say?

"One more thing," I said. "Care to comment on the spelling situation?"

"What do you mean?"

I pointed at the gate that protected Heaven. At the top center point, which floated in front of us, was a sign with the words "Heaven's Pearly Gates" delicately engraved in cursive script. However, a makeshift, hand-painted wooden sign hung over the center word so that it read, "Heaven's *Pearlie* Gates."

"Oh. That's because of her." Akari smirked and pointed at the sky. "See the one with the blue glow?"

I looked up.

We'd teleported here, so I only now noticed the slew of angels forty feet overhead, each with a workspace on his or her own private cloud. They were pretty far, but I noted the glow of their halos, crystal desks, and at least a dozen floating, shimmery screens per station. The "office clouds" shone faintly with different shades. Following Akari's finger, I spotted the angel working at the blue glowing cloud. She appeared to have long, midnight black hair and currently stood in front of her screens, interacting with several while she held a tablet device in her hands. Also . . . it could have just been my imagination combined with distance, but it looked like there was a goat beside her, ripping off pieces of the cloud and chewing on them.

"Pearlie!" Akari called.

The angel lowered her tablet, lifted her round spectacles, and glanced down. "Akari!" She spread her wings and descended gracefully. It was quite the entrance.

"I heard you were back on duty," the angel said, addressing Akari once she'd landed.

Pearlie was slender and pleasant faced, maybe thirty-five or so. Her glasses had caramel frames that matched her amber earrings. She wore elegant, flowing white robes like a Greek goddess with golden tassels and a pattern of crystals. Overall she looked more akin to the traditional representation of an angel one would expect, as opposed to Akari's white tank top and cargo pants combo. Also, Pearlie's halo remained visible over her head and her wings outstretched.

"Grace Cardiff, meet Pearlie Han," Akari said. "That's P-E-A-R-L-I-E. She is the most senior gatekeeper so God fondly renamed the area after her a few decades ago. Nothing bad gets past her."

"Nice to meet the new GA everyone has been talking about," Pearlie said, extending her hand to me. Her accent was Australian, but with a deeper twang.

"Um, thank you, ma'am," I said, shaking her hand. "Nice to meet you too." I examined her wings; they were the backpack kind I'd seen the IDS angels use. "You don't have your own wings either? I would think as a senior gatekeeper you'd have already been enlightened enough to earn them."

Pearlie gave Akari a pointed but amused look. "Your new charge doesn't beat around the bush, does she?"

My face flushed. "Sorry, ma'am."

"I'm joking," she responded. "And I insist you call me Pearlie. To address your queries, Miss Ninety-Eight, that whole 'earn wings once you're fully realized' thing is strictly for *Guardian* Angels. You 90% good and up souls are the only ones who can achieve permanent wings. Not that I mind—look how nicely these glittery straps accentuate my work robes." She popped her hip like she was posing for an impromptu paparazzi photo.

Just then a goat landed beside us, the one I'd seen on the cloud. Only now I grew wide-eyed as I appreciated his large, black feathery wings and the pearl necklace he wore like a 1950s housewife.

"This is Rowbie," Pearlie said, patting the goat affectionately on the head even as he began to chew her skirt. "He's my angel pet."

Rowbie lunged at me with his mouth open and I took a step back. "No offense," I said to him before glancing over at Pearlie. "I just don't want to show up for my first day of school with a bite taken out of my jacket."

"Fair enough," Pearlie replied. She glanced at Akari. "Listen, lady. I have to get back to work, but my shift ends at noon. Fancy having lunch? I feel like I haven't seen you in forever. It's like you dropped out of the sky."

I noticed Akari flinch and Pearlie's face fell. "I'm sorry. That was a poor choice of words."

"No, it's fine," Akari replied quickly. "Listen, maybe another time? I am sending Grace off right now, but I have a lot of work to do at the office today."

Pearlie nodded. "Okay. Shoot me a text. There's a house party at Harriet Tubman's tomorrow night. Also, the old gang and I are putting together this amazing laser tag tournament with General Patton next weekend if you want to—"

"I'll text you, Pearlie," Akari interrupted. "I promise. I'm just . . . getting used to things again."

A weird lull passed. I tugged anxiously on the straps of my glittery cloth backpack.

Finally the gatekeeper nodded. "Of course. Well . . ." She glanced at me. "We're expecting great things from you, Ninety-Eight. You couldn't ask for a better mentor. Akari is the best of the best in the Guardian Angel business. See you two around."

Pearlie saluted and her wings started to glow. She took off and soared back toward her cloud. Rowbie made a disgruntled snort, then flew after the angel in a much less elegant fashion.

I studied my mentor's reserved expression. "Are you okay?"

Akari snapped out of her daze. Her mask of professionalism secured over her face anew. "Of course I am."

"Really? Because your friend said—"

"Surely you have a different question?" Akari said. "We are on a mystical cloud surrounded by celestial wonder."

"I know you're just trying to change the subject," I said, eyeing my mentor curiously. "But since I don't want to overstep, I'll bite . . ." I approached the edge of the cloud and pointed through the bars. "Do you want to tell me what those things are?"

There was a vast expanse of wide-open sky ahead. However, if you looked far enough to the left and right, past our cloud were floating catwalk platforms that extended into the distance, rimming the portion of sky between the Pearlie Gates and the faraway cloud with three towers. Hundreds, perhaps thousands, of angels were on them, each one glowing lustrously.

Akari offered me her hand. I took it and we teleported to one of the narrow catwalks. A single glimmering railing faced the span of sky between us and the opposite platform. As angels flashed in and out, grabbing hold of the railing caused them to illuminate as it did. They looked stunning—gleaming like suns with the silhouettes of humans. After a few moments each angel would let go of the railing then teleport away.

Curious, I extended a finger to touch the railing, but Akari snatched my hand before I could. "Careful, Grace. You wouldn't want to intrude on someone else's party."

"What?"

"When people die, all their souls get sent to the same place," Akari explained. "We call it the Soul Sewer."

I furrowed my brow.

"A crass name for a beautiful, well-organized system," Akari admitted. "The Soul Sewer is a colossal, cosmic pool of energy. That's what lies beyond the Cloud of Three Towers." She pointed out the beacons in the distance. I leaned out, careful to avoid touching the railing.

"I don't see any Soul Sewer past that cloud. Just more sky."

"Because most of us only see in three dimensions."

"How many dimensions are there?"

"More than there are flavors of ice cream but less than there are reality TV shows."

"So somewhere between sixty and six thousand."

"Exactly." Akari cracked a smiled.

I smiled back. I liked it better when Akari loosened up. It made our relationship feel less obligatory.

"So the Cloud of Three Towers?" I tilted my chin.

"They're divine checkpoints—the black is for Hell, the quartz is for Middleground, and the crystal is for Heaven. Employees from each plane of the afterlife work together in the watchtowers to determine which direction each soul in the Soul Sewer needs to go. It's a pretty fast process in most cases, but there's still a magical time lapse. What feels like seconds to a soul transitioning into the afterlife could take anywhere from a few minutes to a few days up here."

"So Judgment Day, as it were."

Akari nodded. "No one on Earth, no matter how big or small, escapes the consequences of their actions forever." She gestured at the sky in front of us. "Souls headed for Heaven pass through here. You can't see it—different dimensions as mentioned—but churning below us are thousands of divine energy tunnels. One for each new arrival. The tunnels surround inbound souls with peace, warmth, and happiness. The feeling of love that souls experience as they approach Heaven is produced by angels."

Akari alluded to the people continuously appearing around us and taking hold of the railing. "When angels in Heaven receive notice that someone they care for has died, they teleport here instantly, concentrate on that person, take hold of the railing, and voilà. You have your celestial welcoming party—beings of pure love who escort you to that bright white light at the end of the tunnel that you cross through when you make it past the Pearlie Gates to reach our Arrival Center . . ."

Akari directed my attention back to the cloud behind the Pearlie Gates where we'd previously been. My jaw dropped when I saw what was below it.

Underneath the cloud—hanging from it upside down like a bat—was a massive golden cathedral that made St. Paul's and the Vatican look like side projects. It shimmered like a dream and exuded a weighty air of power. The Pearlie Gates stretched to guard the bottom half of the cloud, creating a barrier in front of the cathedral.

I couldn't believe that'd been underneath us the whole time!

Akari's halo appeared and her wings sprouted. No teleporting this time, apparently. We joined hands and she dove off the platform, looping beneath it before flying straight at the upside-down cathedral. When we were fifty meters away, suddenly the world flipped. The cathedral was right side up and everything else was upside down. Or perhaps *we* had flipped. I didn't know. And I didn't care. This was *crazy*.

We landed at the threshold of the majestic compound, the marshmallow fluff of the clouds squishing beneath my sneakers. My mentor and I walked up the cathedral steps. I had never felt so small in my life. Or so astounded. Other angels continually arrived by wings or teleportation, making their way toward the cathedral like it was business as usual.

When we entered, Akari proceeded straight ahead and I stayed at her heels, ogling. Stained glass windows depicted not saints nor biblical lore, but humanity—grand, important, amazing moments in our history. Everything from revolution to invention to compassion. The floor in the foyer was a mosaic of tiles that formed a map of the earth. Pure crystal obelisks shot up like stalagmites around the edges of the floor and hung down from the ceiling like stalactites.

Past the entryway resided a bustling room like a post office on steroids mixed with the ingenuity of an international airport luggage system. Plus some magic. Honestly, it was kind of what I assumed the Tooth Fairy's office would look like.

Hm. I should ask Akari if she's real. Do mystical creatures fall in the realm of Heavenly revelations? The woman still hasn't answered my questions about Stonehenge or Easter Island.

"Grace?"

I'd gotten lost in thought and fallen behind. I trotted up to her.

"Once souls enter Heaven, they arrive like this." Akari directed my focus to the enormous walls, which held thousands of slots like mail cubbies. Glowing envelopes with sparkling seals incessantly appeared in cubbies across the room. Angels in silvery mailman attire with matching silver backpack wings flew around retrieving the letters and placing them in "inbox" trays on one of the thousands of golden desks. Desk angels would then swiftly grab the new letter and type something into their computers. A 3D printer beside them created a rolled-up scroll and a thick folder. The two items were tied together with a glimmering purple ribbon. The desk angels proceeded to slide their glowing envelopes under the ribbon as well, then drop the whole package into an empty "outbox" tray. At that, the entire package vanished in a shimmery flash and the desk angels moved on to the next envelope.

"Dead people arrive as *mail*?" I said.

Akari nodded. "The angels who work here type in the name of the arrived soul printed on the envelope, the system pairs them with the best guide in Heaven, then that information—a file on the soul, instructions for their happy place, and any other important notes—are teleported to the angel chosen to guide them. There's no heads up. The assignment just appears and you have to attend to it immediately."

"Kind of intense to have such a big responsibility thrust at you without warning."

Akari shrugged. "You seem to be managing just fine."

"Glad it seems that way," I scoffed.

"People in Heaven actually tend to enjoy taking on roles as welcome guides," Akari continued. "Like I told you the day you arrived, Grace, there is no better medicine for the soul than helping others and spreading goodness. Any and *every* person in

Heaven is eligible to be a guide at some point." She paused for a curious moment and swallowed. "It's not a job; it's a privilege. And you're only matched with someone whose soul will match with yours."

I looked at her with fresh eyes. "Is that what you are to me? Like, a cosmically approved friend?"

"The easy answer is yes."

"What's the difficult answer?"

Akari sighed. "Souls marked 90% good and up are given guides in the same bracket of goodness. Since souls with these percentages are earmarked to work in the Guardian Angel department, their mentors have to also serve in the same sector of the GA operation."

"Like you."

"Only . . . I'm not a Guardian Angel anymore, Grace. At least I haven't been for a while. Since I was on a leave of absence when you died, you should have gone to someone else. Someone more worthy of your soul's purity. But two days ago, your file just appeared at my home. Along with a note from God."

"Whoa."

"Whoa is correct. I've been dead for a century and a half, Grace. I have only met God three times during my afterlife. A couple days ago was the fourth. God summoned me to his office and asked me to come back to the GAs. He said I needed to help you."

"So God is a he," I thought out loud.

"It depends on the day."

"More explanation please."

"That's not important right now." She huffed slightly and waved her hand as if to wipe our slate of conversation clean. "The point is that the universe thinks we're a good match, but I think you should have paired with someone else. Heaven seems to expect more from me than past events would suggest I can handle."

I crossed my arms. "Well, I suppose that the universe is either way better at its job than we're giving it credit for, or it has an interesting sense of humor."

"How so?"

"Because that's exactly how I feel."

Our eyes met and we exchanged a look of genuine understanding.

For a moment I felt lighter, but then a little scared. Although it was comforting to know Akari also felt like a fish out of water, knowing she didn't feel super up to her role either threw my whole security blanket out the window. To keep myself calm as I approached my GA mission, I'd been convincing myself that if I messed up, I had this epic Guardian Angel to step in and take over. It would seem I couldn't count on that.

I didn't know why Akari had been on a leave of absence, or what had happened with the case she had been working—and evidently failed—before that, but it obviously had affected her deeply. She didn't feel compatible with our situation any more than I did. And looking at her, for the moment I couldn't bring myself to ask why.

I cleared my throat and checked my watch. "Um, my school starts soon. Is there an Angel bus I need to take through your divine sewage system?"

Akari's lips curved to a small smile. "Soul Sewer. And no. Getting around in the afterlife is much simpler than that." She headed back through the mosaic map foyer, which branched into hallways on the left and right.

"To the right is where Guardian Angels arrive when they come back from Earth, like the IDS angels you saw yesterday." She gestured as we passed it. "That's where you'll appear when you return to Heaven. From there, just exit the Arrival Center and teleport where you need to go. Here is the departure hallway." She directed me down the opposite corridor. It was lined with glittery, empty alcoves the size of shower stalls. "IDS angels have ejection tubes in their office linked with special energy that shoots them where they need to be. There are some other jobs in Heaven that have their own temporary exits to Earth. For GA work outside the IDS, we use these ports."

I watched angels ahead of us step into individual stalls, flash their Soul Pulses at a sensor, and disappear in a warm glow.

"So I just jump in and *bammo-flasho*, I'll be where I need to be?" I asked.

"Yes."

"And how do I get back? Are there angelic shower stalls hidden around Southern California that I should know about?"

"No. Getting back is more interesting. All you have to do is grab the door handle of any place of worship and concentrate on returning here."

"Really?"

"Uh-huh. Any church, synagogue, mosque, temple, you name it. If it's a place of faith, just go for the door, focus, and it will become a door to Heaven."

"Neat."

"That's a simple adjective to describe it," Akari mused. "But yes, I suppose it is *neat*." She patted me on the back twice and then guided me by the shoulders, turning me around to face the empty alcove behind us. "Well, off you go."

I glanced back at her hesitantly. "Are you sure there's nothing else I need to know before I go? No other magical architecture or angelic goats or celestial mailrooms that we missed?"

"Sorry, Grace. Tour's over. You aced your quiz on Henry and your cover identity this morning, so no more stalling. Have a nice first day of school."

I stepped into the alcove and looked at my mentor.

"Remember, if you forget any part of your cover you can fall back on your real life to prevent confusion. For anything that wasn't in the file, feel free to wing it too. Just try to keep it vague."

I nodded and gulped. Akari's face softened with sympathy.

"Grace, I know I've given you a lot of rules and instructions, but at the end of the day, if you remember just one thing make it this. The most important edict God has for Guardian Angels is keep your human assignment safe. That person's well-being comes first. Just imprint that at the forefront of your mind and your actions, and you'll be fine. Do you understand?"

"You've reiterated that rule eight times, Akari. I understand. I promise."

"Good." She nodded. "Do me proud."

"I'll try . . ."

I always did.

With a deep breath, I centered my heart and held up my wrist. My Soul Pulse flashed and every part of me—every hair, every freckle—disintegrated into energy. It was like a universe imploding. Every molecule and atom that I was made of twinkled like the stars, and then *WHOOSH!*

I was in a bottomless vacuum of empty silence. Until I wasn't.

Light flashed. I blinked and saw green and gold. Beams of broken sunshine flashed through the thick branches of a tree. I reflexively held one hand up to shield my eyes. My other hand gripped something rough and wooden. The world came into focus and I realized I was sitting in a tree. A giant ficus tree.

I glanced up at the pieces of sky I could see through the branches.

"Really? A tree?"

Good thing I wasn't afraid of heights.

The ground was only ten feet down. I couldn't see much else up here, as the tree was so lush, but I heard street traffic. I began descending the branches. Although I may not have been a graceful dancer, thankfully I was agile enough to reverse climb this thing.

When I swung from the final branch, my sneakers landed in a pile of winter leaves—dead like I was supposed to be.

I took a deep breath. Heaven had fresh air of course, but as I was still getting used to the concept of afterlife, I felt like breathing there was a lot like breathing oxygen from a scuba tank. It wasn't the same and your body knew it.

I turned around with a slew of wonder, sadness, and excitement. I was back. Well, sort of. I had to remind myself it wasn't my life I was here to live; it was Grace *Cabrera's*—my cover identity. And she was only here for Henry, not for another chance at her own happiness.

My hands clenched around my backpack straps and with a steady exhale I recentered. Focusing on the job and Henry would be the respite I needed from the torrent of emotions inside.

I found myself on an arbor-friendly traffic island in a cute residential area. My ficus was only one of many trees planted in a row on this thirty-foot-wide strip of land that separated north and southbound traffic. I'd landed on a pedestrian path that ran down the center of the island.

"Where did you come from?"

I spun around and found a young girl staring at me. Her skin was slightly tan, her short black hair was in pigtails, and she seemed around eight years old.

"I, uh . . ."

Maybe honesty is best here.

"I was trying to find my new school. It should be around here somewhere."

Assuming God didn't think I needed some exercise before class.

"Do you mean the high school?" the little girl asked.

"Yes. That's right."

"It's that way." She said, pointing up the path. "You should see a bunch of kids at a crosswalk."

"Oh, thank you, I—"

"Hana!"

We both turned our heads to look down the path. An Asian woman walked briskly toward us, two rambunctious boxers leaping around on the ends of their leashes. I was impressed the petite woman could handle all that energy.

"Here, Mommy!" the girl called.

The woman caught up with us. She wore chunky sunglasses, a white baseball cap, and a navy tracksuit. "Hana, don't get too far ahead of me," she said, exasperated. Then she looked at me. "Sorry, who are you?"

"I'm Grace, ma'am. Grace Car—" I cleared my throat. "Cabrera. I'm new to the area and your daughter was giving me directions. I'll be off now."

"Be careful crossing the road," the woman warned. "First day of school means a lot of traffic and parents rushing so their kids aren't late."

I checked my watch.

"I'll try not to be one of them," I said. "Have a nice day. Thanks for the directions, Hana." I trotted off.

"Careful with the golf carts!" Hana called after me.

I had no idea what she meant, but it wasn't long before I found the crosswalk Hana mentioned. Kids with backpacks strode from one side of the street to the other. I joined seamlessly, none of them noticing the addition. It was not surprising, as most of them were focused on their phones.

Hm. While I kind of miss Instagram, I'm glad Heaven doesn't have phones. I feel like I've had more eye contact in the last few days than I've experienced in a long time.

I took another long inhale-exhale as I absorbed the world around me.

It was surreal. Everything felt so normal, yet it was as if all my senses were heightened. I heard the jingle of every keychain, the humming of cars stalled at stop signs, and the chirping of birds in the trees. I noticed the sun glinting off each windshield, the glare of every cellphone screen, the glimmer of bracelets and watches and earrings. Overall, I just felt the buzz of life around me. Akari hadn't mentioned super senses being part of my new Guardian Angel skill set. Had I acquired this celestial power too or did I just have a deeper appreciation of everything around me because I didn't think I'd ever see any of it again?

Life was such a precious, fragile thing.

I wished I could send a mass group text to all these kids around me telling them that. Urging them to look up and truly see it while they had the chance.

After the crosswalk we journeyed through a connecting neighborhood. We stayed on the sidewalk as cars drove alongside us, headed in the same direction.

I was very wary of them.

Kill me once, shame on you; kill me twice, shame on me.

Finally I saw the school, marked by a sign that featured a dark blue dolphin wearing a crown alongside the words *Rancho Del Mar High School* in royal blue print.

My group merged with kids walking from other directions to form one large migration that curved beside a fence. Our sidewalk wrapped around until we reached an area where the cars were pulling in. School security and traffic guards ushered people along and sent the heavy traffic in three directions—two parking lots and one drop-off line. The sidewalk continued behind the latter until just past the drop-off zone where a concrete path ran by the library. Then came a myriad of open-air connecting halls and the rush of students split into various routes.

Fascinating.

From what I could tell, this school had an entirely outdoor campus. It featured single-story buildings, stucco walls painted with murals, and lockers that faced large patches of grass. The fresh smell of nature grazed my nose. In the distance I spotted huge trees shading an outdoor lunch area. Flowerbeds even grew by most of the classroom doors. Other than some parts of the hallway that were covered on top—perhaps in case of rain—everything was open.

It was wondrous and amazing. Every school I'd ever seen had been enclosed. Once you set foot on campus, apart from maybe some lunch tables outside, the natural world was solely something to be looked at through windows.

Heaven had a lot of impressive things. But this slice of beauty right here on Earth—

"*Oomph!*"

I stumbled and fell back on the grass. I'd been so entranced by the campus that I'd rammed into another student.

"Oh my, I'm so sorry!" The petite girl offered one of her delicate hands to help me up. It was nice of her, but she was so tiny I worried I might snap her wrist if I pulled too hard. I quickly leapt up on my own and dusted the grass off my pants.

Once done, I looked back at the girl. She was stupid pretty, like she should have been at a supermodel agency rather than a high school. Her shoulder-length, luscious brown-black hair broke into gentle waves by her ear line. Her eyes—dark and rich, and wide like a deer's—were framed by fine eyebrows. Overall, she reminded me of a young version of that actress Kerry Washington from the TV show *Scandal*.

I huffed internally with amusement. My older sister used to make me watch that. Gaby was generally a considerate and amiable person, but when it came to our TV remote control, sharing had not been her forte. I smiled to myself thinking about all the melodramatic programs she'd made me watch over the years. *Revenge, Glee, Grey's Anatomy* . . .

I shook my head, caught off guard by the strong pang of how much I missed my sister.

Focus, Grace. Now is not the time to cry.

In addition to being stunning, the girl I'd bumped into was terribly fashion forward. On the bottom she wore dark, straight-leg jeans and ankle boots. On top she donned a glittery, multi-colored crop top, which looked like something an Aztec warrior princess would wear.

"*Excusez-moi,*" the girl said. She had a French lilt to her accent, which was lovely but seemed out of place here. "This is my first day and I am a bit out of sorts. I'm having trouble finding the starter course on my itinerary."

"It's no problem," I replied in surprise. "I'm actually in the same boat. It's my first day too."

"*Incroyable!* What a wonderful coincidence. I'm Solange." She offered me her hand again, this time to shake in greeting. "Solange Alarie. My father's career has caused our family to relocate from Paris and I just transferred here. I must say, starting at a new school in the final term of the final year is quite jarring. Perhaps it is lucky that we ran into each other. Are you from far away too?"

Just north of the clouds.

"Yes. I'm Grace Cabrera. From South Carolina."

We shook hands. Solange pulled a piece of folded paper from her pocket and glanced at it. "I have physics with Mr. Corrin this morning. And you?"

I blinked, startled. I'd already memorized my schedule. "That's what I have too. Let's walk together." I took a glance at the numbers on the surrounding buildings. "I think it's this way."

Solange and I made our way through the crowded hallway. The pace of the kids around us increased with every second as the minutes to first period dwindled. We rounded a corner and entered through the doorway of the physics lab just as the bell rang.

"Take a seat and eyes forward," bellowed the man who

appeared beside us. He was easily six and a half feet tall and had an egg-shaped head, emphasized by a tight haircut.

The classroom was divided into two sections—a couple dozen desks on the left side of the room facing chalkboards, and lab tables for experiments on the right.

Only a couple of empty desks remained—one in the back row and another in the second row, beside a boy who turned to look in our direction.

Henry Sun's smile fell on me. The heightened senses I'd experienced on the crosswalk kicked in again, this time concentrated specifically on him. While I picked up the gleam of his grin, the spark in his eyes, even—I could've sworn—the pulse of his heartbeat, everything and everyone else hazed around him. It was as if for that moment the world pivoted on his existence. Perhaps since I was his Guardian Angel his soul stood out to me more than all the others.

Solange heeded Mr. Corrin's instructions and swiftly slid into the seat beside Henry before I could. His smile shifted as she said hello to him. I scuttled to the back of the room to claim the last desk.

"Welcome back, seniors," said the teacher in a booming voice. "For those who don't know, I'm Mr. Corrin, and here's how I figure it. You have about five months left of high school, which means I have five months to make a mark on your education. Physics is in everything we do. And since I doubt most of you have the interest or capacity to pursue the subject in college—I mean, why would you when there are so many lucrative jobs for Theater and Art History majors?—I am going to do my best to instill respect for this subject during the time I have to work with. Now, please take out your textbooks and turn to chapter one. Let's talk speed equations."

He began writing on the chalkboard. I fumbled through my backpack for the physics text. Akari had provided me with the backpack this morning—stuffed with several textbooks, a blank journal for taking notes, and a pouch loaded with pens, highlighters, and sharpened pencils.

Did Heaven have an office supply store?

Focus, Grace.

My eyes darted between the board and Henry as I took notes. The notes were supposed to be about physics, but I found myself taking mental notes about the boy as well. His dark hair spiked up around his slightly big ears in a natural way, not because of gel. He wore shorts and a sleeveless tank with blue, black, and white stripes—showing off tanned biceps.

"Who would like to solve one of these practice equations?" Mr. Corrin asked. "How about you in the back with the jacket who keeps staring at surfer Joe in the second row?"

Mr. Corrin pointed at me. The class turned around to gawk. Henry looked between our teacher and me.

Well, this is the worst.

I took a breath.

Nope. Not going to freak out.

I'd had teachers put me on the spot before. The only way embarrassment stuck was if you let it look like it bothered you. It didn't bother me here. This was an arena I felt comfortable in.

I took another glance at the $s = d/t$ formula I'd written down in my journal then stood up and walked calmly to the front of the room. Mr. Corrin pointed at the first equation.

"Solve."

"Yes, sir." I ignored the eyes of my classmates and plucked the piece of chalk from my professor's fingers. I faced the board then wrote out the equation, substituting in the numbers he'd provided for the variables. I solved it pretty fast, doing the math in my head. Once done, I pivoted and crossed my arms.

"Not bad," Mr. Corrin said. "Care to take a whack at the others? You can get a calculator if you want."

"Not needed, sir." I turned around and solved the other four examples on the board just as easily. Then I offered the teacher back his chalk. "Are we good here?"

My teacher inspected the board. "We are."

"Excellent. May I return to my seat?"

He nodded. I strutted confidently back to my chair, making eye contact with Henry on my way. This time I smiled at him.

THE FUNERAL

"That was our fourth class together," Henry remarked. I turned to find him leaning against the locker beside mine, students filing around us as they made their way to lunch.

"Was it? I hadn't noticed." I stowed my books then shut my locker. "I guess you must be stalking me."

He smirked. "I'm Henry Sun." He glanced across the courtyard at a girl with black, wavy hair who was coming our way. "And this is my better half," Henry said as the girl joined us, leaning an arm on his shoulder.

"Girlfriend?" I asked.

Both made fake vomiting noises.

"You wanna open up that locker door and scooch over so I can slam my head in it?" the girl asked.

"This is my twin sister Razel," Henry explained.

"Right. Sorry." I knew Henry had sisters, but my file had their names not their pictures. I smiled at the Sun girl. "I saw you in English this morning."

"You're one of the new girls," Razel said.

"Grace Cabrera. Just started today."

"You certainly came prepared. You didn't flinch an inch when the teacher called on you for an analysis of *Hamlet*."

"I read it last semester at my old school," I replied honestly.

"She's a total book beast," Henry commented. "You should've seen her when Mr. Corrin put her on the spot and she nailed everything he threw at her. He was almost speechless."

I shrugged. "I'm good with numbers and memorization. This is the easy part of my day."

"What's the hard part?" Henry asked.

You.

"To be determined," I answered.

"Hey, do you want to have lunch with us?" Razel offered. "It has to be rough starting someplace new for your final semester of high school."

"That's really kind of you," I remarked, pleasantly surprised. "When these scenarios play out on TV, typically the cool, attractive kids don't go out of their way to accommodate the newbie. Are you part of the school's welcoming committee or am I being pranked?"

"Neither," Razel replied with a grin. "And thank you for the compliment. I do look super hot today, don't I?"

"Actually, sis, she said attractive." Henry elbowed her.

Razel ignored him and linked her arm through mine. "Come on, Grace. I'll show you to the lunch line. Meet you at the tables, Henry," she called over her shoulder as she pulled me away.

The lunch area had some covered seating next to the cafeteria, but most of the students ate at tables and benches on the grass, or picnic-style in the shade of trees.

"So tell me, Grace," Razel said as we settled in the lunch line. "What's your deal?"

"My deal?"

She nodded. "I find that the best way to make friends is the kindergarten approach. You just straight-up introduce yourself, ask a person what they're into, then decide if their whole thing vibes with your whole thing."

I already liked Razel. She had an honesty filter built in and wasn't ashamed of it. I tended to babble truths when I was nervous, but her directness seemed to stem from high self-esteem, a complete security and comfort in who she was.

"Well, as your brother noted, I have a knack for schoolwork, I'm from South Carolina, and I have a dog named Droopy."

We made it to the front of the line. Of the several options on trays, Razel grabbed a calzone. I did the same.

"Those are some good basic facts." Razel shrugged. "Let's try something more personal. What do you want to be when you grow up?"

"I—"

Words caught in my throat. Unexpected emotion choked me as I realized that I was never going to grow up.

"Grace?" Razel turned to me after paying for her food. "You okay?"

"Yes." I gulped, handing the lunch lady some cash. "Thank you, ma' am."

Focus, Grace. This isn't about you. It's about Henry.

"That's a tough question. Can I get a different one?" I asked Razel as I followed her back into the open.

"Sure. How about this: What is one thing you'd like to do with your last semester of high school?"

I thought about it and chose an answer that was very true. "I'd like to live up to the expectations that people have for me."

"Pushy parents?" Razel asked.

"Something like that."

Just God, Heaven, and a few zillion angels who watch public access afterlife TV.

"I get it," Razel remarked. "Our dad is a neurosurgeon, and since Henry has always been crazy-smart at science stuff, there's a lot of pressure on him to perform at school and grow up to be a doctor too. My brother may seem super relaxed, but the guy's stressed a lot of the time, always worried about getting a single answer wrong. That's why he was impressed with you earlier. He's smart, but not good at owning it in front of people. He's shy."

"That guy is shy?" I asked dumbfounded as I pointed across the grass to where Henry was laughing with a bunch of kids. They'd claimed four red benches as their lunch area.

"There's different kinds of confidence, right?" Razel replied. "I mean, we all have parts of ourselves that we're good at showing and other parts that we keep to ourselves because we're not as certain about them."

I nodded. "You're not wrong . . ."

"Hey, Razel!" said one of the boys as we joined Henry's lunch group. My head barely reached his chest. "This must be Grace Cabrera." He slapped me on the back—unexpectedly but amicably. "Welcome to Rancho Del Mar!"

"This is Justin Pope," Razel introduced. "My brother's best friend, if you don't count me. He's as nice as he is indelicate."

"Sorry. Hulk tendencies," he replied. "Have you two met the other new girl?" He stepped aside and I saw the boys behind Justin crowding Solange.

She smiled at me. "Hi, Grace. Hi, Razel."

"Hey, girl, hey!" Razel turned to me and Justin. "We had economics together earlier."

"Doll, come here and sit down. I have some news." Solange beckoned Razel over. The latter pushed the boys out of her way in an endearing, assertive manner. When she sat down, the two girls started gabbing excitedly.

"You *are* smart." Henry suddenly appeared next to me. "The calzone is literally the only edible thing on the Monday menu."

"Yes, I'm basically Einstein in a fitted t-shirt," I replied. I sat at the edge of a bench and Henry positioned himself across from me, a bag of potato chips in one hand. He noticed a coin on the ground, picked it up, and pocketed it. I gave him a look.

He shrugged. "See a penny, pick it up, and all day long you'll have good luck."

"Pardon?"

"It's a thing my mom does. With my fate hanging in the hands of a bunch of strangers sorting through college admissions, I'll take all the luck I can get."

He opened the bag of chips and leaned over to say something to one of the other kids. I stared at him. Akari had been clear in her relatively simple instructions: assert myself in Henry's life; stay close so I'd be in a good place to protect him. I was divine glue stuck to his mortal shoe. She hadn't covered anything in orientation about what our dynamic was supposed to be like during that relationship. Could we be . . . friends? My mentor still had breakfast regularly with Winston Churchill. Were *they* pals?

It hadn't occurred to me that Henry could be more than an assignment. Heaven rigged my course schedule to keep us in close contact for seven hours a day, but that could start to look creepy if we didn't have anything else in common. Plus, what about after school? And once we graduated? Akari had tried to calm me last night, get me to focus on the immediate future so I wouldn't be overwhelmed. But I couldn't stop myself from wondering. As such, this is how I figured it. I didn't know exactly how long my time with Henry was intended to last, or how long I would be able to conceal my angelic identity. However, I reckoned my best chance at doing this job successfully was if he and I shared a bond beyond being forced to share the same space. Friendship seemed like the most plausible option, and looking at him . . .

Well, there were worse things than having to get to know a friendly, good-looking guy who seemed to lack all pretentiousness.

Also, I needed new friends. The friends I'd had on Earth were gone, part of a life that was over. Making friends in my afterlife would be difficult given how everyone in Heaven already had a preconceived notion of this "super angel" I was supposed to be. So this school was really my only chance to make a few friends who didn't know to expect anything from me.

Razel was right. We had different versions of ourselves, some we were proud to show and others we reluctantly kept in the shadows. I'd never been self-assured in original Grace Cardiff—the fiery girl who constantly failed to live up to respectable expectations. Nor was I confident in being Miss Ninety-Eight—the amazingly pure Guardian Angel. As for Grace Cabrera—the normal, book-smart teenager—I could work with her. I felt safe under her blanket of identity. I would try to use it to create a life where I seamlessly fit into Henry's world, did not cross any lines, and . . . did not let anybody down.

"Henry?" I said when his friend walked away.

He turned to me. "Yeah?"

"Your sister told me she's fond of directness when it comes to making new friends."

"Yeah, she calls it the kindergarten approach."

"Can I ask you a question pertaining to that?"

"Go for it."

"What do you want to be when you grow up?"

He hesitated with a frown; his brow furrowed. "A doctor, I guess."

"Like your dad?"

"Razel told you?"

I nodded. "Sounds like a nice profession. If that's what you want."

Henry leaned back and popped another chip in his mouth. "I think it is," he replied following a swallow. "I mean, in general I'd like to grow up to make a difference. Given the subjects I'm good at, it seems like something down the medical or bio route would make the most sense. My dad has patented some major procedure techniques. Maybe that's how I can leave my mark on the world too." He paused a moment as seriousness creased his face; then he let that go and shrugged. "Who knows? The world is weird. It's probably egotistical to assume I have what it takes to do something that really matters."

"I wouldn't say that," I replied. "Maybe making a difference starts with believing that you can."

"Hey, Henry!" Justin called, waving him over.

My assignment excused himself and went over to his friend. I watched him go and took a bite of my calzone.

Mm. Pretty decent.

"The two of us are going to have such a lovely time together this semester," Solange gushed, sitting down next to me as I chewed.

I swallowed hastily. "I admire your positive attitude. You're not intimidated by new surroundings, are you?"

"Please." She waved haughtily. "Was this how I expected the year to go? Of course not. But *c'est la vie*. This is where we are now and though it may be different than what we're used to, I love a challenge. And just look at all the fascinating people we have to work with." Solange gestured at Henry and company then sighed. She leaned back and stared up at the sky. "Grace, you and I are going to have some serious fun here."

The final bell rang, signaling the end of the school day. My last class had been statistics with both Razel and Henry.

"Do you drive, Grace?" Razel asked as we exited the classroom, students flowing around us toward the front of campus.

"I have my learner's permit," I replied.

Though I'm not sure if I'll have to get retested since that was issued to a girl who's dead now.

"Henry and I are going to take our driver's tests later this semester," Razel said excitedly. "School is within walking distance from our house, but sometimes Justin gives us a ride if he doesn't have baseball practice. He and our mom rotate as our designated chauffeurs until we achieve vehicular independence. What about you? Are you taking the bus home?"

My mind snapped to my cover story. "I live with my guardian. She doesn't get back from work until late, so I'm not headed home right now. Actually, do you know if there's a church around here?" I hadn't seen one on my walk to school, and I had no idea where to start looking.

"Are you like super religious?" Razel asked curiously.

"No. I just, uh . . . I lost someone recently and being near a church helps me feel connected to them."

"Oh, I'm sorry to hear that," Razel said.

"Same," Henry said; genuine sadness creased his face. "Was it someone close to you?"

It was me.

"Yes," I replied.

"There's a church between our house and Justin's," Henry said. "He's driving us today. I'm sure he'd be happy to give you a lift." Henry saw Justin walking ahead and called to him.

I smiled. "That'd be—"

"Watch out!"

I didn't react in time, but Henry grabbed me by the jacket and yanked me out of the way as a golf cart zoomed by.

"Are you okay?" he asked. "The school security guards can be pretty intense. You'd think they were making a golf cart reboot of *The Fast and the Furious*."

"Oh, so that's what she meant," I thought out loud.

"Who?" Henry asked.

"Just a girl I met this morning. Anyway, yes, a ride would be great please."

We all loaded into Justin's jeep. Henry rode up front while

I settled in back with Razel. We merged into the hectic stream of traffic exiting campus, which routed over a massive downhill slope. I gazed at the chaos of kids leaving school—buses, cars, skateboards, bikes. It didn't seem like the most organized, or safest path. A waft of instinctive worry fluttered in my stomach, and I glanced between Henry and Razel.

"How often do you two walk home?"

"Usually a couple days a week," Henry responded. "Why?"

"It's just . . . it seems really dangerous. There's a lot of traffic. And everyone is going so fast. Plenty of things could go wrong."

"Woof. Severe ominous vibe, Grace," Razel replied.

"Sorry. I'm—"

Concerned about how many ways a teenage boy can get killed.

As if on cue to increase my anxiety, a bus cut us off and whizzed past.

"Let's just call me a worrier," I responded.

Five minutes later, Justin pulled into the driveway of a luxurious house across the street from where I'd arrived this morning. Henry and Razel said their goodbyes, then Justin motioned for me to move to the shotgun seat. I obliged and buckled up.

"So are we working with a deadline here?" he asked as he reversed out of the driveway. "Do I need to get you to the church on time?"

I tilted my head. "Is that a *My Fair Lady* reference? Like with Eliza Doolittle, Professor Higgins, and so on?"

"I like musicals." He shrugged. "Did you think I was some big, muscular jock?"

"Actually, yes."

"Well, you're only half right." He gave me a quick, cocky grin before returning his eyes to the road. "I'll take tickets to a Lakers game or a performance of *Wicked*. Just depends on the day and who can go with me."

"Is Henry into musicals?" I asked.

"Nah. Razel is though. She's all about the drama department at school. I've spent so much time at their house over the years hanging out with Henry that she and I became friends too. She tricked me into giving musical theater a chance and I realized

I actually like it. There are definitely guys I hang out with who would give me a hard time about it, but we've all got layers, right?"

"Right." I nodded. "I was obsessed with the first *High School Musical* movie when I was little. There was this song about not sticking to the status quo that I listened to so many times my sister almost went crazy. The writers of that song would be fans of yours, and going off first impressions, so am I."

"Well, thank you, ma'am." He tipped an invisible hat, one hand remaining on the wheel.

I smiled and rested my elbow on the window as we drove in silence for a few minutes. Crisp wind blew my hair back and I stared out at the ocean that glistened peacefully to my right. My eyes shifted to the clouds in the sky. I wondered how far they were from Heaven.

Maybe my new celestial home wasn't even part of this realm of existence, and I wasn't so much a girl coming from another place as an alien arriving from another universe—

"And we're here," Justin announced. He turned left and pulled uphill into a sloped parking lot. He put the car in park but didn't turn off the engine. "The church is at the top of those steps." He leaned over and pointed. "You sure you're okay here? Do you have a way to get home later?"

"I do," I said. I hopped out of the car and closed the door. "Thank you for the ride. I appreciate it."

"You're welcome."

"And thank you for, well, being so nice in general. All of you have been surprisingly kind today. There must be something in the water here."

Justin shrugged. "I'm sure our school has its share of jerks. Every place does, right? I'm glad we found you before they did." He winked. "Happy to show you the ropes."

"How Professor Higgins of you," I responded. "And honestly, I could use the help as I get used to this new place, and this new life."

"Whatever you need, Miss Doolittle." He extended his hand. "Toss me your phone. I'll put in my number in case you have questions about school, basketball, baseball, or musical theater."

"The basics?" I smiled, digging into my backpack and removing the Earth-issue phone that came with my cover. It had zero frills, zero apps, and other than the ability to text and make calls, zero features the average teenager would want.

"Speaking of basic," Justin teased, looking over my phone once I handed it to him. He input his digits. "I'm gonna guess Henry and Razel gave you their numbers already? They have a thing about looking out for new kids."

I nodded. "Yeah, they texted me their info earlier."

"Cool." He lobbed the phone back to me. "Alrighty, see you tomorrow, Doolittle." Justin mock-saluted before pulling out of the parking lot. I waved at his departing vehicle then turned my attention uphill. I couldn't see the church from here; it was well hidden in the trees.

My sneakers reached stone steps. The more of them I scaled, the more serene I felt. This place was rich in tall, lush nature that shielded it from the outside world. The temperature even dropped a few degrees thanks to the shade. Finally, it came into view—a small, stunning glass church.

Enormous pines shrouded the church's front panels. I approached the set of double doors and peered in. Elaborate wooden framework mixed with magnificent triangular glass fragments to create a striking work of vision. The few souls inside were absorbed in their own thoughts and prayers. They didn't notice the teenager gawking from the outside.

I glanced around to ensure no one would witness whatever was about to happen, then placed my hands on the door handles and concentrated. My Soul Pulse shimmered. I closed my eyes and pushed, stepping forward with resolve. From beneath my closed eyelids, I sensed a rush of light and felt a warmth like the SoCal sun shining upon me. When I opened my eyes, I stood in an alcove just like the one I'd departed from this morning.

Other angels continued appearing down the hall in their own stations. Based on their glittery wing backpacks and rapid, purposeful pace, they must've been IDS angels. I took it slow as I exited my chamber and walked to the foyer.

When I exited the building, I watched as other angels raced

past me then teleported away the second they crossed the threshold of the Arrival Center. Back to work, no doubt. Hopefully to save *other people* before it was too late . . .

I sauntered down the steps of the magnificent golden cathedral and wandered to the edge of the cloud just in front of where the Pearlie Gates hovered.

"Hello there, Ninety-Eight."

I turned and found Pearlie herself trotting over the steps with Rowbie the goat in tow. He managed to keep pace with her enough to chew on the hem of her dress without slowing her.

"How was your first day as a Guardian Angel?"

"It was actually pretty easy. I mean, I didn't do much in the way of guarding, but I got to know the guy I'm assigned to. That's something, right?"

"Absolutely," Pearlie agreed. "I may not know all the ins and outs of the GA operation, but I do know two things for certain. First, from my line of work, I know the importance of souls connecting with one another. All good souls may go to Heaven, but they get here faster and more peacefully because of the people who show up to give them love and support. Second, from everything that Akari has told me, I know that the trust between Guardian Angels and the souls they protect is pivotal when things get hard."

I glanced at Pearlie curiously. "Have you and Akari been friends for a long time?"

"We have," Pearlie said, her tone a little sad. She stared off at the sky, then met my gaze with kind eyes. "You'll have to go easy on her, Grace. She's not the same angel she used to be, but I know she takes her job very seriously and will always try her best to be there for you. You should trust her."

"Because the divine universe says we're a good match?"

"No. Because she's a good person. That doesn't mean she's beyond mistakes or beyond learning, but it does mean she will always keep trying to grow from the former and evolve from the latter. Keep that in mind, Ninety-Eight. People may expect a lot of your pure soul, but that doesn't mean we don't expect you to be human too."

I sighed and crossed my arms, speaking my vulnerable

thoughts into existence. "How can a person be pure but also flawed?" I shook my head, doubts swallowing my heart. "How can a person be wholly good if they've done things that are objectively bad?"

Rowbie hacked abruptly. Pearlie bent to pat him on the head as she pondered my questions. "I don't know, Ninety-Eight. But it's obviously possible; otherwise, everyone would end up downstairs. Maybe the universe grades on a curve? Or maybe the goodness of an action depends on the eyes of the beholder?" She checked her watch. "I need to take Rowbie to the groomer. You should probably get back to Angel Tower."

I nodded. "See you, Pearlie."

"Until another date, Ninety-Eight." Pearlie grabbed hold of Rowbie's left horn and they vanished with a flash of her Soul Pulse.

I followed her lead and concentrated on Akari's office. A moment later, I was on the balcony outside of Angel Tower. My mentor had explained that for security purposes, teleports didn't get you into this building, or work once you were inside because not everyone had access to every floor.

I liked teleporting to this spot. It was where Akari had first brought me. The views were impeccable. Plus, considering my Ninety-Eight status was still fresh in the minds of the angels, I preferred arriving in private up here versus entering the lobby and being gawked at by hundreds of people before I rode the elevator a zillion floors up. I'd tried that this morning and had not cared for it.

I made my way to Akari's office and knocked.

"Come in, Grace."

"How'd you know it was me?" I asked as I took a seat. Akari shoved some papers she'd been reading back in a folder.

"Never mind that. How did your first day go?"

"Surprisingly well," I admitted. "Being back on Earth was weird at first, and emotional, but the more I concentrated on being in the moment—getting to know Henry, meeting his friends, immersing myself in my classes—the easier it was to move forward."

"I'm glad to hear it," she said. "And I'm happy that you even seem a little happy too."

I mused on the notion. "I guess I am. I think being at school today helped me get some of my confidence back. The people were so nice, and shining in academic settings was a boost to the ol' self-esteem. Actually, while I'm riding this wave of energy, if you're ready with a fire extinguisher and angelic first aid kit, I'm ready to try more halo training. Maybe I can actually get that discus trick right before Leo and Monkonjae join us."

"While I appreciate the enthusiasm and thinly veiled masochistic humor," Akari replied, "you actually have another appointment right now. Leave your backpack here."

I set my bag beside the chair and followed Akari out. We rode the elevator about thirty floors down. My head crooked in confusion when the name of the level shimmered into view as the lift came to a stop.

"Animal Transformation?"

"A very popular destination for the newly deceased," Akari explained as we stepped out. "It's by appointment only. On this floor, angels can be transformed into animals, birds, and even insects. Once changed, they return to Earth temporarily to visit loved ones in those forms."

"*That's a thing?*"

I stared with wonder as we made our way through the corridor. The walls were covered in climbing ivy, soft moss, and entwined branches. Boughs of different flowers created the ceiling— bougainvillea in one hall, jasmine in another, roses after that. The entire floor was carpeted with real grass.

"For plenty of people, yes," Akari replied. "After someone has experienced a loss, sometimes they see a white dove, or a butterfly, or a cardinal, or some other kind of creature that objectively would seem insignificant. However, when that person sees this creature, they're filled with an overwhelming sense of faith and peace. Something inside tells them that this creature is the spirit of their loved one, and most of the time, they are right."

"That's wonderful," I said, taking in the signs on different doors along our route that other angels were headed toward. *Blue Butterflies*, *Goldfinches*, *Ladybugs*, *Falcons* . . .

Akari stopped me at a door marked *Funeral Crows*. Seventeen people stood in line ahead of us, and another angel queued behind me almost immediately. When it was our turn, Akari flashed her Soul Pulse on the door scanner and indicated for me to do the same. After two confirmation flashes, we entered the room.

The floor in here was also made of grass, but the walls . . . Well, it didn't look like there were walls. Though the floor and ceiling suggested where they should be, churning gray skies surrounded us on all four sides. The virtual reality even gave off real wind that caused my skin to grow goosebumps and my hair and jacket to blow around me.

Across the room were dozens of sparkly platforms wide enough for two people to stand on. I watched an angel step onto one. When he did, his body shimmered and he transformed into a crow! The bird flapped its wings a moment, cawed, and then vanished with a flash.

"Have you ever wondered why there are always crows around cemeteries and funerals?" Akari asked to my bewildered expression. She gestured at the platforms. "In Heaven, angels can transform into crows and attend their own funerals in those forms." She checked her watch. "Hm. I just hope your family—"

The door opened and my Grandma Robin, Grandpa Jim, Abuela Lupe, and Abuelo Rolando hurried in.

"Sorry we're late," said Grandpa Jim. "We got off on the wrong floor."

I opened my mouth, but Akari answered my question before I got a word out. "Yes, Grace. They're all here because we are going to your funeral. Yours and your mothers. It's happening right now in South Carolina."

"But . . . I . . . You . . ."

Take a breath, Grace.

I gulped and found footing on one important query. "What about my mom? Shouldn't she be here?"

"I wish she could be," Akari said sympathetically. "But her

assigned time in Heaven didn't fall on the day of your funeral. There's nothing we can do to postpone that."

"Oh." I felt my heart deflate. Then I paused. I scratched the back of my neck anxiously.

"Grace?" Akari said.

I sighed and glanced between her and my relatives. "Do I really *want* to see this?"

"You don't have to, Nugget," Nana Robin said kindly. "But I recommend it. We all attended our own funerals. They're sad occasions, of course, but they gave us closure."

"But you didn't die when you were young!" I snapped.

I blinked in stupor after the words came out. Emotion had overwhelmed me unexpectedly. My hands were even trembling. I took a steadying breath. "I'm sorry. I'm feeling a lot of feelings. Mom always said I shouldn't let those get the better of me."

"Grace," Akari said softly. She put her hand on my shoulder with genuine care, not like an assigned guide but a concerned friend. "I don't know your mom, and if that's something you agree with, then I don't want to contradict your beliefs. But you shouldn't worry about emotions getting the better of you because emotions are the *best* of you. There's validity in what you're feeling. And if you don't want to do this, you don't have to."

I thought on it. My Abuela Lupe stepped forward. She changed her youthful appearance to that of the familiar elderly woman with silver, braided hair I'd known as a young child. She took my face in her soft, cold hands. "We are here, *mi cariño*. Whatever you decide."

She let me go and I stood still for a moment. Then I nodded. Maybe I did need to do this. At the very least, it was a chance to see my dad and sister.

"Fine. Let's go."

My two sets of grandparents stepped onto the nearest platforms while Akari shared one with me.

"Is there a specific place I'm supposed to concentrate on? Like an exact cemetery?" I asked warily.

"Not a place. Focus on the people you left behind," she said quietly.

I closed my eyes tightly. My clenched fists tensed and vibrated and the heat increased in my cheeks. My insides lurched. Then my eyes snapped open and I saw black feathers before a flash blinded me. When my vision settled, I found myself perched in a tree.

Five other crows stood on surrounding branches. Somehow, I knew they were Akari and my relatives.

My beady bird eyes took in the world with an interesting tilt—it was like looking through binoculars. I zeroed in on a funeral happening downhill and leapt from the branch, flapping my wings like I'd been flying my whole life. Their midnight sheen cut through the twilight sky as I soared over the cemetery, countless headstones blurring together. I tried to ignore them. It was like when you viewed innumerable ant-sized buildings from the window of an airplane. Though they were the ones that looked minuscule, you felt smaller in your soul when you realized just how many people were a part of this world . . . and in this case, how many people had left it behind.

I alighted onto a branch of the tree nearest the grieving gathering, attendees dressed in attire as dark as my wings. The other crows in my pack landed in the surrounding branches. I eyed the proceedings with a heavy heart and icy veins.

Not twenty feet away were the centerpieces of the assembly: a pair of cypress wood coffins laden with lilies. I recognized friends from school, teachers, and neighbors . . . so many people that I used to know filled the rows. Toward the front was my family—Grandpa Thorston, various aunts, uncles, and cousins from my father's side. The two most important people in the congregation were so close that I felt like my heart might crumble.

My focus fixated on my dad and older sister Gaby in the front row. The former sat unmoving. His eyes were glassy and his face paler than I'd ever seen it. My father Frank was a high-spirited man, a man hardly ever seen without a smile. Looking at him now, I wasn't sure if a smile would ever grace his face again.

Gaby got up and brushed a strand of her blonde-highlighted

oak hair from her face with a sniffle. She walked to the podium, took a deep breath, and spoke into the microphone.

"I keep going over it in my head. All the moments, the days, hours, even minutes I could've cherished my time with my mother and sister more. That's the cruelest thing about death, isn't it? It forces you to realize how precious someone's life is, but that life is already gone, so you can't do anything with the lesson. There were so many times when I chose to have dinner in my room watching some dumb TV show rather than joining my family at the table because I didn't want to hear my mom lecture us. So many times when I could've gone to a concert or a movie or coffee with my little sister when she asked me to, but I didn't because I was busy with my own thing and didn't want to choose quality time with her over convenience for me."

She gripped the podium tightly and shook her head. "If I could go back, I would do it all differently. Because every moment with someone you love—no matter how small or stupid or seemingly insignificant—is a moment *with* them. And that's what matters in the end. I would give anything to be with my mother and sister again. I know they're at peace . . . somewhere. It brings me a little peace too, having faith that they have gone someplace better. I just hope that they know how much they were and are still loved, how much they will be missed, and that wherever their souls have gone . . . a piece of them will always be right here." She held her hand to her heart. "Until we meet again."

I felt my chest crack in half and a caw burst from my beak. It was a powerful, painful cry that made Gaby look up. We stared at each other for a moment. Then my sister went to retake her seat with my father, gripping his hand in hers.

I leapt from the branch, not by choice but instinct, and flew toward the sky. My wings flapped and flapped and flapped as I aimed for a ray of pink streaking through the clouds then—

FLASH.

I was on my hands and knees in a lush room, different than the place where I'd been transformed. Every inch of floor, wall, and ceiling was covered in undergrowth except the shimmering platforms. An exit door was marked across the space. I couldn't go for it though. I just sat there in shock, breathing heavily and slowly.

Other crow-angels arrived around me. When they morphed back to human form, they also remained where they'd landed—digesting the crushing gravity of what they'd witnessed. Akari and my grandparents appeared a second later and approached me warily. I refused to meet their eyes and instead diverted my gaze to the vine-covered floor as I sat and stared vacantly.

After a moment I felt someone's hand lovingly caress my head, smoothing my hair. I sensed others crouch on either side of me too, holding my arms or shoulders to try and comfort me.

I still couldn't look at them. Everything felt like a dream. The only thing that felt real was the cold tear that ran down my cheek then fell and hit my hand—so small but so full of feeling that it may as well have been a barrel of frigid water splashing on my skin and shocking me into accepting the truth. A truth I knew but had kept emotionally at bay for the last few days.

I was dead.

Heaven had blessed me with a lot of new opportunity, but there was no going back on that. And as the true weight of that reality set into my soul, I knew it was finally time to cry.

7

RIDESHARE

"Are you doing okay?" Monkonjae asked me.

We stood next to each other in the training center, aiming our halos at distant targets. He released another perfect shot—slicing through a dangling punching bag so that it fell to the ground. I aimed and threw my halo as well, but instead of going where it was supposed to, it shattered the glass in one of the training center's doors.

Irritation pulsed through me and I summoned the halo back to my head before using my Soul Pulse magic to fix the door. Akari had downloaded another app for each of us this afternoon—Fixer Upper, which put things back together. Needless to say, I was using it a lot.

"I'm making do," I said bitterly.

"Do you need to talk about it?" he asked, magically reattaching his bag. "We've been at this an hour and you haven't said much. I can tell you're upset."

Monkonjae hit his target flawlessly again. My discus veered off course—bouncing off the bleachers before spiraling back and getting stuck in my punching bag.

Oh, that is it.

I scowled in frustration as my feelings boiled up unhealthily. Instead of summoning my halo, I stomped over to the bag. My halo had returned to normal ring form and was lodged in. I grabbed it and yanked it free. Then in a temperamental impulse I kicked the punching bag.

It was ill-advised. The kick was powerful and rocked the bag significantly, but it hurt my foot like all heck.

Monkonjae was behind me when I turned around. My cheeks

flushed with shame. I took a deep breath and made my halo vanish—wringing my hands as I stared at the floor.

"I'm sorry you had to see that. I didn't mean to freak out. It's been a tough day and my feelings overpowered my composure. Regrettably that's an ongoing struggle for me. I hope you don't think less of me for it." I finally met Monkonjae's eyes, feeling like I owed him an explanation. "I went to my funeral today."

His expression shifted to empathy. "Oh. I'm sorry. I died a week ago and attending my funeral was rough. I know exactly what you're going through."

I crossed my arms and hugged myself. All afternoon there'd been a relentless question circling my thoughts with the repetition of a carousel and crushing pressure of a Panini press, but I hadn't known who to ask it to. After some brief consideration as I looked into Monkonjae's warm eyes, I felt safe enough to squeeze out the tormenting thought.

"How did you deal with it?" I asked sadly. "How *are* you dealing with it? Death, I mean."

Monkonjae fidgeted and looked around at nothing in particular. Then he sighed. "To be honest, I kept to myself for a couple of days after my funeral. I was in a pretty dark place . . ." He looked over the halo in his hand, lost in thought. Then he shook his head and met my eyes. "But I chose to come out of it. That's the thing about dark places—there's not always someone to send a lifeline or offer a hand to escape. Sometimes you just have to decide you don't want to be there anymore and pull yourself out. Then you can see what kind of new beginning you can create from there."

I rolled my head back. "I know you're right. I do. Maybe I just need to wallow in the dark a little longer."

"Maybe. Like I said, I did the same thing." He hurled his halo, winding his arm like a baseball player throwing a pitch. His halo hit a target on the other side of the training center.

"Just remember," he said. "A little wallowing can be therapeutic; a lot of wallowing sucks you down deeper. It's like eating ice cream. A bowl makes you feel good; a carton makes you feel awful."

I smiled softly. "You know, when I didn't make it onto my middle school's debate team, I ate an entire carton of mint chocolate chip ice cream. I immediately regretted it when I upchucked all over the couch my mom had just bought. The couch was already mint colored, but even after washing the pillows ten times, they always looked stained, and I—"

I fell silent. "Sorry," I said. "This Heavenly honesty filter combined with my normal blather is not doing my image any favors. I really need to rein it." I huffed and shook my head. "Story of my life."

Monkonjae summoned his halo and fidgeted with it again. "Would it make you feel less embarrassed if I told you about the last time I threw up? Spoiler alert, it involves my cat and a set of golf clubs."

I chuckled mildly. "Thanks, but I'll pass. Our relationship probably works better if only one of us is terribly awkward."

"Sorry we're late!" Ana called as she and Leo entered the training center. "We've been doing some basic skills training."

"Basic skills?" I repeated as the pair came to join us. Deckland and Akari—who'd been off to the side chatting—approached the group too.

"Leo passed away at a young age like me," Ana explained. "He didn't learn how to drive, swim, or even ride a bike."

Leo self-consciously touched that spot on the bridge of his nose. "I was sick a lot while I was alive. Didn't get around to it."

"As Guardian Angels, you have to be ready for anything," Ana continued. "So in addition to supernatural skills, we teach the basic ones. Things get crazy in the field and until you earn your wings, you need to have plenty of other getaway options in your back pocket. I know how to maneuver everything from a forklift to a helicopter."

Akari glanced at me. "In keeping with that, one of these days we'll prep you for an Earth driving test. You'll need your license if you're going to keep up with Henry."

"I figured as much."

"While we're on the subject of new skills," Deckland announced heartily. "Today we're introducing you to another basic use of the halo—the handheld slice. It's a great tool in your arsenal with a lot of offensive and defensive applications. Throwing your halo is a good distance move, while slicing is great for up close situations, like cutting the lock off a cell in a prisoner-of-war camp, which your mentor has done." Deckland looked to me. "Or slitting the tires of mafia enforcers like *your* mentor has done." He flicked his eyes to Leo.

The kid glanced at Ana. "You really get around, don't you?"

"Just because I'm small doesn't mean I can't save the world."

Deckland's Soul Pulse flashed and an assortment of different targets appeared—everything from watermelons on stakes to concrete cinderblocks stacked on top of each other.

"Maybe this skill will come naturally to you, Grace," Deckland said optimistically.

He meant no offense, but the comment perturbed me. I was at the end of my rope for the day in terms of patience and inner peace.

"The first thing you need to understand," he continued, "is that grabbing your halo alone doesn't change it into anything. It's the action after that and focusing on the intention that bring out different powers. Like how flinging the halo transforms it into disc form, if you grip the halo tightly and focus on slicing, the side you're not touching will become sharp. The more focused your intention, the more powerful that slice, allowing you to cut through things with greater density."

Deckland pointed at the fruit targets. "Go for the watermelons first. They should be easy to slice up. Then you can move on to the harder options."

I called my halo to my head and gripped it firmly. Monkonjae and Leo did the same.

Okay, maybe this will be my time to shine.

Calm mind. Composed heart. Collected demeanor.

I can do this.

An hour later, I sat in Akari's office with my head in my hands.

"Oh my goodness, I suck."

My mentor patted me on the back. "You don't suck, Grace. You're just experiencing . . . a really tough learning curve."

"I don't understand." I sat back in the pink chair with a huff. "I could barely cut through a salami, let alone a watermelon. I may as well have been coming at it with a rusty butter knife."

"It's probably hard for you to focus because you've had such an emotionally exhausting day. You'll get the hang of this soon."

"And what if I don't?" I replied earnestly, looking her dead in the eyes.

"You will."

"How can you be so sure?"

"I'm not sure. But I have faith."

I crossed my arms. "That may earn points with the boss upstairs. For regular folk, faith isn't quite so reassuring when you feel like the world is in flux around you." I stood abruptly. "You don't have any more surprises or drills for me today, do you?"

"No."

"Good. I have homework to do." I grabbed my backpack and went for the door.

"Do you want me to escort you to the Pearlie Gates tomorrow?" Akari asked, a touch of concern in her voice.

"I can find my way. Good night, Akari."

"Good night, Grace."

I exited Angel Tower. I paused at the edge of the balcony, taking a long look at the seemingly infinite landscape of Heaven sinking into night. Then that magical energy hiccup happened again, touching everything in sight and rising to the sky. I don't know why seeing it helped calm me—I didn't even know what it was—but somehow, it did. For a moment, the painful feelings that I'd been struggling with all afternoon softened. I inhaled the night air—sweet like flowers, comforting like pot roast in the oven, calming like lavender incense.

A shooting star darted across the heavens above Heaven. I imagined it was an angel cutting through the sky with a daring use of wings—not falling, but charging ahead . . .

I gulped and teleported home. Droopy got up to greet me

when I walked in, which was a nice surprise. I used my Soul Pulse to summon a plate of lasagna and some milk. Meal in hand, I headed toward the couch, but hesitated in front of the framed photo of my family on the wall.

My dad loved lasagna—my mom's lasagna in particular.

She cooked on Sundays. Although she worked a lot and made no compromises where her job was concerned, she and Grandpa Thorston always had dinner together on Sundays when she was growing up, so she continued the tradition with us. In our household the meal was usually accompanied by a side dish of arguing—typically between me and my mother—but I had a sudden longing for Sunday night dinner anyway. If I closed my eyes, I could see every inch of our kitchen behind my father, who sat across from me at the table for every family meal of my entire life . . .

A wad of emotion built in my throat. I cleared it and turned away from the picture.

With a small sniffle I settled on the couch, putting my feet up. Droopy tried to clamber up beside me, but when his tiny limbs didn't cut it, he used his wings to assist him. I gave him a chunk of meat that fell out of the lasagna, then turned on Memory Prime.

"Continue previous stream," I said into the remote.

"Activating shuffle mode for previous search of: Why am I here? Why did they choose me as a Guardian Angel?" announced the automated voice.

The TV fluxed with color and a new scene filled the screen. I was still young, but a tad older and a bit chubbier. Maybe third grade. The bow in my hair matched my glittery capris.

Real me ate a forkful of lasagna and watched little me waiting in line at the handball court during recess. When the next kid was up, little me began to move forward, but a tall blonde girl with sharp eyebrows and a posse of two more friends stepped in front.

"Hey, no cuts," little me protested.

The blonde girl didn't say anything. She simply turned around and shoved little me to the ground then bore over her with hands on hips. Little me blinked in shock. The blonde girl's cruel face was emphasized with shadow from the sun behind her.

Little me stared up at the bully, then glanced at her hands that'd been scraped by the blacktop. Something shifted in her face.

Little me stood, took a step forward, and punched the blonde girl square in the nose.

It was satisfying to watch. It made me feel warmer inside than the lasagna did. But I also felt sad, for I knew what happened next.

"Don't celebrate yet, Droopy," I said, pointing to the TV with my fork. His eyes didn't leave my plate.

I sighed and shook my head dejectedly as I watched one of the teachers on the playground blow a whistle and escort little me to the principal's office. The scene shifted to her sitting in a far-too-large chair, facing the authority of a man in a suit.

My mother entered the room. "I'm so sorry, Mr. Keegan. I would have come sooner, but I was in a meeting. Please accept my sincerest apologies for making you wait, and for my daughter's appalling behavior. I don't know what came over her. She wasn't raised like this."

"I trust not, Mrs. Cardiff. Your daughter Gaby was always so well behaved. I expect more from Grace."

"As do I." My mother shot me a cutting glare. It looked like disappointment mixed with detestation. Not for me perhaps, but for what I had done.

"I've already given Grace a firm talking to about her aggressive action," the principal said, standing. "She will need to stay late after school every day next week in detention. And apologize to Miss Wilson, the young lady she assaulted."

Little me bit her lip. "But I don't want—"

"Grace." My mother gave a silencing finger then readdressed the principal. "Anything else?"

"No. You may take her home now."

My mother grabbed little me by the arm and led her out of the principal's office into the hall. Once alone, she bent over so they were eye to eye.

"Young lady, what you did today was absolutely unacceptable. Good girls do not throw punches or react so senselessly. I am ashamed of you. If there was any doubt about enrolling you in that after-school etiquette class at the community center, there isn't now."

"Mom, you don't understand," little me protested. "That girl deserved it. She was being mean and I—"

"Thought you should punish her? Thought violence was the answer?"

"No, I just—I didn't want to be pushed around."

"Well, young lady, I can tell you that no one here sees it that way. To everyone else, it looked like you attacked her."

"But I'm the victim!"

"Tell that to the girl with the bloody nose, dear. Now come on." She took little me by the hand forcefully and pulled her out through the school main doors. "You made me miss work, so while I'm at home calling to apologize to the people I let down, you are going to stay in your room and make a list of every *sensible* way you could have handled this situation, and repeat the rules of a lady fifty times out loud."

They reached the curb and waited for the crossing guard to signal them.

"Mom—"

"You can start right now."

Little me looked like she was about to cry. She crunched her lip nervously, then ultimately hung her head. "A lady never talks out of turn. A lady restrains her impulses. A lady doesn't create, inspire, or escalate conflict. A lady must remain level-headed and proper in all situations . . ." Little me bit her lip.

Real me spoke what she was forgetting. "A lady respects her parents by obeying her parents." I sighed and paused the TV.

The screen fluxed with color and the automated voice returned. "Shall I play another video?"

"Hard pass," I said. My stomach felt queasy. I handed my plate to Droopy and he lapped up the lasagna as I rolled my head back on the couch and glowered at the ceiling.

My "aggressive behavior" was the thing my mother hated most about me. Other authority figures had judged me harshly for it too. I felt shame for how often I let it get the better of me—letting them all down—but also . . . I was ashamed that I didn't feel *more* ashamed about it.

Every time I got in trouble for "acting out" I partially regretted whatever I'd done, but not entirely because there was something in my character that couldn't condone doing nothing. It hurt way more to be that little girl who let Victoria and Katcha push her around than it did to be the little girl getting admonished in the principal's office for taking a swing at a bully.

I just wished other people, my mother in particular, didn't make me feel like a monster because of it.

I wiped my hand across my face.

This had been an emotionally taxing day and watching Memory Prime was only adding to the distress. My heart was becoming too heavy.

With a rough, but long exhale, I sat up straighter on the couch. I couldn't keep sinking like this. I decided to take Monkonjae's advice and try to pull myself out of my funk. No one else was going to.

I spoke into the remote. "Show me something that will make me happy."

Another flux of color and then actor Dylan O'Brien's face appeared on the screen alongside the movie poster for the second *Maze Runner* film. His hotness was so profound it shocked me out of my stupor a bit. I couldn't help but laugh to myself from the surprise of that.

"Well, okay then."

LA-LA-LA-SHMING! LA-LA-LA-SHMING!

"Yipes!" I woke with a start.

The angel-issued alarm clock in my room—a sparkling golden harp the size of a blender—floated above my head. The strings magically strummed the same melodic cascade of notes over and over, louder and louder. I reached for the mini-harp, but like a dog playing keep-away, it zipped out of range. I harrumphed and threw the covers off.

"Come here, you." I pursued the flying harp across the room. I had to give it to the Heaven tech folk; between the Soul Pulse and an alarm clock that physically wouldn't allow you to hit snooze and forced you to get up, the afterlife had a handle on efficiency.

I thought I had the harp cornered, but it darted to the left. I dove and tackled it to the ground. "Got you!"

I smacked a glowing button on top and the thing shimmered, shook, and then powered off. Once I set it back on my nightstand, I went about my morning: first cereal at the table, then Droopy and I went for a walk. Turns out dogs didn't produce excrement in Heaven; when they approached a tree or bush to do their business, only a rainbow of butterflies fluttered out.

Last stop on my morning routine was my closet. My house had come stocked with the exact clothes I had in my wardrobe on Earth. Literally every sock and shirt I owned was perfectly pressed and put away. However, I had also discovered the Quick Change app on my Soul Pulse. I just needed to think of an outfit and I was dressed in an instant. I felt like a cartoon character transforming from a regular kid into a superheroine with a *sparkle-sparkle-gleam-pop!*

Today, I used that app to dress myself in mauve bell-bottom jeans and a gray t-shirt. Then I picked up my backpack and waved to my dog. "See you, Droopy!"

"*AAWWWHOO!*"

To the tune of my dog's howl, I used my teleportation app to get to the Arrival Center at the Pearlie Gates, journeyed to one of the alcoves, and . . . I was in a tree again.

I glanced up at the sky poking through the branches. "Really? Is this going to be a regular thing?"

I climbed down, landed at the base of the ficus tree, and strolled down the traffic island to the crosswalk next to my school. I made it to physics with plenty of time this morning, arriving in sync with Henry actually.

"And she's back," he declared, motioning for me to enter the classroom ahead of him in a ladies-first manner.

"It's not like I could get out of it," I jested.

Even though it was true.

We slid into adjacent seats. Solange arrived a moment later wearing a turquoise tank, short-shorts with sparkly embroidery, and silver heeled sandals with long straps up her shins as if she were an ancient Roman empress. She claimed the desk on the other side of Henry.

"*Bonjour*, you two!" she sang. She slung her leather backpack over her chair. "So, Henry. I was wondering. I am looking to get an after-school job and Razel mentioned you both work at the mall. Care to point a girl in the right direction?"

"We both work at the movie theater," he replied. "It's not as lame as it sounds, but it isn't very glamorous either."

"Who said I require glamour?" she replied.

I blinked at her. "You're wearing glitter shorts and sandals that Cleopatra would envy."

She waved her hand. "Don't judge a book by its cover, Grace. Can't a girl look one way and be something entirely different inside?"

"Fair point," I replied. "I'm sorry to interrupt. Continue, Henry."

"I don't know if they're hiring, Solange, but you're more than welcome to come with us after school today and ask the manager. As long as you don't mind an also non-glamorous ride in a minivan, courtesy of my mom. She drops off my little sister for dance at the mall at the same time."

"Sounds wonderful," Solange gushed.

"Can I get in on that?" I asked.

They both turned to me.

"You need a job too?" Henry asked.

No. But I need to keep an eye on you, and this seems like a win-win excuse for how to stay in proximity during after-school hours.

Akari may be dodging my questions about this, but it can't hurt to be proactive, right?

"Could be fun," I responded with a shrug. "I like movies, and my life is all about trying new things lately."

The morning bell rang as the last of the students filed in.

"Okay. I'll text my mom to check if she's cool taking on a couple extra passengers." Henry whipped out his phone, but a nanosecond later Mr. Corrin plucked it from his hand.

"Thank you for volunteering, Mr. Sun," our teacher said, towering over us. "I have set up different gravity resistant mechanisms outside, along with pillows and air mattresses. To the roof, everyone! If you paid close attention to your assigned reading last night, you will be familiar with the formula for gravitational force and can calculate how to keep the items we throw off from getting obliterated on impact."

Henry grimaced.

I raised my hand. "Does the school have insurance for this?"

Mr. Corrin threw his head back and laughed like a mad scientist. Then he started ushering kids out the door, back into the sunshine.

"He didn't answer the question," I thought out loud.

Henry shook his head and groaned as he stood. "I just got that phone. Why did I take it out once class started? Mr. Corrin is known for doing stuff like this."

We moved for the door with the other kids. "Razel told me you're super smart, Henry. You'll be fine. You read the chapters, right?"

"Yeah, but unlike you, I get nervous when put on the spot with school stuff."

I gave him a look. "How nervous are we talking about?"

"Have you seen *Star Wars*?"

I nodded.

"Help me, Grace Cabrera, you're my only hope."

I laughed lightly. "Well, I know *that*, Henry."

"Hey! You're the girl who fell out of the tree."

When Henry pulled open the door of his mom's navy minivan, I discovered the driver—his mother—was the Asian woman I'd met yesterday. She wore the same chunky sunglasses, but her hair was down. The little girl riding in the seat directly behind her was Hana.

I froze as Henry turned to me. "You two know each other?"

"When did you fall out of a tree?" Razel followed up.

The bus behind our stalled car honked and a golf cart bobbed and weaved between students and vehicles to pull up next to us.

"This is the loading zone, not the socializing zone," barked a guy in khaki shorts and a red windbreaker. "In and out, kids." He tipped his floppy hat to Henry's mother. "Mrs. Sun."

We hustled inside the minivan. Razel jumped into the seat up front. Henry sat next to Hana. Solange and I settled in back.

"So what's the story, Hana Banana?" Henry asked, patting his little sister's head affectionately.

She'd been chewing contentedly on a lollipop, which she drew from her mouth and pointed at me. "This is the funny girl I was telling you about. She was lost and climbed up one of those epic trees on the traffic island to figure out where she was."

"How resourceful," Solange mused. "Christopher Columbus would be proud."

Hana looked at her and blinked. "You're pretty."

Solange smiled. "Thank you, *ma chérie*."

"Resourceful, yes, but Christopher Columbus was a massive a-hole, so I'd hope he *wouldn't* be proud," Razel remarked from up front.

We came to a halt in a long line of cars approaching a stop sign.

"Right, well, I'd like to introduce myself properly this time," I said. "Mrs. Sun, it's nice to see you again, ma'am. And a pleasure to meet you in less strange circumstances. Thank you for the ride."

The woman glanced at me in the rearview mirror and nodded. "Nice to see you too. We are headed that way, so it's no trouble. Your name is Grace, yes?"

"That's right," I replied. "And may I introduce Solange Alarie. She's also new to the school."

"Pleasure." My new friend gave a wave.

At the bottom of the hill there was a big intersection that divided the traffic into a handful of directions—no streetlights, just stop signs. Our car started to creep through the intersection when Mrs. Sun abruptly slammed the brake. A bus whizzed by.

Mrs. Sun cursed under her breath before easing onto the road again.

"See, kids. *This* is what makes me nervous about you two driving."

"Mom, we'll be careful," Razel groaned.

"I know *you'll* be careful; it's the other drivers I'm worried about. We can control a lot of things in life, but there's no accounting for stupid things other people will do."

"She's right," I found myself saying.

Henry and Razel turned to look at me.

I blinked, flustered. The comment had just slipped out. I needed to explain myself to some degree. My cover identity stated that I'd moved across the country to live with my guardian, and Akari said if I needed to fill in the blanks I could pull vaguely from my real life to make the story simpler to stick to. Maybe some honesty was just what the doctor ordered.

I leaned back against the leather seat with a sigh and admitted my burden. "Remember how I said I lost someone recently? It was actually two someones. And it was in a car accident."

The mood of the vehicle darkened, and I stared at my hands.

Perhaps that had been a mistake. I barely knew these people and I probably shouldn't be so vulnerable with—

I glanced up when I felt a warm touch. Hana had twisted around and put her little hand on my knee. "That's so sad. Is that why you moved here?"

I nodded.

"Grace . . . I'm sorry," Henry said sympathetically.

"Let's not talk about it," I replied, nodding my head once in decision. "I'm trying to pull myself out of the wallowing hole. Fresh start and all that."

"But—"

"Please."

He nodded and the ride continued in silence.

THE GIRL IN THE MIRROR

"Sorry, ladies, but we're not hiring," said the theater manager. "Thanks for your interest though. Razel, Henry, come to my office. I'd like to get your shift schedule straight for the semester."

"Sure, Tina. Give us one sec," Razel replied. The woman trotted off and Razel turned to me and Solange. "Sorry that was a bust. But there are a lot of clothing stores and restaurants at this mall you could try."

"Good plan," I said. "Thanks."

"We'll be done at seven if you want another ride," Razel said.

"Yes please." I nodded.

Solange glanced at her phone, texting as she responded. "Thank you, sweetie. But I have a way home today."

"Okay, see you." Henry gave us a wave and the Sun twins headed to work while Solange and I wandered outside. The mall was an open complex with shops set around wide paths and palm trees dotting the perimeter. The cloudless blue sky was visible from every vantage point, and lawn chairs were set up for shoppers to take a load off and enjoy the sunshine.

We trotted down an out-of-order escalator. When we reached the next floor, I stopped. Directly across from me was the dance studio. That must've been where Hana had gone.

"I shall go inquire about the retail employment opportunities across the plaza," Solange said. "And you?"

"I . . ." My heart beat a bit louder, voicing its opinion. "I think I'll check out the dance studio. Good luck with the job search, Solange."

"Thanks, angel." She gave me a wave and headed off.

I released an amused huff at the unintentionally appropriate pet name.

When Solange was out of sight I had a weird staring match with the dance studio—striding closer to it, then pausing, then pacing back and forth. It was a busy place, with people constantly coming in and out. When a couple kids noticed me through the glass doors, I veered away toward an alcove to contemplate my decision in private.

I had a little less than ninety minutes until I was supposed to return to Angel Tower for training. But maybe I could proceed with an alternate course of action, something that worked for my job *and* my soul.

I activated my Soul Pulse, which passed for a regular smart watch on Earth, and pressed the conch communication icon. I chose Akari's name from the contact list. Three options came after: voice call, video chat, full hologram. I selected video chat and the Soul Pulse started ringing. My mentor had mentioned that while most people's Soul Pulses could only make calls within the same realm, GA Soul Pulses could connect with any soul anywhere. I still had my doubts that this thing had a signal strong enough to connect Southern California to Heaven though. Then on the fourth ring, Akari answered. Her face filled my watch screen.

"Hello?"

"Akari, can you hear me?!" I said loudly as I raised my wrist close to my face.

"Yes, Grace. No need to yell."

"Oh. Sorry." I paused and garnered my nerve. "So listen, I had a thought. I know you encouraged me to just worry about staying close to Henry at school for now, but if my whole thing is protecting the guy long term, I think it would be a good idea to do other activities near him. He has an after-school job. Can I skip training with Monkonjae and Leo on those days and meet you for late night private sessions to make up for it? That way I can stick around Earth longer and make sure he gets home safe."

"That's smart thinking, Grace. GA schedules always adjust based on the assignment's needs and patterns. The only reason I

was encouraging you to focus on school for now is because that's
where he's most vulnerable to anyone who'd want to hurt him."

"For example?" I eyed her a bit suspiciously.

"Walk before you run, Grace. We'll get into more specifics as
we expand on your duties. The point is, stay after school if you
have the opportunity. I'm impressed with the initiative."

"Thanks . . ." I said, still a tad bothered by what Akari was
clearly leaving unsaid. So many questions, so little time.

"So how do you plan to do it?" Akari asked. "Stay close to
Henry after school I mean. You'll want to be careful with how you
proceed—you don't want to appear like a stalker."

I raised a brow. "You folks at Angel Tower are the ones who
put me in all of his classes."

"I'll give you that. So your plan?"

I raked my nails against my pants anxiously. "I thought I
would check out the dance studio his sister goes to. It's only an
escalator ride away from the theater where he works."

"A dance studio?"

My face warmed and I tensed. "Please don't judge."

Akari blinked. "I wasn't going to. Though it seems like you're
judging yourself pretty harshly. Why don't you feel comfortable—"

"Do I have your approval to stay here or not?" I cut her off.

Akari nodded. "Fine. Just stop by my office once you return to
Heaven. I'll give Monkonjae and Leo your regards. I take it you
realize this means you'll miss more halo drills with them?"

I shrugged innocently. The thought may have crossed my mind
a dozen or so times. This was a win-win situation in all senses. In
addition to maximizing my time near Henry, I definitely needed
a break from failing and flustering in front of an audience.

Akari sighed. "Be careful, Grace. I'll see you when you get
back."

"Will do. Thanks."

I hung up the call, stared at the dance studio, then with a final
deep breath charged forward and pushed through the doors.
The place was packed with parents and dancers of all ages. Some
waited outside of studio rooms down the hall; others bided their

time in the lobby waiting in line to speak with a receptionist at the front desk.

I gawked at the space for a moment before a Hispanic woman wearing a black baseball cap and a sweatshirt tied around her waist spotted me. She finished a conversation with a redhead, then trotted over purposefully with a clipboard. "Can I help you?"

"Yes. Hello, ma'am. My name is Grace Cabrera. I'm new in town and was wondering if I could rent some studio space to dance after school a couple times a week?"

I offered her my hand to shake, but she studied her clipboard instead. "Sorry. All the rooms are booked for group classes after school. You can join one of those though. Are you novice, moderate, advanced, or pre-professional?"

"Um, I— I'm not sure."

The woman waved at someone before darting her eyes back to me. "Okay look, our studio is passionate about helping dancers of all ages reach their potential. *However*, we don't want any one student to slow the rest of a class. So what we do is have new students complete an assessment with an instructor and then get placed from there. All our instructors are booked for the day, so we'll have you join Miss Kelsey's novice class that just started and based on how you perform she can recommend what level you belong in from there. Sound good?"

"Um . . . honestly, group classes aren't really in my comfort zone."

They're as much in my comfort zone as Puerto Rico is in Russia.

"Oh, come now. We don't know what we can do if we hide away from trying new things. Be brave. Have some fun. Try it." The woman put her hand on my back and ushered me down a busy hallway, darting around different dancers.

"I . . ."

"Here we go. Studio A. Class just started five minutes ago so you can slide right in. There's a mix of ages, so no need to feel embarrassed. Only good vibes here." The woman pushed the door open. Pop music poured out. "Kelsey, I have another one for you! This is Grace!"

I stepped into the room. The platinum blonde teacher—five

feet tall and possibly younger than I was—turned off the music
and came over to greet me.

"Hi there. I'm Kelsey." She shook my hand.

"Give her an assessment, will you," the woman said to Kelsey.

"Will do. Go on and join the others, Grace."

"Grace!" Hana squealed.

Henry's little sister waved at me excitedly from the other side
of the room. She was one of seven girls taking the class. They were
all under ten years old and wore tiny crop tops and sequined
shorts or leggings. I doubted my arm would even fit through one
of those pant legs.

Embarrassment and anxiety rose inside of me like thermometer
temp in a vat of frying oil. This was not where I should be.

I pivoted around. "Yeah, I don't think I'm—"

"Have fun! Let me know if you need anything," said the woman
in the black baseball cap, slapping me on the back enthusiastically.
"I'm Leanne Suarez, by the way. I'm happy to have you with us."

"All right, back to business!" Kelsey called. "Grace, you can
keep your shoes on or off. Your choice." She turned the music on
again and motioned for me to join the line of girls. I hastily kicked
off my sneakers, then hurriedly crossed the studio to stand next
to Hana. We faced a wall of mirrors. It was the silliest, strangest,
most self-esteem cringing thing to see the way I towered over the
rest of the class. I had never stuck out more.

Also, it was kind of sad to accept that despite the height, age,
and experience I had on these tiny people, they clearly had
more confidence in themselves than I did. You could tell by their
posture. You could see it in their eyes. There was no fear there,
no inhibitions. My mint-green eyes hosted self-doubt as easily as
pie supported whipped cream.

Sigh.

I tried my best to hold my head high and continue to look in
the mirror.

Part of assuming a new identity on Earth meant I couldn't
have the same appearance as original Grace, at least not to the
humans down here. God couldn't let one of his Guardian Angels
be photographed and have people freaking out because there was

suddenly a teenage girl in California who looked identical to a teenage girl who'd just died across the country.

Akari had explained that I would look like my original self to anyone from the afterlife, but every mortal on Earth would see me in the form of a girl who had a slightly different appearance. Only when I concentrated on my reflection could I see what they did. I focused on that now and watched my hair transform from straight chestnut to pecan waves, my skin tan faintly, and my face narrow.

My build remained similar. Also, my eyes stayed the same. Akari told me that the expression about eyes being windows to the soul wasn't just accurate; it undersold the truth. Turns out eyes were tied to a person's soul, and would never change no matter what plane of existence we were in.

I released my concentration and the image of my "new self" faded as normal Grace returned to the mirror. So much fear in her face and tension in her posture.

"Eyes up here!" Kelsey called, taking position at the front of the room as a Shawn Mendes song played through the speakers. "And fan kick, pirouette, sashay, leap!"

Wait, what—YIPES!

"You look like a zombie," Henry commented as I exited the dance studio with Hana. She skipped over to her brother and sister, giving each of them a hug.

"That's not a bad comparison. I feel like a creature risen from the dead," I groaned as I met the twins under the lamplights of the mall. Night had set in while I was indoors, and now the Southern California sky swirled with purples and navy-grays.

"So were you with Hana in the studio this whole time?" Razel asked. "Weren't you going to look for a job?"

"I thought I'd give this place a try instead. I . . . like to dance."

It was difficult for me to say that out loud. My family had been aware I practiced sometimes, but they didn't know just how special it was to me, or how vulnerable it made me feel. Entwining this layer of myself into my Guardian Angel routine was a huge step, and being okay with Akari and my new friends knowing this part of me was just as colossal. Maybe it wouldn't seem like a big deal to other people, but everyone had pieces of themselves they preferred to keep private. And when you were a girl used to being reprimanded when fire lit her heart, you were cautious about letting people truly see you.

"I was planning to just take one lesson, but the teacher insisted I stay for the entire afternoon of after-school 'dance camp' so I could be properly evaluated and placed in the right level. Four hours of twirling and leaping with a break in the middle for snacks and homework." I looked at Hana, exasperated. "Do you do this every day?"

"Yup. Isn't it awesome?"

"That's not the adjective I would choose."

Although talking about my fondness for dance had been a step forward, hours of group instruction had me wanting to tuck into my shell. So much for spending the afternoon not failing and flustering in front of an audience. I'd traded feeling inferior in GA training for feeling six steps behind in dance class.

"So what was the diagnosis?" Henry asked. "Of your dance evaluation I mean."

All the way back into my shell.

I sighed. After hours of trying my absolute hardest, our teacher said I was exactly where I belonged. "Novice," I replied. "*Very* novice. I am at the same rank as the tiny dancer here."

"Grace is the oldest girl in my class," Hana piped in matter-of-factly.

Henry and Razel grinned in unison. "And how old is the youngest person in your class, Hana Banana?" Razel asked.

"Five."

Razel's smile widened and she looked at me. "Wait, hold on. Isn't there a novice class for older students? Are you telling me you've been dancing all afternoon with little kids?"

"To quote our teacher, I am not ready to keep up with the other teenagers." I huffed. "Hence the *very* novice in my evaluation." I clenched my jaw slightly. "And yes, I have been dancing with little kids."

"How'd that go?" Henry asked.

"I kept up . . ." I said, rubbing my arm self-consciously.

"She didn't point her toes enough," Hana interjected. "And she doesn't jump very high for someone who's so much taller than the rest of us. But don't worry." Hana gave me an excited smile. "I'll help you. I'll be your dance mentor."

"Oh. Yay . . ."

We climbed the up escalator, which was also out of order, and proceeded past the theater across a large ramp to a rooftop parking lot.

"So how far is your house from here?" Henry asked as we walked. "We'll need to give our mom directions."

"When I told you my guardian works late, I meant *really* late," I lied. "Most days she wants me to go to the library after school, but with the day I've had, I could use a lift to another church. Is there one nearby?"

"Yeah, there's one just up the hill. Our mom can drop you there instead." He gave me a concerned look. "Are you going to be okay, though? Is she picking you up later?"

"Don't worry, Henry. I have a way home. And sorry for being a burden. I'll get my license soon and then I won't need to bug you."

"Looking forward to the same thing," Henry said. Then he paused and corrected himself. "Not the you-bugging-me thing; you're not. You're great, and I owe you one for saving my cell phone in class today. I just mean that I really want to get my license so I can go wherever I want without needing to rely on anybody, especially my parents."

The headlights of Mrs. Sun's minivan glowed red in a parking spot and we loaded in. Henry, in the front seat, asked his mother to drop me off at the nearby church while Razel looked at her phone. "Solange says she got a job at a clothing store on the second floor of the mall."

"Good for her," Henry commented as his mom put the car in reverse and pulled out of the space. He twisted around to look at us. "I guess we're all going to be mall rats, assuming Grace doesn't flunk out of dance school."

I narrowed my eyes, which surprised him.

"Sorry. Not a topic to joke about?" he asked.

"Definitely not."

"Understood."

We rode in silence for all but five minutes. The church Mrs. Sun took me to was barely a mile away. That'd be convenient for my schedule.

She drove me right up to the front. The church was epically tall and ovular with weird extensions like a spaceship. Long strips of stained glass glowed from within. Lampposts lined the path up to the main entry.

"Are you sure you're okay, Grace?" Mrs. Sun asked, putting the car in park. "I don't feel very comfortable leaving you here without a parent."

"It's a church, Mom, not an alley downtown," Razel responded. "You worry too much. She's fine. See you tomorrow, Grace."

"I am fine. Thank you, Mrs. Sun," I said with a respectful nod.

From the sidewalk I waved goodbye to the crew. Once their vehicle was out of sight, I trotted across the pavement to the church doors—there were eight of them, all grand and made of metal. Seeing no one around, I grabbed the heavy handles of a door to the left of center.

A second later, I was back in Heaven. Then I teleported to Angel Tower and made my way to Akari's office. I knocked. There was no answer, but I tried the handle and the door swung open. Inside there was no sign of Akari, but Chaz the angel panda slept in the corner so I knew she had to be close by.

Not feeling like sitting still as I waited, I stepped back into the hall and wandered. The bustling of the main command center behind me kept up a steady hum of noise. Heaven never seemed to sleep and the GA operation always had angels on duty. It's not as though you could nicely ask chaos to clock out at a reasonable hour so the good guys could go rest and regroup for the next day.

I was ten doors from Akari's office when I heard her voice. It was coming from just feet away—Deckland's office. His door wasn't closed all the way and their conversation escaped through the crack.

"You don't think it's strange that their Plot Points have both vague *and* very explicit things in common?"

"Of course it's strange," Deckland replied. "We could be looking at a group effort situation like when you had Churchill, Mason had King George VI, and I had Roosevelt."

I looked both ways down the empty corridor. My mother would not approve, but I leaned closer to better eavesdrop.

"There hasn't been one of those for years," Akari said. "The ripples are enormous. Not just humanity impacting, but humanity altering." She sighed. "I hope I'm just overreacting and this is all a coincidence. I don't think I have it in me to try and save mankind from another world war, Deck."

"If Monkonjae, Leo, and Grace are really facing a group effort, I wouldn't worry about that, Akari. Classic wars aren't really a thing on Earth these days. I think we may be looking at something very different. Maybe the boss will clue us in when we get closer, unless things reveal themselves on their own."

A pause.

"I should get back to my office," Akari said eventually. "I received a notification on my Soul Pulse. Grace returned through the Pearlie Gates and came back to Angel Tower a few minutes ago. She's probably waiting for me."

Akari can track me?

I started to draw away from the door.

"How's it going with her?" Deckland asked. I stopped. "She seems really nice, but I can't understand why she's not taking to training like the others. It's weird, right? Usually the purer the soul, the easier the powers."

"It's not an exact science, Deck. Great power isn't *created* by purity. It comes from strength of soul—what's there naturally *and* what she adds to it with her own confidence. That's where she's lacking right now. But I don't want to push her. She has to figure it out for herself or she won't stand a chance."

"You're running out of time though . . ." I could hear the concern in Deckland's voice and pictured his brow pinching taut. "If she doesn't feel strong right now, imagine her reaction when we go on our field trip this weekend. I don't mean to stress you out, Akari—I know that you didn't volunteer to come back—but it's not just this kid Henry's soul that's in the line of fire. God doesn't let people with potential off the hook. You're the perfect example. Grace is in this, regardless of how ready each of you feels. And if she doesn't improve soon then she could be in as much danger as her assignment."

I pushed away from the door and hastened up the hall. Tangled questions filled my brain. What were these Plot Points they were talking about? How could Akari claim to have faith in me, but openly express to Deckland that she didn't believe my soul was strong? You couldn't lie in Heaven. So, what, she didn't think current me was worthy but believed I could turn into someone who was? Was that encouraging or insulting?

Also, what kind of field trip could we possibly take that would make my situation even more hopeless? And how could *I* be in danger? I was already dead. Heaven and the afterlife had been providing me with plenty of emotional sucker-punches thus far, but I assumed nothing could hurt me *physically* at this point. Akari had certainly never mentioned anything.

I closed the door to my mentor's office and sat in a hurry. Chaz remained asleep. I pulled out one of the textbooks from my backpack. When my mentor walked in a minute later, for all she knew I'd been studying awaiting her return.

"There you are," she said upon entering. "Who's ready for another attempt at getting her halo moves on point?"

I closed the book and studied her. "I'll keep trying, Akari. But I hope there isn't some final exam for this stuff because otherwise *I won't stand a chance.*"

She gave me a look. "Are you okay?"

I shut my text, stowed it in my bag, and stood. "I'm processing a lot of new information," I said, choosing my words carefully to oblige Heaven's honesty filter.

Akari softened. "Right. Of course. Actually, on that note, I was thinking that maybe after tonight's session you should take the next couple of days off from training altogether. Focus on getting acclimated to school and your new identity. Then come back on Friday when you're feeling refreshed. Perhaps too much new at once is what's causing your learning block."

"Is that what we're calling it?" I shook my head with a sigh. "Fine. That sounds good. Maybe by then I'll have a clearer grasp on all this. And know what questions to ask you."

She gave me a confused look. "Have you been holding back?"

"I didn't think so. But now I'm realizing maybe I haven't been asking *the right* questions."

WHAT THE HELL?!

Without angel training, for the next few days my focus remained grounded on Earth versus up in the clouds of Heaven. Most of that was good for my confidence and allowed me to build myself back up a little, get used to this new life.

I had the safety of textbooks and chalkboards, where I thrived. Plus, who knew it could be so simple to make friends after returning from the dead? Henry and I had only known each other a few days and it already felt like we'd been friends for ages. Were all Guardian Angel assignments this pleasant to be around?

I was also grateful for Razel, Justin, Solange, and even Hana, who had been trying her best to convince me not to drop dance class. That activity had ended up being the only element of my Earth acclimation that truly stressed me out this week.

On Thursday I went back for another helping of Ms. Suarez's after-school dance camp, and it made my self-doubt curdle. It was discouraging to be placed in a novice class with tiny kids—some a third my age. It was extra embarrassing to not even be at their level.

My leaps and turns were not as controlled as the other young girls'. I stumbled and got dizzy from so many spins. My body seemed to move a half second slower than everyone else's. And my agility and, frankly, grace were notably less refined. It was clear, even if they were all too nice to say it, that I was not cut out for this.

Sigh.

I didn't think I had the heart to return to the studio next week. I loved dance, but consistently trying and failing in front of an audience made me not enjoy it. In fact, the whole endeavor made me feel like a fraud. Like I was trying so hard to embody a role and be someone who just didn't come naturally to me. I'd had enough of feeling that way in my old life and was already dealing with a dose of it in Heaven thanks to my Ninety-Eight status. I would prefer to avoid any additional situations that made me feel that way.

Which meant if I wanted to continue to stay in close proximity to Henry after three o' clock, I'd have to find another activity that could fill my time.

When I asked Akari again yesterday how necessary it was for me to be around Henry outside of school, she skirted direct answers like always. However, this time she at least promised she'd explain more over the weekend, which led me to wonder if the answers I sought had to do with the field trip she mentioned to Deckland. I couldn't ask her about that without admitting I'd eavesdropped though, so I would have to wait and see. Maybe in the meantime I'd ask Solange if that clothing shop where she got a job was still hiring, just in case.

The final bell rang, setting us free for the weekend. Henry, Razel, and I exited our classroom together. As kids poured into the school hallways, I spotted our French friend nearby.

"Solange!"

She paused and waited for us to catch up.

"Are you walking home too?" I asked.

"Not exactly," she said. "My ride is around the corner from school."

"Why did you need a ride to the mall this week if you have a car?" Henry asked.

"Oh no," she laughed. "I don't have a car. Even if I did, I would have welcomed your kind offer, as I am still getting used to the area. Now I am more confident with what I have to work with around here. And as a bonus I was able to meet your mother and younger sister, and that's just grand."

Solange nodded toward the downward sloping hill where half the school traffic spilled to exit campus. "If you all are walking out to the street though, I am happy to join the stroll. That's my direction too."

"Well, come on then!" Razel replied. "It's utter nonsense to be at school any more than necessary on a Friday afternoon."

The four of us waited on the curb to let several cars and a golf cart and a bus whiz by. Henry bent down to pick up another lucky penny as we waited.

We crossed onto the sidewalk that lined the epic hill. The traffic seemed more chaotic than usual. Maybe with people itching to leave for the weekend drivers were being less respectful of who had the right of way.

Razel and Henry walked slightly ahead of Solange and me, getting into a conversation about college tours.

"I have to say," Solange said, breaking my focus as I tried to hear their conversation over the traffic. "It has been really nice getting to know you this week, Grace."

I smiled at her. "Same. I was nervous about starting this new life here, but between you, the twins, Justin, and a lot of other nice people, it's been a smoother transition than I expected."

"What did you think life here would be like?"

"I'm not sure . . . I didn't really have any expectations past expecting to be overwhelmed."

We neared the bottom of the hill and I found an explanation for the extra gridlock—a fire hydrant had burst across the street. A huge geyser shot straight up from the hydrant, and the busy intersection at the foot of the hill had already flooded a couple inches. Mix in vehicles vying for the right of way, students on foot, bicycles, and skateboards—some of whom even had the audacity to keep looking at their phones while crossing this bedlam—and you had a recipe for mayhem.

The four of us paused.

"Yikes," I commented.

Solange nodded. "Perfect chaos."

"We'll be fine," Henry said. "Come on." He and Razel continued toward the intersection, Solange and I following.

"I felt the same way coming to this new world, Grace," Solange said, picking up where we left off. She looked at me kindly. "It's *très difficile* to wake up one day and have to start fresh with no idea of what's in store or who you'll be on the journey with."

There was a break in traffic and we hustled across the street with some other kids.

"I mean, yes California is infinitely better than the bowels of hell where I came from," Solange continued as we hastened through the hydrant's ankle deep flooding. "But high school can be a minefield no matter where you attend."

Our feet splashed as we hopped onto the wet sidewalk. The fire hydrant was fifteen feet away, its powerful geyser shooting straight into the air. I released a short sigh of relief as we turned to leave that mess of vehicular pandemonium behind. Henry and Razel hadn't slowed their gait after we'd crossed and were already ahead of us, absorbed in conversation.

"You know, girl," I said, picking up my pace as I tried to overhear the twins, whose dialogue seemed to have taken a heated turn. "Most people wouldn't describe Paris as hell."

"I'm not talking about Paris, Grace." Solange put her hand on my arm and stopped walking. I paused and glanced over her shoulder at Henry and Razel getting farther away.

Solange suddenly took both my hands in hers and looked me in the eye. "I'm talking about *actual* Hell."

I blinked at her. "What?"

"Checks and balances, Grace. Hasn't your mentor explained it to you yet? Guardian Angels try to positively impact humanity. But how unfair would it be if good didn't have anything to keep it on its toes? Challenge it a bit?" She released my hands then looked past my shoulder a moment. "On that note, I just need to move a few steps back."

She took three swift strides away while keeping eye contact with me. Then she whipped out her cell phone.

"Hold on, are you telling me you're a—"

All of sudden I was hit by a massive rush of water from the hydrant. The burst of water had abruptly, *unnaturally* changed directions and knocked me off the sidewalk—plowing me into the middle of the street. I rolled to a stop, totally soaked and my hands scraped up by gravel.

Ow.

I coughed and cringed. Maybe I'd been wrong the other

night. Maybe things *could* still hurt me physically despite being dead, at least when I was on Earth—

"Look out!" someone screamed.

I glanced up just in time to see an oncoming school bus. Ten feet away from me.

SPLASH!

For a second it felt like I was trapped in an intense waterslide, tumbling in blackness with a downpour all around me. Then my body impacted against smooth metal flooring. The two feet of liquid that covered the floor lessened the collision. It still hurt though.

Encore ow.

I scrambled to sit up in the pool, coughing. The liquid I'd landed in was shimmery and fluxed with colors like the digestive acid of a unicorn. I sat in it, transfixed.

"Grace!" My eyes darted up. I was in a thin, exceptionally tall cylindrical chamber with a steel ladder built into the side. The ladder led up a dozen yards to a platform, where Akari stood. "Are you all right?" she called.

I assessed my state. Now that the shock of impact had faded, I was astounded to say I was. "Um, yes!" I called back. "Where am I?"

"Climb up. The Soul Pulse doesn't work here."

Not an answer, but I nodded and hoisted myself up the ladder. When I reached the platform, Akari grabbed me by the shoulders. "What the heck happened?"

My brows raised and I swatted her away, a little offended she was interrogating *me*. "That's my question, Akari. A second ago, I was on Earth. Then this new girl that I made friends with at school tells me she's from Hell and knows I'm a Guardian Angel. A deranged fire hydrant blasts me into the street, a bus comes at me, then *whoosh* suddenly I'm in this—" I glanced around "—supervillain silo. What is this place? What's going on?"

"Son of a—" Sparkly bubbles escaped Akari's mouth.

I blinked, startled. "Is that what happens in Heaven when we curse around people who aren't into it?"

"Basically." Akari took a quick calming breath. "Look, this is a long conversation, Grace, but to begin with, do you remember the Cloud of Three Towers that I showed you on Monday? Where the planes of afterlife sort through the Soul Sewer and decide who goes where? Right now, we're in Heaven's tower. You died again, Grace. You got hit by that bus, the tower alerted me, and I came over here and helped the angel technicians find and fish you out of the Soul Sewer. Hence the splash down."

"Wait. I died again? *How can I die again?*"

"Grace, we don't have time for a ton of questions."

She started for the door, but I reached out and grabbed her arm.

"*Make time.*" I held her gaze firmly for a moment until I realized how aggressive I sounded and looked—and felt—then I hastily withdrew my hand.

Akari sighed. "Fine. Maybe 'dying again' is the wrong way to phrase it. It's better to say that your soul took a hit. God uses divine power to allow Guardian Angels in our department to exist on Earth in human forms rather than forms of pure energy that other GAs, like IDS angels, typically take. But if the body your soul has on Earth gets mortally damaged, you get separated from it. That wavy-haired girl you become when you're down there is not necessarily a skin suit; she *is* you, but your soul just got yanked out. At this moment that part of you is a husk—lying in a hospital in California, flatlining. We have to send you back immediately so your soul can reconnect with that body."

She took me by the hand and threw open the door. "Come on."

The setting raced by quickly as Akari pulled me along—so many doors and windows and colorful lights danced in my peripheral vision. I understood the urgency, but my feet subconsciously begged me to stop and check out the wonders of the building, particularly when Akari led me across an enclosed bridge that overlooked a portion of what must've been the Soul Sewer. In that brief glimpse, I felt the name didn't do the place justice. It looked like the dreams of the universe, the spillage of the cosmos, and the DNA of rainbows.

"Whoa . . ."

"*Grace.*" Akari yanked me forward.

After another minute she pulled open an emergency exit and we were on a balcony overlooking blue sky. In the distance, I could see the golden cathedral upside down.

"The Soul Pulse teleport doesn't work this far from the Pearlie Gates," she explained hastily. "People who work in the towers take stationary teleports directly back to their homes, which means you and I have to fly to the Arrival Center. Hang on." She glowed, her halo and wings appearing. Then we shot into the air.

"*YIPES!*"

I had no idea Akari could fly fighter-jet fast. Reality twisted and my perspective flipped so the cathedral wasn't upside down anymore. We sailed straight past the gates, up the steps, and through the front door. Akari alighted in the foyer but didn't let go of my hand. We sprinted toward the transport chambers.

"Listen to me," she said, grabbing my shoulders when we reached an empty alcove. "I know you have a lot of questions. I have a few myself. But here's all you need to know right now. The towers can create magic time lapses when people die if necessary. To the humans, your body was only unconscious while we were fishing you from the Soul Sewer, and everything that has happened for us in the last five minutes has happened in the seconds your body has been flatlining on Earth. But that cushion is gone and we have to act. Getting sent back will fuse your soul to your Earthly form again. You're going to wake up, make a miraculous recovery, then I'll come get you when the time is right. Don't leave the hospital alone or it will be suspicious."

She almost pushed me into the alcove.

"But—"

"Go!" she ordered.

I obeyed and my Soul Pulse shimmered.

GASP!

I sat up straight in bed as my eyes burst open.

"She's alive!" someone yelled. My vision was a blur of people in medical gowns; my ears were overwhelmed with beeping machinery and heightened voices.

"Grace Cabrera. Grace Cabrera, can you hear me?"

I blinked and held up my hands. The blinding fluorescent lamp above was like a bargain brand version of the bright white light at the end of the tunnel to Heaven. I took a deep breath. I was alive again.

I guess third time's the charm?

"Yes," I said. "I can hear you. I'm okay."

I glanced up from my physics textbook when a knock came at the door. Henry and Razel entered, their faces wrought with concern and confusion.

"Honestly, everyone, I am okay," I assured, setting the book beside me. Being stuck in this hospital cot until Akari showed up wasn't ideal, but the bed was comfy and I was getting a lot of homework done.

"How is that possible though?" Razel came over and sat on the edge of my bed, shaking her head. "You got hit by a *bus*. The nurses said you flatlined, but then just came back. And now there's nothing wrong with you apart from a few scratches?"

I held my hands up in surrender. "Hey, I know as much as you do. I guess I'm just lucky."

"Absurdly lucky," Henry said, still looking at me with worry. "You should be dead."

"Don't let my modest Southern charm fool you. I'm a lot tougher than I look." My gaze narrowed. "Speaking of which, where is Solange?"

"She said she would get her own ride to the hospital, but we haven't seen her," Razel replied. "I just texted to ask what's up."

My fists clenched around my sheets but I took a steadying breath. I couldn't let the twins see how angry I was.

"How did you two get in here, anyway?" I asked. "Aren't hospitals usually pretty strict about visitors? We're not family or anything."

"This is our dad's hospital," Henry said. "We convinced him to let us see you once you were awake and stable. It's not procedure, but he made an exception."

"An exception that only lasts so long as it does not interfere with the patient's rest . . ."

A tall man in a white coat stood at the door. He had graying hair and a well-groomed goatee. He walked over to my bedside and offered me his hand. "Dr. Joshua Sun. You gave us all quite the scare, Miss Cabrera."

"Nice to meet you, sir. Were you one of the doctors who treated me?" I asked, shaking his hand.

"No, I only came because of your recovery. My colleagues tell me that despite the serious collision, your organs and brain activity were unharmed. I had to see for myself."

"So what's the diagnosis?" I asked.

"Miraculously, you are perfectly fine. In fact, you can leave the hospital whenever you feel ready. Though I'd advise that you stay the night for observation."

I glanced down then gave a smirk. "Thank you for the offer, but hospital gown chic is not my preferred slumber party attire. And the only thing I need to observe is my notes for the physics test on Monday. I'll be leaving as soon as my ride gets here."

Dr. Sun turned to his kids. "You two told me you didn't need to study this weekend. That's the only reason I said you could go to the beach."

"Dad, it's fine," Razel protested. "It's just a quiz. And I doubt it will be that hard; we've only had five days of coursework."

"Henry, you know better," Dr. Sun said. "Just because you already submitted your college applications doesn't mean you can slack off. Schools can withdraw offers of enrollment if students fail to live up to expectations."

I cleared my throat awkwardly.

"Apologies, Grace," the doctor said. "My children have a lot at stake this semester but don't focus as much as they should." He patted Henry on the back. I guess I would say it was with affection, but Henry's face suggested he didn't see it that way. It reminded me a lot of the expression on my face when my mother apologized to other people for my behavior—guilty, dispirited, and irritated.

"Given your dedication to schoolwork, perhaps you're just the new friend they needed this final semester," the doctor said. "You seem like you have a good head on your shoulders."

"Well, it's certainly secured there pretty tightly if that school bus didn't knock it off."

Razel huffed, but smirked. "Morbid much?"

"You said you were waiting for a ride?" Henry interjected.

"Yes. I, uh, made a call when I woke up. Though I'm not sure when she will—"

There was another knock and a blonde woman with the haircut of a young Ringo Star came in. I tilted my head at her. Though her physical appearance was unfamiliar, I recognized those golden-brown eyes instantly. When I focused on them, the woman's form shimmered and was replaced in my mind's eye with someone I recognized. Since we were both creatures of the afterlife, once my brain adjusted, I saw my mentor for who she truly was.

I addressed the Suns. "Everyone this my—"

"I'm Grace's guardian Akari," my mentor interceded. She looked at the twins' father. "If you don't mind, can we have some time alone? I already signed Grace out and I'd like to get her ready to go home."

"Of course. Kids, out you go."

Razel and Henry got up reluctantly. "Call or text us if you need something," Henry said before exiting. "Like literally anything."

"I'll be fine," I said. "I'm going home now and both of you should do the same. I'll see you Monday."

They waved goodbye. When the door shut, I threw the covers off and leapt to my feet. I'd only been lying there to play the part. Dr. Sun said I was perfectly fine and I felt it too. Despite some scrapes on my forearms and knees, every part of my body felt at full strength. Plus, seeing Akari charged me up; I was angry, confused, and hungry for answers.

But first—

"If Solange really is from Hell, before we leave I need to make sure she doesn't go near Henry and Razel. They're not safe with her nearby."

"There's no need to worry about that right now. Trust me," Akari said as she gathered my books and loaded them into my backpack.

"*Trust you?*" I repeated, grabbing my jeans from the table and sliding them on under my hospital gown. "You didn't tell me there were going to be people from other planes of the afterlife messing with me as I do my job. You didn't tell me I could die again. What the *literal* Hell, Akari?"

She zipped my backpack and sighed. "I didn't think it was relevant yet. Deckland, Ana, and I were going to explain the whole deal about Hell to you, Monkonjae, and Leo after training tonight."

"There's a *whole deal?*"

She tossed me my jacket and I pulled my arms through the sleeves with agitation.

"Let's get back to Angel Tower. Exposition is more efficiently given in groups and bad news is easier to take with a support system."

Akari handed me my backpack and exited the room. I pursued her down the busy hospital hallway. After a few turns, we ended up in a much quieter corridor and stopped in front of a door. I peered through its thin window and saw an old man bent in prayer.

"This is the hospital's nondenominational chapel," Akari explained. "All hospitals have at least one so that people of any faith have a quiet place to rest and reflect. You'd be surprised how often these have come in handy during my time as a GA."

"I'm not sure that anything you could tell me would surprise me at this point."

Akari glanced both ways, grabbed my arm, and took hold of the door handle, sending us straight to Heaven.

"Well, I stand corrected. Or I suppose, I sit corrected." I leaned back in my chair and took a swig of my "Out of the Woods" latte.

In light of today's events, regular training had been cancelled and our mentors had decided to meet with me, Monkonjae, and Leo in a coffee shop within Angel Tower for a serious talk. No one ever got truly tired during the day in Heaven; you had all the energy you ever needed. Therefore, instead of shots of caffeine, beverages were prepared with shots of emotion. Each item on the coffee shop menu was named after a song because the beverage made you feel the way that song did. The warm latte in my hand named after the Taylor Swift number, for example, tasted like coffee, milk, sugar, deep reflection, sadness, longing, and a glimmer of hope.

I needed that last sentiment desperately, given what Akari had just revealed to me and my fellow newbies.

Maybe I shouldn't have requested a Taylor Swift–themed latte in retrospect.

Was that girl ever truly happy?

Leo sat forward on the white sofa that he, Monkonjae, and I shared in the glittering shop. "So as long as we're down there protecting our assignments, a demon is also around trying to destroy them?"

"And not just any demon," Monkonjae added. "A demon specifically chosen to serve as our foil?"

For once, I was the calmest of the three of us. When Akari had claimed me from the hospital I was still super upset, but in the time since, I'd shifted. It was like I'd used up my allotted shock and awe for the day and now, in the aftermath of being hit by a bus and ejected by a divine sewer, my soul was just processing all the info. I sat disturbingly quiet as I absorbed the unsettling facts and stared at our trio of mentors sitting across from us.

"They're your counterbalances," Ana replied. "Everything GAs learn to protect their assignments and help them fulfill their potential, demons are trained to undo or override with their own intervention."

"But why?" Leo insisted.

Ana sighed. "Hell is just as interested in the downfall of humanity as Heaven is in its success and growth. If the only divine forces interfering on Earth were angels, it would be too easy. Good would always win and the world would turn forevermore without

ever being in any real danger. The demons offset that. Just like
Heaven has many different departments to interject goodness
into the world, Hell has different departments to infuse evil.
There are demons with long-term assignments who are given the
same targets we are. Those are Class One demons. There are IDS
demons who try to cause spur of the moment trouble: Class Two
demons. And then there are Class Three demons."

"Which are?" Monkonjae asked.

"Remember your tour of the various levels of the GA
operation?" Deckland said. "Two floors before the museum is the
Counterthreat Department."

"You said we'd come back to that later," Monkonjae said.

"And here we are," Deckland replied. "In Hell, there is a
Threat Department. That is where demons work to analyze the
best places, people, and circumstances to inject chaos and evil.
Which politicians to corrupt. Which criminals to evolve. What
bullies to breed. Our Counterthreat Department tries to figure
out what Hell is up to and diffuse, counteract, or prevent the evil
the demons intend to unleash."

"Like secret agents trying to find and foil terrorist threats,"
Ana suggested, looking to Leo.

Deckland took a sip of his iced "All Along the Watchtower"
coffee. "It's GA mentor tradition not to bring up Hell and demons
until a full week of training is completed so we can ease you into
the stakes of your job. We don't want to scare you."

"Grace, you're being unusually silent," Akari said then.

Everyone turned to look at me. I took another sip of my
beverage, my expression cool and unreadable. "Do you *want* me
to ask a question?"

"Of course," Ana interceded. "We want everyone to be on the
same page here."

I set my drink on the glass table, leaned forward, and looked
directly at Akari.

"*Why didn't you warn me?* In a case like mine, where you sent
me to Earth immediately without the typical month of training,
tradition is irrelevant. You should have told me there was a demon

strutting the same school hallways. It's your fault I got killed today. You didn't prepare me!" My voice raised an octave, turning almost vicious at the end. I guess I wasn't as out of emotion for the day as I thought; I'd just buried it deep. Or maybe this was emotion over another issue—not the demons or today's incident, but my mentor's behavior.

For most of the week I'd known her, Akari had been an informative, professional guide. I'd say I liked her so far. Her past raised a lot of questions, but even though it went against my natural curiosity, I'd had enough faith in her until now to let most of those go because I believed she would fill in the blanks when it came to important aspects of my afterlife. After today though, that faith was cracked. She'd let me down in a big way.

I took a breath and pushed the bubbling emotions down, leaning back again and crossing my arms instead. A moment of silence between us, then—

"You're right. It is my fault," Akari said.

Her response surprised me; and the genuine sorrow in her tone piqued my attention and weakened my frustration.

"I thought you were safe. There usually isn't a reason for GA mentors to introduce Hell and demons right away because they're not supposed to be able to touch you. The ratio of Guardian Angels to demons has to be equal—one for one. Only when we train a class of new recruits is Hell allowed to do the same. Then you're both sent to Earth simultaneously. It used to be that demons weren't allowed to make any moves against human targets, and had to keep away from Guardian Angels entirely until one month had passed since their deployment. I . . . didn't know the rules had been amended."

"Akari has been out of the Guardian Angel game for three years," Deckland said steadily. He glanced at my mentor, who sat quietly with eyes fallen to the floor. When he realized she wouldn't pick up the explanation, he continued. "Two years ago, the month rule was amended. Demons still cannot harm targets during the first month, but now they can 'interact with' GAs."

"I didn't know," Akari said, her voice despondent. She looked up and met my gaze. "I'm sorry, Grace."

It was one of her rare real moments—no professional mentor mask. Seeing the regret and hurt in Akari's eyes, the suspicion I'd held previously now felt likely. The reserved, all-business vibe she preferred when on the job was not actually for my sake, but hers.

Heaven seems to expect more from me than past events would suggest I can handle. That's what she'd said when I first left for Earth.

Most of the time Akari presented herself as my expert mentor with all the answers, here to metaphorically hold my hand and help me handle my crises and adjust. What if this—that pain and remorse I saw flickering in her eyes now—was actually her truth? Eyes were tied to the soul, right? From what I saw, my mentor had a lot weighing hers down.

"It's not completely your fault," Ana tried to reassure Akari, patting her on the knee. "The demons fought for the amendment so their people could have time to see how ours would be inhabiting the lives of our assignments. For the last two years they've done nothing but observe us more closely. This is the first time a demon has exposed a loophole in the amendment. *We were all* foolish for not realizing that they could interpret 'interact' as a means to cause harm to one of us. Grace is just the first Guardian Angel to be victim of that."

"Lucky me," I snarked. "Do I get a spot in the museum for it?"

"This won't go unanswered, Grace," Ana asserted. "We're going to give the Hellions a piece of our minds tomorrow."

My eyes widened. "That's the field trip, isn't it? You're taking us to Hell."

Akari tilted her head. "How did you know we had a field trip planned?"

I didn't blink. "Don't let all the questions fool you; I'm not as clueless as I may seem. I ask a lot of questions because I like to learn. When I'm not asking, I'm observing. Learning on the down-low."

This time it was Akari's turn to lean forward, temporarily risen from her state of sorrow. She clasped her hands together over her knees and studied me critically. Then she addressed me with a statement, not a question.

"You're trying to avoid Heaven's honesty filter."

"I'm trying to figure things out, Akari," I said bluntly. "Considering you three are the ones who decided not to tell a pack of brand-new angels that we're going to have a long-term working relationship with Hell, maybe my evasiveness shouldn't be the issue on the table."

Akari and I stared at each other until Leo awkwardly cleared his throat, pressing that spot on the bridge of his nose.

"Right then. So . . . we're going to Hell," he mused. "I wonder if I'll see my Uncle Sal down there. My mom always told him that's where he should go whenever the *schmendrick* called to ask for money."

10

INTO THE FIRE

"What do you think Hell will be like?" I whispered to Leo as our team approached the obsidian orb to the left of the Pearlie Gates. It shined darkly like a secret. This was going to be the weirdest Saturday morning I'd ever had.

"I once had food poisoning on a flight from Australia to Canada. So I'm imagining a similar kind of discomfort and misery," he whispered back.

We arrived at the front of the orb. The buff angels guarding its golden entrance nodded to our three mentors. Ana stepped forward and raised her Soul Pulse to a scanner beside the gate. The watch flashed. The entrance shimmered and then creaked open like the rusty gate to a haunted cemetery. Darkness reigned past it. I had *no* desire to step into its grip.

Interestingly, a second later a small flash went off and a jewelry box like the kind someone would hide an engagement ring in appeared. Ana grabbed it and stashed it in her jacket pocket.

"Not to poke holes in a divine system," Monkonjae said hesitantly, "but is this really necessary? A field trip to the infernos of Hell seems like asking for trouble."

"It's the demons who are asking for trouble," Deckland said.

"There, there—no need to be nervous," Ana said, patting Monkonjae on the arm. She could only reach that high given how he towered over her. "All GA mentors take new recruits on a field trip to Hell. We want you to have an up-close and personal understanding of who our enemies are and how they work. It'll light a fire under you. Pun intended. Beyond that, it's important for the demons to see you and realize that you're not intimidated by them or their chaos. If they create problems, you will respond

in kind. Show them you are not afraid to walk through the fire to
do what's right and get the job done."

"Literally or figuratively?" Leo asked.

Ana shrugged. "Depends on the day."

"Come on, guys. It'll be fine," Deckland said encouragingly.
He nudged Monkonjae to join him and the two stepped through
the gate. Ana took Leo by the hand and led him in next. Both
pairs vanished from view a couple steps past the entryway. Akari
came beside me. I hadn't spoken to her all morning.

"Are you still upset with me?"

"Do you really need an honesty filter to know the answer to
that question?"

Just because I knew Akari was sorry about what happened
didn't make up for me being blindsided. Dying in *another* vehicular
accident was traumatic, and it could have been prevented if I
knew about all the variables working against me. It would take
some time to get over that.

She sighed and gently took my arm, guiding me forward. I
gulped as we merged into the darkness past the gate. It was like
walking through a cave without a flashlight. After a few moments,
a wicked luminescence threw the others into silhouettes. When
Akari and I caught up with them, we stood on a large platform
that glowed deep, chilling blood red. The kind of color that all
horror writers idealistically tried to describe at some point in their
careers. Above, around, and below us though, was nothing but
black void.

While our mentors congregated in the corner, my fellow new
recruits and I stood still on the epic slice of sanguine. I tilted my
head a moment and thought about the humor of that word.

"Why the bemused expression?" Leo whispered. He looked
creepy in this light. We all did, more so because we all wore crisp
white—custom, apparently, when angels visited Hell so their
people could know we didn't belong.

"I was just thinking about a term I learned in English class
this week," I said quietly. "As an adjective, sanguine means being
optimistic, especially in the face of a difficult condition. But as a

noun, it means a blood-red color. I just think it's funny because the word could easily apply to a situation in Heaven or Hell."

"You're such a nerd and I am into it," he replied with a smirk.

"Here it is!" Ana declared. Our mentors had found a hatch in the floor. Monkonjae, Leo, and I wandered over as she opened it. Inside, there were three things: a button with an UP arrow, a button with a DOWN arrow, and a button with the words STOP IN EMERGENCY.

Ana removed the small box from her pocket, revealing a thumbtack inside. "I'll do it," she volunteered.

Leo raised his eyebrows. "What are you—"

Ana pricked her finger and a single drop of silver blood escaped, which she angled to fall on the DOWN button. When the droplet landed, the button lit up in vibrant orange and suddenly the perimeter of our platform ignited with crackling, knee-height flames. The reflection off Ana's heart locket made it look like there was a glistening ember on her chest.

The Guardian Angel stashed the thumbtack back in the box and stowed it in one jacket pocket, then took a small circular bandage out of the other and slapped it over her minor prick. She'd come prepared. I raised my hand to ask several questions, but Akari filled in the blanks before I needed to.

"This is the Hellevator—a direct ride from Heaven to Hell, solely activated by Guardian Angels when we have direct business there. Souls who have a timeshare that involves both Heaven and Hell go through Middleground and arrive at the rose quartz building outside. Only souls in our department have direct access from the bottom floor to the top floor, if you will."

"Should we be worried about the flames?" Leo asked, throwing a thumb sideways.

Ana shrugged again. "They're just decorative."

"And the blood?" Monkonjae asked.

"It's a two-step process to ensure only authorized personnel use the Hellevator," Deckland responded. "Our Soul Pulses need to be accepted at the gate, and you need a drop of Guardian Angel blood to operate the platform."

"I was actually more curious about how Ana could even produce blood," Monkonjae said. "We're dead. Grace's accident showed us what happens if we get killed on Earth. But up here in the afterlife, I assumed we were beyond human biology. That we couldn't be harmed."

"Harm exists everywhere," Ana said flatly. "We try our best to be clever or strong enough to minimize it, but it always persists. I suppose it's the universe's way of keeping us alert, and keeping us humble."

She took out the thumbtack box again and opened it, holding it up. "This is Divine Iron. The only thing that can *truly* harm a creature of the afterlife. It's an ancient metal that God, the Devil, and all the founders of the universe used when battling out the tug-of-war that was the creation of humanity. There's barely any left—fossils of an era that even time has forgotten. What does remain is in safe hands. Like this tack GAs use when going to Hell. While Divine Iron can cut any person of the afterlife, as mentioned, only Guardian Angel blood can pay the toll for this elevator. On that note . . ."

Ana put away the box then slapped her hand on the elevator's glowing DOWN arrow. The hatch closed automatically and our platform shook. The flames crackled and shone more vibrantly. Then the Hellevator sank into the abyss.

With black void all around us, it was hard to gauge exactly how fast we were going, or how far we descended, but after a few minutes, burning shades of crimson and tangerine came into view, and I took my first gaze upon Hell.

It felt like we were lowering into the heart of a volcano. A volcano covered in bumper-to-bumper freeway traffic. A massive lake of glowing, goopy lava lay beneath us, spouting the occasional geyser of fire. Set over the lake were countless freeway overpasses and busy highways that curved and twisted and overlapped needlessly, creating a tangled mess. Every car in that terrible gridlock was beaten up, decades old, and pumping out plumes of gray smoke.

"You know how souls in Heaven who've passed through the Pearlie Gates arrive neatly in those envelopes that are immediately transported to angels for welcoming?" Akari addressed the group as a whole but focused her eyes on me at the.end. I nodded. "Well, after passing through the Gates of Hell, souls end up in one of those cars. The set-up was actually designed by the same people who created the 5 Freeway in Los Angeles. So try and stay away from there during your time on Earth if you can, Grace."

"Noted," I responded warily.

Our elevator started to move sideways, gliding over the mess.

"This has been Hell's first wave of torture for decades," Akari continued. "No air conditioning. Uncomfortable seats. The only entertainment options are podcasts about the economy, accordion medleys, and a radio station run by demons. It doesn't play any music; the station only provides useless traffic updates, detailed discussions about the Top Tortures of the day, and Sad Fun Facts."

"What are Sad Fun Facts?" Leo asked.

Ana crossed her arms. "The number of people wrongfully fired from a job this week. Amount of times adults crushed children's dreams last month. How many puppies died today."

Leo's face contorted with horror and disgust. "*Oy vey.*"

I gazed out at the massacre of traffic. "I'll second that *oy vey.*"

Halfway across the lava mayhem, a city started to come into view. It was rare to describe something as both scary and beautiful. Like Miami. Or Rihanna. But that was the gist of the landscape ahead.

The sky above the city seemed to be in a perpetual state of flux. Like a wicked version of the Northern Lights on Earth, contortions of cherry, dark gold, purple, and magenta filled the air. Below that masterpiece of unsettling color loomed innumerable skyscrapers. The architecture initially reminded me of The First City; the towers were just as tall and assorted in shape as those in our afterlife home. But the similarities ended there. The obsidian edifices were sharp and jagged, like the incisors of wild beasts. Everything seemed to be mildly offset by that perfect blood-red color and threatening shades of violet. Perpetual olive smog hung over the lower buildings like a wraith.

Deckland pointed at an astonishing structure in the center of the city. "That's the Hell Beacon. Their version of Angel Tower. That's where we're headed—the heart of The Second City."

My eyes locked on the destination. Structurally, the Hell Beacon was a dark exact replica of Angel Tower. My gaze drifted up to where a pulsing red orb crowned the top. My breathing and heartrate slowed as I stared at it. After a moment, I turned to my mentors.

"I can look at the top office," I said. "It's not forcing me to look away like God's domain." I glanced back at the ruby sphere "It's actually *hard* to look away . . ."

"Evil has that kind of effect," Akari said steadily. "It's easier to see than goodness. And it gets a much firmer hold on those who let it capture their attention."

I hastily darted my eyes away from the building.

Our ride completed its journey over the lake of fire and began to pass through the city. At this speed, we'd reach the Hell Beacon soon.

Monkonjae seemed to be trying to see through the windows of the buildings we passed. "Deck, who exactly lives in this city?" he said. "I assumed that bad people were tortured in Hell. This place has an ominous Gotham-City-meets-*The-Matrix* vibe, but it doesn't seem so terrible."

"That's because not all people are so terrible," Deckland responded. "Everyone in Hell is tortured in a unique, customized way. While truly awful people who are here full time—serial killers, corrupt leaders, war lords, and so on—are tortured in horrific ways on a daily basis, even they need some time to regroup so they can reflect on that horror. Those people spend their nights in straight-up prison cells. However, moderately awful people who are on timeshare programs—cable repairmen, cyberbullies, anyone who ever owned a pet snake—spend their nights in moderately terrible accommodations across Hell."

"Like my mother . . ." I thought aloud. The others turned to me. Emotion bubbled in my stomach like the lava we'd passed. I gulped and forced myself to keep steady. "Will she be staying somewhere in this city when she's down here?"

Akari attempted to put her hand on my arm, but I subtly stepped out of reach. Her expression looked a little hurt, but she proceeded anyway.

"It's possible," she said gently. "But Hell is as expansive as Heaven in terms of real estate; this is just the main hub. And truthfully, many of the dwellings in this city belong to the demons who work here." She tilted her chin to indicate for me to turn around. "Get ready to land."

Our flaming ride approached a section of the Hell Beacon that bulged outward. From the balcony a runway began to extend, its edges engulfed in flames too.

When the runway reached our platform, you could hear the snap and suction of the two pieces connecting. Once locked in, the front rim of flames on our lift disappeared so we could walk up the newly formed dock to our destination.

"And you're sure no one's going to steal a ride on this?" Monkonjae asked.

Deckland shook his head. "The demons may be able to call the Hellevator back to the Hell Beacon as it's partly a product of their realm, but it doesn't matter. If a passenger is onboard, GA blood has to be used to make it move. They don't even have Divine Iron in Hell."

"Now, on to the tour," Ana said, stepping in front of us author-itatively. "Stay close. Your GA powers work anywhere, but aside from the basic functions, your Soul Pulse changes per realm. In Hell, that means no fancy apps and unless you're a demon, you can't teleport. Ergo, we don't want to get separated."

Ana, Akari, and Deckland dismounted our platform and began striding across the bridge. Leo followed hesitantly. I found myself taking a slight step back and accidentally bumping into Monkonjae. He glanced down at me and I grimaced.

"Sorry."

"Don't be," he said. "I'm scared too."

We exchanged a small smile, crossed the bridge together, and united with the others. The moment we set foot on the balcony, a woman exited the building. She was a few inches shorter than Monkonjae, about thirty, and no more than a size 2. Her sunflower-blonde hair was wavy in a grunge sort of way, as if she had gone swimming in the ocean and it just dried that way. And she wore incredibly straight-leg black jeans, a black V-neck tee with the front slightly tucked in, and a black leather jacket. An edgy black watch was strapped to her wrist.

"Hello, Ithaca," Deckland said, crossing his arms.

"Deck, looking cut as always." She winked at him then strode over and took a good gander at Leo, Monkonjae, and me. "Oh my God, they're so cute," she cooed condescendingly. "I swear, your new recruits look more innocent every cycle. Hi, kids, I'm Ithaca Trask. Senior Guardian of Chaos."

"Come again?" I said.

"Guardian of Chaos is a fancy name for a Class One demon," Akari said, clear hatred in her voice. "The kind that messes with Guardian Angel assignments."

Ithaca turned slowly. A wicked grin bloomed across her face when she looked at my mentor. "Akari Brown. I thought you quit. All that nasty business with the explosion . . ." She took a few confident strides closer and put her hands on her hips. "Given how excellent you are at getting people killed, maybe instead of reenlisting with the GAs you should've come play for our team. Your department must be short-staffed. What other possible reason could you have for coming out of Heaven's hiding?"

Akari's face was hard to read, but I saw glassiness in her eyes— vulnerability. Something kicked in, and I stepped between my mentor and the monster in tight pants. "She came for me. She is *my* mentor. God asked her personally."

Ithaca's expression shifted for a second. Then she gave me a cruel, tight-lipped smile. "You must be Grace Cardiff. The infamous Ninety-Eight."

I didn't back down. The confrontational fire I so often tried to suppress blazed inside of me and I looked up at Ithaca with steely resolve. "I think you mean famous. Infamous implies something bad. That's your area. Not mine."

"We'll see," Ithaca replied. Then she bopped me on the nose with her pointer finger. "You are just too precious; I can't take it."

The fire inside of me flared, and I opened my mouth to

respond, but then Ithaca's attention shifted toward the sky behind me.

"Aw, here comes another person dying to meet you."

We turned around and a shadow cascaded over our faces. A man in a dark-wash, button down denim shirt with its sleeves rolled up descended from the fluxing sky. Huge, magnificent midnight wings—three times bigger than GA wings—extended from his shoulder blades like he was part raven, feathers edged with sparkling onyx.

"Show some respect for your fearless tour leader, kids," Ithaca said.

With a final mighty flap, the man alighted onto the fire-lined runway. When he landed, his eyes glowed red before his wings vanished with a flash of lightning. *Like literally*. A giant crack of electricity burst from the sky, the blinding flash caused me to blink, and when I looked again the man's wings were gone. A few loose black feathers floated in the air, falling into the flames around the man and burning to a crisp.

He stepped forward confidently. He was probably in his late forties, around 6'4", and had well-defined arm muscles and rugged five o' clock shadow.

Leo stared. "Actor Joel McHale?"

The man laughed. "No. But I get that all the time. It's the charismatic smile and swagger. Now then." He rubbed his hands together enthusiastically. "Which one of you is our Ninety-Eight?"

Ithaca shoved me forward. I stumbled a step before catching my balance and gazing up at the man. I wish I hadn't gulped. But I did. I wish he hadn't noticed. But he did. Then he smiled at me—teeth brilliant white and navy eyes glimmering with intrigue. "I have really been looking forward to meeting you."

I straightened up and tried my best to mirror his self-conviction. "I can't say the same. But then, this place is so literally and figuratively beneath us, I'm not surprised I didn't even know you existed until yesterday."

I thought the comeback was pretty good, but it only seemed to amuse him. Then he returned volley with a remark that sent a chill through my bones.

"Oh, we're going to have some fun with you."

He walked past me and joined Ithaca by the doors. "Kids, I'm Troy Bellview. I'll be leading your tour today. Please keep all arms, legs, and halos on the path at all times. Otherwise they may get eaten by a monster."

"He's joking," Ana said hurriedly.

Troy shrugged. "Are you *sure*, Anahita?" He cocked his head. "Hey, have you gotten shorter since the last time we saw each other? When was that, 2011? Seeing you get blasted off that roof is still one of my favorite moments of the decade. It's actually my Facebook profile pic."

"You have Facebook in Hell?" I couldn't help but ask.

"Of course. It only makes sense we work with it down here since a shocking amount of people who work on it up there are headed our way." Troy winked deviously before raising his black watch—the Hellion version of a Soul Pulse, I presumed—to a scanner on the door. "You should see what we're building for the Twitter folks. That torture dome puts the construction Beijing did for the '08 Olympics to shame."

The scanner turned red and a buzzer sounded, unlocking the entrance. Like a gentleman, Troy opened the door and ushered us in with a bow. Inside was an exact replica of our GA command center with a few Stephen King and Edgar Allen Poe style alterations.

The ringed layout remained the same, but every item in the room was shaded in a *Stranger Things* color palette: soulless black, off-putting red, and sleek chrome. The gleaming computer monitors, sharp-edged desks, even the demons' business outfits all matched this dark, edgy vibe. I had to be careful not to stumble, as the floor was made of uneven purple amethyst tiles. And my skin crawled completely when I realized every inch of wall was decorated with stenciled renderings of people's faces screaming in agony or wide-eyed with fear.

What stood out the most though, was Hell's pure black Angel Oak. The tree at the center of their operation looked like it had been decimated in a great fire and all that remained was skeletal branches—spiky, gnarled, and hauntingly bare.

"So then! Welcome to the main hub of our Guardians of Chaos division," Troy announced, walking backward like a tour guide as he spoke to us. "Once humans are paired with GAs on your floor of the afterlife, the information comes to us. Desk demons in our division proceed with observing, analyzing, and breaking down the best way to break those humans before they achieve their big destiny or whatever."

Troy paused when a dark-haired demon in a tight leather dress passed by. She smiled at him and he winked at her. "Looking *very* nice today, Sylvie."

He continued around the edge of the command center; the rest of us followed. "We also keep track of you angels," he went on. "Studying your movements, habits, tendencies, yadda yadda. Basically our job is to find the best way to mess with you and your assignment until one of you fails."

"And by *fails*," Ithaca interjected, pivoting to address us, her blonde hair bouncing around her shoulders. "He means either your assignment gets pulled off course and will never reach his or her potential, or you aren't able to protect them from getting destroyed."

"And by *destroyed*," Troy tagged in with a spring in his step, "she means killed, murdered, drowned, blown up—"

"We get it, Troy," Ana cut in.

Our group exited the command center and entered a corridor made from lustrous steel.

"Which brings us to the rules," Ithaca said, pausing at a large ebony plaque mounted on the wall. The gold calligraphy on the plaque drastically contrasted the cold metal surroundings. The title at the top read: *"Demon Code of Conduct."* I was gob smacked at the oxymoronic idea of these people having rules of ethics. One of their kind pushed me in front of a bus yesterday.

"Because the laws of the universe insist that we take it easy on you," Ithaca said, leaning against the wall, "these rules have been instituted since the beginning of the dance between our two departments."

She counted off on her fingers as she read the rules aloud. "One, a demon must never directly harm or attack a human on

Earth and can only directly harm an angel on Earth if the angel initiates the attack. Two, a demon must never reveal the identity of any angel to any human, nor can an angel reveal the identity of a demon. Three, a demon may never be in the same room with a human assignment unless the human's Guardian Angel is also present. Four, no demon may ever set foot in the home or private dwelling of a human. And five, only a single selected Class One demon may work to negatively impact the fate of any human assignment."

Akari, who stood at the back of the group with me, leaned over and whispered. "This is why I told you not to worry about Henry outside of school so much."

I didn't make eye contact with her, but nodded. Rules three and four. I supposed it would have been difficult for Akari to answer my questions without explaining the rest of this.

"These are the *main* rules," Deckland interrupted, stepping forward and exchanging a sizing-up glance with Troy. "Obviously there have been some amendments and clarifications. For example, an angel or demon may reveal his or her *own* identity to a human assignment."

"And a demon can now *interact* with a Guardian Angel from the beginning of an assignment," I said with a glare.

Troy and Ithaca shared an amused glance.

The blonde whipped out a phone from her pocket—apparently Hell had those—and started texting rapidly as she continued. "Classic Solange. The girl seems all priss and proper, but I'd watch out for her, Ninety-Eight. She has a piñata personality: when you crack her open, you don't know what's going to come flying out. She is easily my favorite demon mentee in the last fifty years. Love her."

"You know we're going to be hashing out that amendment," Akari asserted crossly. "I sent a memo to God *and* your superior last night. Your loophole is getting sealed tight."

Troy shrugged. "We'll see."

"What does it mean by not being able to harm a human directly?" Monkonjae asked, alluding to the first rule on the plaque.

"Thank you for the question," Troy said enthusiastically. "It's Mockingjay, right?"

"Monkonjae," he said flatly.

"So you're *not* going to dazzle us with archery skills? What a letdown." Troy rolled his eyes. "But your question does actually bring us to my favorite part of the tour."

"You mind if I catch up later?" Ithaca said to Troy, finishing her text and stowing her phone. "I'm needed in the Confederate Army Punishment Annex."

"Sure, and if you see Tim, tell him he still owes me a favor for losing that bet about Stalin's bowel control."

She chuckled evilly then turned to the rest of us. "See you later, kids." She patted me on the head as she passed. For a split second I flashed back to being eight years old and decking that awful blonde on the handball court. Fire crackled inside of me.

Troy beckoned for us to follow him. I started to, but suddenly felt Akari's hand gently on my arm. "Grace," she whispered in my ear.

"What?"

She glanced down at my hand. Without realizing it, my fingers had curled into a tight fist.

I gasped ever so slightly.

Embarrassed, I rushed away from Akari to catch up with the others at a bank of elevators. Each transport was glass, but with flaming edges like the platform we'd taken to get here.

Also . . .

When I looked down, I was so startled I jumped and crashed into Leo. Which was not that awkward since the kid also leapt in panic and crashed into me. We held onto each other as our eyes fixed on the live swarm of insects buzzing directly beneath our feet—separated from us by merely a sliver of glass.

Troy smirked as he pressed a button on the elevator panel. We descended a few dozen floors. Then *Guardian of Chaos Training Center* lit up over the doors. We strode first into a little entry area like outside our center, then stopped in front of a pair of steel doors.

Troy motioned for me, Monkonjae, and Leo to go ahead. Our

mentors nodded to confirm it was okay. I pushed through the set of doors with the boys and froze.

Demon training was a feat to behold. There were a few dozen of them in here—all dressed in black, leather-accented athletic attire surely found in the Lululemon "Wicked" collection.

In a matter of seconds I saw so many mind-blowing things. Demons phased through walls and obstacle courses. A man in mid-combat with a colleague avoided a roundhouse kick by sinking through the floor. At my two o' clock a woman stood in a chamber of fire directing the size and spread of the flames. Way across the room a pair of men on elevated platforms over a pool seemed to be creating small tsunamis. On the mat closest to us, three sparring women went at it viciously with daggers. Suddenly, one of them vibrated and four identical versions of her appeared. Her opponents didn't know which way to turn.

It was all outlandish and fantastic and intimidating. But I think the thing that surprised me the most was the giant message spelled out on the tiled ceiling:

THE ASSIGNMENT COMES FIRST

It was just like the edict in our training center.

"All your little powers are linked by the same tool," Troy said, moving to stand in front of us. "Your halo." He traced a circle over his head. "And all those powers are derived from one thing: light. Meanwhile, all our powers are rooted in manipulation."

He gestured around him proudly like a dean showing off the marvels of his institution. Then he drew closer to us, locking eyes with my handsome classmate. "See, Mockingjay, demons don't cause chaos. That's a misconception. All we do is take advantage of it."

We stared blankly. Troy leaned around Monkonjae and addressed our mentors. "Hey, angelic types, your recruits aren't getting it. Care to enlighten them in simpler terms?"

Deckland furrowed his brow at Troy before crossing his arms over his chest and focusing on us. "It would be too easy for evil to win if demons could operate freely. Our jobs would be impossible if they could cut the brakes on your assignment's car, or start a fire in their office, or just walk right up and stab them. So that's why they aren't allowed to directly harm humans, a.k.a. create dangerous chaos out of nowhere. They can only manipulate chaos that already exists as a means to hurt people. If a fire is blazing in an apartment, a demon can make that spread to another apartment, the whole floor, or even the entire building depending on how powerful the demon is. If a bar fight breaks out, a demon can manipulate the tensions and anger in the room to cause that fight to escalate into a violent brawl. Get it?"

Understanding sunk in. "So, if a fire hydrant explodes and causes a geyser of water to spout uncontrollably, a demon can manipulate the direction that water shoots?" I said.

"Bingo," Troy replied. "I have to give Solange credit for that one. She's creative. And she's strong. Her powers are developing rapidly." Something buzzed and he drew out his phone. He laughed then typed a text in response. "That's one of the reasons we picked her, Ninety-Eight," he said after he hit send and looked up. "Only the best for you."

"I don't—"

Akari put her hand on my shoulder. Her eyes shot me a stern warning.

"Grace is like no other recruit I've seen before," she said to Troy firmly. "The strength of her powers right now would shock you. So your little demon better watch it. She doesn't know what she's dealing with."

I tried to keep my face blank, but curiosity coursed through me. That was a really weird, accurate, though misleading way to describe my skills.

"There's the Akari I remember," Troy sneered. "Loving the protective mentor vibe. This one's personal for you, isn't it?" He stepped closer to her and lowered his voice. "Someone can't afford another failure."

Akari's lean form tensed. She locked eyes with Troy for two seconds, then she blinked.

He smiled.

"So as I was saying," Troy continued, stepping back to address the group. "Blah blah blah, our people can only bring down your people by controlling whatever chaos is already out there. Blah Blah. Which means they need to be smarter than you and observant of any and all opportunities. Blah blah blah."

"And the intangibility and cloning and dagger fighting?" Leo asked, waving at the training center full of demons in activewear.

Troy checked his phone again, only half paying attention. "Your halos can project beams of light and shields of light and other fancy nonsense. Our powers of manipulation let us warp environments, including controlling fire and the elements when they're already in chaos. Class One demons can also phase through solid objects. What you're seeing there isn't cloning; we can create illusions by manipulating perception. And the daggers are just part of our basic combat training." He glanced up. "We just prefer to do it with sharp, stabby objects."

His eyes returned to his phone. "And on that note, who wants to join me in the Guillotine Room to meet your matches?"

He stowed his cell and gave a half smile. "I don't mean the flammable kind of matches, by the way. The Burning Alive Building is a few blocks from our offices."

FOILS

We heard laughter.

The corridor was reminiscent of an upper-class, aging hotel. Dusty gold molding crowned the ceiling. Crème paint peeled from the walls. The intricate floret design of the crimson carpet had probably once been rich and majestic but was now worn and faded. Chandeliers with melting wax candlesticks like something out of *Phantom of the Opera* hung from rusty chains.

As we continued along, Troy pulled out his phone and sent a quick text, glancing over his shoulder at me after he'd done so.

Then he turned around and did his walking backward thing as he addressed us. "The six of you happen to be here for one of our quarterly team-building activities. Today is Clip Day. It's like a movie night only everyone sends in their favorite YouTube videos, TikTok clips, and Insta stories from Earth. I advise you goody-goody types to brace yourselves. Some of the videos are messed up. Or hey, maybe you'll enjoy them. It's not like you're *one hundred percent* good." He specifically gave me a look that made my skin crawl.

Troy thrust open the doors to our destination. The ballroom-sized space was packed with demons lounging on beanbag chairs or picnic blankets and staring up at a large screen. It cast an eerie glow over the darkened space and elongated the shadows.

A clip was currently playing that ended with a man injuring his private parts in some stupid stunt involving a skateboard, a railing, and a burrito. The audience laughed and clapped heartily. At the conclusion of the clip, a slate flashed that noted the video was provided "Courtesy of Luca Brent." Then the screen flickered and the next video began.

It took me a second to register what I was seeing.

What the . . .

It was me on screen. I was in the outfit I'd worn yesterday, standing on a wet sidewalk with plenty of street traffic and a geyser in the background.

The me on screen looked flabbergasted. "Hold on, are you telling me you're a—"

I watched myself get slammed sideways by a jet of hydrant water. My body flew into the street and flailed about like a fish thrown on the deck of a boat. Then someone off-camera shouted, "Look out!" as a bus barreled toward me in the video.

I covered my eyes just in time. Laughter filled the ballroom.

Someone patted my shoulder. "It's over," Leo whispered. I lowered my hands cautiously as a slate that read "Courtesy of Solange DeCoutere" flashed on screen. I guess that was Solange's real last name. She'd assumed a fake one on Earth just as I had.

Troy strode around the edge of the room to the front and picked up a mic from the podium beside the projector. He gestured to a man operating a laptop. The man hit some buttons, which paused the screen and powered on a sinister red spotlight that shone on Troy.

"Hope everyone's having fun. I just thought I'd interrupt to let you know that the star of the most recent clip is actually here today. Everyone, say hello to Grace Cardiff!" He gestured dramatically to the back of the room and a red spotlight cast down on me too. I froze in place. All the demons twisted around. Part of me expected them to laugh; another part expected them to boo. All they did was smile. Dozens and dozens of white teeth aimed directly at me.

Monkonjae, Leo, and Akari moved in front of me protectively. They thought I needed guarding—that I felt embarrassed or afraid. Had they seen my face, they would have realized the only feeling that pulsed through me was fierce irritation. The fire that'd ignited inside of me when I confronted Ithaca came back. It creased my brow, narrowed my eyes, and pulled my mouth into a tight frown.

The spotlight over me shut down and Troy clapped his hands to recapture the room's attention. "Solange, Jimmy, Oliver, let's go. Baby GAs, head to the Demorale; your mentors know the way. We'll meet you there in ten. The rest of you, as you were."

Three shadowed bodies rose from the crowd near the front of the room. My mentors ushered us into the hallway and began leading us back toward the elevator bank.

"I'm sorry you had to see that," Akari said to me.

"They've been singling me out since I got here." I tried to take slow and steady breaths to calm myself. That had always been my mother's suggestion when I got heated. "Did I do something to these people?"

"You exist," Deckland replied. "That's all the reason they need to come at you."

"Demons find joy in the failure of goodness—chaos, corruption, hatred—*and* the failure of others," Ana said.

"Schadenfreude," I interjected. "It was on my vocab list in English class this week. It means the experience of pleasure or satisfaction from the failures and misfortunes of others."

Deckland nodded. "Demons actively try to get evil to succeed on Earth. It's their main prerogative, which fulfills their sense of purpose. However, they also like to mess with angels on the side, bait us into falling from our moral high ground."

"Is that even possible?" Leo asked. "I mean, we're all 90% good and up."

"But none of us are 100% good," Ana responded as we approached the elevators. "Every person has some darkness in their soul, which means they are vulnerable. Even Grace. Her soul may be 98% pure good, but that still leaves 2% unaccounted for. Troy, Ithaca, any demon here really, would like to provoke that weakness. With Grace having the highest percentage of pure goodness ever, I assume they're seeing it as a personal challenge to get under her skin."

"Lucky me." I punched the elevator call button.

Challenge accepted.

The elevator doors opened. I cringed when we loaded in.

Below the glass floor of this lift were dozens of scorpions crawling all over each other. I tried my best to keep my eyes up for the remainder of the ride.

Deckland selected a large burgundy button at the bottom of the number panel, and we glided down in silence. The doors ultimately opened to an underground train station. It was huge and had the normal sketchy elements: graffiti, litter, low concrete ceilings. The initial spookiness went even further with flickering lights—burnt orange like the sun behind a veil of smoke—spiderwebs sporting arachnids the size of strawberries, and a massive spray paint rendering of a three-headed Doberman with spiked collars.

All of this did not hold a candle in comparison to the horror of the train lines. I'd have been impressed if I wasn't so unsettled.

At least three dozen tracks were laid out before us, the platforms busy as trains arrived and departed and demons bustled about their business. The tracks were all on fire, but that didn't freak me out anymore. What bothered me was the design of the train cars—literal giant human hearts lying on their sides.

Each transport was the size of a coffee shop and modeled perfectly after the vital organ. Every shade of red possible glistened around the curvatures of the cars, from garnet to currant to cherry. The front of each car—resembling the bigger side of the heart, or the cava if I remembered ninth grade biology correctly—was transparent, acting as a window for passengers.

I wasn't a cardiovascular expert, but it seemed like every vein, artery, and valve that was supposed to be there, was. One train car came to a stall near us; it throbbed mildly as if still beating.

"Are the aortas being used as *smoke stacks*?" Monkonjae gulped, pointing to the top part of the nearest car.

It appeared so.

Another elevator opened nearby. Troy stepped out, followed by four others—an Asian woman in her forties with cruel eyes and dyed blonde hair, two younger guys, and Solange.

"Grace!" she exclaimed with glee.

I opened my mouth, but the Asian woman cut me off with an aggressive handshake. She nearly fractured my hand before moving on to do the same with Leo and Monkonjae. "Welcome, kids. I'm Megan Liu. Happy to have you with us. We'll do introductions first then get going. We have a busy schedule to keep with today."

It was so weird to hear words that sounded friendly and were accompanied by a smile, but somehow made you feel terribly on edge. It was like when you watched a movie and something about the sharpness in a grin or the extra honey in a character's voice let you know that person couldn't be trusted. It was a trap.

Megan stepped to the side and gestured at my nemesis, who wore a tight black mini-dress. "Here we have Solange DeCoutere, paired with your Ninety-Eight, as you already know. *This* is Jimmy Fung. My mentee." She put her hands on the shoulders of the trendy Asian boy in his mid-twenties standing beside her. "He will be paired with your Leo Wells."

Jimmy had a smug look, gelled hair, and a small silver hoop piercing his left ear. He wore a tuxedo-style blazer in an elaborate black-and-white pattern. It deviated from the all-black dress code of his four colleagues, but I guess no one said anything because he was pulling it off. The demon accessorized his outfit with a crisp black bowtie that was more Academy Awards chic than nerdy or ironic.

Jimmy nodded at Leo. "Pleasure to meet you."

Leo raised an eyebrow. "How old are you?"

"Twenty-seven."

"Well, that's a bunch of *mishegas*," Leo complained, looking to Ana. "He's almost double my age. Shouldn't I have a match that's the same age, like Grace does?"

"Actually, Grace is four years younger than me," Solange replied. "I'm twenty-one."

"*Really?*" I said, genuinely surprised.

She nodded. "I'm just so hot people don't question how old I am."

"We pair people in terms of personality first and age second," Megan explained. "Purity and goodness wear away as you age, so demons are often older than their angel counterparts. Sometimes we find youthful candidates that check all the boxes though. Like these two." Megan gestured at Solange and the remaining demon yet to be named.

"That brings us to my mentee," Troy announced proudly. He put his arm around the last member of their group. This boy was about my age but a few inches taller. He wore a hoodie under a leather jacket. His hair was a dirty shade of blond, his eyebrows slightly darker. Those brows—which furrowed when Troy touched him—framed the most interesting feature of the boy's face. His eyes.

He put those eyes on me for a moment and I studied them closely. They were deep blue like the ocean. Bluer even. And they were soft. At first observation, I couldn't see the arrogance, self-assuredness, cruelty, or condescension so obvious in the eyes of every other demon here.

"Oliver Evans," Troy declared. "He's eighteen and he'll be working with you, Mockingjay."

"*Monkonjae*," my friend corrected irritably.

Oliver didn't say anything.

Troy glanced at his Soul Pulse and then at the heart pulling up on the tracks two train lines over. "Here's our ride. We can continue the meet-and-greet on our way. This tour has to be over by noon. All aboard the Demorale."

"It used to be called the Demon Rail," Megan explained as we headed toward the heart. "But once, in a drunk game of Words with Enemies, someone mushed the words together and realized it sounds like *De-morale*. That name suited our MO, so Hell's PR folks launched a rebranding."

"You have a PR office?" I said.

"Well, of course, Ninety-Eight," Megan replied. "Evil and high-volume media are kissing cousins."

A section of the heart slid inside itself, creating a door. The demons climbed right in. Monkonjae, Leo, and I hesitated.

Troy glanced back. "No need to be afraid, kids. It's not real. Just a bit of fun design. Now come on." He patted the side of the heart. "I only booked this private car for an hour."

"It's okay," Ana urged, stepping on board to reassure us.

Cautiously, my fellow recruits and I joined the rest of the

group. The lighting inside the train car cast us all in a shade of pinkish red. Two benches lined opposite sides of the transport. Vertical rails and ceiling straps took up the center aisle.

As the door sealed I reached for one of the rails, but the car took off with a jerk and I lost my balance. I rammed into Oliver, my cheek planting against his leather jacket.

"Um, sorry." I quickly pushed away from his chest and grabbed the silver rail, straightening up.

"It's fine," he said simply, taking hold of an overhead strap.

"Our newbies are really excited about taking you to their favorite spots," Megan said, sitting with her legs crossed on a bench between Jimmy and Solange.

"In Hell?" Leo asked.

Megan nodded. "That's a part of the tour. Hell is so vast and has such a colorful array of tortures that a girl could spend weeks touring the highlights. So, when Guardian Angels come down for their introduction, we let each of their counterparts select a destination to show off."

"And not just any destinations," Troy chimed in. I watched volcanoes spewing lava through the cava window behind him. "Ones *they* designed. Part of new recruit training is creating your own type of torture. You pick an infamous person or group of people from history that you'd like to target. Then for one month your design becomes their fate. Jimmy, Solange, and Oliver are looking forward to showing off what they've come up with."

Ana scoffed from behind me, seated on the bench beside Leo. "So what's on the schedule today?"

"Jimmy is going first," Megan said proudly, squeezing both his shoulders. "He requested a dual torture of Christopher Columbus and Edward VIII."

"The guy who abdicated the throne of England?" I asked.

"Precisely," Jimmy said. He leaned back, crossing his arms and tilting his chin up. "You've heard of the game *Chutes* and Ladders? They'll be competing in daily games of *Shoots* and Ladders—that's S-H-O-O-T-S. This is more of an obstacle course. Eddie and Chris have to climb ladders as fast as possible while demons fire shotguns at them."

I blinked.

What?

"I decided to stick with my national roots for my design," Solange piped in elatedly. "Have you ever heard the infamous quote attributed to Marie Antoinette? Legend goes that when told the peasants of France had no bread to eat, she said 'Let them eat cake.'" Solange shrugged her slender shoulders. "I thought I would have a little fun with the lore and am torturing her and King Louis XVI by having them force-fed cake around the clock."

I looked up at Oliver, barely a foot away. Even this close, his blue eyes still failed to hold any wickedness. I was jarred by how dramatically they contrasted the cerise hue that soaked us.

"And who are you torturing?" I asked.

Oliver brought down his gaze to meet mine. "Hitler," he said bluntly. "I had some ancestors that didn't escape Nazi Germany. It felt like a good fit."

"This guy's too modest for a demon," Troy declared, striding across the moving car to slap Oliver on the back. "A little backstory, Ninety-Eight. Hitler used to love art, and actually tried to make it a career until his dreams were squashed when he failed to get into art school—courtesy of *my* demon mentor. See, the unstable little man could draw a mean landscape, but what sunk his chances at art school was that his work couldn't capture the complexities of people; he couldn't get human faces right." Troy slapped Oliver on the back again, harder this time. I noticed the kid wince. "Tell them about the torture you designed."

Oliver sighed. "Every half hour of every day, Hitler will see the face of someone murdered by his regime. Specifically, he sees the look on their faces when they died, but he only gets to see it for thirty seconds. After that, he has to spend the next half hour replicating every detail of that person's face in a painting—every ounce of suffering engrained into their expression. If it's not an exact match, he experiences what it was like to die the way they did." Oliver's gaze dropped to the floor. "Then he starts over."

Troy shook his head in amusement, unaware of the suffering in *Oliver's* expression.

"This guy is the most creative protégé I've had in a while. He'll do great things here, *and on Earth*. Watch your six, Katniss," he said pointedly to Monkonjae.

"Come on, man," Monkonjae protested.

Troy ignored Monkonjae's frustration and took out his phone, texting again as he made his way back to his area of the car.

The train sped on. We'd left behind the volcanoes. Lightning crackled outside the window now. The black skies swirled with charcoal-and-purple clouds, releasing startling golden bolts that would send Zeus under the covers.

"So, Grace," Solange said, pivoting in her seat. "I'm dying to know how you're doing after dying. I hope you didn't mind me sharing the video with my team. It was just framed too beautifully to ignore."

"Grace—" Akari began.

"I'm physically okay," I blurted. "But it definitely brought up some PTSD given the way I died. I'm probably going to be extra anxious around street traffic for a while, which I'm worried will affect my ability to get my driver's license, and I—"

I stopped. I processed. I panicked. *"Why am I telling you this?"*

"*Grace*," Akari tried again. I glanced at her. "Hell also has an honesty filter."

"What!" That's why Akari jumped in to respond for me in the training center. My eyebrows raised and I turned to the demons. "*Why?*"

"Honesty is more efficient no matter what team you play for," Megan replied simply. "Humans can have lies. They're messy, problematic things that delay the inevitable one way or another. While they're fun to toy with when we cause trouble on Earth, lies only waste time and Hell can't condone that amongst its demons. Evil is more effectually spread when the ones trying to spread it are on the same page."

"Teamwork makes the dream work," Jimmy summarized.

I glared at Akari. "Well, thank you for giving me the heads up about *that*."

The train passed through a tunnel for a few seconds then emerged onto a bridge running hundreds of feet above a churning onyx ocean.

"Anyone have any other questions?" Troy asked, checking his phone again. "We'll be arriving in three minutes."

A beat passed.

"I do," I said firmly.

The heads of every demon and angel turned toward me. Oliver's piercing eyes were distracting, so I focused my attention on the others. First looking at Troy, then moving my gaze to my mentor. "If *we* are 90% good and up, what does that make *them*?" I threw a thumb at Solange and Jimmy. "Are they 90% bad and below?"

"Oh, Hell no," Troy replied with a scoff, leaning against the side of the car with his arms folded. "Anyone who is more than 90% bad is a waste of soul—they're monsters, even by our standards. People who are that evil stay in Hell for their entire afterlife getting what they deserve, no timeshares."

"But don't you want the most evil people on the front lines?" I pressed. It seemed like the more evil the demon, the greater the chaos.

Megan shook her head. "Senseless evil is a useless thing. There is no reasoning behind it or reasoning with it. Guardians of Chaos need to be clever, creative, and sympathetic enough to the human condition that they can understand what makes people tick and how to properly bring them down as a result. We never choose recruits with less than 20% good in them. Jimmy is 23% good. Our little lady Solange is 24% good. And Oliver is 32% good."

I glanced at the eighteen-year-old again. He was gazing out the window at the dark sea.

"Why would they want to be demons then?" Monkonjae asked. "I mean, they have some good in them. Don't they have a conscience?" He looked to Solange and Jimmy sitting across from him. "You guys can't *want* to hold back humanity or harm innocent people. You know it's wrong."

"Here's what I know," Jimmy said calmly, voice as smooth as the silk of his sleeves. He stood and rebuttoned his blazer like a gentleman as he strode closer to our side. "It's wrong *and stupid* to doom yourself to an eternity of suffering if there's another door to take. We all had one, so we took it. Not everyone has the luxury of an afterlife filled with harps and fluffy clouds."

Solange nodded. "People who get sent to Hell are tortured the entire time they're down here. The only way out of that is if they are offered and accept the job of a demon. Unlike you lot, who automatically get a Guardian Angel job if your goodness meets the threshold, all types of demons are individually selected by our superior." She gave me a look then raised a finger to each side of her head to simulate horns.

"What about timeshares?" Leo asked.

"Timeshares can be worth your while if you get to spend time in Heaven," Solange replied. "But you have to be at least 50% good to live any amount of afterlife up there. None of us meet that qualification. So our existences would be divided between Hell and maybe a couple days in Middleground. Being a demon is a better move if you're given the opportunity. The job comes with *many* perks."

"Perks?" I repeated.

Troy nodded. "If chosen as a demon—if you've got the right stuff in your personality and past—you spend all your time in Hell and agree to relinquish any time you would've been granted in Middleground. But you have a sweet set up in The Second City, and since your job is serving Hell's purposes on Earth and against angels, you can escape torture. Class Two and Three demons serve minimal torture time while Class One demons like us avoid torture entirely. It's a free pass. You'd be a fool not to take it."

Troy glanced out the window a second—cruelly smiling at a memory—then looked back at us. "Example, I was a doctor on Earth." He threw his head back and released a short, self-satisfied laugh. "I got sued *so* many times. If I hadn't been picked as a demon and accepted the job, I'd be spending five days a week getting operated on by drunk sailors or having catheters incorrectly inserted. Instead, I get to mess with people professionally. It's awesome. And humanity deserves it. People suck."

He tilted his head at me and my fellow recruits. "You kids know what I'm talking about. I *know* you do."

There was a moment of silence.

"Agree to disagree," I said.

The heart started to slow as we left the sea behind and our tracks entered a plain of tall sawgrass blowing ominously in the wind. My hands squeezed tighter around the metal rail as I braced myself against the changing speed.

Troy laughed as if I'd said the funniest thing in the world. "You, Ninety-Eight, are definitely my new favorite." He cocked his head at my mentor. "Train her hard, Akari. We don't want any more mistakes on your record."

Akari remained seated but elongated her neck and straightened her posture in a manner to show utter confidence. "You don't scare me, Troy."

The train car came to a stop and the door slid open. The instant it did, I began hearing the loud crack of shotguns in the distance.

"Alrighty," Troy said rubbing his hands together. "Let's go see some Shoots and Ladders."

Everyone began to file out. As I released my hold on the metal pole to exit behind the angels and demons, there was a hand on my arm.

"Hey," Oliver said.

I paused and looked at him. We were the only ones left in the car.

"Your mentor may not be afraid of Troy, but trust me, *you* should be."

I plucked the boy's fingers off me. "You're an employee of Hell. That guy is your mentor. Why should I believe you, demon?"

"Aside from the honesty filter, which you know means I'm telling the truth, because *I* am afraid of him. All those cocky grins and the charisma he flashes aren't who Troy is. You need to watch your back, Ninety-Eight."

Ugh. I was so sick of people referring to me like I was just a dumb number.

"*Grace*," I said firmly. "My name is Grace. *Not* Ninety-Eight."

"And my name is Oliver. *Not* demon."

I blinked, startled. Then I nodded. "Fine."

He nodded back. "Fine."

"Grace?" Akari called, poking her head back in the car.

"Coming!" I cantered toward the door. Before stepping out though, I stole a final glance at Oliver. I hoped to see a momentary flash of mischief or wickedness in his expression that would confirm that he was just like the rest of them. But the calm blue of his irises remained steady and entirely unreadable.

12

PLOT POINTS

"Check your rearview mirror," Akari instructed from the passenger seat.

I did and glanced out the driver's side window for good measure. There were no other vehicles or angels behind me—just blushing, wide-open sky.

"Now put it in drive," Akari said.

I grabbed the gearshift of the powder blue convertible that Akari had parked on the puffy cloud for me. It was actually the last blue thing left in the sky as sundown washed over Heaven.

"Okay, go," Akari said, indicating for me to drive off the cloud.

My hands clenched the wheel at ten and two, but my foot did not move.

"Grace. *Go.*"

I exhaled sharply, nerves clenching my stomach. "You know, when you told me you'd help me get my license, I thought we were going to practice on solid ground. Not in the sky."

"It's the same thing, only up here there's less chance of you hitting anyone or anything. I thought you'd prefer that, given . . ."

"How I died both times?" I sighed. My fingers tightened on the wheel, then I returned the gearshift to park and adjusted to face her. "I get where you're coming from, but the fear of dropping through the sky in a car seems to be outweighing whatever residual trauma I have about driving on the road. Are you *sure* this is safe? I mean, the idea alone would make my physics teacher implode."

"It's a Heaven car, Grace. The laws of physics aren't relevant here. The tank is full of rainbow sprinkles and this car can fly as smoothly through the clouds as it can drive on land. All you need to do is engage the hover function." She pointed to the silver, illuminated button on the dashboard with a pair of wings on it. "That aside, since when are you overly concerned with what's safe? I can't say if I was more proud or dismayed by your behavior in Hell today—the way you held your ground and stood up to those demons when they challenged you was . . . something."

"Isn't that what I'm supposed to do? I mean, you, Deckland, and Ana didn't take their baloney either."

"That's true. But we're used to them and that place. You're not. Past that . . . given your timid performances during training, I wasn't sure when I would see that more aggressive, bolder side of you."

My gaze wandered forward and rested on the clouds as conflict rested on my shoulders. "I try to keep that part of me reined in. It earned me nothing but trouble in life." I shook my head and pushed past bad memories that tried to come out.

Trying to forget them, I leaned over the side of the car and peered past the edge of the cloud to the seemingly endless drop. My stomach flipped again and I tried to prolong the inevitable. "I thought you said Heaven didn't have cars. That's why there's no traffic, right?"

"First off, we're in Heaven, so if you want a car, you can have a car; you just have to drive it where it doesn't bother anyone. Second, I know what you're doing. You have two kinds of questions—those meant for understanding, and those for distracting. Drive the car, Grace."

Busted.

I moved the gearshift to drive again then pushed my foot on the accelerator. The car moved toward the brink of the cloud. I closed my eyes at the last second and grimaced, instinctively feeling like we were about to drop to our doom *Thelma & Louise* style.

WHOOSH!

We plunged for a second and a slight scream escaped my lips, but then—

WAHOO!

I opened my eyes as we shot into the clouds. The wind blew through my hair. The edges of the car glowed with soft golden magic. In the rearview mirror, I saw we were expelling rainbow light instead of fumes.

"Left, right, and reverse will work the same as in a regular car!" Akari shouted over the wind. "But to go up and down keep your foot on the accelerator, *both* hands on the wheel, and just focus on the direction. It works by telepathic command like your Soul Pulse!"

I gave it a try.

"*Wahoo!*" I shouted aloud this time as I darted around, under, and over clouds in the increasingly pink sky. As I got closer to The First City, I had to execute sharper maneuvers to avoid the glowing lanterns. The color-flux clouds at this level were getting increasingly bright too, blinding me a bit. I didn't mind until a cloud directly in front of me took on a red glow and déjà vu struck. My brain flooded with flashbacks of red headlights charging toward me in the blackness of night an instant before my mother and I were hit by that—

I abruptly swerved the steering wheel to the right. Our angel car spun like an out-of-control top.

"Grace, let go of the wheel!" Akari shouted.

It took me a second, but I managed to unclench my grip. The moment I did, the car settled and slowed its spinning until we were just floating in the sky again.

My heart pounded.

I took a breath and then returned my hands to the wheel, lightly this time.

"I'm sorry." I stared forward before bringing my forehead to rest on the wheel dejectedly. "I thought I could handle this."

"You can, Grace. I'm not upset and you shouldn't be either. Mistakes happen. I forgive you." She paused. "Do you forgive *me?*"

I raised my head slowly and looked at my mentor. A few lanterns drifted by, their lights glistening on the windshield. I closed my eyes a moment and let out a deep exhale before reopening them. When I did, I settled back in my seat and stared ahead.

"I'm not mad at you anymore, Akari. After seeing so much in Hell today, petty personal grievances seem so trivial. It's just not worth the time given how much we have at stake and how big this world really is. But I feel like we're approaching a point where you need to be honest with me."

"Grace, all I can be is honest with you. The filter."

"Then maybe forthcoming is a better word." I said, turning to face her. "You claim to know everything important about me from having read some detailed file. But despite the hundreds of questions I've asked since I got here, I still feel like I don't know you. Or everything that's going on here."

"Grace—"

"Am I wrong?"

Akari sighed. "You're not." A lantern bopped into our car; my mentor gestured at a nearby cloud. "Why don't you park there?"

I gently guided our ride over and put the vehicle in park upon the cloud. I continued to hold onto the steering wheel though. The car wasn't going anywhere, so perhaps it was to keep myself steady.

"Will you ever tell me everything?" I asked a bit sadly.

"I'll give you every piece of the puzzle, Grace. But one at a time. Being a Guardian Angel in Heaven is no different from being a human on Earth. You can't just have all the answers at once. For them to mean something you have to earn them, and grow enough to be able to handle them. Today was a big test for you, Monkonjae, and Leo. Tomorrow you'll be ready for the next phase of your journey."

I perked up. I opened my mouth. Then my lips tightened.

Questions were useless if the person with answers didn't want you to have them. Akari was keeping me on a very controlled leash. My mother had done that my entire life—claiming it was for my own good like Akari was doing now. Even if they were right, it didn't quell the fire in my soul that so often desired to be bolder, but I so often repressed out of fear of seeming too aggressive, and disappointing those around me.

Sigh. How did I get stuck in the same cycle?

I swallowed the quiet yearning for freedom and dealt with the truth. Heaven's honesty filter couldn't affect my internal thoughts, but I felt no desire to lie to myself.

I meant it when I told Akari I wasn't mad at her anymore. I knew she didn't intend me any malice and regretted the harm that her oversight had caused. And although overhearing her conversation with Deckland made me question what she thought of me in her heart of hearts, I knew that sometimes you did your best learning when you just listened. So I should listen to her.

Moreover, the way the demons talked to her in Hell finally confirmed my theory that Akari's aloof, professional behavior was a means to cope with whatever happened in her past.

Like me, she had sides to herself that she wasn't keen on letting people see. I would try to respect that because I understood how conflicting it felt to live that way. Moreover, I understood that sometimes living that way—suppressing elements of your personality and past that others didn't appreciate—was the only manner to exist without being judged.

The sky had fallen into a lavender color palette by then. Resolutely, I put the car back in drive and decided to go forward— both figuratively and literally.

"So how fast can this thing go?" I asked Akari.

"Grace, just because we're in the sky doesn't mean I want you speeding."

I shrugged. "Call a cop." Then I punched the gas before she could stop me.

WHOO!

"So . . . have you ever full-on fought anyone before?" I asked Monkonjae, teetering anxiously on my heels.

It calmed me a little to see he seemed equally apprehensive. "I was in a boxing club in high school," he said. "But I've never done *this* kind of fighting."

I nodded. I thought my weekend couldn't get any weirder after spending Saturday in Hell. Yet here we were, spending Sunday on the sidelines of an angel fight club.

One level below the Angel Tower training center was our sparring center. Our mentors had reserved two octagons for us today, the type the UFC used for pay-per-view fights. Currently

Akari and Deckland were making good use of one, giving us a demonstration of how our halos could be used for combat. They both wielded their respective halos as they dueled like total bosses. Leo, Monkonjae, and I stood outside the octagon with Ana.

My mentor moved with the agility of the acrobat she looked liked. Deckland deftly handled everything she threw at him with some kind of Muay Thai action that utilized all parts of his body—fists, elbows, knees, shins, etc. My eyes were wide as Oreos as I watched. Their general combative skill and athleticism was impressive, but those abilities still didn't top the featured weapon in the fight—their halos. Troy and the demons could keep their stabby daggers. This was way cooler.

Every time the halos collided they shined with extra brilliance and made a *SHMING!* sound. With the speed our mentors moved, the glowing accessories struck each other almost too rapidly to keep track of like body-slamming fireflies.

"This is some fantasy action nonsense right here," Monkonjae whispered as Akari blocked Deckland's halo with hers then did a backflip.

He was right. The spectacle reminded me of this show called *Shadowhunters* based on a book series—hot, powerful people fighting like it was no big deal.

"I think it looks fantastic," said Leo, his eyes glued to the duo. "I watched this show on Earth called *Shadowhunters*, and engaging in a spicy training montage became a top to-do on my bucket list. Sadly, that is not an option provided by the Make-A-Wish Foundation."

I tore my gaze away from the arena and stared at Leo. It was surprising that he and I were on the same page with the TV reference, but the kid just raised a WAY more important issue. "Leo, did you—"

SHMING!

"Get him, Akari!" Ana cheered, cutting me off.

My mentor flicked her wrist and sent her halo spinning toward Deckland. He ducked and the glowing discus ricocheted back to Akari's hand. She side-stepped to avoid Deckland's jab and cross. He kept coming at her again and again. Akari was quick, but he was hammering her into exhaustion with his continuous follow through. She was running out of steam and room.

He threw a right hook at her temple. In a moment's reaction, Akari ducked under his fist moving her arm in a scooping motion, then thrust her hand at his chest. Her halo contorted into a ball of light and blasted Deckland ten feet back. He hit the fence of the octagon.

What the—

"Sorry! Sorry!" Akari dashed over to him.

Deckland shook his head as the shock of impact began to fade. "I thought we said no other powers besides the discus and hand-held halo."

"We did. Again, I'm sorry, Deck. It's been a while since I sparred and I just . . . reacted. You came at me and that was a reflex."

"*THAT* was awesome; that's what that was!" Leo declared. "I'm *plotzing* so hard right now I may actually erupt. Did you just produce a laser beam like Iron Man?"

"It's a beam of light," Akari said as she and Deckland stepped down from the octagon. "It's one of the more advanced powers. We'll teach it to you when you're ready."

"So Troy was right," I commented. "All our powers are derived from light."

Ana shivered. "Ugh. Grace. Never say Troy was right, please. I feel like he can sense it and is grinning down there somewhere."

"Sorry," I said. I wrung my hands together with a touch of insecurity.

"You don't seem hurt," Leo commented, looking Deckland up and down then poking him in the arm. "Are the blasts more bark than bite?"

Akari shook her head. "Our powers pack a punch, but as they're meant to defend good, we can't hurt mortals or angels with them past initial impact like you saw with Deckland."

"We can get hurt in other ways though," I said, trying not to be overcome by the image of that speeding bus. "Look at what happened to me on Earth. And Ana told us about Divine Iron. So how immortal are we? Really?" My voice started to heighten. "I mean, what happens if I am accidentally impaled by a unicorn up here or fall down a Heavenly staircase?"

"All right, settle down," Ana said, holding up her hands. "Yes, we can be harmed, but only temporarily. When Guardian Angels get hurt in our immortal bodies, we sort of dematerialize into sparkly goop and then reform. It's . . . unpleasant, to tell you the truth. And it can take a week on average. But we're fine after that."

"Hold on. I want to go back to what our powers can do," Monkonjae interjected. "They can't harm humans or angels, but I assume they can harm demons, right?"

Deckland nodded. "If you hit any creature of demonic origin with a solid blast of light or discus throw or halo slice, they go back to Hell. You have to aim for center mass if you want all of them sent there—I'm talking a direct and 'fatal' hit, which will cause the full reform Ana mentioned. Just hitting their hand will only send that body part back."

My face puckered. "Sounds kinds of gross."

"And sounds like a bandage on a problem," Leo added. "Wouldn't it be better for the universe if we could just wipe them out? Or is that also too easy?" He glanced at Ana.

She shrugged. "Yes and yes. However, we're not in the business of harming anything with a soul, which demons still have even if they are terrible."

"We're getting off track," Akari said with an assertive wave to call our attention. "The point of this wasn't to preview advanced powers. It was to introduce you to general sparring."

"Like the demons we saw practicing with those knives," Monkonjae said.

"Why do we even need to learn this?" I asked. "Don't get me wrong, I love expanding my skillset. But are fantasy action fight scenes really relevant to this job? My assignment is in *high school*. I can't foresee challenging some fellow to a fight if he cuts Henry in the lunch line. And with the Demon Code of Conduct in place, it's not like Solange is going to try to jump Henry in our school parking lot."

"It's about being prepared, Grace," Akari said. Her Soul Pulse flashed and a water bottle appeared in her hand. "You don't *know* what kind of dangers could compromise your assignment, or what threats your demon will send your way. Then there's the Dark Breeds . . ."

"The what now?" Leo asked.

Akari took a long drink of water. I think she was hoping one of her coworkers would answer. The gambit worked. Ana's Soul Pulse flashed and three thick books materialized in her arms, which she distributed to Leo, Monkonjae, and me.

"You love hitting the books, Grace. Here is your own copy of *Dark Breeds: A Complete Guide*."

I flipped the text open to a random page.

It was the wrong page.

A rendering of a six-armed beast with the veiny, buff limbs of a body builder, the chest of a gorilla, and spiny dragon wings stared up at me.

"Whoa!" I slammed the book shut and looked at Akari. "What the heck was that?"

My mentor paused. She took another extended sip of water. Ana glanced at Akari then answered on my mentor's behalf again.

"Three types of creatures live in Hell—the demons who work there, the normal people who get tortured there, and the Dark Breeds, which are sometimes used to terrify and torment the people but in general just roam around. See, unlike the souls who arrive in Hell when they die, Dark Breeds are born there. They're monsters molded from fear, fire, rage, and wretchedness. We don't include them on the tour because we don't want to frighten you."

My eyes narrowed into a glare. "What a considerate thing to do when you take someone *to Hell*," I remarked. I took a breath and re-centered, but my fists remained clenched. "Sorry, that was too rude."

"But fair," Leo chimed in. "If I know my fantasy drama, I'm guessing you are trying to ease into telling us that we have to fight those things at some point?"

"Don't be ridiculous," Monkonjae said. Then he caught a look at our mentors and his expression sank. "*Seriously?*"

"It's not a regular thing . . ." Deckland said, trying to placate us. "Dark Breeds can't cross over to Earth on their own. They have to be summoned by an extremely powerful demon, and even then they can only exist on Earth for a short time before they are drawn back to Hell. Our enemies can mask the true appearance of the monsters with a mirage so they look like something else once on Earth, but most demons don't have the skill to conjure Dark Breeds anyway. It's like one in fifty, so I wouldn't worry . . ."

We stared at him.

Deckland rubbed the back of his head uneasily. He knew we weren't buying what he was selling. "Also, if it helps—and playing more to your point, Leo—Dark Breeds don't have a soul, so with a good shot you can completely blast them out of existence."

I stood stupefied.

After a moment I decided to crack open my book again, but when I saw a spider monster with tongues for legs, I closed the text forcefully.

"Nope. I'm out."

My heart thudded faster as fear and anger contorted inside me. No deep breaths would save me now. It was too much.

"What do you mean, you're out?" Akari asked.

"I covered my eyes during half of *Stranger Things*." My fingers tensed around the book. "I've been trying here, but with the demons, and Hell, and now these monsters . . . Well, just tell me where to return my halo, because I don't want to do this anymore."

"Grace—"

"*I'm done.*" My face filled with heat and I shoved the book back at Ana before storming out of the sparring center. The hallway connecting to the elevator bank was silver and frigid. I felt that cold on my skin, but my cheeks still felt flushed from getting so worked up.

What part of being good meant I had to be *insane*? I couldn't fight horrifying monsters even with some after-school training, and I wasn't going to delude myself into thinking otherwise. I wasn't ready for this. I was never going to *be* ready for this. The potential just did not exist.

There were still moments when I tripped up and stumbled

doing a simple dance move I'd executed a thousand times. How was I supposed to battle a spider-tongue monster or dagger-wielding demon?

I wanted to live up to the expectations that Akari, and Heaven, and the whole universe seemed to have for me. And I cared about Henry and didn't want anything bad to happen to him. But it all felt so . . . unrealistic. I was not an epic magical heroine. I was just a girl who wanted to keep her head down, stay in her lane, and find some peace.

I pressed the up button next to the elevator bank and waited. I heard the door to the sparring center open and close with a soft *whoosh*.

"Leave me alone, Akari."

"It's not Akari."

I turned around as Ana approached.

"What are you doing here?" I asked, arms crossed tightly over my chest.

"I told Akari I think it'd be best if I spoke with you."

"Why?"

"Because I get it. Some people take to all this surreal Guardian Angel stuff naturally. Leo was practically exploding with excitement when he was watching that demo. On Earth, he didn't get a chance to live as action-packed as he would've liked. Here, he can be his true self. About half the souls who enter the GA department are that way—fierce and ready to fight, like Akari or Deckland. I didn't feel that way when I died and met my fate here."

A second later the elevator arrived and the doors slid open. Ana tilted her head toward a bench against the wall, giving me a choice to let the elevator go and join her instead. I glanced between the tiny angel and my ride out. Then I allowed the doors to close.

"Even without Hell's honesty filter, I know Akari meant it when she told Troy she isn't afraid of him," Ana remarked as we sat down. "She's always been incredibly brave. Until a few years ago, I would've said she wasn't afraid of anything. Me? I am completely the opposite. Don't let the assertiveness and crazy stories of my past assignments fool you. I'm ten years old, Grace. *I don't like fighting monsters.* I would prefer not to even look at them in a book. But they are a part of this insane, intense, wonderful job. After a while, I found the strength to accept the bad with the good. Like people are supposed to do in life." She put her small hand over mine. "It's all fresh now, but you will get the hang of this job and find a way to deal with the scary stuff too. Trust me."

I hung my head, wanting to believe her but feeling totally overwhelmed. "*But I can't do this,*" I said adamantly.

I stood suddenly and paced. "I appreciate that you're empathizing with me, Ana, but I've spent most of my existence overwhelmed by doubt and I've never been the person others expect me to be. On Earth that caused this constant struggle between resenting feeling lesser-than while wishing I didn't constantly have to hide who I actually am. I've been facing the same issues since I got to Heaven, but I can't juggle those emotional demons with *real* demons."

I paused and shook my head sorrowfully. "I don't think I have it in me to be a GA. I'm not strong enough in a *lot* of ways. And I am not the person I'd need to be to change that. I thought I could skate by under the radar, keep Henry out of trouble and count on Akari to swoop in if I needed her. But I know I can't rely on that, and every day you all keep adding more elements working against me. Demons, Hell, Dark Breeds—there are too many variables. Too much material and not enough time to study. My soul is already spent and it's only been a week. I can't see myself doing this long-term."

A hard moment passed with Ana's eyes upon me.

"Do you know what I think you need?" she said, studying me. "A purpose."

"Isn't that what these jobs in Heaven are supposed to give us?"

"Grace, a job can't give you purpose if you don't feel like your heart is fully in it."

"Yes, but in fairness I didn't choose this job."

"Just because you don't choose a path doesn't mean it isn't the right road. Try focusing on the reasons this job matters to you. I know that it does. I saw your reaction in the museum during our tour. I heard the tone of your voice when you didn't back down to those demons in Hell. You feel connected to this role. Your heart—your soul—*is* in it, but you need to understand why, otherwise you won't be able to handle the challenges or fears that come your way."

Ana removed her locket and handed me the heart-shaped accessory. "Open it."

I obliged and found two names inscribed inside. "Debra and Richard Messenger. Your family?" I guessed.

"Actually, I've never met them."

I gave her a puzzled look.

"A few months before I died, I was travelling by plane to meet my mother. I was seated next to an old woman named Nancy. I love people—always have—so despite our age difference, we struck up a conversation. She told me all about her daughter Debra and son-in-law Richard—their careers, their home, their latest vacation. I asked Nancy if they had any kids; older people love to talk about grandkids. Do you know what she told me?"

I shook my head.

"She told me that Debra and Richard never wanted to have kids. That's totally fine, but it was their reason for it that bothered me. They believed our planet was on an unalterable downward trajectory and didn't want to bring new life into the world and subject them to that. So they were just going to live for themselves without worrying about the consequences for future generations. That comment has always stuck with me because it rattled, saddened, and angered me to my core. Debra and Richard had given up on humanity and when you do that it becomes second nature to live selfishly and destructively. I know those are two strong words, but the fact is that people who believe doom is inevitable and that what happens after they're gone is inconsequential only take from the world with no regard for securing the future for others."

Ana closed her eyes as she let out a long, frustrated breath. "From billionaire oil tycoons who ignore safety updates on rigs, to the average person who throws trash on the sidewalk instead of bothering to find a trash can. People like that don't bother thinking about what we owe to each other or the next generation because they figure, Hey, we'll be long gone by the time things get really bad, so who cares? We're not going to save the world, so let's just ride the ride for everything it's worth now and screw whoever and whatever comes after we're gone. *The world lives and dies with us . . ."*

Ana's eyes had never been so intense, not even when she was talking to Troy, Megan, and Ithaca. She gestured for the locket and I returned it.

"Debra and Richard are just names, and there are obviously way worse people out there, but I keep them close to my heart because they remind me of why *my* heart is in this job," Ana said as she reattached the necklace. "I know humanity has a ton of flaws, but despite the madness and cruelty and foolish conflict, our world is beautiful and human beings have the potential to shine as brightly as any light in Heaven. I fight for *them*. I fight so they can have a chance to keep trying to learn and improve and make the world better, even in the face of the Debras and Richards who are satisfied with the idea that doom is inevitable. *It's not.* And plenty of people know it. Those people deserve a chance to prove that and live brilliantly. With that as my core—recognizing this as my purpose as a Guardian Angel—I am willing to face any monster the universe throws at me."

The small warrior for good stood up. "I know it's frightening. I know it's overwhelming. And I know you haven't felt very strong lately. But heed your heart, Grace. You may not be sure why it wants you to stay, but I believe if you listen to it, and are honest with yourself, you know that it does. We'll figure out why in time. I promise."

She extended her hand to me, nodding in the direction of the sparring center.

I stared at her, then at the door.

My heart tensed with reluctance, so I did as Ana had advised. I listened to it. After a beat of self-reflection, despite logic, fear, frustration, and a thousand other things . . . I was amazed to discover she was right. I didn't *want* to stay, but I *had* to stay. Not

because she, or Akari, or God told me to, but because my heart—
the crux of my silly, elusive soul that had gotten me into this
situation—required it. It felt right. And I had to *do right* by that
instinct otherwise I'd be failing myself as much as I'd be failing
these people. And Henry.

I took Ana's hand and let her guide me back into the room for
another try.

At least for the rest of the day I didn't embarrass myself during
GA training. Nor would I—hopefully—for a few weeks. Our
mentors announced that for the next month we would focus on
the drills and skills required for basic combat training, no halos
or powers. What a relief. I'd be happy to learn the fundamentals
of fighting alongside Leo and Monkonjae. It would just feel like
really intense gym class.

At half past one o'clock, we split into private meetings with our
mentors with the promise that afterward we'd have the rest of the
weekend to ourselves. I sat in my usual chair in Akari's office with
the Dark Breeds book in my lap. I ran my hand over the embossed
black cover, a twisting pattern of gold, silver, and red framing the
edges. Held at certain angles, a holographic silhouette of some
beastly creature sprang into view on the front. I turned the book
a smidge counterclockwise and it vanished. I turned it another
way and the monster reappeared, shimmering like liquid metal.

"I'm sorry I wasn't more help this morning easing you into
those monsters." Akari used her Soul Pulse to summon a steaming
mug of tea into her hand. The mug had a picture of a cartoon
panda holding a revolver in each paw.

"You did try to warn me," I replied. "When we were in the
car last night, you told me I'd learn about the next phase of my
journey today."

Akari took a sip and set her cup down. "Yes, but I wasn't referring to the Dark Breeds. I honestly didn't consider that you might
need a more delicate introduction to those creatures. When
I went through training, I wasn't that dismayed to learn about

Dark Breeds after seeing Hell. I'd been to the bowels of evil, so knowing a few more monsters existed didn't ruffle me."

"Ana did mention that you're epically brave."

"I don't know if I would go that far." Akari took another sip from her mug.

Her beverage smelled nice—like jasmine—so I used my Soul Pulse to summon a cup of English Breakfast tea. My mug featured a picture of a llama wearing a sombrero under the words *Como Se Llama?*

"Our day is almost over," I commented after taking a sip. "If the Dark Breeds conversation isn't the next big step in my journey you were referring to, then what is?"

"Before we get into that, I do just want to talk about your driving briefly. And what we're going to do about that."

I sighed and set the cup down. "Let me guess, you're taking away my angelic learner's permit? Give me another chance, Akari. Other than my PTSD moment, and those few lanterns, and that near accident with the balloon, I think it went pretty well. And in my defense, how was I supposed to know that Pierre and Marie Curie like to fly their hot air balloon over Heaven in the evening? Anyway, it's not like the balloon popped; they just got bopped around a bit."

"Actually, I was going to tell you that it's imperative that you keep driving. You need to pass your driver's test as soon as possible. We are going to keep practicing a few nights a week."

"Oh."

Wariness sparked in Akari's eyes as she took her next sip of tea; she was nervous about how I would take the news that came next. I had one more drink then addressed her straight on.

"Now what's the real shoe you want to drop?"

Akari put her cup down then opened her desk drawer. She pulled out three simple notecards like the kind I'd use to study for a test and handed them to me. Each one had a single short phrase on it, which I read out loud.

"*Avoid driver's license until high school graduation. Pick USD. Be in the elevator on the left off the Main Galeria at the Biltmore at 9:04 p.m.*

on Saturday, May 28th." I raised an eyebrow and looked up. "What are these?"

"Henry's first set of Plot Points," Akari explained. "I told you that God doesn't like to immediately divulge the full scope of our assignments and their potential. However, as their paths become clearer to the angels monitoring them, we are informed of key things that will change the course of our humans' lives. We call them Plot Points because they are pivotal events in the stories of the people we are protecting—the make-or-break moments, the forks in the road, the choices that end up altering a person's entire life *and* what they achieve. A few days ago, these were finalized for Henry."

I took another glance at the notecards.

"These are the most important to-dos for Henry between now and his high school graduation. After that, eventually you'll get more Plot Points. The good news is that demons don't get access to any of these, so at least there's that working in our favor."

I shuffled back to the first notecard, realizing the implications. "Henry and Razel are taking their driving tests this semester. How am I supposed to stop him from getting his license? How am I supposed to keep any teenager from getting a driver's license?"

"You'll have to figure it out. The angels who prep Plot Points predict there is an 87% chance that Henry gets into a fatal car accident if he drives on his own before he graduates high school. Hence the urgency for you to get *your* license. You can be one more person he relies on for rides."

My stomach did a flip. "And the other cards?"

"USD is the University of San Diego. Henry needs to choose it as his college. As for the last notecard, I'll admit it's odd. We don't usually get such specific instructions, but at least you know exactly what you're supposed to do."

I took a breath. Then went for my tea again.

"Are you okay?" Akari asked kindly. I'd noticed her tone had more of that these last few days. Either emotionally-detached professionalism was becoming too tiring to sustain, or we were getting to a place in our relationship where she was actually starting to care about me as a person, not just as the assignment God forced her into.

I nodded slowly and unconvincingly. Then I set the cup on Akari's desk, stashed the cards in my jacket pocket, and my Soul Pulse glowed.

Three Labrador puppies appeared on my lap—warm, soft, and wriggly. "I downloaded Puppy Palooza from the app store," I explained to a surprised Akari, scratching the ears of the pups. "You were right in the beginning. They do soften the blow of bad news."

OPPOSING FORCES

Feeling hungry, I strolled down the streets of The First City until I came across a shop called Bake It Till You Make It. The name made me smile; the goodies inside caused that grin to expand to my ears.

I ended up purchasing a six-inch-round chocolate ganache cake. "Your eyes are bluer than the sky in California," I told the woman at the counter to pay for the baked good.

"Aw, thank you, sweetie."

I carried my cake outside to enjoy it at one of the patio tables. It wasn't a lunch that any nutritionist would recommend, but I couldn't have been happier with the choice. I was eight forkfuls in when I looked up and saw a woman with red hair wandering the sidewalk. Her back was to me, but I recognized her instantly.

My heart did a flip that would stun an Olympic gymnast committee.

"MOM!" I leapt from my chair, tipping it over as my mother turned.

"Grace!"

I dashed over, ready to go in for a hug when my mother abruptly held up her hand. "Dear, you're a mess. Your face is covered in chocolate. Hold still." She reached into her little white purse and removed a handkerchief, then took my chin in her hand like I was five and wiped my cheek.

"Um, thank you," I said, swatting her away after a second. "Can I hug you now?"

"Yes."

As I embraced her, my mother stiffened slightly. She really wasn't a touchy-feely person, but I was glad to feel her arms around me. I squeezed her hard until she withdrew and patted my head.

"How are you?" I asked eagerly. "I know you wanted some space, but I couldn't ask for a better fate than running into you. So much has happened that I need to talk about. I've seen the Pearlie Gates, and I've been back to Earth, and just yesterday I went to Hell and saw—"

My mother held up her hand again, notably stressed. "I have been to Hell, dear. I'd prefer not to discuss it in Heaven."

"Oh, right." I shifted my weight back and forth on my feet. I probably should've been more considerate about that topic. Who knew what my mother had endured down there on Friday. I was curious, but she very clearly didn't want to get into it.

"Well, why don't you tell me about how your time in Heaven has been? Would you like to join me for lunch?" I gestured at the table where I'd abandoned my cake.

My mother raised a judgmental eyebrow. "You're eating cake for lunch?"

I shrugged. "No calories."

"And apparently no restraint," she replied wistfully. "We can work on that though. If we're going to be together on weekends, that's two days a week when I can continue to help you make the right decisions. With that in mind, I *would* like to join you, dear." She nodded firmly and released a sigh that clearly held regret. "I've been thinking about you since I arrived, Grace, and I owe you an apology. It was selfish of me to want to be alone during this time. Despite the blame I'm digesting over the accident, I should've been there for you."

I was surprised and impressed. My mother rarely apologized to me.

She gestured forward and I escorted us back to the table. I hastened a few steps ahead to right the fallen chair, then dusted off the seat and offered it to her. As she sat, I brought over another chair from a nearby table. Once we'd settled I extended my fork to my mother so she could try the cake, but she turned me down with a demure wave.

Instead, her Soul Pulse flashed and a steaming teacup with

saucer appeared in her hand. The china was delicately painted with wildflowers, like the set she had at home on Earth. Or at least used to have . . .

"I see you downloaded an app on your Soul Pulse," I commented.

"Yes, quite clever, wonderful things. None of Heaven's applications work in the other planes of the afterlife, but I intend to make good use of them here." She looked me up and down— hazel eyes judging my white jacket, tee, and yoga pants combo over the brim of her cup. "Might I suggest you download Dress for Success. It can create a custom wardrobe that is an upgrade from what you're used to. If you're going to be a Guardian Angel, I think it is best you start dressing more professionally."

"This is the same look I wore on Earth, Mom. I'm not pretending to be something I'm not in Heaven."

"Are you certain of that, dear?"

I swallowed my current bite of cake and looked at her pointedly as I put my fork down. "What's that supposed to mean?"

"Only that the people here currently see you in an elevated . . . *idealistic* light. So if you are going to continue to convince them of that persona, a more ladylike wardrobe would help make the image last longer."

My fingers curled with anxiety. "Mom, I'm already dealing with enough doubt about my new job. *Please* don't make me question my fashion choices too. I'm not Gaby, okay. I didn't want to wear cutesy dresses every day on Earth and I don't want to do it here."

"I know you're not Gaby, dear, believe me. But I am only trying to help. I'm worried for you, Grace. The expectations they have for you . . ." She paused, choosing her words carefully. "I was watching Heaven's local access channel last night and learned that the angels believe you are pure as snow."

I gulped. "You heard?"

"I believe the show is *Heaven't* You Heard?"

This time it was my mother's turn to fidget, conservatively though. Just one finger scraped the design of her teacup.

"I realize you and I disagreed on a lot of things in life," she said after a moment. "But I know you are not a liar, Grace. That is one part of your personality I am proud we got right. Given that, I trust you came clean with the angels and told them that you . . . shall we say, are not perfect?"

"I did."

"And?"

"There's no mistake. Apparently I am 98% good."

My mother raised her brow in true shock. "How can that be though?"

I crossed my arms. "Do you have to sound *so* surprised? I mean, I was too, but still."

"I'm sorry, Grace. Goodness knows I love you." She cringed and set her teacup down. "But I also *know* you. Please do not take offense and get riled up like you always do," she said softly and steadily, "but people who are 98% good aren't as naturally aggressive and audacious as you. I've tried to train that out of you; thankfully it seems I did it thoroughly enough that you ended up here. However, whatever progress I made improving your demeanor on Earth is not a résumé for sainthood."

I did take offense, and I definitely got riled up. "Should *you* really be the judge of that? I mean, I am the one in Heaven. You got timeshared."

"See? There it is again, creeping out," my mother replied calmly, pointing a manicured finger at me. "That hostility in your tone, the belligerence in your posture. *My well-intentioned, quick-fused child*," she mused sadly, taking another sip of tea. When she set the cup on the table, she sighed. "Do you *always* have to fight me?"

"Mom, you're the one picking a fight. It's like I tried to tell you so many times on Earth; you—other people—shouldn't judge me so harshly for reacting defensively."

"You're reacting *antagonistically*, dear. I am not picking a fight now, nor have I ever. You take constructive criticism as an attack on your character."

"Only because you make me feel like my character isn't enough."

My mother paused and asked pointedly, "Do *you* feel it is enough?"

Her words now, like so many times when we spoke, held a double meaning. She was asking and answering for me at the same time. If I were enough for her as a daughter—as a person—I wouldn't always be disappointing her. She wouldn't constantly be criticizing me and admonishing my behavior. And if I were enough for myself, then I wouldn't feel so hurt when she didn't understand me and where I was coming from.

"Grace . . ." my mother said. "I know you are good-hearted, and I am so relieved that you ended up in Heaven full-time. You are my daughter and I do not wish any suffering on you, ever. I want you to be happy and safe, and fear of something happening to you tortures me more than you will ever understand—"

She paused and took a breath. "All I was trying to say is that I am having difficulty understanding how someone who got into so much trouble on Earth can earn the status they've given you here."

I sighed and sat on my hands to keep myself from wringing them raw. "Yeah, so am I," I admitted, eyes falling to the table. After a beat passed, I looked up again. "I am trying though. I want to be better, Mom. I want to be the person they think I am and meet everyone's expectations. Even though I couldn't do that in life—even though you've had doubts that I could change—it would mean a lot to me if I know that you believe I can do it here and now. Being honest . . . I'm scared and overwhelmed. Feeling like I'm not enough in the eyes of teachers and school counselors is nothing in comparison to feeling like I'm not enough for angels."

I swallowed roughly. "My mentor may think I can do this, but her reading a file about me isn't the same as her *knowing* me. Not like you do. So if *you* tell me you wholeheartedly believe I can be this 98% perfect angel of goodness . . ." I gazed at her desperately. "That would go a long way in helping me convince myself of that."

I saw a strange flux of emotion cross my mother's face—sorrow, pain, and also uncertainty. After a moment, she gulped like I did when trying to stomach something conflicting. That act alone sent a tremor of worry up my spine.

My mother extended her hand across the table. I hesitantly took it, and she looked me in the eyes.

"Grace. I don't want to negatively affect your self-esteem. And I am glad you intend to work so hard on being a better person and are also very aware of the areas you need to improve on. I would be more afraid for you and your wellness here if you weren't being honest with yourself."

My heart beat a little faster. "*But . . .*"

She took a deep breath. "But Heaven has an honesty filter so I can't say what you want me to."

I blinked in surprise, hurt, and confusion.

"*Why?*" I said, taking back my hand.

"You know why, dear. All the incidents in your life, every time I had to pick you up from the principal's office, every time I received a call from a coach or a Girl Scout troop leader. The list goes on."

"But even if I let you down all those times, even though you never understood why I acted the way I did, you never stopped pushing me to improve—believing that I could be more like you, more like Gaby. No matter how many times I came up short, you never left the matter alone. Why is our afterlife situation any different? Why don't you believe I can be better now?"

"Grace, please don't make me answer that. I can only be completely honest and I do not want to—"

"*Tell me the truth,*" I urged. "What's changed?"

"What's changed is that I am angry with you, Grace."

It came out so suddenly I think it stunned us both. My mother blinked. I stared at her and tilted my head. "Why are you angry with me?"

She let out an extended, pained exhale. "I have always hoped that given enough time, and help, and molding, you could stay on the right path and not turn into—" She cut herself off and shook her head.

"Mom?"

My mother wiped away whatever thought had occurred with a brusque wave of her hand. "The point is that spouts of detention or fights at school are not irreversible scars on your potential. I always had faith that your aggressive and impulsive behavior would not lead to true harm if I just kept being your mother and pushing you to be better. But my faith was broken when that very behavior is what led us to be *here*."

It took me a long moment to process the implication of the statement. I looked at the cake and felt sick. The angels strolling down the street in my periphery were a nauseating blur. Everything focused on my mother, the eye of the storm in this moment—as in every moment when she and I were about to have it out.

"Hold on. Are you saying you blame *me* for us dying in that car crash?"

"Yes, Grace," she said solemnly. "I do."

"But you were the one driving!"

"Dear, lower your volume," my mother said, glancing around uneasily. "You're a lady, not an air traffic controller."

I frowned but lowered my voice obediently. "*But you were the one driving*," I hissed.

"Picking *you* up after you got into that fight with your stage manager."

It took all my human and angelic powers to keep the very aggression my mother worked so hard to beat out of me from boiling over.

"Mom. I got into that argument with the stage manager because I was trying to delay the dance recital because you said you would be there. It was going to be the first time you ever saw me dance. That *anybody* saw me dance. It was a huge deal for me . . ." My voice cracked on the last bit. I shook my head, feeling uncomfortably tingly just talking about that vulnerable side of me. I had to take a deep breath to force myself to finish.

"The stage manager said some terrible things about my lack of talent and you 'not missing anything,' so I got in her face. She's the one who called you a bad word. I was just standing up for you. The director overreacted when he punished me for shoving her."

"*Oh, Grace*," my mother sighed.

Those two words again—so much power in so few syllables.

"You always had a talent for making picking fights sound so noble. While I appreciate your desire to defend my name, I did send you a message that I was not going to be able to make it. It's not my fault that you don't check your voicemail. I sent Gaby a text to pick you up afterward, but when your director insisted on speaking with me about your behavior, I had to abandon my meetings early. Hence why we were on the road in the car at that time. It is because of you, dear. I just didn't want to say anything before to burden you with guilt."

My soul felt like a deflating balloon as I realized there was a stronger, more shocking blow that a girl could receive than being hit by a bus.

"When you were apprehensive about us seeing each other right away, I thought it was because *you* felt guilty that you got us both killed. That you blamed yourself," I thought aloud. "But you were mad at me this whole time. You think I let you down in the ultimate way . . . that my aggression got us both killed."

My mother looked at the table. "I'm sorry, dear. But yes. And that is why I can't honestly say that I wholeheartedly believe you can be the Ninety-Eight the angels expect—this symbol of utter perfection. By the very nature of everything you've done, and how we ended up dead . . . I love you and always will, dear, but in *that regard* . . . I don't think you are *good* enough."

All my soul burned. Though I felt speechless, one more question came out anyway. "For you, or for this place?"

My mother's face was blank. "Do you believe there is a difference?"

Double meaning again. She was asking, but also answering. She'd always asserted that her way was the right way. The only way. I went along with it because I wanted to do her proud and have at least a modicum of harmony in our relationship. At this moment though, I was so upset with her that I genuinely didn't know if I could ever have that—*in any life*. She would never understand me. And I was tired of making her try to. I couldn't do this anymore.

We sat in silence for a long, long time until eventually I spoke my truth, even knowing it would fall on deaf ears. "You're being too hard on me, Mom. You can't blame me for the accident."

"It's not as though I want to feel this way, Grace," my mother replied earnestly. "I think given time I will forgive you, but right now I am *also* afraid and overwhelmed. I can't stop worrying about all of this, the future, and what is going to happen to you, but through it all . . . I'm sorry, I do blame you for what has happened to us, and for the greater tragedy of being separated from your father and Gaby for the rest of their lives."

Another extensive pause and then—

"I disagree, Mom. I disagree strongly."

"You always do, dear. But that does not mean I am not right."

My mother's Soul Pulse began to buzz. She glanced at the flashing reminder. "I have a check-in with my angel guide, so I'm afraid I must go. If you need me, or my counsel on your decisions as you move forward in your job, *please* reach out to me, dear. Despite my feelings about how we landed in this situation, I *am* your mother. I have only ever had your best interest at heart. And while I regret that I have my doubts, and as such couldn't affirm my full faith that you'll succeed in your quest to be good, I still want to do everything in my power to help you work toward the goal. I genuinely, honestly, would love nothing more than to be proven wrong and protect you from falling."

She reached for my hand across the table, but I pulled away. This seemed to hurt her, however for arguably the first time I cared very little about that. I was carrying too much hurt in my own heart to also worry about hers.

After a moment, realizing I would not budge, my mother stood and smoothed out the wrinkles of her white dress. I got up too. She checked her watch once more.

"I have to go."

She came around the table and gave me a quick side hug—which I didn't reciprocate—then patted my hair with caring and kissed the top of my head.

"I love you," she said.

I didn't return the sentiment either. I didn't even look at her. To see myself reflected in my mother's eyes would only fill me with more conflict.

Seventeen years of trying to do everything right so that she and the conservative world I grew up in would approve of me. Seventeen years of hoping that when I messed up, my mother would understand me. Seventeen years of burying every "inappropriate" instinct. It all had led me right here—different plane of existence, same circumstance. I felt like I wasn't, and never would be, enough. And the woman who I most wanted to believe otherwise didn't.

So what was I supposed to do?

How was I supposed to make peace with that and believe I could do a job that revolved around saving others and making the right choices?

With a final "affectionate" touch to my head, my mother drifted away from me. After a few seconds, I eventually turned to see the last of her red hair disappear in the crowd of angels.

I grimaced as the weight of multiple worlds crushed me. Then the floor of Heaven lit up and that golden hiccup spread over everything. People smiled upon seeing it. I couldn't.

My nerves hadn't been this shot when I'd looked demons in the eyes.

When I first returned to Earth last week, I'd felt so conscious of everything around me—every detail crisp and calling for my attention. Now that I had been to Hell and back, and knew the true stakes of the situation, as I walked to physics Monday morning, hugging my textbook close to my chest like a teddy bear, I felt even more aware.

Perhaps aware wasn't the right word for it. I was alert. Existing was scary enough when you were just trying to make it through. When a veil of innocence was lifted and you realized there were actually people out there who actively wanted you to fail, your perspective sharpened.

"You okay?" Henry asked as I sat down at the desk behind him.

"I think so. I just—"

I glanced up as Solange entered in tight gray jeans and a white crop top. She saw me and smiled. "Good morning," she chirped.

"Hey, Solange," Henry replied.

There were no seats near us, so she took a desk in the back. The bell rang and Mr. Corrin approached the front of the class.

"Okay, first thing: today's quiz. Once you're done, there's an assignment waiting for you in the lab area. Group up and see how fast you can solve the speed and distance puzzles I've laid out. Each station is a different superhero theme. For example . . ." He trotted over to one of the lab tables with a giddy grin. "This is the Spider-Man table. In that first movie with Tobey Maguire, he jumps off the building to save Mary Jane Watson. You get to use math to determine what speed and distance factors would need to be in place for Spidey to realistically reach her before she splats on the pavement. Cool, huh?"

The room stayed silent. I actually did think the experiment was cool though. And practical.

Mr. Corrin began distributing the tests. I looked over the paper then felt that weird instinct when you know someone is watching you. I glanced back. Solange was three seats behind and one row over, staring at me contentedly. It reminded me of the way a hawk shrewdly watched a dove mind its own business in a bird feeder. The dove thinking, *Everything's fine*. The hawk thinking, *You're mine*.

It made the hairs on the back of my neck stand up, but I narrowed my eyes and nodded at her as if to say: *I see you*.

I was the first to finish the three-page quiz. I liked physics. I was good at it. While my Heavenly life was basically a dumpster fire, at least I had the ease of school and academics to make me feel confident. I was grateful that my GA assignment still allowed me that world. I needed the reprieve of feeling strong at something. Had Henry been a deep sea fisherman or a fashion model I would have been doomed.

I journeyed to the lab table our teacher had referenced in his example and began looking through the Spidey assignment. I smiled as I tapped my pencil. I secretly really liked Mr. Corrin. He may have been a few steps off center and kind of intense, but he loved math and nerdy stuff as much as I did.

I did calculations on my own for a few minutes until Solange's voice interrupted my focus. "Hello, angel."

My brow furrowed. Before I could respond, Henry appeared beside her and picked up a copy of the assignment. "So, Spider-

Man," he said. "What's the first step to figuring out how this hero comes out a winner?"

"Maybe he doesn't," Solange suggested. She leaned against the table and casually picked up her own copy of the worksheet. "Movies can be so unrealistic. This may very well be a trick question and there's nothing the hero can do to save him."

"*Her*," Henry corrected. "Spidey is trying to save Mary Jane."

"Right, of course," Solange said. She shot me a quick smirk before rudely reaching over me to grab a pencil.

My glower intensified. Sadly, there was nothing I could say or do here. My entire relationship with Solange had changed since Henry saw us last Friday, but it's not like I could alert him of that.

The three of us worked on the experiment as our other classmates finished their exam and picked their own lab tables. I wasn't afraid of a challenge, but much to my regret, I didn't have time to solve the current one. After a while Mr. Corrin used a tiny mallet he kept at his desk to bang a miniature gong, bidding us to switch stations. I was a bit perturbed to move on without solving Spider-Man's predicament, but Henry and Solange went on to the next challenge, so I did too.

The rest of the class period went surprisingly without a hitch. While I was glad to solve the rest of the superhero physics puzzles, it was uncomfortable working side by side with Solange so normally. Demon rules aside, I guess part of me had been expecting her to whip out a dagger and tackle me at some point. No such dramatic turn of events occurred though. She, Henry, and I collaborated easily, compared notes, talked about the cafeteria lunch menu. It was super weird.

At two minutes to the bell, Mr. Corrin rang his gong a final time and called for our attention. "Read chapters six and seven tonight. That's all for homework. Also, Drum roll, please, Kyle." He pointed at one of the students. The kid was startled, but obliged and thudded his hands against his desk to create the drum roll effect.

"Get your sunscreen and slide-rulers ready," Mr. Corrin continued. "The senior class physics field trip to Magic Mountain is set for the second Friday in February. More details to come in the next few weeks!"

The bell sounded and all the kids hustled back to their desks to pack their bags.

"What's Magic Mountain?" I asked Henry as I loaded my notebook into my backpack. "It sounds like something out of a YA fantasy novel."

"It's a theme park," he explained. "Six Flags Magic Mountain. Mr. Corrin takes his classes there for a field trip every semester. He has everyone do physics problems involving roller coasters for half of the day. For the second half, we get to hang out."

"That sounds fun. Mr. Corrin may be intimidating, and he plays it a bit fast and loose with other people's cell phones, but I like his style." I glanced at our teacher who sat at his desk, staring at a worksheet while eating a large, plain celery stick—no peanut butter or anything.

Henry followed my eye line. "He's definitely one of a kind." My friend tilted his head toward the door. "Now come on. We've got another class." He nodded to Solange down the aisle. "See you in history."

We sure would. Thankfully Solange was only in three of Henry's courses. However that still meant three hours of class time plus lunch when we were stuck together. I had no idea how long it would take me to get used to that.

Each time Solange met up with us during the day, I was so on my toes I may as well have been wearing ballerina pointe shoes. She'd killed me three days ago. Yet, to my confused amazement, she was the essence of nonchalance. During class she took notes, raised her hand if she had a question, and participated in group assignments. At lunch, she laughed with Razel, flirted with the boys, and pecked at a green salad.

When the final bell finally rang, Henry and Razel bid me a quick farewell then rushed off to the parking lot to meet Justin for a ride. I headed in the other direction. Toward Solange's locker. I spotted her innocently putting away books like a regular girl as the other kids migrated around. When the last one near Solange closed his locker and hurried off, I approached.

"So what's the deal?" I said, leaning against the wall of lockers. I felt my confrontational side brewing.

Solange glanced sideways. "Oh, Grace. I didn't see you there." She smiled sweetly before going back to focusing on her locker mirror—fixing her hair and applying a fresh coat of lip gloss. "And I believe you know what the deal is. You. Me. Henry. A triangle of doom if I do my job right."

She smacked her lips and then stowed the gloss.

"No, I mean what's the deal with *this*," I replied, gesturing at her dramatically. "You acting like everything is hunky-dory and being so . . . normal."

Solange turned to look at me directly, putting a hand on her hip.

"Grace, what did you expect—for me to set Henry on fire during a physics test?" She huffed with amusement. "Please. I am not so tacky, and Guardians of Chaos have rules to follow. That being said . . ." She took a confident step closer to me so we were barely a breath apart.

"I *am* going to make a move on him. You can count on that. Just in my own time. And I will keep making moves against him until I succeed in destroying his future. If I have a spare moment and the right opportunity, I'd love to kill you a few more times along the way too." She shrugged. "That's more just for fun, not business. But whether it's you or him, you know the rules prevent me from simply attacking either of you directly—no matter how efficient that would be—so calm down."

Solange stepped away and returned to her locker, taking one more book to store in her bag.

"Plus, I am not even allowed to work against Henry in *any* way for the first month we are here." She zipped her bag and flicked her eyes back to me. "You'll be happy to know that means no more surprise assaults on you either. Your bald mentor followed through and God had a talk with our superior. I will be the first and last demon to expose that loophole in our realms' dealings with one another."

"Good," I said with a firm nod.

"That's your game, Grace," Solange said. She grabbed a pair

of huge, jewel-rimmed sunglasses from her locker and put them on. "Mine is evil. Remember that."

She slammed her locker door and gave me a final smile as she strutted away. "See you tomorrow, angel. *Salut!*"

GAMES

"Try to think of it like doing the splits in the air," Hana explained as a half dozen tiny dancers whirled across the studio. "You kick your back leg into it while doing a half turn."

Hana demonstrated—throwing her weight down, spinning on her heel while extending one leg to the ceiling, then rising up smoothly. "And that's an illusion. Remember, as you're throwing your leg up, your hands need to end up in the opposite direction from where they were originally aiming."

"Uh-huh," I said.

"Now you try."

"Yeah, I'll just do that," I said with a huff.

I raised my arms and went for it. Leg up. Twist. *Stumble*.

"Yipes! Sorry!" Though I kept myself from falling, I'd rammed into a nine-year-old. She gave me a curious look that read the way most of these girls' expressions did every time I'd shown up for class in the last two weeks: *What are you doing here?*

I considered it a miracle that I'd found the courage to keep coming back. I really didn't think I had it in me to continue, but now that I knew about Solange's identity, and she had gotten that job at the mall, this seemed like the simplest way to stick close to Henry after school.

Plus . . . I don't know, something compelled me to stay. It was like that day I learned about Dark Breeds and had returned to training even after I felt sure my soul couldn't handle the stress any longer. Listening to my heart then, I knew I had to keep going. The same thing went for dancing at this studio. Being here was as much of a lesson in humility as it was in movement, and yet

I just couldn't tear myself away. I needed to be here. It mattered to me.

Maybe subconsciously I saw it as a metaphor for my role in the afterlife and how out of my league I felt with that identity and its insane standards. Maybe I felt like if I could master this, I could master anything. Or maybe I was just too stubborn to give up without a fight.

"Did you pull a muscle?" Hana asked, trotting over.

Is self-esteem a muscle?

"No," I replied sheepishly. "I just need practice."

"Okay, ladies!" Kelsey called, clapping her hands. "We'll end today with some improv. Line up!"

"What does that mean?" I whispered to Hana as we filed against the back wall.

"Miss Kelsey puts on a random song and one at a time we dance however we want for a minute in front of the entire group."

"*What?*"

Kelsey powered on the stereo and the first girl in line sashayed forward. She kicked her foot over her head, grabbed her ankle, and spun while holding on to it.

I gulped.

Seriously, how was I supposed to compete with that? I went to school in South Carolina, not Cirque du Soleil!

The next girl did a running leap to take center stage. Despite only being ten, she jumped as high as my collarbone.

My heart started thumping louder. Flashbacks of my epic fails with my halo filled my mind. The line moved up.

As I watched the next girl twirl without a care in the world, I realized it was probably for the best I hadn't gotten to perform in that recital the day of my accident, and that my mother hadn't seen me flopping about on stage. I just thought maybe sharing such a vulnerable part of myself would help my mother truly see me. But it was a foolish idea. She didn't even come, and if she had, I would've probably let her down like with everything else I did.

Hence why I usually danced alone. There was no judgment. No fear of looking stupid. No worrying about what others think of you.

The next girl did a flawless illusion as her opening move. The line inched forward again. Hana was next and I would be right after. I ground my teeth with nerves. Soon enough Hana danced to center stage. My stomach twisted. I glanced at the line of girls behind me. What would they think of me if I let myself be seen?

The music heightened and suddenly I found myself moving, but not to the dance floor. I jogged off to the side, whispered "bathroom" to Kelsey, then booked it out of the studio. When the door closed behind me, I leaned against it and took a deep breath.

Nope. No thank you.

I just wasn't ready to serve myself up to the judgment of others without crumbling to doubt. I didn't know if I ever would be.

I hastened to the cubbies, grabbed my bag, and went outside to wait for Hana. Class let out a few minutes later and she met me by the escalators that led up to the movie theater. Still out of order.

"Where'd you go?" she asked curiously, her sparkly bag slung over her shoulder. "I finished my dance and you were gone."

"I didn't feel good. I had to get some air."

Both completely true statements.

Hana tilted her head. "You weren't scared, were you?"

I scoff-laughed unconvincingly. "Why would I be scared?"

"Well, I don't know, Grace. There's no need to be. Yeah, other people are watching, but when you go out there it's not about them; it's about you. Who cares what they think? They're not the ones on stage."

"Hey, prima ballerinas!" Razel yelled from atop the escalator. She raced down the steps with Henry in tow. "How was class?" She gave Hana an affectionate hug.

"Grace ran off," Hana said.

"Hana!" I shot her an embarrassed look.

"Well, a fleet of little girls in leotards can be terrifying," Henry said in mock seriousness. "We're all surprised you lasted this long, Grace."

"Oh hush," I said shoving him playfully. Then I tensed. Was

that too familiar? Too aggressive? I took a step back. "What are you doing down here? Hana and I usually come up to meet you."

"Our mom is going to be late today," Henry explained. "We were going to walk across the street and get some boba."

"Yay!" Hana pumped a fist in the air.

"What's boba?" I asked.

Razel put an arm around my shoulder and made an elaborate rainbow gesture with her other hand. "What dreams are made of . . ."

Boba was two things:

1) Squishy, little balls of tapioca liberally loaded into an icy, milky tea to form a beloved Taiwanese beverage.

2) Definitely *not* what dreams were made of.

I coughed violently as one of the boba balls shot up the straw and punched my uvula. Hana patted me on the back with concern.

"You three actually like this?" I asked once I managed to swallow.

"Duh. It's amazing," Razel responded. "We come here at least once a week. Just don't suck up so many boba at once."

The four of us sat at a yellow table outside the busy beverage shop. The color definitely stood out against the navy night that had set in. Plaza lamps glistened all around us.

"So how was work?" I asked the twins, stirring my straw and eyeballing the boba swirling in my cup with distrust.

"Fine." Henry shrugged. "Weekday afternoon shifts at a movie theater are super slow. The only customers we get are really old people coming for senior discounts."

"I like it when it's slow," Razel chimed in. "On weekends when we're super busy I sweat through the polyester uniform and go home with popcorn kernels stuck in my hair. On weekdays, sometimes I get to watch bits of movies from the projection rooms or eat popcorn when our manager isn't paying attention."

I glanced at Henry. "Do you do the same?"

"Him? Please." Razel rolled her eyes, answering on her brother's behalf. "Henry doesn't relax. Anytime he's not busy at work he's doing homework or extra credit. You should have seen him during college application season a couple months ago. I felt like I didn't even have a brother anymore."

"You applied to all your schools as an undeclared major," Henry protested, putting his drink down. "That's much easier than trying to get into a specific program, let alone science-focused majors. Pre-med tracks at any serious university are beyond competitive."

"BLAH!" Hana threw her head back in aggravation. "If you guys are going to talk about college again, can someone give me a phone so I can watch Netflix?"

Henry gave his sister a sympathetic look. "Sorry, Hana." Then he glanced at me. "Our parents have pretty much talked about nothing else for months now. It's a lot of pressure. I don't blame her for being tired of it. I'm tired of it."

"Then let's talk about something else," I proposed. "I know you like science, Razel likes theater, and Hana likes dance. You all share a love of dangerous Taiwanese beverages. Tell me something random about yourselves, something I don't know."

Razel, Henry, and Hana exchanged a look.

"I really love vacuuming," Razel volunteered.

"*Really?*" I asked.

She shrugged. "It calms me."

"Look at what I can do," Hana said, shoving her whole fist in her mouth.

Razel patted her sister affectionately. "Now that's a skill you can take to the bank."

The ladies and I pivoted to Henry.

"Your turn, Henry," Hana said.

He fidgeted for a bit then sighed deeply. "Um, I'm a pi champion."

I perked up. "What flavor?"

"No, not the baked good. Pi the number, you know, 3.14 infinity? I won a contest in middle school for memorizing 598 numbers in a row."

"You must get all the ladies with that trick," I teased.

This time Henry shoved me playfully.

Razel smiled and turned her gaze to me. "What's a random fact about you, Grace?"

I took a cautious sip of my milky tea drink, wondering whether I should share something specific about my former life with my new friends. The stuff about the car crash had just slipped out. If I shared any truths about Grace Cardiff now, it would be a choice.

"Actually, you and I have that in common," I said, looking to Henry as I opened up a real piece of myself. "In middle school, I won a pi contest too. We had a tournament every March 14th and the winner won an actual pie."

"*Seriously?*" Henry replied.

I nodded. "What? You think you're the only nerd at this table?" I knocked my knuckles against my head twice. "Not just a hat rack, my friend." I took another careful sip. "Except I memorized *611* numbers."

"HA!" Razel laughed and smacked her brother on the shoulder. "She kicked your butt!"

Henry smirked as he crossed his arms and leaned back in his chair. I held his gaze with an equal smirk as I sipped my drink, playing it cool. At least until another boba shot up my straw and assaulted my windpipe.

"BLECK!!"

"Here comes that balloon again," Akari warned as I maneuvered my angel car through the clouds.

Pierre and Marie Curie were enjoying their evening hot air balloon ride. This was my sixth time driving with Akari, and the Curies had been a frequent obstacle for me, popping out of the clouds when I least expected it.

Tonight, I was ready. I turned the steering wheel and angled my vehicle around the couple. Then—just as we passed—I cupped one hand around my mouth and yelled out the window. "Thank you for your service!"

"Grace, eyes on the clouds!" Akari urged.

"Sorry." I returned my hand to the wheel. "They gave us polonium *and* radium. I had to say something."

"Just focus."

"Yes, yes. Are we doing turn practice around The First City's skyscrapers tonight? Should I go lower?"

"Actually no." Akari pressed a button on the dashboard and a part of the console flipped around, revealing a touchscreen. "AGS," Akari explained. "The Angel Guiding System. It's an app on Soul Pulse, but I'm connecting it to the car. In lieu of regular training tonight, Ana, Deck, and I are taking you three to a special event."

I flicked my eyes to Akari suspiciously. "Please tell me this isn't another field trip that involves an inferno?"

"No, Grace. This is a *fun* excursion." She held her watch to the console and both flashed simultaneously. "We could teleport there, but you need as much driving practice as possible. Driving through an AGS wormhole requires hard focus, which sometimes you lack in the non-school departments. So this will be a good test for you. Just don't freak out."

Akari hit enter on the AGS.

"Why would I—"

Whoa. A round golden portal the size of a gardening shed opened in front of us. It shone as brightly at the sun.

"All you have to do is drive into it and concentrate," Akari instructed.

"Yeah, I'll just do that."

Why do people keep asking me to do crazy things like it's no big deal?

Following a short exhale I punched the gas pedal. The wheels of the angel car spun and we shot into the portal. The second we entered, I felt like we were driving through some sort of hyperspace *Star Trek* reality. Not the original *Star Trek*, mind you, the reboot movies with Chris Pine looking super hot in all those uniforms—

"Grace!" Akari grabbed the wheel and corrected my drifting trajectory.

"On it!" I clutched the wheel and concentrated.

Thousands of vivid colors whizzed by in straight lines, constructing the equivalent of a cosmic freeway tunnel. I just had to keep the vehicle steady center as we flew down the celestial pathway, brilliant sparklers going off all around us.

Eventually I spotted another portal as brilliant as the one we'd originally entered. I aligned the car and drove through it, ejecting us into regular sky again. The First City was nowhere in sight. In fact, if it weren't for all the angels and other flying cars, I wouldn't have even suspected this was a part of Heaven. A massive, roofless arena stood in a lush green field. Ten times the size of the largest sports venue on Earth, the stadium was dotted with the color of innumerable spectators.

"What was that?" I asked Akari, gesturing back at the portal as it snapped shut. "And what is this?" I waved at the arena below.

"When we travel by teleport, we as people end up in different parts of Heaven. If we want to travel somewhere by means of a car, flying with our wings, using a hot air balloon, etcetera—we use the AGS to connect us by portal. As for this . . ." She alluded to the arena. "We're going to watch tonight's featured match of the Guardian Angel Games."

Once we'd parked on a nearby cloud, Akari spread her wings and flew us down. We descended through the open dome alongside other fully realized Guardian Angels headed for the stands. I pulled my eyes from their magnificent wings and below me saw periodic flashes of light that preceded the appearance of regular angels teleporting in.

My mentor landed on a stretch of cushioned benches maybe five hundred rows back from the arena main floor. The rest of our group was already waiting.

"Hey, Grace!" Leo called over the noise of the arena. Monkonjae waved.

"Hi!" I replied.

"Now that we're all here, what's the deal?" Leo said, glancing at our mentors. "I'm getting a Super Bowl meets Ed Sheeran concert vibe from the angels in the stands, so these Guardian Angel Games must be good."

"That's understating it," Deckland said eagerly. "You three

have only seen the beginning of what Guardian Angels are capable of. We have a solid number of powers that we hone over time, and when you combine them with combat training and creative thinking, you get the greatest sport known to the different dimensions."

Ana clapped her hands excitedly, glancing at the arena. "Guardian Angels compete in these games for fun once a week. In the spring, we have tournaments that end with a championship in the summer."

"Like the NBA playoffs," I suggested.

Monkonjae nodded and offered me a high five, which I gladly exchanged.

We both like the music of Queen and basketball. That's two things in common!

"How are we supposed to see though?" Leo asked. "Everything looks tiny from here."

"You just need to download the Preferred Seating app on your Soul Pulses," Akari replied. She gestured for us to proceed. Once all three of us had finished the download, she gave us an encouraging nod. "Okay, now focus on the main event," she instructed, pointing forward.

Monkonjae, Leo, and I pivoted to face the arena. For a moment it continued to look far away, then—all of a sudden—it was as if someone shoved super-powered binoculars into my eye sockets and everything zoomed in. The arena looked huge, anyone standing in front of me blocking the view vanished from sight, and the crowd surrounding us was merely a blur in my periphery.

"*Whoa!*" the three of us gasped in unison.

Fourteen enormous gold rings like the halos of giants floated over the arena floor at different heights. The seven on the right glowed with a faint outline of metallic green, and the half on the left were rimmed with radiant cobalt blue. A line divided the floor in two, round craters dotting the ground on both sides. The craters pulsed with white light as if keenly anticipating the moment when they could unleash whatever power they currently kept hidden.

I turned to address Akari and my eyesight abruptly switched back to normal. I blinked rapidly, trying to adjust to the change.

"It can be dizzying at first," Akari said, seeing my disorientation. "You'll get used to it."

The entire stadium filled with cheers and I whirled around again. *BAM!* My vision altered once more and it felt like I had the best seat in the house.

Two teams of seven players entered opposite ends of the arena. Matching the mega halos, one team wore sleeveless metallic green jumpsuits with shimmering gold detailing and the other sported glistening cobalt uniforms with silver accents. The outfits felt like a cross between a 1980s track-and-field design and a Britney Spears backup dancer costume.

The teams took their positions, each player crouching as if about to attempt a sprint. Once settled, they sprouted sets of flawless white wings and sparkling halos.

"Only fully realized Guardian Angels can compete in the games," I heard Deckland say.

A gargantuan scoreboard appeared overhead. The team names were displayed there in colors matching their uniforms.

"*The Four Noble Truths*," I read aloud from the green half of the scoreboard. Then I glanced at the blue side. "And *The Pentateuchs*."

"Religion isn't the foundation of Heaven; faith and goodness are," Akari said. My eyes shot back to normal as I looked at her. "As I explained when you arrived, angels experience the afterlife individually; there is no right and wrong regarding personal beliefs. We do like to pay homage to different beliefs in fun ways though. For example, every team name in the Guardian Angel Games is a tribute to some aspect of religious culture. The Four Noble Truths are the essence of Buddhist teachings. Pentateuch translates to 'the five books,' which Jewish people call the Torah."

"Genesis, Exodus, Leviticus, Numbers, and Deuteronomy," Leo said, counting off on his fingers. "*Boom.* The five books. Can a Jewish nerd get a high five?"

I gave him one gladly.

"Anyway," Akari continued, "In Heaven angels leave behind the 'them vs. us' mentality in all forms. So it's not like you have to be a certain religion to play for any of these teams. Deckland was a Catholic on Earth but competed on The Four Noble Truths last year."

"I think you mean I *dominated* on The Four Noble Truths last year," our tattooed mentor friend corrected. "MVP, baby!"

"And *that's* the truth," Ana chimed in.

She exchanged a fist bump with Deckland.

I returned my gaze to the arena as the audience enlivened. An angel in full, majestic robes had appeared in the center of the gathering. His frock seemed to be covered in ivy, and he held two flags that shimmered as if woven with diamonds. For a moment, the entire stadium froze, and then he whooshed his flags in opposite directions.

The cheers grew so loud I had to cover my ears.

With a running start the competing angels leapt into the air. Some targeted the halo rings opposite their side of the court while others darted to protect the rings behind them. The halos were *goal posts*! I watched in awe as angels on the offensive attempted to chuck their halos discus-style through their opponents' rings.

"*GO! GO! GO!*"

At the chanting, my attention hurried to a buff, dark-skinned angel in blue just as he scored. The crowd went nuts. He summoned his halo back as the score for The Pentateuchs went up by one.

My eyes darted to another part of the arena where a blonde angel in green released her halo with a flick of her wrist. An angel from the opposing team zipped in and used his halo to project a shield of light. The halo ricocheted.

Whoa! We can project shields?

Colossal bursts of air began shooting up from the craters in the floor, challenging the players even further. Just then a wind geyser impacted a redheaded angel, dramatically blowing her off course. An opposition player took advantage, bolted forward, and scored.

"A match has four quarters of fifteen minutes," Akari said in my ear. "It's purely a numbers game. The team that gets the most halos through the rings at the end wins. All powers are on the table.

Like energy shields," she explained as two green players used the ability simultaneously to block shots. "And energy beams." A blue angel got blasted backward with a ray of light. "Obviously, the players constantly use flight and combat skills." She alluded to the range of mid-air sparring as angels challenged one another for control of the space. "And short-range teleportation . . ."

Two green angels had cornered a blue angel against the stands and were getting ready to blast him. At the last moment, he created a small version of the portal we'd driven through. The angel darted into the portal and it snapped closed just as the energy beams reached it. A second later, a new portal appeared twelve feet behind the assailing angels and the guy in blue popped out with an energy beam of his own—firing at them.

"Hey, Monkonjae?" I leaned over, keeping my eyes on the game.

"Yeah?" he said, sounding in a daze.

"You spoke too soon. *This* is some fantasy action nonsense right here."

―――――――

"Don't forget, class!" Mr. Corrin announced as we packed our things. "One week from today is our Magic Mountain field trip. Your teachers are all aware of the adventure, but you're fully responsible for making up any work, getting any notes, and turning in any homework for the classes you'll be missing that day."

The bell rang. I stepped between Solange and Henry as we walked out of the room. I was getting used to putting myself into this position. For weeks now, any time that she and he were both present, I made a subtle but intentional effort to create a physical barrier between them. I figured it was good practice for when her hands-off month passed, which was only days away.

"I have to meet Justin for a minute," Henry said to me. "I'll see you in our next class." He gave a quick wave before hurrying down the hall, leaving Solange and me together. I half-expected her to shove me off the path and into the bushes.

"So, how's dance class going?" she asked as we walked side by side.

I hugged my books protectively against my chest as we maneuvered through the crowd. "None of your business."

"Seriously, Grace," she sighed. "Must you *always* be so aggressive?" My body tensed at the word—my Achilles' heel. "I am just trying to get to know you."

"So you can have a better idea of how to destroy me." I rebuked.

She gave a haughty huff. "What does the intention matter? For someone who is 98% good, I would expect you to be civil to others in basic conversation."

"I'll add that to the list of things I'm expected to be," I muttered.

Solange looked at me then smiled innocently. "Is someone feeling overwhelmed with the responsibilities burdened on her shoulders?"

Oh no. I probably shouldn't have said that.

I hugged the book tighter. "That's also none of your business. But FYI, things are going great. I'm totally ready for your month of sitting on the sidelines to be over."

Solange studied me critically as we continued down the path. "You do realize that I don't need Heaven or Hell's honesty filter to know that you're lying? Your facial expressions and body language give you away just as easily."

"Thank you for the critical analysis, Sigmund Freud," I said snappishly.

Grateful to finally arrive at my next classroom, I pivoted to enter, but then Solange stuck her arm in the doorway blocking my entrance. I narrowed my gaze.

"Your time is up at the end of the week, Grace. Yours and Henry's. For your sake, I hope there is some truth in your claim that you are ready. Because there's something you should know about me. I don't hold back. I have a bet going with some of the other demons for how long it will take me to kill Henry, and I intend to exceed *my* expectations."

My fire flared and without thinking I grabbed Solange by the collar of her bomber jacket and yanked her out of the doorway—shoving her against the row of adjacent lockers.

The move definitely surprised her. It surprised me too.

I quickly released the girl and glanced around. By some miracle no one had noticed—or maybe nobody cared because the bell was about to ring. Either way, embarrassment over losing control flooded through me. Normally that, and my mother's voice in my head, would've been enough to cause me to back down. But not today. Protective instinct consumed me and I bore over Solange as belligerence got the better of my behavior.

"What do you mean?" I growled.

Solange huffed, ignoring me as she dusted off her jacket and cursed under her breath in French.

"*Hey.*" I snapped my fingers under her nose. "Eyes up here."

She looked at me.

"What do you mean *kill* him?" I said in a hushed tone. "You're just supposed to keep him from reaching his potential."

Solange gave me an amused scoff. "Demons are allowed to operate in any way we see fit, Grace. Some of us prefer a more subtle approach. My mentor and I believe when it comes to an enemy, don't wound what you don't kill. If things simply go wrong in a person's life and they are knocked off their path, there always remains the possibility—*the threat*—that they will find their way back. And as such, we think that it is more effectual to destroy a human target by eliminating them completely. So let us be clear: when I move to take Henry down, I will be aiming to take Henry *out.*"

I froze as I absorbed this. I knew that GAs saved their human assignments from death on occasion. Just as I knew that the humans in the "Gone Too Soon" and "Lost" sections of our museum had died prematurely. But given that Henry was a kid, I was a kid, and even *Solange* was a kid . . . I guess I didn't think things were going to get so serious so quickly. At least I'd hoped they wouldn't. But I suppose hope was a fragile resource when your opposition was literally straight out of Hell.

The halls had emptied around us. A couple kids scurried through the doorway behind me.

"Better go, Grace," Solange chided. "I'm sure you have a lot to learn." She turned on her heels and sauntered away.

I opened my mouth to say something after her, but nothing came to mind. Was part of demon training mastering the art of having the last word? I hated how small I felt every time our interactions ended. She was such a—

"Grace?" Henry jogged up to me. "Why aren't you inside? Are you ready?" He tilted his head toward the classroom door.

I gulped, gazing at Solange as she disappeared around the corner. "No. But I guess I have to face the music anyway."

"Dramatic much? It's just English class." He patted me on the backpack and urged me forward. "Come on. I'm right there with you."

Back atcha, Henry. More than you know.

"Sorry, Nugget, I can't chat!" my Nana Robin shouted, her face projecting from my Soul Pulse. She wore snow goggles and a rainbow-striped beanie. Snow caught in tundra winds swirled around her. "Grandpa Jim and I are climbing the Celestial Mountains today!" She angled her Soul Pulse so I could see Grandpa Jim waving.

"Hi, Grace!"

The sound of blenders in the background caused me to bring the watch closer to my face. In recent weeks I'd found the coffee shop in Angel Tower to be a decent spot to get work done. The energy of the place fueled my productivity without blowing my concentration. It was clearly not the best place to make calls though.

"Why don't you come join us?" Nana Robin shouted over the winds.

"I can't. I have Guardian Angel training soon."

"Ditch it! Training is boring! How often do you get to go magical mountain climbing with your grandparents?"

She had a point, and I was tempted to follow the fun impulse—goodness knows it would feel liberating to throw caution to the wind and abandon responsibility. Heaven was supposed to be paradise. It hadn't escaped my notice that people like my grandparents had gotten the better end of the deal where that was concerned. The dead had their "afterlife purpose" jobs wherever they spent the majority of their time. So Nana Robin and Grandpa Jim did their jobs while they were in Middleground, then when they got up here they could just enjoy themselves. I was in Heaven for my full afterlife, but mine was a job I couldn't take a day off from. Maybe I *should* ditch and claim some well-deserved me time . . .

I shook my head. That wasn't me. "Maybe another day, Nana Robin. Can you please just call me back when you're done? I'm feeling a bit overwhelmed and could use someone to talk—"

I heard an excited shout in the background. "Sorry, Nugget. Gotta go! Grandpa Jim just saw a reindeer!"

Nana Robin ended the call. I sighed. Of all my relatives in Heaven, Nana Robin and Grandpa Jim were the only people I had established relationships with. Everyone else had either died before I was born, died before I was old enough to form lasting memories, or I'd just never connected with much in life due to age or distance.

I'd been excited to bond with Nana Robin up here, but every time I reached out, she was off on some fun adventure. She could never talk to me about any of the serious matters I could've really used help with.

With my mother and my relationship not just on the rocks, but thoroughly impaled by them, I had hoped my Nana could be a replacement maternal figure. She did say we were alike right? But what good was being alike if she wasn't there?

I needed someone I could rely on.

My mother had been adamant that I could reach out to her. However that meant forcing myself to be something I wasn't. That didn't seem like the healthiest path right now. On Earth I'd chosen to deal with feeling inadequate in exchange for having a relationship with her—feel that parental warmth and support a kid naturally craved. Here, with my GA role needing me to be strong, I wondered if it was better to be alone than put myself through that.

Sigh.

My sense of duty, my conscience, and my need to feel good about myself would have to sort things out before I decided—if I decided—to contact her again.

"What are you working on?"

I raised my head. Leo stood beside me with an ice-blended beverage in his hands. Caramel swirled atop the whipped cream and a metal straw stuck out at an angle.

"I have an English test on Wednesday and Solange goes into full demon mode tomorrow, so I'm brushing up on two different worlds." I gestured at the pair of textbooks on the table in front of me, separated by my notebook. "Over here we have Hamlet dealing with internal monsters." I pointed at the splayed open novel. "And here, we have actual monsters."

Leo sat down and spun my Dark Breeds book toward him. His brow went up. "You covered all of the pictures with sticky notes."

"I am studious, not self-destructive. I'm going to learn as much as I can but try not to be traumatized and scarred along the way."

"Good advice for studying, and for life. *Mazel tov* on the innovation." He took a sip of his beverage. "I'll borrow that idea when I eventually crack the book. Haven't had the time yet. I start on my Earth assignment next week and the books I've been brushing up on are legal in nature. My human is a lawyer."

"Interesting that you and Monkonjae were both assigned professionals," I commented. He'd started with his doctor assignment the week before. I tilted my head as something occurred to me. "You know, Monkonjae didn't mention what time zone his assignment is in. Should we have a meeting to figure out our schedules for training? I've been running on California time, but my five o'clock could be two in the morning for him for all I know."

Leo shrugged. "I wouldn't worry about it. Ana said that for

our first assignments GAs are given humans in the countries we feel most comfortable in. For all three of us, that's the US since we lived a good portion of our lives there. So our assignments don't have time zones that are crazy incompatible. For whatever differences we do have, Heaven's time zone adjustment will take care of the rest. No need to break out the Google calendar."

"What do you mean?"

He looked up from his straw. "You don't know? In Heaven people live on whatever time zones they want. It's kind of a combo of Heaven's language filter and how what we see here shifts depending on our Earth religions. Like, okay, what does the sky look like to you right now?"

I glanced left at the windows. "There are a lot of pinks and oranges from sunset."

He nodded. "If you say so. To me, it's pretty dark purple because my assignment is in New York and it's already night there. Our internal clocks adjust automatically without the impact that time changes have on Earth. What's cool is that, like with the language filter, we hear what works with our timeline. For instance Ana told me if someone in Heaven sends you an invite to a party, whatever time is listed will magically alter to your time zone."

I blinked. Then frowned. "Seems like you got a mentor who is up front about all the facts." I took a slow, steady sip from the steaming mug near my hand. "I think I need something stronger."

He nodded toward the cup. "What are you drinking?"

"A chai 'Give Your Heart a Break'."

"Demi Lovato is a solid beverage choice for someone who's stressed out. Which I guess you are?"

"Very much." I sighed and shook my head. "What about you? That's looks like a fun drink."

"It's a white mocha 'Can't Stop the Feeling!'"

"Someone is in a good mood," I mused. "Don't tell me that's because you're excited to start your GA assignment?"

"I wouldn't say excited is the right word. I'm a pasta salad of anxiety over that . . ."

He shook his head and repressed the stress I saw crinkle his expression, touching that spot on the bridge of his nose. "I've got an extra spring in my step because I just spent the day with my dad. He died in a car accident like you when I was five. I've spent a lot of time with him since I got here. It's been great getting to know him."

"Oh, wow," I said, setting my pencil down. "That's . . . heavy, Leo. I'm happy for you."

He smiled to himself and took a long sip. "You know," he said eventually. "Because my dad died when I was so young, I didn't really have any memories of him; yet I missed him my whole life. Sometimes I used to wonder if that was dumb or fair—to miss someone you couldn't even remember, to feel sad about losing someone you didn't know. My mom and my older brothers would share things about him—*your dad would've loved this place, your dad would've been so proud, your dad would've thought that was funny*. But I never had anything to contribute. I just had to wonder—would he have loved the places I loved, been proud of me, thought *my* jokes were funny. I didn't know. I could only ever imagine . . . Until I got here."

Leo stared out the windows of the busy angelic café. "I have the truth now. It wasn't dumb or unfair to miss my dad even though I didn't remember him because, having spent time with him, I know I always needed to. Feeling connected to a parent—to hear them and feel heard by them, to know why you love them and also come to actually like them too, it's incomparable. And worth all the *mishigas* that drives you nuts and small things you don't see eye to eye on."

I felt a lump form in my throat. Leo sipped his drink, unaware of the pain regarding my own parental problems. What I wouldn't give to reach that kind of peace with my mother.

"Have you spent time with your mom since you got here?" He asked, unaware he was poking the exact subject I least wanted to broach. "You said she died with you, right?"

My body tensed. "Yes. And yes. I have seen her, but it didn't go great."

He wiped whipped cream from his upper lip. "Can I make a suggestion?"

I gave him a curious look. "*Okay . . .*"

"This afternoon, I took my dad to my favorite place in Heaven so far, and he took me to his. Maybe next time you see your mom, you could take her someplace where you feel super happy and the feelings that place gives you will make connecting with her, *and* having patience with her, easier."

I rapped my fingers against the table. "You know, I'm not sure I have a favorite place in Heaven yet . . ." I liked a lot of the restaurants, but given what happened when I tried to break cake with my mother, I didn't think this route would accomplish what Leo was suggesting. I sighed. "I'm not sure it would work anyway, but thanks for the advice, Leo. It's not a bad idea."

"Of course it isn't, *bubbeleh*," he said. He took another sip of his sugary drink then lightly slammed it on the table. "Now come on, Miss State of Grace. Move that *tuches*. Just because we're both a delight doesn't mean they'll keep forgiving us for being tardy to training."

Very true. The two of us rode the elevator to the sparring center.

"Who's ready to try some combo moves?" Deckland bellowed as we entered.

As I practiced the different jab-cross-hook-uppercut combinations we'd been learning the last few weeks, I tried to ignore my mother's voice tsking in the back of my mind. To my surprise I had actually really enjoyed learning these self-defense moves, and I had taken to them quite well. Despite that, I constantly felt myself holding back. My mother's opinions on my aggression haunted the base of conscience with each punch I threw. As a result, every move was always a bit restrained.

Thankfully my desire to master these skills in case I ever needed to defend myself or Henry allowed me to work through her shadow. When I managed to focus on listening to that protective instinct, the power of my strikes notably increased.

Having been raised to be reserved, and having lived through the trouble my fiery instinct had gotten me into, in those moments I almost felt guilty about how satisfying it felt to have my fist make that smacking sound in the punching bag. Yet, I let myself lean into it a little more every day. It was the only thing that drowned out the doubt, and I *needed* to drown out the doubt. Second-guessing myself in a gym meant I wouldn't advance as quickly. Second-guessing myself out in the world when enemies were coming at me was a good way to get taken down.

"When are we going back to halo training?" Leo asked, loud enough for the whole group to hear as we continued our drills. "I'm dying to mix it up like at the Guardian Angel Games."

"I second that," Monkonjae said as he blocked and countered Deckland. "I want to try that awesome teleporting trick."

"You will eventually," Deckland replied, taking another swing at his partner. "But trust me, you guys aren't ready for that stuff. And we prefer new recruits to advance as a team so you all learn at the same pace."

"In other words"—I launched an angry fist into Akari's glove—"when I can finally keep up, the rest of the class can move on."

"Grace, it's not—"

"It's fine," I cut Deckland off, releasing another jab-jab-cross combo. "I think it would save time if we didn't beat"—hook, cross—"around"—cross, jab—"the bush." Akari stumbled back from the force of my final punch. I felt bad. That wasn't protective instinct; that was fury and frustration.

"Sorry." My ferocity ran and hid when I saw the surprised look on Akari's face. "I'll tone down the aggression."

I pivoted to address Deckland and the whole of the class, putting my hands on my hips. "I don't want anyone getting held back because of me. So please teach Leo and Monkonjae whatever you think they're ready for and I'll do my best to keep up and not get in the way. I'm getting pretty good at that on Earth." A side effect of being in a dance class with way younger, way more talented kids. "I can eat humble pie here too."

Akari walked up to me, removing her padding. "That's noble, though worryingly self-deprecating, Grace."

I waved her off. "It's neither. I'm just being practical. So what do you all say?"

"As it happens, we were only planning on doing basic combat training for another week," Ana responded. "In mid-February, we'll give that a break and go back to working on your powers."

"Any chance of a preview?" Leo asked, lowering his fists.

Akari glanced at her co-mentors, who nodded in agreement. "Fine. Gather round."

We met on a shared mat. For once, Akari held up a hand to Deckland and Ana. "I've got this."

I was taken aback. Whatever had happened in Akari's past had sunk her spirit like the iceberg did the Titanic. Hence her controlled behavior around me, the distance I'd seen her keep from her friends, and why she deferred to Ana and Deckland in our sessions. Recently though, I'd noticed her decorum shift here and there. The more time we spent together, the more comfortable we became around each other. Hopefully all this was a sign that she was on her way to healing and letting me in. Both on her secret, and as a friend. I'd like that.

I didn't have a true confidant right now, no one who made me feel totally safe, at ease, and most importantly, like I wasn't being judged. With the current void I felt in terms of a maternal figure, having a mentor to understand and accept me would have been great. But if Akari didn't feel secure enough to trust me with her whole self, and didn't feel like I wouldn't judge her for the mistakes in her past, how was I supposed to feel like I could do that with her?

"Next week we'll start working on the shield of light," my mentor said as we formed a circle around her. "It requires a lot more focus and strength than turning a halo into a discus or blade." She summoned her halo. "As noted when you learned about slicing with the halo, your will allows you to use your different powers, but activating them is based on your movements. For the shield, remove the halo from your head. Then bring your forearm parallel with the ground, keeping your elbow as close to a ninety-degree angle as possible. Punch your elbow back in a sort of pumping move, then reverse that and jab your fist forward in any direction."

My mentor demonstrated. When she thrust her fist forward,

a fantastic shield of light four feet in length materialized with the halo acting as a handle. Akari repeated the arm pump and the shield disappeared.

Her halo vanished too and she crossed her arms. "The more soul strength and will power, the greater the energy, and thus the bigger and firmer the shield you can create."

"Can we try?" Monkonjae asked.

"In another week," Ana replied. "For now, back to regular training." She lightly punched Monkonjae in the side. "You still seem kind of soft to me."

MAGIC MOUNTAIN

"It's a beautiful day for high caliber equations!" Mr. Corrin declared, competing with the sounds, colors, and smells of Six Flags Magic Mountain. Not an easy task considering there were seventy teenagers in our group, plus a handful of adult chaperones.

We stood just inside the park. I was normally extremely attentive when a teacher spoke; however, the holler of people enjoying the roller coasters was decidedly distracting. Also, a nearby stall called the Funnel Cake Factory was giving off a *very* inviting scent.

It's a good thing our teacher was so tall; no one could wander off without being spotted.

And believe me, it was tempting.

"These packets *will* be graded," Mr. Corrin continued. "In fact, they're worth 10% of your overall grade. So take your time. Don't rush through the work so you can enjoy the park sooner."

Justin passed me a stack of documents. Standing next to him provided ample shade from the sunny California day. I couldn't believe *this* was their February. Apparently CA didn't have respect for Groundhog Day's verdict; winter was over when SoCal said it was over.

I took a stapled set of papers and passed on the rest to Razel. She'd come prepared for the bright day. Her tight ponytail poked out of her baseball cap and a smudge of un-rubbed-in sunscreen still remained on her nose.

"All right, everyone. Good luck!" Mr. Corrin announced. "You can work in up to teams of five, and remember, in addition to a good grade, the winners get a coveted mystery prize!"

The assembly of students broke apart and forged into the wonders of the amusement park, free to go wherever we liked for the entire day until our bodies were due back at the buses at three o'clock.

"Can something really be coveted if no one knows what it is?" Razel thought aloud. "Mr. Corrin changes the prize every year."

I flipped through the packet briefly. There were half a dozen pages of equation-based questions. I smiled.

"Someone's excited about the workload," Henry commented.

"These equations do seem fun, but I'm smiling because there are six pages in this packet. You know, like an ode to *Six* Flags."

He raised an eyebrow.

"On that enthusiasm alone, I definitely want you on my team, Doolittle," Justin said. "If you make sure I don't fail this assignment, I'll make sure you don't get lost in this sea of churros and roller coaster riders."

"I feel like you're getting the better end of that deal."

"I'll also buy you a funnel cake," he offered.

"You drive a hard bargain, Professor Higgins, but I accept." I took the pencil out of my pocket and stuck it behind my ear.

"We've got our team then," Razel declared. "Two Suns, two fans of *My Fair Lady*, and one smokin' hot French girl." She nodded to Solange, who was texting a few feet over.

I rolled my eyes. I had been trying to avoid my demon archnemesis, and it wasn't just because the sparkle of her black sunglasses and matching tank top were blinding in the sun.

Her time on the sidelines was over, and I nervously awaited her first move. I didn't know how advanced Solange was in her magical mastery of manipulation. But her control of that hydrant, and the way she'd taken me my surprise, made me very aware of one cruel, important fact: Right now, this girl was probably more powerful than I was. And despite the confident face I put on when confronting her, I didn't know how I would handle it when she used that power again.

My gaze drifted to the demon. Although she'd been uncharacteristically late to catch the field trip bus this morning, she'd sat with us during the ride. I would have to keep a close eye on her today as we—

"Actually, I already have a team," Solange said, waving to a few nearby kids who were looking through their physics packets.

My eyebrows shot up. "Really?"

Solange glanced at me. "I'm sorry if that disappoints you, Grace. My group and I made plans earlier in the week."

"Want to meet for lunch?" Razel offered. "Hopefully we'll be done by one."

"Lovely," Solange responded. "*Au revoir*, everyone." She went to join her team as my friends waved goodbye.

I was flabbergasted.

What was she playing at? This had to be a trap, right? Or a test? Or—

"So here's my vote," Justin declared. "For every page we complete, we go on a ride. That way we still have fun while getting the work done."

"I'll vote for that," Henry said.

"Me too," Razel agreed.

My eyes remained on Solange as she drifted further into the throng of theme-park-goers.

"Grace?" Henry said.

"Um, yes. That's fine," I answered quickly. "Let's get started."

Our team of four forged into the amusement park. I was the only person on our team not amused in the least. I was downright scared. And not of the rides.

Okay. Now I was also scared of the rides. Gazing up at the metallic construct of insanity and genius, I felt more bewildered than I ever had.

"You must have a death wish," I commented.

After completing the first page of the packet, my friends and I approached CraZanity. This wasn't even a roller coaster. It was an epic disc attached to a long metal extension. Passengers were strapped along the disc's outer rim. The ride's mission: rise 170 feet in the air then swing back and forth like a pendulum at 75 miles per hour.

I had to remind myself that I couldn't *really* die again. As for my friends . . .

"Is that your way of saying you don't want to go?" Justin asked me.

"HA!" was my response.

"You want to wait for us down here?" Razel asked.

I glanced at Henry, extra concerned. "Are you really going to go on that thing?"

"Well, yeah. I love freaky, daring chiz like this. Razel and I are roller coaster addicts."

Perfect. Why couldn't I get a GA assignment with a fear of heights and an affinity for knitting?

I looked over my shoulder. Solange was several hundred feet away and collaborating with her group. Henry seemed safe from her demonic threat for now.

"I'll wait here and continue working on our assignment if you three don't mind. It'll distract me from thinking about all of you swinging to your doom."

"Calm yourself, Grace," Razel said jokingly. "No one lives forever."

Don't I know it.

I let the group go and found a picnic table nearby to sit at, keeping the trio in sight as they waited to be strapped into the maniacal mechanism. I looked around for Solange. The girl had wandered away from her group and seemed to be consoling a young guy in a park maintenance uniform. He was crying while she patted him on the back supportively. Weird.

My watch rang. I answered in video chat mode and Akari's voice came through, her face on my watch screen. "How's it going, Grace?"

"Um . . ." I glanced at Solange again. "*Unusually.*"

"Should I be concerned?"

I looked at my mentor. "You sound concerned."

"Well, perhaps I am. Your demon is free of the month waiting period, you are in an unfamiliar setting, and Henry is more exposed than he would be on a normal school day. I was worried that you may be panicking about how to protect him."

"To be honest I was at the start of the day, but Solange has been keeping her distance from us since we got here. I don't know; maybe she's trying to rattle me."

"I wouldn't take comfort in distance, Grace," Akari advised. "Have you heard the saying, 'Keep your friends close and your enemies closer'?"

"Yes, I'd actually added Sun Tzu's *The Art of War* to my reading list this year before the death thing. Does Barnes & Noble have an app through Soul Pulse? Because maybe I could read it between—"

"*Focus*, Grace."

"Right. Sorry."

"Speaking from personal experience, I worry way less when my counter demon is close by. Remember, Solange can't hurt Henry directly. Most of her work will come from manipulating situations. That goes beyond her powers."

"What do you mean?"

Akari cleared her throat. Her eyes left me for a moment.

Oh boy, this wasn't going to be good.

"Listen, Grace, demons have to file reports when they complete a plan. After your incident with the hydrant, I put in a request for a GA warrant to review the report that Solange sent to Ithaca. The warrant finally came through this morning and I learned how Solange did it.

"She went to the coffee shop near your high school at lunch, where a rude man cut the line in front of another man. They got into an argument and Solange used her magic manipulation to escalate their anger. One guy shoved the other, causing him to spill his hot coffee on himself. When he leapt back, he hit a cyclist. The cyclist crashed into a car, setting off its alarm. The alarm scared a dog being walked nearby and it ran away from its owner. Eventually, the dog crossed the street near your school and an SUV swerved to avoid running it over. That SUV hit the fire hydrant and caused the damage. All Solange had to do was wait for you to go near it and magically manipulate the chaos of the geyser and traffic."

My imagination tried to visualize the dominos falling one by one. Then my eyes drifted to Solange across the park. I saw her buy the weepy amusement park employee a coffee. Her charitable action was uncharacteristic and now *troubling*.

The weight Akari's information carried soaked into my brain like soup into bread. I knew Solange would be a threat, but I didn't realize the ripple effect even the slightest move on her part could cause.

She had to be plotting something. Something possibly as elaborate as the picture Akari had just painted for me . . .

Excited screams drew my attention up. I shivered despite the warm weather. CraZanity swung at a colossal height and scary speed. The ride didn't just graze the clouds; it scalped them.

I turned my eyes down. Back on Earth, Solange bid adieu to the amusement park worker and returned to her group, pointing at a waterfall-based ride. There was a child throwing a tantrum near the line.

"Grace?"

"Thanks for calling, Akari. I have to go." I hung up.

I crept closer to my nemesis, using the crowd for cover. Once she and her team were by the ride, while two of the kids were distracted by their phones and the others studied their packets, I watched Solange pivot and gaze at the complaining child. Suddenly his tantrum escalated and he started wailing. Was she manipulating his mood to enhance his distress?

The Earth phone that I'd been issued buzzed with a message. It was from Razel. They were done and wondering where I'd gone. Since I couldn't very well tell them that I was stalking a demon plotting Henry's demise, I came up with the easiest excuse.

Had to find a bathroom. Be right back, I lie-texted.

Lexted?

It was lucky that Earth didn't also have an honesty filter. Spies, lawyers, and reporters would all be out of a job. And I would be committed for saying crazy things.

Reluctantly I abandoned my pursuit of Solange and reunited with my friends. We continued with our morning as before—solving equations and picking attractions. Now that Akari had made me realize that being next to Henry didn't assure his safety, I didn't feel as bad about opting out of the rides. I wasn't afraid of heights, but I didn't like the idea of insane speed mixed with loop-de-loops and abrupt drops. After all, I wouldn't be able to do my job effectively if I was dizzy or nauseous.

When we had completed the fourth page of our work, Razel insisted that the team ride some crazy twisted thing that loomed nearby.

I sighed. "I'll pass on this one too."

The others nodded—used to my refrain—and lined up. I glanced around. Last I saw, Solange and her team were boarding a coaster. With any luck, demons also dealt with nausea, possibly vertigo? They did live way below ground. Maybe great heights were a shock to the system.

I took a gander at the next question in our packet. It actually dealt with the coaster I was currently in front of. My mind shuffled through the formulas required to solve the problem. One piece of the puzzle was the width of the track. I glanced up.

How was I ever going to get that measurement? The gift shops likely didn't sell measuring tapes. Even if they did, it's not like the theme park employees were going to let me climb down onto the track before the next car pulled into the station so I could measure it.

Hmmm . . .

Elated screams called my focus. There was an area close by where the coaster track passed over the sidewalk maybe twenty feet above ground level. The coaster cars whooshed over the crowds every thirty seconds or so.

I trotted to the spot. The sun was hitting the track at just the right angle that its shadow shot straight down on the sidewalk. I glanced around. My mother would never approve of this. Maybe that's why the idea seemed intriguing.

I carefully got onto my hands and knees then lay down so that my body rested over the shadow. Once I was fully on the asphalt, I tried to guesstimate how much shadow still went past my head.

"What are you doing?"

I turned over to find Henry looking down curiously at me. I actually wasn't embarrassed. I'd made this choice in the name of science and a good grade so I stood by it.

"Since I can't get near enough to measure the track itself, and we don't have measuring tape, I'm measuring the shadow," I explained, gesturing at the darkened area of asphalt. "I know that I am five foot six. If I use my body as a unit of measurement, I can calculate the answer."

Henry blinked. "That's brilliant."

I knocked on my head twice. "Like I said, not just a hat rack."

The roar of another car approached. I lay down on the ground again, this time on my back so I could still see Henry. "How much longer is the track's shadow than my body?"

"I'd say about a foot and a half," Henry said. He glanced up and then quickly lay next to me.

"What are you doing?" I asked.

"The coaster is coming. Seems like an awesome view."

He looked up. So did I. Seconds later, the roller coaster car went zooming by at top speed. Gazing up at it from underneath *was* awesome.

Henry and I grinned at each other before he got up and offered me his hand. I accepted, dusting myself off once returned to my feet.

"Why aren't you on the ride?" I asked. "Growing a sense of prudency?"

"Not today," he responded with a smirk. "I'm bummed to sit this one out, but that double fudge milkshake I had ten minutes ago isn't sitting right."

"I told you not to drink that after eating a giant kosher pickle," I lectured.

"Yeah, yeah." Henry rolled his eyes. "It looked good, so I ate it. For the record, you'll also be wasting your breath if you try to talk me out of having chicken wings for lunch."

"Henry, is that the smartest decision?"

"Who cares. I have to watch every move I make at school so my grade point average doesn't dip a decimal and my dad doesn't lose it, so I do what I want and take chances when he's not looking. Eat junk food, ride roller coasters, surf the roughest waves—that kind of thing."

"To spite him?"

He crooked his brow. "No, of course not."

"But you're doing things he wouldn't approve of, going against his expectations. With gusto. Isn't that a middle finger to your father and his wishes?"

Henry shook his head. "My parents may drive me crazy and stress me out at times, but I love them and know they've sacrificed a lot for me. I want to make them happy and I owe it to them to try. But that doesn't mean I have to always blindly follow their lead to maintain a good relationship with them. I have my own soul that I have to be true to, which sometimes means doing things how my mom and dad wouldn't. That's not acting against my parents; it's acting *for me*. I try to do justice to that, and them. Which means sometimes I'm responsible, focused Henry who fulfills my dad's expectations and studies all the time. Other times I'm risk-taking, adventurous Henry who likes to push limits and take chances. Neither is right or wrong, good or bad. I respect my parents, so I often heed their advice. And I respect myself, so I listen to what I want too. What I do next depends on the situation. I think that's fair." He shrugged. "I can't grow into my own person if all my choices are based on someone else's perspective."

"So you let yourself be two different people—one version around your mom and dad, and another when they're not looking."

"No, I'd say I'm just one person who is open to exploring different ways of living life. I'm not going to feel bad about testing other sides of my personality because my parents or anybody else has certain expectations of me. After all, who's to say anyone else knows what's right for me more than I do? I definitely won't know who I really am or who I'm supposed to be if I don't give other parts of my personality a chance, let them breathe from time to time."

He gazed up at one of the coasters. "It's about balance. And maybe it's a test in humility too—trying to accept when my parents know what they're talking about, even if it's annoying, versus knowing when to stand my ground on stuff we don't agree on. Stuff that feels like me and feels right, even if others don't see it that way."

I thought on the idea. Henry's take was very different than the ride-or-die mentality I always believed I had to endorse to maintain a relationship with my mother. And the carefree way he allowed his character to breathe was nothing like how I forced myself to conform to people's expectations and apologized when pieces of me that others didn't understand escaped. For someone so young, Henry was incredibly grounded and insightful and—

"Oh cool. A churro cart!"

My introspection fractured as my friend headed for a vendor across the sidewalk.

"Henry, your stomach!" I protested.

He shrugged and grinned as he jogged backward. "You only live once!"

I shook my head but smiled—amused by the inaccuracy of his statement, and also him. I liked Henry. He was silly for a science nerd and softhearted for a strong surfer. We had a lot in common, on the surface and on a deeper level—specifically our changeable natures.

When under scrutiny, I always tried so hard to be what my mother and other adults from my childhood wanted—proper, ladylike, restrained. When I was alone or acted on impulse, sometimes sassier and bolder parts bled through.

Henry shrunk in the presence of his father and could be shy in front of our teachers despite being smart—so afraid to make a mistake he didn't want to put himself out there. Yet, once unsupervised he suddenly became comfortable throwing caution to the wind as his character pulsed with daring.

We both changed depending on who was watching. The main

difference between us though, was that he felt no inhibitions about letting himself off the leash to be true to diverse parts of himself. He didn't feel any shame about it, and believed he could live that way while having a strong, respectful relationship with his parents.

Was it possible for me to unlearn the guilt I felt when I acted true to myself? The fiery part of my soul had always been in the shadows, caged by every conversation I'd had with my mother and other authority figures.

It made me feel bad.

And it made me feel like *I* was bad.

Henry was self-assured and trusted himself to know what was right for him above all others' judgment. He inspired me to wonder if my soul could grow that strong—evolve to a place where I confidently made choices that I knew were right even if they clashed with my mom's vision.

Was it possible to find peace in divergence? Respect for one another in disagreement? Pride in character even if that courted conflict?

If you acted with goodness in your heart and the sole intention to defend yourself, others, and what was right . . . wasn't that enough to hold your head high?

I sat down at a picnic table as Henry waited in line for his churro. I smiled to myself. I felt like he would understand why I ate cake every day in Heaven. Unlike my mother, he'd probably tip his hat to me.

With a sigh I smoothed the papers of my physics packet on the table. That was enough introspection for now. This field trip was supposed to be fun, wasn't it?

While I awaited Henry's return I worked out calculations with the new shadow length data. I could do some of the math in my head, but for other things I had to break out the trusty multiplication tables and long division.

When Henry got back, he tore off a piece of his churro and offered it to me. That made me like him even more.

We munched away as I showed him my work and he double-checked the math. From partnering with him on physics and

statistics assignments this last month, I trusted his ability to calculate in his head too.

"Justin and Razel will be stoked we got through another
page while they were having fun," Henry commented when we
finished. "You know, you didn't have to keep working on your
own. You're way too nice to us."

I laughed. "You three are the ones who are too nice to me." I
leaned back and tapped my pencil on the sheet. "I have another
math problem for you, Henry. Given the number of kids in our
high school and the percentage of people who go out of their way
to help others, what are the odds that I—a transplant from across
the country—just happen to find a trio of unusually kind kids
who make me feel at home on my first day and embrace me as a
friend in the weeks after?"

Henry shrugged. "There is no equation for that. It's probably
an outlier. We have values that are very different from the rest of
the data set."

I tilted my head at him.

He sighed. "In math, even though outliers don't affect the
most frequently occurring mode they can still influence the mean,
the arithmetic average. When it comes to people—to use your
wording—the 'unusually kind' way we treat others is comparable.
Razel and I were raised to believe that even if we can't affect how
the masses do things (the mode), by deviating from the norm
we can still influence some people and some things, making the
world a little better one gesture of goodwill at a time. If you add
up all that kindness, over time you can alter the mean yourself.
You can change the average of the world around you."

I blinked. "That was a very specific analogy, Henry. I'm impressed."

"I used it for my college entrance essay," he admitted. "I took
a prep course last summer and the guy in charge told us that most
kids make one core mistake with their essays. They think they
should write about whatever hardship or challenges they've faced
and this is what admissions officers want—to hear a sob story. But
that's not it at all. It's not about your weaknesses or the adversity

you've faced, it's about how you've handled them and how you approach life as a result. Not the problem, but what you did and are still doing about it.

"When my family moved to the US, Razel and I were ten years old. It was a difficult transition. Neither of us spoke much English, and we were scared about being transplanted someplace unfamiliar. Things were hard at first. I mean, it's not like *no one* was welcoming. There are three types of people, right? Those who go out of their way to be kind, those who go out of their way to be jerks, and those who don't go out of their way to do anything—they just exist."

What a spot-on way to break down the kinds of people who go to Heaven, Hell, and Middleground.

"I hated feeling like I didn't belong just because I came from a situation and place that people didn't understand. So regardless of how others want to go about treating strangers, Razel and I have always made an effort to be kind and welcoming to new kids, especially ones who are new to our town. It's the Golden Rule, right? Do unto others as you would want them to do unto you."

"Empathy and understanding," I said.

"They're two of the most important traits a person can have," Henry agreed.

"You're absolutely right." I smiled softly, remembering a similar conversation with Akari when I'd first arrived in Heaven. The third important characteristic that my mentor had explained was the part of Henry that still remained unclear: his true purpose.

Now I was more curious about it than ever before.

Connecting with Henry today had felt like the finishing hot fudge on the sundae image of him I'd been constructing over the last month. He was a genuinely good person with a lot of potential. I didn't need God to prove that to me with facts about his future. *Anyone* with this much of an open heart and mind had endless potential. And in realizing that, I felt a renewed sense of energy in my role.

I'd griped about the responsibilities, fears, and ludicrous challenges that came with my GA job, but in this moment I looked at it another way. For the first time, all my dreads and reservations were pushed from the forefront of my mind. A more powerful, positive idea had moved into that prime real estate.

Being Henry's Guardian Angel—protecting him while he found his purpose—would be as much my pleasure as it would be my privilege.

I'd become genuinely invested in seeing how this boy turned out, *who* he turned out to be. I wanted to know and help him find his purpose. It had to be something grand to warrant the intervention of God, the protection of a Guardian Angel, *and* be worthy of someone as unique and wonderful as Henry.

"Empathy and understanding *are* two of the most important things people should have . . ." Henry repeated, his tone introspective.

I glanced at him. His eyes had narrowed and his brow furrowed like the gears in his mind were turning in a new direction.

"Henry?"

He shook his head and came out of the stupor. "Too bad not everyone has the capacity for that, am I right?"

I huffed. "Hell would definitely be less crowded if they did."

16

SOMEHOW

"Cheers to a job well done!" Razel toasted, holding up her soda cup.

The four of us clinked our cups together. It was nearly one o'clock and our physics packet was complete. We were free for the next two hours. Our first stop: lunch at High Octane Wings.

Razel suddenly waved, her focus behind me. I twisted around to see Solange strutting over. Justin immediately got up to make room between him and Razel. The too-eager reaction caused Razel's expression to briefly flicker with annoyance. Mine probably did too.

When the demon sat down, she ended up right across from me.

"Sorry I am late." She shifted her huge sunglasses to the top of her head. "My group still is not done with our packet, but we agreed to take a break for lunch." She glanced over at the elaborate chicken wings menu. "What's good here?"

"We already ordered three dozen wings for the table," Justin said.

"Six different sauces," Henry added. "We figured we could share."

"Lovely," Solange said, though her tone suggested she felt anything but lovely about the idea. She drew a compact mirror from her bag, which she quickly checked her hair in. "Do be sure to tell me my share for the bill and I will pay you back."

"It's not much. Don't worry about it," Henry said.

"Aren't you sweet." She snapped the compact closed and smiled at him. "But I don't care how little. I insist, sir."

"Have it your way." Henry shrugged. "You can Venmo us later."

I eyeballed Solange from across the table. Though she played it cool, checking her phone absentmindedly, I couldn't contain myself anymore. Curiosity and suspicion were bursting like the buttons of pants after Thanksgiving dinner.

"So how has this field trip been for you, Solange?" I asked, swirling my soda cup.

Solange shrugged. "It's been . . . educational. Believe it or not, I've never been to an amusement park. This place and all its precarious coasters are fascinating. Take that beastly ride just outside. It's closed today, but it executes loops 160 feet in the air, then comes crashing down at phenomenal speeds. I spent the morning getting a lay of the land to learn about *all* this park has to offer that way I can make the most of the second half of my day."

"I like the strategic thinking," Justin commented. "Eventually when you're done with your work, you can be more efficient and have optimal fun."

"Exactly." Solange smiled.

"NUMBER THIRTY-TWO! YOUR ORDER IS READY! NUMBER THIRTY-TWO!"

"That's us," Henry said. He nodded to Justin. "Give me a hand?"

The boys got up and made their way across the busy establishment.

"I'm going to use the bathroom," Razel said. "BRB."

Before I could think of a reason for her to stay, she'd abandoned her seat, leaving Solange and me alone. I rapped my fingers on the table. The demon blinked at me expectantly.

"Well," she said after a moment. "Ask me."

I raised an eyebrow. "Ask you what?"

"Come now, Grace. You're always full of questions. I know you have one for me; it's practically burning in your eyes."

I looked over at Henry and Justin. They were talking with a cashier about something. I turned back to Solange.

"What else have you been up to today?" I said quietly. "Akari read me your report about the hydrant incident. I've been watching you around the park and I know you're planning something."

"That's correct. And I'm not going to try to hide it. In fact, I'll tell you *exactly* what I have been up to today." Solange reached across the table, grabbed my soda cup, and took a long sip from the straw. When she set the cup back down, she folded her hands over the table.

"I was late this morning because I had to make an anonymous call to the California Division of Occupational Safety and Health, and on my drive to school I went out of my way to cut off a woman in traffic. No one was hurt, but she did get a flat tire when she ran over some nails. I'll spare you the details of how they got there. Skipping ahead, since arriving at the park I have contributed to someone being fired, consoled a maintenance worker over a broken heart, distracted an ice cream vendor with a screaming child, bought a snow cone for an old woman, got a tourist to throw up in a roller coaster car, and put a coin down on the sidewalk."

I opened my mouth, but she held up a hand.

"In case you were wondering, I only used my magical powers once this week—my ability to phase through solid objects. I have to be conservative with my divine tricks for now, as I am nowhere near as powerful as the great Ninety-Eight."

Solange reached into her backpack and took out a wrench, which she placed on the table between us. "There. Now you know what I have been up to. So in return I have a question for you. What are you going to do about it?"

I stared at her. She gave me a wicked smile that oozed superiority.

Solange put the wrench back in her bag and three seconds later the boys returned, setting baskets of sticky wings in front of us.

"Okay, so half of these are spicy, but the server forgot to label the extra hot ones," Henry said. He settled onto the bench beside me again. "She offered to remake them, but I said we'd figure it out." He rubbed his hands together. "Who's ready for some danger?"

Solange gave me a pointed look.

Being in a classroom with your demon archenemy was already pretty weird. Eating hot wings with your demon archenemy was bizarre beyond measure.

Our group of five easily demolished the three dozen wings, making casual conversation about upcoming driving tests, musicals, and roller coasters. When Solange spoke, I was torn between tuning her out and paying extra attention. I wasn't sure if the details she shared about her life were real or not. She talked about her sweet tooth, seeing the Paris Ballet perform, how her secret to staying in shape was eating a banana a day, and her penchant for glass figurines—hence the crystal flower with an aquamarine stone that she'd bought at one of the Six Flags gift shops.

Sigh.

Even if any of that was true, it was hardly information that would help me understand or foil her. And having no idea how to do the latter, my soul was troubled through the meal.

I would've thought that seeing my prissy nemesis with barbeque sauce on her face would have humanized her and calmed me, but I was wrong. Solange had given me a literal play-by-play of every domino she'd set in motion and taunted me with the challenge of figuring out her end goal. But smart as I was, I was not the Miraculous Ladybug (not embarrassed to admit I love that cartoon). I didn't have the experience to take a bunch of random fragments of information and tools to see a perfectly formulated plan in a nanosecond.

The best I could figure, Solange had done something to one of the rides.

"Hand me that little celery stick will you," Solange said to Henry, nodding to the basket between them. "I'll have that and you may have the last wing."

"Are you sure you don't want it?" he asked.

"Not even a little. I insist, sir."

My brow furrowed. I felt like Solange had said that exact

phrase—*insist, sir*—at least half a dozen times since we sat down. Was she making fun of me? Calling people sir and ma'am was a reflex I had from growing up in the south.

"So, you guys ready for the Viper?" Justin asked as he wiped his mouth with a napkin. He'd been talking about that ride since the bus this morning, insisting it would be the coaster we celebrated with after finishing our packet.

"Why don't we all do something a bit safer for a while," I suggested, eyeing Solange. "For our stomachs' sakes I mean."

Justin groaned but Razel chimed in to support my suggestion. "I would like to do some shopping. Our mom's birthday is the first week of March and I want to get her something nice. Solange, where did you get that crystal figurine?"

"There is an artisanal glass shop just to the left of here," she responded.

"Ugh. A shopping break?" Justin complained.

"For like fifteen minutes," Razel said. "You don't want to throw up on a ride. That's probably why several of them are closed."

"*Fine*," Justin grumbled. We started to get up from the table. Henry, Justin, Razel, and I had already efficiently shoved all our trash into our individual wing baskets. To my surprise, my normally prim nemesis had all sorts of napkins and fallen fries around her place setting.

Goodness, she was acting strangely today. What was she playing at?

Solange checked her watch, which I assumed was her own disguised Soul Pulse. "I have to get back to my group," she said. "I'll walk out with you though. Just give me a moment to tidy up this mess."

We waited patiently as the demon cleaned up obnoxiously slowly. Finally, as we headed out, when Solange was in the middle of checking her watch she suddenly tripped, rolling her ankle. Henry grabbed her arm and kept her from falling.

I hadn't seen anything that would cause her to fall, and she walked in heels flawlessly. Between that and the lengthy clean up . . . was she trying to delay our leaving?

"You okay?" Henry asked.

"Yes, I'm just a little embarrassed." She steadily righted herself, holding on to Henry's arms. "Thank you for the assist. Certainly don't worry about me." She let go of Henry and glanced at her watch again.

Time.

Whatever she was planning had to do with time. Now I was sure of it.

The sound of a thundering roller coaster not far from our lunch spot echoed through the air. There was no delighted screaming accompanying it though. I'd seen the CLOSED sign on that ride before we'd entered the restaurant. When we moved outside I spotted the cars of the coaster high above—empty. Park maintenance must have been running a test on it.

"I have to go," Solange said, lowering her Lady Gaga sunglasses to conceal her eyes. "Happy shopping!" She trotted off into the crowd.

"Well, I'm going to the glass shop," Razel announced, pointing left.

"You go, Raz," Henry said. "I saw a candy store on our way over here. Hana Banana will be super mad if we forget to bring her something."

"Good thinking," Razel said. "Justin, Grace—glass crafts or candy?"

"I'll go with you," Justin said to Razel. "Don't want candy to keep me from riding the Viper ASAP."

"I'll go with Henry," I responded.

The empty roller coaster screeched. I held up my hand to block the sun and saw the train of connected cars go over one of the ride's multiple peaks before plummeting out of sight. Sections of its track hovered over the surrounding sidewalk.

"Grace?" Henry called to get my attention.

"Coming." I trotted after him.

"Nice of you to think of Hana," I commented as we walked to the candy shop. "That's very thoughtful."

"I should probably think about her more than I do. Razel and I will be leaving home next year and I worry about her. I'm not sure why I started thinking about Hana while we were eating, but hearing Solange talk about her sweet tooth reminded me that I'd seen this candy shop on our walk over here." He pointed ahead.

This got my attention.

My brain started to churn. I thought about how many times Solange had checked her watch. Her various shares—*candy, ballet, glass gifts, bana*—

"Oomph." I accidentally bumped into a man. "Sorry, sir."

He nodded at me in forgiveness. I didn't break stride from Henry's path, but suddenly my mind wandered off when I saw a family buying some fruit from a cart in the shadow of the roller coaster track. One of them was eating a *banana*.

My eyes widened.

Miraculous Ladybug instinct kicked in and puzzle pieces started snapping into place.

Hana *Banana* was Hana's nickname. Solange talked about dancing at length—Hana's favorite hobby. How many times had she said "little" in conversation? A lot, right? And of course, the topper—Solange's unusual phrasing. I'd watched a neurology special on the Discovery Channel once about manipulation through subtle word association

"I insist, sir" ended with *sist-sir*. That sounded like *sister*.

There were other cases of this. "Thank you for the assist. Certainly"—*sist-certainly* . . . *sist-cer* . . . *sister*. And so on.

Had Solange been planting Hana in Henry's mind since the moment she'd arrived at lunch? What if *everything* Solange said or did at lunch was to lead us in directions of her choosing? The candy shop, which clearly Solange had inspired Henry to visit, was a walk to the right of the restaurant. Maybe my nemesis told me her plans because she wanted to scare me so I'd veer my friends away from Viper, which involved heading left. Maybe she'd shown us that glass figurine with the aquamarine stone to trigger Razel on the idea of shopping for her mom. Aquamarine was the birthstone for the month of March.

Oh no. My fear and Razel's inspiration had caused our group's plan to change—giving Henry an opportunity to head this way at this exact time . . .

Just then I saw Solange—far off and only for a second between the crowds of people. She leaned against a tree, watching us from a distance.

"Henry!" I grabbed his arm. "We can't go to the candy shop."

The roller coaster rumbled louder. I saw it plummeting in my peripherals, picking up speed.

"Why?" Henry asked. "It's right there." He pointed.

I'm pretty sure our classmate orchestrated doom for you inside.

A French demon manipulated us to going there through subconscious suggestion.

Neither answer would do. I didn't have a good excuse prepared and couldn't explain without sounding nuts.

"Hold that thought," Henry said. He knelt to pick up a glistening penny from the asphalt.

Someone screamed bloody murder.

"*LOOK OUT!!!*" another person yelled.

I whirled around.

The train of empty roller coaster cars rushing downhill had come loose from the track and was flying through the air in our direction at full speed.

Henry!

My instinct and senses sharpened and I suddenly felt incomparably alive. In the two seconds it took the train of cars to bridge the distance to Henry and me, my halo emerged with a flare of light, I grabbed it, pumped my arm back, and shot my fist forward.

FLASH! I projected a shield as bright as a supernova and as wide as a minivan.

WHAM! The runaway roller coaster collided with my energy shield.

CRASH! The cars careened off my shield and into the asphalt beside us.

The world no longer felt crisp and clear; all was a blur. Everything in the vicinity felt quiet. Or maybe I just couldn't hear anything over my drumbeat heart pounding in my chest.

BUM-BUM. BUM-BUM. BUM-BUM.

I blinked—stunned—and properly looked at the massive

energy shield projecting from the golden handle in my hand. While my senses were all currently consumed by haze, what I *did* sense was power. *Strength.* Pulsing through my veins like audacious lightning.

I quickly repeated the arm pump move Akari had shown us and my shield vanished; only my halo remained.

What the—

I finally started to hear the screams and panic. I willed my halo away. Then I turned to see Henry on the ground behind me. Staring up at me.

His eyes were wide and his chest heaved up and down from the near-death experience.

Then he asked me the question I dreaded was coming.

"What was that?"

Henry and I sat on a bench in the shade. Razel hugged her brother for the third time in the last two minutes. Mr. Corrin talked with theme park personnel nearby. Security guards shooed away spectators snapping pics and videos of the roller coaster crash site.

"Man, I can't believe you're both alive," Justin said, his face still pale with shock. "We saw that coaster headed straight for you and then it just . . . changed directions. It's *crazy.*"

"It's a miracle," Razel said.

No. It was me.

Nobody seemed to be aware of that though.

I stared at the roller coaster cars in the asphalt. They'd made a huge indentation, like a meter collided with Earth.

I'd heard multiple witnesses recount the incident the way Justin just had. Everyone who saw the roller coaster headed for me and Henry said that all of a sudden it just veered left— trajectory changing in the nick of time to spare us from death. Some people mentioned seeing a flash of light, but no one saw or described seeing a shield.

I thought about when Monkonjae, Leo, and I took our tour of the IDS and witnessed that angel intercede with the truck and car. In one view you saw magical interference, but in the other it looked like pure chance that neutralized the accident. Could humans not see our magical intervention?

"Kids . . ." Mr. Corrin came over to us. "Do you want me to call your parents to come get you? There may be some legal options you want to take."

Henry stared off into space. After a moment Razel nudged him. He cleared his throat and addressed our teacher. "No, Mr. Corrin. On both counts. We're fine. *Somehow*, we're fine."

Razel squeezed him again. I nodded in agreement.

Somehow was the optimal word.

I gazed back at the accident site and noticed Solange in the crowds checking out the damage, sunglasses pushed atop her head. She sensed my gaze and looked up. Our eyes locked briefly before she disappeared into the throng.

I gulped, curling my fingers anxiously as my mind filled with flashbacks. I remembered the train of cars coming toward me. I remembered grabbing my halo. I remembered the wall of intense light that appeared.

No. It hadn't appeared. I'd *created* it.

Somehow I'd managed to generate massive angelic magic without meaning to. It just happened. After weeks of futility, I'd done something amazing and I didn't even know how I did it. Apparently it had been inside of me all along though . . .

I glanced down at my hand, recalling the powerful feel of the halo glowing in my grip.

A sigh drew my attention to Henry.

"I honestly can't believe that just happened," he said, shaking his head again.

I took another glimpse of my hand, focusing on that powerful feeling, and released a deep exhale of my own. "You and me both."

TRUE COLORS

"I don't understand," I said. "I *had this* today."

I stood awkwardly in front of Monkonjae, Leo, and our mentors in the training center. My brow furrowed as I concentrated and pumped my arm again. With focus and will, I attempted to create a shield as epic as the one I'd unleashed this afternoon. I wanted them to see what I could do, and recognize my strength, and just take me seriously. And yet . . .

The energy shield activated, which was good, but it was the size of a placemat—barely enough to protect someone from an angry raccoon, let alone an incoming roller coaster.

"That's actually pretty good, Grace," Deckland said supportively.

"Uh-huh," I mumbled, lowering my shield and crossing my arms.

"Seriously," Deckland tried again. "You guys haven't practiced that move at all and you only saw Akari demonstrate it one time. The fact that you created any shield is really impressive, especially considering how rough the other powers have been for you."

Akari cleared her throat and shook her head slightly at Deckland.

His expression took on regret. "What I meant to say, Grace, was—"

I waved him off. "It's okay. We all know it's true. But this time, I really did it." Frustration twitched beneath my brow then with a sigh I looked at the group with desperation. "You have to believe me."

"I do believe you," Akari said. "Because I saw it happen. God can see everything, including every human *and* every angel on Earth. That endless influx of info is filtered through different GA departments monitoring humanity."

"Egads," Leo commented. "That's disconcerting."

"Not at all," Akari replied. "It's not like anyone is watching every move you make on Earth constantly; there's so much going on that we don't see everything in real time. Hence why the IDS can't save everyone. But we can request usable footage after the fact to see important things we might've missed. After Grace told us what she did today, I requested access to footage from the amusement park."

I thought on this critically. "Did you do that for the hydrant incident too?"

Akari nodded. "But it didn't do any good. The only thing we can't see in Heaven are demons. They're invisible to us up here, and they make it hard for us to see the humans and angels they get near. Solange was too close to you during the hydrant incident so when I tried to review that footage, it was a useless blur. Today she was far away when the roller coaster went off the track. Which is why we were able to see this . . ."

She raised her wrist. Her Soul Pulse flashed then a large hologram projected from it like a flickering drive-in movie.

I watched in awe as the Magic Mountain incident replayed. Everything happened as *I* remembered it—not how the humans did. A split second before the roller coaster would've annihilated us, I defended Henry with a massive energy shield.

The others' mouths hung agape.

"*Whoa!*" Leo exclaimed.

"Grace, that's incredible," Monkonjae said.

Deckland rubbed his hand over his face. "That's . . . I mean, for your first attempt . . . That's just not possible."

Ana smacked me on the arm. "I knew you had it in you."

That makes one of us.

The projection ended and I looked to Akari. "No one seemed to see the shield though. Not even Henry. Some people saw a flash of light, but *everyone* saw the coaster change directions on its own. They think it was luck."

"GA magic is concealed on Earth from most mortals," Akari explained. "Only about one in every ten million people can see what is really happening when we intercede. Unless we want them to see us of course, which we usually don't."

"Now it makes sense why you're so frustrated," Leo interjected. He patted me on the back sympathetically and I looked at him. "If you can do that *mishigas* under pressure, why *can't* you do it now?"

"Maybe it was an adrenaline thing," Monkonjae suggested. "At least you know you can do it. Focus on that. You're on the spot now, but if you relax and just concentrate on unleashing the same intense power, I'm sure it'll come back."

I sighed. "Unless it was a fluke."

"Don't think that way," Akari said. "You know what, we weren't going to start working on energy shields until next week, but why don't we concentrate on them today? We can build on your momentum."

I nodded in agreement and hoped she and Monkonjae were right.

Momentum was a double-edged sword wasn't it? On the one hand, it could help you run faster, hit harder, and jump higher to achieve a goal. In other cases, like avalanches and rockslides, momentum could lead to a large crash. That's how my pride felt now—like it had crashed into the training center floor.

For the next couple of hours we intervaled between energy shield training and basic combat drills. At one point, I managed to transform my shield to the size of a boogie board, but that was the extent of my progress. It was so maddening. Why couldn't I be strong now that I was in a place to show it off?

At six o'clock, our mentors gathered us around.

"We have some news," Ana announced.

"Do we need to sit down?" Leo jested. "Usually news from you lot means we're about to get punched in the face with GA information."

He and I exchanged a smirk. Then Ana's Soul Pulse glowed

and three wooden chairs appeared behind me and my classmates, causing our amusement to fade.

"What is it now?" I sighed as I took my seat.

"It's time to return the favor. Pay the piper. Feed the mongoose," Ana said cryptically.

We turned to Akari and Deckland for clarity.

"It's an exchange program situation," Deckland explained. "Hell gave our new recruits the lay of their land. Tomorrow, we have to do the same for theirs."

I couldn't help myself. "HA!"

"I'm going to second that 'HA'," Monkonjae said more conservatively. "Isn't it a *terrible* idea to invite demons into Heaven?"

"Yes," Deckland responded. "But we'll keep as close an eye on them as they did on you when we visited their turf."

My friends and I gave him a doubtful look.

He held his hands up. "I get how this sounds. But it's tradition. It's fair. And it's only for a day."

"Don't some religions believe that Earth was made in six days?" Monkonjae commented. "You don't need a lot of time for big things to happen."

"Valid point," Akari said. "But we have our Soul Pulses to ensure a mischief-free field trip." She raised her wrist. "These things can't be taken off. Ever. And every person in the afterlife has one. God and our GA feeds may not be able to see demons, but their Soul Pulses track their movements. So none of our demon guests will be able to access anything they're not supposed to, or wander off."

"Wait, go back a second." I leaned forward attentively. I'd been meaning to follow up on this since overhearing Akari and Deckland. "So you guys know where we are *all* the time?"

Leo glanced at his mentor. "Is that true?"

"Well, yes," Ana explained. "But it's not like we are obsessively watching you every minute of every day. Just like with the video footage Akari requested, it's just info that God and the GAs have access to if they need it. It's not intended to sound creepy."

"Is there a way that magical, all-knowing tech permanently strapped to your wrist doesn't sound creepy?" I posed.

"Not if you say it like *that*," Ana retorted. "Look, Soul Pulses provide every angel in Heaven with a convenient means to access everything they could ever need. And for Guardian Angels, knowing where we are can be a huge benefit if we ever need to help each other."

Leo, Monkonjae, and I remained silent—absorbing.

"So moving on," Deckland said authoritatively, and clearly trying to change the subject. "Your homework today is to plan a portion of tomorrow's field trip. As part of their tour, each of your demon counterparts took us to a special part of Hell they designed. Each of you will take the tour group to your favorite part of Heaven."

"Oh good," I mused. "I was really hoping to take the girl who tried to decimate me with a roller coaster on a day trip."

Leo snorted.

That made me smile a bit. I was glad the kid appreciated my sense of humor. Unlike a lot of people in my mortal life, my mother included.

If I had to sum up the general reaction my preferred brand of comedy had earned on Earth, I would use two words: *rough crowd*. Getting a different response from my colleagues in Heaven and my new cohorts in California filled me with overdue satisfaction. I liked to be sassy, even—*dare I say*—snarky in my dealings. It was a lighter form of aggression and fieriness that didn't earn me punishment most of the time, just disapproving looks.

I'd been happily surprised that I hadn't needed to worry about that here, especially with so much to be sassy about. Making jokes when I was uncomfortable or afraid was reflexive habit. It may not have been terribly ladylike, but I thought it added levity to a situation.

Thank goodness I was finally around people who accepted that. I did not miss the cutting looks my mother used to give me when I was sarcastic. According to her, sarcasm was the Devil's cadence. I didn't think that was true, but maybe someday I could ask him. Or her. I was still unclear about the gender assignments relating to the all-powerful divine folk we were dealing with . . .

My classmates and I said goodbye to our mentors and headed

for the training center exit—walking in sync at first and then Leo jogged a bit and started walking backward in front of me and Monkonjae. "Hey, kids! What say we have a team dinner?"

"Like a bonding activity?" Monkonjae replied.

"Well, yeah. Just because we're technically coworkers doesn't mean we can't be friends too, right? Break bread, share our struggles, *kvell* about one another's successes."

Monkonjae and I exchanged a look. Then I glanced back at Leo and nodded.

"Let's do it."

"How about Dinner is a Movie?" Monkonjae suggested as we exited. He held the door open for me with a warm look on his face. "After you, madame."

It felt like a tiny grenade of glitter exploded inside of me and I did a small curtsey in return. "Thank you, sir."

Was that cute or lame?

"Also, do you mean dinner *and* a movie?" I clarified as we walked to the elevator bank.

Monkonjae pressed the DOWN button and shook his head. "Nope."

The massive restaurant had a mash of themes—jungle, dystopian, sci-fi space adventure, under the sea, sports fans, fairytale realms, and more. I lost count of the settings we passed when the hostess escorted us to our section of the restaurant, the "Political Intrigue" room.

Our tabletop was a giant chessboard. All four walls held beautiful murals of famous government buildings from across the world. The wait staff wore suits and ties. And like the other guests seated here, Monkonjae, Leo, and I had each been given a fedora upon sitting down. The classiest and most clandestine of all the hats.

I glanced over the menu in my hand, the restaurant's name printed at the top in bold dramatic letters: *DINNER IS A MOVIE*

"So every dish here makes you feel how the movie it's named after makes you feel?" I said.

"Exactly," Monkonjae replied.

"I'm ordering off the action section for sure," Leo commented.

"Magical combat training isn't doing it for you?" I said, flipping to another page of the menu. The brim of my scarlet fedora came down. It was a bit big. I pushed it up.

"Not yet," he replied. "I can't wait to fight my first Dark Breed."

"That makes one of us," I muttered.

"What can I get for you this evening?" asked a Hispanic woman with pulled back, curly hair. Her purple pantsuit and dark green tie reminded me of a refined, non-threatening version of the Joker.

"I'll have the . . . *Lambshank Redemption*," I replied, handing her the menu.

"*Hamhawk Down* for me," Leo ordered.

The waitress raised an eyebrow. "That's an intense dish."

"I'm an intense person," Leo responded with a cheeky grin.

"Have it your way, kid. And you?" the waitress asked Monkonjae.

"I'll have *In the Lime of Fire*," he said, turning over his menu. The waitress trotted away as Leo and I stared at him. "It's a citrus curry dish," he explained. "Named after the movie *In the Line of Fire*."

"*Booo*," Leo and I said in unison.

Monkonjae blinked. "You guys don't like Clint Eastwood?"

"Oh, I like him," Leo said. "And that's why I hate that movie. It sucks, whereas he doesn't."

"Agreed," I said. "And dude can certainly work a cowboy hat."

"Agreed," Leo replied with a nod. We high-fived.

"Does team bonding mean having to deal with getting served smack talk?" Monkonjae said with an amused expression, glancing from Leo to me. "Even from you?"

"What, you think that just because you're tall, dark, and handsome I'm going to agree with everything you say? Hard pass. I may be a lady, but I'm a lady with strong opinions."

"And to that, I say cheers." Monkonjae raised his glass. "This job of ours looks like it could get weird and hard. Our mentors seem pretty in sync, so chances are that we'll work better if we're there to help each other keep both feet on the ground too. Metaphorically speaking since we're currently in the clouds," he corrected. "So here's to strong and frank opinions amongst friends. Honesty filter or not. Always."

Our trio clinked glasses in the center of the table.

"*L'chaim!*" Leo exclaimed.

The glass of our goblets had barely finished reverberating in our grips when the food arrived. I gazed at the steaming hot supper in front of me then took an eager, but ladylike-sized mouthful of *Lambshank Redemption*. It tasted . . . well, it tasted like redemption. And also somehow like perseverance and the soothing sound of Morgan Freeman's voice.

I looked over at Monkonjae. When he swallowed a bite of his citrus curry, his face soured with distaste like mine did when I saw the film it was named after. I smirked at him. "You regret it, don't you?"

"Eat your redemption, Grace."

I continued to enjoy my meal with a small but smug smile. The food was five stars. I was definitely adding this place to my list of favorite eateries in Heaven.

"So here's a question," Leo said eventually. "Are you two *actually* cool with knowing these Soul Pulse things don't come off?"

"I can understand the practical value," Monkonjae began, stirring his food with weighty reflection. "It's like at a hospital; patients wear their wristbands to maximize efficiency—get them what they need and where they need to go."

"Practicality is for professors and professional trainers," Leo said. "I know hospital wristbands too, MJ, and they're basically thin plastic shackles. What about you, Grace?"

"I understand the logic too. We need our Soul Pulses to do anything and everything up here . . ."

"But?" Leo pressed.

Oh, boy. Here comes the babbling honesty.

"But on Earth I didn't even want to get those dumb earpod things for listening to music after I saw this episode of *Doctor Who* where everyone in a parallel universe walked around with these metal earpods that ended up sending a mind control signal that made all the people walk to their death and get turned into metal monsters called Cybermen. So . . . yeah. Hard pass on tech you can't take off. Too creepy."

Monkonjae blinked at me.

"You think I'm nuts now, don't you?"

"Nope," he said simply. "You're just . . . an interesting girl."

"Don't make my head inflate from such flattery," I muttered. Then I sighed. "Let's change the subject to something that makes me sound less crazy. Do you boys have any idea where you're taking our demon guests tomorrow?"

"I think so," Monkonjae said. "I can show you both after dinner if you want. Deckland took me there last week and it has become my favorite place to unwind."

"I'm intrigued," I said. I swallowed the last bite of peas that came with my dish then dabbed the side of my mouth delicately with my cloth napkin. "I am all done, so whenever you're ready."

"Me too," Leo seconded. He flicked his eyes to our friend's curry, which Monkonjae had hardly touched. "Should I get you a to-go box?"

I smiled.

Monkonjae rolled his eyes.

"Who's ready to paint the sky?"

The angel standing before us with her hands on her hips had short, walnut-brown hair, a sprightly nose, and a spark in her smile that glistened with confidence like the bright stars prolifically decorating the sky.

I didn't think I would ever get used to the breathtaking nature of being in the grip of the heavens—night and universe all around us.

Leo, Monkonjae, a few dozen other angels, and I stood on a cloud outside a glowing bungalow. The structure reminded me of a beachside stand where one might rent a kayak or swim fins. Only, instead of aquatic gear, there were racks of shimmery golden backpacks, colorful water guns of various sizes, and innumerable cans of spray paint.

Since the sky was dark with evening, glancing around, it was easy to see hundreds of other clouds that featured a shining bungalow. They were all part of the same operation. This was just the cloud Monkonjae had brought us to.

"My name is Ellis Cartwright and I am your group's design leader," the angel at the front continued, gesturing for us to make a line in front of the bungalow. We did so and the angels working there began distributing backpacks and tools.

"If you're a returning artist, welcome back. If this is your first time, it's very simple. This is the Sunrise | Sunset Department. Our job is to design the sunrises and sunsets in every sky above every town, city, country, and continent in the world. As a result, we have the largest employment force in the afterlife and encourage you to come here and volunteer as often as possible to help out and have fun."

A mustached angel with hair as long as mine, just possibly more shine, handed me a golden backpack. I followed the lead of the other volunteers and slung it on. It had straps in the front that buckled over my chest like a parachute harness. There was a glittery emblem on the right strap in the shape of a crescent moon cradling a sun.

"Hit the emblem on the strap to activate your wings and goggles," Ellis explained. "Once triggered, the wings respond to telepathy like your Soul Pulses. For this excursion our team will be designing the sunset over Oahu, Hawaii. Most of your painting tools today are loaded with shades of orange, but a few of you will have pink and cherry."

An angel with gelled silvery hair handed Leo a flamboyant, lime green water gun. Monkonjae was given a purple bazooka. I was assigned a pair of neon-blue pistols.

We approached the final angel distributing equipment. This beauty with braided hair gestured for each of us to turn around. She latched a paint canister to both sides of my backpack, then sent me on my way with a friendly slap like a farmer sending a cow to pasture.

"Everyone onto the mass transport pad." Ellis pointed to a glowing platform. "These pads have been energized with divine power to beam you to a skyward location on Earth. Unlike visiting the mortal realm through the Pearlie Gates, the effect of this transport is partial and timed. You will be invisible to the human eye on Earth. And you'll be zapped back here after exactly one hour wherever you are. So make the most of your painting time. Your artwork will soak, sink, and fade into the skies of Earth once we're gone. Eventually, twilight will naturally take the colors away as night settles in."

I climbed aboard the platform. There were stickers across the floor, spaced out every eight feet indicating where we should stand. I chose a place near Leo.

"Okay, activate your wings!" Ellis instructed.

We pressed our emblems in unison.

BLAM!

My golden backpack sprouted lustrous golden wings. They weren't made of feathers like Akari's; these seemed to be constructed from fleecy wisps of sunlight. A second later, old-timey aviator goggles like Snoopy's magically appeared on my face.

"Newbies, press the button on the side of your goggles to operate the guide display. It'll help," Ellis beckoned. She checked her watch then leapt up to an available space on the platform. "Transport!" she commanded, pointing at the silver-haired man in the bungalow. He yanked on a dramatically large lever. Then light shot up from each of our standing stickers and consumed us. The next thing I knew, I was levitating in a crisp blue sky with a hypnotic turquoise ocean swaying hundreds of feet beneath me.

Most angels immediately began flying off in different directions. I flapped in place for an extended moment—watching in wide-mouthed awe as "paint" of various colors ejected from their backpack canisters and water guns.

Once my initial wonder over that calmed down, I was stunned by something I hadn't fully appreciated yet. *I was flying*.

No Akari to hold my hand, I was floating in the sky—totally untethered for the first time my soul could remember. I did a flip in the air and then shot up higher as streams of tangerine and cerise expelled from my backpack canisters.

I felt freedom like when I danced, only better. There was no gravity to obey. Four walls and a ceiling didn't restrain me. The limitations of my sometimes-uncoordinated body couldn't get in the way. Most importantly, neither the stares nor judgments of others—or my own insecurities—could hold me back. No one could catch me up here. No one could drag me down. Not even me.

Eventually I paused and just floated again, relishing it all.

"There you are!" Monkonjae called. I turned as he flew over. "I wanted to give you and Leo a few tips, but you took off so fast."

He pushed up his goggles to look at me properly. I did the same.

"Is Leo nearby?" I asked, glancing around.

"I already gave him my pointers. Now he's speeding through the clouds again. Here, let me show you too. So if you just want to rely on your backpack and do some hands-free flying . . ." He pressed an emblem on his bazooka. It shrunk to a tiny bazooka-shaped keychain, which he latched onto the harness of his backpack.

"Convenient," I commented.

"You want to try one of the design guides together?" he asked, gesturing to his goggles.

I nodded.

Monkonjae pulled his goggles down and pressed a button on the side. I mimicked his move and a display filled the inside of my eyewear—recommending where to fly and where to aim my pistols to maximize my impact. The display moved as I did.

"Let's go this way," I said, pointing to the right where my display indicated a serious need for color.

Monkonjae unclipped his keychain and clutched it tightly. It expanded into a bazooka again. We flew side by side to a cloudless portion of sky—the flaring Hawaiian sun on our backs and its beaming reflection creating magical streaks on the ocean at our feet. Together, we began decorating the world: golden winged and color at our beck and call. He made more of an impact on the sky than I did, as his bazooka had a much heavier stream than my pistols.

"Can we switch?" I asked after a while, wanting to unleash beautiful, heavy streams of color like he'd been doing. "These petite pistols are kind of lightweight compared to your artillery."

Monkonjae flitted over to me. "All paint pistols can create thick streams of color if you squeeze your triggers hard enough." He miniaturized his bazooka and latched it to his harness. "Shrink one of yours too and I'll show you."

I pressed the emblem on the pistol in my left hand and attached the cute keychain to my backpack. When I glanced up, he was suddenly hovering a *lot* closer to me.

"May I?" He gestured at my general person.

I wasn't completely sure what he was asking at first. I nodded and Monkonjae closed the distance between us. When he did, our wings merged. Their energies combined to create a single set of massive wings that supported us both—one wing stemming from his backpack and the other from mine. His left arm around my shoulder, he placed his right hand over mine on the trigger.

My breathing picked up slightly. Was this really happening?

I thought this kind of thing only transpired in those romantic Hallmark movies that my mother and sister watched together. The flicks had always been a little too mushy-gushy for my taste, but at this exact moment I felt like a hypocrite for ever making fun of them because currently my insides were *all* mushy-gushy.

"Together on three," Monkonjae said. "One, two, three—"

We squeezed the trigger of my pistol tightly. A huge beam of orange burst out and continued to blast forth as we started to fly. With our hands joined, and my back in the crook between his arm and his chest, we kept our eyes on the sky as we flooded the area with warm color. Well, I *mainly* kept my eyes on the sky. When temptation grew too great, I sometimes glanced up at Monkonjae's face. He didn't notice and I was glad. It gave me a chance to appreciate him without worrying about saying something stupid. I could only look for a moment though—like staring at the sun, it was too much for me.

I'd never had a proper crush on a person before. Being

distracted by cute actors, musicians, or that tall guy who worked at the Olive Garden was one thing. They were like jewels in a luxury store window; you looked but didn't touch. You admired but didn't require a connection. It's not like I felt a need to hold Chris Pine's hand or have a lengthy conversation with the guy in the *Maze Runner* movies. I just liked that they were there. Seeing them and feeling a tiny flutter inside was enough.

Monkonjae was different. I liked the feeling of his hand over mine. I liked talking to him and wanted to get to know him more. It was exciting, but also foreign, distracting, and weird to have a swarm of butterflies inside whenever I took him in and . . . I could only experience it in small doses for now. That was enough out of my comfort zone for today.

I cleared my throat. "I'm good to go solo now. Thanks for the demo."

He glanced down and nodded. "Okay. Have fun. I'll see you back in Heaven in . . ." he checked his watch. "Thirty minutes."

He withdrew and our wings diverged into two separate sets again. I returned my second paint pistol to its original form and clutched one tool in each hand.

"See you!" I called, nodding appreciatively at him then taking off on my own.

THREATS

"I keep feeling like one of them is going to pull a demon knife on me any second," Leo whispered as we kept to the rear of our tour group.

"I wouldn't put it past them," I whispered back.

Troy, Ithaca, Megan, and their three baby demon charges had arrived at the Pearlie Gates a couple of hours ago. We'd accompanied our mentors to retrieve them, and since then had been giving them a tour of the various departments within Angel Tower.

Jimmy glanced back. Leo and I stiffened. Had he heard us?

The twenty-seven-year-old demon smiled, then returned his attention forward as Ana finished explaining the different sections of the museum.

"Can we see the 'Lost' section first?" Solange asked, raising her hand like we were in class.

Ana shot Troy a look. "Why is it that the demons in your training classes always want to start there?"

"Because I train them right," Troy said with a shrug.

We proceeded into the harrowing section of the museum to once again be humbled by the devastating number of people who hadn't gotten the chance to reach their full potential. The individual demon mentors escorted their mentees around, pointing at photos on the wall.

"And that's how I turned a burnt bag of popcorn into the train crash that killed her," I heard Ithaca explain to Solange as I walked by. They were standing in front of the picture of Ariel Woo, that girl Deckland told us once had the potential to cure cancer.

I shuddered.

Deckland and Monkonjae were deep in conversation near the entrance. Leo warily looked at photos. Akari and Ana stood off to the side keeping a vigilant eye on our guests. I joined them and crossed my arms, trying my best to look imposing as I watched our demons. Once again they all wore black—their uniform, as ours was white when on official business. Except, like last time, Jimmy's outfit bent the rules. His velvet blazer was adorned with kisses of silver fireworks.

He asked Megan the occasional question as they perused the museum. Every now and then, Solange and Ithaca whisper-giggled about something. Then my eyes drifted to Oliver.

Troy had an arm around him like a big brother. However, while the older demon seemed engrossed in whatever story he was telling his young charge, Oliver's attention was never focused on the pictures. I noticed his eyes occasionally drifting to the floor, to the ceiling, and then at one point, to me.

He gave me a subtle nod in greeting. I averted my eyes without returning it.

Sorry, but I will never be on a casual "What's up?" basis with a demon. Even one with eyes like the Oahu sea.

"All right, that's enough of that," Ana said, clapping her hands together to draw our attention. "We're heading to the other sections of the museum now."

"Sweetie, what's five more minutes?" Ithaca said. Based on the skin-tight jeans she wore, I assumed demon Soul Pulses also had fashion apps, as there was no way even someone as slender as Ithaca could get into those pants without magic.

"Out," Ana said, pointing at the door. "And you've known me for two decades, Ithaca. You know my name is Anahita, not sweetie."

Ithaca shrugged. "It's a term of endearment."

"It's a term of belittlement," Ana countered. Ithaca did not refute her.

We exited and proceeded with the rest of the museum tour. I played it cool, trying to emulate Akari's intense, authoritative vibe. I was not great at it. Solange didn't say a word to me in the "Fully Realized" section of the museum, but she sidled next to me at the back of the group in the "Gone Too Soon" section as Deckland guided us around the Martin Luther King Jr. exhibit.

"You know, I have been reflecting on the roller coaster incident," she said, her voice pitched low. "Deciding how to proceed with you kept me up most of last night."

"Let me help you with that," I replied sarcastically. "I accept apologies in the form of fruit baskets and pastry boxes."

Solange's thin lips crept into a smirk. "I have to be open with you, Grace. I truly thought you were bluffing when you said you were ready for me. Your Ninety-Eight status may exude power, but you hardly do."

"Okay, that concludes our tour of Angel Tower," Deckland announced, coming to a stop at the front of the exhibit. "We'll take elevators to the ground floor and then teleport to our next destination."

We began filing through the museum curtains, headed for the glass elevators.

"Anyway, I underestimated you," Solange continued as we exited.

"Go ahead and keep doing that," I replied, locking my gaze with hers. "It'll be more fun for me to see the look on your face every time I foil you."

"Here's the thing though . . ." Jimmy abruptly appeared on my other side as we walked—body *uncomfortably* near mine. His cheekbones were astounding this close, sharp and defined like a marble statue. "Solange and I wanted to ask you if that was the first time you were able to conjure that much power. Because according to her, you seemed quite surprised when you created that shield."

Careful with your answer.
Remember the honesty filter.

My brain whirred, searching for the right response as I stepped into the elevator. "Well, the extent of my powers constantly surprises me," I ventured. "I never know just what—"

"Grace, wait!" Akari called.

It was too late. Distracted, I hadn't noticed that I'd boarded an elevator full of demons. Troy pressed the lobby and close-doors buttons before any of my own people could join the transport. The doors sealed and the elevator sank beneath the floor line.

Suddenly I felt very, *very* small with Troy and Jimmy on one side of me while Solange and Oliver stood on the other, blocking access to the button panel. Our lift plummeted down at a decent pace, but the museum was on an upper floor. There were hundreds of floors below and nowhere to escape in the meantime.

Do Heaven elevators have an emergency brake?

I reflexively backed up closer to the glass until there was nowhere left to go. Troy stepped closer and leaned one arm against the wall just above my head, bearing over me.

Rather than dart my eyes to the floor, I kept eye contact—my glare hard and unyielding. Just because Troy put me on edge didn't mean I was going to let *him* know that. Demons were only as powerful as you led them to believe they could be.

"What Jimmy here is getting at, Ninety-Eight," Troy said, "is that Solange doesn't think you knew what you were doing yesterday. You can hold your head high, choose your words carefully, and stand as tall as you want. But you know what, kid? I believe her. Eyes act as windows to our souls. And I can see fear and uncertainty in yours. You know what I *can't* see?" He leaned down. "Real strength."

I fumed. Whatever fear and unease my current company filled me with, for a moment it was not a top priority. Anger had a way of telling anxiety to take a hike.

I crossed my arms and gave Troy a defiant look, gesturing at the congregation. "Is this supposed to intimidate me? We're in Heaven. This is my turf. You can't hurt me. And I'm smart enough not to tell you anything you could use against me. Honesty filter or not."

"I don't doubt you're smart, Ninety-Eight," Troy said with a shrug. "But that doesn't mean you can't also be misinformed. Oliver?" He glanced at his charge.

Oliver tensed. "Troy, won't the GAs retaliate? I mean, there are rules up here, right? And what about God? And—"

"Oh, I'll do it," Jimmy huffed.

"Do wha—" I didn't get a chance to finish my question.

Jimmy grabbed my jacket collar and thrust me back. I should've slammed against the glass wall of the elevator, but instead I phased through it, as did Jimmy's arm.

He was using his demonic power to turn intangible and phase through things. Evidently he could extend that ability to whatever he touched and the skill worked in Heaven just fine.

Jimmy's limb was coated in a glowing, red aura that had spread over me too. While he and the other demons remained within the safety of the descending elevator, my body from my hips up dangled outside the transport, only Jimmy's grip keeping me from falling.

My head turned a bit and I took in the *shockingly high drop* awaiting me.

Suddenly Jimmy yanked me back inside. The glow faded and he let me go. My heart pounded.

"We can't *kill* angels," Solange said. "We learn that on day one. But you can still be hurt. If you fell a hundred stories to the ground in Heaven, your body would be smushed. What do you think, Troy? How long would it take her soul to reform?"

"Maybe a week." He shrugged and turned to me. "A very unpleasant week."

"And in the meantime, it would be open season on Henry," Solange added with a smile.

My lips parted to protest, but Troy abruptly grabbed my jacket and shoved me through the elevator again. He leaned forward so his upper body was through the wall too.

I flailed my arms, completely helpless.

"Tell us the truth, Ninety-Eight. We've heard rumors. You're not that powerful, are you? That roller coaster was a fluke. You're nothing. You don't really have the power to protect your assignment, let alone yourself."

My peripherals detected golden haze over my head. Out of

nowhere my halo had appeared. Perhaps it was instinct—like a nightlight powering on when you flicked off the bedroom switch.

The crown of my designation shone over me, but it did little to help the situation. I felt like one of those guys that mafia hitmen dangled off rooftops to get information.

Is this what my afterlife had come to—a celestial shakedown?

Troy hauled me inside again. "Well?" he asked. "Are we making an angel pancake or are you going to be straight with us?"

My pulse thumped wildly. I glared at him and my lip quivered, but I swallowed down the panic and refused to answer.

Troy sighed. "You may think you're special, Ninety-Eight. But Ninety-Seven thought she was special too. I guess we teach you the hard way that there aren't enough angels in Heaven to truly keep anyone safe." He nodded at Jimmy across the elevator.

"Troy—" Oliver tried.

Jimmy moved toward me, raising his hand to grab me again.

All of a sudden, I reacted. I gripped my halo before Jimmy's foot completed a step, moved my arm in a scooping motion, and thrust my fist toward the demon. The halo instantly contorted into a ball of light that blasted Jimmy back.

CRACK!

A large, spidery fracture in the glass erupted where the blast of light slammed Jimmy against the wall. He reeled from the impact, then *freaked out* when he noticed one of his arms was missing. Well, it was disintegrating.

I'd hit his right arm with my blast, and now we all watched it crumble into golden particles that drizzled off him into vanishing. There was no blood or gore. We were immortal forms of ourselves, after all. However, when the disintegration stopped it was like his arm had been entirely erased from existence, jacket sleeve and all.

The demons froze with their mouths agape. I no doubt held similar awe on my face as I stood there, halo returned to its normal form and radiating in my hand. I composed myself quickly though. My enemies didn't need to know how surprised I was to have conjured a power I'd only seen up close once when my mentor accidentally demonstrated it weeks ago.

I put the halo back atop my head and crossed my arms. "Any other questions?" I asked Troy pointedly.

The demons stared at me.

"Okay—*seriously*—where the heck is my arm?" Jimmy exclaimed.

"Calm down," Troy said, annoyed, still keeping his eyes locked with mine. "It'll grow back eventually when we get to Hell."

"But—"

Troy huffed with a scary kind of irritation. He tore his gaze away from me and turned to the kid. "We get sent back to Hell to reform when angels hit us with a solid attack. She only got your arm, so stop whining. You're only down a limb. Mirage it. *Now*. Can't have the other GAs knowing what went on here."

Jimmy closed his eyes and his form glowed. Then a limb— sleeve and all—appeared to replace the one I'd blasted off.

Solange reached out to touch it and her delicate fingers went right through. The arm was just a trick. Another extension of the demons' powers of manipulation.

I felt the elevator slowing down. I was still in shock regarding what happened, but I knew three things.

1) I didn't want the GAs to know about what went on here either. Last time I tried to show off my power I'd only looked like a fool when I couldn't follow through.

2) I had zero idea how I'd just pulled that off. Until I did, I should play things close to the vest.

3) Just because I was rattled, baffled, and totally out of my element didn't mean I shouldn't try to capitalize on the situation.

"Go ahead. Mirage your arm. Don't tell the others what happened," I said to the group. "I don't plan on telling them either because I can handle this—*all of you*—myself." I panned a finger across the four demons. "There's a saying on Earth. Ladies don't start fights; we finish them. My mother never liked the phrase, but I was rather fond of it. And I think an amended version suits our situation quite well. Angels don't go looking for trouble; but they enjoy putting a stop to it. You want the truth? Maybe I am afraid. Maybe I don't know what I'm doing. But if you come at me . . . I *will* come at you."

The elevator doors dinged open on the lobby floor. I extinguished my halo and stepped out without glancing back. It was more dramatic that way. Plus, I didn't want Troy to get a good look into my eyes again. While my words held nothing but might, and each sentence felt at home in my voice, for now my soul was fragile and I couldn't afford to let him, or any of my enemies see that.

At least until I understood how to connect those heart-spoken words with the uncertainty I felt in my ability, strength, and purpose. Demonstration of power aside, all three were as up in the air as the city of Heaven.

Hopefully this episode bought me some time before my foes tried to expose that again.

The demonic crew exited the elevator behind me. Countless souls migrated around us—headed for our elevator bank, one of the other elevator banks across the massive, train-station-sized lobby, or Angel Tower's main exit that connected to the streets of downtown. While the walls were paneled glass, the lobby ceiling forty feet up was covered in blooming jasmine that dangled down in thick bunches. The expansive floor was patterned with gold-flecked white marble. A single crystal fountain gushed at the center of it all.

A minute later, another elevator opened and my mentors and classmates, as well as Ithaca and Megan, exited.

Akari hurried over to me. "Everything okay?" she asked.

Nope.

"They didn't hurt me, if that's what you're wondering," I replied.

She gave me a somewhat disbelieving look, then Ana clapped her hands to summon our attention. It was an effective and authoritative tactic, like something a schoolteacher would use on children. But as Ana was a child, it was always oddly cute and commanding when she did it.

"Okay, up first, Monkonjae's Heaven excursion," she said. "We need to go outside for our teleports to work. Come on, everyone. Hustle." She herded us through the lobby and to the sidewalk outside of Angel Tower. The fresh air embraced us like a cool hug scented with snickerdoodles.

As we exited the skyscraper, I noticed Oliver's eyes darting over the crowds anxiously like he was searching for something or someone.

Ana pivoted to address us. "Angels, grab a demon partner and take them to Ellis's cloud. "She's expecting us in"—Ana checked her watch—"thirty seconds. Crud, we're cutting it close for the sunset we booked."

"My lady." Troy offered Akari his arm in a sarcastically chivalrous fashion.

"Shut up." Akari rolled her eyes, grabbed his arm gruffly, and teleported them in a flash. Megan slinked her arm through Deckland's next while Solange made her move on Monkonjae. He looked uncomfortable as they flashed away.

"Let's go, sweetie," Ithaca said condescendingly. She offered Ana her hand, bending over unnecessarily. "Can you reach?"

Ana scowled, snatched Ithaca's hand, and disappeared. Now it was just me, Leo, Oliver, and Jimmy. I looked at the latter.

"Shall I hold your good arm?" I asked with a smirk.

"I'll pass," Jimmy replied, taking a nervous step backward. It was the first time I'd seen him fazed. I kind of loved it. Was that bad?

Jimmy took hold of Leo's shoulder. "All right, kid," he said. "Do your thing."

Leo rolled his eyes and beamed away.

I paused and glanced at the demon in the hoodie and darkwash jeans next to me. "I guess that just leaves you and me," I said to Oliver. The kid was still looking over his shoulder, scanning the faces in the crowd.

"Don't sound so disappointed," he said absentmindedly.

"Actually, I'm not," I replied, stepping closer to him, which got his attention. "Make no mistake, I will *never* be cool enough with what you are that you and I, like, share a quiche or something. But out of all your Hellion buddies, you're currently the one I loathe the least. You're at least the one who confuses me the most.

Troy wanted you to dangle me outside of the elevator, didn't he? He addressed *you* first when it all went down. You didn't want to."

Oliver took an awkward step away from me. "I just hesitated."

"Why?"

"Does it matter?"

"If it didn't, you wouldn't be answering my question with a question."

We stared at each other.

Both our Soul Pulses buzzed.

"I hate these things," he commented.

"Me too." I sighed. "It's like eternal parental supervision." I glanced at the caller ID as the buzzing persisted. "It's my mentor."

"Mine too," Oliver seconded, looking at his.

"I guess they're wondering where we are."

"Best not to keep them waiting."

Oliver looked me up and down uncomfortably, like he was trying to decide what to do. Then he awkwardly placed his hand on top of my head. "Okay, teleport us or whatever."

I gave him a bewildered, offended look. "I'm not a genie or a crystal ball. Stop being ridiculous." I grabbed his hand off my head and held it normally.

I hadn't thought it was weird when I did it. But then there was a moment of stillness, a lingering pause when I looked into his blue eyes and he looked back and I kind of forgot what I was supposed to be doing . . .

Focus, Grace.

I diverted my gaze and concentrated on Ellis's cloud. A flash of light consumed us and we appeared on the busy cumulonimbus. Oliver let go of my hand and we joined the group as Ellis was giving the same instructions speech as last night.

"Why didn't you answer?" Akari said, gesturing to my Soul Pulse as she came to meet me. I kept a side eye on Oliver as he walked away. "Grace?"

I huffed. "Akari, stop worrying about me."

I moved past her to merge with the group of people waiting to paint. There were several dozen of them reporting for duty on this shift.

As Ellis spoke, Oliver once again seemed distracted and an-xious. He wasn't paying attention to her instructions, and he certainly didn't seem impressed, let alone interested, in the idea of painting a sunset.

Our GA-demon tour group got separated for a moment in the excited rush of angels moving to claim equipment, get strapped in, and climb atop the platform. Oliver disappeared in the mass and I found myself looking around for where he had gone. I wasn't sure why I cared, but there was something about his behavior that seemed . . . off.

For a second I thought I spotted him by the equipment bungalow. Then he was suddenly a few meters to my left on the platform, standing next to Monkonjae.

"Okay, everyone." Ellis called out. "Activate your wings now!"

We did as she commanded, and she launched into her final directives. I was half-listening to her until I saw Oliver. Not the one to my left. *Another* Oliver. Just for a split second, I noticed him, or certainly someone who looked like him, slip around the side of the equipment bungalow.

What the hell? Or Heaven?

"—and just press the side of your goggles to operate the guide display," Ellis continued.

"Akari," I whispered to my mentor, standing on my right. I glanced at the Oliver on the platform, then held my tongue. For whatever reason, I backed down on my initial thought and came up with something else that would satisfy the honesty filter. "I, uh . . . I have this strange feeling in my stomach."

It's called gut instinct.

"Can I stay behind?"

So I can investigate what the heck is going on here.

"Um, sure. We'll be teleported back here in sixty minutes. If you leave this cloud, make certain you're back by then."

"Got it."

"Are you sure you don't need me to—"

"I'm fine. I can handle this on my own." I gave Ellis a wave as I hastily stepped off the platform. "Sorry. I have issues."

True in so many ways.

I waited for the group to teleport. Once they'd all vanished, I made my way around the bungalow—trying not to seem conspicuous to the angels working there. I checked behind the structure. No one was there.

Then came that weird feeling again.

It compelled me to take several steps forward and look down over the edge of the cloud. Below, golden wings caught the sunlight. The person flying wore all black.

I dashed around to the front of the bungalow and gestured to my loaner wings. "May I borrow these briefly? I'll be back soon. I promise."

"Sure, Ninety-Eight. Do your thing," said the silver-haired angel. "Big fan."

Geez, does everyone know who I am?

"Thank you!" I called over my shoulder.

I ran around the side of the building.

Well, here go the laws of physics. Again.

Somewhere Mr. Corrin's ears were burning.

I leapt off the cloud and spiraled down like a falcon in pursuit of prey. The wings I was after were much farther away now— shimmering specs. Thankfully, my experience flying yesterday allowed me to make up the distance between us quickly. When I was a few dozen feet away from the black-clothed figure, I confirmed what my instinct had been telling me. It *was* Oliver. He hadn't noticed me. It was time he did. I cupped my hands around my mouth.

"Hey, demon!"

Oliver visibly startled, wings jerking sharply to the side. When he regained control, he twisted a bit to see who had called him. I waved. His eyes widened and he made a run for it. Or I should say a plummet for it.

"Hey!" I shouted, pursuing him through the clouds. His glowing wings made him easy to track, as did his dark clothes against the pale palette of the sky. We kept descending and I kept gaining on him. Then we broke through some clouds and The First City came into view. He bee-lined for it. I zoomed after him, bobbing and weaving between the colorful lanterns.

He made it to the streets before I did and had a rough landing in a park downtown. The cherry blossom trees were in such full bloom it looked like they were coated in cotton candy.

Oliver's wings shrunk into his backpack and he stumbled to his feet, moving toward the bustling sidewalk. I landed six seconds later, stowed my wings, and followed him. No one paid us any mind; they were happy in their own paradises, and flying teenagers were hardly the most magical sights in town.

I darted around anxiously. For a moment I thought I'd lost him. Oliver was a lot lighter on his feet than I was. Catching up to him had been much easier in flight.

Oh, what the heck.

I activated the wings again and soared fifteen feet above the ground. My eyes searched the crowds. Eventually I saw him near the end of the block.

Got you.

I rushed after the boy until I was flying directly above his shadow. With a speedy spiral I dove and landed right in front of him. He rammed into me with an audible *oof*.

"Funny bumping into a demon like you in a place like this," I said, vanishing my wings and planting my hands on my hips. "Care to explain?"

"Not really," he said, pushing past me rudely.

"Let me rephrase that," I continued, keeping pace with him. "Unless you want me to yell really loudly that there's a *demon* loose on the streets of Heaven, you'll explain. *Now, Oliver.*" I grabbed his wrist to get him to stop. That's when I noticed that his Soul Pulse was missing.

"Where is your Soul Pulse?"

He thrust off my grip. Though his huff was angry, his expression was nervous. Oliver diverted his eyes. Something about his worried—even sad—look changed my approach. I was a curious person by nature, and Oliver was a big question mark. Every interaction we'd had so far only triggered more enigma. I needed to understand what was going on with him and why he seemed so concerned.

"*Oliver?*" I looked at him with more softness. "Tell me what's happening. You didn't hang me out of that elevator today. You hesitated. I owe you at least a moment's hesitation too . . . before I turn you in."

His eyes darted around uncertainly. There were tons of people in the area, so I zeroed in on a brunch spot across the street. I sighed and shook my head. "Come on. We need to talk."

19

FRIEND AND/OR ENEMY?

I couldn't believe I was having quiche with a demon. Even after declaring I'd never engage in that specific activity, like, a half hour ago.

Maybe I shouldn't use the word *never* in the afterlife. So many crazy, illogical things happened here. Planting my foot in the ground could be a waste of time.

"Are you actually hungry?" Oliver asked as I stabbed at my slice. The diner whirred with activity. Glasses of orange juice clinked, hot coffee steamed, servers moved with such grace and coordination it was like they'd choreographed a dance.

"So what if I am?"

"Didn't all that flying upset your stomach?"

"Ugh, is this what I'm like?" I said, putting my fork down. "You ask a lot of questions to avoid talking about issues other people want to discuss. Spill the tea, Oliver. We're throwing a lot of protocol out the window and possibly breaking, like, a commandment or something by having this little Heaven-Hell brunch date."

"Brunch *date*?"

My face probably turned redder than the fires Oliver came from.

"You know what I mean." I leaned forward and lowered my voice. "Seriously. First off, what's the deal with your missing Soul Pulse?"

Oliver raked a hand over his hair then leaned forward too so our noses were only a foot apart over the small table. "Look, I needed to run an errand, but those things track us. I took mine off and hid it in Monkonjae's jacket pocket when the loser wasn't paying attention. I'll swipe it back from him later. For now, it will seem like I'm still with the group."

I paused a moment and digested this info before digging further. "So the mirage of you with the others . . ."

"We take to our demon powers differently," Oliver said. "Mirages are my strength. I created one of myself to go with our tour. Mirages aren't tangible, so as long as nobody runs into it, that version of me will fly around with your sunset painters and no one will notice the difference."

My eyes fell away for a moment, my mind wild with curiosity that I had trouble articulating. Though Oliver was a huge mystery and I was a girl motivated to find answers, I found it difficult to form succinct questions when looking directly into his eyes, as if their aquatic nature short-circuited my train of thought, like a cell phone falling into the ocean.

Kaput.

I rapped my fingers on the table until I had the right query. "How did you get it off?" I asked, pointing at his bare wrist. "Soul Pulses can't be removed."

"I'm not going to tell you," he said, leaning back in his chair.

"But you have to," I argued. "Honesty filter."

"And I'm being honest with you. There is literally nothing you can say or do that will make me answer that question."

I huffed in exasperation, then leaned back in my own chair and crossed my arms. "You do realize you are giving me *zero* reason not to call my mentor and drag you back to Hell. I'm sure the folks down there would also like to know how you got your Soul Pulse off. And I doubt they would ask you nicely over brunch."

The lines on his face tightened. That spark of fear I'd seen in his eyes when he'd warned me about Troy in Hell shone for a moment. It was like a glimmer in a lake—only visible in the right light, but notable if you looked.

It caused me to feel bad about threatening him, but what was I supposed to do? It's not like he was a good guy. By definition, Oliver was a *bad* guy, and I wasn't being a very *good* Guardian Angel if I let him get away with this. I should hang him out to dry. Even though he had hesitated in the elevator, it's not as if he stopped the others from trying to hurt me. He just didn't get his own hands dirty. That wasn't enough of a reason to let the fox in the henhouse as it were, and that's what was happening now. He was a demon wandering around unsupervised in Heaven. I had a responsibility to my GA job. I had to—

"Please don't," he said.

The earnest sincerity in his voice caught my attention.

I sat forward again and spoke with candor but caring. "Give me a reason not to."

He drummed his fingers on the table. Then he sighed.

"It's my mom," he said. "She's up here. I wanted to see her."

"Your mom?"

He nodded. "She died when I was seven. When I died, I found out she landed in Heaven, *full time*. The timeshare I ended up with would've gotten me four days a week in Middleground and three days a week being tortured in Hell. Then I was made the demon offer." He gulped, frown tightening as he looked down at the table. "Since the only thing I cared about in the afterlife was my mother, and my timeshare wouldn't even let me get in the same afterlife realm as her, I chose this. Partly to avoid torture, but also because . . . I knew demons get to visit Heaven on occasion. Like this field trip. I thought it was my chance to find her."

I sat there dumbfounded as I studied the demon sitting in front of me. The diner buzzed merrily around us, and yet Oliver and I may as well have been on another plane of existence. Much to my dismay, he suddenly didn't seem very demonic. He seemed human. And I felt bad for him.

"Oliver . . ." I said. "All joking aside, you could get in serious trouble for what you've done. I haven't been in the afterlife long, but they seem to take rules very seriously. This was a dangerous plan. You were so young when your mother died. Do you even remember her?"

"She's my mom, Grace. I may not remember her favorite color or song or what she liked on her pizza, but I remember that I loved her. She was the only good thing in my life. She was good in general, which is why she got sent up here. I wanted to see her. Even if it was just once. Even if it was just for a little while, and

. . ." He sighed and shook his head. "Even if she's disappointed in who I turned out to be."

"A demon?" I said.

He gave me a look. "No. The worst version of myself."

My brow raised. "Isn't that the same thing?"

"More juice?" a waitress interrupted. Oliver and I both straightened guiltily, like two kids caught eating chocolate before dinner.

"No, thank you," I said hastily. The waitress left and I readdressed Oliver. "Before your Soul Pulse *mysteriously vanished*, did you try calling your mother? Normal Soul Pulses can only contact people on the same afterlife plane. Now that you're in Heaven, you should have no problem contacting someone else who lives here."

He looked at me like I had to be kidding. "Hell Soul Pulses are different. If you're a normal person being tortured you can't make any calls and can only take calls from demons. If you're a demon, your Soul Pulse can only be used to reach out to other demons or regular people in Hell." His expression still held surprise. "I can't believe your mentor didn't tell you all this."

I frowned. "GA rules are unique; we can call anyone from anywhere. She must have just chosen to give me the information I needed."

"Does your mentor do that often? Tell you partial truths?"

Yes.

"This isn't about me or my mentor." I waved my hand dismissively. "This is about you and what I am going to do with you."

He raised an eyebrow as he crossed his arms. "Have you decided?"

I thought long and hard, absentmindedly poking my quiche into a million bits of egg and pepper and crust. Then—

"That is literally all you wanted out of this stunt, the only reason you broke away from our group—to see your mom? Nothing else? You're willing to risk some kind of horrible punishment I can't even fathom, just to reach her?"

He nodded again.

"Well then, come on." I stood up.

He blinked. "Where are we going?"

"We have thirty minutes before our group gets back. Let's find your mother." I strode purposefully toward the exit. After a pause, Oliver followed. He caught up with me by the door.

"Ninety-Eight?"

I paused and crooked my brow at him.

"Sorry. *Grace*. Why are you helping me?"

I sighed and shook my head. "I honestly have no idea. It just feels like the right thing to do. And I'm a Guardian Angel; that's my schtick, isn't it? Doing the right thing?"

We left the diner and I opened the app store of my Soul Pulse. "I know I saw a directory app on here somewhere," I thought aloud, scrolling. "Ah, here it is."

I quickly downloaded it and a shimmering search bar appeared over my watch with a space for a name. I glanced at Oliver.

"Marian Evans," he said.

"Find Marian Evans," I said to the screen. A rainbow wheel turned as the search loaded. Then a response appeared. "It says there are 276 Marian Evans in Heaven. Let's narrow the search a bit. How old was she when she died?"

"Thirty-five."

I returned attention to my Soul Pulse. "Find Marian Evans, mother to Oliver Evans, died at thirty-five."

Rainbow wheel and then *TA-DAH!* one result revealed itself. "Looks like she has her Soul Pulse privacy settings on so we can't call or teleport to *her*, but the location of her residence came up so we could go there and hope she's home."

I learned about Soul Pulse privacy settings in week one. Unfortunately, GAs couldn't utilize them the same way as other angels. If we were needed, our mentors would always be able to find or call us.

I scrolled through the search result. "Her home is . . . It's an apartment in The First City!" I smacked Oliver on the arm excitedly. "She's not that far away. I can teleport us there!"

His eyes glimmered. "Well, do it then."

I shot him another look.

"Sorry. *Please*."

"That's better." I took his hand in mine. Again, I hadn't thought anything of it at first, but then we experienced another awkward, lingering moment.

I cleared my throat, concentrated on the destination, and in a flash we were in the well-lit hallway of an apartment building.

Oliver and I stood in front of a pale pink door with a floral doormat. A giant, fancy *M* decorated the mat. Real flowers— yellow tulips—bloomed in twin sconces on either side of the door.

I glanced at the demon. He seemed in awe and also a little scared. "Go ahead and knock," I urged.

He gulped. "I need my hand back for that." He flicked his eyes down. I was still holding onto him. Embarrassed, I let go speedily and brushed my hand off on my pant leg.

Oliver took a deep breath, stepped up to the door, and knocked. We waited five seconds. There was no answer. He knocked again, more intensely this time. Still nothing.

"Can't you teleport us inside?" he asked.

Now it was my turn to give the you-must-be-kidding look. "Oliver that would be rude. Just as important places like Angel Tower don't allow teleports, we can't just appear inside people's homes. We teleport to their front doors for the sake of privacy. For the same reason, we can't teleport directly next to someone. If we're looking for a specific person, we have to know where they are and then the Soul Pulse will take us near that location if it's not off-limits and if the angel doesn't have privacy settings on. Unless you're a GA . . ." I grumbled at the end.

Oliver scowled. "You angels have so many rules." With a huff he knelt down in front of the door and reached inside his jacket.

"What are you doing?" I asked.

"Breaking in," he said.

My brows shot up. "Oliver, that's not—"

"Good?" he asked, glancing back. "How do you think I wound up in Hell, Grace? Selling Girl Scout cookies?"

He took out a couple small lock-picking tools that I guess he just kept on him, and went for the door. Then I had a thought. I walked up and turned the knob. The door opened easily.

Oliver blinked, then stared at me.

"Homes don't seem to have locks in Heaven," I explained. "I suppose it's because angels trust each other."

"Suckers," he replied.

Oliver stepped inside the apartment. When he saw I was stalled, he waved me forward. "Come on, Grace."

I hesitated at first, quickly looked both ways, then followed. He closed the door behind us. It was a gorgeous dwelling—much more spacious than I had imagined. The kitchen had distressed brick walls and the cutest breakfast nook that overlooked the city. Vases of fresh flowers decorated every flat surface. The living room featured robin's egg blue curtains, smooth wooden floors, and a violin racked in the corner.

Suddenly a tiny terrier appeared. She wore a pink collar with the nametag "Daisy" and wagged her tail excitedly as she looked up at me.

"Oliver, your mom has a dog and—" The demon was nowhere in sight. "Oliver?"

"In here," he called. I pursued his voice into a bedroom. The bedspread had an intricate floral pattern, and the chandelier held real candlesticks. Daisy trotted after me obediently, not yapping or bothering us, just following like she wanted to be a part of the team.

Oliver stood in front of a dresser, holding a picture frame in his hand. I walked over slowly. The photo showed a beautiful woman with short blonde hair kneeling in a garden. I couldn't see her face; a floppy sunhat covered everything but the tip of her nose and mouth. However, she had her arm around a young boy, who I could see very clearly.

"Is that you?" I asked.

He nodded.

"When was that taken?"

He sighed. "Would you think less of me if I told you I don't remember?"

I took in the sadness in his eyes.

"No," I replied. "She remembers you. That's what is important. Your picture is in this apartment, Oliver. The where and when captured in this photo don't matter. The fact that this memory happened, and that it clearly meant something to her, does."

He put the frame down and glanced around the room. "Part of me never thought I'd get this far. Now that I have, and she's not here . . . I genuinely don't know what to do."

I checked my Soul Pulse. "We only have fifteen minutes left. I can teleport us at the last second, but I'm not sure if that's going to give us enough time to find her. I wouldn't even know where to start looking."

"We have to try," he insisted. "Help me search the place for any sign of where she might be. A clue or something."

Oliver moved back to the living room, me right behind him. He started opening desk drawers and rifling through their contents.

"Um . . . I feel kind of weird about this, Oliver. The trespassing on its own felt morally dicey. Now we're going to search this apartment like the police on a raid?"

"Calm down, *Law & Order*. We're not ransacking the place. Just looking around."

He continued with his search. I reluctantly headed for the kitchen with Daisy at my heels. Then I heard another *CLICK* and the door swung open.

Oliver and I jumped like salmon heading upstream. A man wearing a newsboy cap, a purple argyle sweater, and a matching bowtie came in. He carried a baguette and a small grocery bag. He blinked in surprise when he saw us. "Oh, hello. What are you kids doing in here? Are you friends of Marian?"

"I know her from a while ago," Oliver interceded when I couldn't form a sentence. He hurriedly joined me. "How do you know her?"

"I'm her neighbor Portrow. She asked me to take care of Daisy while she's away for the weekend."

Oliver enlivened. "Where did she go?"

"Um, a botanical garden. I can't remember which one." He chuckled. "Heaven has as many botanical gardens as Disneyland has souvenir stands. She'll be back on Monday."

The boy beside me completely lost heart—whatever kind of heart a demon had. He deflated like a helium balloon after a party.

"I don't mean to be rude, but is there a reason you're in Marian's apartment?" Portrow asked. He turned to me. "You look familiar, young lady. Do I know—Oh hello, Daisy." He bent over to pet the dog.

"*Lie*," Oliver whispered tersely in my ear, forgetting the rules.

"*I can't*," I replied under my breath. Then a light bulb went off in my head. "And luckily, I don't need to. Honesty gets you way further."

"Sir, I look familiar because I'm Grace Cardiff," I told the man as he straightened up.

"Oh, you're Ninety-Eight! How exciting to meet you!" He came over and shook my hand enthusiastically.

"Nice to meet you too. My associate and I were looking for Marian, but I guess we're not going to be able to find her today, are we?"

"Or call her either. Marian always turns on her Soul Pulse privacy settings when she goes on her nature excursions. I don't suppose you have time to randomly check every botanical garden in Heaven?"

I sighed. "Sadly not. Thank you for your time, sir. Let's go, Oliver."

The two of us exited the apartment. Once we were in the hall with the door closed behind us, I felt the urge to do something ludicrous: comfort a guy from Hell.

I couldn't help it. He looked so downtrodden that on impulse I put a hand on his shoulder. "I'm sorry. You risked so much for this."

"It's not about the risk," Oliver said. "I just can't believe I lost my chance. I'd risk way more if I had another opportunity to see her."

"Really?"

"Well, yeah. She'd probably be ashamed of what I turned out to be; I'm so different from the kid in that picture. But even if we're a million miles apart in who we are, she still matters to me, so I'd do whatever it takes to make things right between us. Wouldn't you do the same for your mom?"

"Honestly . . . I'm not sure," I admitted. "We don't have the best relationship. I've tried so hard my whole life to bite back parts of my character that she and other adults don't agree with. But I slip up—a lot. When I do, she makes me feel so small and is super tough on me. I just wish she'd see me as—" I paused, noting his intense interest and realizing I'd been talking a while. My cheeks flushed with embarrassment. "Sorry. I babble sometimes."

He shrugged. "I like it. It lets me know you're being real."

"Isn't that what honesty is for?"

"I think we both know telling the truth doesn't mean you have to be fully upfront about what's on your mind. Honesty doesn't reveal character unless there's vulnerability involved."

I paused again. Then I looked up at the demon. "Oliver?"

"Yeah?"

"You're a lot different than what I thought you would be. Is it normal for a demon to be so . . . nice? And to care about people the way you do about your mom?"

He thought about it. "I don't know. Is it normal for an angel to break rules and go out of her way to *help* a demon?"

"I doubt it." I crossed my arms. "But to be fair, no one ever specifically told me not to help a demon, so I wouldn't say I've technically broken a rule. This is just a weird situation."

He shrugged. "I wouldn't say I'm technically nice either. *This* is just a weird situation."

I checked my watch. "Well, whatever *this* was, it's over. Time is up." I started to offer him my hand but paused when we locked eyes. I felt a twinge of . . . *something* tingle my spine again. "You know what. Just put your hand on my head."

He did as he was told and we flashed away, returning to Ellis's cloud.

"You'd better hide," I told him once we arrived. "Can't have your doppelganger show up with you in plain sight."

"Agreed." He began heading toward the equipment bungalow, then stopped and turned around. "Thank you for helping me, Grace. You're a lot different than I thought you'd be too."

I tensed. "Please don't tell your demon friends that."

"We're not friends. And don't worry, I won't. I owe you one, Grace."

"Oh, goodie. A favor from a demon," I said in jest. "Just what an angel wants."

He shrugged. "You never know." He smirked and started to walk away again, but then I called after him.

"Oliver? One more important thing . . ."

He gave me a curious look.

"I know we just had brunch, but for the sake of appearances, grin and bear it when we visit *my* supposed favorite spot in Heaven. I don't really have one, so I'm just taking everyone to a cake shop . . ."

20

DRIVEN

This was by far the sketchiest thing I had ever done.

Crouched in the school parking lot, I hurriedly used my halo to slice through the front left tire of Justin's jeep.

One of the benefits of being top of most classes meant that teachers trusted me if I needed to leave for a few minutes. For example, this afternoon in statistics class I'd finished my work early, so the teacher let me go to the "library."

I'd come here instead.

My GA powers were still fighting me, so the simple task of cutting a tire, which should have taken a second, was taking forever. Halo in-hand, I sawed through again and again with the effort of someone cutting down their own Christmas tree, anxiously checking over my shoulder periodically. The final school bell would ring in ten minutes and school security had already whizzed by on golf carts several times since I'd been here. I was totally on edge that they would catch me in the act.

Come on. Come on.

With a final slice, my glimmering tool finally cut deep enough. Air began escaping from the tire. It would be deflated soon, just like the other front tire I'd already cut. Justin kept a spare attached to the back of his jeep so I couldn't afford to damage only one.

I vanished my halo and started to stand, but then heard the golf cart coming and threw myself to the ground, rolling under the jeep. When the coast was clear, I crawled out and scurried back to class. My teacher gave me a pleasant nod as I resumed my seat.

The bell rang shortly after and Henry and Razel hastily shoved their things into their backpacks. They were out the door before most of the kids had put their pencils down. I waved goodbye to our teacher and jogged after my friends.

"Wait up!" I called.

"Sorry, Grace," Razel said. "We're in a rush. Justin is taking us to our driving tests!" She waved as Justin approached from down the hall.

"You both are going to kick butt today!" he said as we reached the end of the sidewalk. We waited for a break in the stream of cars before crossing. "The only thing you'll have to decide is who gets to drive us home when you're done."

We entered the parking lot. My heart beat faster. Keeping Henry from getting his driver's license before he graduated high school was one of his Plot Points. I had to be creative to execute that—hence the tires—however the action came with guilt. He was my assignment, but he was also my friend. He'd been nothing but nice to me, and I felt bad taking away something he wanted so desperately.

A *very* loud curse word shocked me out of my introspection.

Justin had discovered the first flat tire.

"What the frack? Someone slashed my tire!" He opened the door and threw his backpack onto the front seat, then took a deep breath and tried to calm down. "It's fine. I have a spare. It'll just be five minutes."

"Um . . . Justin?" Razel said from the right side of the car. The two boys rushed over and discovered the other flat.

More cursing ensued.

Razel groaned, face pinched with stress. "Our DMV is the worst; they fail you if you're a minute late. What are we going to do?"

"I'll call Mom," Henry said. "She'll be picking up Hana from school right now. That's not too far. I bet she can get us."

I waited to the side. Justin was kicking his tires, muttering about towing and tire costs, making me feel even worse. Thankfully, as part of my human cover, I could *cover* him. The backpack Akari had given me on my first school day was a literal Godsend. Every GA got a magic supplies bag that took on a form to match our cover identities—a briefcase for a businessperson, a duffel bag for an assistant coach, etc. Inside was anything we'd need to maintain our human identities, including money. It was like having a Mary Poppins bag crossed with an ATM.

Later in the week, I'd take out a few hundred dollars and leave them on the street where Justin could find the cash, reimbursing him for the damage.

"What do you mean there is a *goat* pile-up?" Henry exclaimed into his phone.

I hid a smile. This part of my plan I felt less bad about. Mainly because it was funny.

I'd done a good amount of research at Angel Tower's GA library this past week. Beyond our own shrewdness and magical powers, Guardian Angels could seek assistance from any non-GA department in Heaven to help with our missions. It had taken a lot of research to find an idea for this specific situation, but eventually I'd come up with something clever.

Henry hung up the phone and shook his head incredulously. "So apparently a bunch of petting zoo animals got loose around Hana's elementary school. While the kids are having the best time, all the adults are trapped in massive traffic."

Heaven's Animal Awesomeness Department added extra bits of animal-related wonder to the world. The angels who worked there made dolphins pop out of the ocean when people were kayaking. They encouraged hummingbirds to build nests near windows so you could watch baby birds being born. They had deer run across your path when you took a hike. And they caused Instagrammable "Hilarious Animal Shenanigans" to occur—such as a petting zoo driving through town, breaking down, and all the goats and llamas breaking free to graze and frolic in the neighborhood.

It had only taken a few quick calls and meetings with different members of the department to set up this silly situation, which I engineered to keep Henry and Razel's mom from reaching them quickly.

Razel checked her phone. "The closest Uber is thirty-five minutes from here," she wailed.

No one was surprised, least of all me. I'd checked every ride-sharing app I could think of every day for the last two weeks, and half an hour was the typical wait time for a pick-up from our school. We were in a secluded suburban community; plus, with all the schools in the area, traffic at this time stunk.

Henry and Razel texted a few of their friends, but no one could give them a ride to the DMV. I'd been nervous about this, as I couldn't delay everyone in their contact lists, but I'd had faith that very few teenagers had last-minute free time on a Friday afternoon to spontaneously drive across town to the closest Department of Motor Vehicles.

I stayed with my friends as they settled down on the sidewalk to await roadside assistance for Justin's car and the twins' mom. When the time the latter's tests were supposed to start passed, I gave my friends a grimace.

"I'm sorry you missed your appointments."

Henry sighed. "Getting an automatic fail for not showing up is such an ego blow. We literally failed without trying. Now we have to wait two weeks before we try again."

That gave me two weeks to think of another way to get him to blow it. I needed to do some more research and hopefully find another cunning solution.

The cavalry arrived about an hour later. I checked my watch as Mrs. Sun pulled up in her minivan. I needed to report to my own test ASAP.

"Hi, Mrs. Sun," I said. "If it's not too much trouble, can you please drop me off at the glass church?"

"Welcome, everyone, to the DMVD—Department of Motor Vehicles for the Dead."

The female angel greeting us wore a navy tracksuit with glittery silver wings embroidered on the back. Her fanny pack said *Get Your Eyes off My Fanny.*

She met with us in the waiting room of the department, which was *extremely* different to any DMV I had seen on Earth. Every seat was a massage chair with a magical tray that produced your favorite beverage. The walls were calming murals of lavender fields. Bunches of fresh daisies decorated every worker's desk. Most notably, all workers wore happy smiles as they answered old-timey rotary phones and gave thorough answers to questions received.

"I'm Donna," the woman said. "We're really excited to conduct your driving tests. Once you have your license, you will be cleared to operate vehicles where they are permitted in Heaven. I'm told we also have a Guardian Angel in the group today." She gestured at me. "Honey, when you pass, your license will be valid on Earth as well."

"Ma'am, don't you mean *if* I pass?"

"Oh, honey. You're Ninety-Eight. Of course you'll pass."

Great. So there's that.

No pressure.

"Your name will appear on the screen when it's your turn," Donna said, gesturing to a prompter overhead.

I glanced around. The other angels waiting to be tested consisted of adults, teens, even a few kids. Heaven didn't have a traditional age limit for things because people didn't age here. If you'd died below the Earth-required age for a license, you could apply for a learner's permit after a certain period and take classes at the Heaven Driving School.

"Your test car will pull up just outside the main doors and then you'll proceed on a course designed to evaluate whatever driving environments your type of license will cover," Donna continued. "Let me know if you have any questions. And help yourself to the licorice whips on the table there."

"What flavor?" asked an angel with an afro.

"Confidence!" Donna replied with a dazzling grin. "The recommended flavor before any basic skills test in Heaven. Good luck, everyone! I'll be over there at the front. Feel free to use any of your relaxation or calming apps while you wait if that will put you in a better mindset."

Donna trotted away and sat down at her desk as her rotary phone started ringing. She smiled and picked up the phone. "Thank you for calling the DMVD. How can I make your day more pleasant?"

Yup. Nothing like the DMV on Earth.

The name "Damian Crane" flashed on the prompter and a man in a suit and tie leapt up from his massage chair and exited through the main doors.

I sipped my blackberry-flavored iced tea as I reviewed two different books in my lap. Balanced on my left thigh was *Heaven Driver's Manual,* and on my right thigh rested the *California Driver's Handbook.* Akari had been giving me regular lessons for weeks and I felt pretty confident . . .

My gaze fell to the container of licorice.

But an extra helping doesn't hurt.

I grabbed a piece of candy and chewed as I reviewed the basics of four-way stop signs. I wasn't sure how long I'd have to wait to take my test. According to Donna, I was number eleven on the list. If I was in an Earth DMV, that meant I could wait up to three hours. Just as I calculated the math of my theoretical wait time, the second person's name came up on screen.

Hm. That was fast.

An eight-year-old in a pink frilly dress jumped from her massage chair and went to take her turn.

By the time the ninth person was called, I'd eaten four licorice whips and my jaw was starting to hurt. They did their magical work; I did feel confident in my driving. But they hadn't removed my fear of failing. A lot was riding on this. Both literally and figuratively, considering that if I was going to prevent Henry from getting his license, I had to be able to give him rides.

I set down my tea, raised my Soul Pulse, and started scanning through relaxation apps on Wonder. I paused on Kitten in a Laundry Basket. The icon was a picture of a smiling cat poking its head out of a pile of laundry.

What was this? An app that produced a basket of warm kittens? I was normally a dog person, but with a shrug I clicked to download. My Soul Pulse dinged with success a moment later, and I activated the app. My watch glowed then—

An enormous pile of clean laundry fell from the sky, burying me. Every garment was the perfect toasty temperature. It would have been wonderful had I not been in public, and the load not rained down on me so abruptly. I dug my way up through warm sweaters, shirts, pillowcases, and towels, until I poked my head out of the cozy enclosure, a crisp white sock on top of my head.

The other waiting angels at the DMVD didn't pay me any mind, but Donna quickly came over.

"Apologies, ma'am. I didn't mean to cause a disturbance. New app."

"What? Oh, honey, it's fine. Kitten in a Laundry Basket is one of my favorite soothing apps. I love sitting in a private mountain of clean, warm laundry when I have my Fine Wine Friday movie nights. I just came to get you because it's your turn." She pointed at my name glowing in neon on the prompter.

"Permission to tidy up?" Donna asked, gesturing at the pile swamping me.

I nodded and her Soul Pulse flashed, causing the laundry to disappear. I picked up my books and swung on my backpack. Donna walked me to the doors.

"Next time you use that app, I would recommend that you try the 'gently surround' option. It makes the pile appear around you instead of directly on top of you."

"Good tip. Thank you."

"Best of luck, honey. Not that you need it." Donna gave me a pleasant wave and returned to her desk as I made my way outside. The blue convertible I'd been practicing in was parked out front. I was pleased we got to pick the car we took our test in.

"Hello, Ninety-Eight." A man with darker skin and a tweed jacket came around the side of the car and shook my hand.

"Grace Cardiff, sir."

"As you wish. My name is Simon and I will be your driving exam proctor." He glanced at the clipboard in his hand. "Now, I see your mentor Akari Brown has registered you for three different license categories today—Celestial, Traditional United States Vehicles, and Unusual Circumstances."

I tilted my head. "She didn't mention the last one to me."

"Oh, it's standard procedure for every GA taking a driver's

exam to pass this kind of test. It focuses on improvisation and instinct, assuring us that you can take care of your assignment in a vehicular emergency. Your mentor probably just didn't want you to worry. After all, there's no need to. If you have general driving skills and good Guardian Angel instincts—which, of course you do—then you'll be fine."

"Of course," I said with a sigh.

I settled into the front seat of the car. Simon got in beside me. Once we'd buckled up, he pivoted to address me. "Now, before you get started—"

"I know, sir. Check my rearview mirrors, adjust my side view mirrors, and disengage the emergency break."

"No."

"No?"

"Before you get started, it's time for positive affirmations." He put his hand on my shoulder and looked me in the eyes reassuringly—speaking in a slow, calm voice. "You can do this. You are a great driver. You're ready for this. *I believe in you.*"

I blinked—stunned—as he removed his hand and faced forward in his seat.

"Now you can go ahead with normal procedure, Miss Cardiff. When you're ready, pull forward off this cloud and consider the glowing rainbow ahead as your first street."

"Yes, sir." I nodded.

I put the car in drive and went for it. The convertible eased off the cloud and we glided along a rainbow track that twisted and turned through the sky. It felt like I was in some sort of magical racecar game from an '80s video arcade.

I turned left and right—the different colors of the rainbow acting as lanes. At some points my driving proctor had me use the up and down flying options of the car. I parked on various clouds, used turn signals, drove through AGS portals, and so on.

Eventually Simon removed a gadget from his pocket and attached it to the dashboard. "Miss Cardiff," he said as he checked another box on his clipboard. "Congratulations, you have passed the Celestial portion of your driving test." He tapped the gadget on the dash. "We're going to be using this sub-dimension creator going forward to enter pocket dimensions of Heaven that simulate conditions for the two other classes of license you are applying for. Are you ready?"

My fingers tightened slightly on the wheel then I nodded. My proctor pressed a button on the gadget and it lit up. Then the whole car lit up. With a flash we were transported to a highway, ocean on my right. I was on the streets of Southern California. I easily recognized the combination of sun and palm trees.

The test proceeded normally enough. After twenty minutes, Simon gave me my second helping of good news. "Okay, that completes your Traditional United States Vehicles test. Congratulations. Are you ready for your final class of certification? Once I hit the situations modifier on this gadget, it will begin a random series of evasive GA scenarios. I don't control them. You have to be brave and power through. Use your best judgment and reflexes. Understand?"

"Um . . . yes, sir," I said. My hands tightened further.

Simon twisted the gadget on the dash and hit its main button again. The car lit up with another flash, but when the light faded, we were still on the streets of Southern California.

"I don't understand," I said, stealing a quick glance at my proctor. "Weren't we supposed to—*YIPES!*"

I jerked the wheel and pumped the brake, narrowly avoiding being plowed by a truck that had run a red light at an intersection. Our car spun to a stop. As it did, my mind filled with flashbacks from the day I died, causing my heart to pound. It took me a solid moment to catch my breath. When I did, along with air, I was filled with anger.

"What the heck, Simon?!" I said.

"Keep driving, Miss Cardiff. We're in the middle of an intersection."

"But—"

"Demons can orchestrate all kinds of different dangers for you and your human assignment. Normal danger also threatens you and your charge every day on the road because bad drivers and people who make bad choices are everywhere. You need to be able to handle all kinds of scenarios. Now drive."

Though my nerves were still shot, I gulped and merged back into traffic. Two seconds later, a sudden flash overtook the car again. The sunny, busy street was ripped away and I found myself driving through a dark alley. Then . . . then I heard gunfire! A vehicle with tinted windows abruptly turned into the alley a ways back and began driving in my pursuit. I looked to Simon, but his eyes were on his clipboard.

Okay, fine! I've seen action movies.

I punched the gas and flew at top speeds as the other car gave chase. Eventually I shot out of the alley and made a hard right, only instead of speeding on, I put the car in reverse, timed it, and then hit the gas again. My car flew backward and brutally rammed into the pursuing car the moment it ejected from the alley. Simon and I slammed back in our seats. The enemy vehicle was utterly smashed. I quickly changed the gearshift back to drive and sped forward to escape.

Geez, I didn't know I had that in me.

My mother would never speak to me again if she saw that level of violent aggression.

Was it wrong that I enjoyed that a little?

FLASH.

Our car was on the freeway now. One vehicle after another cut me off, but with an agile hand and a light foot, I avoided every potential accident.

FLASH.

This time I was driving downhill when a cute dog ran across the road. I swerved. The car spun. I hit the brake and barely kept our car from colliding with a wall to my right.

FLASH.

I was on another freeway, going over a grand bridge constructed of mint-green iron hundreds of feet over the sea. Also . . . Simon was gone.

"Simon?" I called.

"Grace, look out!" I glanced over my shoulder and saw Henry in the back seat. I also spotted dark, mangled shapes rampaging toward us from the side of the bridge we were driving away from.

Were those Dark Breeds?

Cars honked and panicked drivers floored it, trying to escape the inbound nightmares. I snapped my eyes forward in time to avoid a collision, and changed lanes again and again, picking up speed.

I kept my eyes on the road but caught glimpses of the creatures in my rear and side view mirrors—a gorilla with bat wings and a human face, a rhinoceros with eight legs and a horn the length of a didgeridoo, and a shockingly large demon porcupine. They were gaining on us.

Suddenly a scream pierced the air. I glanced right. Just behind our car, Razel was riding with Justin in his jeep.

In my mirror I caught sight of a menacing shadow. The gorilla Dark Breed was only yards from both our cars. I jerked the steering wheel to the left and avoided its taloned paw. However, the gorilla's massive bat wing caught Justin's jeep and caused it to flip over. The car tumbled until it rammed into the edge of the iron bridge. There it lay on its side, liquid spilling from a severed gas line.

"Razel! Justin!" Henry shouted.

The end of the bridge was in view, the road clear. I could punch the gas and speed away from the monsters. Instead, in immediate instinct I put the car in reverse and rammed into the gorilla monster the way I had that car in the alley. The back of my ride hit the top-heavy gorilla's legs with incredible force, sending it flying forward and flipping over the car.

I swerved around the collapsed creature. In my mirrors I saw the other Dark Breeds getting closer—leaping around terrified cars. I also saw that Razel and Justin hadn't escaped their wreck.

"We have to go back for them!" Henry insisted, grabbing my shoulder.

"I know, I know!"

Even as the gorilla monster started to get up, and though the other two Dark Breeds would be on us soon, I spun the wheel and started to drive in the direction we'd come. I bobbed and weaved around cars. My heart pounded faster, faster, faster—

FLASH.

Simon and I were back on the cloud in front of the DMVD.

I blinked, adjusting to the change. My knuckles were white from clenching the wheel. It took some effort to pry my fingers off. Like removing a cat clutching a tree after it'd been spooked by a Rottweiler.

I took a deep breath and glanced at Simon. "So did I pass?"

He sighed and looked at his clipboard. "As I said, you passed the Celestial and United States driving exams. But speaking candidly, Miss Cardiff . . . I am not sure I can pass you on that last section. Which puts me in a difficult position because something we are not supposed to mention at the start of your exam— *again, to not worry you*—is that if GAs don't pass the Unusual Circumstances portion, we aren't supposed to give them any kind of Earth license because they aren't capable of taking care of their assignments on the road."

I felt crushed. My shoulders slumped. "I don't understand. What did I do wrong? Should I have used my signal to change lanes when I was escaping *monsters*?"

"No, Grace. It's nothing technical like that. The only scenario you failed for this test was the last one. At the last moment. You went back for your friends."

I tilted my head. "Of course I did. They're my *friends*."

"But your job isn't to protect your friends," Simon countered. "Your job is to protect Henry Sun. By going back for the others, you put him in significant danger. The correct move would've been to make a getaway while you had the chance."

I unbuckled my seatbelt and twisted to face Simon more directly. "But that's so . . . wrong."

Simon sighed. "I think it's best if we get your mentor up here. Wait in the car for a moment." He exited the convertible and wandered far enough away that I couldn't hear what he was saying, but I saw Akari's hologram appear from his watch in my side mirror. After they talked for a minute, my mentor magically teleported to the cloud in person.

I got out of the car and leaned against the trunk with my arms crossed. Simon removed a sheet from his clipboard and handed it to Akari before returning inside the DMVD office.

Akari walked over to me.

"*So?*" I said.

"We came to an agreement. Since you did so well on the other two portions of your exam, and because he trusts that your Ninety-Eight status means you generally know what you're doing, Simon has agreed to pass you . . . Assuming you confirm that you understand what he was trying to tell you."

"But I *don't* understand," I replied. "I'm a Guardian Angel. I couldn't leave Justin and Razel. Like I told Simon, that's wrong."

"Grace, you know the first rule for a Guardian Angel: the assignment comes first. Henry is your one and only priority on Earth. I know that will be difficult to remember at times, and your service in this department may bring you face to face with incredibly hard choices, but trust me—nothing good comes from gambling with life and fate . . ." She paused a moment, clearing her throat with a slight shake of her head.

Akari released a deep breath. "That's what you did when you went back for your friends in that simulation. Henry could have easily been killed along with you and both those kids if that were a real situation. You may have lost him, and humanity would have lost his amazing potential. Then *you* would have to live with that."

Though the lecture had the tone of a scolding, my mentor's eyes carried desperation. It didn't feel like she was telling me what to do so much as warning me what *not* to do.

"It still *feels* wrong though," I ventured.

Akari sighed. "I know. Believe me, I do. But rules exist for a reason, Grace. God and all the Guardian Angels who have more experience than us made those rules so we would have the most success and create the greatest good. No matter what happens, your assignment needs to come first, always. I need you to promise me that you'll engrain that principle into your head and heart as firmly as it's engraved in the ceiling of our training center. Do that, and you can have your license."

She held up my driving evaluation. It had the word *Approved* scribbled on the top in red ink. All I had to do was agree and the pass was mine. All I had to do was go along with the prescribed way of thinking and we could proceed without turbulence.

It was tempting.

I knew from experience that challenging authority never went well. If you followed the rules, went with the flow, and adhered to proper procedure, it was generally smooth sailing. It was easier to get things done and advance in life when people found you agreeable. If you got in people's faces, ruffled feathers, and defied convention to follow your truth, then well . . . you ended up in the principal's office, or the guidance counselor's office, or worse.

For years now I'd marveled how pop culture and the media made it *seem* like thinking differently and fighting for your beliefs was something to be encouraged on all fronts. But I'd gotten in enough trouble to know that in real life, society applauded the idea of boldness but was annoyed when someone executed it. And that was because—to borrow Henry's term—outliers were disruptive.

Sigh.

When I was younger I had hope for a more understanding world. On Earth when I wasn't reading books for school, I was geeking out over awesome fiction literature and cinema. The play-by-their-own-rules protagonists were always so dynamic and inspiring. It broke my heart long ago when I realized that these aggressive heroes were not realistic role models. If you did any of that insubordinate stuff in real life, you got in crazy amounts of trouble.

No one liked a rebel. Even if she did have a cause.

And yet . . . as I weighed all this and considered simply nodding my head to Akari to make things easy, my heart tensed. I knew my defiance was never well received. I knew that acting outside of conventional parameters was courting trouble. And I *definitely* knew that paying heed to that fiery voice in my soul only drove me off course from a comfortable, agreeable existence. But in this moment, like in so many unruly moments in life, I couldn't stomach the passive reaction. Awareness of the inevitable backlash had never been able to fully warp the core of my character. For that reason, sometimes I had to make things difficult.

It seemed the wings of my inherent character that my mother, many others, and even I had tried to clip kept growing back.

I pushed my hair behind my ears and held my mentor's gaze.

"I'm not going to dodge the honesty filter with clever wording or questions here, Akari. I hear you. I respect what you're saying. And I understand that rules are important and listening to superiors who know better is important. You're right; God knows what he or she is doing and it's not my place to question the principles he or she sets. But I just . . ." I swallowed and held firm. "The truth is that I don't know if I can do what you're asking. It doesn't feel right, even if you're telling me it is."

Akari studied me—a small, frustrated frown curving her mouth. After a moment, she released a calming exhale and addressed me with partially strained patience. "Given what I know about your past, Grace, I can understand why you feel that way. It's *dangerous* for you to feel that way, and the sooner you can come to terms with what I'm telling you the better. But for the sake of your GA role, how about instead of me continuing to try and force you to adjust your way of thinking now, you meet me halfway?"

"How so?"

"You love reading and research. Instead of an ultimatum, I'm giving you homework. Visit the Greater Good section of the library one of these days. Learn for yourself why assignments must come first and about the angels who've sacrificed to ensure that they do. Promise me you'll do that, and that you'll *try* to understand and embrace this rule, and I'll let you get out of here with what you came for."

I nodded. "*That* I can do."

"Fine then." She extended her hand to give me the document. I reached out, but at the last second Akari pulled it back.

"In all seriousness, Grace, this is our most important principal. I'm trying not to push you right now, but if you go against this rule in real life versus in a simulated test, we'll have a problem."

I pointed a finger between the two of us. "You and I?"

"No. Us and the divine being who created us. This isn't my rule, Grace. It's God's. I trust you understand that carries a lot of weight. Some things, and some superiors, are beyond questioning."

I reluctantly nodded again.

Akari finally handed me the approved form. "Now go inside and take your driver's license photo," she said. "They have a dozen different filters and six different photographers to choose from. You have an hour to settle on a photo you like. How's that for service?"

Sitting on my living room couch, I looked over the gleaming new driver's license in my hand. It was made of magical reflective material. In a certain light, I could see Heavenly information—my GA status, the DMVD winged car logo, and the year of my death. When I slanted the card, I saw what humans on Earth would—a normal California driver's license with possibly the cutest photo ever taken thanks to the highly professional angel photographers. Not even *Vogue* had their patience and artistry. I looked like a movie star, unlike in most pictures I'd taken on Earth.

My eyes drifted up to the framed photo of me and my family on the wall. I wished I could show my license to them. My dad and sister had been taking turns teaching me to drive since I got my permit last fall. They would be so proud.

My throat tightened and I turned my attention to the TV to avoid the painful longing.

Memory Prime had been streaming in the background— playing on shuffle mode through different scenes that apparently all contributed to why I'd ended up as a Guardian Angel. The clips I'd watched over the last few weeks had not shed the light I'd hoped for. In fact, seeing these somewhat emotionally traumatic memories had only brought me more unrest as my hunger for understanding increased by the day.

Coming to terms with why I was a GA was no longer just a personal journey. I had enemies now, formidable ones. And accidental demonstrations of power weren't going to hold them off forever. I needed to crack my code—figure out what God and Akari saw in me, and solve Ana's riddle of why my heart was invested in this job. If I accomplished both, perhaps I could finally remove the mental block around my powers and stand a chance against the demons who wished Henry and me harm.

A girl could hope anyway.

Suddenly a knock came at the front door of my cottage.

Droopy leapt up and scurried for the door with a long howl. "*AAWWWHOO!*"

I pocketed my license and followed him. When I opened the door, I found Leo standing there, the night a wondrous background behind him.

"Evening, *bubbeleh*." He tipped an imaginary hat.

"Hi, Leo. What are you doing here?"

"I had a late-night training session with Ana and it kicked my butt. I thought I could come to you for moral support."

I put a hand on my hip. "Because I'm so familiar with what that feels like?"

He grinned. "Exactly."

Droopy scampered past me onto the lawn, intrigued by the fireflies frolicking in the night air. "Go on in, Leo. I'll be right there."

I let Droopy enjoy the fireflies a little longer before I scooped him up and carried him inside, kicking the door shut behind me.

"Would you like a hot chocolate or a tea or—"

My heart froze when I saw Leo in my living room, watching Memory Prime. I'd forgotten to pause it! I recognized thirteen-year-old me onscreen. The setting was my middle school. Young me sat at a lunch table with a couple of friends. Beside her on the bench was a sparkly two-foot baton, glittery tassels on each end.

I hastened for the couch to grab the remote, but Leo snatched it first and held it out of my reach.

"Leo, turn it off!" I bobbed around, trying to take the control from him, flashing back to my sister and I bickering over our own TV remote. The stakes were way higher here though. I couldn't let Leo see this part of my past. *What would he think of me?*

"No way, Grace," he said, continuing to evade my grasps by passing the remote from one hand to the other. "This is gripping stuff."

"*Move away from the cool table.*"

Both Leo and I darted our attention to the screen where

half a dozen thirteen-year-old boys had gathered ten feet from the table. Young me grabbed her baton and stood to face them, addressing the boy who'd challenged her. She jutted her chin up.

"No way. This is the cleanest, shadiest table on the lawn. You and your friends kicked me and my friends out yesterday, and we ended up having to eat in the *literal* bushes by the dumpster. Not today. We were here first. *You* find another table."

"Don't make us move you," said a boy with dusty-blond hair at the head of the pack.

Young me wielded the baton in front of her body, pointing it at the lead boy's chest. "Go ahead and try."

He took a step toward her, but then young me did some sort of crazy spinning twirl move with her baton, passing it between both hands like a girl who'd watched too much *Avatar: The Last Airbender*.

The lead boy and his friends took several steps back—weirded out and a little afraid—then someone blew a whistle off screen.

I finally snatched the remote from Leo and paused the video.

"What?! Grace, no," he protested. "I want to see what happens next. That was amazing and hilarious. You were about to go all *Avatar: The Last Airbender* on those guys."

I raised an eyebrow. Leo and I always seemed to be on the same page with our pop culture references.

"Sorry to disappoint your love of fantasy action, Leo, but I actually wasn't. I don't know how to fight with a staff. That's absurd. I'm not Avatar Aang or Crisanta Knight or even that buff guy from *Pacific Rim*. That baton was plastic, hollow, and filled with glitter. I bought it at a party supply store and I only brought it to school that day in case I needed to scare those boys off. What you just saw was as good as that clip was going to get because that whistle you heard was a school security guard ending the exchange. Following my bold stunt, I was sent to the principal's office, suspended for a week for aggressive force and bringing a 'weapon' to school, and grounded by my mother for a month."

I swallowed the large lump in my throat. I wasn't sure I'd meant to tell Leo all of that.

With a sigh, I plopped on the couch and abandoned the re-mote, staring at the screen and the frozen look of fear, shame, and conflict on my young face.

"But that's not fair," Leo said carefully, sitting down next to me.

"Of course it's fair," I told him. "I was aggressive and that's wrong. Even if I wasn't actually going to hurt those boys, or even touch them, that was still a stupid move. I just got so worked up. Those kids bullied me and my friends. I had told the teachers and security guards about it the day before, but they didn't do anything. So I took matters into my own hands. I shouldn't have done that. We're not *supposed* to do that. I don't know what I was thinking."

"Well, I do," Leo said. "You have *chutzpah*, Grace. You were defending yourself and your friends. That's an honorable thing to do."

I shook my head. "I didn't do it the right way, though. Clearly. Those boys barely got a talking to whereas I got julienned into pieces—punished like some problem child."

"The *right way*." Leo gave a haughty wave. "That term is a pain in the *kishkes*. Take it from a fellow nerd, Grace. The *right way* isn't a hard fact, like a date from history or a physics formula. It's changeable and differs based on the eye of the beholder. It's actually like the term *chutzpah* when you think about it. That word means nerve or gall or audacity, but those three things can mean very different things depending on who you're asking and what you're doing with them." He harrumphed. "That's why the criteria that should measure what's right isn't the way we accomplish it, but what we accomplish."

Leo spotted my US History textbook on the end table beside me. He stood and strode over to pick it up. "Perfect example. Technically, the guys who founded the US were all traitors, weren't they? I mean, that's what they were doing when they declared independence a couple hundred years ago—committing treason against England. Back then, the Brits probably thought the founding fathers were the bad guys, but the founding fathers were just trying to build a better world for their people and had to get aggressive and bold to do it."

I leaned back on the couch with a huff. "You know, 'aggressive' and 'bold' are two of my mother's least favorite words. And although your historic analogy is accurate, and the founding fathers did have a lot of *chutzpah*, I don't see her coming around to a different way of thinking, Leo. Most people aren't capable of that." I gestured at the TV. "Most people see that as inappropriate aggression that needs to be driven out of a person. And as a result, they see people like that—people like me—as bad stock, a problem child, a person who is . . . no angel."

Leo swayed on his feet anxiously. He touched the bridge of his nose and put the book down. "Is that why you were watching Memory Prime? To figure out why you got picked as a GA?"

I looked at him seriously for an extended moment. Then I chose to answer honestly for me, not because the universe was forcing me to. I nodded. "Now you know my shameful secret. The great Ninety-Eight has no idea why she's a Guardian Angel and doesn't think she deserves to be one."

I sighed deeply. "God, it feels good to say that out loud. It's embarrassing, but I feel like I've been hiding in plain sight around you and Monkonjae. You two are so good at being good. Every time I wear my halo, I feel like a piece of me is dying inside because I still can't make peace with how *that*," I gestured at young me onscreen, "earned all *this*." I magically summoned my halo, grabbed it, and held it up to make my point. Then in a pang of frustration and angst, I flung it across the room. It lodged in the fireplace like a ninja throwing star.

"You know . . ." Leo ventured, coming over to sit beside me again. "This may come as a shock to you, but we're in the same boat."

I sat up a bit straighter. "Pardon?"

"I don't think I deserve to be a Guardian Angel either. I definitely don't understand how I earned my 94% rating. I didn't do anything grand or great with my life like our human assignments are supposed to. I barely did anything at all. I got cancer when I was six and spent a huge chunk of my life in hospitals. So it seems kind of unfair and ridiculous that I get to spend eternity in paradise doing an epically important job for God when the most action and acts of heroism I experienced on Earth were those I watched on TV. At least you did *something* with your time on Earth."

Sympathy *and* empathy welled up inside of me. I couldn't relate to the suffering Leo had experienced on Earth, but I understood what he was going through here and now.

I took his hand. "Leo, I didn't realize the extent of your illness. You never said anything."

"I don't like to be a *kvetch*."

"I don't know what that means. But I am really sorry, Leo."

He nodded, exhaled, and now it was his turn to lean back on the couch. "Anyway, I've also been watching snippets of my Memory Prime when I get up the courage, hoping to feel better about why I belong here too. So don't be embarrassed." He glanced at the TV and alluded to young me. "And don't be so hard on her either."

I huffed. "Want to tell my mother that for me?"

"I think that's part of your journey, Grace."

"Then mine is a journey fraught with peril and probably an unhappy ending. My mother's perspective is annoyingly, impossibly different from mine. She'll never come around to my way of thinking. At this point it may be a waste of time to keep hoping and trying to get her to."

Leo shrugged. "People have different perspectives. That's not a bad thing; it's actually a wonderful thing. Frankly, it's a miracle that billions of beings from the same species can all see stuff uniquely. Heaven clearly celebrates that. It's why this place appears differently to people. And it's why God and our mentors can see potential in us that we don't see in ourselves. I'm sticking with my advice to not be so hard on yourself, Grace, but maybe you shouldn't be so hard on your mom either. Maybe if you want her to see you in a different light, you should try exploring the one *she* lives in. Seek to understand before you seek to be understood."

I looked at him.

"That's what my *bubbe* used to say," he explained. "I don't know the whole backstory between you and Mama Cardiff, but maybe she grew up learning a different definition of what's right and that's why she doesn't get yours. It doesn't mean either of you are wrong; you just don't understand each other. Maybe if you did, she wouldn't work so hard to change you and you wouldn't be so damaged and bitter about her trying to. Since you're supposed to be the angel here, I would try bridging that gap by making the first move. Try and understand *her* first."

I mulled over the thought then looked over at my friend. "You say some fun Yiddish words sometimes, Leo. Is there a term for having a lot of wisdom and insight? Because that's what you've got."

"You could say I have a lot of *sechel*." He shrugged. "And you're half Hispanic, right? What's a Spanish word for fighter?"

"Um, I guess you could say *luchadora*. Why?"

"Because that's what both of you are." He pointed at the live version of me on the couch and the past version of me onscreen. "And my *amigo*."

"*Amiga*," I corrected. "Feminine ending for that word since I'm a girl."

"Okay, calm yourself, professor."

He grinned at me and I grinned back. Then Leo picked up the remote. "So, seeing you act like a boss with a glitter baton has me hankering for an action movie. I already rewatched all of *The Last Airbender* recently. Have the Crisanta Knight books been made into movies yet?"

"No," I responded. "But hopefully soon."

"Then *Pacific Rim* it is," he announced. He looked at me. "Unless you have pre-existing plans for your Friday night?"

My Soul Pulse flashed and a bowl of buttery popcorn appeared in my lap. I smiled at him. "There's no place I'd rather be."

BEACH DAY

A loud buzzing on my wrist woke me up. It was a call on my Soul Pulse.

I groaned. Leo and I had stayed up way too late. After we watched *Pacific Rim*, we'd continued our Charlie Hunnam marathon with his King Arthur movie and that remake of *Papillon*. I didn't think audiences were kind enough to those films; they were awesome, he was hot, and I enjoyed them. I certainly *did not* enjoy waking up at such an ungodly hour on a Saturday after binge watching all three.

"*Hello . . .*" I grumbled, answering the call.

"Get dressed, Grace," Akari said. "You're going on a beach day."

"Wait, what?"

"I'll be at your door in five minutes. Hurry up."

I rubbed my eyes and sat up in bed. Droopy had not moved; he was deep in a Saturday morning coma like I should've been. Lucky dog.

With another groan, I rose from bed. I remembered seeing an app on my Soul Pulse called Adventure Ready. I downloaded it and watched as options for all sorts of exciting outings began to load. A holographic list shimmered above my watch face, categorized by climate. Under warm and sunny, I clicked on the icon for "Day at the Beach."

FLASH.

I was now ready for a seashore outing. I wore a bright yellow one-piece bathing suit under a pair of raggedy jean shorts. My toes poked through sandals. A floppy sunhat rested on my head.

In my left hand, I held a wicker beach bag stuffed with all sorts of goodies—chips, water bottle, beach blanket, and so forth.

I heard a knock in the distance. I left my bedroom and went to open my cottage front door.

"Good morning, Akari," I said to my mentor, standing on my welcome mat. I held up the supplies in my hand. "Are we having some sort of mentor-mentee seaside escapade?"

"No. You're going back to Earth."

My brow furrowed. "Really? You've only had me keep an eye on Henry on weekdays."

"That's because Solange always returned to Hell on the weekends. Until now. We may not be able to know what she's up to once she's on Earth, but our Counterthreat team monitors when demons return to the mortal realm. And she went back this morning."

"Doesn't the third demon rule say Solange can't be in the same room with Henry unless I'm also present?"

"Your demon loves loopholes. Henry technically isn't in any kind of room right now. He and his friends have surf team practice. I assume Solange is headed to the beach to see what kind of mischief she can cause. Hence your needed presence."

I yawned. "Alrighty, I'm on it." I glanced toward my bedroom. "Do me a favor? Stick around until Droopy wakes up and give him breakfast and a walk? I don't want to wake him yet. He had a late night."

I yawned again.

"Seems like you both did," Akari said. "But yes. I'll wait around for your dog. Also, before you go, I have a gift." She waved her arm grandly and stepped aside. Parked on the curb was the blue convertible we'd been using for my driving lessons. It looked especially shiny today. Did Heaven have a car wash? Did it even need one?

Akari held up a set of car keys on a sparkly key chain shaped like a pair of angel wings. She tossed them to me. "It's all yours."

My eyes widened. "Seriously?"

"Yup. You've heard of an all-terrain vehicle? This is an all-dimension vehicle; only GAs can apply to have one. Press the green button on your keys and the car will appear or disappear, whether you're on Earth or in the afterlife. It will change shape to best accommodate whatever dimension you're in too."

I walked around the vehicle in a daze, then stopped at the custom license plate.

NINETY8

I looked up at Akari with a crooked eyebrow. "*Really?*"

She shrugged. "I couldn't help it."

"As if that number doesn't already follow me around." I reined in my vague annoyance and focused on gratitude for the gift. "Thank you, Akari. This is great. In fact, I think I'll drive to the Pearlie Gates this morning instead of teleporting to test it out."

I tossed my beach bag in the back and buckled up, adjusting the mirrors.

"Remember, eyes on the clouds and be careful," my mentor nagged.

"Yes, yes. I've got it." I turned on the engine, put it in drive, and activated the flight function.

"And, Grace, *no speeding.*"

I glanced at her. "Call a cop." I punched the gas and took off into the sky, leaving a trail of rainbow-colored exhaust behind me.

"Where's the sun?" I asked, squishing across the sand to join a surprised Razel.

For the first time since being transplanted to this land of palm trees, Pilates studios, and gluten-free restaurants, I didn't see the bright cosmic bauble that always lit the skies and scared away the clouds. Today was actually gray and hazy. It made me feel like I was in a cinematic flashback for a dramatic movie.

My friend lowered the gossip magazine she was reading. She had quite a nice set up with her plastic chair, striped beach blanket, and a cooler full of sodas.

"Hey!" she called, perking up. "What are you doing here?"

"You and Henry talk about the beach all the time. I've been a California girl for a month and a half and the fact that I haven't been to the beach is probably some sort of crime in this county." I laid my own blanket beside hers, then glanced around. I spotted Henry with several others in the water. The ocean was much darker than normal and seemed to churn with anger. The waves weren't huge, but they were rough.

"I'm sorry your introduction to beach life has to be on a day like this," Razel said. "We don't get rain or storms often, but when we do, we barely get any warning. Henry still has surf team practice though, so here we are, enduring the surprise winter weather." She shivered as a slight wind blew, slipping on a hoodie that'd been hanging over the back of her chair.

"No need to exaggerate," I said with a laugh.

She blinked at me. "Sorry?"

"Oh, you're not joking? Razel, it's sixty-eight degrees."

"Right. California winter." She nodded seriously, her teeth almost chattering.

I smothered another laugh with a cough and sat down, gazing at the sea. Henry caught a wave and glided on its curve. When he finished the ride, he glanced in our direction and waved when he saw me. A second later, he waved again. I pivoted and found Solange traipsing across the sand. She wore neon red shorts and a skimpy black bikini top. Her eyes were covered by those huge bejeweled sunglasses she always had with her.

Razel saw her and groaned when my enemy reached us.

Solange put a hand on her hip. "Well *bonjour* to you too."

"Sorry," Razel said. "It's just you both have terrible timing. I don't want you telling your buddies back in Paris or South Carolina that California is not all that. I swear we usually have better weather than this at the beach."

Solange pushed her glasses up on her head and smiled, setting down her sequined beach bag. "No worries. I actually like storms. There's beauty in their kind of chaos, don't you think?"

I took a fresh gander at the cloudy sky and agitated waves. Thunder rumbled in the distance. "Ohhh, so that's why you chose today."

Both girls looked at me, Solange slightly amused and Razel confused. I glanced at my watch, trying to change the subject.

"Razel . . ." I cleared my throat. "How long does Henry have practice for?"

"Another hour. This storm isn't supposed to get bad until the afternoon. We'll be home drinking hot chocolate by then."

"It's only sixty-eight degrees," Solange commented in surprise.

"That's what I said!" I replied with accidental enthusiasm. So weird that a demon and I were on the same page about something.

Solange glanced at me before settling on her own blanket. Razel offered her a spare magazine and the girl accepted, lowering her sunglasses and flipping through it.

Razel also handed me some reading material. I only pretended to peruse the articles inside. My eyes flicked between my nemesis and Henry out on the rough water.

It was a bit unnerving to just wait. Demons manipulated chaos that already existed. Unlike the hydrant and Six Flags incidents however, which required a lot of planning, I was fairly certain Solange was winging it here. I assumed my nemesis intended to magically manipulate the brewing storm in some way. I had seen those demons at the Hell Beacon controlling waves and fire, so I knew it was possible. What I didn't know was what she was waiting for.

Every now and then she looked up from her periodical and focused on the sea. Panic would rise in my chest and I'd get ready to intervene by either running to the water to get Henry out, or kicking sand in Solange's face to break her concentration. But other than a few moments when the waves Henry rode rose from six feet to maybe eight feet, nothing crazy happened. And that's when I realized something that genuinely made me happy.

Solange scowled in frustration and tossed her magazine aside. Razel raised an eyebrow. "You okay, girl?"

"Yeah, you okay?" I didn't do a good job of concealing my smile. For the first time since meeting Solange, she didn't seem confident or in control. Considering the air of superiority she regularly tried to suffocate me with, this tasted sweeter than the lushest cupcake in Heaven.

"I've just developed a cramp from sitting here so long,"

Solange lied. She turned to Razel kindly. "I had hoped to do more at the beach than fail to get some sun." She tilted her head up at the sky. The clouds had grown thicker since I'd last checked.

"You know what, that's fair," Razel said. "I have an idea. Are you sure you're not cold?"

"I run hot," Solange replied.

"That's what she said," Razel joked, standing up. "Okay. BRB."

When our friend had traipsed out of earshot, I pretended to casually look at my magazine while maintaining a very amused smirk on my face. As I'd hoped, it perturbed my nemesis.

"What's with the stupid grin, Grace?"

"You can't do it, can you?" I said, smile persisting while I turned the page. "You were hoping to cause some sort of chaos by manipulating the storm. That's why you came to Earth today. Because of the weather."

She harrumphed. "Congratulations. You figured me out. What do you want, a medal?"

"Nope. This"—I finally pivoted and gestured up and down at her person—"is all I need. You've been harassing me for weeks about how you don't think I'm powerful. I didn't realize it was a diversion tactic. You're not that strong yourself, are you?"

She pushed her sunglasses up on her head and locked eyes with me. "You *know* that's not true. Let's not forget I've already killed you and come incredibly close to taking out our assignment. And all within my first two months on Earth."

"Yet you can't make any real waves," I taunted. "Don't tell me you're at the bottom of your demon class? I noticed that Troy turned to Oliver first when you all roughed me up in that elevator."

Solange's face soured. "We all have some things we take to better than others. Oliver is excellent at mirages, but Mr. *So Not Perfect* can't phase through things to save his afterlife. Troy didn't know that at the time. Otherwise, he definitely would have asked me to deal with you, not his precious protégé."

Wait. Was that why Oliver hesitated?

I thought it was because . . .

Well, I don't know what I thought.

"I may not be great at manipulating the elements," Solange continued, "but I'm learning, and in the meantime I have natural ability in . . . other areas."

"Picking out sparkly outfits?"

She was unaffected by the comment. Her confidence was returning. I could feel it like heat rising from a stovetop. "You know what, I'd rather wait to unveil it to you. It's as surprising as it is full of possibilities. Let's just say you're not the only new kid on the celestial block this world should watch out for."

My eyes narrowed.

"I promise to give you a challenge worthy of you soon." Solange glanced past my shoulder. Now *she* smiled. "Manipulating the elements is much easier the closer we are to what we're trying to affect."

"Okay, who's ready for a surf lesson?" Razel declared. I turned and discovered her carrying two surfboards, one tucked under each arm.

Solange winked at me. "Time to get in the thick of things."

"Have you ever done this before?" Razel asked as she set down the boards. She removed her hoodie and shorts, revealing a turquoise tankini.

"No, but I'm a quick study," Solange assured her *and me* with a side glance.

"So am I," I declared. I directed my gaze to Razel. "Mind teaching a lesson for two?"

"Uh, sure. Let me grab another board from the rental shack."

Razel scampered across the sand to the aquatic equipment hub. I returned my attention to Solange, trying to keep the essence of an upper hand as best I could. "I don't know what you hope to accomplish, but controlling strong and unpredictable open sea isn't like temporarily redirecting water from a fire hydrant. You've been in the field for less than two months; you're out of your depth. Also, have you forgotten how I blasted off your demon buddy's arm in that elevator? I'm warning you, Solange. Don't test me."

We both noticed Razel receiving another board from the rental counter and starting to head back to us. Solange began to unbutton her shorts. "I thought you liked tests, Grace. You certainly obsess over school enough."

I removed my jean shorts as well. "I like to be thorough in all things. Studying, taking notes, keeping my enemies in line."

We stood before each other in our bathing suits, hands on hips.

"Someone took the banana in Banana Boat Sunscreen too seriously," Solange snickered.

I crossed my arms, unintimidated by her and her itty-bitty bikini. I liked my bright yellow bathing suit; it was as if a sunflower was about to go swimming.

"Well, we can't all do our swimwear and underwear shopping simultaneously. I hope that top is good quality. One rough wave and you'll be exposing these innocent humans to more than just your malevolent agenda."

Razel returned. "Okay. We've got three surfboards, two brand new Californians, and a dream," she announced, sticking the third board upright in the sand. "Let's do this."

My friend put on a long-sleeve swim shirt then adjusted her gaze to the lifeguard stand a few dozen feet over. She raised her fingers and unleashed one of those piercing whistles that fans fired off at sporting events. The lifeguards glanced our way and Razel signaled at our beach bags and blankets. "Grady! Cora! Can you keep an eye on our stuff?"

"Sure, Razel!" the girl Cora replied. "Heads up though. With the storm brewing we're probably going to call everyone back to shore in the next fifteen or twenty minutes."

"Fine," Razel responded. "But you're telling the team." She waved at Henry and his surfer friends. "Prom season is in a couple months and I can't have a slew of my shirtless, muscular classmates thinking I'm a buzzkill. A girl needs a date." Razel pointed a finger at Grady. "This guy knows what I'm talking about."

The cute guy cracked a smile. Razel winked at him before helping Solange and I strap on the leashes from our surfboards. The tethers were the same length as the boards and wrapped around our ankles with Velcro. Fully fastened, we grabbed our boards and trotted into the water.

Okay, *that* was cold.

The iciness caused my entire body to tense. The sensation got worse the deeper we delved. I felt like crying out from it. Bunches of seaweed, disturbed by the developing storm collided with my legs underwater, tangling around them to almost cause me to trip a couple times. When we were up to our chests in water, Razel advised we just rip off the bandage. The three of us dunked ourselves fully under the waves.

COLD! COLD! COLD!

I burst back to the surface. After a moment, I adjusted to the temperature. Solange and I followed Razel's lead and climbed onto our boards and began paddling out to sea. There were no big waves inbound for the moment. Razel led us about a hundred feet from shore. Henry and his friends were a lot closer to us now, sitting on their boards and laughing while they waited for the next decent wave to come along.

A tumble of seaweed wrapped itself around my leg again. I carefully detangled it and gave a couple good kicks to shake it off. Suddenly we heard a distant rumble of thunder. It was only a prelude to the small crack of lightning that lit up a distant smudge of clouds. The sky was more frightening than the water for now. The storm was only teasing us; all bark and no bite.

I didn't know how much stronger Solange's power would be now that we were, quote, "in the thick of things." I hoped before she focused her powers enough for me to find out, the lifeguards would call us back to shore. With any luck, I could get through today without a demon incident and be back in Heaven by lunchtime. After soaking in this freezing water, I was more than ready to give Kitten in a Laundry Basket another try.

Razel proceeded with her surfing instruction—teaching me and Solange how to stand up, keep our balance, catch a wave, etcetera. On more than one occasion moderate waves came our way and we tested our skills. I actually wasn't terrible at it. In fact, I was amazing at it, which Razel seemed surprised by. I was surprised too. But then, maybe Leo was right; I was too hard on myself. Between dance and GA physical training, my balance, agility and strength were noticeably improving. I may not have been refining much in terms of magical powers, but I was getting a lot more athletic. I guess that was something.

Solange had a bit more difficulty with the surfing endeavor. That was a point in my favor. It was hard to concentrate on magically manipulating the elements when so much of your focus was being devoted to not falling off a board and face planting in the water.

Another grumble of thunder.

The waves were getting choppier.

Come on, lifeguards. Call us in.

Demons could only manipulate chaos. I figured for something to fall under the chaos umbrella it had to have elements of trouble, danger, or unruliness. Speaking of umbrella . . .

A raindrop hit my nose.

The storm was gaining, the waves increasing in size on their own. The latest eight-foot swell got the better of me and I tumbled off my board into the water. Something brushed my leg and I opened my eyes. It was lucky I did. The salt stung them, but I avoided a huge wad of knotted seaweed and kelp rushing toward me, caught in the wave too.

I looked down. Deep below, a thick kelp forest stretched up in long strands from an unseen ocean floor.

It was super creepy and reminded me of that Black Lake scene from *Harry Potter & the Goblet of Fire*. If I didn't already have my own kind of pretty monster on the surface to deal with, I would've worried about evil mermaids popping out and trying to drown me.

My board's leash yanked my leg sideways. With some effort, I righted myself and swam for the surface. When I burst through, I grabbed my board and took a few big breaths.

It was drizzling now, and the lightning no longer felt like foreboding possibility; it was coming. As were bigger waves in the distance . . .

The second I lifted my body onto my board, a whistle blew.

"TIME TO COME BACK IN!" one of the lifeguards called into a megaphone at the edge of the shore, hundreds of feet away now.

Geez, when did we drift so far out?

Henry and his team, a few dozen meters away, started to head in, as did Razel. Solange was farther out to sea than I was. She sat unmoving on her surfboard. Despite my board bobbing in protest against the rough surf, I paddled toward her.

My enemy's dark hair matted against her face and neck. Her eyes were trained on the rising water in the distance. They were big enough to be considered troublesome, dangerous, *and* unruly. I knew they were her last chance to use her powers for the day. She was going for it.

Lightning cracked, and when that flash lit up the water, I made it close enough to Solange to see the red energy in her eyes.

That's why she liked wearing those sunglasses all the time! When she used her powers, her eyes shone cherry red the same way my halo glowed gold.

I glanced over my shoulder at Henry and the others. Then I looked ahead. The large waves building in the distance were getting pretty close. I didn't know how much more Solange could add to them, but as is they'd already catch Henry before he reached shore. I just needed to make sure they weren't too big for him to handle. Fixing my eyes on Solange, I did the only thing I could think to do.

I shoved her off the board.

"Whoa!" Solange flailed her arms and I saw the red leave her eyes just before she toppled into the water. As a result, the nearing waves dropped several feet. They'd grown too much to be completely discouraged, but at least this helped.

I started paddling forward as Solange resurfaced. A moment later she began to paddle too. After a few seconds the sound of rushing water filled my ears and I looked back.

Oh no.

Solange had regained her focus. Her eyes glowed as a massive wave rose behind her. It was bearing down at about twenty feet. She looked angry now. Perhaps it had been a bad call to push her; emotions could be one heck of a power boost. Inspiring negative feelings in a demon may have been like fanning the magical flames.

I leapt to my feet on the board at the same time as Solange. We rode over the water as the waves kept growing behind us. She was in the zone now.

Double or nothing?

All the other kids had their eyes forward, focused on the beach, and the lifeguards weren't looking our way. Seizing the moment, I sliced through the water at an angle and came up behind my nemesis. "Have a good swim!" I shoved her again and then cut away as fast as possible. The demon and her surfboard got caught and buried in the wave.

SPLASH!

With Solange's focus broken, the wave decreased in size again. Unfortunately, it'd already picked up a lot of speed and size. I cupped my hands around my mouth.

"Incoming!"

Henry and several of the kids heard me, glanced back, then hopped on their boards when they saw the wave.

WHOOSH!

The wave got a hold of them like it had me, still moving with the powerful speed Solange had inspired. There was no way to slow it down and there were too many of us sharing the space. Me and a couple of boys veered together and tumbled off, crashing into the water.

I bounced around under the surface, tethered to my surfboard above. Dark water and kelp balls whirred around. For a split second before I freed myself of the shadowy depths, I saw two faraway glowing red dots. Solange?

I returned to the surface and glanced every which way. There were no more giant waves approaching. The one that'd taken me down had completed its course and was now crashing onto shore.

Some of the kids were safely on the sand. A good number of them were still out here though, recovering from the wave.

"Henry!"

I turned. Razel stood on the edge of the beach, hands cupped around her mouth as she shouted. "*Henry!*"

My pulse quickened. "Hey!" I called to one of the nearby guys. "Did Henry get taken out by the wave too?"

"I don't know!" he responded.

"Here's his board!" a kid yelled in the distance.

But there was no boy or leash attached to it.

"I don't understand! Where's the leash?" I shouted.

"Not all of us were riding with one today," he responded. "It's an optional thing!"

Razel had now run into the waves and was paddling out at a shocking speed despite the bumpy seas. Members of the surf team were searching the water and shouting to the lifeguards for help. At my eleven o' clock, Solange's head popped out of the water and she started heading for shore.

My panic rose higher than the last wave had. I ripped the Velcro strap from my ankle, abandoned my board, and dove into the water. I could hardly see anything except the shadows of the kelp forest—growing denser as the ocean got deeper. I swam in the direction Solange had come from, kicking and stroking. It was so dark.

Idea!

I summoned my halo and created my own private ring of light. I grabbed the magical accessory from my head and held it out in front of me. After a few seconds of frantic searching, I saw a figure deep in the clutches of the kelp forest. It was Henry. He'd gotten his legs tangled in strands of thick kelp. I darted over like a minnow. Bubbles were escaping his mouth as he desperately tried to free himself.

Before I even consciously acknowledged the choice, my grip tightened around my halo, its light tripled, and the opposite end changed to blade form. In two slices, I cut through the entire mess of seaweed holding Henry.

Oh my God, how was that so easy for me this time?!

My friend kind of made eye contact with me, but his attention was shattered—eyes starting to close as he struggled to stay conscious. I vanished my halo, put his arm around my neck, and kicked us to the surface with the strength of an Olympic swimmer. When we reached the air, sweet oxygen flooded our lungs and Henry coughed and hacked up water. I tried my best to keep afloat, but the ocean was choppy, the kid was heavy, and adrenaline-induced super strength could only last so long.

"*Hang on!*"

I turned my head and saw Grady the lifeguard paddling over on his surfboard. Seconds later, he was beside us. The guy tried to help me first, but I shoved Henry toward him.

"I'm fine. Help *him*."

Grady nodded and lifted Henry, still coughing, onto the board. Grady offered me his hand next; however there was barely any room for me and my added weight would slow down getting Henry to safety.

"Paddle to shore," I urged, waving Grady off as I bobbed in the water. "I'll swim behind you. Go."

Grady seemed reluctant, but agreed. He started paddling toward the beach. I took a few more big breaths to enliven my tired body, then followed. My arms cut through the water one stroke after another. After a few seconds I heard something. It sounded like Razel shouting. I caught words every time I came up between strokes for air.

"GRACE—"

"LOOSE—"

"BOARD—"

I stopped swimming and came to a float, glancing around. Razel was several dozen feet away, hastily paddling toward me. When she saw I'd surfaced she opened her mouth to yell again, then paused when she glanced behind me.

"Look out!"

I pivoted in the water just in time to see my loose surfboard— caught in a rush of current and coming straight at my forehead like a missile.

SPLASH!

My body bounced off smooth floor, impact cushioned by a swell of rainbow-colored water. I sat up, coughed, and realized where I was. The tall silo where I'd landed after the hydrant incident.

"GRACE!" Akari yelled from the platform.

"*Seriously?* Again?" I shouted.

"I'm afraid so! Hurry. We don't have a lot of time."

I couldn't believe I'd gotten killed *again*. And by a surfboard. Did that make me the lamest angel or the lamest Californian of all time?

I hoisted myself up the ladder and Akari and I raced through the magnificent tower. "Any questions this time?" she asked as we bolted.

"Nope. Just get me back."

Her wings sprouted on the balcony and we flew toward the golden cathedral. I hopped in the alcove and with a flash I was back in the SoCal ocean . . . underwater. It seemed while my soul got shot back to Heaven, my human body had sunk deep into the dark kelp forest—by miracle, not tangled just surrounded.

Alive again, I kicked and stroked with all my might until I pushed through the surface.

GASP!

I had drifted far from the shore and from where my friends and I had been surfing. Everyone else was way off to the left, calling my name. The lifeguards were on jet skis now, searching the waters. How long had passed since I'd been taken down?

I swam toward the lifeguards and when I was close enough gave a wave. "Hey! I'm fine!"

Five minutes later, I was back on the sand, a dozen people gathered around me.

"You disappeared under the water fifteen minutes ago," said Cora, the female lifeguard, as she checked my vitals.

Razel stood just to my right. The poor girl looked totally shaken. "We thought you were . . ." She gulped.

I gave her a soft smile. "Well, I wasn't." I addressed the whole assembly. "After that board rammed into me and I went under, the current dragged me down to that cliff area." I pointed in the distance. It was far enough away that they wouldn't have seen me, but close enough that a current could've plausibly carried me there. "I got a cramp in my leg, so I couldn't swim back immediately. I'm honestly fine though. Not cuts, bumps; I didn't even lose consciousness."

"You're very lucky," Cora commented.

"You're also a hero," said one of the guys on the surf team. He spoke to the entire group. "I was swimming around under the water looking for Henry when I saw this chick using some sort of light-up Swiss army knife to cut him free. It was awesome. I didn't even know they made those. Can I see it?" He pivoted to me.

"I, uh, lost it at sea."

My eyes turned to Henry. He'd been quiet for these last few minutes. Though he seemed physically fine now, his face was painted with fear.

"Are *you* okay?" I asked.

He paused, his eyes warbled with stupefaction. "It's a lot to take in."

Once all health checks were completed, things quieted down. Henry and I swore we were okay and people began to head home. Eventually Henry and Razel's mom showed up. They offered me a ride but I declined, saying I had my own. Henry—still in a daze—thanked me for saving him then my friends solemnly got into their vehicle and drove away.

I wondered if they were going to tell their parents what happened. Henry had insisted on not freaking his parents out over the Six Flags incident. He didn't want to give them extra reason to worry about him or restrain his freedom any more than they already did. By that logic, I had a feeling the twins were going to lodge this secret away too.

I was walking through the parking lot when I heard a familiar voice.

"I'm thinking of getting a tattoo." I turned around and found Solange and her sparkly beach bag. "Actually, two tattoos. They could be like little tally marks—one for each time I get you killed."

"Did you always intend to use the kelp as your main strike instead of the waves or the lightning?" I asked directly.

"It's like when I put that wrench on the table at Magic Mountain, Grace," she said, crossing her arms. "You're the one who decided what to be afraid of. That afternoon you made the choice to keep your friends from going on their intended roller coaster; *you* changed their course. Today you focused on the obvious threat too—the one above the surface, if you'll pardon the pun."

She sighed and shook her head with a slight smile, like an amused dog trainer addressing a puppy who just wouldn't learn.

"At Magic Mountain, you helped me steer Henry right where I wanted him. Today, once I realized my power for manipulating the waves alone wasn't enough to best such a strong swimmer, I came up with another plan to drown Henry—manipulating the chaotic seaweed beneath us too."

"Well hooray for you," I said with a huff. "You can feel as proud of yourself as you like, Solange, but you still lost today."

She shrugged. The demon didn't seem as perturbed by her failure as she had been at Magic Mountain. Perhaps she was trying to mess with my head.

Solange reached into her bag and removed a set of keys. Her key ring had a black bat bauble hanging from it.

I raised an eyebrow. "Your mentor gave you a car too?"

"Not exactly." She pressed the button on her keys and a sleek, black motorcycle with giant wheels like something Batman would ride appeared in the empty parking spot behind me. My jaw just about hit the floor.

Solange mounted the bike and revved the engine.

I glared at her. "Dead or not, I hope you got a proper license to drive that."

She shrugged. "Who's going to stop me if I didn't? You?" With a snide smile and another rev of her engine, she sped past me, wheels screeching.

My annoyance was at max capacity.

With a frustrated huff, I claimed my own keys from my bag. After driving to the Pearlie Gates this morning, I'd pressed the green button and the car had vanished. When I teleported to Earth, I'd arrived in the changing room of a hair salon right by the beach, so I hadn't needed the car again until now. I pressed the designated button, expecting my glorious convertible to form in the empty parking spot. Instead, a vehicle the size of a clown car appeared. It had the same baby blue color and license plate as my convertible, but it was barely bigger than a Jacuzzi.

"What the—"

I got into the tiny car and called Akari on my Soul Pulse.

"*What happened to my car?*"

"Grace, you just got your license. This little car is much more practical, agile, and safe for Earth streets."

"Oh, come on," I complained.

"I'm doing this for your own good. In Heaven, everyone is already dead. Considering your sporadic episodes of losing focus and your fondness for speeding, you really think I'm going to let you loose with a powerful V8 engine convertible on Earth where everyone is still alive?"

"But I passed my test!"

"Take a breath and calm down. The car will transform into a convertible in Heaven, but on Earth you'll have this extremely safe, compact, and sturdy model. No muss or fuss—just a secure way for you to get from Point A to Point B. Now, if there's nothing else, I have a meeting to get to."

"Ugh. Fine."

I hung up the call then leaned my head against the wheel, sounding off the horn by accident.

Worst beach day ever.

MIRACLES

With a whoosh, I glided across my cottage's living room floor. The song ended and, having danced out my feelings thoroughly after the exhausting beach day, I pressed the button under my fireplace mantle. The white wormhole reappeared and spat out my furnishings, returning them exactly where they belonged. The lighting in the room reverted to normal.

Droopy sauntered over from his basket and used his little wings to propel himself onto the couch. I plopped down beside him. My eyes fell on that framed picture of my family again. I felt a tug in my chest, my heart straining like it always did.

It was strange. Even though I was the one who had died, when I looked at pictures of Gaby and my father, it felt like they were the ghosts. Like *they* no longer existed.

Hence why I never let myself look at these photos for long. While I loved my father and Gaby dearly, it was too painful. Seeing them at the cemetery had almost broken me. I was glad I had gone—even my brief visitation had provided an important mental separation. The event cemented into my soul that *that* was not my life anymore and I had to move on. Unfortunately, accepting this meant experiencing soul-crushing heartache whenever I thought about the people I was forced to move on *from*.

Yet, after this whirlwind of a day, I felt I needed to see them, to hear their voices. Even if it did hurt.

I turned on Memory Prime and asked it to show me fond memories of my sister and father. This triggered montage mode rather than full scenes. The screen fluxed with color and my life began to play out.

I saw my father teaching me to play chess. Gaby and me

chasing Droopy around as a puppy. My father and me sipping iced teas on lawn chairs in the backyard. Gaby and me giving each other makeovers as little girls. My father and me at the grocery store, him pointing out the freshest fish in the case. Gaby and me messily baking muffins together.

A tear escaped over my cheek. I sniffled, wiped it away with the back of my hand, and turned off the TV.

I was grateful to have made great connections in the afterlife. Henry and I shared more than a destiny; he was a true friend, as were Razel and Justin. Leo had been a surprising confidante and I appreciated the bond we were forging. Monkonjae's handsomeness made it hard to focus, but he was kind and I felt safe when I was with him, which was no small feat these days. All my new friends were a blessing and I knew that if not for them I likely would have crumbled by now. GA responsibilities, Ninety-Eight expectations, and generally dealing with death were a lot to handle. I was a fighter, but without anyone in your corner your resolve weakened faster.

I gulped and couldn't resist my eyes going back to the picture.

As grateful as I was for the new people in my life, no friendship could supplant the loss of family. A bond with a father or sister was special and had no replica.

Sigh.

I so wished I could talk to them right now.

My father was kind and pragmatic. The man didn't sweat the small things, so he had an easygoing relationship with everyone in our family. He never made me feel bad no matter how much trouble I was in. He never minded accommodating my mother's need for tradition, order, and structure. Even to the extent that because "Cardiff" was an old family name, and my mother was an only child, he was fine with her keeping the last name and passing it on to me and Gaby.

What I loved most about my father though, was his calm and patient nature, which made him a great listener. When I vented about my mother he never took sides; he advised me to remember that she always had my best interest at heart, but heard me out in full. I appreciated that. Sometimes you didn't need someone to say that you were right and the other person was wrong; you just needed someone to assure that your feelings weren't falling on deaf ears.

If my dad was my go-to listener on Earth, who I went to when I wanted to spill my thoughts and feelings, Gaby was my rock—a warmhearted, reassuring presence that I could entirely be myself around. That was a beautiful thing I was missing in the afterlife. New friends took an adjustment period. They didn't know everything about you and vice versa, so you had to be on your toes a bit as you sussed each other out. Siblings already knew your full deal, so time spent together carried no pretense; it was freeing and personable.

Oh, Gaby.

Of the million things I missed about my sister, more than anything I just missed being in the same room. What I wouldn't give to turn my head now and see her standing there, walking through the door, coming up behind me smiling.

I shook my head as I felt another tear press on my iris. I wiped my eye with my hand before this one could fall.

Gaby had expressed regret at the funeral about us not spending enough time together. I regretted that too, but I didn't hold it against her. Some distance had grown between us when she started at our local university a couple years ago. She was changing, maturing, and finding her own way, and little sisters who asked a ton of questions could be a burden. I tried not to let that distance bother me when I was alive, just as I'd always tried not to be bothered by how much better she and our mother got along. That wasn't Gaby's fault. She was just the lady our mother wanted us both to be. The girl didn't speak out of turn, she never got in trouble, and—to quote Mama Cardiff—she didn't "raise hell" like I did.

My fingers tightened around the decorative throw pillow I'd been clutching.

It made sense now why my mother hadn't wanted to talk about my father or Gaby when we'd first died. She'd been separated from the man she adored and the child who filled her with pride. While I did not believe the accident was my fault, and I was still angry with my mother for putting that on me, I felt guilty that the daughter she was stuck with could only bring her frustration.

I always knew that our mom liked Gaby better than me because of that. I didn't think she *loved* Gaby more, but obligatory parent-child love was not enough for me. Despite all the ways that our mother drove me nuts, I wanted her to like me too. Or accept me as I was at the very least. It mattered. I wished that it didn't, but it did.

That's why shame and guilt came so easily when my character flared with ferocity and I acted in ways she disapproved of. When I got in trouble, it felt like I broke her heart a little. And doing that to my mother . . . it broke my heart a bit too.

Overall, I guess the doubts that haunted me weren't solely about regretting my aggressive actions and personality. A lot of remorse came from disliking the discord that it caused with my mom, and the polite society way of thinking she came from.

Droopy whined in his sleep. I glanced over. While I'd been in deep reflection, he'd fallen into a deep slumber. I rubbed his belly gently and in response he stretched out even more.

My mother, my mother, my mother . . .

What was I going to do about my mother?

Leo had told me to try and understand her perspective. After seventeen years, I was pretty sure I already understood her perspective. The woman was harder to please than Gordon Ramsay at a BBQ. She liked order and discipline. She didn't like shenanigans or rudeness. She wanted me to grow up to be a prim and proper Southern woman like her. Someone who polite society and my upstanding Grandpa Thorston would highly regard.

That being said . . .

Even though I thought I had my mother all figured out, in the name of personal growth I made room for the idea that *maybe*, just maybe, I didn't know everything about her. The issue became though, how to confirm or deny that. How could I get fresh perspective?

Directly asking my mother to open up wouldn't work. On Earth she'd avoided talking about her feelings and her past; I doubted being in the afterlife would change that. More importantly, after our devastating last interaction, I still wasn't ready to face her. Which meant if I was going to learn anything new about my mother, I would have to talk with someone else. There was only one person up here who could fill in the blanks.

Nana Robin, please answer this time.

I tried calling her, but like most of my attempts to phone my grandmother, it proved unsuccessful. Hmm. Her Soul Pulse privacy settings weren't on, and she was in Heaven today. Maybe if I went to her in person she would make time to talk to me.

I brought up the search directory on my Soul Pulse and immediately thought of the last time I'd used this app—trying to help Oliver find his mom.

Oliver . . .

I shook my head. I could easily waste my evening wondering about him, his strangely likable nature, and how he'd gotten off his Soul Pulse. Right now I needed to focus—no more introspection; time for action.

"Find Robin Lecord, my grandmother," I vocally commanded the app. Droopy stretched, stirred by my voice.

The app made a pleasant *DING!* when it found her. My nana was at some place called "The Strip – Ian Fleming Palace."

I patted Droopy. "I'll be back, boy. As you were."

I teleported away. The place I landed was a surprise to say the least. It was like Las Vegas in the clouds, only no one was trying to sell me something and I didn't have to close my eyes to avoid the inappropriate billboard content.

Glittery buildings with flashing neon signs shot up from pristine, white sidewalks. Dinosaur-sized marble fountains were at the center of various plazas, each filled with either dark brown or golden liquid. I walked up to the nearest one—carved in the shape of four mermaids pouring the contents of their seashells into the fountain's pool. The embellished signage at the front of the fountain read *RACLETTE*.

It was a cheese fondue fountain! And surrounding it was a serve-yourself, wrap-around bar of French baguette, veggies, chicken, beef, apples, and more. I watched in awe as angels grabbed ladles to scoop bubbling cheese into their own dishes and then helped themselves to toppings on a buffet tray.

I counted three other massive fountains ejecting liquid hot cheese in the area, and I assumed the two with dark brown contents were chocolate fountains.

Oh, where to begin, where to begin . . .

Wait. Focus, Grace.

Across from me stood Ian Fleming Palace. It was a Monte Carlo styled casino with grand Corinthian columns, innumerable rooms, statues of angels and cherubs, and countless luxury sports cars parked out front. Very different from the two hotels beside it: The Bachelorette—decorated with so many sparkly jewels and sequins I could barely look at it—and The Hangover—dark blue with a giant wolf mural and a rooftop pool party.

I approached the Palace feeling out of place in my yoga pants and t-shirt, but the moment I stepped onto the gold-gilded threshold a wave of dazzling energy passed over me. Mirrors at the entrance revealed I now wore a forest green strapless gown and a necklace-earring set made of *real* emeralds! My hair looked like it'd just gotten a blow out and full makeup decorated my face—lipstick, mascara, the works.

"Welcome, Miss Cardiff."

A butler-type man appeared next to me offering a silver tray with a brochure and a champagne glass filled with bubbly liquid. "My name is Anders. I am your magic host for this evening."

I raised an eyebrow. "You mean you're not real?"

"No, miss. Not all jobs in Heaven are filled by angels. In places like The Strip where many service industry folk are required, God has staffed them with magical assistants such as myself. You can think of me as a Celestial Program."

"*That brings up a whole mess of questions . . .*" I muttered to myself. Then I shook my head and refocused. "I am looking for my grandmother, Robin Lecord. Can you take me to her?"

"Of course, Miss Cardiff. Right this way." He offered up the tray again, but I waved my hand to pass.

"I don't drink."

"I know. It's apple cider, miss."

"Oh. Well okay then." I took the champagne flute and the brochure and followed Anders through the bustling casino. Every patron was as fabulously dressed as I was. The number of jewels in here would have given Cartier a heart attack, and the tuxedos looked like they came out of James Bond's personal collection.

I had a realization and glanced at Anders. "Is that why it's called Ian Fleming Palace? Because everyone in here is dressed like they belong in the 007 franchise?"

"More or less, miss. Every Miracles Casino and Hotel on The Strip has a specific theme that emulates a unique type of experience. This entire building is modeled to create the debonair, high echelon feel of sophisticated *Casino Royale* moments à la James Bond. Without the villains of course. Meanwhile, The Bachelorette next door is designed to mimic the wild frivolity of bachelorette Las Vegas fun. Feathered boas and margarita machines abound, Britney Spears impersonator performances every night, and so on."

I raised an eyebrow.

"A description of every Miracles Casino and Hotel can be found in that brochure," Anders indicated as we migrated past the blackjack sector of the casino. I noticed there were no noisy change machines—only roulette, baccarat, poker, and blackjack tables were interspersed among various sleek bars. I *also noticed* that the chips angels played with resembled those gold-wrapped chocolate coins you could buy at candy stores around Hanukkah.

"Ah, here we are." Anders directed me to a poker table where my Nana Robin and Grandpa Jim were seated. If Anders hadn't pointed them out to me, I wouldn't have recognized them; I still wasn't used to seeing the pair in their much younger forms. Did anyone ever get used to seeing their grandparents looking hot? *Ew.*

Even describing them that way felt weird, though it was true. My nana wore an orange halter-neck gown and Grandpa Jim sported a velvet purple sportscoat with black bowtie.

"Nugget!" my nana declared. "How lovely to see you."

Anders offered me the tray again and I set down my empty

glass. "If you need anything else during your stay at Ian Fleming Palace, please let me know. When you entered, the Casino Caretaker app automatically downloaded on your Soul Pulse. You simply need to summon me."

"Um, okay. Thank you, Anders." I saluted him and to my surprise he copied the gesture before vanishing. I settled onto the empty stool beside my nana.

"I raise," she told the dealer. The dealer nodded then pivoted to the next of the six players around us.

I stared at the two dazzling chips that Nana Robin had just pushed to the center of the table. Curious, I picked one up. These were definitely not chocolate. The coin felt and looked like gold except that each piece glowed vaguely like our halos did. *ONE MIRACLE* was imprinted on one side of the coin, while a crest of angel wings was emblazoned on the other.

My grandparents studied my confused face. "Hasn't your mentor explained about miracles yet?" Grandpa Jim asked as I set the coin down.

"Um, no."

"Oh, Nugget! You'll love this. Jim, keep an eye on the game for me."

Nana Robin grabbed my wrist and brought up the main screen with the five original icons Akari had showed me—a halo around a globe, a conch shell, a gold coin, a folder, and a glowing W.

I bit my lip, remembering. "Wait, Akari did mention that the coin icon kept track of a miracle balance or something. I've just had so many things to think about since then that I never followed up."

"I fold," said an angel across the table.

The dealer exposed her cards, which revealed that a woman in red was the winner. The dealer passed her all the chips. Nana Robin pouted a bit. Then the dealer started distributing new cards.

"Nana Robin . . ." I said, trying to get her attention back.

She put a single chip in the center as new bets were placed before returning to me. Still holding onto my wrist, she pressed the coin icon. A loading symbol came up.

"While we're on Earth, our good deeds earn us points in Heaven," she explained. "Once we get here, we cash those out as miracles that we can use on behalf of loved ones on Earth. You remember when your father had that kidney surgery and there were complications? The reason those complications didn't turn deadly was because your Abuela Lupe and Abuelo Rolando used miracles to make sure everything went smoothly. Or how about that time you and your friends went river rafting at summer camp? The only reason you didn't get smashed against the rocks when you made a wrong turn was because people who love you on this plane of reality spent miracles to bring you home safely."

I blinked, astounded. Then my Soul Pulse made a *DING!* and I saw *+16* appear beside a question: *Claim miracles?*

"It's not that many," I commented. "I know I died young, but I feel like I did more than sixteen good deeds while alive."

Nana Robin was back to concentrating on the game, studying the other players' faces intently. I took my wrist back and cleared my throat.

"It's not a one-to-one ratio," said Grandpa Jim on my Nana's behalf, glancing up from his cards. "I'm not really sure of the exact math, but I think every five hundred small good deeds—such as holding a door open for someone—is equal to one miracle. Whereas more big-ticket good deeds, like rehabilitating an injured sea otter, earn you a whole miracle on their own." He shrugged and returned his eyes to his cards. "There must be a department in Heaven for that somewhere. Probably a bunch of angel accountants." His Soul Pulse flashed and his Celestial Program butler appeared, offering him a large cocktail.

I powered down my Soul Pulse and glanced around. "So this place . . ."

"At Miracles Casinos, we can literally bet our miracles," Nana Robin said. She gave me a wink. "It's just like Vegas."

"I raise," Grandpa Jim said to the dealer, throwing in three of his five remaining miracles.

"Me too." Nana Robin pushed her final three miracles into the center of the table.

"Nana Robin—" I protested.

"No more bets," the dealer announced. She flipped over her cards and revealed that both my grandparents had lost.

"Those were your last miracles!" I said to my nana.

"Nope," she responded sassily. The segment of table in front of her flashed and another chip appeared. She held it up for me. "Since this is Heaven, the casinos here have two adjustments: the house never wins, and no one ever loses everything. Even if you bet your last miracle, a single one always reappears after you lost it. So I can keep playing and trying to increase my count without ever worrying about the repercussions."

I tilted my head at her as the dealer laid out another round of cards. "How many miracles did you start with?"

"Today? Seven."

"But isn't that irresponsible?" I argued. "You still have one granddaughter on Earth. What about Gaby? Wouldn't you rather help your family with the miracles you do have instead of losing those possibilities?"

"Oh, Grace. What's life if you never pull your skirt down and slide on the ice? A little boldness never hurt anyone."

"But doesn't *this* boldness have consequences?"

My nana waved dismissively. "Oh tosh. You sound like my ex-husband. And your mother."

I made a face but swallowed the distaste in my mouth. I was already in discord with my mother; I didn't want to quarrel with my Nana Robin as well. Maybe I was being too hard on her. Who was I to judge how she enjoyed herself in Heaven? I should just be grateful I got to spend time with her.

I used to adore when she and Grandpa Jim came to visit from whatever exotic travels they'd just returned from. Without warning the pair would suddenly blow into town and take me on wild escapades of our own. Since my mother didn't care to be around Grandpa Jim, it was the few times I got to be as bold as I liked without anyone admonishing me for it. Those were some of my happiest memories and I'd been devastated when my grandparents had died. Given all that, I figured I shouldn't be so critical now and just appreciate the chance to get to know them on a deeper level.

"Speaking of my mother . . ." I said to Nana Robin. "Do you mind taking a break from the game? I have something I want to talk to you about."

"Nugget, I'm a little busy."

"*Please*. It's important."

To my surprise, Nana Robin huffed like an impatient child told to pack away her toys. "Fine, Nugget. Jim, keep the table warm for me." She kissed his head and left the card table.

We sat down at one of the sleek bars. It was kind of an odd place for a grandmother and granddaughter to have a heart-to-heart, but nothing about this day had been orthodox. I had started it reading magazines on the beach with a demon and now I was in a casino with my hot grandma. Oh, and somewhere in between I had died again.

Nana Robin ordered a cocktail. The bartender made it by hand, rather than having it just magically appear. I guess that added to the James Bond atmosphere of the place. The barkeep looked at me next.

"Ginger ale please. Shaken, not stirred."

The man behind the sleek steel bar prepared my soda, stuck a metal straw in it, and handed me the drink. I took a sip, then gathered my non-liquid courage.

"I was hoping you could tell me a little more about my mother's childhood."

"Why the sudden interest?" my nana asked. She took a drink of her cocktail then signaled a passing waiter and plucked a shrimp from his tray.

I sighed. "We have always had trouble getting along, but when she and I met up here in Heaven, we had one of our worst fights ever."

"Ooh, what happened, Nugget? Did you flip a table? Did you yell and scream? Your mother is so much like her father and goodness knows I let *him* have it back when we were together."

"Um, no. Nothing quite so dramatic."

"Shame." She stopped another waiter and grabbed a tiny crab puff.

"*Anyway*," I tried again. "The reason the fight was so bad was because she hurt me emotionally more than she ever had. I don't know what to do with those feelings. I've tried to ignore them and focus on my job, but I think it's finally time I figure out how to fix this. Fix us."

My nana sighed and her expression turned serious for the first time since our conversation started. She patted my hand. "Nugget, if you and your mother make each other this upset . . . perhaps you both *should* keep some distance between you. Only see each other occasionally that way there's less chance for conflict. That's the best suggestion I can make."

I shook my head, resisting the unsatisfying solution. "Maybe it *would* be easier for us to avoid each other for the rest of our afterlives, but I can't stomach that. I don't want to feel so much resentment for my own mother. I need to find peace with her. I . . . *have to.*"

My eyes fell to the floor. I thought of what Oliver had said to me that day we searched for his mom, and I sighed as I realized I felt the same way.

"Even if we're a million miles apart in who we are, she still matters to me. So I'll do whatever it takes to make things right between us." I looked up at my Nana Robin. "I just don't know how."

"Nugget . . ." My Nana Robin was at a loss for words. In that void of silence my sadness bubbled with my bitterness. A long sigh escaped my lips and my shoulders slumped from crushing memory.

"I spent my life thinking that the best way to maintain peace between me and my mother was following her rules and reining in audacious impulses. But that hasn't worked because A) it made me resent her, and B) I'm not particularly good at it. When push comes to shove, I push back. I *am* aggressive even if I shouldn't be. And my mother will always like me less because of that. What I was hoping you could tell me is *why*. Is it really just her being too much like Grandpa Thorston? Did she always love order and follow that conservative Southern lady archetype? Or was there ever a time in her life when she made room for other possibilities?"

My Nana Robin looked at me sorrowfully. "I'm sorry, Nugget. I can't help you."

"*Why not?*" I said a little loudly. A few patrons passing by stared. I took a calming breath before continuing.

"Nana Robin. Please. My relationship with my mother has always been characterized by letting each other down. With Gaby and my dad on Earth, and just the two of us facing this new world together, we need to end the vicious cycle and build something better—a relationship based on acceptance and respect even if we don't always see eye-to-eye. It's a tall ask, I know, but I've gotten to know humans, angels, and even demons who demonstrate how important meaningful bonds with parents can be. I want that for myself. And the first step is understanding my mother more. You're *her* mother. You're the only person who can enlighten me—help me find a different approach to understanding and thus possibly reforging my relationship with her. You must have some insight into the years when she was defining her character . . . Like I'm trying to do now."

Nana Robin reached across the bar and took my hand. "Nugget, you misunderstand me. I would love to give you that insight. Goodness knows I also wish I had a better relationship with my daughter. Unfortunately, I don't know her well enough to help either of us. Darla Cardiff—my straightlaced, strict, goodhearted but hardhearted daughter—has been a mystery to me for decades. When I didn't want to be a part of Thorston's rigid world of high society and proper procedure, we divorced, and he got main custody of her. I followed my own path and was away for long stints of time after that. It was what was best for me and my life, but sadly, it meant I wasn't around a lot when your mother was growing up. When I did return, she wanted very little to do with me. We were just too different. Like you and her, it would seem."

My heart felt like it weighed more than a fountain full of fondue. I leaned against the bar and took in the wide spectacle. Countless shimmering coins littered the card tables but I knew there were not enough miracles in the afterlife to magically fix my problems with the woman who had given *me life*. This would require a lot more work.

I sighed. "Well, if you can't help me understand my mother better, who can?"

"I think that only *your mother* can," Nana Robin replied gently. "And no, before you ask, I'm not sure how you're going to get her to open up. She has never been a sharer. If you do ever crack that walnut though, please keep me posted. I would genuinely like to fix things with her as well. Whenever our Heaven timeshare days intersect I keep hoping she'll reach out to me."

I nodded. "I haven't heard from her since our spat either."

"She's a stoic, proud woman, that one."

We sat in silence.

"Nana Robin . . ." I looked up at her after a moment. "What does your timeshare look like? You never mentioned the specifics and I'd love to be able to meet up in person and talk with you more meaningfully like this."

To my surprise, Nana Robin waved her hand dismissively. "Oh, Nugget. Don't worry. You're very important to me and I promise I'll make time for us to be together more."

It wasn't an answer to my question, but Nana Robin slapped her hands against her thighs and stood. "Come on. No more wallowing. Let's have some fun. Maybe spend some of your miracles?"

I gave her a look. "Spend them on what?"

Nana Robin grinned. "Oh, there are so many things to choose from."

23

SECRETS

"I did it! I did it!" Razel came bounding over to our lunch group, full of unusual enthusiasm for a Monday. She held up her cell phone. "I got acceptance emails from Loyola Marymount *and* Fullerton during class this morning."

She did an intense victory dance with a lot of wiggly arm movements before Henry gave her a hug. Then she ran around high-fiving everyone like a pro football player entering a stadium on game day.

I was glad to see Henry smile. He'd been in a weird mood all day, especially toward me. Granted, he had almost drowned over the weekend. But he'd partnered with someone else on our physics lab assignment, hadn't walked with me to any of our classes, and had been brusque when I tried to strike up conversation. It kind of hurt, and I wondered what was going on with him.

"It's official then," Justin remarked. "College admission season is here." He sighed and shook his head. "I wasn't going to say anything today, but I got a physical letter from the University of Florida on Saturday. It was a no."

"Oh, I'm sorry, man," Henry said, patting his friend on the back.

Justin tried to play it off with a shrug. "It's fine. Plenty of other schools have solid baseball programs, including right here in California."

"What are your top schools, Henry?" Solange asked interestedly, forking her salad.

"I'm trying not to get my hopes set on any one school, but ideally UCSD," he said. "University of California San Diego," he clarified at her confused look.

This made me pause.

"Not the University of San Diego?" I asked. Henry's Plot Points had directed *that* was the school he needed to attend.

He gave me a curious glance. "I applied there too, but UCSD is in the top ten college programs for microbiology, cell biology, and molecular biology and genetics. It's a better school for a pre-med track, and it's where my dad wants me to go."

Well, that's a problem.

Our group continued discussing the different schools. I traipsed over to the trashcan and threw out my remaining lunch. It was called a "Chalupa Boat" and I was not into it.

My watch started buzzing—Akari. It was a good thing smart watches had become such a norm on Earth otherwise talking to my wrist would've been conspicuous. I wondered what the GAs did to communicate before the high tech era—walkie-talkies maybe, magic carrier pigeons?

"Hi, Akari."

"Grace. How's your day going?"

"Could be better," I responded, sensing an ulterior motive. "How can I help you?"

"I wanted to check in." Her tone stiffened, like she wasn't fond of nagging me but was going to do it anyway. "I was fine giving you the weekend off after what you went through at the beach, but I want to make sure you can come to training today."

"Yes, yes. I'll be there." I saw Solange chatting with Henry. "Anything else?"

"Have you had a chance to research the Greater Good section of the library yet?"

"Akari, as noted, I had a busy weekend and I have a lot of stuff to sort out right now. You know me. If I'm putting off studying, it's important."

"Fair enough," Akari said, a bit friendlier. "Don't be late."

"Considering you downgraded my car because of my fondness for going fast, that doesn't exactly encourage me to hustle," I said pointedly.

"Goodbye, Grace."

She hung up and I sauntered back to our group. When I sat

down next to Henry, he got up almost immediately and went to talk to one of his other friends. I furrowed my brow, feeling puzzled.

What's going on with him?

Akari took a swing at me with halo in hand. I easily ducked and spun to her other side. She spun too, extending her leg in a high kick. She didn't turn as quickly as I expected though. I blocked the kick with my left arm while my right hand went for my halo. I made the correct scooping motion and shot my hand out, but the ray of light I was hoping for was only a small sputter. I had to withdraw rapidly—leaping back and vanishing my halo while sidestepping to avoid another of Akari's jabs. However, like most of her strikes, it seemed wide, like it would have missed me even if I hadn't moved. She was going easy on me; I could tell, and I didn't like it.

We fought for a while longer until I managed to shove Akari back with a kick and simultaneously summon and grab my halo. She scooped her arm and fired a beam of light, then another, then another—though again, I felt like the shots weren't aimed right at me.

I bobbed and weaved around the octagon, then evaded her final shot by doing a forward roll and ending up at her feet. Akari's still-glowing hand was primed to fire at my face. I pumped my arm with halo in hand and concentrated on projecting a large shield, but it barely grew to the size of a textbook before flickering out of existence. Akari's eyes filled with panic and she changed her aim at the last second. The beam of light she'd loaded plowed into the floor beside me like a small crater.

"Time out!" I called.

Akari's Soul Pulse glowed as the scorch marks from her beams repaired themselves.

Frowning, I turned to her. My angel classmates and their mentors looked up at us from outside the octagon.

"I want you to attack me," I told Akari flatly.

Over the last few rounds of magical sparring practice, I hadn't managed to get my shield or beam of light to work as well as Leo or Monkonjae had. Thinking about the times when I *had* yielded great power—the roller coaster incident, the demon elevator ride, underwater over the weekend—a reason for why had started to form.

"I *am* attacking you," Akari said, looking surprised.

"No, you're not. Not really," I said. "I don't believe you're actually going to hurt me."

"Well, of course I'm not going to hurt you, Grace."

"Then it's not real. I've been racking my brain trying to figure out why I'm strong when it matters, but not in training, and I think it's because of my state of mind. The three times I've been able to fully utilize my powers were when something truly bad was about to happen."

Akari gave me a look. "Don't you mean two times?"

Oh, right. No one here knows about the demon elevator ride.

"Right. Anyway, my point is that I think my powers are stronger when I am afraid, or at the very least when I feel a rush of adrenaline. That's not going to happen if I don't believe there's anything at stake."

Akari glanced at her colleagues. Deckland shrugged. "It's a decent theory."

"Maybe," she agreed reluctantly. "But I don't think there's a way for us to test it, Grace. No matter how hard we train, I think we all know, deep down, that no one is in any real danger here. We'd pull a punch at the last moment, adjust aim if we didn't think you could handle a blow, yield. Mentors, angels in general, aren't ever going to hurt each other intentionally."

"What about the Guardian Angel Games?" Leo chimed in. "People constantly get smacked, blasted, and land on their *tucheses* in those."

"Yes," Ana responded. "But as you've seen, though it looks impressive, that kind of hit isn't hard for us to shake off. Mortal peril just isn't something we're afraid of when angels fight each other."

"Well, someone needs to attack me and mean it," I urged. "I'm fairly certain that's the answer to my learner's block. And if it is, how am I supposed to overcome it and enhance my skills if no one here can give me the alarm I need?"

"We're just going to have to find another way to inspire your powers," Akari said, more stern than sympathetic. "Fear and adrenaline aren't the healthiest means for relying on strength anyway."

I shrugged with arms crossed. "Says you. I've seen superhero movies. When people are all worked up, they channel more power."

"Movies aren't real life, Grace," Akari said more crossly. "Trust me. If you let emotions influence how you use your powers, you are more prone to not seeing things clearly. You can lose focus on the big picture and make mistakes."

"Again with the trust me," I muttered, scuffing the mat with my shoe. I looked right at Akari and spoke firmly. "*This* is what I believe I need to do to train better. So unless you want to elaborate further with an example of why this isn't a good idea, or have a constructive suggestion, I'm not about to throw my one lead out the window."

A long, uncomfortable pause ensued. Akari didn't budge. Neither did I. We squared off—more might in our gazes than had been in the punches we'd been throwing.

"Why don't we call it a day . . ." Ana said eventually. "I have plans with some folks from the IDS, and if you're all okay with it, I had hoped to end training early."

"Fine," Akari said curtly.

"Fine," I seconded.

My mentor and I climbed out of the octagon. I hopped down to join the others and went for my water bottle on the floor.

"You have some sort of fancy schmancy business dinner?" Leo asked Ana as he grabbed his backpack.

"No. Gentry is good buddies with Shakespeare, who's hosting a '90s movie night at his place. We're watching the 1996 *Romeo + Juliet* with DiCaprio and 1998's *Shakespeare in Love* with Gwyneth Paltrow."

Leo's brows shot up. "Can you bring a plus-one?!"

Ana shrugged. "I don't see why not."

"Bye, everyone." Leo looped his arm through Ana's and practically dragged her out of the room, flooding her with inquiries. "Do we dress in costume? What's the leotard policy? Is there going to be a spread? Should we bring something? I make a mean salmon dip—"

As they exited, Deckland turned to his charge. "Do you want to come to my office and workshop ideas for your next Plot Point?"

Monkonjae nodded. "Definitely."

The boys waved and headed for the exit. I followed, but stopped short when Akari called after me.

"Grace—"

I waved a hand to cut her off. "Yes, yes. I know. The library. Greater Good. I'm on it."

"I hoped you'd still be here."

I glanced up from my book and found Monkonjae gazing down at me from the other side of the short bookshelf I rested my back against. I'd created a small nest on the floor of the GA library: texts I had already flipped through on my right, and those that I still intended to peruse on my left. I'd been sitting amongst them calmly until I saw my angel friend's face. That guy literally looked flattering from any angle.

"I, uh, you . . ." I took a breath and pulled myself together. "What are you doing here?"

"Looking for you."

Really?!

Play it cool, Grace.

I shrugged nonchalantly. "How come?"

"Well, after brainstorming Plot Point options with Deckland, the thought of going back to my house to read medical textbooks by myself was not a tempting plan. Keeping up with my assignment Dr. Wang has been exhausting lately."

"Your cover identity is a hospital intern, right?"

He nodded. "An intern training to be a resident. On Earth I wanted to be a doctor and was pre-med at university before I died, but with this cover I'm pretending to be someone who has already finished college *and* medical school. I have to study for hours every night to keep up with the other interns."

"Goodness, way to put things in perspective," I remarked. "I will never complain about having to balance my GA duties with history and physics homework again."

He smiled and came around the side of the bookshelf to join me properly. In the seconds I had before I was in his sights again, I ran my fingers through my hair and dusted crumbs from my shirt, courtesy of the half-eaten cake sampler plate beside me.

What? A girl needs nutrients to study properly.

"You have no idea how tired I am of feeling like I can't keep up with brilliant people." Monkonjae sat down on the floor, leaning against the bookshelf across from me. "Deckland's advice is to continue studying and act confident. Ana told me to wing it. Leo said that when someone at the hospital asks me for an opinion, I should just say 'I concur' and nod."

I smiled. "It's a *Catch Me if You Can* reference."

"Yeah, I know." He sighed. "Anyway, when I finished meeting with Deckland, I decided to come look for you instead of going home."

"To distract you from your work?" I raised an eyebrow.

Monkonjae's eyes widened slightly. "Oh no, I'm sorry, I didn't intend it to sound that way. You're not some random distraction."

"Darn straight," I said, shutting my book.

"I meant that I could use your help," he corrected. "I don't think I mentioned it, but my assignment is also in California, just a different part. Since you and I are on the same time zone, I thought maybe we could study *together* sometimes. You're so focused when it comes to schoolwork and honestly, I've never been great at studying alone. I thought it may go better with some company."

"It may go better for *you*," I replied. "But I'm hardly going to get any work done with that face distracting me." I pointed at him briefly. Then realization hit and I felt my cheeks flush and I groaned. "Sometimes I really hate this honesty filter." I knocked my head back against the bookshelf. A moment passed, and then—

"My pillowcases have dinosaurs on them."

I raised my head and stared at Monkonjae. "What?"

"When I was little, I was obsessed with dinosaurs. Everything in my bedroom was covered with them. They don't exactly make dino-print things for people nineteen years of age, so I packed my dinosaur pillowcases when I went off to college to remind me of home. They appeared in my house in Heaven too, and I've been using them the whole time we've been here for the same reason."

My heart melted like chocolate in the sun.

"Monkonjae, that's really sweet." I paused. "But, um, why are you telling me this?"

"I'll make you a deal. Every time you say something to me that you think is embarrassing, I'll tell you something that makes me embarrassed. Even playing field that way—no one is the uncomfortable one in our relationship. An eye for an eye."

I blinked twice. "You would do that?"

"Why not? We're dead, right? I don't think we should let foolish things like pride keep us from being happy or from being around people we like."

I smiled. Our eyes held each other for a whole three seconds before I felt awkward and had to dart them away. That was improvement.

I grabbed the plate beside me and held it out to him. "Cake?"

"I'm good."

I set the plate down and pushed some loose hair behind my ear. Then I gestured at the book in my hand. "So . . . I would be glad to study with you, and maybe you could help me in return? Akari wants me to learn about how Guardian Angels prioritize the Greater Good when making tough choices in the field. Has Deckland given you any useful reading material about that? I'm trying to find examples specifically related to sacrificing life in the name of protecting your assignment . . ." I'd tried to keep my voice emotionless, but I couldn't help frowning remembering the argument with my mentor at the DMVD.

"Deckland hasn't assigned me that kind of reading." Monkonjae scooched next to me. I held my breath as he picked up some of the texts on the ground. "And I haven't read these, but my advice would be to look through a wider selection of material."

"These are literally all the books in the Greater Good section of this library."

"Why don't you try Heaven's Public Library? There's probably a way bigger collection of books on the Greater Good there."

It took me a full four seconds to process the information. "*Heaven has a public library?*"

"Haven't you been there? I assumed you knew."

"*No!*" I leapt to my feet. "I thought this GA library in Angel Tower was all we had to work with. This is where I've been coming since our mentors pointed it out on our tour."

Now it was Monkonjae's turn to stand hastily. "What?! Grace, you're going to love this. We have to go right now."

"Give me two seconds to clean up." My Soul Pulse flashed and all the books rose off the ground and zipped back to the shelves where they belonged. I grabbed Monkonjae's hand with a hundred percent excitement and zero percent awkwardness. "Lead the way."

Monkonjae's Soul Pulse lit up and in a flash we appeared in front of a dazzling marble building that made the New York Public Library look like a sloppy LEGO construct. Towers and turrets projected from different levels. Immense owl statues perched all over the roofing. The staircase leading up to the main entrance resembled a giant scroll that had unraveled onto the street. Floating lanterns—each bigger than a dining table—floated over the steps.

I completely forgot about Monkonjae and raced up the stairs two at a time.

The main entrance had no doors; it was a wide-open archway, as if to symbolize that no one could close the door to knowledge. It was available twenty-four seven to anyone and everyone. I *loved* that.

Inside, I was immediately overcome with emotion. The closest thing I could compare it to was how Belle must've felt when she first admired the Beast's library. Now multiply that by five hundred and you'd come close to understanding the rapture this place inspired.

Reading and learning were my happy place. Studying and

school had always come naturally to me, and of course I enjoyed fantastical fiction like Leo did. Really, I just adored absorbing information no matter the genre. There was so much to understand out there—history, human nature, science, psychology—and the more you understood, the greater your perspective of everything and everyone. At heart, I was a girl who asked a lot of questions because I loved answers. Books, libraries, lessons—they were all tools to get me as many answers as possible to questions I had, as well as those I'd never thought to ask. And fundamentally . . . I believed everything *had* an answer. No matter how complicated the puzzle, twisted the dilemma, or painful the challenge, there was always a way through. A library like this only reminded me of that, and dared me to assert the due diligence to find it.

Monkonjae caught up with me. "You're fast," he commented.

"When properly motivated." I gazed around at the impressive building. There were no fewer than fifty floors. Books magically flew across the space, heading to the waiting hands of readers or back to their original shelves. Many sections of the ceiling had been built like an atrium—large, open-air skylights complemented by thick branches that live owls perched on. Rose gold emblems were carved so intricately into the balconies that it looked like the banisters had enchanted tattoos. Black floor tiles with shimmery question marks were spaced out every twelve feet while the rest of the tiles resembled book covers.

I spun slowly in awe. "I don't know where to start." My eyes lingered on a corridor on the second floor with a sign that read *Secrets of the Universe—Earth Archives*.

Once again, without thinking, I grabbed Monkonjae's hand, this time yanking him across the lobby to one of the elevator banks. Forget teleportation; these things looked awesome.

The lifts were like something a steampunk junkie would dream up, with exposed gears and wires, bronze platforms to stand on, and shimmering ropes. I pressed the button for the second floor and when we got there I bolted to the hall I sought.

BAM!

I bounced backward and slid on my butt across the marble floor.

"What the—?" I wasn't hurt so much as I was stunned. Monkonjae helped me up and I approached the hall again, slowly this time. A glimmering, previously invisible force field stood between me and Earth's secrets.

Through the barrier, I could see plenty of angels in the stacks, so why couldn't I get through? I gazed longingly at the *A Section* just beyond my reach. The headers above the nearest four shelves read: *Alexandria* | *Aliens* | *Antarctica* | *Assassinations*.

Monkonjae raised his hand and pressed forward. The force field stopped him too. "Strange," he said. "I've been to this library a couple of times but haven't tried this section. I don't know why it's blocked off." He closed his eyes a moment. His Soul Pulse flashed but nothing else happened. "Hm. The teleport won't take me inside. Let's ask a librarian."

He strode to one of the question mark tiles and tapped his foot on it twice.

"Yipes!" I jumped back.

A full-sized librarian's desk had popped into existence in front of us. The smiling librarian sported a blonde bob and wore a green turtleneck. A huge golden owl necklace with opals for eyes rested on her chest.

"Hello there. I'm Gladice. How may I help you?"

"Why can't my friend and I access that section of the library?" Monkonjae asked, gesturing at the tantalizing hall behind us.

Gladice opened her mouth and a ray of angelic light shot out and scanned us from toe to head. The light vanished and she smiled again.

"Monkonjae Seoul and Grace Cardiff. As you are both Guardian Angels, you are forbidden access to the Secrets of the Universe sections in Heaven's Public Library."

"*WHAT*. Ma'am, that can't be right," I protested.

"I am not a ma'am. I am Gladice. And this is the correct information. You are not allowed access to this section of the library. You are, however, permitted to ask one question regarding the Secrets of the Universe and I—Gladice—am permitted to answer it for you."

I pouted in annoyance and decided to call Akari. When she

answered, I selected the option that allowed her hologram to emerge from my Soul Pulse so I was conversing with a full-size version of her.

"Hey, Grace. Are you okay?"

"Not really," I replied. "First off, why didn't you tell me that Heaven had a public library? Second, why are the Secrets of the Universe off-limits to us?"

"Calls are frowned upon in the library," Gladice said with a smile.

"I'll be just a minute," I told her.

"Grace, I assumed you knew about the library. I must've mentioned it. Did I really forget to tell you?"

"Yes. You really forgot to tell me."

"Well, I'm glad you know now. That is where I meant for you to go do your research on the Greater Good."

"Fine and dandy, Akari. What about my other question?"

"Excuse me?" Gladice said, raising her hand. "Calls are frowned upon in the library."

"Almost done, I promise." I whipped my attention back to my mentor.

She sighed. "I didn't want to overly bum you out when you first arrived in Heaven, but one of the only downsides of being a Guardian Angel is that we don't get to know the answers to all the mysteries of life. It's too dangerous. GAs are trustworthy, of course, but we spend so much time on Earth that there would be too great a risk of these secrets being revealed. If you know the answers, they may spill out unintentionally and alter the course of humanity."

I was about to blow up at her when she interrupted.

"To keep our recruits from getting too upset, like I see you're about to, GAs can ask one question regarding the Secrets of the Universe every year. One secret is much easier for the mind to digest and keep silent about. So choose wisely."

I glanced at Monkonjae as an idea formed.

"GAs aren't allowed to share their chosen secrets with one another," Akari said, reading my thoughts.

"Pardon me?" I glanced up to see Gladice waving pleasantly from behind her desk. "Calls are frowned upon in the library."

I sighed. "Bye, Akari." I hung up and looked over at Monkonjae. "Do you know what you're going to ask?"

"I'm deciding between the pyramids and Area 51. You?"

I took a longing look at the hall behind me, filled with angels deeply engrossed in books. I swallowed my frustration and decided to go with instinct. There were so many things I wanted to know; it would drive me crazy to overthink and prolong this.

"I have my question," I said to Gladice.

The librarian nodded. "Answers to Secrets of the Universe for Guardian Angels must be shared privately. Monkonjae Seoul, please take two steps back."

He did and a magical, semi-translucent dome fell around the desk, caging me and Gladice inside. "Should you try to share your secret with another Guardian Angel, this dome will reappear around you," the librarian said sweetly, like that wasn't a super creepy fact. "What is your question?"

I took a deep breath. "What's the deal with Stonehenge?" I said decidedly.

It was one of the first questions I'd asked when I'd arrived in Heaven, so it seemed like a good place to start.

Gladice held up her hand and a blank envelope appeared between her fingers with a flash of light. She offered it to me.

I opened the envelope carefully, withdrew the notecard inside, and read. After a moment, I glanced up in surprise.

"Jenga for giant aliens? *Really?*"

Two main things of note characterized the next ten days.

The first—I still couldn't bring my powers to the level they'd been at during those fearful adrenaline moments, and I couldn't find a single GA who would jumpstart those feelings. Though some of them did try attacking me with more gusto, I guess after our conversation the other day my subconscious irrevocably knew the angels wouldn't hurt me if it came down to it, and even if they did land a solid magical blow, I would be fine.

Second—Henry continued to act strangely around me. We still had lunch in the same group and occasionally worked together on assignments in class, but he avoided one-on-one moments. It bothered me tremendously. At Magic Mountain we'd been closer than ever and now he seemed wary of my presence. Had I done something to offend him?

"I was hoping you could give me a lift to my driving test next Thursday," Henry said to Justin at lunch. "I have to work a super short shift at the theater to help my manager with snack inventory, then bolt for my test at 4:30. My mom was going to drive me, but some PTA thing came up at Hana's school."

"I'm sorry, man, I've got a baseball game. Raz, are you taking your test then too?"

"The day after," Razel answered as she cracked open her soda. "Mom *is* taking me."

Justin turned back to Henry. "Can you reschedule?"

"We got the DMV's only available slots for the next few weeks. If I don't take this one, I'm screwed." Henry sighed. "I guess I could schedule an Uber in advance. It's better than nothing."

"I could drive you," I volunteered.

"That's a great idea!" Razel said, putting an arm around my shoulder. "That little toy car of yours fits two people, right?"

"Ha ha," I said dryly.

Henry gave me an ambiguous look. "Uh . . ."

"You're supposed to say, 'Thank you, Grace'," Razel chimed in. "What's the matter with you, bro?"

What *was* the matter with him?

"Gather around, everyone!" Kelsey turned off the music and clapped her hands. My much shorter cohorts and I abandoned our pirouettes and circled around the teacher. As always, I stood in the back so I wouldn't block anyone's view or draw too much attention to myself.

"I wanted to let you know that our spring recital has been set for the middle of May. Starting next week, we're going to work on a group number that you'll all perform together."

Hana shot up her hand excitedly. "Can we invite our parents?"

Kelsey nodded. "You can invite anyone you want. I should mention that just because we're going to be working on the routine in class as a group, participation in the recital *is* optional." She flicked her eyes to me then readdressed the class. "Okay, everyone, go get some water and a snack before your next session."

While the little girls went to their cubbies and got out bags of carrot sticks and PB&Js, I grabbed my backpack.

"Where are you going, Grace?" Hana asked, taking a sip from her juice box.

"I'm taking your brother to his driving test," I replied.

"But you'll miss the rest of today's classes! The more you practice, the better you'll be at our recital."

"I wouldn't worry about that . . ." I gave her a quick wave as I exited the studio and jogged up one of the still-broken escalators. Henry was waiting for me outside the movie theater, checking his watch.

"Hey," he said.

"Hey."

Without another word, we walked across the bridge to the rooftop parking lot where I'd left my tiny angel car. Henry got in the compact passenger seat with some effort and soon we were merging onto the street. We drove in silence for fifteen minutes. The radio hummed on low volume and he focused on his phone.

"Henry," I said eventually. "Is something wrong?"

He looked up and out the windows with slight panic in his voice. "What's going on? What's wrong?"

"Calm down. I'm not saying something is wrong out there. I'm asking if something is wrong *here*." I gestured between the two of us. "You've been acting weird since that day at the beach. Did I do something?"

A long beat passed before Henry sighed. "I don't know."

"Well, that's not a particularly helpful answer."

"I'm aware of that. It's just . . . The sketchiest thing that ever happened to me before this year was when I got stung by a half dozen jellyfish while my family and I were on vacation. Then you come along, and I've almost died twice in a matter of weeks."

I gulped, staring forward as I processed. "You think I'm a jinx or something. Is that why you've been keeping your distance?"

"No. That's not it at all. I think you're my Guardian Angel."

"*WHAT?*" I tore my eyes from the road to look at him, abruptly driving into another lane. Loud honking pulled me out of my stupor and I jerked the vehicle back on track.

"Geez, Grace! Get a grip!" Henry said, clutching the armrest.

"Sorry. Sorry. But what do you mean you think I'm your *Guardian Angel?*"

God, it was hard to have this conversation without looking at him.

"I just mean you're like a human good luck charm. I almost got mowed down by a roller coaster and drowned. Both times I *should* have died, but I didn't. Both times you were there and by a miracle I was saved. That coaster changed directions; somehow you found me in the middle of the ocean and cut me free. That's more fortune than most guys get in a lifetime."

I thought long and hard as I drove without saying anything. When I came to a complete stop at the next traffic light, I finally turned to Henry. "If that's what you think, then why act weird around me? If you think I'm good luck, wouldn't that make you want to hang out with me more?"

He scratched the side of his head anxiously. "See, that's the awkward part of this. You're going to think I'm crazy. *I* think I might be crazy."

"What is it, Henry?" Now he had me really concerned.

My friend hesitated. Then he released a rough exhale. "Okay, you know how some witnesses of the Magic Mountain incident said they saw a flash of light just as the sun bounced of the coaster when it switched directions? Well, I saw a giant *wall* of light. It was like a force field. The coaster was coming at us, and then the light completely blocked it. Next thing I know, the coaster is on the pavement." He fidgeted in his chair, not meeting my gaze. "And you remember how my buddy Matt said he saw you use a glow-in-the-dark knife to cut me free? To me, it looked like you were holding a big glowing ring in your hand . . ."

A car honked loudly behind me. The signal had turned green and traffic had begun to move. I was forced to redirect my eyes back to the road and drive forward.

Henry exhaled deeply. "I think I may be having some sort of stress-related nervous breakdown. Razel teases me about that sometimes. She says a human being can't pull so many all-nighters studying, and work a job, and do all my different activities while dealing with the immense pressure my dad puts on me. I thought I was keeping it together, but apparently not, because now I'm seeing things. I'm sorry if I've been acting weird around you because of that. I just got freaked out. For a minute, I even had myself convinced that *you* had magical powers." He snorted. "Anyway, being around you lately just reminds me of how easy a guy can lose his sanity when he's under a lot of stress. It's a reality check for me to handle my life better."

"Oh, Henry . . . I don't know what to say."

"Please don't say anything, and please don't tell anyone. I'm going to try to get more sleep and maybe join Razel for some of her weekend yoga sessions. It just looks like elaborate stretching to me, but she says it helps to calm the mind."

I saw the DMV sign and chose my words carefully as I turned into the lot. "Henry, I don't think you're crazy." I selected a spot and parked. Once I switched off the engine, I adjusted to face him again. "You're my friend. And if you want to think of me as your lucky charm, that's fine. But don't push me away because you're dealing with something. You should have just told me why you were freaked out. I would have understood."

He crinkled his brows. "You would have understood if I told you I was seeing things?"

I shrugged. "I would have preferred that over the cold shoulder."

"Yeah, that's fair." Henry sighed again. "Look, I'm sorry. How about we both try to forget all the bizarre stuff that's happened and move forward?"

"I think that's best."

In more ways than one.

We both stepped out of the car and gazed at the DMV—a short, beige, rectangular building with a slumped roof speckled with bird poo and a few traces of graffiti on the side. If only the people who worked here could see the DMVD upstairs.

"Well. This is the moment of truth," Henry said.

Also in more ways than one.

I was about to cash in my first miracle.

You know how there's a prize redemption area at Chuck E. Cheese's and carnivals where you can exchange tickets or tokens for prizes? Picture that. But then visualize a bunch of prize booths gathered in one grand outdoor space—farmers' market style. If you wrapped your imagination around that, you could start to picture Miracle Marketplace, the locale where angels cashed in their miracles.

After our casino encounter, Nana Robin and Grandpa Jim had taken me to Miracle Marketplace, where booths were full of symbolic objects that represented all kinds of miracles. For example, if you bought an expensive miracle to ensure someone pulled through a tough illness, you might receive a commemorative stethoscope. If you bought a medium-priced miracle to help a lost cat find its way home, you'd collect a stuffed animal. A cheap miracle like getting someone to work on time would provide you with a plastic toy car.

Just as the number and kinds of good deeds you did in life were weighed differently to determine how many miracle coins you earned in the afterlife, the number of coins you needed to buy a miracle varied too. Helping someone get into a state school required less miracle coins than getting someone into Yale. It cost more miracles to save a relative suffering from cancer than it would to help a dog with a urinary tract infection. Promotions at work, winning contests, making it home safe, having a dream or prayer come true—they all had values. Knowing that, I understood why some angels could become obsessed with our magical casinos. The temptation to increase one's miracle count was immense.

Working a booth in Miracle Marketplace was a popular job for angels who'd enjoyed sales in their lifetimes, and for those who loved being in busy environments. Vendors hawked their wears enthusiastically as angels shopped.

"Two-for-one miracles on marriage proposals for your kids!"

"Do you know someone who wrote a book? New discount on miracles to help them find a publisher or agent!"

"Have a loved one waitlisted for a university? Our miracles can help them get in!"

A girl could never have enough spending money around there.

Anyway, on my excursion with my grandparents I discovered the perfect way to use my first miracle coin—at the "Teenage Boy Dream Come True" booth. The recipient of my miracle: Justin. The intent: keep Henry from passing his second driver's test. I'd gotten a commemorative mini basketball as a souvenir in exchange for the purchase.

Henry started walking toward the DMV and I followed close behind. I watched him go through the motions. He checked in at the desk, signed some forms, and was told he'd have to wait a while because they were running behind.

Typical.

We took a seat in the designated area—bland as a saltine cracker with a perfect view of the many sour-faced employees sighing at their desks. Then Henry's phone rang. He took it out of his pocket. Justin's name and picture lit up the screen.

"What's up, man?"

I leaned in closer. I only caught every other word, but I knew what was being communicated.

"You're kidding! That's nuts." Henry's voice had risen an octave and several people glared at him.

"Justin, I'll call you back in a sec," Henry whispered into the cell and hung up. He looked at me incredulously. "Someone who works with Justin's dad just gave him three courtside seats to the Lakers game tonight. With locker room access to meet the players afterward!"

More people glowered at us, so I kept my voice low. "That's amazing."

"It's a frickin' miracle," Henry said, eyes wide and excited. "That kind of access is only for the super-rich and famous types." Then he slumped in his chair. "But if I go, I'll miss my driving test. Justin ditched his baseball game because this is a once-in-a-lifetime opportunity, and he said that if I want to come his dad can pick me up from here in twenty minutes. I don't know what to do."

"Henry, you can get a driver's license any time. This kind of miracle doesn't happen every day. Go to the game with Justin. Bail on the test."

"You think so? This will count as my second fail before I even get behind the wheel. That leaves me only one more chance. If I fail next time, my permit would be revoked and I'd have to start the process over. It would take months to get my license."

"I'm sure you'll be fine. What are the odds of that happening?"

He glanced nervously at the desk, tapped his foot anxiously, then called Justin back. "Hey, man. I'm in."

Perfect. Two fails down. One to go.

I was that much closer to checking off this Plot Point on my to-do list. Spending my first miracle on Justin had proven very effective. I *was* still nervous about how I would stop Henry from getting his license a third time though.

A problem for another day . . .

24

THE FAVOR

Well, it was another day. Now I had to deal with the problem. I sat at one of the study tables in Heaven's Public Library. I'd assumed the wide selection of books—every single book known to man, and thousands they didn't know existed—would provide answers for any issue. Alas, would you believe there wasn't a single book in here that offered creative ways for Guardian Angels to keep teenage boys from getting driver's licenses? I guess it'd never come up.

GAH! Frustration!

I sighed and laid my forehead against my current text. No books could be checked out of the library, so I'd been coming here for days. Henry had his third and final driving test in less than a week. I was running out of time to come up with an idea for how to stop it. Between that worry, the continued block with my powers, and the constant uneasiness about when Solange would strike next, I was really getting stressed.

How I envied my mortal friends. They were probably spending their Friday afternoon watching TV or hanging out at the mall. Meanwhile, I was surrounded by unhelpful books and owls that occasionally stole my snacks.

"Hey, get your own," I said, shooing away a bird that suddenly swooped in to take a pretzel from the bowl beside me.

Needing a break, I stood from my table and went over to the railing that overlooked the library's open floor plan. I gazed around at the vast, impressive space. It was as full of wisdom as my soul felt empty of inspiration. Very.

I could sure use someone to talk to right now—someone who could workshop ideas with me, hear out my stresses, perhaps provide encouragement. I suppose that's why GAs were assigned mentors, but I didn't feel comfortable opening up to Akari. I knew she cared, but things between us could be tricky. Recently there was our whole Greater Good disagreement and the mounting strain of my powers block. Those areas of dissonance only highlighted our ongoing issues regarding trust, expectations, and willingness to be upfront with each other.

No, Akari was definitely not someone I felt like I could be vulnerable with at the moment. That meant my other GA confidante options were Leo, Monkonjae, Deckland, and Ana.

Monkonjae was still on Earth at some sort of banquet honoring his doctor assignment, and I didn't think trying to workshop things with him would be the most fruitful since I could only look at the guy for shorts stints. Leo may have been a solid option, however our assignment time differences made it difficult to connect regularly, and I knew he was hanging out with his father all weekend. Deckland was nice, but he and I weren't close yet. And though Ana had offered great support that day I had my meltdown in the sparring center, I felt reluctant around all our mentors given how drastically their expectations differed from my progress. The two had been mismatched from the start, but as time went by it was a growing shadow. Our mentors were good souls, who maybe didn't judge me. Nevertheless, as I judged myself harshly for the shortcomings, it was hard to look at them— just another group of people I was letting down.

I decided to call Nana Robin, the next most reasonable— though remarkably unreliable—choice for a sounding board. By some miracle after three buzzes she answered, but only her voice came through. Weirdly I didn't have the option to see her.

"Nugget? Is this really you? Is this a trick?" she sounded out of breath and surprised.

"Um. Yes it's me and no it's not a trick. I just wanted to talk to you. Are *you* okay though? You sound strange."

A pause.

"Nugget, there is no delicate way to say this. Today I'm in Hell. When we're down here, we can't make calls and usually can only take calls from demons."

Another pause—this time by my doing as I processed the information. I addressed the easiest part of Nana Robin's comment first.

"Guardian Angels can call anyone in any realm. I guess that supersedes your rule. As for the rest of that . . . I'm sorry, I didn't know."

A flash went off in my peripherals. Gladice's desk had appeared behind me. She smiled. "Excuse me. Calls are frowned upon in the library."

I huffed and returned to my Soul Pulse. Before I could say anything, Nana Robin spoke. "Nugget—not that your voice isn't a welcome break from this . . . horror show—but I don't want to know what happens if a demon catches me breaking one of Hell's rules."

"I understand." Then a thought occurred to me. "Nana, seriously, what is your timeshare? You didn't answer me the other day, and if I had known—"

"Don't worry about it, Nugget. I'll see you soon."

She hung up.

I turned around and held my wrist up to show Gladice the call had ended. The magical librarian gave me a thumbs-up then disappeared with her desk.

Left alone again, I leaned on the railing deep in thought. If there was one thing I disliked more than people not answering my questions, it was when they tried to avoid the questions entirely. Why didn't my nana want to tell me about her timeshare?

I went over to one of the question mark tiles and tapped it twice. Gladice and her desk returned. "How may I help you?"

"Is there a section of the library that breaks down timeshare plans for all the souls in the afterlife?"

Gladice's eyes turned neon blue, her body perfectly still. Then she reanimated with a smile. "Timeshare assignments are kept in the Timeshares Bureau of each of the three planes of the afterlife. Copies are stored in section 12-19-2798-alpha of Heaven's Public Library. Please touch the owl icon to proceed."

A glowing owl symbol the size of a typewriter hovered in the air in front of me. I touched it. A second later, I was standing in an unimaginably huge corridor of books. The hall was deserted, and a bit darker than the other sections I'd explored. By the looks of it we were in a sub-basement level, which brought up the question of how big exactly was this library?

The shelves here were easily five times the height of the impressive Christmas tree my hometown put on Main Street every year. They extended so far back I figured I could probably walk the corridor for hours and not reach the end.

The sign above the hall I'd been deposited in designated it as *Timeshares*. I walked up to a shelf and pressed the nearest shimmering button with a ladder icon. A rolling ladder appeared beside me, attached to the bookcases. I hopped on and wrapped my hands around the glistening grips. The whole ladder flared with magic energy.

"Robin Lecord—timeshare assignment please," I commanded.

I closed my eyes and hung on tight. I'd tried this search method a few times in the last week to find a book. It was intense. The second my eyelids shut, the ladder whooshed down the corridor. It wasn't a Six Flags roller coaster, but it certainly had a mastery of speed.

When the ladder came to a stop, it transformed into an escalator. I rode it to a shelf ten feet up where a book was glowing. Once I pulled the text from the shelf, the escalator carried me down and morphed into an armchair with a built-in reading lamp.

I settled into the armchair contentedly. Heaven's Public Library had left the Dewy Decimal System in the dust. This was *exactly* how a person should fetch a book.

I flipped through the alphabetically organized pages until I found my nana's name. Her schedule detailed that she was in Heaven two days a week, Middleground three days a week, and spent *two days a week* in Hell. Was that why Nana Robin hadn't wanted to tell me about her timeshare—embarrassment, shame?

Talking to her a few minutes ago, I'd been surprised to learn someone I loved and looked up to since I was a little girl spent any time in Hell at all. Discovering she spent two days there every week for all eternity to pay for her sins . . . that was a lot to digest.

Although I considered my Nana Robin a wonderful, warm

person and only had fond memories of our time together, she spent one more day a week in Hell than my mother. What had she done in life to deserve that? Also . . . in retrospect, what had my mother done to deserve Hell? I didn't think she was the greatest person in the world—goodness knew she'd made my life Hell plenty of times—but was that really enough to get a person sent to the bowels of the underworld? What was it like for her down there?

Concern, guilt, and something else welled in my throat.

When I arrived in Heaven, Akari had told me not to think about my mother's time in Hell and to let it go because we were all assigned where we were supposed to be. I'd accepted that at the time—partly because I was so distracted by other huge revelations that kept flying at me. Now, the need to know more resurfaced. And if I couldn't count on Akari for answers, I would seek them out myself.

The only thing to decide was *how*?

I stomped twice on another question mark and Gladice returned.

"Is there a section in the library for Hell? Specifically what each person faces there?"

Gladice froze and her eyes turned blue again before she answered. "Heaven's Public Library has a Hell section. This is limited to a general history, demon class descriptions, demon powers, history of demons, and descriptions of Dark Breeds. Tortures are customized for each soul and are updated at the discretion of torturers. Therefore, information about individuals in Hell—what they face and what they did to deserve their sentence—is not in our records. Footnote: additional information may be found in the Public Library of The Second City."

Gladice vanished. I stared down the empty, shadowy corridor. Then I pulled my car keys from my pocket as an idea formed in my head. It was a little bit good, and a little bit bad . . .

After I teleported to the Pearlie Gates, I tried to act as casually as possible. I was just an angel who happened to be wearing all black, minding my own business. Nothing to see here.

I made my way toward the obsidian orb that led to Hell. As always, a pair of buff Guardian Angels stood by the gate. I didn't *think* they'd be a problem. Other than those off-limits floors at the top of Angel Tower where God dwelled, and the Secrets of the Universe section of the library, GAs had maximum security clearance with access to everything and anything we wanted. Our souls were the "purest" or whatever, so who was going to question us?

With a deep breath, I tilted my chin up and held my head high, giving the angel guards a nod as I passed. When I reached the gate, I gulped and held my Soul Pulse to the scanner. My watch flashed and the gate creaked open, inviting me into the darkness. The same jewelry box as before popped into existence and hovered in front of me. I plucked it from the air then stepped into shadow.

Once on the chilling, dark red platform, I opened the Hellevator hatch, removed the tiny piece of Divine Iron from the box, and pricked my finger. A single drop of blood made the elevator DOWN button shine. Flames flared to life along the periphery of the platform. I pressed the button and the Hellevator jolted into motion.

Eventually a warm glow blanketed my body. The lake of fire freeway came into view—as gruesomely gridlocked as I remembered. My platform traveled across the turmoil. However, when The Second City started to come into view, I went back to the hatch in the floor and hit the STOP IN EMERGENCY button. The platform halted in midair, hovering over the bubbling lava. I rummaged through my bag for my car keys and pressed the button.

Whoa.

A pure black convertible with graffiti-style blue flames painted along the sides appeared on the platform beside me. Akari had told me the car would change forms based on the realm I was in. As hoped, my ride was now Hell ready. With the exception of one thing . . . My *NINETY8* vanity license plate would not help me keep a low profile.

I summoned my halo and with some effort used it to slice the plate off, then threw it face down in the backseat of my car.

No turning back now.

I hopped in the driver's seat and made the call. "Redial Oliver Evans." I told my Soul Pulse. The device buzzed and then a hologram of Oliver's face formed above my wristwatch.

"So, you made it?"

"Yes. And the car disguised itself as hoped. Now where should I meet you?"

"Do you see the Hell Beacon?"

I glanced up at the intimidating tower with the red orb at the top, pulsing with power. I tore my eyes away with difficulty. "Yes."

"Drive toward it. Hang left at the building with neon purple lightning. You'll see a blade sharpening store, a poison production facility, and a taco stand. Park in the alley behind the taco stand. I'll meet you there in ten."

"You can get tacos in Hell?"

"You can get tacos anywhere, Grace. And for God's sake, don't talk to anyone, don't look directly at anyone, and don't do anything to call attention to yourself."

I huffed in amusement. "That's kind of an odd thing for a demon to say. *For God's sake.*"

Oliver scowled and ended the call. Time to go.

Since the Hellevator was only used for occasional meetings between Guardian Angels and Guardians of Chaos, it was strictly designed to go from the Pearlie Gates to the Hell Beacon and back. Thank goodness that all elevators had an emergency break. And thank goodness I had wheels. The plan was to leave the lift here while on my mission, then fly my car back to the platform and ride it home once I was done. Easy as pie in theory . . .

I revved the car to life. Instead of the rainbow energy it emitted in Heaven, flames shot out the exhaust.

So much for not calling attention to myself.

I drove off the Hellevator, looking in my rearview mirror to ensure it stayed exactly where I'd left it.

Suddenly I heard screaming from below and made the mistake of glancing down. The orange and red hues of lava eerily illuminated the rims of my car. It seemed like the swirls of lava were forming sinister faces.

A crack of thunder whipped my attention in the opposite direction. Above, the sky churned with throbbing veins of purple, magenta, dark gold, and horrid red.

When I made it to The Second City I lowered from flight to the streets, reducing my speed. This caused my flame exhaust to settle down a bit, but that hardly mattered. Other vehicles on the road also projected flames, plumes of smoke, and even lightning when they picked up velocity. They each had vanity license plates too, and I spotted plenty of off-putting bumper stickers in use, such as:

Go to Hell ☺

Team Zack Snyder

I was in Tiananmen Square in 1989 and all I got was this lousy bumper sticker.

Demons were messed up.

Wicked buildings in shades of onyx, violet, and scarlet stretched around me. Soon they consumed my view of the sky almost entirely. After driving through the edifices for just a minute I felt like I'd never escape the city for a breath of fresh air again.

I spotted a black tower with neon purple lightning running up the course of its spine and made a hard left. Every hair on my arms stood straight as I continued to drive through the demonic domain—anxious that at any moment I would be jumped. I'd been pretty confident in my idea to come down here, reckless as I knew it was. Now that I was actually *in Hell*, my view of the decision had changed. It wasn't reckless. It was stupid.

I drove by the blade sharpening shop Oliver mentioned— scythes, machetes, and daggers in the window. The poison production facility came next, showcasing as many colorful products in its display as a jellybean factory. I imagined whereas the latter melted in your mouth, anything manufactured in this building would probably melt your insides.

My eyes darted from road to sidewalk, looking for my next marker—the taco stand. In doing so I noticed that the cement blocks that made up the sidewalk were inlaid with shimmery red inscriptions. I couldn't make any of them out from my car though.

So many strange sights in such a short time. And yet, one of the oddest things was that aside from the darkly comical, freakiness of the city, it wasn't that dissimilar to any other metropolis. People (demons, I suppose) walked the streets. Traffic was abundant. There were shops, restaurants, even dogs out for a stroll. Granted, they were three-headed dogs, or dogs with lizard bodies, or dogs with alligator faces.

Egads!

Finally, I found the taco stand. The menu board advertised a special on ghost pepper queso dip and vegan-friendly options. The long line waiting beside it was made up exclusively of people dressed like they were extras in *The Matrix*.

I pulled into the shadowy alley and waited, drumming my fingers on the steering wheel. All was still and quiet except for a lone pigeon pecking at grime on a dumpster.

"Hey."

"*Yipes!*"

Oliver had suddenly appeared in the passenger seat next to me.

"Keep it down," he said, putting a hand over my mouth in reflex. I roughly pushed his arm away.

"Maybe don't sneak up on someone *in Hell*," I responded irritably.

"I wasn't trying to scare you. Demon Soul Pulses work differently than yours," he said, also irritably. "There are no privacy settings. We only get a ten-second warning when another demon is incoming. And when we're within city limits, they put you right next to the person you're after. Unlike your kind, we don't care about privacy."

"Or personal space," I replied. "Angel or not, you grab my face like that again and I'll break your hand. Got it?"

Oliver smirked. That caused my skin to crawl a bit, but I chose to let it go. I needed him, after all. I put the car in reverse, prepping to exit the alleyway. "So which way to the library?"

"I have a better idea," he said. He abruptly put his hand over mine—clutching the gearshift—and returning the car to park. "I don't think we should go to the library to find the files on your mom."

"Oliver, that's why I'm here." I slipped my hand out from under his. "When I called you to cash in the favor you owe me, you said you'd help."

"The library is full of demons, Grace. Your Ninety-Eight status makes you the second most infamous angel around town. I thought about it more after we spoke, and this is not a good plan."

I adjusted in my seat to better face him. "*One*, how many demons could there possibly be in a library? Don't you all get your jollies torturing people, not delving into literature? *Two*, why am I the *second* most infamous angel? Who's number one? And *three*, obviously this is not a good plan, Oliver. If I were looking for *good*, I would not have come to Hell, or to you."

He narrowed his gaze. "*One*, bad people can be just as smart and well-read as good people. Sometimes even more so. If they weren't, why would evil so often have the upper hand? *Two*, we're not allowed to say the name of that infamous angel to your kind; Heaven has a policy of pretending she doesn't exist. And *three*, I don't need to be good to do something right. You came to Hell to find out more about your mom and what she's going through. Since taking you to the library will be a celestial suicide mission, and we can't check out any texts, the best way to get you what you want is to have you see it for yourself. Now get out of the car. I'm driving."

"Oliver—"

"Grace, I know how to drive *and* I know the way. Just settle down. It'll take way longer if you drive, and more time that you spend in Hell is just more time for us to get caught. Do you really want to increase your risk of being found here—an angel alone in Hell?"

No.

No, I did not.

My stomach knotted. With a huff I got out of the car. Oliver and I switched seats. "Just don't ding the car. It's new," I said as I buckled up.

He smirked again and powered the convertible back to life. We drove out of the alleyway at a surprising speed—cutting off cars and motorcycles and nearly causing six accidents within six seconds of us being on the road.

I clutched the edge of my seat. "What happened to keeping a low profile?"

"For a demon, chaos is low profile."

We drove for a bit in the scary traffic. My eyes meandered to more sinister shops and occasional eateries. Every sidewalk we passed continued to be made of those bricks with inscriptions, but they went by too fast for me to read them.

"What is written on the sidewalk bricks?" I asked Oliver.

"They're all different," he said. "They're intentions."

"Come again?"

"Have you ever heard the expression, 'The road to Hell is paved with good intentions'? Well, it literally is. Each of those inscriptions is a good intention that someone who wound up in Hell once had."

I sunk back in my seat, feeling mortified. After a moment I took a breath, then twisted and leaned forward to gaze out the window again. The curiosity was too great. I stared for a while until—

"Ow!" I yelped as I felt something slice the back of my thigh.

"You okay?" Oliver asked, glancing over.

"I think something cut me." I adjusted in my seat but didn't see anything. And yet, my leg still stung.

"Is this for flight?" Oliver asked, taking my attention as he pointed at the button with wings on my dashboard.

"Yeah. But since you've never—"

"I have a car too, Grace. It's got a button with black wings; I was just making sure yours worked the same." He slammed the button and our car rose off the streets. We started to whiz through the city. Sharp, gleaming towers flashed past in a blur. My hair blew around me and the wind beat against my black leather jacket.

The underside of my leg still hurt but when I looked again and couldn't find anything to blame for it, I assumed it must've been an electric shock or something. I'd experienced weirder.

Finally we soared out of the congestion of skyscrapers. Soon after we left the city behind entirely and flew over a plain of seemingly infinite sawgrass. I began to see a network of huge buildings like sporting stadiums.

"They're different torture annexes," Oliver explained, glancing at my bewildered expression. "For group torture." He pointed left. "That one is for low-level Nazis. The place next to it is for anyone ever involved in the slave trade. At our two o'clock you have domes for trashy reality TV stars—your Real Housewives, your Jersey Shores, and so on. Oh, and that—"

"I get it, Oliver. You torture bad people. You don't have to sound so excited about it."

Olive raised his eyebrows and looked at me. "I'm not excited about the *concept* of torture, Grace. I'm happy because those terrible people are where they should be. On Earth, even bad people who get caught don't always get what they earn. Humankind is too *civilized* for real justice. Not in this place though. Hell is no different to Heaven in that way. Up there and down here, people get what they deserve."

"And what's that?" I tilted my head.

"Exactly what's coming to them."

We drove in silence for a stretch, our car flying immeasurably fast. The annexes petered out eventually and were replaced by small towns of crumbling buildings, the type you'd expect to see in war-torn villages or post-apocalyptic movies. Following that came barren wasteland, then a gruesome lake of tar. Big streaks of lava ran through it—boiling, bursting, and clawing at the surrounding shoreline like a possessed, burning tide.

"So how's it going with your assignment?" Oliver asked suddenly.

I eyed him. "Oliver, I don't think it's a good idea to talk shop with each other. We are on opposing teams, after all."

"In most senses." He shrugged. "Though personality-wise, I

couldn't be further from the people on my team. I can't stand Jimmy or Solange. I was hoping to hear in more detail about how you wrecked her plan to drown Henry this past month. I have a feeling she drastically underplayed how thoroughly you crushed her."

Intrigue overcame me. "You aren't friends with Jimmy and Solange? But you're in the same training class."

"So? I grew up with an abusive father and spent half my time on the streets. Solange was the spoiled daughter of a CEO. Jimmy was a former Instagram influencer—whatever the Hell that means. Just because we have the same job does not mean we're anything alike. Don't tell me you get along perfectly with the guys in your training class."

"Actually, I do. We get along great. I'm really happy to have them to support me."

Oliver rolled his eyes. "Give it time. Trust me. I've been spending a lot of it with Monkonjae at our hospital and the guy is a complete drag."

"You work at the hospital too?"

"As a high school volunteer. It's a much simpler cover than pretending to be a doctor. Your boy better watch it in that regard. If he keeps acting so clueless on rounds with the other med-heads, people are going to figure out he's not what he says he is."

"Monkonjae is not clueless and I'm sure he'll be just as good at foiling you as I am at foiling Solange. Who—*by the way*—says you're no perfect student, either. I hear you can't phase through things to save your afterlife."

His grip tensed on the wheel. "What, you've never struggled to be good at something?"

I chose not to answer for the sake of Hell's honesty filter. A moment passed and another question lingered on the tip of my tongue. I hesitated to ask it. Was I afraid of the answer?

"Oliver . . . Is that the reason you didn't hang me out of the elevator in Angel Tower? You didn't have the power to?"

A long pause ensued. Oliver's eyes never left the sky and I saw not a trace of flux in his expression. He had as good a poker face as the best gamblers and more mystery than a shadow.

"No," he said.

And that was all he said.

We flew over an expanse of forest peppered with homes that were actually nice—condos, houses of varying stories, even mansions. Parts of the forest shook every so often like something big rushed through the trees. My whole body tingled when I heard a far-off roar. It was like a bear crying out for vengeance. A flock of green ravens burst from a copse of pines and soared past us.

A minute later, Oliver lowered our car into a clearing with just enough distance between the trees for us to fit. It was a pretty impressive parking job to be honest.

"Press the button on the keys to make the car vanish," I instructed as I got out. "I'll hit the button again later and the car will appear wherever we are."

"Nope," he said. "We have to keep the car like this. Teleports of any kind—including a car suddenly appearing next to you—don't work past city limits. It'd be too easy for humans to escape torture if they did. That's why we have the Demorale train line. If we make this car disappear, we're walking home. Got it?"

He tossed me the keys.

"Got it."

He walked around the car to meet me but stopped at the back of my vehicle. "No license plate?"

"I got rid of it."

"I don't think a car is street legal if you don't have a license plate."

"Call a cop." I shrugged. "Now, lead the way. I thought you were a demon, not a traffic controller."

Oliver frowned and pushed past me, bumping my shoulder intentionally. I turned and followed. The ground was a combination of broken pavement and rotting leaves. The trees swayed uneasily in the chilling breeze. Spider webs as thick as wedding veils clung to branches.

Another roar echoed in the distance. I gulped.

"You know," I said walking brusquely behind Oliver while keeping an eye on my surroundings. "If this were Earth, or a movie, this would be the part where I find out you're a murderer or a monster and are leading me into a trap or haunted mansion."

Oliver slowed his gait, allowing me to catch up. "You already thought I was a monster, Grace. You haven't been afraid to get close to me before, so there's no sense in retreating now. And the mansion I'm leading you to isn't haunted. It's your mother's."

ISSUES & BREAKTHROUGHS

Oliver pushed aside some branches and I stepped past my demon escort.

Wow.

Right in the middle of this secluded, creepy forest was a beautiful, Southern-styled home with three stories, a navy roof, crisp white paint, and perfectly polished windows.

I recognized the place instantly. I'd seen it in photo albums. This was the house my mother grew up in.

"This is my Grandpa Thorston's home," I said.

"It's your mom's Hell House," he clarified. "This forest is full of personalized Hell Houses for the recently deceased. The demons that design the Hell experience like to keep a close eye on the newly dead to see how they respond to different types of suffering. That way experiences can be better customized so sins evenly match consequences."

We took three steps closer and a ripple of shimmery air passed over us. I gazed up and watched the magic wave trace the perimeter of the house, revealing a dome shape for just a moment.

"It's an energy field designed to specifically keep your mom in the house and other things out," Oliver explained.

"Other things?"

"Don't worry about it."

"Oh, I'm worried about it." I gave him a suspicious look.

"Back to business . . ." Oliver said dryly. "Full disclosure—before you got here, I went to the library by myself to find out where your mom was and what her torture entails. I just figured if you really want to understand what your mom is going through, me reiterating some bullet points wouldn't do it."

"So you know what's in there?" I pointed ahead.

"I did a thorough read of her file, yeah."

"Because you like seeing people get what they *deserve*?" I shot him a condescending glare, but my gaze softened when I realized he looked confused.

"Sorry," I felt compelled to say.

"Don't be. I do appreciate appropriate consequences, but in this case I was thorough because I wanted to make sure this wouldn't be too painful for you. I'm supposed to be helping you, right? I'm not really doing that if I traumatize you."

"Oh."

That was weirdly considerate.

He offered me his hand. I raised my brow.

"I'm going to use the cloaking app on my Demon Soul Pulse," he explained. "It allows us to check on tortured souls without them noticing. Your mom won't be able to hear or see us, but you have to hold onto me if I'm going to spread the cloak over you too."

"Fine," I said. I clasped my hand in his and he led me up the steps to the house. Though we were in Hell, I felt cold as ice. When he pushed the door open, I was met with a long corridor. Dark shadows spilled from some rooms while warm light flooded out of others. I heard voices coming from each of them, pouring into the hall.

"Hell Houses are designed for ordinary people who spend time in Hell," Oliver explained, leaning down a little too close to speak in my ear. "They are not criminals or the truly cruel, just people who have hurt others. Their torture is intended to hurt them to the same degree."

Oliver gestured to the first room on our right. I peered in and saw a younger Nana Robin and Grandpa Thorston arguing. A fireplace roared in the corner—bathing both my grandparents in heated light and causing my nana's orange hair to burn with color.

"They're not real," Oliver whispered. "Just holograms."

"You embarrassed me in front of my entire staff!" Grandpa Thorston yelled.

"Your pig of a vice president came on to me. What was I supposed to do, take it? He deserved to get slapped, Thorston. I should have hit him harder!" Nana Robin shouted, waving her arms dramatically.

Grandpa Thorston pursued her across the room. "You could have been the bigger person. Just once, you could have reined it in. You're out of control—you're *always* out of control—and you probably got me fired."

Oliver tugged on my hand and took me to the next door. There I saw a young redheaded girl rocking nervously in a chair. Her locks were wavy and she had a massive bow atop her head that matched her lavender lace dress. It was my mother. My mother as a little girl. The entire room was *covered* with postcards and letters. They flooded the floor in rolling waves that came up to her collarbone and could've drowned her.

Careful not to let go of Oliver's hand, I bent down and picked up two documents near my feet. The first was a postcard from Mexico.

Sorry, Nougat. I won't be able to make it to that Girl Scout Jamboree after all. I got held up in Guadalajara. See you when I'm back stateside!

Lots of Love, Mom

I scanned the second document. It was a letter with the same handwriting, but there was a seal on the top that indicated the paper had come from a state penitentiary.

Hi, Nougat. I'm sorry I missed your birthday. I meant to call. Got into a bit of a mishmash involving a bar fight. Shortsighted cops couldn't see that those guys were asking for it. Anyway, I'll come visit soon! You're very important to me and I promise I'll make time for us to be together more."

Lots of Love, Mom

I put the documents back in the pile and stepped away from the door, pulling Oliver after me. The next room featured a version of my mother in her pre-teen years. She stood in front of Grandpa Thorston. Her expression was notably stressed while his was unyielding.

"Say it again, child. Repeat *all* the rules. Then you can go with your friends."

My mother took a breath and held her head high. "A lady never talks out of turn. A lady restrains her impulses. A lady doesn't create, inspire, or escalate conflict. A lady must remain level-headed and proper in all situations. And, um—"

"No stuttering."

My mom's brow flinched. "I wasn't—"

"No backtalk. *No aggression.* You don't want to end up like your mother, do you?"

Pain flecked my mother's eyes. "No, Father."

"Exactly. Now, chin up and shoulders back. The final rule. Out with it, child."

My mother stood up straight and stared past her father at the wall. She swallowed visibly. "A lady respects her parents by obeying her parents."

"Oh my God . . ." I whispered, backing away.

My heart rate had increased and my brain fuzzed with tension like after spending too many hours staring at a textbook.

The subsequent room waited several strides up the hall. Its door was closed, and it was one of four rooms left on this floor before the grand wooden staircase at the end.

In a daze, I opened the door, expecting to be shocked and distraught by another slice of my mom's past. But to my surprise, the following room featured a segment of mine.

This room formed a portal that overlooked the front lawn of my middle school in South Carolina. From the doorway, Oliver and I watched a teacher hold me by the backpack and present me to my mother, waiting by the flagpole.

"How many days of detention this time?" my mother asked sadly.

"Three," the teacher responded. "For fighting."

I retreated from the doorway and yanked Oliver roughly to the next one. This room was no less uncomfortable to visit. It displayed my former high school principal's office. He was on the phone. A recent version of me sat in the chair across from his desk, shame weighing down her face.

"Yes, Mrs. Cardiff. I'm afraid suspension is the only option at this point." He nodded as my mom said something on the other end.

"She claims she was trying to stick up for some kids in the theater club," he responded. "I'm not sure of the details, but she gave her classmate Miss Houston a black eye, and that can't be permitted." He glared at my hologram.

"You got detention *and* suspended?" Oliver whispered, giving me a stunned look. "I thought you were supposed to be an angel."

I waved him off, annoyed but also embarrassed and shocked. "Detention, yes. But this—" I alluded to the scene. "This never happened. I never got into enough trouble to warrant suspension. That's my principal, and that's me. But this isn't a memory like the other rooms. I don't know what this is."

Oliver studied the situation and then nodded with understanding. "It's a *fear*." He glanced over his shoulder—two doors left to check. "Come on. Let's test the theory."

In the second to last room we discovered an older version of me—around college age. It made me sad to see her. Being dead meant I couldn't age. I would never look like that. I would forever and always look exactly as I did now.

The sorrow over that soon melted to concern, however, because this older version of me stood by the front desk of a police station. My mother filled out paperwork with a bitter expression while twenty-something me leaned against the desk with her arms crossed. As soon as my mother put the pen down, older me stomped out the doors of the station. The grand hologram of the room shifted and we followed the women outside.

"Grace Cariño Reyes Cardiff, get back here this instant!" my mother declared. She was angry, but I noticed something else in her expression. Oliver was right. It was fear.

"Get off my back, Mom. I'm not sorry for what I did and if

these were the consequences, so be it. *This* is who I am." Older me gestured at herself. "I'm not going to let you try to control me anymore. I'm done!"

Once again, I backed out of the room. My heart rose in my throat like a hot air balloon headed for the sky. There was only one final room I needed to see. I turned up the hall toward it, but then stumbled back when I saw my mom coming down the staircase. I glanced at Oliver. "Is that—"

"Yeah, that's really her. See the Soul Pulse on her wrist?"

Not only did I see it, I was disturbed by it. The watch glowed a powerful red. The wrist that it was attached to was stretched out in front of my mother like a half zombie walk. She seemed to be struggling against it, and I realized the watch was forcing her forward.

There was anguish on her face. Her other hand raked against the banister of the stairs, trying to slow herself down.

My mother was drawn to the same room we'd been headed for. I peered in after her. This room was a portal to . . . The First City in Heaven! Angels walked around, the outdoor seating in front of restaurants and cafes was full, a mirage of the perfect blue sky and color-pulsing clouds shone hundreds of feet above our heads.

When my mother entered the room, an armchair appeared and she was forced to sit down. It was a strange sight, my mom sitting in an easy chair in the middle of celestial downtown. The Soul Pulse seemed to lock into place on the armrest.

Oliver and I watched from the safety of the doorway.

Heaven didn't normally have advertisements, billboards, etc., so when a huge holographic screen appeared above the city, I was surprised. Smaller versions of the same screen popped up all over downtown. The logo for the *Heaven't You Heard?* news program flashed across them and a smartly dressed pair of reporters appeared.

"Hello and good afternoon, I have some sad news to report," said the male reporter. "Grace Cardiff—the pride of our after-life community and the Guardian Angel with the highest percentage of goodness the GA department has ever seen—has fallen."

I backed up roughly into Oliver's chest.

"After going rogue and betraying the covenant of goodness required of a Guardian Angel, she has been stripped of her wings and will be changing teams immediately. More on this story as it develops . . ."

The news show started showing B-roll footage of me at the Pearlie Gates being escorted toward the obsidian orb to Hell by multiple winged angels, including Akari, Ana, and Deckland.

I stepped forward in a daze, gazing up at the main screen. It felt like a block of cement had settled in my stomach. I let it sit there for minute before it crushed me too much to continue.

"I'm done here," I said to Oliver. Without another word, I exited the room, pulling him behind me. I couldn't get out of the house fast enough. Once the door was closed behind us, I let go of Oliver's hand.

I ran down the steps and then paced, crushing the rotting leaves. "That was horrible."

"Torture is intended to be."

A roar of rage echoed in the distance. It shook the trees and caused the ground to tremble. In normal circumstance that would have caused me great concern. However, all of my concern was currently occupied by other matters.

I crossed my arms tightly across my chest. "So my mom's Hell is two parts. Being forced to relive traumatic episodes from her childhood, specifically what her parents put her through, and facing the fear of what she thought *I* would turn into."

"Of what she still fears you could turn into, based on that last room."

I bit my lip. That was probably the most upsetting five minutes of my life. And I was dead. I couldn't believe the horror psychologically haunting my mom—the pain and fear that had warped who she was on Earth and continued to plague her like a malevolent nightmare here.

What she still fears I could turn into.

That last room bothered me in more ways than one. My mind was pulled back to our last interaction.

"I'd love nothing more than to be proven wrong and protect you from falling . . ." I thought aloud.

"What?" Oliver said.

"My mom . . ." I said, still thinking. "The last time we saw each other and were arguing about whether or not I could cut it as a Guardian Angel, she said she wanted to protect me from *falling*, not failing." My curiosity sharpened. "Oliver . . ." I turned to him. "I know that room was just a mirage, but can angels really fall? When Troy threatened me in that elevator, he said I may think I'm special, but Ninety-Seven thought so too. Akari also mentioned an angel of 97% goodness to me once. However I looked it up in Heaven's library and there is no record of any angel with that percentage. Today you commented I was the second most infamous angel. Was Ninety-Seven the first? Is that who you were talking about? Is she real?"

Oliver's face was unreadable—it lacked sympathy but it wasn't cold either. A study in pragmatism. "Grace. I get why you want honesty here. But I don't think you want it from me. Whatever info I have about Ninety-Seven is probably slanted because it was told to me by demons. If you want trustworthy answers, ask an angel. Ask your mentor."

If only my mentor was always trustworthy. She shared things with me when they became relevant. She wanted me to grow but kept me on a tight leash. I needed help with my personal problems, but she seemed to have plenty of her own to deal with.

"My mom seems to know," I commented. "About fallen angels."

"As part of her torture, she may have been briefed on certain things so the fear makes more sense."

"She's afraid I'm going to blow it as a GA—get in trouble and not live up to Heaven's expectations for me just like I failed to live up to hers on Earth. In her book I'm too aggressive and impulsive and unruly to be an angel."

Oliver sighed. "I read your mom's file, Grace. Everyone's parents mess them up to some extent; she's no different. *Her* mom's behavior made her look down on and resent people who are aggressive, impulsive, and unruly. Your grandma's personality is entrenched in those traits, and as a result, her marriage broke up, she had trouble with the law, she was a flighty parent, and she never found a place to settle and live peacefully in life. Your Grandpa Thorston made your mom believe that the way to avoid that kind of chaotic cycle was order, decorum, and restraint."

Oliver gestured at the house. "Now she's tortured half the time with memories that fill her with the anger, sorrow, and bitterness that still lie in her heart because of her parents. The rest of the time she's tortured by the prospect of what you could turn into if you follow in your grandma's footsteps. According to her personality profile, at her core, your mom is driven by the fear that if you act 'aggressive, impulsive, and unruly,' you'll turn out like *her mother*—who broke her heart, lived selfishly in a lot of ways, and never quite fit into society."

I swallowed roughly, then paced a few steps. Another roar sounded. A green raven rushed out of a dying pine and headed for the murky sky.

"I never knew," I whispered out loud—not to Oliver, or anyone, just the trees.

Finally I turned to face my demon guide. "I always thought my Nana Robin was amazing and spirited and my mom was rigid and cold. This doesn't undo how my mom made me feel over the years, but it does give it context. And . . . it makes more sense why she would be this way."

I shook my head angrily. "That means my grandma either lied to me or is too self-absorbed to really know what my mother has been through. Nana Robin seemed genuinely sad about not having a relationship with my mom when I asked her about it. How could she *not* know? How could she not see how her actions are responsible for my mom's unresolved issues?"

Oliver shrugged. "Because she has her own. Out of curiosity, I looked up your grandma's file too. Like I said, everyone's parents do some damage; some just get off easier than others."

He tilted his chin toward his eleven o' clock. "See that path in the woods? It's a five-minute walk to your grandma's Hell House. Demons like to keep relatives close together in case we ever want to try a synergy cross-torture effort. After reading about *her* issues . . . I get why your grandma became who she is."

My eyes boggled. "I need to see it. Now." I took off at top speed toward the path, passing through the shimmery ripple of the house's energy dome.

"Grace, hold on!"

I was already far ahead—moving with the power of desire, desperation, and curiosity. I dashed through the forest, following the naturally worn trail. Eventually Oliver caught up with me and grabbed my jacket so I was forced to stop.

"Grace. *No.*"

I jerked myself free. "Oliver, you have no idea how much perspective I just gained seeing what plagues my mom. It's going to take me days, maybe weeks to sort through that. Today my nana is in Hell for her timeshare. I should take the opportunity to see her truth too. I may never be here again."

Oliver glanced around nervously. "I get it. I do. But one, we're currently not under the protection of a Hell House force field, and that's dangerous. Two, while I fully understand why you want to see this, you shouldn't. *Trust me.*"

A roar shook the trees but it didn't shake my resolve. "Nope. I have to do this." Before he could blink, I took off again. I managed to get maybe forty feet down the path before Oliver reached me again. I was quick, but his legs were longer.

He snatched my arm. "*Grace*, stop it. I'm serious. Look, your grandma was not a great parent. But it was a trickle-down effect of how she was treated when she was younger."

His eyes drifted behind me for a moment and I pivoted to see the glowing window of a tall building just through the trees— Nana's Hell House. My eyes lingered on it until Oliver firmly took my shoulders in his hands and turned me to face him. He looked down at me earnestly with his piercing blue eyes.

"The truth is, as a kid, your grandma dealt with some abuse. She was meek and scared and just let it happen—taking it when people talked down to her, even smacked her around on occasion. Those are the things you'll see if you go into that house, and as someone who lived through that himself . . ." He cleared his throat. "Believe me, it's not something you want to see."

My chest fluttered with sympathy and more curiosity. "Oliver—"

"Your job is all about guarding people. Let me guard you from this," he said, cutting me off. His eyes turned glassy, then he abruptly let me go and waved halfheartedly toward the house. "There are two kinds of kids with troubled pasts—those who grow up acting a certain way because of it, and those who act a certain way in spite of it. Your grandma became aggressive and refused to ever rein herself in as an adult because she hated feeling so powerless as a kid. Maybe it's not an excuse for how that negatively affected your mother, but it is a reason. Her reason. That's what you wanted to know, right?"

I nodded.

"So do you still need to see it, or can you take me at my word?"

A big question.

I stole one final glance at the house then locked eyes with Oliver again. "I trust you," I said. After a second, I cleared my throat and added, "In this case."

Oliver's mouth started to curve into a smirk, but then every part of his face stretched with fear—eyes widening and mouth going slack. In my peripherals I saw branches trembling. Heavy steps sounded behind me. I spun. The forest was undergoing a minor earthquake as something surged through the trees toward us.

"Run!" Oliver urged.

We took off up the path. The footsteps thumped closer, the forest's rustling sounds mimicking a hail storm. More green ravens shot into the sky.

"What is that thing?" I called, leaping over a log.

A roar rattled my eardrums.

"Dark Breed," he panted, not looking back. "This land isn't just for Hell Houses. The forest itself is a kind of torture. Animal poachers get sent here to be hunted by monsters."

"And you're just telling me this now?!"

"I didn't think you'd go wandering off the path! We just have to get back to your mom's house. The force field is for keeping *them* out."

My mother's dwelling came into view just as an enormous, dark shadow leapt over our heads. It landed on the path in front of us. The elephant-sized creature was orangutan-shaped with black fur and *no face*. The place where it should be was creepily flat and smooth. One giant eye blinked in the center of the creature's chest just before it raised its fists and tried to Hulk smash us.

Oliver dove left and I threw myself right. I barely looked up in time to see the monster's fist hammering down again. I rolled out of the way. Suddenly a pair of black sneakers appeared in front of me. My eyes darted up to find a full replica of myself standing there. I glanced over at Oliver as his eyes flashed red. He'd created mirages of us both. They started running around the orangutan, distracting it. The monster released a piercing screech. That confused me at first, as I hadn't seen a mouth, but as the Dark Breed thrashed wildly trying to smash our doubles, I realized it had a huge mouth taking up the back of its head.

Real Oliver got up and so did I. We escaped into the trees.

"Get to the car," Oliver said. "Those mirages will vanish if they get hit or—down!" Oliver grabbed my jacket and thrust me to the dead leaves. It prevented me from getting smacked by a giant stinger, but not Oliver.

"Oomph!"

Another Dark Breed the size of a Hummer had rushed out of the woods. It looked like a bear with the legs and tail of a scorpion. Thankfully Oliver hadn't gotten stabbed, but he did get thwacked against a tree.

Another orangutan screech assaulted my ears and I glanced back to see that Oliver's mirages had vanished. His concentration had been broken when *he'd* gotten hit, and thus the spell was broken too.

The scorpion bear scuttled around, snapping its stinger in our direction. It was taunting us while deciding its next move. I could see the shimmering rims of my car through the trees, but the creature prevented access. Meanwhile, the orangutan clambered closer, blocking the way to my mom's house.

My fists clenched and I rose to my feet.

Halo.

Light shone powerfully above my head and I grabbed my celestial ring. This seemed to enrage the beasts. The scorpion bear roared and the orangutan pounded its chest.

Oliver got up, but then the orangutan ripped a tree from the ground, roots and all. The Dark Breed hurled the tree at my demon.

"Oliver!"

I bounded in front of him.

WHABLAM!

Reflexively I pumped my arm and summoned a shield as strong and wide as the one from Six Flags, protecting us both. The tree bounced off and dropped to the forest floor. I lowered my shield a moment. The scorpion bear rushed in. I activated a smaller shield to whack away its inbound stinger then smack the creature's head when it spun around to tear at me with its teeth.

The scorpion bear whirled its stinger at my head a second time. I dove into a forward roll, accidentally dropping my shield in the process. The scorpion bear chased me closer to the car while the orangutan pursued Oliver, trying to grab him.

I made it to the car and my halo reformed reflexively above my head. I snatched it and threw it at the incoming scorpion bear. The halo transformed into a disc and sliced off the Dark Breed's entire tail in one shot.

WHOA. Did I do that?

The halo spun back to my waiting hand. For a moment the monster continued thundering toward me—I backed up against the car—then it stiffened. Its tail stub oozed out goopy liquid that glimmered like the tears of a mutated sun. The entire monster turned purple. It roared in agony then . . . disintegrated completely.

I exhaled, but relief was cut short by Oliver's panicked shout. The Dark Breed orangutan held the demon boy up to its chest so the monster's tire-sized eye was staring into his fear-filled blue ones.

I raced forward with my arm scooping the air. The halo transformed into a ball of light. Then I fired.

Again. And again. And again.

Trees exploded in half as the orangutan dodged my light with dexterity. Finally I hit the monster's arm and it dropped Oliver with a screech. The orangutan didn't go down right away like the scorpion bear, but I took advantage of its delay and released two more beams at the monster's chest. Direct hits in the eye both times. The creature unleashed a terrible ultimate shout as that oozing, glowing substance secreted in gushes. Then the beast vanished too.

My ragged, adrenaline-filled panting was the sole sound in the woods for a minute. I stared at the trees, mind blank. Or maybe there were so many thoughts and questions rushing through my head that my cerebral circuits had become overloaded, unable to process anything. Eventually I turned to Oliver, who was staring at me. Another roar echoed in the distance.

"We gotta go," he said.

I nodded and we hopped into the convertible. This time, I drove. We rose above the tree line and sped forward. Oliver and I flew in silence for a beat. Then, with one hand on the wheel, I turned and smacked Oliver on the arm. Hard.

"What the Hell, Grace?" he scowled.

"Back atcha, *Oliver*. You parked the car in a forest full of monsters? What is the matter with you?"

"The force fields around Hell Houses keep Dark Breeds out and prevent them from seeing or hearing us. We were safe there. If you hadn't gone running off and been so dramatic, we could've just gotten in the car and left."

"Don't turn this on me. We had a long car ride over here. You could have said something like, 'Hey, Grace, we're going to be parking the car in monster-infested woods, so don't scamper off.'"

I huffed in annoyance, glancing at the lava-tar lake below us. Silence hung thickly in the air for a lengthy pause until—

"You're right," Oliver said, to my disbelief. "I'm sorry. You helped me when I was searching for my mom on your turf. Part of returning that favor should've meant keeping you safe on mine."

I let a moment pass before responding. "I'm sorry too." I sighed. "Even if I didn't know what was out there, it was stupid of me to go running off in unknown terrain. Keeping me safe wasn't part of the deal and you didn't need to."

"That's for sure," he said with a scoff. "Troy was so adamant that you were weak. After that elevator ride, he didn't know what to make of you. None of us did. But you really are powerful for someone so new to this job."

"I'm figuring it out," I said truthfully. I rapped my fingers on the wheel. "Also . . . in addition to an apology, I think I owe you a thank you for that monster incident back there."

Our car began to soar over the wastelands.

"*Why?*" he asked.

"My power seems to come from fear. I haven't been able to test that in Heaven because there's nothing and no one to be afraid of. Facing those Dark Breeds confirmed my theory. Now I know that fear is the source of my strength, and hopefully knowing that will help me find a rhythm for how I harness my power."

"Grace . . ." Oliver responded. "Not to challenge your big moment of enlightenment or whatever, but I think you're wrong. I *know* fear. It's a way of life, a calling, and a tool for every demon down here. It can definitely save a person in circumstances like you're suggesting, but it's also an erratic emotion and a weakness that can compromise judgment. I saw your face when you saved us from those Dark Breeds—there wasn't any fear in your eyes. Not even a hint of it. You just jumped in to defend me and defend yourself. No weakness, only strength. No impulse, a choice. I get that we're on different teams, but in the name of—I don't know—sportsmanship or something, I think you may be looking in the wrong place for what gets you going. Power-wise, I mean."

I didn't say anything for a while, ruminating over Oliver's critical analysis as we passed wasteland, ruins, and annexes. As The Second City limits loomed before us, I finally swallowed and nodded. "You may be right."

He laughed and I glanced at him. "What?"

"That may be the first time an angel has ever said that to a demon."

I couldn't help but smirk.

We entered the ominous metropolis and I kept the vehicle up high until Oliver indicated for me to descend. "I can't teleport outside the city, freeway of fire included. You can leave me there." He pointed toward a congested area of buildings.

I nodded and parked in an alleyway. Oliver got out of the car and came around to my side, leaning his hand on the door and looking down at me.

"I guess this is it," I said.

"Unless you plan on breaking into Hell again."

"Let's see how many vacation days I get on my Guardian Angel employment plan."

We exchanged a spark of amusement. Then Oliver looked at me sincerely.

"I hope you got everything you came for," he said.

"I did. You've given me all the answers I was looking for on this trip." My eyes fell to the car floor. "And answers I didn't even know I needed. For that . . ." I looked up at him, "I thank you."

"So no other problems you'd like help with?"

I shook my head and smiled vaguely. "Unless you also happen to know a way to keep a teenage boy from getting his driver's license."

"Your human assignment?"

I nodded.

"Why don't you just break his leg?"

I blinked. "Sorry?"

He shrugged. "That's what I would do."

I narrowed my gaze. "Thank you, Mr. Demon."

"You're welcome, Miss Ninety-Eight." He gave me a mock salute and then without another word his Soul Pulse flashed and he disappeared. I put the car in drive and rose above the streets. Eventually the freeway of fire came into view. I flew over that for another five minutes before I saw a looping overpass that looked familiar. Then I spotted the Hellevator. I parked the car, got out, and pressed the button on my keys. The convertible vanished.

Then I paused.

I gazed across the inferno at the Hell Beacon and The Second City, wondering where Oliver had gone next—training, his home, someone else's torture environment?

That demon . . . that *boy* was never going to make sense to me. He had a cruel shrewdness to his mind and tongue at times, but if the rules of the afterlife hadn't told me he was evil, I'm not sure I would've immediately noticed.

I unzipped my jacket pocket and took out the Divine Iron thumbtack as I returned to the Hellevator hatch. With another drop of angel blood the UP button was charged and I powered on the platform.

Hell moved farther and farther away from me. The bubbles of the lava palpitated like my own self-reflection.

It seemed strange to accept that a person, let alone an angel, could learn so much from a trip through Hell. But then, weren't there plenty of sayings on Earth about character being found through adversity, strength being forged in fire, and phoenixes being born out of flames and ash? That's what I felt now—stronger from the answers I'd obtained. Transformed in a sense. New understanding and perspective on my mother, my grandmother, and me flooded through my system like a powerful cleanse.

My ride eventually came to a halt and I shielded my eyes from the blaring light of Heaven as I exited the obsidian orb.

When I moved past the gate the small box that held the thumbtack vanished from my hand—magically returned to whatever pocket dimension it was stored in for safekeeping. With a flash of my Soul Pulse, I teleported home. I ditched the demon-wear black clothes and settled on the couch in a comfy pair of sweats and a t-shirt. My Soul Pulse summoned an iced tea to my hand and Droopy started to trot over from his basket.

Then there was a knock at the door.

I got up gradually. Droopy was way more enthused—refreshed from his nap, it seemed. He scuttled to the front door of our cottage. When I opened it, I found Akari with her arms crossed. Droopy sniffed her excitedly and wagged his tail.

"We need to talk," my mentor said sternly.

"*AAWWWHOO!*" Droopy howled.

WHY CATS HAVE IT BETTER
THAN ANGELS

"I can't believe I have to ask this," Akari said, barging into my cottage. "But what reason, in the name of all that is good, could you possibly have for *willingly* going to Hell?"

Panic tensed my body. "Who says I went to Hell?" I said as nonchalantly as possible, shutting the door.

Akari grabbed my wrist and held it up.

My Soul Pulse.

I felt an explosion of worry in the pit of my stomach. "*SH—*" sparkly bubbles escaped my mouth as Heaven cut off my first curse word in a year.

I didn't like bad language. I didn't use it often. In place of the soap some parents used to wash their kids' mouths out after saying a bad word, when we were little my mother would feed Gaby and me a spoonful of Tabasco hot sauce. As a result I forever associated bad language with burning pain. The fact that I had tried to swear just now despite that was a clear sign of how frustrated I felt. For a smart person, I had been an utter fool. I'd been so focused on my plan I had completely forgotten *the tracker* on my wrist. Akari had caught me red-handed.

And yet, instead of feeling guilty about what I had done and begging for forgiveness, my distress turned to indignation. I narrowed my eyes and pulled my wrist away, striding to my kitchen and leaning against the counter.

"Let's be very clear," I said bluntly. "I get that these Soul Pulses *can* track us. But are you *actively* tracking me all the time? Do you have some sort of Grace Alert app that tells you when I go someplace you don't want me to? Would you know if I missed a class at school? Checked out a department in Heaven you thought I wasn't ready for? Ate at a restaurant you didn't approve of?"

"Don't go getting upset with me, Grace. And don't try to distract me with questions. You're the one who made a mistake today."

Droopy started to whine. I picked him up and carried him to my bedroom, closing him inside. His ears were big and sensitive; I was not about to subject them to the shouting match I felt brewing.

"First off," I said, spinning back to face my mentor, "maybe I wouldn't have so many questions if you told me everything I needed to know. No half-truths, no incomplete picture, no I'll-tell-you-when-you're-ready nonsense. Second, what gives you the authority to say what I did today was a mistake? I went to Hell to get a better understanding of my mother and my grandmother so I could make peace with them. That's *my* personal journey and path, which is none of your business or the GA department's business. Furthermore . . ."

My *chutzpah* was growing and I couldn't tell if it was in a positive or negative way. "If I'm 98% good, and you're 93%, wouldn't that mean I know better than you do?"

Akari raised a brow. "Really? You're going to play that card?"

"It's the card *you* gave me," I retorted. "You know I've never fully accepted the number I was assigned. I don't think I'm this epic force for good; my family and no one on Earth ever thought so either. But God and all of Heaven believe I am. Even you believe I am. You've told me so since the beginning. So if you all are right about me, doesn't my ratio alone literally mean I can do no wrong? That I'm not capable of it?"

"*Everyone* can do wrong, Grace. Being fundamentally good doesn't mean you're immune to a bad decision."

"Like Ninety-Seven?" I crossed my arms and didn't blink.

"What?"

"On my first day in your office, you told me the angel with the highest percentage who'd come before me was 97% good. Troy and Oliver have both referred to her on separate occasions. Tell me who she is."

Akari seemed genuinely uncomfortable. "Grace . . . we're not supposed to talk about her."

"Balderdash," I said. "This is Heaven. Can't we do what we like here?"

"I didn't say we couldn't. This is about shouldn't."

I began to pace. My anger was fading as my frustration and desperation rose. "Akari, you're my mentor. You can't keep doing this to me. This may not be Hell, but this world that I've become a part of *is* scary. I can't keep running in the dark hoping you turn on lights as I go. I need to be able to find my own way, and I can't do that with you making me wear blinders. You're supposed to be my guide, but you're also supposed to be my cosmically approved friend, right? Be both by being real with me. Stop treating me like a child."

Akari's expression fluxed with sadness. That took some of the air out of my sails while also annoying me. When you were all worked up, you wanted someone to meet you with equal fire. You didn't want to confront a person who looked so . . . broken.

She walked toward my living room, then paused—keeping her back to me a moment. Eventually she turned to face me and leaned against the couch. "You're always asking for answers, Grace. You think they will fix you and make the world easier to understand. It's not always so simple. Sometimes knowing more makes living harder. Because when you remove shadow and shade to reveal things for exactly how they are your perspective changes, and you can never go back."

She shook her head with a sigh. "Most people think that time is the most valuable resource. It's not. As you've seen, time isn't limited to life. *Childhood* is humanity's most precious resource, and it is not renewable. Innocence allows us to run fearlessly through the dark—learn, grow, and explore without apprehension. Take that away and you'll never be as surefooted again. And even if you do find the courage to run, you'll always be looking over your shoulder and to the sides and underfoot because you know just how many things can go wrong and hurt you . . ."

Her words sunk in. They meant something. But my impudence couldn't fully accept them yet.

"But Akari—"

"Your soul can die, Grace."

I paused. My heart did too. "What do you mean?"

"Nothing is permanent and nothing is without weakness. When celestial beings were created, so was Divine Iron. For every Guardian Angel, there is a demon. You know that our bodies can still get damaged in the afterlife, and that you can die again on Earth. There's more to it than that."

She stopped leaning against the couch and stood up straight. "Guardian Angels can only die so many times on Earth before our souls can't take it. Dying is a lot for a soul to handle. If it happens too many times, the soul disintegrates. Like a shoe that's been worn too much, it can't hold itself together anymore. It falls apart."

My eyes widened. "Why didn't you tell me that?! Had I known—"

"You would have acted differently? Done your job differently? Proceeded with greater caution because suddenly you're aware of just how much you have to lose?"

She strode closer, walking around me like an art collector appraising a statue. "Would you have jumped in front of that roller coaster or dove into that ocean as swiftly if you knew death meant something to you? Now that you know it does—that you have something to lose—aren't you going to be a little more careful every time you return to Earth, a bit more afraid of Solange, a tad more hesitant about stepping into danger to protect Henry?"

I stared at the floor.

Akari stopped in front of me and crossed her arms. "That's another big answer for you, Grace. It's what you wanted from me. Do you feel fixed? Do you feel stronger? Or did the world actually just become even scarier from hearing a truth I was protecting you from until I thought you could handle it?"

A beat passed.

"How many times?" I asked finally. "How many times can angels die on Earth before our souls can't take it?"

"Eight."

My eyes buggered. *"Seriously?* Even cats have nine lives. We get one less than cats? I've already died twice!"

Akari sighed and gestured toward the couch. I was hesitant, but realized the weight of this confrontation was taking its toll. It was getting hard to stand.

I sat on the center cushion. Akari positioned herself on the table in front of me.

"This is your first assignment, Grace." She spoke reassuringly. "I died twice during my first assignment too. Once we get the hang of our GA work, demons don't harm us as easily. We become skilled at outsmarting, outrunning, and outdoing them. I've been a Guardian Angel for a century and a half, and I've only died four times."

"I *guess* that makes me feel better . . ." I said in a small voice.

So many conflicting feelings battled for control of my temperament and perspective. Ultimately, I adjusted on the couch and looked at my mentor seriously.

"Akari, there's merit in your caution with telling me things. I understand your point of view better now, but you're not *my* Guardian Angel. Protecting me has to come second to helping me make sense of this world and this job. At the end of the day, I have a responsibility to Henry and you have that responsibility to me. If you want me to keep trusting you, I need you to tell me the truth, even if it's hard. What's on the higher floors near God's office? Who is Ninety-Seven and what happened to her? And . . . what happened to you? Why did you leave the GAs? What went wrong?"

Akari and I locked eyes for a long moment. Then she got up and headed for the door. I leapt to my feet and followed her.

"So that's it? You're going to give me the silent treatment instead of being honest?" My tone had heightened, but I was more hurt than angry.

My mentor abruptly spun around when she reached the door. Her Soul Pulse flashed and a thick file appeared in her hands. "I can't stop you from searching for answers, Grace. But I can't—" Her voice cracked. She seemed more hurt than angry too.

She took a deep breath. "There are some things I never want to talk about again. That's not about you; it's about me. Trust me. Don't trust me. That's your choice. Truthfully, I'm sure you can find the story of my failure in the library somewhere. However, since I know I can't stop you from learning the truth about me on your own forever, here."

Akari held up the file. "This is my own report on the incident that made me leave the GAs. And this . . ." Her Soul Pulse flashed again and a second file appeared atop the stack. "There's nothing about Ninety-Seven in the public library, but senior GAs have access to our department's private records. This will tell you her story. If it means that much to you, disregard my advice and wishes and discover the answers for yourself."

Akari extended the folders toward me. I stared at them. They tempted me until I met my mentor's eyes. She'd told me a person's eyes were tied to their soul. When I looked into Akari's, I saw the pain permanently stained there. And for the first time . . . I realized some answers weren't worth the cost to acquire them.

I'd been mad at my mentor, and frustrated with her too. But despite my big confrontational speech and the secrets she kept from me, my mind flashed back to what Pearlie had told me months ago when she advised me to trust Akari.

She's a good person. That doesn't mean she's beyond mistakes or beyond learning, but it does mean she will always keep trying to grow from the former and evolve from the latter.

I knew Akari was good. Not because of some number, or her celestial residence, but because of the time I'd spent with her. I'd compared her to my mother—someone who tried to keep me on a leash in the name of what she believed was in my best interest. But there was so much more to her than that.

Everyone had reasons for doing things. Oliver was right; they weren't excuses, but they did lend perspective if you allowed them to. If you put aside your own anger and pride and desires for a moment to empathize with someone else's situation, you may not see eye-to-eye but you would see *them*. And in seeing them, you could proceed more wisely, more forgivingly, and—dare I say— more humanely.

This afternoon I'd seen my mother in a new light. Not because my mother chose it, but because I chose it. I had elected to try and understand her perspective. Unexpectedly, I was being offered the same opportunity for a second time today—the chance to put aside my own hurt feelings and yearnings to be right in favor of trying to understand Akari, and then judge her less harshly because of it.

In that instant, as I stared at her and those files, I knew this was an opportunity too precious to ignore.

I wasn't perfect. My mother and Akari weren't perfect. *No one was perfect.* It was inevitable that we hurt each other and make mistakes. But as Pearlie had noted, we could learn and evolve. I felt like the best way to do that was by giving other perspectives a chance at being valid alongside my own perspective. It was a win-win situation. If I cut others some slack they'd feel less guarded and judged, *and* I wouldn't have to force those in my life to be a certain way to make me happy. Maybe I could hold my head high even if they questioned my character, feel strong even if they didn't agree with my choices, and accept them for who they were—imperfections and all—even if they annoyed or hurt or doubted me. And by lending them that understanding first, taking that initial humble step . . . perhaps in time they could *see me* too, and return the understanding.

I took a step back and held my hands up, refusing the files. "Keep them," I said. "I lost my cool for a minute. It's been a long day, as you can imagine. But that long day did teach me something and I need to be smart enough to heed the lesson."

I took a deep breath. "You're supposed to be my mentor and my friend, Akari. I shouldn't be pushing you to do or be anything you're not comfortable with. I only want the truth from you if you're offering it freely, not because I force your hand. While I do wish you would trust me—with not just the full truth, but *your* truth—I respect your wishes. And I appreciate you trying to protect my innocence, and doing everything in your power to keep my world from being too scary all at once."

I nodded firmly, confidently. "I may not see things the same way, or want to follow the same path, but I understand where you're coming from. And though you may not like it, I think you understand me too. So how about if instead of those perspectives continuing to butt heads, we just try to coexist with them, starting with giving each other the benefit of the doubt. Don't track me everywhere, don't ask me about why I do certain things, don't question my every tactic when it comes to navigating this crazy afterlife. Let me be me. And let me figure out who that is for myself. In return, I won't keep pushing you for answers about the GAs or any other secrets you're not ready to share."

With chin tilted up, I held my hand out to her. "Deal?"

Akari was silent for a beat—staring at me with surprise and . . . perhaps also some pride. Then the folders vanished. "You've started to find your way, haven't you?"

"Let's say I'm winging it."

The edges of Akari's mouth turned up slightly.

She clasped my hand and sealed our new attempt at understanding each other.

"Before you all trot off, I have an announcement," Mr. Corrin said.

The bell had already rung but we stopped packing our things to look at our teacher.

"I've graded the packets from the Six Flags field trip, and the winner is"—he pointed at the back row—"Drum roll, Kyle." The kid obliged like always, thudding his hands against the desk. Mr. Corrin held up the packet in his hands proudly. "Team Funnel Cake!"

Henry and I looked at each other. That was our team!

"I know teenagers find secrets taxing, so you can tell Razel and Justin the news before I see them in class this afternoon if you like," Mr. Corrin said to us. "And you can tell them your prize. You all get the day off from school this Friday and thus get to skip our next test."

"*What?*" a kid in the back said.

"No fair!" another student protested.

"Rigged," someone coughed into their hand.

"It is fair and most certainly not rigged," our teacher responded indignantly. "And for those of you who are no doubt thinking it, I am not simply being nice to this team because these two almost died." Mr. Corrin pointed at me and Henry, which made us shrink with discomfort.

"Let this serve as a lesson to all of you," he continued. "Particularly the team that drew a picture of a bear riding a horse for the extra credit question. Work hard and you get to play hard. Dismissed. Enjoy the rest of your Monday."

Several students grumbled on their way out. Solange caught up with me and Henry as we exited. "I suppose congratulations are in order. I should have accepted Razel's offer to join you."

I shrugged and looked at her sassily. "I guess you picked the wrong team."

Solange was not amused. I was though.

"Razel is going to flip out. Justin too. I can't wait to tell them," Henry said. "This is turning out to be the best week of the semester. A day off in the near future. No studying for a physics test. Razel already got her license. I have my driving exam this Thursday. And we've all gotten a ton of college acceptances. Things are looking up."

"That's the plan," I said. I gave Solange another pointed gaze.

I couldn't help letting a little extra spunk shine through. As Henry noted, things were going well. Since my trip to Hell and deep talk with Akari, I felt different. I felt stronger, freer, and more confident. And I was eager to see if that renewal would leak into all parts of my afterlife. In training these past few days we'd been focusing on individual combat drills again, but I was itching to try out my powers. With the way I was feeling, for once, I wasn't worried about looking stupid. Oliver's insight about fear *not* being my source of strength made a lot of sense. Reflecting on everything he'd said and everything I'd done, I had a new theory and I wanted to test it.

Beyond that, also pumping me up was finally deciding how to reconnect with my mother. Something had to give and in a sense that was going to be me, but not to the extent that I went back to old patterns and compromised who I was for her sake, or anyone else's.

Relationships involved give and take.

I loved my mother. I respected her. It was important to me that she knew that. It was equally important for both of us, and our relationship, that she realized loving and respecting her didn't mean doing everything exactly as she wanted or apologizing for acting in ways she disagreed with. Likewise, now that I understood my mother's perspective better I couldn't demand that she simply change and think differently. That would've been shortsighted of me. And that wasn't love.

Love was not forcing someone to see or be a certain way. Love was about coming to peace with the fact that two people could be and think very differently, but still care about and support each other.

I was at a place where I finally felt ready to confront and reach a new understanding with my mother—my understanding of *her* would be the peace offering, and her understanding of me would hopefully be the outcome.

The only thing that remained was the courage to set this endeavor in motion.

It seemed I wasn't the only one with a grand plan on the brain. At lunch, after Henry gave Razel and Justin the good news, he revealed what had been brewing in his mind since the morning.

"So I was thinking . . ." he said as he slid onto the bench next to me and his sister. He waved Justin over to join the conversation. "I got into USD and UCSD. Razel got into the former. Justin got into the latter. And you said you got into both." He pointed a finger at me.

I nodded, keeping with my lie from last week.

"Our college decisions are due at the end of the month, and none of us are one hundred percent sure where to go. Why don't we use our day off to take a road trip down to San Diego for the weekend and check out those schools in person?"

If a road trip meant nudging Henry in the direction of choosing USD, then I was absolutely in. "I love the idea," I said.

"Ditto," Justin and Razel both seconded.

"May I join you?" Solange asked, popping up behind me. She startled me so much that I spilled a bit of milk from the carton in my grip.

"Solange, you didn't win the prize with us," I said flatly, dabbing myself with a napkin.

"I'll get my parents to write me a note or call me in sick," she lied with a casual shrug. "I also was admitted to both universities in San Diego and have never seen them."

"If your parents are cool with it, the more the merrier," Justin said. "All of us will have a license by then, so we can take turns driving."

Razel shot her hand in the air. "I'll make the playlist."

"Oh, no," Henry said. "It'll be nonstop showtunes. I get enough of that at home hearing you sing while doing dishes."

"I have to keep my instrument sharp," she said, putting her hands on her hips. "The school musical opens in three weeks and I have a reputation of theatrical excellence to uphold."

"So we're all in for Friday?" Justin confirmed, cutting off the arguing siblings.

"We can meet at our house in the morning," Henry said.

"And we'll take my car," Justin suggested. Then he gave me a sympathetic look. "No offense, Doolittle. Your ride may not be equipped for—"

"Human adult use?" Razel offered.

"Oh, hush," I said.

It was hard to rewire your brain.

Even if you learned something that changed your perspective, even if you desperately wanted to infuse that change into yourself, a lifetime of feeling a certain way was not so simple to undo. It was like one of those fancy ribbons on gift boxes—tied tight and quadruple-knotted. Pulling at it did not mean it would give easily.

Nevertheless, pull at it you did, knowing that eventually you'd get the goods inside.

I was sparring with Akari in the octagon again. She swung at me and instead of ducking, I firmly blocked. Then came another block, then a shove. Akari stumbled back. Combatively speaking, I had the upper hand. I should've kept pushing.

Yet, I hesitated. The voice in my head that had nagged me for seventeen years not to be aggressive surged and filled me with reluctance instead of desire to press on. I missed my opening and Akari fired a beam of light. I skittered out of the way and summoned my halo.

You're not attacking; you're defending, Grace.

It's okay to fight back.

I grabbed my halo and sprinted forward before Akari fired another shot. We sparred with glowing rings, making *SCHMING* sounds when they collided like two chefs having a knife fight.

The pair of us violently danced around the octagon. Fire pulsed in my heart and suddenly without thinking I leapt sideways and kicked her hard in the calf. In the spilt second Akari was off-balance, I snatched her arm and thrust her to the ground. I scooped my own arm and a large ball of light started to form in my hand.

"Whoo! Destroy her, Grace!" Leo shouted from the sidelines.

My conscience and muscles froze as the weighty shadow of doubt and learned timidity took hold. The light in my hand vanished like a startled bird and Akari whipped her leg around, taking my feet out from under me. My halo fell from my grip as Akari spun to standing. She bore over me and scooped her arm.

Defend yourself, Grace!

I seized my halo from the ground and pumped my arm at the exact moment a ball of light appeared in Akari's hand.

BLAM!

An energy shield the size of a beach umbrella blocked Akari's shot. I lowered my hand a second later and—to Akari's stunned expression—followed up with a pump and arm scoop that changed my shield to a beam. I blasted her in the diaphragm before my conscience could provide further admonishment. The light plowed her into the net surrounding our octagon.

I panted heavily then regret reflexively grasped my tongue.

"Akari, I'm so sorry!" My halo disappeared and I scampered over to her as my classmates and their mentors climbed into the octagon.

On the ground, Akari blinked—still surprised—then rubbed her chest before accepting my hand up. "Don't be, Grace. That was—"

"A long time coming," Ana said proudly. She turned her chin up at me. "Something's changed in you."

"Something is trying to," I admitted. "I still have work to do, but I may be finally finding where my soul gets its strength from. My purpose—the reason my heart is in this job—was never about fear; my magic is stronger when I act defensively. My power lies in my protective instinct to defend others, defend myself, and defend what's right. But . . ."

"*But?*" Ana prodded.

"I just need to stop getting in my head so much."

Leo gave me a knowing look. "It's not really *your* head that's the problem, is it?"

I sighed. "No. No it's not."

It was my mother's.

I'd get through that obstacle soon enough though. Hopefully.

I held myself tall and nodded positively. "But I'll take this win and build on it."

"Good attitude," Deckland said.

"Can you work here and have any other kind?" I jested.

Monkonjae and Deckland began warming up in the octagon as the rest of us returned to the sidelines to observe.

Leo nudged me on the shoulder. "Are you going to talk to your mom soon?"

"Yup," I said, eyes forward as I watched my angel crush celestially spar with his mentor.

"Movie night this Friday?"

"Next weekend please. I have a roadtrip this Friday."

The boys' halos sparked when they collided—again and again and again.

I took a pensive breath. Every deep conversation I'd ever had with my mother had been a sparring match. While in the octagon I wanted to get over the stigma holding me back and fight harder, with her, it was time for the fighting to end.

"Mom?"

"Yipes!" My mom dropped her book. She'd been resting on the couch in her home when I called from Heaven's Middleground Viewing Center. A teacup steamed on the end table alongside a plate of finger sandwiches.

She picked up her book and set it aside as I sat up straighter on the couch in my Viewing Center room.

"Grace, I am . . . surprised to see you."

"Happy surprised or Grandpa-Thorston-dropping-in-for-an-unannounced-visit surprised?"

"Grace, don't speak ill of your grandfather."

"Sorry." I sighed. My eyes drifted to the floor for a second, then my nerve came back and I looked at my mother. "Mom, I think it's obvious that we have some things to straighten out between us. It's been weeks, and I don't want to keep avoiding each other."

To my astonishment, my mother sighed too. "I feel the same way."

"Good." I nodded.

A moment passed.

"There's a lot I need to say, but I don't think this virtual conference thing is the right setting for it," I continued. "We need to see each other in person. I know what a fan you are of formalities. So I want to formally invite you to meet me in Heaven next weekend. We can go somewhere and talk." My eyes flicked down for another moment and I gulped as I worked up the courage to re-raise them. "I would like to speak openly and honestly with you. Does that . . . is that something you'd like to do?"

My mother looked at me, expression a mix of sorrow and vague disbelief. "Do you think you can control yourself long enough to allow that, dear? You get quite upset whenever I speak to you 'openly and honestly'."

My fists clenched the couch cushions.

Seek to understand before you seek to be understood, I reminded myself.

"Yes, Mother. I can."

"Well then I would very much like to talk with you, Grace," she said. "Just one thing, I cannot do next weekend. I have joined Heaven's Tea Enthusiasts Club and will be spending next Saturday and Sunday at Heaven's Tea Blossom Botanical Garden."

"Sounds tranquil," I commented.

"Do you have availability this weekend?"

"Actually, I'm touring colleges. It's part of my Guardian Angel cover."

My mother's face shifted in a way I didn't recognize and she glanced at the floor. When she raised her head again, I saw sadness in her expression, and longing. "I wish I could be there with you."

"*You do?*"

"Of course, Grace. I went with Gaby on college tours when she was a senior. I was planning to go with her again this spring if she got accepted into any of the schools she wanted to transfer to. I had intended and hoped to do the same with you."

"But it's *us*." I gestured between my mother and me. "You and Gaby are like two peas in a pod. We're not like that. You really wanted to spend all that time just you and me anyway?"

"Grace dear, I don't say this to draw your ire, but just because you drive me crazy does not mean I don't want to be with you."

I mulled over her comment. The idea of my mother and I going on such an adventure together still seemed absurd. I had trouble believing what she was saying.

"I can't imagine you and me traveling cross country together on tour schools," I admitted carefully. "That's asking a lot of you, Mom. And no offense, but you've never missed work for any of my activities. Not soccer games, or class field trips, or . . . a dance recital."

"Grace," she said firmly, clearly a bit offended despite my best efforts. "I don't apologize for making work a priority. It put food on the table and a roof over our heads while helping a lot of people. But despite how you view me as an 'absentee parent,' I would always be there for you when it mattered."

"*Mom*," I said, shifting in my seat, clutching my hands together. "If I invited you to something, then *it mattered to me*. The truth is, what you just said means a lot because I've always felt the same way—just because you drive me crazy doesn't mean I don't want to be with you. I want you to be proud of me and share things with me. My heartaches, my triumphs, the things that are closest to my soul, *like dance*."

I took a deep breath and went for it.

"I know you don't understand, but dance is a very vulnerable thing for me. I've spent so much of my life feeling boxed in and embarrassed to show my true colors. Dancing is the one place where I can let all that go and be me in my purest form, for better or worse. Inviting you to that dance recital was my way of inviting you to see the real me."

We sat with that revelation for a long moment. It was strange how exposing a truth that you'd never fully put together could make you feel so much freer and yet more afraid. My fingers fidgeted in the heavy silence until my mother uttered three words I didn't expect.

"Then I'm sorry," she said.

I blinked. "What?"

"I'm sorry I missed your recital, Grace."

I paused a moment. Then I nodded and said something I had no idea would be this easy to voice. I guess I really wanted to say it. "I forgive you, Mom."

She fidgeted like I did and glanced down. "Can you do it a second time?"

I tilted my head. "Do what a second time?"

"I shouldn't have thrust blame on you for the accident, Grace." She met my eyes; they held the same spark of guilt mine so often did when I disappointed her. "For all the times I have told you to handle your emotions and control your anger and self-destructive aggression, I did not practice what I preach when we reached the afterlife. I did not know how to handle the loss of your father and Gaby. The sorrow overpowered my good sense and I blamed it on you. It was cowardly, it was shameful, but it was easier. For that, I am truly sorry, dear. And I hope you can forgive me."

"Mom . . ." I was speechless. "Thank you."

"Do not thank me, Grace. I only gave you something you were owed. I cannot believe I acted so out of character—so selfishly impulsive and aggressive toward my own daughter. It's reprehensible. I swore I'd never be like that, like—"

She cut herself off, but I knew what she was going to say.

That was a conversation for another day though.

We sat there for a beat and then she half-smiled and released a light huff. I gave her a curious look. "What's so funny?"

"Nothing, dear. I am simply optimistic about our get-together in Heaven. Correct me if I'm wrong, but I believe we just defied our typical expectations for one another and proved that we can speak openly and honestly without claws coming out, so to speak."

Now it was my turn for a huff with a small smile. "I didn't even have to spend any miracles," I jested. I drummed my fingers against my leg. "So how about the weekend after next? The last weekend of April?"

My mother nodded. "I shall put it in my calendar. Where would you like to meet?"

I'd been wondering about that but didn't have an idea that thrilled me yet. "Can I get back to you?"

"Yes, dear." She glanced at her watch. "If there's nothing else, it is getting late here and making supper in this kitchen is always quite an endeavor."

"Have a good night, Mom."

She got up from her couch and began to smooth the wrinkles in her dress as I moved to press the off button on the side of my TV monitor. Then I paused.

"Hey, Mom?"

"Hay is for horses, dear."

I rolled my eyes. "*Mom*."

"Yes?"

"In case it doesn't go without saying . . . I love you. In spite of everything, but also because of everything. I hope you know that even if I've disappointed you over the years, and even if you've always been afraid of me turning out poorly, nothing I've done that you don't approve of has been because I don't love you."

My mother stood still. I wasn't sure I'd ever seen her look so stunned. So . . . caught off guard.

"Thank you, Grace," she said eventually.

"Don't thank me," I replied. "I only gave you something you were owed. Something I should have made clear a long time ago."

"Are you sure?" I asked Monkonjae via Soul Pulse.

"I'm sorry, Grace, but I have no idea how to make someone fail a driving test. If he's really as committed to getting his license as you say, I think you're going to have to do something while he's taking the test."

I sighed and leaned back against my chair in the public library. "Like what? Put on a fake mustache and a baseball cap and impersonate a DMV test proctor?"

Gladice appeared at her desk a ways in front of me, wearing a turquoise turtleneck today. The color of her top changed daily, but the massive owl necklace remained the same. "Excuse me, calls are frowned upon in the library."

I wasn't sure if magical librarians could get annoyed, but I was sure I had to be pushing her limits. Gladice would just have to deal with it though. As my comfort with myself grew, I found my comfort defying authority when it mattered also increased. *And this mattered.*

In three days Henry would make his third attempt at a license. He had to fail in order for me to check off that Plot Point and secure his future. But despite plenty of research and brainstorming since his last blown test, I still didn't have a good idea for how to stop him from passing this one.

I huffed, thinking aloud. "Not that it would matter. Even if I could impersonate a proctor, I'd have to follow DMV rules. If Henry doesn't make a mistake, I'd still have to pass him."

"Oh, how about this—I recently read about a Department for Random Weather that GAs work with sometimes. What if you make it harder for him to drive with rain or something?"

"I don't know, Solange already manipulated a storm once when she tried to drown Henry. I feel like that's not the safest—"

Gladice's desk appeared *directly* in front of my study table, startling me. Several owls alighted onto the edges of her desk and glared at me. The librarian's smile remained on her face, but it seemed more forced now. *"Calls are frowned upon in the library."*

"I have to go," Monkonjae said, noise in his background. "My boss—my assignment—has a medical conference on Saturday that we're traveling for, and I need to help him prep."

"So we both have working weekends." I glanced up at Gladice. "I have to go too. Before Gladice feeds me to the owls."

When I hung up, the librarian nodded at me and vanished. The owls alighted to various bookshelves nearby.

I sighed and gazed over the books spread out on the table. Literally the only idea I had at this point was Oliver's suggestion to break Henry's leg. And I couldn't do *that*.

Right?

My eyes fell upon a textbook entitled *The Greater Good: The Practical & The Painful.*

I shook my head.

No way. That's crazy.

I felt like such a creeper.

Henry's mom had given him a lift to his driving test after school. It seemed too pushy for me to volunteer to take him. There was a fine line between providing moral support and being a stalker. I had to be there to intervene though, so here I was in my tiny blue car, parked under the voluminous shade of a weeping willow—stakeout style.

Since I hadn't found a solution for this conundrum in Heaven's hallowed books, I'd taken to the streets—quite literally—and decided on a hands-on course of action. Over the last couple of days I'd missed dance and spent my after-school time dedicated to memorizing the routes of the DMV's driving test by trailing cars.

I took a sip of orange juice and looked through the binoculars I'd brought with me as people exited the DMV across the street.

All I needed was The Police's "Every Breath You Take" to play on the radio, and a bag of corn chips, and I would have all the lurky vibes going.

The DMV doors opened again.

Finally.

Henry got into his test car as the proctor—a middle-aged, heavy-set woman—settled in the passenger seat. When they took off, I pursued them slowly. While I enjoyed speeding in wide-open Heavenly skies, I'd seen enough secret agent movies to know a steady pace would be best in this situation. I needed to keep up, but not draw attention to myself.

As I merged into traffic, I took another quick glance at the piece of notebook paper taped to my dashboard. It was a breakdown of the different streets, turns, and lane changes that I'd observed proctors test their licensee hopefuls with. All I had to do was make Henry miss enough points on this test and he'd fail.

Sorry, Henry.

I followed for a while as Henry drove along at a moderate pace. There was a sharp left turn coming up. I changed lanes so I was at my friend's four o'clock, leaving enough distance between us that he wouldn't see me.

"God, please let this work," I thought aloud. Then I glanced up at the sky. "That wasn't an expression. I'm really talking to you, if you're listening."

Halo.

The glowing ring appeared and I snatched it with my left hand.

Only one in every ten million people on Earth could see GA powers as they manifested; annoyingly, Henry just happened to be one of those people. I'd been lucky that he'd been too distracted to accept what he'd seen during both the roller coaster and drowning incidents. He'd chalked it up to trauma messing with his mind. I had to be careful with my magic around him now. Hence another reason to allow appropriate space between our cars.

There were only seconds until the turn.

I took a deep breath.

My GA powers had been getting stronger as I'd been getting stronger internally, but my performance could still be spotty. During combat training I still hesitated at times, which led to getting knocked to the floor. I couldn't afford to falter here.

I had to defend Henry.

I held the wheel tightly with my right hand while scooping my left arm. My left hand extended out the window as a ball of light formed in my palm and then—

BAM!

I released a blast of energy at the front right fender of Henry's car as he veered left. The blast rammed the car enough that when Henry turned, he drove onto the curb with a loud *kerklunk*. To the proctor, it would've looked like my friend had drastically overshot the turn. She was definitely marking his evaluation with red pen as consequence.

No time for me to celebrate though. I'd driven past the turn and had to circle back. My eyes darted to the cheat sheet on my dash. I switched my blinker on to indicate my intention to make a U-turn at the next light. I had to catch them quickly.

I didn't doubt my memory or strategy—I'd studied these streets thoroughly in preparation for this plan—but I couldn't control the traffic lights, and the longer Henry and I were separated the fewer opportunities I had to mess him up.

I came to a stall as the next signal turned red and anxiously drummed my fingers along the ten-and-two position where I clenched the wheel. That is until a tall man with shoulder-length blond hair strode across the crosswalk in front of me. His locks bounced hypnotically.

My eyes widened.

Whoa. That hot guy looks like a young Chris Hemsworth. Hm. Chris Hemsworth . . . I'm still on the fence about whether he looks better with short or long hair. I wonder if—

HONK! HONK!

The light had turned green and the car behind me was blaring its horn.

Focus, Grace!

I spun the wheel and made my U-turn. After navigating through a few side streets, Henry's car fell into my sights again. The game resumed.

That's how we spent the next half hour. Henry would innocently be driving along then at the right time I would give his car a little long-distance blast and it would look like he jumped a curb or scraped a bush; I even got him to hit a mailbox.

Finally his route was coming to an end. I thought I'd *probably* done enough to get him to fail, but uncertainty churned my gut. There was no room for error here. Henry could not get his license. That Plot Point made it very clear. With an 87% chance of him getting into a fatal car accident if he got his license before he graduated high school, I couldn't leave anything to chance. I'd attempt one more infraction to be on the safe side. Something bigger.

I recognized the residential street we were approaching. Before heading back to headquarters, the DMV proctors always brought their students here. After a few more turns, Henry would come upon a steep road that inclined upward San Francisco style. There was a tricky intersection near the top of the hill with an ill-placed stop sign. I say ill-placed because it required cars to suddenly stop and hold still at a *very* steep incline.

When Henry reached it, he would need to speedily go from acceleration to hitting the brake. He would then need to swiftly reverse the action without allowing his car to roll back in the half-second that his foot went from pedal to brake and back.

My memory rapidly ran through my knowledge of surrounding streets and came up with a plan.

I'd been driving behind Henry, but when the light glowed green, instead of turning with him, I accelerated and continued straight ahead. While the proctor took him the long way, I would get to the perpendicular street at the top of the hill that crossed in front of where Henry was meant to stop.

I sped to my destination and parked my car. Then I bolted on foot to the dreaded stop sign. The epically thick branches of a grand tree on the curb stretched across the road, casting it in shadow. A large limb grew over and slightly in front of the stop sign.

Henry's vehicle turned onto the street at the bottom of the hill, several cars behind him. I jogged past two houses and ducked around the corner of the second one. My heart thumped nervously.

Henry's car was inbound. When he passed the house where I was hiding, I scampered out, keeping to the cover of trees on the sidewalk. The other cars behind Henry went by too. I got into position and summoned my halo.

Henry was seconds from the stop sign. He pumped the brake.

Defend him. Do what needs to be done.

I let the halo fly. Sailor Moon would've been proud. The glowing discus sliced through the hefty branch above the stop sign. The halo returned to my waiting hand as the branch fell toward the car. Henry's reflexes reacted and he released the brake to avoid being struck. When he did though, his car rolled back on the steep incline and collided with the car behind him. Immediately his vehicle shot forward again—he must've pumped the accelerator—but then he rolled back a second time and hit the car once more. Angry honking ensued.

That really ought to do it.

I bobbed around the backs of houses and returned to my car. Then I drove to the DMV, parked in my stalker spot, and settled there in wait. I was 99.9% sure he'd failed, but I needed to see it with my own eyes. I needed to see the proctor hand Henry his failed test.

When Henry's car finally pulled into the parking lot, I sat forward and whipped out my binoculars. Surprisingly, *the proctor* stepped out of the driver's side and walked over to Henry's mom, who was reading a book on a bench outside the DMV waiting for her son. They exchanged a few words, then Mrs. Sun rushed to the car as the passenger door opened. Henry emerged, but he grabbed his mom's arm and she had to help him out of the vehicle. He winced as he put pressure on his foot. He seemed to have a limp.

I lowered my binoculars.

What did I do?

27

ROAD TRIP

Heaven's Wi-Fi network was extremely good quality; it even took calls from other realms of reality. While I was typing up my English paper in my cottage, a loud ringing overtook my screen. I had an incoming video call from Henry and Razel.

I clicked accept and saw the twins sitting next to each other on a couch. One of their boxers had its face on Razel's lap; the dog was drooling on her pajama pants, but she didn't seem to notice.

"Henry! How are you doing?" I asked. "I was super worried when Razel texted me you got hurt during your driving test, but she didn't give the details. What happened?"

"See for yourself," he said, irritated. Henry adjusted their screen so I could see the cast on his foot.

"His big toe is broken," Razel said as he tilted the screen back up.

"There was an accident during the uphill part of my test," Henry explained. "This tree branch fell and I backed into the car behind me. Then as I tried to move forward, my foot slipped off the pedal, so I ended up hitting the car behind me a second time. And then I was freaked out and my proctor was shouting so I slammed my foot into the pedal so hard that I snapped the bone."

Guilt did an impressive triple flip in my stomach. "I'm sorry, Henry. That's terrible."

"It's dumb is what it is," Henry replied. His mom passed by in the background. When she'd gone, he continued in a lower register. "All that stuff we've lived through recently and a dumb tree branch is what puts me in a cast. Talk about adding injury to insult. Not only did I fail, now I have to wear this stupid thing for four to six weeks."

"You couldn't retake the test for a while anyway," Razel said. "Now that you've failed a third time you have to start the process over."

"Thank you, Captain Optimistic," Henry huffed.

"I guess that means our road trip to San Diego this weekend is off," I said.

"Actually, no," Razel replied. "Hang on, I'm gonna call Justin and Solange too."

My laptop screen split again and Justin's face took up a third of the view.

"Hey," he said, waving.

"Solange isn't answering," Razel muttered.

Hell probably doesn't have a particularly good Wi-Fi signal.

"I don't think there's a lot of reception where she lives," I said. "The video call may not work. You can just text her later. Now what's up?"

"We talked to our parents," Razel said. "Given that we need to make our college decisions soon, we convinced them going is vital. Henry obviously can't drive and will be on crutches, but we're determined to do it. You both in?"

"Sure," Justin said. "You sure you're going to be okay, man? Campus tours involve a lot of walking."

"I'll be fine," he insisted, somewhat irritably. "This is important. The only thing that's changing is that we're not leaving until the afternoon. Our parents only agreed to let us go if we take their minivan. It's 'safer'." He used air quotes. "My mom needs the car until three o'clock, so if it's cool with you two, we'll drive to San Diego tomorrow afternoon and be there by dinner. Then we can do tours of both campuses on Saturday before we head back on Sunday."

"Are we still staying at Justin's uncle's house?" I asked.

"Yep," Justin confirmed. "He's expecting us there for Friday night. I booked us one of those overnight housing experiences at UCSD for Saturday. We'll sleep in the dorms and get the full college vibe."

"I'm bringing shower shoes and batteries," Razel chimed in. *I'm bringing a halo and hand sanitizer.*

At half past three, Solange rode up on her motorcycle. I guess the others hadn't seen it yet.

"Whoa! Sweet ride," Justin said, jogging over to admire it as my nemesis parked in the driveway beside Mrs. Sun's minivan. We'd all been waiting on the Suns' porch. Henry strode over with his crutches. Razel stayed beside me with her arms crossed as the boys drooled over the motorcycle; Justin maybe drooled over Solange a little too.

"Why do guys think girls who give off intense vibes and ride motorcycles with leather jackets are so appealing?" she asked.

I shrugged. "I don't know. I blame Scarlett Johansson and action cinema."

Razel sighed. "I'll go tell our parents we're ready to go. Justin!" she called. "Help me get the cooler."

He trotted into the house after her. I got up and sauntered over to Solange and Henry. "Late again," I commented to Solange. "Traffic must've been Hell."

She narrowed her gaze at me.

"Henry!" Dr. Sun beckoned to his son as he and Mrs. Sun stepped outside. Both their boxers bounded onto the front lawn.

"Be right back," he told us. He moved across the lawn on his crutches. For only just getting them, he maneuvered with surprising agility. Maybe it was his excellent arm muscles and the strong core he'd gotten from surfing. I was glad for that; it meant he'd be okay for the next few weeks as his foot healed. A tad unhappy, but okay.

"Are you going to keep making those Hell innuendos for our entire relationship?" Solange asked, vaguely exasperated.

"Yup. One, I enjoy it. Two, I can see that you don't. You're more than welcome to join in the sly divine discourse if you can keep up." I gave a quick, close-lipped smile and walked away.

"Son, I still say this is a waste of time," I heard Dr. Sun say to

Henry. "You should just declare your college decision now and spend the weekend studying for your final—"

"Dad. We talked about this." Henry groaned. "I'm going. I have to be sure that this is the right choice."

I felt awkward arriving at their huddle when I did, but it was too late. Dr. Sun cleared his throat and checked his watch. "I have a video call with a patient. Drive safely, everyone." He gave Henry a side hug and Razel a more open one.

Hana scampered out of the house with a half-eaten cookie in one hand as Mrs. Sun said goodbye to the twins.

"Bye, Hana Banana," Henry said, rubbing the small girl's head while he balanced on his crutches. She threw her arms around his torso and hugged Razel too. Then she looked up at me.

"Grace, why did you miss dance class this week?"

"I was busy after school," I said.

Not a lie.

"Kelsey got the final interest list for our dance recital. If you're gonna be in it, you should let her or Ms. Suarez know."

"I, uh, already told Kelsey I'm not doing it," I said, feeling uncomfortable with all my friends' eyes on me.

"But you're good, Grace! Maybe not the best, but you've gotten so much better. You shouldn't be embarrassed to show people what you've got," Hana urged.

"Leave her alone, Hana Banana," Razel said. "Being in the spotlight is hard. If she doesn't feel comfortable letting people see her like that, that's her choice."

"Right . . ." I said.

"Speaking of choice," Henry interceded. He put his hand on my shoulder for a second to show compassion as he changed the subject. "We need to decide who's driving the first shift."

"Actually, Solange volunteered to drive the whole way," I piped in before a surprised Solange could interject. "She *loves* to drive and she is already eighteen, so she's had her license for over a year." I turned to Mrs. Sun. "She'd be the safest bet on the freeways."

"Oh, that makes me feel better," Mrs. Sun responded, smiling.

She pivoted to Solange. "Thank you, dear. That's very kind of you to offer."

"I, um, you're welcome," Solange said. She was so caught off guard that she was unable to form words or reason to deny the lies I'd just spilled out.

Mrs. Sun handed her the keys appreciatively and everyone moved toward the minivan.

"Shotgun!" I shouted.

"*Grace*," Razel protested.

"She called it, Raz. That's fair," Justin said. "Your luggage, Madame?" He held out his hand to Solange and she handed him her small overnight bag.

As he went to load it in the trunk with the rest of our stuff, Razel rounded the dogs back into the house with Hana. To his chagrin and protests, Mrs. Sun helped Henry get settled in the car with his crutches; the guy did not like looking weak. But then who did?

With them all out of earshot, Solange turned to me. "What was that?" she hissed. "You know I'm two years younger than you."

I shrugged. "So Ithaca will have to make you a different ID. Big deal. You were already lying about your age so you could drive the Batcycle over there."

"But why volunteer me for all that driving?"

"Your rules state that you can't hurt Henry directly. Which means you literally have to be a good driver because you can't just take us all out with a head-on collision. *I checked*. Akari told me more about the limits of our GA souls the other night. It made me want to look into yours. I spent a lot of time in the library this week and learned your whole deal. Demon rules aren't just rules. You don't choose to obey them; *you have to*. If you break a rule, your soul disintegrates. It's a part of your deal with the Devil. So I know you're going to get us there in one piece. And since you have to do that—and keep your eyes focused on the road because of it—you can't concentrate on magically manipulating any chaos we may encounter. I watched you at the beach, Solange. You need to focus for your powers to work. You're not strong enough yet for distractions. Just to be on the safe side, I'm riding up front in case you need a few extra."

"You guys, let's go!" Razel urged.

"Coming." I nodded to Solange then went to situate myself in the front passenger seat. A moment later, a clearly perturbed Solange got into the driver's seat beside me.

I twisted around to address our friends as she buckled up. "Would you three agree that the driver should get to pick the tunes?"

"I guess so," Henry said.

Justin shrugged.

"Awesome. Solange was too shy to say anything, but it turns out she's a huge musical theater fan. Razel, hand me your phone. We're putting on your ultimate showtunes playlist."

Henry groaned. Justin shrugged again. Razel could not have been more enthused. Her grin shone brightly whereas Solange shot me a *very* irritated glare as I powered on the music. I winked at my nemesis as the opening ballad of *Oklahoma!* blasted from the speakers.

At about half past six, we arrived in San Diego. Justin suggested that we get something to eat before we head to his uncle's house. Our friend recommended a restaurant in the Little Italy area of downtown.

I thought it was going to be difficult finding a parking spot with the Friday rush of folks out for a night on the town. I at least expected for us to have to circle the block several times. But I guess there were some advantages to having a demon as your chauffeur. Solange wasn't a bad driver. She was a brutal driver.

My friends and I clung to our seats as she bobbed and weaved through traffic—cutting off cars, zipping across crosswalks milliseconds before people stepped off curbs, and abruptly stealing a parking spot from a red sedan.

"Geez, Solange, what are the driving tests like in Paris?" Razel commented as the red car honked angrily before leaving.

We got out of the minivan and the twinkling lights of dozens of restaurants and bistros shone in my periphery.

"If it's all the same to you," Solange said to the group, "I am going to tap out on driving for the rest of the trip."

"Fine by me," Justin said. He accepted the keys from her then led the way across the road to a worn-looking building with paneled windows. "Welcome to Ironside Fish & Oyster, one of the best restaurants in San Diego."

It was a busy, beautiful restaurant with tiny white tiles on the floor and a surprisingly high ceiling. On the right was a bar with gold-painted metal stools, a lot of iron framework that curved overhead, and the tallest backbar I'd ever seen. My eyes widened when I realized the left wall was comprised of hundreds of fish head skeletons—one skull after another in perfect rows.

Yipes.

"How many?" the hostess asked Justin.

"Five."

"It'll be about an hour wait."

Razel smacked Justin on the arm. "I thought you made a reservation?"

"I forgot, okay?"

"Well, I'm too hungry to wait an hour," Henry said. "Why don't we—"

"*Oliver?*" Solange said.

My heart tightened and I spun around. The demon in question was at my two o'clock. This wasn't a planned run-in. Both he and Solange looked genuinely shocked to see each other.

Oliver walked over to Solange. "What are you—" He stopped cold when he saw me.

"We're on a road trip to tour colleges," she said hastily. "What are *you* doing here?"

"I, uh . . . you know I volunteer at that hospital. There's a big medical conference this weekend and I asked if I could tag along to learn from all the speakers. We're just having a team dinner." He pointed to a large table with about ten people.

Wait. Does that mean—

I glanced over and sure enough Monkonjae was there, chatting with his colleagues.

"How do you two know each other?" Razel asked, gesturing between Solange and Oliver.

The pair exchanged a quick look.

"Study abroad program," Solange jumped in. "Last year I stayed with Oliver and his family for a semester. We have a lot in common and have stayed good friends." Oliver tried to hide a cringe as Solange put her hand on his shoulder.

"Maybe your good friend won't mind adding some extra chairs to his table?" Justin piped in, looking over at the large party. "Looks like you guys haven't ordered yet, so what's a few more people?"

Solange glanced at Oliver. She was about to say no, but then she looked at me. My nemesis saw the panic and confusion all over my face and readdressed the group. "I think that'd be lovely." She smiled sweetly. "We could catch up. *Right, Oliver?*"

"I . . ." He looked at me too. "I can't think of a reason why that's not a good idea," he said truthfully.

"Is that okay?" Henry asked the hostess.

"Of course," she said. She summoned a busboy to add some more place settings and chairs. My friends followed him to the grand table. Henry moved between Oliver and me on his crutches. Oliver glanced down and saw the cast. When he looked back up at me, his smile made me uncomfortable. He looked like someone had just told him a dirty joke.

The demon opened his mouth to say something, but my glare told him to back off. Thankfully he did just that. He strode over to the table to explain the situation to his colleagues.

"Isn't this bad for you?" I said to Solange as we stood by the hostess podium, observing the others interact. "You'll have to come up with tons of lies on the spot and remember them in case our friends bring anything up again."

"Perhaps," she shrugged. "But it's a worse situation for you. I know Monkonjae is playing the role of someone years older than he actually is. You both have to act like you don't know each other or weave an elaborate web of lies for why a teenage girl from South Carolina is friends with a medical resident in Southern California. Plus . . ."

She unexpectedly drummed her fingers delicately on my bare arm, which made me shiver. "Oliver makes you uncomfortable."

"All you demons make me uncomfortable."

"But there's something about Oliver specifically, isn't there?" She stepped fluidly in front of me. "I saw it. I don't know what *it* is. But seeing you looking so off-balance and annoyed is the perfect revenge for having to drive for *three hours* straight and listening to non-stop musical numbers. Enjoy your dinner, Grace." She spun on her heels and went to join the table as Oliver beckoned us over.

I took a deep breath and followed. When I arrived and met Monkonjae's gaze, I could tell he was stunned. My friend and I had a silent conversation with our eyes. For all intents and purposes, we didn't know each other.

Solange slid into an empty seat as Oliver finished the introductions to the medical folks that were at dinner. "And finally, this is Dr. Liam Wang," Oliver said, gesturing at the head of the table.

"Nice to meet you, kids." Dr. Wang provided a kindly nod. He was in his mid-forties, with a pleasant face and thin, round-framed spectacles. "We're happy to have you join us. Oliver said you're on a college tour. Which universities will you be visiting?"

"USD and UCSD," Justin responded.

"Really?" Dr. Wang perked up. "They're both fine schools, but if I may input bias, I hope you choose USD. That's my alma mater."

"*Really?*" Henry said. He sat at the opposite end of the table from the doctor, a couple feet from where I stood. His crutches were tucked under the booth lining one side of the table. Chairs lined the other side.

"I did my undergrad there and then med school at John Hopkins," Dr. Wang replied. "That's where my passion for brain development research started."

"That's the topic Dr. Wang is presenting on at the medical conference tomorrow," Monkonjae offered, stealing a glance at me.

"That would've been really cool to go to," Henry commented. "Of all the topics we've covered in our school science classes, the brain always fascinated me the most."

"Too bad we're busy," Razel piped in quickly.

Dr. Wang took a sip of water. "I'll give you my card before you leave. Email me and I'll add you to my newsletter list. I send one to the local med community every month talking about recent breakthroughs, updates on my hospital's research studies, upcoming conferences, things like that."

"That'd be great!" Henry said.

"And if you do decide to go to USD, let me know. As an alumnus, I stay pretty involved. I've helped students with internships and research grants in the past." Dr. Wang winked at my friend, then turned to the waitress who'd arrived to take orders.

Monkonjae and I exchanged a very different look this time—full of curiosity and confusion. Our human assignments were making a connection. Was that okay?

"Grace, why are you still standing there?" Razel asked.

Because I'm in shock.

I took the chair beside Henry as Oliver came back over to our side of the table. He paused and frowned when he saw where my demonic nemesis sat. "Solange, you're in my chair."

"Just take the one next to Grace." She shrugged.

He had no other choice. It was the last one left so he sat down—placing himself between me and his demon colleague while I was sandwiched between him and my human assignment.

Lovely.

"Anything to drink, kids?" the waitress asked.

We placed our beverage orders and lively conversation ensued across the table as people casually continued checking out the menu. While Henry was deep in conversation with Justin about some sporting match, Oliver leaned closer to me.

"So, you took my advice?" he whispered in my ear. "You broke his leg?"

I clenched the menu and turned to meet his eyes. Their aqua

shade went well with the nautical elements of the restaurant. "I did not," I whispered, heart beating a little faster. "I broke his big toe. And technically, it was an accident. I didn't mean for it to happen."

"You must be happy though. With that injury I'm guessing he failed his driving test. That's what you wanted right?" He flicked his eyes to Henry. "Plus, your GA job just got easier. He won't be able to surf or do any other more dangerous activities Solange could take advantage of for the next couple months."

Oliver was right. I hadn't thought about that. Was it messed up for me to be happy realizing it? Was Oliver trying to tangle me up inside with conflict over the matter?

I stole a quick glimpse at Henry. He was still wrapped up in conversation, not paying us any attention. Razel chatted with Solange. Monkonjae, however, was watching us.

"That was not my intention," I said quietly to Oliver. I leaned away from him then cleared my throat and redirected my gaze. "So, Justin?" I said loudly. "What's good here?"

For the rest of the evening I tried to ignore Oliver and Solange and Monkonjae as best as possible. Thankfully, the food provided welcome distraction. I concentrated my attention on the lobster roll that Justin had recommended. The contents were juicy, the bread was buttery and toasty, and the crispy shallots added a salty crunch.

Near the end of the meal, Solange invited Oliver outside to talk. Monkonjae and I sat up a little straighter on high alert. After ten minutes had passed, I decided to investigate. I excused myself from the table, ducked around the hostess stand, and took a quick peek through the paneled windows. Oliver paced along the curb by himself. He looked frustrated.

Without thinking, I went outside and came up behind him. "Where's Solange?"

Oliver turned, not surprised to see me. "She went around the corner to call Ithaca."

"I don't suppose you'd like to tell me why?"

"Only if you give me a list of Monkonjae's weaknesses," he joked.

"Right. Different teams." I sighed and crossed my arms, staring at him seriously. "You didn't tell anyone about—"

"Our adventure? No, Grace. It's hardly returning a favor to a person if I sell them out afterward."

"That's true, but I was just making sure. I didn't know demons and codes of honor went well together."

He shrugged. "Maybe it's like how some people like dipping French fries into milkshakes. It doesn't make sense, but once in a while it works."

We looked at each other. The San Diego nightlife twinkled around us. After a beat, Oliver laughed. "Before we go back to pretending we don't know each other, can I just say that what you did to Solange is hilarious. She told me how you forced her to drive for three hours straight so she couldn't concentrate on using her powers. Aggressive first move. I approve."

I flinched and Oliver noticed.

"What?" he said.

"Nothing. I just hate that word."

Oliver gave me a curious look. "Why? Being aggressive isn't a bad thing."

I raised a brow. "Are you really the best authority for deciding what's good and what's bad?"

"Point taken. But if you ask me, being aggressive isn't a quality unique to either team. Aggressive just gets things done and is unafraid of what weaker people think. Sure you can use it for evil, but the good like you can also use it to enforce what's right."

I gazed out at the nighttime traffic, watching the cars go by one after the other. "I was raised to believe doing what's right and good had nothing to do with being forceful," I said, solemn and thoughtful. "To attack is to be hostile. To fight is to incite conflict. Confrontation is an unagreeable person's game."

"Who wants to be agreeable?" Oliver huffed. I pivoted to look at him. "A person who's liked by everyone is as impossible as a unicorn. And honestly, having enemies means at some point in your life, you stood for something."

I paused. "Winston Churchill said that."

"Well, there you go." He shrugged. "We demons take advantage of aggression, but like everything that falls into human hands—weapons, technology, all that stupid social media Jimmy is obsessed with—it can be used for bad or for good. Don't let smaller, more timid minds brainwash you. Sometimes the world needs a little confrontation. Conflict isn't wrong if it's in the name of stopping those with no regard for what's right."

I stood there for a beat and really let myself process the information. My eyes didn't leave the demon's. "Oliver," I said. "Are you sure you're playing for the right team?"

The question surprised him. The fact that I felt the need to ask it surprised me too, but I was sincere. Oliver's face contorted with confusion and we remained gaze-locked another moment until Razel stuck her head out of the main door of the restaurant. "There you two are! We're ordering dessert. You want in?"

Oliver broke from my hold. "Um, yeah. Thanks." He quickly followed Razel but glanced over his shoulder at me just before going inside.

After visiting Hell, I felt sure the demon would never make sense to me. Now I wondered if he even made sense to himself. As someone who'd spent a great deal of life trying to force character and embody a role that didn't fit, the more I spent time with him, the more I thought I recognized similar holes in Oliver's performance.

You must be joking?

I stared at our hostess, mouth agape.

Justin's aunt and uncle had two guest rooms and two kids of their own—a nine-year-old boy and a fifteen-year-old girl. Razel had volunteered to bunk with their daughter, which left a pair of rooms to be split among four teenagers. As our group had a set of girls and a set of boys remaining, guess who my roommate was?

"I set up a rollaway cot beside the bed," said Justin's aunt Mrs. Burke, pointing to the corner as she showed Solange and me our room. "You ladies will have to decide who gets what. There are fresh towels in the bathroom." She alluded to a door by the window. "Please let me know if you need anything else."

"Thank you, ma'am," I said.

Mrs. Burke nodded and closed the door. Solange put her bag on the main bed.

"Don't even think about it," I said.

"What are you going to do?" she asked. "Zap me with one of your little energy blasts?"

"Don't tempt me." I thought for a moment. "Rock, paper, scissors?"

"Seriously?"

"It's either that or a celestial battle. Did you bring your dagger?"

She huffed. "Fine." We got our hands ready.

"On my count," I said. "One, two, three, shoot. Boom!" I grinned. "Eat that, demon."

Solange opened her mouth angrily, then a knock cut off whatever curse she was about to utter. The door opened and Justin popped his head in. "It's movie night in the Burke house. I'm making popcorn. You gals want to join?"

"Coming!" we said in unison.

Ten minutes later, we had settled on a couple of couches in the Burke's family room.

"What are we watching?" Henry asked.

"The first *Maze Runner* movie," replied Justin's nine-year-old cousin.

My eyes widened. Then—

"I love those movies!" Razel exclaimed.

I pivoted to my friend, seated beside me. "*Really?*"

She nodded. "The main guy is my flavor. He's cute and he's so fast."

"He is *SO* fast!" I agreed eagerly.

Razel and I high-fived.

Henry groaned. "Play the movie please, somebody."

It was nearly midnight when my Soul Pulse rang. Solange rolled over in her cot and glared at me. "Do you mind, Grace? You have no idea how early I got up today."

"Calm yourself," I said.

The call hadn't woken me. I'd been reading a textbook by lamplight as there was too much on my mind to sleep. However, I think I'd reread the last paragraph a half dozen times and it still hadn't sunk in. Death had been swirling around my mind—finding meaning in my own, preventing my friend's at the hands of the demon sleeping beside me, wondering how my father and Gaby were dealing with mine and my mother's . . .

Eager for a distraction, I answered the call and smiled at Monkonjae's face. I kept it on my watch screen rather than projecting it as a hologram.

"Did I wake you?" he asked.

"No," I responded. "I was just studying."

"You woke *me*, you tall, dark, and annoying angel," Solange grumbled.

"Who's that?" Monkonjae asked.

"Solange. We're sharing a room tonight."

"She's not going to kill you in your sleep, is she?" Monkonjae asked worriedly.

"Only in my dreams," Solange groaned, getting up and heading for the bathroom.

When she shut the door, I turned back to my friend. "It's against the rules for demons to harm angels directly on Earth unless we attack them first, remember? She can't just stab me while I'm asleep. And since there doesn't seem to be much chaos in this suburban bedroom for her to manipulate, I'm pretty sure I'm safe. That doesn't mean she's not eavesdropping though . . ." I clambered out of bed and went into the corridor. The house was dark. I opened the door to a large linen closet and ducked inside.

"I don't think we should talk long," I said. "Too many mortals around."

"Same on my end. I just thought I'd check in with you. Tonight was . . ."

"Bizarre?" I offered.

He shook his head. "You're the math whiz. What are the odds of us running into each other on Earth? And what are the odds of our assignments making a connection like that? Henry and Dr. Wang talked for a while during dinner, and your guy took my guy's business card. They could keep in contact."

"I don't need math for that, Monkonjae. Odds don't matter when the formula was rigged from the start." I sighed. "I never told you and Leo, but months ago—before I knew what Plot Points were—I overheard Akari and Deckland talking about how you, me, and Leo have assignments with Plot Points that share things in common. Apparently sometimes GAs have assignments that intersect to create huge impact on the world together."

"How huge?"

"Akari referenced a World War, but Deckland believes it's something else."

"That's massive, Grace!" Monkonjae exclaimed. "Do you know anything else?"

"That's all I have. But at the end of their conversation, your mentor said something like, 'Maybe the boss will clue us in when we get closer, unless things reveal themselves on their own.'"

Silence for a moment.

"Well, thanks for telling me," Monkonjae said eventually. "We should tell Leo too."

"I agree. He and I have been hanging out for the occasional movie night recently. I'll bring him up to speed."

"Hanging out without me? Did I fail the friendship test during that first group dinner with my poor taste in curry and Clint Eastwood films?"

I smiled. "There is *nothing* you could do wrong in my book, Monkonjae."

A beat passed.

Darn. I couldn't blame Heaven's honesty filter for that one. I felt hot and panicked. I started to open my mouth to say something to save face when—

"Your smile sets me off balance."

I stared at Monkonjae. "What?"

"Eye for an eye, remember? Our deal—one piece of embarrassing honesty for another."

"Right. Wait, *what*? Hold on—"

There was noise in Monkonjae's background. He turned away from the screen for a second. "Sorry, my roommate for the conference is coming back. Good night, Grace."

And just like that, he was gone. I sat motionless in the linen closet for a minute. Did Monkonjae like *me*? I mean, the way I liked *him*?

No. That's absurd.

Is it absurd?

I stood hastily. I needed to pace or get some fresh air, neither of which this tiny room accommodated. Upon exiting the closet, a ghostly flicker caught my attention. Someone was in the family room. Feet treading on cold marble, I followed the flicker and found Henry flipping TV channels. The spectral glow of the screen washed over him and cast strange shadows across the room.

"You couldn't sleep either?" I said, sitting on the couch across from his.

"I was thinking about that doctor we met at dinner," Henry said, not startled by my presence. He muted the TV and adjusted to face me. "You?"

"Honestly, I was thinking about death."

"Geez. Morbid much?"

"Maybe for some. Death is a concept I can't escape anymore, so I don't run from it; I run with it."

A long, *long* pause ensued. The TV light shimmered hauntingly over us.

"Grace, you mentioned a car accident once," Henry said quietly. "Who did you lose?"

I gave him a pained look. "Henry . . ."

"I'm sorry," he said quickly, suddenly appearing self-conscious. "You don't have to answer, or talk about it with me."

I hadn't really spoken about the accident with anyone besides my mother. It didn't fill me with the urge to cry or wallow anymore. Following Monkonjae's advice, I'd pulled myself out of that hole of despair a while ago because I was useless there—it was a place where light and hope and meaning couldn't grow, and I *needed* to grow. For my own sake, and my mother's, and the boy sitting across from me.

Henry asking about the accident now didn't hit me like a hard blow the way it would have months ago. Instead, it felt like a piece of ice held against my skin—a cold, dull pain that made my body stiffen and heart shiver. The fact that he cared though, was a warmth that made me feel safe enough to answer.

I exhaled deeply and crossed my legs on the couch. "I lost my father and older sister."

It was the truth. Gaby and my father may not have been the people who had died, but they had been taken from me. That was one thing the living didn't realize—the pain they felt in their souls when loved ones died was shared by their loved ones, mourning the loss of *them*. We were all victims to death, no soul escaped unscathed.

I lay back on the couch and stared at the ceiling. "I'd give anything to see them again in person, spend time with them, even just hug them for a moment. I've tried to find peace and move forward, and friends like you have helped. But I don't think you can ever fill the space in your heart that death vacates when it takes someone from you."

The TV flickered meditatively.

"I'm sorry," Henry said. "You've been through a lot. I guess you must think I'm a whiny jerk for always complaining about dumb problems like what college to go to and getting my driver's license."

"They're not dumb problems, Henry. You care about those things, so they matter. I'm not going to compare our lives or our problems; friends don't do that, and people shouldn't either. You have your world and I have mine. I respect that as much as I respect you."

Henry looked impressed. "That's deep, Grace. You're really smart. Has anyone ever told you that?"

"Constantly."

I smiled. He did too. I cleared my throat. "So, the doctor? Why were you thinking about him?"

"I just, well . . . All the logical reasons say UCSD is the best school for me. I get why my dad wants me to go there. It's his alma mater, it has amazing opportunities, the programs are perfect on paper for what I need to study, and I think it's a smart choice."

He ran a hand over his eyes. "But I'm drawn to USD. I wanted to go on this trip because I'm hoping that by checking out both places in person, I can find enough of a reason to convince my dad and myself that it's a better choice. Meeting Dr. Wang is another point I can use in USD's favor. With the doors he could open if I went to USD . . . Maybe it was fate that I met him."

I sighed and looked at the glowing TV, thinking aloud. "You could be right, Henry. You could be right."

THE SPECIALTY

As we strode across the sidewalk, I glanced at the optimistic kids around me. Thoughts of the future burned as brightly in their eyes as the sun illuminating our USD campus tour.

The University of San Diego was an impressive institution. From an academic standpoint, there were dozens of majors and minors to choose from, research opportunities (which Henry seemed excited about), honor societies, and so on. From a physical standpoint, the college had an open campus with sixteenth century Spanish Renaissance architecture, plenty of palm trees, and an unobstructed view of the California blue sky.

Our tour guide, Tiana—a peppy Indian girl who expertly talked and walked backward at the same time—escorted us down a wide path lined with blooming jacaranda trees.

"Some people think that what makes us stand out as a school is our beach city appeal or the contemporary Catholic values that the university was founded on. But I assure you, we have plenty of students who don't swim and plenty of students from different faiths. We welcome and include people from all backgrounds and emphasize building a sense of community with others to form life-long friendships. Our focus on encouraging students to make connections is part of what makes us strong as a college. Our other great strength is commitment to creating an environment where students and faculty are partners in learning. Those are not just words on our website; it's the bread and butter of this campus. Since we are a small university of about 10,000 students, if you are looking to really collaborate with a professor on your academics or private research projects, this is the school for you."

"That could help convince your dad," I whispered to Henry

as we kept up with the group of wide-eyed prospects. He nodded as our guide came to a stop.

"Before we proceed to the library, does anyone have any questions?" Everyone shook their heads. "Okay, great. So off we—"

"*Wait!*" a voice yelled from behind.

The whole tour turned as a girl raced up the path and made her way around the edge of our herd. Henry and I were wedged in the middle of the group, so all I saw were traces of a flowery dress and wavy, oak hair with blonde highlights.

"I'm sorry I'm late, ma'am," said the girl, her voice so familiar. "My dad and I just flew into town this morning. We got a little lost."

The hairs on my arms stood up and I started pushing my way past the crowd. I broke through to the front just as the girl held out her hand to our tour guide.

"I'm Gaby Cardiff. I'm a possible transfer student for next semester."

I staggered backward and bumped into two kids. Gaby and Tiana turned and stared at me. My sister wouldn't recognize me, which meant my awkwardness and shock were completely one-sided.

"I . . ." My mouth opened to voice a thousand thoughts, but no words came out.

"Are you okay?" Tiana asked.

No. No I am not.

I nodded and slipped back to hide behind a few people, still gawking at Gaby.

Tiana readdressed my sister. "Welcome, Gaby. Will your father be joining us?"

"No, it's just me. I know I'm late, but may I please still join your tour?"

"Absolutely. And when we break for lunch, feel free to ask me any questions you may have about what you missed. Everyone, this is Gaby Cardiff from—" Tiana turned to Gaby with a questioning look.

"South Carolina," Gaby replied.

"South Carolina!" Tiana announced. "Let's make her feel welcome in our lovely group. On that note, on to the library!"

Gaby settled into the pack near the front. I gaped at her as we walked. After a moment, she tilted her head at me curiously.

"Um, hi there. I'm Gaby." She offered me her hand. Before I could take it, Solange pushed through the group and wedged herself between us.

Solange stared at Gaby then at me. Her smile was as big as a banana.

"No way," she said.

I fell back into the crowd without shaking Gaby's hand. All the kids filed past me, blurs on either side. Except for Solange. In my distraction, she suddenly grabbed me by the t-shirt and yanked me to the side.

"That's your sister!" she gushed in a low voice.

"What? I don't . . . You don't—"

"Save it," Solange said with a wave of her hand. "If her name and home state weren't enough, your face is all the proof I need."

My emotions in the next two seconds could not have been more dissimilar.

First: dismay, panic, fear.

Second: pure, angry fire.

My gaze narrowed. "Leave her alone, Solange."

"Oh, I won't touch her. You know the rules. But I have to say—I thought I'd seen some imaginative tortures in Hell; this is just delicious. *Now* who is going to have trouble focusing?"

"Come join us, Gaby," Solange beckoned with a smile. Our tour had finished at midday when we reached the school dining pavilion. The ornate stone architecture was elegant and kept with the style of the rest of the college. The thin metal chandeliers hanging from the ceiling reminded me of halos.

My friends and I had decided to eat lunch here then head over to UCSD for our afternoon tour. I couldn't say if I was more looking forward to or dreading departure from this school. I had been in a nauseous, tormented daze since Gaby joined our group. What was I supposed to do? What was I supposed to say? As much as I wanted to, I couldn't exactly embrace her and tell her I was her dead sister. Solange was spot on; this *was* torture.

My whole body tensed as Gaby came over with her tray of pizza and joined me, my friends, and my demon. She sat down directly across from me. My hands tightened so hard around my burrito that some of the contents squirted out the top and bottom.

"So what did you think of the school?" Solange asked Gaby.

"It's great," my sister replied, pushing her hair behind her shoulders. The sunshine spilling through the ceiling-high window behind her made her blonde highlights glow. "It's very different from my old school. Converse College is also wonderful, but last year I decided to expand my horizons and apply to transfer out of state. You know, spread my wings."

I choked on my water.

Razel patted me on the back. "You okay, Grace?"

Gaby stopped. She stared at me and her whole face paled. "Your name is Grace?"

I swallowed roughly. "Yes. It's . . . nice to meet you."

Her brown eyes stared into my mint ones. "Nice to meet you too," she said distantly.

"So, South Carolina, huh?" Henry said. "That's a pretty big coincidence. Grace is from there too. What part, Grace? I'm not sure we ever asked."

"Um, Bluffton," I lied quickly. It was the hometown listed in my GA cover and thankfully pretty far from Spartanburg.

"Where are *you* from, Gaby?" Solange asked eagerly.

"Spartanburg, it's, um—I'm sorry." Gaby laid her hands flat on the table and looked directly at me. I suddenly wished I had the demon power to phase through things; I'd melt straight through the floor right now.

"Have you ever been to Spartanburg or Converse College? I've never been to Bluffton, but I feel like I've met you. Your eyes are so—"

"Familiar?" I cut her off. I had to get it together. I made an effort to change the cadence of my voice in case Gaby recognized that too. "I actually get that sometimes. I have one of those faces. But we've never met."

We stared at each other for another moment. Then Gaby shook her head.

"You're right. Apologies for staring. I think you just . . ." Emotion filled her eyes and she cleared her throat. I understood; the same pain was creeping up mine—building with every minute I was this close to her.

"You just remind me of someone," she said. She took a sip of water and looked away.

"So what other schools are you thinking of transferring to?" Razel asked Gaby, trying to lead us away from the awkwardness bearing down.

"A couple in Texas, one in Florida, one in New York, and three more in California," Gaby replied. She took a deep breath. "I didn't really have a preference before—I just wanted to go to a good school someplace different from where I grew up. But now it's a choice my father and I are making together. We went through a tragedy earlier this year and could both use a fresh start somewhere."

My eyes widened. "You're moving?"

She glanced at me again and nodded.

I looked down at my burrito and took a bite.

"Are you all visiting any other schools in the area? I'm headed to UCSD after lunch," Gaby said to my friends.

I choked again.

"Grace?" Henry looked concerned, but I held up my hand.

"I'm fine," I said weakly.

"Assuming we don't have to take our friend here to the hospital," Justin said, eyeing me, "do you want to ride with us, Gaby? Our minivan may not be the hottest ride in the beach city, but we have room and we're headed to UCSD for a tour right after this."

Gaby blinked. "Oh, that's very kind of you. I'd love to."

Solange glanced at me and laughed to herself as she went back to her salad.

"So how much divine wrath are we talking about?" I asked Akari. Our tour at UCSD was about to start, but there were still a few kids signing in with our guide, Lee, so I'd ducked around the side of the admissions building to call my mentor.

"Grace, while Guardian Angels sometimes find good reasons to reveal themselves to their assignments, there is *no* protocol to tell a random human your identity."

"But she's not a random human; she's my sister," I argued desperately.

"She *was* your sister. On Earth you are no longer Grace Cardiff; you are Grace Cabrera. I'm sorry, I can only imagine how painful this is for you, but you can't tell her the truth. God *will* punish you if you do, and the scary thing is that I don't know how. Don't be the angel that finds out what happens if you break one of our celestial parameters. Remember that talk we had about respecting God's authority and heeding the principles of our work? You have to do the right thing here. Even if the right thing is hard."

I groaned. "Leo says the right thing is relative. It depends on perspective."

"That's an interesting but dangerous idea," Akari warned. A silence passed between us. Then she sighed. "Grace . . . you know you have to let her go, don't you?"

I gulped. My heart felt like it was cracking. "I do," I said softly. I hung up and came around the side of the building just as Lee was calling us to gather.

"Who's ready to check out the coolest campus on the West Coast?"

Depression sunk in as I glanced at my sister. We were so close and yet, like at my funeral, she was completely out of my reach.

UCSD was a fascinating campus. Whereas the University of San Diego had an open, tranquil feel, this place was mysterious and edgy.

First to note, the award-winning architecture that Lee boasted about. I'd never seen anything like it—the epic columns of the glass-walled Great Hall, the marvel of hexagon-patterned outdoor corridors known as the Bonner Hall Archways, and of course the sci-fi majesty that was the Geisel Library. I found it almost as hard to look away from as the head office of the Hell Beacon. It was wondrous and terrifying at the same time. Named for Audrey and Theodor Seuss Geisel (the latter better known as Dr. Seuss), the concrete-reinforced structure at the top of the hill looked like a cross between an alien spaceship and a massive piece of honeycomb.

Currently we walked the snake path that stretched from the library's east side. And I used the term "snake" not just because the route was winding; it was actually modeled to resemble a massive serpent.

"This 560-foot-long tiled work of art is courtesy of Alexis Smith," Lee explained. Our group passed a small garden of fruit trees and a massive granite statue of the book *Paradise Lost*. Lee paused to read the inscription aloud:

"*Then Wilt Thou Not Be Loth To Leave This Paradise, But Shall Possess A Paradise Within Thee, Happier Far.*"

"This place is so cool," Razel gushed as we continued.

"More like creepy," Henry said, still miraculously keeping up with the tour despite his crutches and the downhill slope.

I glanced down at the beige, black, and bronze tiles beneath my feet that matched the scale colors of a common desert snake. "I'm going to side with Henry on this one."

Offsetting the extremely modern architecture in some parts of the school were patches of thick, creepy forest that looked like something out of *American Horror Story*, Roanoke edition. Goosebumps spread over my skin as we walked through the tall, thin trees. They seemed to transport you to another world—the kind that murder mystery writers construed in their darkest imaginations.

"I would not want to be walking here alone at night," Razel whispered.

Solange nodded thoughtfully. "Seems like a good place to get murdered."

"I was just thinking the same thing," Henry said with a smirk.

"Please don't joke," I protested.

I stole another glance at Gaby. If I couldn't tell her who I was, I was going to use every moment I had to memorize every detail about her—the sheen of her hair, the smell of her coconut lotion, the dimples in her cheeks. This was probably the last time I'd ever see her in person. Each fraction of a second mattered.

As a result, for most of the tour I was distracted. Solange never drifted farther than a few feet from me, so thankfully I didn't have to worry about her scampering off and plotting against Henry. However, I barely heard a sixth of what our guide said. No offense to Lee, but I had a lot of personal things going on right now.

It wasn't until we passed Revelle College that he got my attention.

"Did he just say *Watermelon Royalty*?" I whispered to Razel.

"This is one of UCSD's favorite traditions," Lee explained to the tour. "We celebrate the end of spring classes with our school's selected 'Watermelon Royalty' running up the seven stories of Urey Hall to drop the fruit and attempt to break our splat record. The tradition was started by physics professor Bob Swanson in 1965 when one of his exam questions asked students what would be the terminal velocity of a watermelon dropped from the seventh floor of Urey Hall and how far would it splat."

"Sounds like he and Mr. Corrin could've been best friends," Henry whispered to me.

I raised my hand. "Was the weight of the watermelon and height of the building provided on the exam?"

Lee blinked at me.

"I, uh, I'm not sure. But back to the tradition!" he said, dodging my question. "Every year, Revelle College holds a pageant to elect the student or faculty member who gets the honor of dropping the watermelon—our Watermelon Royalty. If any of you are staying here tonight for the freshman experience program, you're in for a real treat. The pageant for electing this year's Watermelon Royalty is happening tonight. Although you can't vote, you should come down and enjoy the party. It's a blast."

Lee motioned for us to follow him as he resumed the tour.

"That's so weird and I am *into it*," Justin commented. "I want to chuck a watermelon off the top of a building with a college full of kids cheering me on."

"It's important to have dreams," Razel teased.

He amiably smacked her on the arm.

I smiled as my thoughts drifted to how Gaby and I used to feast on watermelon in the summer. It was the perfect treat on a hot South Carolina day, and the juice would run down our chins and hands—

"My sister and I used to love eating watermelon," Gaby said suddenly. She cleared her throat. "It's too bad I'm going to miss the party, but my father and I have a plane to catch early in the morning."

"I'll have a slice in your honor," I said, meeting her gaze seriously.

She regarded me a moment and nodded. "Thank you."

The tour continued for another half hour but it felt like less than five minutes. Probably because I didn't want it to end. Gaby's presence had started to feel more akin to the anguish a spicy-food lover willingly endured when eating the hottest chilies—you enjoyed the experience enough that the pain was worth it. The nausea and heartache I'd stomached earlier had taken a backseat to appreciating this miracle I didn't pay for. I may not have been able to reunite with Gaby as my sister, but at least she was right here.

For another minute anyway . . .

"Well, it was really nice meeting all of you," Gaby said, bidding us farewell once the tour ended. We stood in front of one of the school's main drives. My heart rate sped up as I realized I only had moments left with her.

"Maybe we'll see you at one of these schools next year?" Justin said brightly.

"Anything is possible," Gaby replied with a shrug. "To be honest, I'm still waiting to hear back from my first choice. I'm a math major, you see, and I'm waitlisted at Columbia in New York. I'm really excited about the program there."

"Well, in that case I hope we don't see you again," Razel offered kind-heartedly. "It sounds like you deserve a win. I hope you get into your dream school."

"Thank you," Gaby said with a sad smile. "Though getting into Columbia would require a small miracle at this point. Anyway goodbye, everyone."

My sister exchanged a high five or handshake with each of my friends and Solange. Then she stood before me. "Bye, Grace." She offered me her hand.

Screw it.

I wrapped my arms around her in a huge, tight hug. I only let it last a moment; it was all I could afford without coming across as too much of a weirdo, and without falling apart.

"Sorry," I said, pulling away from her. "I'm a touchy-feely person."

"Um, it's okay," Gaby said, though she seemed a bit shaken.

"Okay, kids!" Lee called from under a nearby tree. "If you're staying for the freshman overnight experience, come see me for your dorm assignments."

As if on cue, Gaby's Uber honked its horn. My sister gave us a final wave before she got in the car. As my friends walked back toward Lee, I watched the vehicle pull away with the solemn, heavy understanding that this was the last in-person view of my sister I'd ever have.

I turned my head to see Solange snapping a picture of my face with her phone.

"For my department's newsletter," she explained. "There's a weekly contest for which Guardian of Chaos made his or her angel suffer the most. I think your face will easily place me in the top three."

I narrowed my eyes at her. More anger than I think I'd ever felt burned inside. "I hate you, you know that?"

"Then I'm doing my job right." She pocketed her phone. "And on that note, I hope you had a nice vacation these last twenty-four hours. Remember when I told you at the beach that demons are gifted at different skills? I've been dying to show you my specialty. After months of practicing, I'm finally ready to debut it, and I think we're in the perfect place for me to do so." She patted me on the back before turning to trot away. "Stay on your toes, Grace. It's going to be one Hell of a night."

The campus became more and more alive as dark descended.

My friends and I wandered the thriving afterhours scene of UCSD. Being Saturday, there were plenty of students heading to parties and dinners. Then there was the added frivolity of the Watermelon Royalty pageant. Shades of pink, peach, and green dominated many outfits and décor across the campus in honor of the fruit.

A trio of boys in bright green leggings, dark green boardshorts, and hot pink tank tops charged by with coolers on their shoulders, hooting loudly. Music played from large speakers. Snack stands and activity booths lined the pedestrian paths.

Razel walked at the head of our pack with her nose buried in a brochure. "There's a Freshman Fun Dance around the Silent Tree, which is being put on specially for those of us doing the overnight experience, of course there's the pageant here at the Student Center, and *ooh*, an improv show over at—"

"Nope," Henry interrupted, keeping up on his crutches. "No improv."

"Agreed," Solange said.

"But it's an underappreciated art," Razel complained. "Can't we just—"

"VOTE ASHLEY S. FOR WATERMELON QUEEN!" A swarm of sorority girls in pink crop tops and lime short-shorts accosted our group and bestowed us with plastic beaded necklaces before continuing on their way in fits of giggles. I guess they didn't know we weren't college students.

I held up one of the necklaces I was now adorned with. A tag with the words *Vote Ashley S.* dangled from the end.

Justin's eyes wandered over to a table where similarly dressed sorority girls were hawking Ashley S. merchandise and offering free watermelon.

"You know, I'm kind of hungry," he said. "I'm going to check out that watermelon."

"Yes, I'm sure you're checking out the *watermelon*," Henry said, laughing.

"Shut up," Justin said, smoothing his hair as he walked over to the table.

Razel sighed and turned to Henry. "It's okay if you want to investigate the 'watermelon' too, I wouldn't hold it against you for ditching me."

"Maybe later," he said. "I think I'll go look at some of the other booths." My friend pointed with one of his crutches and strode off into the crowd.

I kept an eye on him. From a tactical standpoint, staying overnight on campus left me and my charge vulnerable. Solange's threat had me on edge, and the after-dark atmosphere turned the school into a threatening funhouse full of twists, turns, and disorienting shadow shapes.

I glanced at my demon, texting on her phone. If she was up to something it was impossible to tell. What could her specialty possibly be? Was she a master at mirages like Oliver? Maybe phasing through things was her jam? How could she use either of those to manipulate the environment on campus tonight? The vibe was rowdy, not chaotic. Though if I'd learned anything from watching movies about college, it was that things could get crazy without warning, so I had to keep my guard up. And I had to keep Henry away from any potentially dangerous, stupid stuff.

Like that . . .

Henry had joined several boys who were preparing a catapult to launch watermelons at pyramids made of plastic red cups. I had a sneaking suspicion that the boys were not drinking sodas as they set up the contraption, making the situation even dicier.

Oh blerf. This was *college.* There was potentially dangerous, stupid stuff everywhere.

"Henry, get away from there." I grabbed him by the shirt, yanking him from the catapult device as the boys wound it up to the whooping encouragement of others.

Henry stumbled on his cast and hissed in pain. "Grace, what the heck?"

"I'm sorry, Henry. You're on crutches and those guys don't exactly seem delicate, pragmatic, or sober. I know you like to take the occasional risk, but maybe you should put some distance between yourself and anything too crazy tonight."

He rolled his eyes. "Grace, if I wanted a chaperone, I would've asked one of my parents to come on this trip."

"She's just trying to help, Henry. Calm down," Razel said, trotting over. "This scene *is* too crazy. Let's go to the freshman dance instead. It's not like we can vote for Watermelon Royalty anyway. And if we stick around much longer, we could end up like him." She waved at Justin who made his way toward us with a big, dumb grin on his face. He wore a *Vote Ashley S.* jersey over his shirt, *Vote Ashley S.* snap bracelets on his wrists, and a *Vote Ashley S.* watermelon-shaped hat on his head.

"I think the redhead likes me," he said turning back to the booth and giving one of the sorority girls a wave and smile.

"I think that girl is old enough to be your babysitter, Justin," Razel said. "Now come on, let's go party with people our own age. There'll be plenty of time to evolve into these creatures when we're in college next year."

She patted Henry and Justin on the back, urging them forward.

Thank you, Razel.

Our group crossed the campus to the alien-honeycomb library. The area in front was decked out with lights, speakers, and tables of food and drinks for visiting kids who were staying in the dorms. The centerpiece of the gathering was the "Silent Tree" that the DJ had set up by.

I *had* paid attention during that part of the tour. Lee had explained that back in the '80s, an artist named Terry Allen was tasked with creating a unique work of art for UCSD. For his subjects, he chose three massive trees that had been cut down by the university to make room for new buildings, and he preserved them with a protective lead skin.

Two were placed in the eucalyptus woods surrounding the library and were wired for sound. One played music and the other projected spoken poems or stories. They played their recordings at random, and because lead absorbed light, they blended in with the trees seamlessly.

The third artsy tree, meanwhile, stood alone—planted in the floor of concrete at the front of the library: the "Silent Tree."

So weirdly fascinating.

My group and I joined the dance party and socialized with the other kids for a while. I was absentmindedly eating a pretzel when I realized I'd lost track of Solange. My eyes darted around the packed area. Razel was dancing. Henry and Justin talked with kids by the food.

Where did you go?

I would have missed her in the shadows of the woods if not for the sparkly hem of her miniskirt. Solange was at the edge of the library. She suddenly turned and looked in my direction. The demon stood still, eyes locked with mine like she was waiting for me. Then she walked into the woods. I took another glance at my friends then followed her.

Armed with suspicion, defensive instinct, and a dash of fear, I entered the shadowy grip of the eucalyptus grove. The music and lights of the party faded into the background as I tracked Solange's silhouette until—abruptly—I lost her. One moment I saw the demon and the next she was gone.

I turned around in place, trying to locate the girl and orient myself. Gothic fog layered the earth with an airy, eerie gray carpet. For a second I forgot that over thirty thousand students went to school on these grounds. I felt like I was completely alone. A scared explorer adrift on a quiet, secluded state of reality.

YIPES!

Loud classical music suddenly belted out from behind me and I jumped two feet in the air.

I staggered away at first, then approached the nearest tree

and put my hand on the trunk, feeling its cold metal. It was a Singing Tree.

Hmm, I wonder if . . .

A menacing cherry glow lit up the fog at my eleven o' clock. I headed toward it in a trance. When I found the source of the light, I found Solange.

"I needed to find the right place," she said from twenty feet away, speaking to me with her eyes fixated on the earth. "Somewhere isolated where I could focus and humans wouldn't be around to witness the emergence. Divine intervention may keep most of them from seeing the truth of our powers, but just in case, I couldn't have anyone interfering or panicking prematurely over what's about to happen."

She finally looked up. Her eyes were red like a Terminator without a skin suit. I opened my mouth to speak, but shut up when the ground split open between us. The jagged crack grew wider as Solange's eyes glowed brighter. I grabbed hold of one of the trees as the earth shook. Bloody light shone out of the widening crevice.

A pure black hand with seven long talons shot out of the opening and clawed at the dirt. The ground trembled as the rest of the mighty creature emerged—head and torso of a bull, limbs and wings of a vampire bat, overall the size of my car. When it rose out of the crack and screeched, its mouth opened too wide and I saw at least two hundred teeth spread over four rows.

The bull-bat huffed clouds of smoke and flapped its wings, levitating three feet above the forest floor.

What in the—

Without warning the ground seized up as curtly as it had opened, leaving no trace the crack had ever been there. Just as suddenly, the bull-bat morphed into a human, taking on the appearance of a skinny kid with glasses in a yellow t-shirt. He snorted the same smoke as the bull-bat, then took off running through the trees toward the library. My mouth hung agape.

"I . . . you . . . *What was that?!*"

Solange staggered a little as her glow faded. She looked like she was about to faint, but she found enough strength to smile at me.

"That's my specialty. Ithaca says it's been decades since they trained a demon with this much talent for summoning and controlling Dark Breeds. I've been practicing a great deal. I had to match your greatness, after all. That thing should last twenty minutes before Hell sucks it back, which is plenty of time for it to find and kill Henry like I asked it to."

"But you can't directly kill Henry!"

"*I'm* not going to. The rules say nothing about Dark Breeds. Most demons don't have a knack for this kind of power; for those of us that do, it's a huge advantage. Miraging it as a kid should make it even easier to take out Henry—much less running and screaming as my creature draws near."

My brain seized a bit as her words sunk in. I shot my gaze in the direction the kid had run then darted my eyes back to Solange. She waved me ahead.

"Good luck, Ninety-Eight. I'd like to see you get out of this one. Better hurry."

YIPES!

I ran faster than I ever had. My feet pounded the foggy grounds as the irregular thud of my heart clashed with the high-pitched classical music belting from the Singing Tree.

I summoned my halo and grabbed it mid-run. In seconds the lights and music of the party crowned the area ahead. I burst through woods and touched down on concrete again.

The crowd in front of the library had grown thicker with kids dancing and mingling. I started shoving my way through them, looking everywhere for the skinny kid in yellow. No one gave my halo a second glance.

Just as I squeezed between a buff guy and a blonde girl, I spotted the skinny kid emerge from the dancing mosh. Henry was directly ahead of him, maybe ten feet away. Smoke escaped the creature's nostrils and he rushed forward. Monstrous talons extended from his miraged human fingers, reaching for the neck of my distracted friend.

THWACK! I chucked my halo, and it sliced off the skinny kid's arm.

SCREECH! The kid roared like the monster it was and everyone turned to see its bull-bat form rip through its skin suit.

SCREAM! That one's pretty self-explanatory.

A huge uproar of panic seized the crowd as my halo returned to my hand. Everyone started running in different directions, blocking Henry from view. With all my might, I bobbed and weaved around the frantic kids. Through momentary gaps in the masses I caught glimpses of the monster and my assignment trying to get away on his crutches.

"Henry!" I shouted, pushing forward.

I broke through a surge of people as the bull-bat grabbed my friend by his cast. The creature hinged on its hind legs and dangled Henry by his bad limb. Its other taloned-hand rose— about to julienne my friend. I got ready for another halo throw, but then Henry shoved one of his crutches into the creature's mouth, jamming it down the monster's throat.

The bull-bat dropped Henry and staggered a few feet before ripping the crutch from its throat. Panicked people knocked me back as the monster made a hacking sound.

The Dark Breed returned its attention to my fallen friend as I forced my way through. It released a screech and loomed over Henry with talons extended and teeth barred.

"HEY!" I shouted.

I scooped my arm and released a *massive* ball of light. The creature dodged, but not far enough. The blast plowed into its shoulder and caused it to go sailing backward—knocking over the DJ equipment and colliding with the Silent Tree.

I dashed to my friend, taking a knee. "Henry! Are you okay?"

Henry groaned, but rolled to his side to face me. I quickly looked him over; he seemed okay except for a few scrapes where he'd hit the concrete. The creature's grip had also shattered the cast protecting his foot.

SCREECH!

We whipped our heads in the direction of the monster. It

flapped its wings and began to ascend. My halo returned and I leapt in front of Henry. The bull-bat's red eyes locked with mine as it hovered twenty feet above. Then it swooped down, talons extended. With great force and concentration, I pumped my arm and rammed my shield up at an angle, thrusting the beast over us. A split second later I spun and shot another ray at its backside.

This beam pierced the right wing and the Dark Breed lost altitude and crashed to the ground. It tried to flap its wings again, but the hole I'd created was too big. Flight was no longer an option. Unfortunately, that didn't stop it. The monster screamed in anger then took off down the path from the library toward the greater campus, chasing after innocent students.

"No! No!"

I bolted from Henry's side. The monster was fast, erratic, and dark. Between the dim lighting and the freaked out kids fleeing the scene, it was hard to keep track of. I paused and turned around in place.

Where'd it go? Where'd it go?

Shrieks called my attention to the woods. Halo in hand, I raced through the trees until I spotted the bull-bat cornering a pack of watermelon sorority girls.

I narrowed my gaze and fired a beam of light. The creature must've had a sixth sense because it stepped to the side and avoided the ray. Then it took off again. I fired as I ran, one blast after another like some kind of angelic machine gun. Every single shot missed, but at least it deterred the monster. The Dark Breed tried to slash or bite the kids as it passed them, but having to run from me and dodge my attacks kept it from laying a claw or fang on anyone.

My heart pounded wildly as shadows and screams blurred past. I had no idea where we were or how far we'd run. The Dark Breed broke free of the woods and I leapt out after it, sneakers thudding on some other part of campus abundant with abandoned snack booths and turned over tables. And then—

I glanced around, hand still glowing, but the area was deserted. The bull-bat was gone.

A snort caused me to turn and look up.

Oh no . . .

The bull-bat launched at me from a nearby tree it was perched in. I moved a moment too slow and the Dark Breed's talons cut into my torso. Together, we tumbled over the concrete amongst trampled plastic red cups and loose fliers.

Owwww.

I attempted to sit up and regain my magical concentration, but I was hurt. *Really* hurt. I grunted and tried to pull myself together. I needed to defend myself, defend these kids, defend Henry!

A dozen feet away, the bull-bat shook itself and clambered to its feet, snorting.

Halo.

Halo!

Faint light flickered above my head before fading out. I was too panicked and in so much pain. I clutched my side, then glanced down in alarm when I felt wetness. Shimmery silver blood dampened my t-shirt.

Oomph!

The bull-bat knocked me onto my back, its torso feeling like a million pounds on my chest, its taloned hands pinning my arms down to the concrete. Hundreds of tiny teeth bore over me and a drop of green drool fell beside my face. I seized with fear—

SPLAT!

With brutal velocity, a whole watermelon smashed into the side of the monster's head and sent it tumbling over. My eyes darted to the right. Among the abandoned tables and booths, Henry stood by the watermelon catapult. He wound up the mechanism again as the bull-bat got back to its feet.

Henry launched a second melon at the monster, but this time the creature saw it coming and slashed through the fruit with its talons. Four pieces of melon went spinning in different directions. The Dark Breed snorted, losing interest in me now that it'd been reminded of the purpose Solange had summoned it for. *Henry.*

The bull-bat bounded toward my friend.

My entire body surged with emotion and I jumped to my feet. My halo formed. I scooped my arm and—

WHAAAMMM!

A beam of light as wide as a lap pool and as strong as the blast from six landmines exploded from my halo. It was like nothing I had even seen in Heaven—obscenely powerful and all consuming. When the blinding light subsided, all that remained of the monster was a large puddle of purple goo.

My breathing was heavy and ragged as I stumbled over to the carnage, clutching my injured side with one hand. The ooze bubbled, shrank, then finally vanished.

"Grace . . ."

I looked up. Henry stood by the watermelon catapult, one foot bare.

With a gulp I walked closer to him.

"So . . . what did that look like to you?" I asked warily.

"It looked like a monster tried to kill me. Then you fought it off with a glowing disc that kept changing shapes. Now you blasted the thing out of existence with a magical beam of light."

I took a shaky breath. "That's about right."

29

MY MORAL COMPASS

It wasn't easy to explain the entirety of the afterlife, and my role in it, in under ten minutes. Considering everything, I thought I did a pretty good job. I got through all the basics in an orderly fashion—big concepts first, then specifics without getting too specific. Henry was still human, after all. Plus, a surplus of info would overload his brain. It'd taken me months to learn about my GA deal, and even that had been rushing it.

"In sum, the celestial struggle is real," I said. "Good versus evil. Dark versus light. Essentially, some negative forces in the universe want to keep you from reaching your potential. I'm here to stop them and protect you." I took a deep breath. "I take it you have questions?"

The two of us sat together in the dorm room at UCSD that I'd been assigned. We'd helped each other back to it at my suggestion. I'd wanted a quiet place to have this conversation where we wouldn't be overheard.

I perched on one of the two twin beds, side wrapped with bandage tape I'd found in the dorm's first aid kit. My injury was aching terribly.

Henry sat in the swiveling desk chair across the room—his mind no doubt swiveling madly with the details I'd just shared with him. My friend's face was puzzled and ashen. His eyes were blank.

Oh no. Had I broken him?

"Henry?"

"Sorry, yeah. I just . . . I have so many questions I don't know which to ask first."

I sighed. "I know the feeling."

He took another moment to chew on the truth and then met my eyes. "Why am I so important?"

"I honestly don't know," I said. "As Guardian Angels, we aren't told out the gate why our assignments are chosen. My job is simply to keep you safe until you fulfill your purpose and accomplish whatever grand thing you have the potential to do."

Henry thought for a few seconds. "So the accidents with the roller coaster and at the beach . . . Not accidents?"

I shook my head. "Not accidents."

"And that monster . . ."

"Dark Breed," I offered.

"It was another strike from some sinister mystical force trying to off me?"

"I'm afraid so. Evil has taken an interest in you, as it does in anyone that threatens its goals." I paused. I wasn't allowed to reveal the identities of any demons to humans, but I suppose I could warn Henry of their existence. We'd already come this far. "And it's not some mystical force. Demons work for Hell in the same way angels work for Heaven. I don't want to scare you, but I think it best at this point that I'm straight with you. There'll be more danger in your future. It's only a matter of when."

Henry was silent for a long time.

He got up suddenly and tried to pace, but when he put pressure on his bare foot, he cringed and almost fell over. I stood, but he waved off my help.

"*I'm alright*," he said harshly.

He sat back down. I adjusted my bandage slightly, then wished I hadn't as the cuts burned fresh from being touched.

Until now I'd believed only Divine Iron could pierce angel skin, but maybe my mortal angel skin was different. I'd have to bring it up at our next training session. Monkonjae and Leo needed to be aware of the threat. I glanced at the dried silver blood on my t-shirt.

How long would I take to heal?

Henry wasn't doing much better. After the bull-bat had crushed his cast, he'd pried it off and clambered across campus until he found me and saved me. His toe was enormous and a dark shade of blue-black that radiated up his foot in swollen red. The skin around it was puffy. He was clearly in substantial pain, but like me he was too proud to address it. Anyway, at the moment he was distracted trying to process a platter of mind-blowing things.

"You know," he finally said, "I really thought I was going crazy. You made me *feel* like I was going crazy. Those things I saw when you saved me—"

"I didn't know you saw what happened until you told me that day on our way to the DMV," I interrupted. "Most humans can't see angelic powers unless we want them to. Their minds sort of filter the magic out and they see things that make more sense."

He didn't respond. His face held resentment and distrust.

"Look. I wasn't trying to make you feel crazy. I'm supposed to keep my identity a secret for as long as possible. But because of what you *can* see, and what happened tonight, it made sense to tell you everything now. You can't tell anyone else though. Not your parents, Justin, or even Razel."

"But—"

"No one can know, Henry," I stated firmly.

He clenched his jaw. After a bit, he nodded and exhaled a deep breath. "Fine. I get it. You're my cosmic babysitter. This whole thing with us being friends, that's—"

"That's real."

He stared at me, disbelieving.

I clasped my hands together like in prayer and sat forward. "We *are* friends, Henry. I'd do my job even if we weren't, but the fact that we've become close is a blessing to me. You may need me as a Guardian Angel, and I've saved you a few times, but you've done just as much for me without even realizing . . ."

I took a deep breath and leaned back, staring at the ceiling with my hands planted on the comforter. "I was vague about the truth when I told you that I'd lost my father and sister." My gaze drifted back to Henry. "I did, but it's because my mother and I are the ones who died in that car accident in South Carolina. It's taken a lot of getting used to, being dead. You've helped make coming back to Earth something to look forward to every day, not something that rubs salt in the wound. I think your friendship *saved me*."

Henry didn't react for what felt like an eternity. Then, unexpectedly, he used his good leg to push the swivel chair across the floor. The wheels squeaked as he rolled until he stopped in front of me. He sighed.

"I'm sorry, Grace. I shouldn't have gotten mad. If anything, I owe you a thank you. You're dedicating your afterlife to me." He smiled slightly. "All I've done for community service this year is volunteer at an animal shelter."

I gave him a small smile in return and met his eyes steadily, garnering the courage to ask the million-dollar question. "So . . . we're good?"

"I have about a hundred more questions, but yeah, we're good."

"In the interest of full disclosure, you should know I'm not going to answer all your questions. I realize that's super ironic considering curiosity and searching for answers are core parts of my character, but the reason God doesn't give Guardian Angels all the details about our assignments is so human beings don't have knowledge they shouldn't. Giving you a full lesson in Afterlife 101 isn't in the interest of that."

"*Grace*," he complained

"*Henry*." I gave him a look.

"Fine," he said with a huff. "But seriously, next time there's a monster on the loose, send me a text or something, will you? So at least I know what we're dealing with."

"What *we're* dealing with?"

"Yeah. Then we can figure out how to fight back."

"Henry, you did save me back there, and I'm super grateful for that. But as I am the one with the magical powers, and I'm already dead, how about you leave fighting evil to me? My job is to guard *you*."

"That doesn't mean you couldn't use someone to watch your back."

"I don't think—"

"Nope." Henry held up a hand. "I'm telling you now, Grace,

I'm not the type to hide until the big, scary monster is gone. You should know that by now. If you're with me, you have to deal with the fact that I'm with you too. Team effort." He pumped his fist up. "Hashtag SaveHenry."

I cracked a smile. "Ugh. Fine. Hashtag SaveHenry. Just be careful and don't do anything too dangerous or heroic on my account. I don't want to see you get hurt."

Henry's eyes drifted down to my silver-bloodied t-shirt. "Same," he said.

The burden of my new job and responsibility lifted slightly. It was amazing how much richer the soul could feel from being heard and cared for. The universe threw so many challenges and enemies at you; it was a miracle that sometimes when you least expected it, someone good would come along and offer to share the load, and also make you feel like the weight of the world was worth bearing.

"I have to say," Henry commented, "the fact that you have superpowers surprised me, but your attitude out there was also unexpected."

I tilted my head. "How so?"

"The way you went after that Dark Breed—blasting it like a boss—that was epically impressive, Grace. It's no wonder they made you a Guardian Angel. I've never seen someone fight like that to defend someone else. And you saved all the kids on campus. I may not know who you were in a previous life, but on that alone I can tell you were a good person. And that my life is in good hands."

I looked at the floor. "Conflict isn't wrong if it's in the name of stopping those with no regard for what's right," I murmured.

"What's that?"

"It's something a . . . friend said to me. He was trying to convince me that being aggressive isn't a bad thing. That *me* being aggressive isn't something to be ashamed of."

I thought about the power I'd been able to manifest against the Dark Breed. I'd fought back hard wearing the hats of both angel and aggressor, two roles I had thought were mutually exclusive. But together, they'd allowed me to stop a monster, protect the innocent, and even rally to save Henry after I'd been injured. I wouldn't have been able to harness that power if I'd been more timid.

"He's right, isn't he?" I thought aloud.

"Your friend? I would say so," Henry replied. "You're aggressive in the name of defending others and defending yourself. You're forceful so you can get the job done. And as far as conflict goes . . . I get that you come from a more conservative background, but you remind me of this girl cat from a Disney movie called *The Aristocats* that Hana was obsessed with. This girl cat said that ladies don't start fights; they finish them. That's kind of like you."

"I know the saying," I replied. "My mother never liked it, but I agree with you. That *is* kind of like me. Only . . ." I thought long and hard then nodded as an enlightenment that had long eluded me finally sunk in.

"Now, I know better," I said firmly. "Ladies can start fights too, can't they? If it's in the name of what's good, and in the name of defending others and yourself, there's nothing shameful about that. Letting bad things happen and bad people win when you could do something about them doesn't make you a lady, or the bigger person. Aggression is like any other kind of strength and power; it's what you do with it that matters."

The doorknob shook as someone started unlocking it from the outside. In panic I seized my jacket and quickly put it on to cover my silver-bloodstained shirt.

Razel burst in and let out a huge sigh of relief when she saw us. *"There you guys are!* Answer a call or a text sometime, huh?"

Henry and I both dug into our pockets. My phone was on silent, and I had over a dozen messages from Razel and Justin. Henry scowled when he took his phone out and saw the screen was cracked.

"Ugh, Dad's going to kill me. I just got this for Christmas."

"I was so worried," Razel said. She gave Henry and me brusque side hugs before plopping down on the comforter next to us. "That was the craziest thing that has *literally* ever happened. How an escaped gorilla from the San Diego Zoo could find its way onto campus and go all King Kong rampagey is beyond me."

Henry and I exchanged a look.

"You saw *a gorilla?*" Henry clarified.

"Well, yeah! Didn't you get a good look at it? It was so scary when it went charging through the dance. I'm surprised no one died. It's all over social media."

She showed us a video on her phone. I guess since the video was captured by human technology, the same mystical veil that protected mortals from the magical truth applied. The gruesome truth had been transformed into a digestible version for regular people.

Henry and I exchanged another look.

"You're in this video a couple times too, Grace," Razel continued, alluding back to the phone. I glanced at it and saw images of me running through the woods. Where rays of light had escaped my hand as I pursued the Dark Breed, in this video it looked like I simply held a big flashlight casting light in all directions. The moments where my beams blasted trees and created craters, those areas looked like they'd gotten smashed by the "rampaging gorilla."

"Huh. That's so strange." Henry glanced at me.

"Not the adjective I would have picked to describe the traumatic evening," Razel replied. Then her eyes drifted down and she finally noticed his foot. "And look at you! What happened to your cast? Are you hurt? Where did you guys go after the attack?"

Henry's eyes widened. "Uh . . ."

"On second thought, hold tight," Razel said quickly. "Justin and Solange are in the dorm lounge downstairs. I think it would save time if we all freaked out about this together. I'll text them." She stood abruptly and texted as she paced.

Henry gave me a worried look and mouthed, *What are we gonna say?*

I held up a hand calmly. "I got this," I whispered.

And I did. Imaginative excuses on Earth were starting to come as easily as embarrassing honesty in Heaven. This was not my first rodeo, and it definitely wouldn't be my last.

When I finally teleported back to my cottage on Sunday afternoon, I could not have been more spent. It had been a draining, enlightening, painful, restorative weekend.

At least I didn't need to worry about Solange. It seemed that using that much power had really taken it out of her. She went to bed right after the incident. Through breakfast, she could barely keep her eyes open. And she slept the whole ride home. I poked her in the arm a couple of times to make sure she wasn't faking it, but the way she groaned and swatted at me confirmed that she was in actual nap mode. The tiny French demon was tuckered out. It would have been cute if not for the fact that her little body was full of pure evil.

All I wanted at this point was to take a nap too—lay down on my couch with my basset hound on top of me. Regrettably, I found a note slid under my door.

Hi Grace,

Please meet me at the Moral Compass at three o'clock. I've been tracking your trip and I know you'll be back by then.

—Akari

I checked my watch. I had less than ten minutes.

"*AAWWWWHOO!*"

Droopy clambered over. I threw my stuff down and knelt to embrace him and massage his ears. "Hey, boy. Did you have a good time with Leo while I was away?" I rubbed Droopy's noggin again then stood.

Ow.

I cringed and clutched my injured side. Just squatting like that had hurt. The scrapes my Earthly form sustained when I was hit by that bus had not followed me to the afterlife. The Dark Breed's claw marks had. This morning when I'd showered the dried silver blood on my skin had come off, revealing four dark gray, jagged lines across my side. I'd assumed they'd vanish when I got to Heaven, but they remained, as did the pain.

I went to the kitchen to drink a large glass of water. There was no time for anything else; I only had five minutes until my meeting with Akari. I'd never heard of the Moral Compass, so I searched for it on my Soul Pulse. It was on a cloud just outside The First City. I concentrated and teleported.

FLASH.

I landed in a beautiful park in the sky. Other angels lay on the grass in the sun, ate picnics, tossed balls to their dogs, and bought ice cream from cute stalls. In the middle of the park stood a gold-and-bronze compass bigger than a barn and mounted atop a matching podium built in the center of a crystal fountain. Instead of the compass having four directional designations, it only had an arrow pointing up toward a G and an arrow pointing down toward an E. Blue light filled a little more than half the compass face while Fuji apple red filled the remainder.

Akari sat on the edge of the fountain, reading a book. The sunlight made her bald head shine, and I realized it was the first time I'd seen her out of her usual Kim Possible uniform of a tank top and cargo pants. I had to say she looked nice in her loose marigold sundress.

She looked up when I neared her. "Hello, Grace," she said. Her Soul Pulse flashed and her book disappeared.

"Hi." I gazed up at the park's main feature "So why are we meeting here and not your office?"

"This is my favorite place in Heaven. I come here when I need some extra peace. It's a special place, particularly for Guardian Angels."

I sat on the fountain beside her. The soothing trickle of water and faint laughter of angels around the park were incomparably serene.

"The percentages of good and evil in people determine where they end up in the afterlife," Akari said after a moment. "The Moral Compass shows the current ratio between good and evil for the whole of humanity."

I glanced up at the compass, shielding my eyes, then looked at Akari. "Wouldn't that bum you out though—to know how much bad there is in the world despite how hard you and the angels work to counteract it? It looks pretty close to fifty-fifty."

"Yes, but never has the goodness percentage sunk *below* fifty. Goodness is always ahead of evil, even if by just a little. Even during Earth's darkest hours when humanity has shown its worst face with wars, genocides, slavery, and political debauchery— even through all that, for as long as humankind has existed there have always been as many or more good people on Earth as there have been bad people. I think it's important to know that. It's a helpful reminder for us as Guardian Angels since we go to war with wickedness every day. And it's healthy for us as people to appreciate this too. Bad people and bad things make a lot of noise and get most of the attention. But good is always out there—beating in billions of hearts and showing itself in a million small ways every minute of every day through love, hope, and kindness."

She sighed and shook her head. "People give evil too much credit. Good may not be the featured player highlighted on the world stage, but it's behind the curtains, and in the audience, and atop the mezzanine—working hard to keep everything together and never giving up, even if it seems the production is going off the rails."

I thought on this and then took another gander at the Moral Compass. The warm light reflecting from it onto me suddenly made me feel warmer too. Akari was right; it was helpful and healthy to remember the good out there. I'd faced death, conflict, demons, monsters, and heartache of every variety. Focusing on those things got me nowhere. It was only when I started appreciating the good things in my new world that I started to become productive as an angel, and as a person again.

Every smile, laugh, good deed, moment of connection with someone—they all worked together to counteract the bad. They were the reason a trip to Hell could lead to a heart-to-heart with my mother. The reason a monster attack could be followed by a stronger friendship with a boy I cared for. The reason I could face off with a demon, get hurt, and drive my body within an inch of exhaustion and yet still be here—sitting in the sunshine with hope in my heart and a calm optimism about where I was going.

"I'm glad you showed me this," I said. "Because of what it means, but also because I can tell it means something to you. You know so much about me, Akari, and yet I feel like you are a stranger to me in so many ways. I like it when you share."

My mentor stared straight ahead. "I closed myself off when I left the GAs. It's hard to reopen your soul when it has been damaged. I wasn't ready to come back to the department. I wasn't ready for you. But *ready* isn't something the universe takes into account when dealing its hands. Anyway, that's why I brought you here . . ."

She flicked her eyes to the compass a moment. "I've watched some video replay of what happened to you this weekend. When I address that, I want you to know that my reasons for trying to convince you to change aren't based on fear that wickedness is too strong. They're based on my own experiences, and my hope to save you from the pain those experiences unleashed while helping you preserve as much goodness as possible."

She cleared her throat and sat up a tad straighter. "A lot of your weekend was a blur to us thanks to your proximity to Solange. But I did see everything regarding your encounter with the Dark Breed."

I looked at her uneasily. It felt like the seconds before a teacher handed me back a graded test. "How did I do?"

"Deckland, Ana, and I are incredibly proud of how much power you were able to call upon. Solange harnessing that kind of demon magic this early in her journey is concerning, but looking at how you performed, I suppose that's why she was chosen as your foil. Hell's superior saw the same potential in her that God saw in you."

My fingers clenched the edge of the fountain. "Potential aside, Akari, if Solange can summon a Dark Breed *now*, I am pretty worried about keeping Henry safe in the future. I can't fight off a monster every weekend."

My mentor cocked her head. "I guess you haven't gotten to the last chapter of the Dark Breeds book yet."

I shook my head. "Sorry. I'm not one to put off reading, but that book is a bit hard to get through."

"I understand. The point is, demons who can summon Dark Breeds can only use that ability once every calendar year. Solange's temptation to show off and jump the gun caused her to act too soon. If I were her, I would have waited until I was stronger and could call two or more at once."

I stared at the sun glinting off the grass. "She'll be able to do that someday, won't she?"

"I imagine so. Thankfully, her cockiness means you have at least a year to prepare for the next attack."

"I'll need that year," I said. "My human form almost died a third time last night." I lifted my shirt slightly to show her the wound where the monster had slashed me.

"I'm afraid it's more serious than that," Akari said. "Since Dark Breeds are made of raw celestial energy, like Divine Iron, they can mortally harm immortal beings."

"Yes. I learned that lesson."

"No you didn't. Not completely at least, and thank goodness for that. Being wounded is one thing—it's pain we can get over and heal from in time. If Divine Iron or a Dark Breed *kills us*, we're as gone as if we had died for our eighth time on Earth."

I blinked, stunned.

Whoa. Heavy.

Akari's brow pinched. "You're going to yell at me now for not telling you this sooner, aren't you?"

"No." I sighed. "There's no point. I can't keep losing my cool over shocking turn of events. I have the information now. I'll approach things with this new understanding."

Now Akari seemed stunned. "Grace, that's so mature."

"Don't sound so surprised." I smiled softly.

"In the spirit of that . . ." my mentor continued after a moment. "I need to talk to you about the Greater Good."

I grimaced. "Akari, I've had a really tough—"

"I know. And I know I've been really hard on you about hammering home the notion of the Greater Good. But I don't want to lecture you right now. I want to tell you about my last assignment . . ."

My whole body tensed. I might have even stopped breathing, subconsciously worried that the slightest shift would startle Akari back to her secretive hole.

"He was a good man," she began in a wistful tone. "Like Henry to you, he was more than a job to me. He was my friend. I ended up revealing my identity to him pretty early in our relationship like you just did, and that made our bond stronger. I protected him for years and though he was the only person I was *supposed* to guard, since he mattered to me by extension I also dedicated myself to protecting what mattered most to him—his wife and four daughters. In the years we were a team I saw him grow, and change, and achieve so much. He meant a lot to *a lot* of people across the world. He inspired them, and actively made an impact on humanity. God eventually told me the extent of what he was meant to do. In addition to inspiring a generation—bridging cultural, religious, and racial divides—he would build an empire that would help children reach their potential and, with his daughters in mind, propel female empowerment to a new level in media, sports, and business."

She paused until I dared to ask the deepest question.

"What happened to him?"

Akari didn't respond right away. Ultimately, she hung her head with the saddest sigh Heaven had ever heard. "I failed," she said simply.

Her eyes focused on distant nothingness. "There was an accident. On a private plane with his family and friends. It's too terrible to get into the specifics, but a chain reaction caused the aircraft to malfunction. I should have gotten him to safety first. I had my wings and my teleporting powers, and decades of experience under my belt. But he was too good a man, you see. He insisted I get everyone else off the plane first. I did as he asked but when I was on the last person, dropping his eldest daughter safely on the ground, that's when it happened."

She swallowed roughly. "He was the only one still aboard when the plane exploded. I can still remember the orange and black plumes in the sky and the debris raining down . . ."

Akari choked on her last words. A single glistening tear

escaped her cheek and fell to the concrete. With effort she took a breath and turned to face me. "He died, Grace. I saved his family and friends, which is what he wanted. But he is what the world *needed*. All those wonderful things he still had the potential to accomplish, and the millions of people he would have inspired . . . all that vanished in an instant and can never be resurrected. It's because of me. It's because I cared so much about people that I forgot about the Greater Good for humanity. The world is a shade darker because of that. And no one and nothing can ever make it right."

Akari put her hand over one of mine. "That's why I want you to understand the Greater Good, Grace. When that Dark Breed ran off across the UCSD campus, you should have taken that opening to get Henry to safety. Instead, you left him there. What if Solange actually had the potential to summon a second creature? What if she'd still had the strength to manipulate the chaos in the area to kill Henry another way? He could've been trampled or electrocuted or a dozen different things. You abandoned him to chase after the Dark Breed and protect the other humans. That's noble, but I'm sorry to have to tell you that it was wrong."

I sat there with the information. The trickle of the fountain seemed so loud now. The world felt heavy and complicated. Dead or alive, one realm or another, I guess it always would be.

With care, I put my other hand over my mentor's. "I can't thank you enough for sharing this with me, Akari. I realize how hard opening up like that had to be and I'm so, so sorry for what happened to you and your assignment." I sighed. "But though I hear what you're saying . . . isn't it in our blood as people— as angels—to care? To protect others? If I were on that plane I probably would've tried to save everyone too. It's our instinct. That's why we're GAs. How am I supposed to unwrite that code in my DNA?"

"You don't have to rewrite who you are, Grace, or change the way your heart and soul are designed. I couldn't. But you do have to be strong enough to choose that which feels wrong *to you* in the name of what's right for others."

"That's the exact opposite of what I've been trying to teach myself though!"

I withdrew my hands and leaned back on the fountain with a huff of exasperation, staring up at endless sky. "I'm finally in a place where I feel confident about doing what I know is right, even if some people may view it as wrong. How can my soul keep that newfound strength and confidence while justifying what you just said?"

We sat in silence a while until Akari spoke again.

"In Heaven, the assignment comes first, Grace," she said plainly. "It's a rule in our line of work. It's a mandate from God. And it's advice from me. *Please follow it*. Don't make the same mistake I did. Heed the rules and listen to those of us with more experience."

I marinated on the warning a bit longer. Then I stood. I took Akari by the wrist and tugged her lightly to her feet. Then I hugged her. Tightly. Her body tensed in surprise at first, but then she returned the hug. No words or further explanation necessary.

When I pulled away, I held her gaze. "I'm not going to let you down, Akari. I don't know if you'll always approve of my choices, but I genuinely understand what you're telling me." I took a deep breath and nodded, internalizing her advice.

I'd learned it was not only okay, but healthy to question what other people believed was best for me and how others and society thought I should behave. I felt like I'd broken free of the chains my mother and cultural expectations had placed upon me, and I was never going back. But I begrudgingly also accepted that perhaps even people who'd broken free, and who'd come to appreciate the value of fighting battles, had to respect that there were some that shouldn't be fought. I was upset about what God and Akari wanted me to do, but maybe there were some rules—some principles—too big and set by beings too powerful to be questioned . . .

"The assignment comes first," I said firmly. "I'll listen, Akari. Even if it's hard, I promise to take your advice seriously. Because it's God-sanctioned and Guardian Angel approved, but also because I know how difficult it was for you to share your truth and you wouldn't have done that if you weren't at your last resort to get me to listen. Thank you for caring enough to do that. I appreciate it. And once more, I'm truly sorry for your loss. It must be so hard to live with that kind of pain every day."

She sighed wistfully. "We all live with pain, Grace. Even angels don't escape that. Maybe it's time I stop letting pain keep me grounded. I miss the person I used to be when I didn't feel so much weight in my soul, when I used to allow myself to fly without being held down by heartache. Maybe it's time I see if that woman can be revived. Mentoring you has certainly made me think it's possible. You've reminded me of my purpose."

"What's that?" I asked.

She smiled softly. "To help other people find theirs."

I returned the smile.

Suddenly a young boy's Frisbee landed at my feet. I bent to pick it up, then winced wretchedly as my side flared with pain. I suppressed the grimace as I handed the child back his toy. When he scampered off, Akari's Soul Pulse flashed and a small purple jar appeared in her hand.

"Your wounds should heal on their own in a few weeks," she said. "For obvious reasons, Heaven doesn't have hospitals. However GAs have several tonics to soothe the pain of Dark Breed injuries and speed along the healing as much as possible. This is the one I'd recommend."

She gifted me the jar.

"Will the marks go away?" I asked.

"Depends on how deep they are. Those tiny pricks from the Divine Iron at the Hellevator vanish, but deep wounds don't necessarily."

"Fantastic." I rolled my eyes.

"There are worse things than having battle scars," Akari said. She turned around and my eyes widened. Her backless dress revealed several faded, dark gray scars that looked like they'd come from a set of large claws. She pivoted to me and shrugged.

"Whoa. Tell me that story sometime?" I asked.

"Perhaps," she said. Her smile returned—soft as the breeze and warm as the sun. Akari patted my arm. "I'll see you in training tomorrow. Sessions are cancelled today. Get some rest, Grace."

My mentor walked away and my eyes followed her marigold dress until she disappeared into the crowds of the park. When she'd gone, I glanced up at the gleaming Moral Compass.

I'd acquired a lot of *chutzpah* and a strong sense of self in these last few months. I finally knew my purpose as a Guardian Angel—to defend. I would live by that purpose *and* heed Akari's advice, God's wishes, and the Greater Good by focusing on defending Henry only.

I guess that could be enough.

I guess that was the right thing . . .

At school on Monday, Henry whisper-asked me questions about my job whenever he didn't think anyone else was listening. After three class periods of this, I had to establish a new rule. No asking questions that weren't related to anything immediately affecting us. If it was a normal day, we were only going to talk about normal things. Henry wasn't happy about that, but I was firm. Our relationship was not going to involve afterlife show-and-tell. He needed to trust me and treat me like his friend, not an angelic Alexa.

Once I had that matter under control, the only topic I had to be careful around was the UCSD attack. Henry rolled with my version of events of what happened on Saturday when I told Razel, Justin, and Solange. We kept up those lies at school when kids who'd seen the "gorilla attack" on social media asked us about it.

Other than those complexities, the day actually went really well. Solange wasn't at school. According to Razel, the demon was sick with the flu.

I knew better though. Between seeing her exhaustion on Sunday, talking to Akari, and reading more of the Dark Breeds book, I knew Solange's summoning had drained her dramatically, even dangerously. She was likely in Hell's infirmary right now, having the demon equivalent of chicken noodle soup—maybe something nourishing like blood stew with eyeballs?

As pleasant as Solange's absence made the school day, after school was even better. In fact, after school was *brilliant*.

It was our four-month training evaluation, and that meant Monkonjae, Leo, and I had to simultaneously combat each other with all the powers we'd acquired. Like an angelic street fight within the boundary of an octagon. Only, the ropes around the octagon had been removed because the last trainee still inside its borders would be the winner.

I was lucky that magic antidote Akari had given me really packed a punch. Though the scars remained, my pain was completely gone. Allowing *me* to pack a punch.

My heart pounded with more joy than adrenaline, and my soul surged with energy as I asserted my full strength. Finally.

I slid under Leo's beam of light and spun back to my feet, releasing a blast of my own. It knocked him back, but not far enough to cross the limits. I turned to block Monkonjae's jab. We exchanged a few traditional strikes and counters before his halo appeared. Mine did too. We simultaneously grabbed them and clashed glowing rings. Movement caught my periphery.

Shield.

I whacked aside Leo's incoming halo discus and then used the same energy wall to shove Monkonjae away. Leo raced in and fired one long blast. I firmly kept my shield up. Though his energy drove me back inch by inch, I held my ground. The second his beam ran out of juice, I converted my halo back to a discus and flung it at his right leg. Since our halo discuses couldn't slice through angels, the impact knocked his leg out from under him.

Leo hit the mat. I caught my halo then hinged back to kick Monkonjae in the chest as he came at me. I whirled around and formed a ball of light as I spun.

BLAM!

My beam drove into Monkonjae, blasting him out of the octagon.

I didn't apologize.

A moment later when Leo was almost to his feet, I spun while summoning another shot and sent my friend flying out of the octagon as well.

BOOM—winner!

I punched the air in victory. "Whoo! I *owned* you two."

Both boys took a second to reorient themselves. When Leo sat up he slow-clapped. "I am *kvelling*."

"I don't know what that means," Monkonjae said, offering the kid a hand up. "But I am impressed, humbled, and really happy for you, Grace. It's never been such a pleasure to be knocked on my a—"

Bubbles escaped his mouth. I smirked then approached him confidently. I popped a bubble with the tip of my finger. "Glad you had such a nice experience."

Our eyes met for a moment; then our linen closet conversation from Saturday flooded my mind and I felt awkward and darted my gaze away.

Dang, I was cool and collected for like thirty seconds.

That was progress, right?

Deckland, Akari, and Ana came to join us.

"We're all proud and impressed, Grace," Ana said. "Seeing one of our own find their purpose is a beautiful thing. You may not believe me, but you look so much more alive now."

"Oh, I believe you," I said, crossing my arms. "I feel it too. I guess that means my wings should be showing up any day now, right?"

"Take a number," Leo said. "I've been having my own story-line over here, and my personal growth hasn't gotten me any feathers."

"Give it time," Deckland replied. "When you are fully realized you'll know it; your wings will just show up. You three are becoming strong in all senses, so keep pushing and you'll get there."

"Speaking of pushing . . ." I said. "I'm going to do that with the metaphorical envelope and straight-up ask. Monkonjae and I told you all about Henry and Dr. Wang connecting at dinner over the weekend. Do any of you three senior GAs want to clue us in on the big secret with our assignments intersecting? I know there's more to it than coincidence."

They were definitely surprised by my directedness. Like *really* surprised.

Deckland exchanged a glance with the girls. "It happens sometimes . . ." he admitted.

Ana nodded. "Once in a rare while, our assignments work together or come together to achieve massive impact on humanity. We don't know for sure that's what's happening with you three, but we're just as curious about it as you are. I'm afraid that's the only answer we can offer right now. We'll all just have to play it by ear. If we push for more answers or look deeper into possible connections, we could accidentally tamper with the fates of our assignments. That's not good for them, us, or anyone."

My angel classmates and I exchanged our own look. Then I put my hands on my hips and answered on our behalf. "I guess we'll all buckle in for the ride and see where it takes us."

The boys and I were dismissed from training. As we headed for the exit, Leo looked at us with a grin. "Team dinner?"

"Can we do Wednesday?" Monkonjae asked. "I have a lot of studying to do."

"I probably should hit the books too," I said. "But I'm good with Wednesday."

"MJ!" We paused and turned as Deckland caught up with us. "Actually, can we talk before you go?"

Our friend nodded and waved us goodbye. Leo and I walked out of the sparring center together, then boarded an elevator.

"I still can't handle you, Grace," Leo said in admiration as we rode down. "You're a true *berye*."

I gave him a look.

"It basically means a master of one's craft," he explained.

"Oh. Thanks. Your Yiddish words don't translate with Heaven's filter. I'm not sure if that's because they're part of a dialect, or because they add flavor to your personality like the occasional French words Solange peppers in. Either way, I can usually deduce the meaning through context, but I've tried on so many personalities lately you literally could've been calling me anything just then."

"Only positive adjectives for you, my friend."

I nudged his shoulder. "Well thanks. And congrats on your internal arc by the way. You said you've been making a lot of progress on yourself too?"

"Yup. I figured out my purpose."

"I thought so," I mused as I watched the floors sail by through the glass of our lift. "Don't think I don't appreciate how much more powerful you've been fighting. I'm not the only *berye* in town if you ask me."

"Thank you, *bubbeleh*." He touched the bridge of his nose. Someday, I'd have to ask him about that tick of his.

"So, what is it? Your purpose?"

He stared at his reflection in the glass a moment, then looked at me. "To help others live life to the fullest."

I smiled at him. "That suits you."

"Yes. Yes it does." Leo sighed and shook his head. "My purpose and the parts of me I needed to understand to fully accept it seem so obvious now. They click with my character and fit like a peg in a hole. And yet, I don't think I could have gotten all the way there without the help and honest perspective of others. Between Ana and my new friends on Earth . . . I needed them to find myself. I'll be forever grateful that they got me here and gave me the great gift of understanding myself without expecting anything in return."

I blinked as I reflected on this. "You're right, Leo," I thought aloud. "The people who helped us did give us a gift expecting nothing in return."

Our elevator reached the lobby. We strode out the main doors into the twilight-soaked streets.

"Are you sure I can't tempt you with a bite?" He nodded toward a nearby café. "Or some movie night shenanigans? I'll let you pick the theme."

"Tempting, but . . ." I gazed up the block. "I think there's something else I need to do."

"Suit yourself. See you tomorrow." He waved and trotted away.

I paused for another few seconds of contemplation, then I concentrated and my Soul Pulse flashed. When the light faded, I found myself in a well-lit hallway in front of a pale pink door with a floral floor mat.

I knocked. For a beat nothing happened and I wondered if I'd missed her again. Then the door opened and I was face-to-face with a strawberry-blonde woman with a red sweater and familiar aqua eyes.

"Hello, dear," the woman said sweetly.

"Excuse me, ma'am. Are you Marian Evans?"

"That's me. How may I help you?"

"I know your son Oliver. Can we talk?"

30

BEING BRAVE

"*Se le va el pájaro*," I said, sitting down next to Henry at lunch on Tuesday.

While everyone else in our group ate and chatted away, Henry had been in a daze—eyes vacant and focused on the distance.

"What's that?" He looked at me.

I chewed a French fry thoughtfully and swallowed before responding. "It's something my dad and my abuela used to say. The literal translation is 'the bird is leaving.' But we say it when someone is staring off into space so much that they look like their brain has left the building. What gives?"

"I was thinking about Sara Bareilles."

I choked on my next fry. "The singer? *Why?*"

"*Razel* wouldn't stop singing along to the radio this morning on our way to school. This song came on called 'Brave' and it got into my head."

I shrugged. "Sara B. isn't your average teen boy's favorite singer, but her songs are catchy, so I respect you're secure enough in your masculinity to admit you like them."

"It's not that." Henry huffed, frustrated. He twisted the cap off his water bottle and took a drink before continuing. "*Razel* was really brave last night. She flat out told my parents she was committing to USD. She didn't ask for their permission or approval or advice. She said the campus spoke to her, she likes the small class sizes, and although she's going in as an undeclared major, she intends to look into taking some intro theatre classes."

"Wow!" I glanced over at my friend who was laughing with Justin and a few others. "That's huge. Good for her." My eyes wandered back to Henry's pensive expression. "And bad for you? What's wrong? You look upset, not like a supportive brother."

"I'm not upset. I'm jealous. I wish . . ." he sighed and shook his head. "I wish I could be that brave." He stared at me seriously. "Grace. I want to go to USD too."

"Henry, that's excellent!"

He raised an eyebrow.

"Sorry. I know that was a lot of enthusiasm. Go on."

"I want to go to USD, but I always come back to that list of why UCSD is better for me. Given what my dad and I want for my life, that school makes a lot of sense. But it just . . . doesn't feel right. The University of San Diego *does*. I like the strong partnerships between students and teachers. I like the extended opportunities available for research. I'd probably have more of a chance to grow and do my own thing since it's a way smaller school. And I like the campus better." He lowered his voice, glancing around to make sure no one else was listening. "And that's not just because a demon monster tried to kill us at UCSD."

"Okay, then . . ." I said carefully. I wanted *and needed* him to pick USD, but I didn't want it to seem like an obligation. Henry had to decide for himself. "So be brave, Henry. Tell your dad what you just told me. Minus the part about the demon monster of course."

"Easier said than done."

"Maybe. If it makes you feel better, I actually have my own emotional confrontation with my mother planned this weekend. If I can manage that, then you can manage this."

"I don't know if—"

"April is over at the end of the week, Henry," I said bluntly. "Your college decisions are due. There's no time left to put this off. If being brave were easy, then everyone would do it. I think you know what you want in your heart, so take a risk. Be the guy who inspired me this semester to take charge of my own life. Do what's right by your character and your dreams; don't sacrifice yourself to please others or live up to your dad's expectations. It's not who you are *and you know it*. Please don't forget that now when your choice is so important."

Henry looked at me for a long moment then took one of my fries. "Does your Guardian Angel job include pep talks? Because that was a pretty good one. I guess I'd be dumb not to follow your advice. You're probably brave in all aspects of your afterlife."

I fidgeted then released a deep breath. "Not all of them," I admitted. My heart pounded nervously at the mere thought. "But like you, I think I'm ready to start living that way, even if it's not easy."

This commitment dwelled in my soul for the rest of the day. It whispered at the back of my conscience and hummed in my head like a song *I* couldn't shake loose. I was preaching to Henry to be brave, but there were still avenues of my life where I was running and hiding. That had to end. I was fight, not flight. And I was tired of limiting my character to the shadows where I could avoid feeling vulnerable or embarrassed. Most people only lived once—on Earth anyway. I had a second go-around and I wasn't going to waste it on old insecurities any longer.

Before dance class started that afternoon, I knocked on the back office door then pressed it open when I heard "Come in!"

"Ms. Suarez?" I said, stepping into the studio owner's den. She sat at her desk wearing the same black baseball cap over her ponytail as always.

I took another deep breath and faced my fear head on. I *loved* to dance. That was the only thing that mattered. Hana had been right when she told me there was no need to be scared of performing in front of others. No matter how many people were watching, it was not about them. It was about the person on stage and the courage and passion it took to be there.

Ms. Suarez glanced up. "What's going on, Grace?"

The small girl had been wiser than I was. Thankfully I *also* loved to learn.

"If it's not too late, I'd like to be a part of the dance recital."

One down, one to go.

After my training session at Angel Tower that night, I knew my commitment to being brave required a final step. This one was different because it wasn't about letting go of something that filled me with dread. It was about letting go of someone who filled me with love.

I strode through Miracle Marketplace, reading the different signs and listening to the angels announcing their miracles for sale as I searched for the right vendor.

"Colleges—both community and four-year! Spend your miracles on ensuring your loved ones get a good education!"

My ears perked up and I turned my attention to a dreadlocked female vendor wearing a gorgeous embroidered shawl.

Heat flushed my cheeks and my heart beat faster again. I opened a photo of my family on my Soul Pulse and stared at Gaby's face.

Seeing my sister the other day had been the most wonderful, painful blessing. The very fact that there existed some version of the future where the fates aligned and she chose USD or UCSD as her college and we could see each other regularly flooded me with such joy. And yet, it also worried me deeply. It was selfish of me to want Gaby to end up at either of those two schools. For one, I should be rooting for her to get into her dream school in New York. Second, the closer we were to each other, the more danger that would court.

Solange knew Gaby was my sister. That didn't bode well for either of us. And even if Solange didn't directly involve Gaby in any plots against me, the demon had brought that Dark Breed to campus, endangering everyone there. Had Gaby not gone back to her hotel, her life would've been at risk because of me and Henry.

Which brought up yet another reason I'd be thinking selfishly if I wanted Gaby to come to California.

Henry was my priority. If I was going to be listening to God's rules, then my friend would always have to come first and that tempted the idea—*the possibility*—of needing to protect him over my sister. That was an impossible situation I never wanted to be a part of.

Past that, Henry was my job and I wouldn't be able to do that job properly if I was always distracted. I'd barely paid attention in either college tour once Gaby showed up. My love for her and the amount I missed her subsumed all my good, wiser intentions. I couldn't risk that long term. I had to keep an eye on Henry and Solange and the universe as it turned around them both. My own heart would have to take one for the team.

Sigh.

It would be so easy, so satisfying to buy a miracle that influenced fate so Gaby and my father ended up in California, allowing me the chance to see and know them as my new self, even if just in fleeting moments . . .

No. I shook my head.

I couldn't have that. I had to be selfless. *And I had to be brave.*

I closed the photo with a nod, summoning as much strength as my soul could bear. Bracing myself, I walked up to the angel vendor and remained steadfast in my choice. "Hello, ma'am. I'd like to buy a small miracle for a transfer student, please. She needs to get off the waitlist for Columbia University."

"How's it going down there?" I asked Oliver, keeping his face limited to my Soul Pulse screen for the moment.

"Grace, you really shouldn't risk reaching out to me. I'm in my apartment right now, but if any of the other demons saw your name on this dumb watch's caller ID, we'd both be toast."

"It was worth the risk last time and it is today too. I have a gift for you."

In our time knowing each other, I had never seen Oliver look so confused.

"*Why?*"

"Because I want to thank you."

He sighed with exasperation. "Grace, we're all paid up in the favors department. You don't owe me anything."

"This isn't about owing you something, Oliver. This is about me being grateful. You really helped me the other night. Our talk in San Diego may not have meant anything to you, but it meant a lot to me. You helped me find a part of myself that I needed. The peace that's given me—it's something I've wanted for a long, *long* time. I want to offer you something that matters to you just as much. Unprovoked. No return favors required. Just a good deed. Now hold on, I'm going to change the Soul Pulse setting so you project as a full-size hologram and I can make a proper introduction."

"Introduction?"

I adjusted my Soul Pulse and Oliver's holographic body appeared. His feet were on the smooth wooden floor like he was actually there. My demon friend turned and then froze. Perched anxiously on the armchair in her spacious apartment, was Oliver's mother. She stood up when she saw him. The light flooding through the windows made her strawberry-blonde hair glow with angelic warmth.

"*Mom?*" Oliver's face wasn't as excited as it was shocked and ter-rified.

"Sweetheart, is it really you?" Marian walked over and ran her hand as close to the energy that composed Oliver's cheek as possible.

Oliver's eyes darted to me.

"I found her," I said.

He kept staring at me so I stood and sighed. "This was the only way I could think for you both to meet. You'll probably never be in Heaven again. You can't call anyone here. And regular angels can't call Hell. The only person who could facilitate this meeting is a Guardian Angel, so here I am."

My demon friend was shell-shocked for another moment. Finally, his eyes reverted to his mother. "Mom, I just . . . I thought about this so many times and . . ." His voice cracked and he shook his head. "I'm sorry. I'm an idiot. I should've known what I was going to say if I somehow found you. Maybe I didn't actually think we would ever see each other again."

Oliver's mom looked at him longingly. "Neither did I, sweet-heart."

I could tell by her anxious body language that she wanted nothing more than to hug him, and it hurt to know that she couldn't.

"I was devastated to learn that our different afterlives meant we would never be able to see or speak with one another," she continued. "How such a wonderful, celestial place could keep a mother from her child is a dismal side effect of the universe."

Oliver gulped—a nervous habit I was very familiar with. "You must be so disappointed in me. With where I ended up and what I chose."

Marian sighed. "I am, Oliver, but it's not entirely your fault. I left you alone when I died. I'm sorry for that. Your father . . . I wish I had been around to protect you."

Oliver cringed. "Mom, please don't apologize for dying. It makes me feel like a jerk. I mean, I *am* a jerk in a lot of ways, and I did a lot of bad stuff, and I hurt a lot of people and I . . . now I'm babbling like an idiot."

Another habit I was familiar with.

"You're not an idiot, Oliver," Marian said. "And I don't care what these afterlife assignments say. You're not a bad person. I know you."

His face turned sad. "You don't know me, Mom. You know a kid who stopped existing years ago."

"No," she said firmly. "I don't believe that. I am saddened by many of your choices, especially that you decided to become a demon and contribute to hurting innocent people and making the world a worse place. However, you're not beyond redemption. I know that in my soul as surely as I know that despite what you've done and where you are, I still love you. I always will. And I hope you know that."

Oliver was glassy-eyed and arguably more astonished than when this conversation started. "I . . . I love you too, Mom."

She nodded. "The rest we can discuss another day, in another way."

"Another day?" He moved his gaze to me.

"I figured there is stuff you and your mother would like to say to each other without a third wheel eavesdropping," I said, gesturing at myself. "Goodness knows I wouldn't feel comfortable with someone crashing an exchange between me and my mother."

I reached into my pocket and removed a sealed envelope. "Your mom wrote you a letter. I didn't tell him what it was for, but I asked Monkonjae for the address of the hospital where you both work. I'm going to mail this letter to you on Earth. When you have a response, send it care of my dance studio in SoCal. The return address is on the envelope. I'll bring it back to Heaven and give it to her." I shrugged. "It'll be slow-moving, but we can work together like that to keep a kind of pen pal relationship between you and your mother. It's unorthodox, but it's the only way for the two of you to connect without me being in the room like this."

Oliver just stared at me, stunned. Then he glanced at his wrist and his brows shot up. "I have an incoming teleport from Troy. I have to go. Mom"—he darted his gaze to her—"you have no idea how great it was to see you. And, Grace." He looked at me. "I . . . I can't believe you did this. *For me*."

"That's my job, Oliver. Helping people. Plus, just because we play for different teams doesn't mean we can't be friends, right?"

He started to open his mouth, then looked at his Soul Pulse again and ended the call. I gazed at the place where his hologram had been. Marian put a caring hand on my shoulder. We shared a smile.

I'd done a good thing.

I stood at the edge of my cloud and stared into eternal sky.

There was nothing here except a wooden park bench. The cloud itself was barely the size of your average bathroom. It was a simple spot for a complicated moment.

Light flashed behind me and my mother appeared. She glanced around at the surroundings, or lack thereof.

"What an . . . interesting place for us to meet, dear," she said.

"Hi, Mom." I walked over to her and we stood a foot apart. I think we both considered hugging but couldn't bring ourselves to overcome the awkwardness.

I gestured to the bench and sat down. She smoothed her skirt and sat next to me, ankles crossed and posture perfect.

"How were your college visits, dear?"

"They were good. My human assignment is supposed to attend the University of San Diego, so if all goes well, I suppose that's going to be my school too." I tucked a strand of hair behind my ear. "I saw Gaby. She was touring the campuses because she and dad are moving."

My mother nodded calmly. "I know."

"You know?"

"I watch them on one of those fancy TV channels when I'm in Heaven. They've been talking about it for a couple of months. Haven't you checked in on them?"

I shook my head. "Not via TV, no. It's hard enough just to look at a picture of them sometimes. After the funeral, I tried to put up some boundaries. I can't do my job if I'm always falling apart."

"I understand. And I respect your decision."

I gulped. "Funny that you should say that . . . Understanding and respect are actually the topics I want to discuss with you."

"*Oh?*" My mother looked a little suspicious.

"My understanding and respect for you," I clarified.

Her suspicion morphed into surprise and confusion. I sat up straighter and clasped my hands together to keep them from fidgeting uncontrollably. I'd done a lot of brave things this week, but this was going to be one of the most important conversations I was ever going to have. It had to work. The two greatest questions to ever cross my mind—which had continuously crossed my mind for most of life—were about to be answered. Could my mom and I find peace with each other? Could we have a meaningful relationship that fulfilled us both?

Here goes everything.

"Mom. I know what you're afraid of and I know what has hurt you. A friend of mine showed me what kind of torture you go through when you're . . . down there."

My mother's eyes widened in horror. "Grace . . . you shouldn't have seen that."

"Maybe I needed to. I've been resentful my whole life, Mom. I didn't like the person you forced me to be, and I hated the disappointment we both felt whenever I failed to live up to those expectations. I always assumed you were being hard on me because you wanted me to be exactly like you. But that was a lazy thing to believe. It's easy to assume a parent doesn't care about how you feel or what you want—that parents in general just give 'my way or the highway' commands without just cause. But everyone has their reasons for doing things. And my stubbornness and desire to blame someone for my unhappiness kept me from doing the mature, empathetic thing and trying to understand yours."

I sighed. "Hell changed everything for me, Mom. I see the truth now. I see *you*. The impulsive and short-fused, sometimes selfish way Nana Robin acted in life made you more susceptible to Grandpa Thorston's strict and proper upbringing. You committed yourself to be disciplined and conservative like him—and nothing like her—because she let you down. Then I came along and you worried I would turn out just like her. That's why you've always been so hard on me. That's why you're still scared of the consequences of me stepping outside of the reserved and restrained ladylike image you want me to live by . . . Isn't it?"

My mother's face had flushed when I mentioned Nana Robin, then had gotten paler as I spoke. She suddenly got up and moved to the edge of the cloud. I gave her a minute. Eventually I stood and slowly approached her, speaking to her back.

"Mom, I understand. And I want to take your fear away. I am not Nana Robin. I'll never be like Nana Robin—not in the manner you resent, anyway."

"I wish I could believe that," my mother said. She turned around and I saw a face burdened by sorrow. "You're so much like her, Grace. I've tried my best to carve the aggression out of you, but it flares up and that will only lead to trouble. You are an angel, dear. You're supposed to be good. How can you be if you lash out so heatedly?"

"It's not about lashing out; it's about taking action, Mom. Being good doesn't mean doing nothing. I understand the 'be the bigger person' mentality you've always advocated when I get into fights. But that doesn't always work. It doesn't always stop the villains and bullies."

My mother huffed. "Dear, bullies only do mean things because it makes them feel strong. Like I always told you when you got into spats at school, when someone does something mean, show them that you're the strong one by just letting it go. Once that bully sees he or she can't upset you, they'll stop bothering you."

"*Sometimes. Maybe*," I insisted. "Every obstacle and enemy we face is different, Mom, which means our responses to them can't always be the same. We have to be wise and mature enough to accept that *and* show understanding to those who stand up for things in ways that are dissimilar to how we would approach them. Conflict is not always shameful and confrontation is not a sign of weakness or emotional instability. It's all relative. My instinct to fight back isn't a bad thing. It's a different kind of aggression: purposeful and protective rather than selfish and misplaced."

She still looked skeptical. The sadness and doubt pinching her brow caused frustration and desperation to overwhelm me. I turned away from my mother and walked a few steps to get some space. I would say I was taking a moment to find the proper words to follow up with, but the truth was that they were all right there—rising out of me like steam from a teakettle. I just needed to pace them out so our conversation wouldn't explode or fall flat.

After a minute, I looked at my mother with sympathetic but fervent eyes. "I feel proud of who I really am, Mom, which is an *aggressive, fierce*, and *strong person*. Our culture prioritizes not offending people. So to you, and for a long time to me, the term 'aggressive' has been interchangeable with rude or inappropriate or wrong. But that's also a lazy thing to believe. And letting the world convince you that whatever is inside of you is something to be ashamed of, *that's* wrong. Whatever qualities add fire and life to a person's character aren't something to be ashamed of or gutted out; they're meant to be harnessed for good. That's what I'm doing."

I swallowed down the very last misgiving about my personality I'd ever have and held firm, fists clenched.

"When we first connected in Heaven, you said that it was your influence on my behavior that made me good enough to be an angel. That's not true. I ended up here because of me. The things I've done that other people—you included—criticized me for were all in the name of defending myself and others. My intentions were never malicious or selfish. There was never any need to try and carve my aggressive instincts out of me. The only thing I needed was someone to help me understand why I reacted that way, so as I grew up I could learn to channel my aggression as positively as possible. Learn how to tell when it's the right time to fight and develop the confidence to do so. I've figured out how to do that now, and I'm never going back."

I took a risk and stepped forward, taking my mother's hands in mine. "I understand your perspective and your reasons for how you raised me, Mom. I don't hold them against you. I respect that you were only trying to do what was right to protect your heart and protect me. But I have to *be me*. And I hope that you can accept that."

My mother hadn't flinched from my hands, so I pressed on. I nodded, sure of myself. "I told you months ago that I could use your blessing. The truth is that while I would like it, I don't need your blessing. You're not God; you're my mother. All I really need from you is you. That's why I picked this place for our talk. A friend of mine told me that when we reconnect, I should take you to my favorite spot in Heaven. I've had trouble picking one; I've seen so many wondrous places in the afterlife. For a minute I considered taking you to the public library. But then this morning, I realized something. The reason I haven't been able to pick a favorite place is because the best place—in any plane of reality—is wherever you feel loved."

I let go of my mother's hands and brought up a hologram of the family photo that hung in my cottage. "I'd give anything to spend my days with Gaby and dad again. But it's just us now. Life is too short for not seeing eye to eye to keep you from seeing someone you love. And as I said the other day, I love you, Mom. You may annoy me and disagree with me and fight with me, but at the end of the day, I'd rather sit on this empty cloud and share a hug with you than be anywhere else in the spread of the universe."

My mother looked at me for a long moment. Her face wasn't flushed anymore, but her eyes were glassy. For such a tall woman, her humbled expression made her seem so small. And for the first time I could remember, her perfect posture faltered as the gravity of so much honesty and understanding came crashing down around us.

She cleared her throat. "I . . . I can try to be different, Grace. I can try to be different for you."

I shook my head. "I don't need that, Mom. I'm secure in who I am and it's okay if you don't always get me. As long as you're willing to *try* and understand, and respect me even if my choices don't always match yours, then I think we'll be okay." I paused a bit. "Okay?"

She gazed at me and I felt so much love without her uttering a single syllable.

"Okay," she said, emotion in her voice.

Now it was my turn to clear my throat. "Well then, I don't know if I was too subtle before, but . . ." I extended my arms out—open wide.

She smiled softly and gave me a real hug. Not a quick one. Not a non-committal side-hug. This was strong, pure, and dare I say, aggressive.

PROM?

"You're back."

Solange and I approached the physics classroom on Monday at the same time.

"Miss me?" she asked, propping her sunglasses up.

"Like blood misses a leech."

Henry was headed our way, making excellent time on his crutches as always. Solange gave him a sparkling smile and a wave. "Good morning, Henry."

"Hey, Solange," he said. Then he glanced at me and crooked his head to the side. "Can we talk for a sec?"

Solange pouted slightly and I childishly stuck my tongue out at her when Henry turned away. She entered Mr. Corrin's class while Henry and I moved under the shade of a tree.

"What's up?" I asked.

"I did it," he said. "I told my dad that I want to go to USD. I stood my ground and stood up for myself—laid it all out there."

"*And?*" I asked.

He unzipped his hoodie and I saw a USD t-shirt underneath. "I bought it at the gift shop, just in case," he said with a mischievous grin.

"Henry! I'm so proud of you!" I tackled him with a huge hug that almost knocked him off his crutches.

"Whoa, easy," he said. "Kind of defeats the purpose of having a Guardian Angel if she knocks me on my butt."

"Sorry." I stepped back, embarrassed but still smiling.

Obviously as his Guardian Angel I was thrilled and relieved that he'd committed to the University of San Diego. With that decision, and his license delayed until after graduation, I'd successfully completed two thirds of Henry's first set of Plot

Points. However I was also ecstatic for Henry on a personal level. I wanted him to be happy. Like Akari had pointed out, I'd come to care about the guy.

"Not sure if you take passengers," Henry said, "but if you want to pop out your angel wings and take me for a victory lap, I feel pretty on top of the world right now."

"I'm sorry to disappoint you, but I don't have my wings yet. They have to be earned."

"Like in *It's a Wonderful Life*," Henry mused. "So if I play bells on my phone, does that mean you'll sprout feathers? You know, like that saying—every time a bell rings, an angel gets it wings."

I cracked a smile. "If only it were that simple." I paused and stared at Henry a bit, taking him in.

He crooked an eyebrow. "What is it?"

"You're just . . ." I laughed to myself. "You're so cool with this. I told you barely a week ago about Heaven, Hell, my magical powers, and the celestial target on your back, and you've taken it in such stride. If you'll pardon the pun, when I realized I had to tell you the truth, I accepted you'd probably need a grace period where you were scared, or at least weirded out and pushed me away. But you seem fine—and oddly into the whole thing."

He tilted his head side to side for a moment, as if he were also searching his brain for the explanation. "Have you ever seen *Doctor Who*?" he asked.

I blinked in surprise. "I was a TARDIS for Halloween last year."

He grinned. "Okay, well you know how the human companions the Doctor finds on Earth are always a little wary initially? They're like, 'Oh my God, he's from another world and there's monsters and time travel—blah!'"

Now I grinned. "Yes."

"Well, whenever I watch that show I always think to myself, if that happened to me—if some super powerful and super smart higher being dropped out of the sky in a magic blue box and was like 'Hey, want to go on an epic, dangerous adventure?'—I'd be like, well, obviously. Sounds awesome. No convincing needed because, despite my love of science, I always hoped the universe could be that nuts."

"So I'm you're super powerful, super smart higher being who dropped out of the sky?"

"More or less. You even come with a blue car. But I'm not calling you Doctor. Given my intended career path, that could get complicated in the long run."

I laughed. "Fair enough." I shook my head. "You really are an outlier, Henry, and I love that. Thank you for being you."

"While we're on the subject of thanks . . ." Henry reached into his backpack and pulled out a burrito wrapped in foil. "You know how I used to stop and pick up loose change for luck? I'm over that now. The only luck I need is you. So I spent all those pennies and nickels and dimes I'd collected on this breakfast burrito."

My brow rose. "How much was it?"

"I got extra guac, so in the neighborhood of ten bucks. Anyway, call it a thanks for saving my life multiple times."

I shrugged. "Sure, that seems fair—you avoid being drowned, smashed, and eaten by a monster; I get a breakfast burrito."

Henry cringed. "Well, when you put it like that—"

"I'm teasing," I said with a grin. I accepted his gift. "Thank you. That's actually very sweet. Now I really wish I could give you an angelic victory lap. You deserve something to celebrate your accomplishments too. How about since I can't provide a tour of the clouds, I treat you and Razel to that God-awful boba you love so much?"

Henry smirked. "What a sacrifice for you."

"That's an understatement. But you earned it and we have plenty of reason to rejoice. Both you and your sister will be going to the same university! The dynamic duo lives on."

"Maybe we should call it the tremendous trio? As part of your cover, I take it you'll be enrolling at USD too?"

"Where you go, I go," I said.

The first bell rang. Henry nodded toward the classroom door. "In that case, you better keep up with me, Grace." He winked. "You're making us late for class."

At the end of the week, when the calendar turned to the first Friday in May, I proudly wore my own USD t-shirt to school. "Commitment Day" was a tradition at Rancho Del Mar High School. Every member of the senior class wore clothing for whatever university they'd committed to.

I was having a great time strutting around campus, and as a bonus, Solange was absent again. Though she'd come to school most of the week, it was clear she still didn't have her mojo back. The girl hadn't just tired herself with that Dark Breed; she'd wiped herself out. We barely exchanged snipes these last few days, let alone any actual conflict. She just didn't have the energy.

Fine by me. I needed a vacation from evil.

Didn't we all?

Anyway, the Sun twins and I happily showed off our USD gear, and at lunch I was pleasantly astonished to see Justin in a UCSD sweatshirt.

"You read right," he said to my shocked expression. "The four of us are going to be collegiate neighbors."

"There goes the neighborhood," Henry joked.

Justin smacked him on the arm.

"I have to say that I'm surprised," I said, settling down on one of the red benches. "Being on campus during a crazy wild animal attack didn't turn you off the school?"

"You can't blame an entire campus for one escaped gorilla," Justin said. "Anyway, UCSD has a great baseball team and they offered me a partial sports scholarship. It's the right move." He shot Henry a devious look. "And the high number of hot sorority girls didn't hurt my decision either."

"Well, you better train extra hard on the baseball team then, Justin," Razel commented. "We can't have you striking out in two areas of your life."

He scowled while the rest of us laughed.

"If you're through taking shots at my swagger, can we talk about something else?" Justin said. He grabbed his pizza for a bite.

"Absolutely," Razel replied. "Actually, I've been dying to spill the tea. My friend Ronnie on student council told me they finally settled on a location for prom. They're making the announcement over the PA system at the end of the day right before the final bell, but guess who's got the inside scoop?" She pointed both thumbs at herself. "This girl."

"Where's it going to be?" Henry asked.

"The Biltmore."

I choked on my fried rice.

"Girl, you need to take smaller bites," Razel commented. "You choke on your food *a lot*."

I took a sip of water and dabbed my mouth with a napkin. Maybe I wouldn't choke if people didn't keep saying such shocking things while I was eating.

I remembered the final Plot Point notecard that Akari had given me:

Be in the elevator on the left off the Main Galeria at the Biltmore at 9:04 p.m. on Saturday, May 28th.

I'd been wondering for a while how I was going to arrange this. I was familiar with the Biltmore. My family had taken several vacations to the historic mansion-museum in North Carolina. I'd assumed I would need to buy plane tickets, get days off from school, and so on.

"The Biltmore Estate is in North Carolina," I said. "How can this school afford to have their prom at a fancy mansion on the other side of the country?"

"What?" Razel looked puzzled. "No, Grace. The Biltmore is a hotel in downtown LA. It's called the Millennium Biltmore."

Wow. I felt dumb.

This is what I get for making assumptions. That's several hours of using Heaven's Wi-Fi to browse Expedia and Travelocity I'll never get back.

At least that made things easier.

"The dance is going to be held on Saturday, May 28th," Razel continued.

And now they were *even easier*.

"And the theme for the prom," Razel finished, "is 'A Date with Destiny'."

"HA!" I said.

"I have something for you both," I told Henry and Justin as we waited outside the school auditorium. Night had hit about half an hour ago and we—and the hundred other people gathered outside—conversed under the light from the lampposts.

I handed each boy a pink flier.

Henry grinned. "You're going to be in Hana's dance recital?"

"Hey, I have seniority," I said in mock seriousness. "Hana is going to be in *my* dance recital."

Justin leaned in and sniffed my head like Droopy smelled my shoes when I walked in the door.

"What are you doing?" I asked, giving him a look.

"That smell of confidence you're giving off, Doolittle. It's noticeable."

I smiled and swatted him away with the playbill in my hand.

"It's two weeks from tonight on the 21st. So if you boys don't have issues spending another Saturday at a friend's performance, I'd love for you to be there."

"My whole family is already going because of Hana," Henry replied. He jutted his chin toward where his parents and small sister chatted with some adults farther off.

"I'll check my calendar," Justin said.

Now Henry and I both swatted him with our playbills.

The side doors opened and we filed in and found seats in the tenth row. I perused the playbill for tonight's school musical. Razel had landed the second female lead and had been working hard for months. She was so passionate about musical theater; I was really looking forward to seeing her shine.

I noticed Justin draping his sweatshirt on the chair beside him, saving a seat.

"Who's that for?" I asked.

"Me," Solange said, appearing behind my friend. "Sorry I'm late. I had some things to take care of and freeway traffic in my area is murder."

Not a lie.

Justin awkwardly jumped up and gestured at the empty chair dramatically.

"Aren't you sweet," Solange commented.

She sat elegantly, crossing her legs. I wondered if Ithaca had gifted her those gray jeans. They were tighter than a witness's mouth at a mafia trial.

"I am also sorry that I have been missing in action this week," Solange continued once she and Justin were situated. "I was terribly under the weather after our trip to San Diego. Then yesterday I had to meet with some people to ensure there were no issues with my next steps."

"Which are?" I posed.

She opened her studded leather jacket and revealed a red tank top with *USD* embroidered on it in gold, glittery letters.

Of course.

"Solange, you also committed to San Diego? Congrats!" Henry said.

"That's right," she replied, shooting a dazzling grin at him. "Our adventure together continues, Henry Sun."

Justin sighed. "Well, I guess the four of you can carpool to visit me."

I patted him on the leg supportively. "There, there, Higgins."

"Anyway, now I am feeling back to my old self and am excited to finish out the year with a bang." Solange glanced around Justin to meet my eyes. "You know what I'm talking about, don't you, Grace?"

"I always do, Solange," I said plainly. "And I couldn't be more ready for it."

She nodded. Then she helped herself to the playbill in my hand with a swift snatch. She raised an eyebrow at the cover. "So what the Hell is *Hairspray*? A musical about hair care products?"

"Can I have everyone's attention?"

We all turned to the stage where Brandon, a boy from my English class, was standing under the spotlight, holding a mic. He wore a gray zip-up jacket and held a scarlet rose. "If I could get Cynthia Moor on stage please."

There was some shuffling in the audience and then a girl with bouncy curls climbed up from stage right, looking confused. The moment she did, four more boys in zip-up jackets stormed the stage. They all stood in line with Brandon and simultaneously unzipped and tossed their jackets aside. The friends each had a huge letter painted on their shirts in glitter paint, while Brandon's shirt had a massive question mark. Together they spelled out P-R-O-M-?

Cynthia gushed. "Yes! Of course!" She hugged Brandon and the audience whistled and applauded.

"And so it begins," Henry commented wryly.

I looked at him curiously.

"Kids at our school get really into prom proposals," he explained. "Now that they've officially announced the date and venue, I'm sure they're only going to multiply by the day." He sighed. "I guess we're all going to need dates."

"And apparently a fair amount of glitter paint," I said.

"So what'd you think?" I asked my mother as we left Dinner is a Movie. The First City's streets were packed with the Saturday lunchtime rush, but I contentedly felt absorbed in the world just between the two of us.

Since our big talk, my mom and I had been making an effort to share a meal together once a weekend. Other than a few vague disagreements about TV programs and books, we hadn't argued at all.

I didn't expect the peace to last forever. We were different people with very different views of the world. However, it seemed that we'd both come to accept that, and thus accept each other. If we always remembered to, then I figured we could disagree about any number of things and still coexist with this new appreciation and affection for each other. That's what we both wanted anyway.

"It was lovely," my mother replied. "My *When Harry Met Salmon* filled me with such wonderful, heartwarming feelings. We shall definitely have to eat there again."

"Agreed," I said. "I'm glad we were able to do lunch instead of dinner today. I have to get back to Earth for my dance recital by four o' clock."

My mother stopped. "Dear, I truly am sorry I won't be there to watch you. *Again*."

"Mom, it's okay. You legitimately can't come in person, and I know you would live stream the recital if your meeting wasn't at the same time."

Her mouth tightened with guilt. "That was my excuse on Earth, Grace. I don't want to prioritize a meeting over what matters to you in the afterlife too."

I waved a hand. "This isn't chatting with donors or your marketing department, Mom. Your Middleground caseworker handles your afterlife livelihood. If she called you in for a 'special review' then it must be important, and you don't want to cancel last minute and risk ticking her off."

"Even so, I feel that I'm letting you down a second time. I know how important this is to you."

"The fact that you understand that is enough for me, Mom." I linked my arm through hers. "Now come on. I want to take you to an ice cream parlor that has literally a million flavors."

"Grace, we just ate!" she protested.

I smirked. "We're trying new things, remember? Girl bonding time, talking without losing our tempers, dessert after every meal?"

She huffed, exasperated, but there was a twinkle in her eyes. She patted my arm with her other hand and let me escort her down the sidewalk. After a few minutes we closed in on the ice cream parlor. It was right next to a disco-themed cardio dance studio. I knew the Saturday afternoon class was taught by Donna Summer, my Nana Robin's favorite singer . . .

I checked my watch. The class was just getting out.

People started exiting the studio. I anxiously scanned the faces as we approached.

Come on. Come on.

The moment my mother and I passed the studio, Nana Robin exited—wearing a black leotard with sparkly gold leggings and a headband over her orange hair.

"Mom!" my mother exclaimed, taking a panicky step backward.

"Darla?" Nana Robin's eyes were wide with shock at first, then they curved upward with delight. "Nougat, I am so happy to see you!"

"Please don't call me that," my mother replied. "I'm an adult woman, not a candy bar."

"No need to get your panties in a twist, Darla. It's a term of endearment." My nana glanced at me. "You understand that, don't you, Nugget?"

"Oh, I understand, Nana Robin." I glanced between the two women. "I understand a lot now. Starting with, it's been almost five months since Mom and I got here and it's ridiculous the two of you haven't seen each other."

"Agreed," Nana Robin said, looking to my mother and swiftly taking her hands. "I kept hoping and waiting for you to reach out to me, Darla."

"Typical," my mother said, raising her voice slightly as she withdrew. "Because *you* couldn't reach out to me? Too busy gallivanting around Heaven, I suppose?"

"And that's probably enough for one day," I said hastily, sensing a big blow-up coming. "Let's go, Mom. Hope to see you soon, Nana Robin."

I hastened down the street, maneuvering my mother forward by our linked arms.

"Grace, did you plan that?" my mother asked, eyeing me as we walked.

"Yes, Mom. If you and I can be brave enough to patch things up with each other and give our relationship another chance, don't you think you could at least try with Nana Robin? I know how she hurt you in life, but trust me when I say that just as you had your reasons for treating me the way you did, she has reasons for her choices and character too."

My mother lifted an eyebrow. "Such as?"

"I think that's something you should discover by learning more about her yourself. She's *your* mother. You two should swap perspectives sometime."

My mother huffed again, this time with distaste. "That woman is too self-involved. She is never going to step outside her little adventure-chasing world to try and understand my perspective."

"Seek to understand before you seek to be understood," I said as we arrived at the ice cream parlor—What's the Scoop?

"Pardon?"

I let go of my mother's arm so I could move in front of her and speak directly.

"It's something my friend Leo told me. People are prideful creatures, Mom. They always want others to come to them because they believe they're in the right. Sometimes they are and they shouldn't have to make the first move, but that's not the point. Maybe Nana Robin is not the type to take the first step to mending things with you. Some people are just too stubborn to bend that way. Plus, she's your mother and parents rarely apologize to their children—you know all about that."

She gave me a look.

I held up my hands to show I meant no harm. "I'm just saying if you genuinely want to mend things with her, I think it has to be you that attempts to understand her first. That has to start with learning to tolerate her in small doses. Hence my reason for the run-in back there."

My mother didn't meet my gaze.

"Are you mad at me?" I asked.

She sighed. "No, dear. I know you were just trying to help. I am not sure if I even want a relationship with my mother, but I'll give your advice some thought. Does that satisfy you?"

I nodded. "Yes. Yes it does."

"Good. Now lead the way and show your mother what ice cream flavors pair best with a stomach full of grilled fish."

I smiled and held the ice cream parlor door open for her. "Happy to, Mom."

"*Ahh! Ahh! Ahh!*" I let out three nervous mini shouts as I pumped myself up backstage.

Hana gave me a look. "Are you having a stroke? My daddy says adults have to be careful of those."

"I'm not having a stroke and I'm not an adult. I'm just

nervous." I peered around the curtain. There were like a hundred people out there, which was about a hundred more than I was comfortable with. Suddenly I felt a small hand slide into mine.

Hana looked up at me, her glitter stage makeup catching the light. "It's okay," she said sweetly. "It'll be fine. You know what I say—Dance like everybody is watching."

I gulped. "Hana, I think the saying is 'Dance like *nobody* is watching.'"

"That's dumb. If you love what you're doing and love yourself, you should be proud to show other people. Plus, that sparkly vest looks great on you." She grinned.

I returned the smile and squeezed her hand.

The performers on stage finished their jazz number and applause filled the theater. The curtains closed and Ms. Suarez came stomping over. "Places, Group J. Places!" She wore the same black baseball cap as always, but she'd swamped out her sweatshirt for a smart blazer. Little Hana, a dozen of her petite peers, and I rushed the stage.

I could do this.

I had to do this.

And . . . I wanted to do this.

As I took my position, I realized Hana was right. I *was* proud enough of who I was to show it off. I was not the same girl who'd enrolled at this dance school months ago. I had changed. Who cared if I made a mistake? Who cared if I stumbled? Who cared if other people thought I didn't belong here? These days the theme of my existence was unapologetically taking center stage in my own life in all senses of the phrase. If I could stand up to a demon, my mentor, and my mother, I could definitely twirl and leap in front of an audience.

The curtains opened to a sea of darkened faces and phone camera flashes. Then the music started and I danced. I danced like everybody was watching.

And after a few nervous bars, I realized that they should.

Because I was someone to watch.

Also in all senses of the phrase.

I knew that now. And it had nothing to do with being the

famous Ninety-Eight. It had everything to do with just being me and understanding how glorious that could feel if I stopped running and hiding from her.

The two-minute performance felt like ten seconds. When the curtains closed, my heart beat wildly. Adrenaline coursed through me like after I'd blasted that Dark Breed. Only this time, instead of panic, that rush of energy was accompanied by grand feelings of pride and joy.

Ms. Suarez shooed us off stage so a team of tap dancers could click-clack into position. The second we were in the wings again, Hana scurried over and threw her arms around me.

"You were so great!" She squealed. I bent down to return the embrace.

"You really were."

I spun to find Henry waiting backstage.

Hana dashed over. He gave her a huge hug and presented her with a small bouquet of daisies. "Awesome job, Hana Banana. I'm really proud of you."

"Thanks!"

"Hey, you mind if I talk to your dance partner for a second?" He gestured to me.

"Sure. I'm going to go change!" She hugged him again then raced off.

Henry sauntered over to me. He'd gotten his cast off earlier in the week and was clearly glad to have full swagger back in his gait. A plastic grocery bag dangled from his hand.

"What, no flowers for me?" I teased.

"Sorry, no. I do have something else for you though." He held up the bag.

I took it and pulled out a plastic container with a Bundt cake inside. I glanced at him.

"It's angel food cake," he said with a grin.

I laughed. "How appropriate. Respect."

"Turn it over," he said.

I carefully turned the small container upside down. A notecard had been taped to the bottom with the message:

Guard Me At Prom?

"What do you think?" he asked with a sheepish grin.

"I think that if you're going to pass our English final next week, you need to remember not to capitalize prepositions."

"Noted. Lesson aside . . . Do you want to go with me?"

"To prom?" I hesitated and winced slightly. "Like as *dates*?"

"What? No, as friends."

I sighed with relief. "Oh, thank God."

Henry gave me a stunned look. "Geez, Grace. I'm no Chris Pine, but way to shoot a guy in the ego."

"No, sorry! I didn't mean it like that." I took a breath. "I just freaked out because I see you as a friend. And technically I'm dead, so dating really isn't a good idea for us."

"We're on the exact same page," Henry assured. "I just figured that since you need to come to prom to protect me, and Justin asked Razel to go as friends, we could pair up. We always have fun together, don't we?"

"Wow, that's so sweet, Henry. Are you sure there isn't some cute girl you'd prefer to ask in a romantic fashion?"

"Well, actually I thought about asking Solange . . ."

My eyes narrowed.

Over my literal *dead body.*

"But even though I think she's hot, she can be a bit uptight sometimes. You and I get along better, and after a semester of driving fails and near-death experiences, I think I just want to have a fun, carefree night with people I can be myself around."

"In that case, I accept." Then I gave him a playful grin. "For the record though, I do expect you to bring flowers *that night*, or at least a corsage. If we're going to do this, we're going to do this properly."

He gave me a gentlemanly bow. "Yes, ma'am."

32

INTERSECTION

"You have got to be kidding me," I muttered to myself.

I stood in the driveway of the Suns' home. Henry and Razel's parents had rented us a limousine, so our group was meeting here. It was incredibly kind of them, and I had been excited to attend the prom in style.

Then Solange stepped out of an Uber with Oliver. In a tux.

"Everyone, you remember Oliver," Solange said. "I asked him to accompany me to the dance tonight. I realize the relationship between both of your pairs is platonic, but I did not want to feel like a fifth wheel. Plus, this fellow looks absolutely dapper in pictures." She touched Oliver's chin and I could tell by the look in his eyes that he barely was able to stifle the impulse to swat her away. Strange how I'd become familiar enough with those eyes to notice even slight changes.

"Didn't eight guys ask you to the prom, Solange?" Razel asked.

"None of them were suitable," Solange replied.

"Kids! Come take pictures," Mrs. Sun called from the porch. My friends drifted over. Justin and Razel posed awkwardly by the tree on the front lawn. He went to put his arm around her waist, but panicked and ended up putting it around her neck so it resembled a loose chokehold. Hana used a pink Polaroid camera to snap pictures of Henry with the enthusiasm of the best paparazzo. I stayed behind and crossed my arms as I confronted the two demons.

"What gives?" I said. "Rule Five of your Code of Conduct states that only one of you can work to negatively impact a human assignment."

"Oliver isn't here to interfere," Solange assured. "We both

know what happens if demons break a rule. If fortune smiles on the wicked tonight and I do find the right way to manipulate chaos, Oliver literally can't assist me or do anything to help harm your precious Henry."

"Then why bring him?"

"Let's get all the boys in one shot!" Mrs. Sun beckoned. Hana raced over and grabbed Oliver by the hand. He could not have looked more startled but didn't resist as she tugged him away.

"Because of San Diego," Solange replied. "I can tell Oliver affects you. I don't know why, but your face and body language shift *ever so slightly* when you see him. I may not be able to enlist him to bring chaos to Henry, but there's nothing in the rules about using a second demon to mess with an angel's focus. This prom will be a whirlwind of four hundred students in a loud, dimly lit, essentially unsupervised downtown hotel in one of the most rambunctious cities in the world. I am *certain* that some opportunity for me to manipulate chaos will arise. When it does, the less focused you are, the better."

"And now all the girls!" Hana called excitedly.

Solange strode past me. I wondered if I could get away with one of those chokehold poses with her . . .

We assembled under the tree. While Mrs. Sun used her phone, Hana worked her Polaroid. She shook the collected pictures then scurried over to show us. "You three look so pretty. Here's one for each of you." She handed a photo to me, Solange, and her sister.

What an excellent addition this will make to my War with Evil scrapbook.

After a few more pictures for posterity, we squished into the limo. Before I could stop it, Solange stealthily engineered it so I was sitting between Henry and Oliver.

"Hi," Oliver said awkwardly.

"Hi," I returned with equal weirdness.

He looked me up and down. I wore a knee-length dress with a sparkly silver bodice and flowy white skirt. "Nice dress. And nice kicks too." He nodded to my silver-sequined shoes. My special occasion sneakers.

"Thanks . . ." The vibrant blue of his tie made his aqua eyes stand out even more. "You clean up good yourself."

"Okay! I made a playlist for the ride," Razel announced, rummaging through her purse for her phone.

"Nope!" Henry said, sliding forward quickly and plugging his phone into the sound console. "We're not listening to any musical numbers this time. Strictly the classics."

"Henry, musicals *are* classic."

"Classic *rock*," he corrected.

Razel huffed. Henry ignored her and tapped on his phone to find a playlist. Oliver and I fidgeted nervously. Around our celestial colleagues, we were supposed to be enemies. In private, we'd formed a strange kind of friendship. And on Earth, we were two strangers who'd only met once. It was hard to figure out how to act around each other.

Solange was right—him being here could really mess with my focus tonight. It was a major problem considering I needed every ounce of concentration not just to counter any threat she posed, but also to make sure Henry was in that elevator at 9:04 p.m. to complete his final Plot Point. I had no idea why this was so important, but given the specificity of the requirement, my timing had to be exact. I didn't want to risk failure and damage Henry's future.

Perhaps the best tactic to diffuse the discomfort with Oliver was banal conversation that had nothing to do with our work. While the twins bickered and Solange spoke to Justin, I dared a glance at the demon boy and ventured an icebreaker. "So . . . do you like classic rock?" I asked in a hushed voice.

He nodded. "It's been kind of a conflict of interest for me given who my mentor is."

"How so?"

"Troy was the demon assigned to the Freddie Mercury case."

"Oh."

Well, so much for that.

"Alrighty," Henry said. "We're all set with the music. Should I keep the volume low so we can talk or louder so we can focus on the tunes?"

"The latter," I said tersely. *"Please."*

Walking through the Millennium Biltmore reminded me of gliding through the Pearlie Gates' cathedral in Heaven. The grand hallways, ceiling, and walls shimmered in every possible shade of gold. Like, if you bought an eye shadow palette called "King Midas is My Man," it would mirror the ombre richness stretching before us.

After proceeding through the hotel lobby, my group and I strode through the wide corridor that connected to the ballrooms, shops, and bar. *This* was the Main Galeria mentioned in Henry's Plot Point. I glanced around and spotted the elevator banks to the left. I had an hour and a half to get Henry back here.

Despite the unusual specificity, I couldn't believe the third Plot Point was this simple. Nothing with my GA job had been simple. It made me wonder if the other heeled shoe had yet to drop.

The Main Galeria was full of regular hotel guests, hotel employees, a large number of adults in smart business attire, and a bunch of dressed-up teenagers. The gowns really seemed at home in this space, like its true purpose was to host lavish affairs.

When I asked the concierge, he'd told me the hotel was built in the 1920s—hence the gilded wall designs, frescoed mural ceilings, crystal chandeliers, and elaborate carvings. However, the shimmer on every curve and corner, and the antiquated designs made the hotel seem so much older—almost ancient and celestial. Like the kind of place God might book for vacation.

I wonder if God ever takes PTO days . . .

"Oomph!"

I'd accidentally bumped into a woman in her mid-thirties wearing a pencil skirt and blazer. It was both our faults. I'd been engrossed in the architecture while she was reading the documents in a folder she'd been carrying, which had now spilled to the floor.

"I'm sorry," we apologized in unison. I bent down to help her pick up the papers. The woman thanked me then hurriedly proceeded on her way toward the elevator bank.

I rejoined my group, and together, we entered the Crystal Ballroom. It was one of three grand ballrooms on this floor and it was fit for the Great Gatsby himself. The ceiling was as tall as a cathedral and the painted fresco over it featured Greek and Roman gods, angels, cupids, and mythological creatures. Both the entire left and right walls had high-up balconies with mauve drawn-back curtains framing them, interspersed with columns and glimmering sconces. The most intricate molding I'd ever seen lined the very top of the room.

Opposite the main doors an enormous purple banner printed with tonight's theme of *A Date with Destiny* hung under a silvery balloon arch over the stage.

It was funny to see this space of old world beauty host the modernity of a DJ, teenagers doing mosh pit dancing, and flashing neon lights that painted the walls erratically.

"This beat is so hot!" Razel said, grabbing Justin by the hand. "Let's go!"

She yanked him into the mosh of sweaty, formally dressed kids. Solange gave Henry and me a little wave then led Oliver around the side of the ballroom. He shot me a look of caution and concern over his shoulder. I remembered that look from when he stopped me from going to my Nana's Hell House. My gaze lingered on the demon pair until they vanished into the crowd of adolescents.

"I hope you don't mind!" Henry shouted in my ear over the blaring music. "But I'm not much of a dancer!"

I gave the mosh a once over. In some areas it was awkward and jumpy while other parts looked grindy and scandalous. "No worries!" I replied. "Because this isn't dancing!"

He smirked and gestured at the refreshments area. I nodded and we wandered over. The two of us hung out there for a while, bobbing our heads to the music, voting for king and queen, making use of the funny photo booth, and spending way too much time by the chocolate fountain. Eventually Henry became engrossed in conversation with some guys from his surf team. I started to get bored and Henry noticed. He leaned closer to speak in my ear.

"You don't have to babysit me *all night*. I'll be fine."

It was a tug-o-war of responsibilities when it came to my instinct for protecting Henry. On the one hand, I felt the need to stay with him; if danger sprung out of nowhere, then proximity to my charge was key. However, Solange was dangerous when left to her own devices. We were in a crowded, unfamiliar space and surrounded by all sorts of people and possibilities, so my time could be equally well served keeping an eye on her.

I checked my watch. An hour had passed since I'd last seen her and Oliver, and I should really check what she was up to. It was also probably a good idea to get a closer look at this elevator that would somehow alter Henry's life.

"Please don't wander off," I said in Henry's ear.

He waved me off. "Calm down. What could happen?"

I literally have no idea. That's what scares me.

I stepped away from Henry and cut through the throbbing ballroom. It was an epic party surging with life. That was great, and beautiful; however if I'd learned anything in my line of work it was that places with the most life were the most dangerous for a Guardian Angel. Every person was a variable. Variables meant more risk, like with the Six Flags and hydrant incidents when Solange used innocents to create chaos. Variables also meant more liability, like when she unleashed that Dark Breed on a campus of students.

I exited the Crystal Ballroom, my airy white dress bouncing around my knees and sparkly sneakers gliding over the polished floor.

I would inspect the elevator bank first. It was just next door to where the prom was being held—housed within a red-carpeted foyer framed by gilded gates. There were four elevators, two on each side. I strode to the elevator my Plot Point had indicated. At that exact moment, the doors slid open. After several people exited, I peeked inside. It looked like a perfectly normal elevator.

A man cleared his throat behind me, and I turned and stepped out of his way. "Sorry, sir."

Passengers boarded the lift and the doors shut again. I stood there with my arms crossed. I didn't get it. Why this place? Why this time?

The other end of the elevator bank led to a balcony. I drifted there and was met by more grandeur. Large crème-colored bricks walled the room beyond, massive arches looming on the left and right, gold accents everywhere. Above the bronze doorway I'd entered hung a fancy clock. Below, a fountain surrounded by flowers flowed delicately.

Suddenly a shadow caught my eye.

My balcony separated into two red-carpeted staircases. Halfway down the left one—paused and staring off in thought—was Oliver. He seemed to sense me looking at him. He met my gaze then tilted his head downward. I understood the message and descended the right staircase opposite him. We met on ground level in front of the fountain.

"Where's Solange?" I asked.

"She wanted to check out some of the other floors of the hotel—the conference rooms, the pool area, the roof."

"Should I be concerned?"

"Probably. She's out for blood, Grace. You guys graduate next week. It's going to be a thousand times harder for her to worm her way into Henry's life during the summer. I think she's hoping to do something big tonight."

"Well, everything seems chaos free in the main areas of the hotel right now—rowdy, but controlled and happy. There's nothing obvious for her to manipulate. Any thoughts on her approach?"

Oliver's face tightened.

"Right, different teams. Sorry," I said.

He sighed in frustration. "You know, as a demon, it makes my skin crawl to have an angel apologize to me. It makes me feel like I'm doing something wrong. I mean, technically my whole purpose is to do wrong, but this feels . . . different."

"Different how?"

"*I don't know.*" His tone turned unexpectedly angry and he paced a couple steps. "You're too nice to me. First in Heaven trying to help me. Then treating me like a person, not the big pile of crud that I am, which is what landed me in Hell and rightfully so. Now this whole thing with connecting me with my mom."

I blinked twice, totally stunned. "You're upset about that? I thought you'd be happy."

"Why do you care if I'm happy?" He turned and took three purposeful strides toward me, stopping inches from my face and bearing down. "Why are you doing this? I'm not a good person, Grace. You should be keeping your distance and treating me like the enemy, *because I am.*"

I looked up at him calmly, unyieldingly. "I don't see you that way, Oliver. Honestly . . . I'm not sure you see yourself that way either."

He angled away from me and planted his hands on the edge of the fountain. "Well, everyone else does. And this is my lot. My role. I have to lean into it, Grace. You being nice to me is messing with my mind and keeping me from focusing on my job. That's dangerous for me."

Oliver shook his head bitterly and released a maddened sigh. "If a Guardian Angel fails, their assignment gets a picture in your fancy museum and the GA gets to start fresh with another human. If a demon fails, we lose our positions and are *destroyed*. Our souls get wiped from existence. It's literally our deal with the Devil."

The gravity of the situation, of *Oliver's* situation, hit me like a ton of bricks. No wonder the demons were so motivated. No wonder Solange had been willing to exhaust herself with so much power raising that Dark Breed. Their souls were at stake. This wasn't just about the well-being of the humans they were trying to derail. This was about their well-being too. Their very existence.

My eyes fell to the floor. "I didn't know. I'm sorr—"

"Don't say it," Oliver cut me off.

A moment passed before he spoke again, this time with more steadiness. "Grace . . ." he turned to face me. "I'd be lying if I said I haven't come to think of you as a friend. Truth be told, you're probably the first *real* friend I've had since I was a little kid, maybe ever. But friends weren't part of the deal I made when I agreed to be a demon. Even if I like you and appreciate what you've done for me, I think it's in my best interest if we don't talk or see each other anymore. You have your war to fight, and I have mine. Magic elevator aside, there's a reason Heaven and Hell are separated by such distance. They weren't meant to interact. And neither were the people who live there."

I paused before replying. "I understand. I'm sad for you. But then, what you're saying reflects the main difference between us, doesn't it?"

"What do you mean?"

I looked at him evenly. "Well, angels make choices thinking of other people first. Demons think about their best interest ahead of all else. Given that, I wouldn't worry about letting your team down, Oliver. You seem rather committed to your role." I patted him on the arm twice then moved toward the staircase. Before ascending, I hesitated and pivoted to him. "I'll tell your mom you sent a goodbye. And consider this one from me."

I climbed the steps and didn't look back. Some sadness flowed inside of me, but not an overabundance because I realized I probably should have seen this coming.

Perhaps it was foolish and naïve of me to think Oliver and I could be friends. I trusted my instincts—I knew he was different from Solange and the other demons I'd met. He'd helped me, protected me, and counseled me. We'd laughed together, fought together, and connected. Angel and demon differences hadn't mattered to us when it mattered most. Unfortunately, he *had* chosen a team. I couldn't ignore that and neither could he, especially given what was at stake for him. While some part of me that I'd never truly understood had always been drawn to learning more about him, I had to accept that his true nature and who he had the potential to be were questions I was not meant to answer.

I started to make my way back to the Crystal Ballroom, however on my way I finally spotted Solange's purple dress. My enemy was at the opposite end of the Main Galeria, inspecting something mounted to the wall. I weaved my way through the crowd. By the time I reached the spot where she'd been standing the demon was gone. I looked up. She'd been staring at an emergency floor plan. My internal warning system started to pulse.

I hastened around the corner and saw Solange descending some stairs into a sublevel part of the hotel. I made to follow her, but stopped short and checked my watch. It was ten minutes to my deadline. As much as I needed to see what Solange was up to, I absolutely could not risk missing Henry's date with destiny.

I hurried back to the ballroom where the party was still going strong.

"Doolittle!"

I turned as Justin jogged up to me. "I know Henry hates dancing, but you don't. Razel is taking a break right now. Thought I'd find you and offer you a partner." He bowed gallantly and extended his hand. "Shall we dance?"

"Justin, I would love to—and love your *The King and I* reference—but I actually have something to do with Henry. Have you seen him?"

"Over by the chocolate fountain."

"Thanks!" I wormed my way through the party. It felt so much warmer in here now due to the hundreds of bodies bopping around.

"Henry!" I shouted, as I got closer to the fountain.

"Is it time?" he asked.

I wasn't meant to tell Henry about his Plot Points, but I had mentioned to him that we needed to take care of a special Guardian Angel task at around nine—no follow-up questions about it would be answered. Thankfully, the guy was learning to roll with the punches.

"Yes." I grabbed him by the wrist and guided him through the ballroom into the Main Galeria. I glanced at my Soul Pulse as we moved. Five minutes to go.

"I know this is going to sound weird," I said. "But we have to take a ride in an elevator."

"To which floor?"

I halted.

In all the time I'd had to think about this moment, I never once considered what button to press once we got inside the elevator. Maybe I just needed to let whatever happened happen.

"Let's play it by ear," I said.

We waited in the elevator bank under the glow of a fancy lantern. When the first elevator opened and people started to board, Henry stepped forward. I held my arm up and stopped him.

"Not that one."

Time ticked by until 9:03 p.m. finally arrived. With a minute to the grand moment, we were the only ones left on the landing. I pressed the up button of my desired elevator and tapped my foot nervously.

At precisely 9:04 p.m., the elevator dinged open. I signaled Henry to wait a second as I checked inside first. It was empty and seemed as ordinary as before.

"Alrighty, let's go I suppose." I gestured for Henry to enter. When we were both inside, I tapped my foot again.

How much can happen in sixty seconds?

The elevator doors started to shut. I glanced at the button panel. I guess I would have to pick one . . .

"Hold the elevator!"

A briefcase and the sleeve of a blazer slid through the closing doors, activating the elevator's sensors and sending the doors open again. It was the blonde woman I'd bumped into earlier. She strode in with *Leo* directly behind her.

33

MY RIGHT WAY

"*Grace?!*" My friend stumbled back and pressed the bridge of his nose.

"*Leo?!*"

Henry and the blonde woman stared at us. "You two know each other?" Henry said.

"It's a long story," I responded quickly. I tried my best to compose myself despite the ludicrous situation. "What floor, ma'am?"

The blonde woman gave me a questioning look. "Um, sixteen please."

I pressed the button and the lift started to ascend.

"Naomi Joseph." The woman offered me her hand. "Are you a member of the same mentorship program as Leo?"

"Um, what mentorship program?" I asked, shaking her hand.

"I'm in a mentorship organization for kids interested in becoming lawyers, kind of like Big Brothers, Big Sisters with more paperwork and gavels," Leo explained, speaking fast from the nerves. "Naomi is my mentor. She and her law firm have rented out several conference rooms at the hotel for the weekend for a legal symposium."

Naomi checked her watch. "Leo, are you *sure* the last place you saw me with my phone was upstairs? I only have five minutes before I have drinks at the bar with the partners."

"Yeah—*gulp*—that's where it should be . . ." Leo said, darting his gaze to me.

The elevator stopped for a moment on the eighth floor and a small group of teenagers from the prom got in. They smiled at Henry and me but were wrapped up in their own lively conversation. When they squished in, Leo and I ended up on one side of the elevator while Henry and Naomi were herded to the other. As the doors closed, Leo turned to me and spoke in whisper.

"Is that your human assignment?"

I nodded. "Is that yours?"

He nodded. "I had a Plot Point for Naomi that told me she had to be in this elevator at 9:04 p.m."

My brain boggled. "That's the same as Henry's Plot Point."

The elevator halted and my classmates emptied out of the lift. We began the final ascent just the four of us again.

"What kind of law do you practice?" Henry asked Naomi, completely unaware of the weirdness of the situation. The floor numbers lit up over the doors as we rose higher.

12 . . . 13 . . . 14 . . .

"Patent law," she responded. She took a business card out of her blazer pocket and handed it to my friend. The number 16 lit up and the doors started to open. "I specialize in—"

And then the world broke.

The four of us were thrust against each other as the entire compartment shook violently. The emergency lights and alarm began to sound, alerting us to the earthquake that we were already very aware was happening.

Yipes!

The elevator rocked back and forth, then plummeted for a split second.

I hit the floor. Leo fell next to me. The shaking was so intense that it felt like my skin was trying to slide off my skeleton. Naomi was knocked off her feet next, brutally hitting her head against the button panel on the way down. Henry clung to the railing that ran along the walls of the car.

Thankfully the quake ceased a moment later. The sound of the alarm stopped, but it continued to flash on the ceiling.

"Naomi!"

I got to my feet as a panicked Leo rushed to his charge's side. The woman looked woozy. She'd injured herself pretty badly on the button panel. A gash on her head leaked liberally; I imagined a concussion was in store.

Suddenly a new alarm started going off. It was the fire alarm for the hotel.

Henry took out his phone and sent several rapid texts. The replies were just as speedy. "Razel, Justin, and Solange are okay, but the staff is evacuating the hotel," he told me. "They're worried about structural damage and there are fires in different parts of the building."

"I don't think we should sit around and wait for firefighters to save us," Leo said, trying to steady his charge. "Naomi is hurt and who knows how long it could take them to reach us."

"Agreed. We need to get out of here STAT." I bit my lip as my mind whirred.

The elevator doors were open about six inches. With the lift having fallen a few feet during the earthquake, through that opening you could see a little over a foot of the fifteenth floor below, a wide concrete band of the internal building structure, and the bottom two feet of the sixteenth floor where we'd been headed. The flashing white lights and moderate, persistent beep of the fire alarm pulsed along the hallways beyond.

"I think if we pry these doors open a bit more we can climb out," I said.

"Let's do it," Henry replied. "I also texted Justin. No one's as fast as him. He's already on his way up the stairs to help us."

Henry and I moved forward and successfully pushed the doors in opposite directions to open them much wider. "The lightest of us goes up first, then helps the others," Henry instructed.

Naomi was standing on her own now, but she was clearly disoriented. Leo hastened forward. "Okay, Give me a boost," he said.

"Shouldn't we give Grace a boost?" Henry suggested. "Girls are usually lighter."

Leo looked at me. "How much do you weigh?"

I stuck out my cupped hands. "Up you go, Leo."

Henry and I boosted him and he pulled himself through the gap.

"Hey!" Justin's voice sounded down the hall. A second later our friend knelt beside Leo.

"Where's my sister?" Henry asked worriedly.

"She and Solange refused to leave without you guys. They're coming; they're just slower in heels. Now come on."

He motioned for the next person to come forward.

"One of you can go," Naomi said to me and Henry. She'd taken off her blazer and was using it to wipe the blood trickling down her injury as she leaned against the elevator wall—pale and wobbly. "You're kids. You take priority."

"No way," Henry said. "You're injured, *you* take priority. Now come on, up you go."

Together, Henry and I carefully boosted Naomi; then Justin and Leo helped her into the hallway.

"Henry?!" Razel's panicked voice rang through the hall.

"I'm in here!"

Razel and Solange reached the group. Then the world tore us apart.

I grabbed the railing as the second wave of earthquake struck. At first it only seemed like a small aftershock, but then I saw Solange's eyes glow red and her smile grow wide.

Oh no.

The opportunity was too perfect. Her magic took to the situation like a seal took to swimming. Before I knew it, the tremor tripled in strength and loud snaps sounded above us. Henry and I were thrown to the floor. As I rolled over to look up at the doors, my friends fell from view.

Because the elevator fell.

A horrible screeching accompanied our descent. We weren't in free fall. Solange may have manipulated the earthquake energy, but either not all the cables had snapped or the lift had some sort of emergency brake system in place.

Henry and I managed to clamber to our feet. We held tightly to the rails as the shaking continued. Our car's lighting became a blurry strobe and the numbers rushed through countdown on the indicator above the button panel. Ground level approached.

"Brace yourself!" I yelled.

The elevator hit with a crunch and we were thrust to the floor again. For a moment I lay there, trying to catch my breath as the elevator continued to shake from the quake. Then everything went still. The aftershock was over. Though the shock of the event still remained.

Henry groaned.

"I second that . . ." I said wearily, lifting my face from the ground. I gradually boosted myself up. "Are you okay?"

"Yeah, I think so. You?"

"Still dead, but I'm fine."

We stood shakily, thinking we'd escaped the worst of it. Then two seconds later a new problem arose. Literally.

"Henry, look." The doors of our lift were still open, but the doors that connected the elevator shaft to the floor beyond were closed. Despite that, smoke was seeping its way through the cracks up to us.

"I see it," he said. "One of the fires must be down here." He checked his phone. "No signal. I can't call for a rescue."

"You already have one." I summoned my halo. Glowing ring in hand, I concentrated, aimed, and with a small scoop produced a powerful beam of light. The doors blasted away. The second they did, plumes of smoke embraced us heartily. It wasn't so thick that we couldn't see, but we coughed immediately.

The sprinkler system had been triggered down here. It soaked us the instant we stepped out of the elevator. We were in a sublevel of the Biltmore. A quick glance at the floor plan mounted to the wall nearby showed us that the kitchens, spa, and fitness center were on this level—along with two emergency staircases.

"The nearest staircase isn't far from here," I said, coughing. "This way."

We ran down the first corridor to the left for a minute then stopped short. That *entire hallway* ahead was engulfed in flames. The paint seemed to practically be dripping off the walls from the heat.

"Other staircase?" Henry said.

"Yup."

We spun on our heels and proceeded back up the corridor to

find the second emergency exit. Henry moved faster than I did. When he banked the next corner ahead of me, a shadow darted across my peripheral vision. I froze and turned around. Solange was a dozen feet behind me.

"What are you—"

She held a finger to her lips. Her eyes glowed red and the fires from the hallway Henry and I had just escaped abruptly roared. They began hungrily surging in my direction like someone had pressed fast forward on a remote control. I backed up in panic as Solange phased through one of the walls. A second later she popped her head out of another wall farther away, a wild grin on her face.

"You'll never escape. There's too much chaos to play with and I've been practicing just as you have. I can masterfully manipulate the instability, the fires, and any aftershocks. And I can phase through every room and floor of this place to spread the damage like . . ." She giggled. "Well, like wildfire really. *Au revoir!*"

"Grace!" Henry called.

Solange disappeared into the wall and I rounded the corner to catch up with my friend. He opened his mouth to ask a question, but then coughed violently. I grabbed him by the arm and urged him forward. The smoke was building and the fire was at our heels.

Unfortunately, at the next turn our path was cut off again by more flames. The doorway to the stairs was visible, but we'd be torched before we reached it. Solange had been through here already.

"I can't believe the fire spread so quickly," Henry thought aloud, panic in his voice. "Why aren't the sprinklers slowing it down more?"

I bent over in a coughing fit. "Short version—the universe *really* wants to kill you, Henry."

And by universe, I mean a devious French demon in a party dress.

Another placard with a floor plan was mounted nearby. I scanned it quickly. "If we circle around we can approach that first emergency exit from a different direction." A few more seconds to memorize the map. "Okay, follow me."

We about-faced and headed down a new path that took us to the Biltmore's indoor pool. The low-ceilinged room had brass trimmings on the doors and railings, blue-and-white striped columns, and Italian mosaic tiles on the walls. The smoke was heavy in here, but that was not the greatest threat. Halfway across, the world rocked as another aftershock struck. The waters of the pool sloshed out, and the teakwood deck chairs skidded over the tiled floor like we were on a cruise ship caught in a storm.

The slippery tile and shaking made it impossible to stay on our feet. A rush of water suddenly collided with Henry like a small tsunami and he fell hard onto a chair. Just then I saw Solange phase through the back of the room. She waved before passing through another wall. The aftershock finally ended as I helped Henry up, and we kept moving.

Finally, we found the hall approaching the stairwell. Plaster crumbled from the ceiling; thankfully there was no fire here. I used my halo as a large shield, holding it over our heads to protect us from debris.

We reached the door. Henry jiggled the handle. It wasn't locked, but something was blocking it from the other side. With another beam of light, I obliterated the door and the blockage. Smoke and heat assaulted my face as if I'd opened the door to a preheated oven. When I blinked away the dryness in my eyes, I hesitantly stepped into the stairwell. Henry did too. We looked up, blinking through the drizzle from the sprinklers. My heart sunk.

The entire stairwell was on fire. Our bodies glowed with red and orange light and sweat instantly began to form on our skin. We backed away into the hall.

"What do we do, Grace?" Henry asked wearily.

"I—I don't know." We'd tried every option, every potential escape route. I . . . I didn't have a solution. I diverted my gaze to him and spoke the truth. "My powers are strong, Henry, but I don't know how to use them to get out of this." I coughed violently.

"What about your shield?"

I shook my head. "It's for blocking things; it's not going to insulate us from the fire."

"We could try to find another way to that second set of stairs," he suggested, then coughed. "Or backtrack to the elevator and try to—*whoa!*"

A third aftershock.

Henry was instantly thrown down. Solange darted by in the corridor behind him. My frustration flared. It was like being haunted by a skinny ghost in formal wear. I angrily summoned my halo and chucked it at her. The shaking threw my aim off and she disappeared into another wall, unscathed, as massive chunks of ceiling fell from above.

Halo!

My accessory returned in the nick of time and I got my shield up to protect our bodies. Regrettably, I couldn't do anything to stop the debris that crashed behind us, blocking the path we'd just come from. Ahead, several wall sconces also exploded, resulting in an electrical fire that began to run along the walls and carpet in our direction.

We were blocked on both sides and our only other exit—the stairs—was an inferno of no return. The tremor stopped and Henry rose on his own.

"Was that quake the universe or California's tectonic plates trying to kill me?" he joked, though there was a tremble in his voice. "I thought this kind of stuff only happened in disaster movies."

"Henry, I—look out!" I shoved him out of the way as a huge chunk of ceiling plaster came crashing. It forced us into the stairwell.

What do I do? What do I do?

"Grace!"

I spun around and looked up. "*Oliver?!*"

The demon raced down the stairs through the fire like it was nothing.

"Dude, *what?!*" Henry gestured dramatically between Oliver and the flames.

"I'm a demon," he said, revealing his identity freely. "I can walk through fire. It's a perk. Now *let's go.*"

Oliver waved us forward. Though doom was near, I couldn't

budge. I was too shocked and stared at him skeptically.

He huffed in aggravation. "Look, when the earthquake hit I had a feeling your," he flicked his eyes to Henry then back to me, "*other half* would escalate things and you might get trapped."

"And you came back for us?" I said. "But what about your role, our different teams, your deal with the Devil?"

"*I don't want to talk about it,*" Oliver scowled. Conflict wrenched his face and he grunted. "Just come on, okay."

"Grace, can we trust this guy?" Henry asked, still bewildered.

I turned to Oliver, studied him another moment, then nodded. "Yes."

Oliver returned the nod then his eyes flashed red and he opened his arms wide. The flames on the next few flights of stairs moved out of the way, creating a narrow path for us to freedom. The demon raced up the steps and we followed him until we reached the door to the next floor of the hotel. It was unlocked. Thank God!

We piled out. There was fire surrounding the door and Oliver cleared that too. We made our way to the Main Galeria. It was empty now—of people, and thankfully also of flames for the most part. The sprinkler system was doing a good job putting out the small fires that had spread here. Without Solange around to make matters worse, the building's safety measures were containing the hazards.

Our trio sped for the exit. Chunks of columns and gold embellishments littered the floor. Two of the chandeliers lay on the ground, shattered.

When we ran past the Crystal Ballroom, I turned my head to see our prom venue in total shambles—chandelier down, tables knocked over, *A Date with Destiny* banner hanging off one end and partially in flames. Very *Carrie*.

Not that I'd ever seen that scary movie. I Googled it after a Halloween episode of *Dancing with the Stars*, which I watched partly for the dancing and partly for Derek Hough, who was so—

FOCUS, GRACE!

Suddenly Henry's phone blew up with messages. His signal had returned. Despite the sprinklers, he drew the phone without breaking stride and glanced down—then he skidded to a stop. "We have to go back!"

We were mere feet from the lobby. Oliver and I both halted.

"*What?*" Oliver said.

"My sister and best friend never made it out. She's been sending me HELP messages." He turned to me desperately. "They're on the stairs—a regular set, not the emergency back stairs. They got trapped by debris after coming to help us"

"I'm sure 911 or the fire department are coming," Oliver said. He glanced anxiously toward the lobby. "We have to go, man."

"No way. They're on the sixteenth floor. This place is full of fire and stuff is collapsing all over. Outside help may not make it in time. You both have superpowers. We have to go back for them. *Now.*" He lunged in the direction of the stairs again, but I grabbed his arm roughly.

"No. We have to go. My job is to protect you, Henry. I have to get you out of here. Now's our chance."

"Forget it, Grace. I'm not leaving." He shook me off.

My halo formed and I leapt in front of him as he tried to make a break for it—projecting my shield to shove him back. He looked shocked. I lowered the shield and stood firm.

"Henry, I get it. They're my friends too but . . ." I shook my head. "I can't. That's not what God and the angels want. I have to protect you at all costs and above everyone else. Those are the rules. That's what the highest higher-ups of the universe have said is necessary. *That's my job.*" Reluctance quivered in my throat. Uncertainties rushed through my head.

I was proud to have developed a make-no-apologies confidence recently. But after I had met Akari at the Moral Compass, I'd also accepted that there were some people who shouldn't be questioned. Some people so far above you in terms of authority and power and experience that you needed to respect their plans and perspectives even if they disagreed with your own. That's what I was *supposed to* believe.

My heart tightened. It didn't like the idea any more now than when Akari had first introduced it. But did I really have the audacity to push back against the established way of powers so much bigger than myself? And if I did . . . did I have the right to use that boldness? *Was it right* to use it?

I vanished my halo and felt something turning inside of me—a conviction.

The right way . . .

This was not it. I felt that cognizance burning my soul and knew those words I'd spoken to Henry weren't mine, or what I believed. I couldn't go on pretending that they were.

Leo's advice from months ago came surging back, this time making hard impact like a long overdue aftershock of conscience. I looked at Henry.

My purpose was to defend others, myself, and all that was good. But *defend* was the cousin of *defy*. And maybe no one was above facing defiance. Maybe *no one* had the right to tell you to stand down, follow blindly without questioning, and abandon your instinct.

Maybe . . . no, *absolutely*, doing what was right meant having the courage and nerve to think for yourself, and judge for yourself what was truly good.

"Henry, get outside," I said firmly.

"But—"

"Listen to me. The rules say I should get you to safety and stay with you to protect you. *I* say I trust you to get clear of the building and take care of yourself while you trust me and Oliver to save Razel and Justin." I stuck out my hand. "In this together?"

Henry paused, then extended his hand and we gripped each other's arms tightly. "In this together."

"Good. Now go."

Henry took off across the connecting lobby and I saw him exit through the revolving door. All of a sudden my entire body glowed with golden light—so bright and majestic it was like I was a Christmas tree angel turning on for the first time. It only lasted for a moment, and left no visible change, but it felt like something changed inside of me. Despite my damp hair and dress, I felt warm within. Like baked bread rising in the oven.

"*What was that?*" Oliver asked, staring at me.

"No idea. And no time to form one. Let's move." I motioned for him to follow.

"I can't believe you're doing this," Oliver huffed as we bolted for the stairs.

"Isn't that the pot calling the kettle hot? What happened to looking out for your best interest?"

"Shut up."

"That's not an answer," I replied.

As we got closer to the stairs my demon sidekick worked to clear the flames, protecting me. Once we reached the stairwell he stayed in front and continued harnessing his magic. He had to pause every few flights to prepare the path ahead, so we sped up the steps in bursts.

"Wouldn't it be faster if you phased us through the flames?" I asked, running up the next set.

"I suck at phasing," he said angrily. "I've tried to work on it, but I can barely phase a coffee cup through a table, let alone a person through a wall."

"Still?" I coughed from the smoke. "You haven't gotten better at that?"

"*Grace.*"

"Sorry."

My eyes tracked the numbered doors as we kept climbing. *9 ... 10 ... 11 ...*

Finally, we made it to the sixteenth floor. It was locked. I summoned my halo and was about to blast it when a thin arm abruptly phased out of the door and yanked me through. I was thrust onto the carpeted floor of the connecting hall.

Solange stood over me. She snapped open the tiny clutch that matched her prom dress and pulled out a small pair of daggers. I clambered to my feet. There were no flames, but chunks of ceiling and broken sconces littered the area.

"I thought you weren't allowed to attack me directly," I said, the emergency sprinkler still drizzling over us lightly as we squared off.

"Unless you attack me first. You did that when you threw your halo at me downstairs. Even if you missed, the loophole formed."

My halo shone brightly and I took the ring in hand. "Well then, why don't we work out our differences?"

She smirked wickedly. Then she lunged, daggers slashing.

My halo deflected one blade, then another. I kicked her in the chest, but instead of thudding into the door behind her, she phased through and fell out of sight. A second later she charged out of the wall a few feet away—dagger extended. She missed my neck by barely an inch.

Shield.

I shoved her away. Oliver banged on the door, but there was no time to let him in. Solange's eyes glowed red and the sprinkler directly above me suddenly burst. The deluge shot down on my head and the water temporarily blinded me. By miracle my reflexes alerted me to dodge a dagger that went spinning through the air.

Solange rushed at me as my halo contorted. I fired one beam of light, then a second, then a third, but she phased through the walls to avoid the shots. It was like a fruitless game of whack-a-mole until she passed through a door and didn't return.

I waited anxiously—hand glowing and ready for her. She didn't come. Oliver banged more intensely. *Was this my opening?* I turned and raced to let him in. Halfway there my nemesis charged out of the wall and nailed me with a full body tackle. I managed to grab her by the wrist to keep her blade from striking me, but her force knocked me over. She activated her phasing powers as we fell. Instead of hitting the carpet, we dropped through the ground then the ceiling of the level directly below us, landing with a thud on the carpet of floor fifteen.

Ow.

Solange, who had been on top of me when we fell, rolled away when we impacted the ground. My halo reflexively flickered back to my head. I blinked, trying to reorient myself. Good thing these human suits were tough.

As I started to sit up, Solange pushed herself to her knees. Her dagger was just out of reach. She went for it. I grabbed my halo. She pounced.

BAM!

Shield in hand, I smacked her in the side of the head when she lunged at me.

Between my magic force and the angle of impact, I thwacked her into the wall so hard that when she collapsed to the floor she did not get up. I'd knocked her unconscious. Captain America would've been proud. And perhaps jealous.

Have a nice nap.

I stood over my downed enemy, took a breath, and went for the stairs. This door was unlocked.

"Oliver! I'm down here!" I called.

He glanced over the railing and moved the fire out of my way so I could get back to him. I took the steps two at a time.

"What happened?" he asked as I met him on the landing.

"I kicked butt and took names, that's what happened."

Halo.

I blasted the locked door and we dashed through. There was a floor plan on the right. Moonlight shone on us from a grand window down the hall as I glanced it over.

In addition to the emergency backstairs that Oliver and I had been using, the hotel had carpeted staircases integrated into the center of the design that guests could take in lieu of elevators. That's what Justin and Razel must've used to find us; that's where they were trapped. When Henry and I were stuck in the elevator, they'd come from the left. I used that as a point of reference to figure out where we needed to go.

"Got it," I said with a nod. "This way."

I navigated us and soon we came upon the elevator doors where Henry and I had last seen the others. They were still pried open, leading to an empty shaft and a sixteen-story drop.

"We're close," I said.

We continued our sprint. Bigger pieces of fallen ceiling and plaster were strewn over the carpet here, as well as shards of a broken decorative mirror and high-heels guests had abandoned in their haste to evacuate.

Oliver and I turned a corner and at last I spotted my friends. An enormous chunk of ceiling had landed on top of Justin's leg.

Razel was desperately trying to pull it off, but she didn't have the strength. The way Justin had been pinned stomach down didn't allow him to assist her. She shouted from despair and frustration. How long had she been trying to do this by herself?

I was about to call to them when I plainly cried out instead. Something pierced my calf. With a grunt, I fell back around the corner before Razel and Justin could see me. A dagger stuck out of my leg. I turned and saw Solange coming up the hall, seeming back at full force and wielding another blade in hand.

How many of those could fit in one purse?

The demon was in the midst of charging toward me when her eyes shifted and she saw Oliver. Solange froze. Her hateful expression dropped to pure shock.

"*Oliver?*"

His face streaked with panic.

I yanked the dagger from my leg and tossed it aside. It hurt like Hell, but the wound sealed itself quickly à la Wolverine. The blade wasn't Divine Iron, and I hadn't been hit in a fatal place that would send me to the Soul Sewer. This strike only hurt in the moment.

Solange's eyes flicked from Oliver to me and back. Her brows narrowed and she spoke but one word. "*Traitor.*"

My halo formed as Solange drew back her arm, poised to throw her dagger. Before she could, Oliver's eyes flashed red and six extra versions of me and him filled the hallway. My copies brandished glowing halos while each of Oliver's held a knife. The dozen mirages ran toward Solange, blocking her view.

"Come on," Oliver said, grabbing my arm. "Now's our chance to get your friends."

I didn't budge. "Are you strong enough to lift that debris off Justin by yourself?"

"Obviously."

"Good." I nodded around the corner. "Go help my friends. Free Justin. Use your powers to clear any fire out of the way and take them to Henry. Too much chaos has been set loose. Solange is only going to keep taking advantage and trying to hurt them. I need to stop her. Effectively this time."

Solange shouted angrily as she slashed at our doppelgangers. Several had already been disintegrated. Soon enough she'd discover the real versions weren't actually anywhere near her.

I took Oliver's lapels in my grip and looked up at him intensely. *"Can I count on you?"*

He hesitated for a lengthy moment that made me more nervous than smoke and fire and earthquakes. Then he nodded. "Yes."

"Good." I released his tux and gave him a simple pat on the chest. "In all senses of the word."

Without further ado, we took off in our different directions. I raced toward Solange as she cut through two more mirages. As I merged into the remaining pack with my halo raised I should've had the advantage, but then Solange looked up the hall.

"Henry!" she shouted.

Instinctively I turned to look. I was the only one who did, giving myself away. Solange stepped forward and punched me in the face. She sliced through the remaining mirages as I rubbed my jaw with my free hand.

"You're too easy," she said.

"And you're too sure of yourself."

I blasted light at her. She ducked and took off running. I pursued the demon as she zigged and zagged through the corridors. My beams created craters and burn marks along the walls each time I missed. Which was every time. Solange was absurdly skilled with phasing and quick on her feet. Soon we were back at the elevators. I lined up a good shot, but she abruptly sank through the floor and the beam of energy blasted out the large window farther down.

I paused and waited, staring at the moonlight-drenched carpet. She'd be back. I assumed by means of the emergency stairs. Then, behind me one of the elevators dinged.

Really?

I approached the elevator bank with my halo raised. One clean shot and I would kill her. Well, send her back to Hell.

The light shone over the first elevator on the right. It was about to open. I backed up across from it, preparing for her to suddenly phase through the doors. Astonishingly, she didn't. The doors opened and she just stood there a moment, normally and calmly with dagger in hand.

BLAST!

She escaped my beam by phasing through the side of the elevator, which deposited her in the hall right next to me. The speedy demon's dagger went for my face. I hinged back and evaded, but she spun around me for another shot. She kept spinning around me—too close and too quick for me to release any kind of offensive ray. All I could do was duck and dodge in the tight parameters of the elevator bank. It was actually making me dizzy the way she whirled and weaved, not giving me a split second to breathe or think. Until—

Finally, in a perfect chance moment I changed my halo to a ball of light and blasted her! At least I tried to. My beam went straight through Solange's chest, and her entire form vanished.

A mirage . . .

Oh no, she'd tricked me.

"Wrong one."

I spun around and real Solange full-body rammed me through the wide-open door of the elevator shaft. I screamed as I plummeted through the dark. My third death and a Grace pancake were seconds away. Or so I thought.

The glow that had enveloped me in the Main Galeria seized me again, only this time I felt a grand whoosh of wind surround me just after. Then I stopped falling.

What the . . .

Gorgeous, glimmery white lit up my peripherals, and I found myself hovering a few floors above my intended doom—my glorious *wings* keeping me aloft.

"*Oh my God.*"

It was all I could say, and it sure seemed appropriate.

But why now? What had I done to be fully realized?

There was no time to ponder. My wings responded to my soul's desire and with a couple powerful flaps I soared upward. My halo *SCHMINGED!* to life over my hair which, like my dress and body, had magically dried when my feathers appeared.

I gripped the ring. Seconds later I shot through the open doors of the sixteenth floor. Solange turned around, but this time she was the one taken by surprise. With a single mighty flap, I zoomed straight at her with halo extended and jammed the ring through her chest, shoving her against the wall.

Solange's face seized with shock. Her gaze raised and I locked eyes with her.

"I'd say see you in Hell, but I don't plan on visiting."

My enemy's mouth hung open, but no words escaped. Her eyes went black and her stunned expression went slack. I yanked my halo out and the demon's limp body fell to the floor. It lay there for a second then disintegrated into black smoke. Her soul returning to her realm to reform. It was over. For today anyway. I'd see her again soon enough. A week, if I recalled my GA lessons correctly.

I headed for the stairwell. Unfortunately, the path Oliver had cleared was no longer an option. Though the sprinklers were doing a much better job of containing the flames, they still burned on many of the steps. This was not a safe way down.

A slight breeze brushed my arms and I pivoted. The window I'd blasted extended an open invitation.

Hmm . . .

With a quick, deep breath and literal leap of faith, I ran and bounded through the window. My wings extended as I fell through the air, then a second later sent me skyward.

"*WHOOOOO!*"

This must've been the kind of victory lap Henry was talking about.

Henry.

I glanced down. The streets surrounding the Biltmore had been blocked off and were lined with fire trucks and police cars. I could see more vehicles with flashing lights across the city. The faint sound of sirens and some smoke carried through the wind. Nothing too terrible though. LA was still standing, and emergency responders could handle it. The ill-timed earthquake had hit everyone unexpectedly. This hotel had just gotten the worst of it thanks to one malicious demon's manipulation. Now that she was out of the way, downtown could catch a break.

I called Oliver on my Soul Pulse. He answered right away.

"Are they safe?" I asked. "Henry? Razel? Justin?"

"They're all okay. Razel and Justin are getting some medical attention, but for nothing huge. Oh, and for the record, I also saw that scrawny angel kid you work with, Leon or Leo or whatever. He got into a car with a woman in a suit. Not sure if you knew they were at the hotel, but just an FYI."

Relief filled my chest. "Good. Everyone accounted for then."

"Are *you* okay?" Oliver asked.

I let the satisfaction of the truth sink in. "I am." I looked at him warmly, gratitude and sincerity filling my soul. "Thank you, Oliver."

"You're welcome, Grace."

"Not bad for a demon."

"Pretty good for the great Ninety-Eight."

We exchanged a small smile, then he looked behind him quickly. "I have to go," he said, and he hung up the call.

I hovered in the sky for a few more wing flaps then flew to the roof of the hotel. With feathers still extended, I landed at the very edge. I stood there a while, my mind blank after experiencing so much in the last hour.

From my radiant vantage point, over the next few minutes the sirens waned as I watched the fires get put out. I didn't know how long I held there, but it was enough time for a semblance of peace to sink over the city—the aftermath of chaos when people looked around, calmed down, and picked up the pieces. They always did, didn't they? *We* always could, couldn't we?

I turned my head up a bit to stare at the heavy night sky before gazing at the contrasting shimmering buildings across Los Angeles. The glow of my stunning wings illuminated the area around me. The City of Angels had never felt more literal.

I couldn't believe I'd gotten my wings, but so many questions remained about the reason they'd appeared. I sighed, then turned my gaze up from the bustling city to the dark sky again.

"Why now?" I asked the half moon and scattered stars, as if they were messengers to the being who'd put me here.

As expected, there was no response. I wondered if, even with my angel status, when it came to the big questions I would spend my entire existence asking "Why?" to someone who may not even be listening. Like everyone else on Earth did.

I guess that's something I still have in common with humanity.

FLASH!

A crisp white envelope with a glowing golden seal abruptly appeared in my hand. I turned it over. On the back were the words: **The Answer.**

I opened the envelope hastily and pulled out the note inside. The message was short and written in sparkling gold calligraphy.

> *All you have to do is ask, Grace. I have ten minutes free in my schedule for you. Come now if you can. If you're strong enough to get there. This is not a place you reach by elevator.*
>
> *— Your "Boss"*

34

THE WHY

I stood at the base of Angel Tower. Heaven's residents milled around, The First City's towers twinkling with wonder in all directions. I directed my eyes up at the stars shining in the cloudless night. Then I glowed.

My wings sprouted lustrously and I took off. Like a rocket bound for the moon, my path was straight and powerful. The floors of Angel Tower whizzed by as I headed for God's office. At first I kept my gaze controlled to just above me—locked on the glass of the building—but when I passed the GA department, I tilted my chin up. The moment my eyes tried to lock onto my destination, I had to avert them. A dozen more floors, then I tried again. I was able to look at the orb atop Angel Tower for five seconds this time before light burned my corneas and I was forced to look down again.

Focus, Grace.

I normally gave myself the mental command snappishly, like I was correcting bad behavior. This time I reminded myself with calm, encouraging energy. Following a cleansing breath and extended exhale, I repeated the words in my head like a mantra.

Focus, Grace.

When I sensed myself getting close, I shot my gaze back up to the glowing, golden orb where the creator of Heaven resided. My eyes watered. My instinct begged me to keep my head down, hold back. I wouldn't do it. That was not me anymore.

The closer I flew to the orb, the brighter it shone until—

WHOOSH!

I crossed an invisible barrier and a rush of tingly wind passed over me. Right after, the burning in my eyes stopped. I looked around. The area surrounding God's office had a force field. It was mainly translucent on this side, but shimmery enough to be perceptible. It seemed that was what caused you to look away, not the office itself. The effect only worked when you were on the other side though. Now that I'd had the strength to get past it, I was fine.

I hovered in the air a moment and took in the city—so small from here. No other skyscrapers came close to grazing the height that Angel Tower reached. It impaled the night so deeply, the stars practically embraced it.

Now that the pain and pressure in my eyes had gone, I flapped closer to God's office freely. It reminded me of that golf ball–shaped dome in Epcot at Disneyworld, only there were glass panels around the top, reminiscent of a greenhouse. I couldn't see inside it. Glowing brilliance emanated from the glass, shielding what lay within from view.

There were no doors attached to the office. However, I noticed the force field also protected one floor directly below the orb that had a U-shaped glass balcony extending from it, much like the skywalk at the Grand Canyon. I alighted onto the balcony, mentally commanded my wings to vanish, and went for the door. It opened automatically at my approach.

My heart pounded as I walked in. Like all floors in Angel Tower, the space I entered reminded me of Doctor Who's TARDIS—so much bigger on the inside than it looked on the outside. The room was huge and airy like an art gallery. It was also full of actual art. Paintings, tapestries, murals, even huge sections of graffiti art decorated the walls. Countless cultures and styles were represented here, possibly all of them. A Rembrandt next to a Warhol, a da Vinci next to a Banksy, a Van Gogh next to an O'Keeffe. It. Was. Incredible.

"Welcome, Grace."

There was so much wonder that I hadn't noticed the woman sitting across the room. She had long hair, thick arms, and a warm smile. Her humble wooden desk looked like something you could buy cheaply at a yard sale.

I crossed the tiled floor, which was a mesmerizing collage of mosaics.

"Hello, ma'am" I said. "I'm here to see—"

"You're expected." The woman smiled at me then reached into a mini fridge and pulled out two glass bottles. "Can I offer you fresh water from Fiji or a bottle of liquid courage?"

"Um, no. Thank you."

"All right then." She put the bottles back and glanced at her Soul Pulse. "Not to be a bermblot, but please try to keep it to a ten-minute visit. He still has a meeting with the Soul Sewer engineers, a brainstorming session with some of the Founding Fathers of America, and a Global Crisis strategy session with Gandhi, Winston Churchill, and an eight-year-old from Croatia named Lucija."

"Wow. Sounds like quite a full evening."

She blinked at me. "That's just in the next hour."

"Oh."

The woman pressed a button on her desk and a pair of twenty-foot double doors magically appeared in the middle of the room.

"As I'm sure you noticed outside," the woman said to my shocked expression, "God's office does not have a traditional entrance. This will take you inside the orb." She gave me an encouraging wave forward. "Go on."

I hesitantly strode toward the doors, took hold of one of the smooth silver handles, and with a deep breath, pushed.

Meeker than I would have liked, I stepped inside. Total awe washed over me. In the center of the office grew a beautiful Angel Oak, similar only in size to the one in the GA department. This tree's screens projected white haze and white noise. Instead of leaves, thousands of butterflies clung to the branches. And its roots—pulsing with golden energy—extended to the blue tile floor and then grew up the rounded walls, clinging to the glass panels.

I closed the door behind me and they both vanished. Dazed with wonder, I wandered out into the space. I didn't see anyone else at first. Then I heard the warmest, kindest, strongest voice to ever bless my ears.

"Hello, Grace."

I turned around and tilted my head in confusion, surprised by who I saw.

"Actor Tom Cavanagh?"

Standing before me in a simple gray cardigan and jeans was a dead ringer for the six-foot Canadian actor who I knew from various TV shows like *The Flash*. Lean and long-faced, he had an easy smile and tussled short, dark hair that showed off his ears.

"Hm. So God is male? And Canadian?" I said.

He laughed. The sound was comforting like calm waves lapping the shore. God walked toward the curved glass wall. The tree roots spreading up that area parted before him, revealing a clear view of the night sky and The First City below.

"Grace . . ." The sound of his voice saying my name was more soothing than warm milk and cookies. "Have you ever heard the expression that God made man in his image?"

He beckoned for me to come closer.

"Yes . . ." I said, doing so.

"The truth is just the opposite. God didn't make man in his image; man made God in theirs. I can appear as anything and anyone you imagine me to be. Gender, ethnicity, height, weight— it's no different than going to a dog shelter and finding you can't decide which animal is the cutest because they're all beautiful and wonderful in their own way."

He turned to face me.

"Just as the mind adjusts what you see in Heaven to suit your soul's preferences and beliefs, so does your image of God change. Based on your expectations for this initial meeting, you would have also felt comfortable with a God that looked like Morgan Freeman, a blonde Emily Blunt, your tenth grade world history teacher, Frida Kahlo, and any member of Netflix's Fab Five."

I paused, then nodded. "Yup, that checks out."

We stood in silence, staring out at the afterlife. It was strange, although I had at least a million questions for him, in that moment, my soul just felt content and safe to stand beside him and share existence.

Eventually, he turned and strode across the office. As he

walked, furnishings magically appeared around the roots—a white marble desk, mighty armchairs, a few gold lampshades.

"So what would you like to ask me?" he said, going over to his desk. When his hand touched it, seven stacks of ancient-looking texts appeared. He opened the cover of one book, read something, and harrumphed.

"I . . . I have so many questions," I said, coming closer. Then I grimaced. "I hope that doesn't annoy you."

God closed the book and looked at me. "Of course not. The strongest souls never stop asking questions."

"And you don't mind? Even if people question . . . *you?*"

"I encourage it. How else will people grow? The buck doesn't stop with anyone, not even me. I know a lot. I've seen a lot. And I work to ensure the best possible future. But I am not to fully thank, blame, or cite for anything. Humans are wonderful, frustrating, wild beings. I learn from them all the time. Every moment of every day, someone shows me the great, surprising extent of what humankind is capable of. Sometimes that's good. Sometimes that's bad. But so long as people question things, question people, and question actions, I have faith that humanity will keep moving forward. I may have contributed to the creation of your universe, and I try my best to guide it and keep things sailing on the smoothest course, but you all are the ones who got yourselves where you are now."

"For better or worse?" I joked modestly.

He shrugged. "Yes. Though I like to concentrate on the better. Anyone can complain about the burnt French fries in the basket. Why not focus on those in the pile that are golden and crispy?"

A small smile crossed my lips. Was it weird to say that God was surprisingly chill?

"So your questions?" God said.

Too many tap-danced across my brain; it was hard to home in on what to ask first. "I know you're on a tight schedule, so I'll try to focus on what matters."

"That's what I always recommend."

I gulped. "How about three questions?"

He nodded and gestured to the armchairs. We sat down. Anticipation drew me to the edge of the seat.

"My first question is actually my newest question," I began. "Why did I earn my wings tonight? Originally I thought figuring out my purpose for serving as a GA would qualify as becoming 'fully realized,' but I discovered mine weeks ago and nothing happened. Now my wings show up in an elevator shaft when I'm falling to my doom, but I earned them in a hotel lobby, specifically after sending my assignment away so I could save our friends . . ." I paused—cringing slightly, but gaze holding firm. "I hope you're not mad about that by the way. No disrespect, but I don't apologize for, or regret it. It was *my* right thing to do."

God smiled. "And that is why you earned your wings, Grace. Discovering strength in your purpose is what drives Guardian Angels to achieve great things, but it's not what makes them fully realized. That kind of enlightenment isn't about understanding and harnessing strength; it's about understanding and harnessing weakness."

He leaned forward, hands clasped together in earnest.

"Grace, you are a kindhearted, loyal, honorable, aggressive person. So, although it took you a while to figure it out, defending comes naturally to you. It beats in your heart and glows in your essence. Fully accepting every way this can manifest inside you provides soul strength, and that's where your power comes from. But while natural strength of heart, mind, and even soul can take you far, true character is forged by weakness. Accepting it. Learning from it. And pushing yourself beyond it."

He sighed. "While you will always be drawn to defending others, and fighting when it matters, Grace, there's a reserved part of you that will also always question if the moment at hand *is* one that matters. This misgiving about whether any here and now is the time to be aggressive is your core weakness. Tonight, for the first time since you became a Guardian Angel, you addressed that doubt head-on in a pivotal moment. Despite the many reasons to shy away and follow the rules—do the conventional, agreeable thing—you chose to find your own way. You questioned. You deliberated. You listened to the crux of your conscience that lies between your head and heart to do what others may have viewed as wrong in order to do what you knew was right. That is what caused you to cross the barrier of your enlightenment. *That* is when you reached a point of being fully realized and why you earned your wings."

I thought for a long moment, trying to process everything. "It's about picking your battles," I said after a beat. "What holds me back is worrying about whether I'm picking the correct ones— fearing how others will react if I do something they don't approve of or don't understand. When I was deciding whether to follow the standard Guardian Angel playbook and God-approved rules to stick with Henry or go back and save our friends . . . it was questioning if anyone else really *has a right* to tell me which battles to pick, to tell me what fights are justified and which aren't."

I nodded. "I overcame my doubts—my core weakness, as you say—when I realized that regardless of power or stature or established order, absolutely no one has that right because no one understands me and my character better than I do. *I'm my own person*. I have to stand tall and act like it—rely on myself first and not let the judgment of others keep me from questioning, fighting, and following my own conscience. And my own path."

God gave an encouraging nod. "I couldn't have put it better myself. So with that, I say congratulations on finding your way. So far that is . . ." He smiled a tad mischievously and winked. Then he glanced at his watch. "What's the next question?"

Goodness it was hard to narrow these down! For a long time one of my top questions was why Henry had been chosen, but I'd actually come to appreciate the benefits of not knowing for now. It preserved a sense of innocence like Akari had proposed. If I knew Henry's exact fate it would be more difficult treating him like a person, and a friend.

I took a breath and focused on something else.

"I guess it's kind of a loaded, twisted-up question. You sent me and Leo to that elevator at 9:04 p.m. tonight. I assume you set that up because Henry and Naomi needed to meet each other, but we were trapped when the earthquake hit. Considering that Henry and I, and our friends, could have died, I just wonder if you anticipated those consequences when you sent us to the Biltmore, and if so, why risk them?" I waved my hand brusquely. "To paraphrase all that, my question is . . . Do you know everything? Do you have a full understanding of everyone's fates?"

"A valid question."

He stood abruptly. "And perhaps one that would benefit from a visual aid." Another floating door appeared in the center of the room. "Walk with me," he said.

I followed God's lead. He held the door open and I was ushered into some sort of pocket dimension. It was a *big* pocket. A massive warehouse lay in front of me; flowers and foliage dripped from inestimable hanging clay, bronze, and glass pots. Every segment of the ceiling itself was covered in ivy interspersed with twinkly lights.

"It's modeled after the Hanging Gardens of Babylon," God explained, noticing how wide my eyes had grown. "One of the Seven Wonders of the Ancient World."

I nodded in a daze then focused on the main feature of the warehouse.

Picture the largest flag any country has ever flown. Then multiply that by 1,028 and you could imagine the massive piece of material hovering parallel to the floor about four feet above it. The material continuously rippled, as if lightly caressed by wind, and all across it countless tiny images flickered—like someone had woven a billion bite-sized iPhones into the fabric.

Hundreds, possibly thousands of angels dawning glittery robes tended to the material, either minding the edges or using loaner backpack wings to fly above it. Most of them wore golden microscope goggles like a biologist or optometrist would use, and plenty scribbled in notebooks as they observed.

I approached the material. In the small section directly in front of me, I saw dozens of small images and scenes rapidly changing one after another with no repetition. People's faces, empty terrain, births, battles, hugs, deaths, a jungle, a courtroom, a sandwich. It was dizzying to look at. It reminded me of this government database called "the Intersect" from the TV show *Chuck*.

Hm. Not a lot of people would get that reference. I bet Leo would.

"This is the Fabric of the Universe," God said proudly, coming to stand beside me.

I stared at him, stared at the material, then stared at him again. "It's *actual fabric*."

He nodded. "This is where a team of specially selected angels— some of the wisest, shrewdest, most tactful yet still compassionate souls—help me sort through everything that has happened, is happening, and could happen on Earth. Because the truth is, Grace, I don't know everything. I retain the information that maybe a million human brains could hold. But even I am not so arrogant to think that's enough. People are too complex, and every second is filled with innumerable possibilities. These angels help me keep an eye on the big picture by analyzing the infinite tiny details."

He stopped and gazed out at the mass undertaking. "We get a lot of chess players, professional sports coaches, book editors, and Girl Scout gold award winners. For example . . . Let me introduce you to a woman you may take a particular interest in." He led me to a woman a short walk away. "This is Olivia Swenson."

When God spoke her name, the woman in question lifted her golden goggles on top of her head. She had brown hair parted down the middle, dark eyes, a pointed nose, and a kindly smile that likely made all who met her feel reassured. She tucked her notebook in her robe pocket and stuck out her hand.

"Pleasure to meet you, Ninety-Eighty. I've been watching you." She gave a cheeky grin and tapped her microscope goggles.

I extended my hand and she shook it once, strongly.

"Pleasure to meet you too, ma'am." I glanced between her and God. "Is that the right thing to call her? I feel like with such an important job, a higher title may be in order."

"These people are my right hand," God responded. "Olivia here is one of our most experienced fabric inspectors and I trust her completely." God tilted his head, thinking something over. "Based on your family's religion, you could refer to her as a Semi-Saint."

Olivia grinned. "That's what my employee travel mug says." Her Soul Pulse flashed and a large silver bottle appeared in her hand. Printed across the side was a thin script that read, *Being a Semi-Saint doesn't mean I want Semi-Strong coffee.*

She took a sip, then the mug vanished.

"Olivia is the Semi-Saint in charge of creating your Plot Points for Henry."

My eyes widened. "Seriously?"

She nodded. "Don't worry; I'll have a new set for you real soon."

I gave a nervous grin and rubbed the back of my head. "No hurry . . ."

God thanked Olivia for her time and let her get back to work as he escorted me to the door he'd left open to his office.

"The Fabric of the Universe and the angels who monitor it don't give me a full understanding of fate, but they provide me with a chance to project, prepare, and protect the world and humankind from the different ripples fate is constantly under-going," God explained as we walked. "The Semi-Saints' diligence allows me to know which tiny thread to pull to alter the overall work. In terms of Guardian Angels, in addition to determining upcoming Plot Points, Semi-Saints help me decide which humans need a GA and pick the best GA matches for said humans."

He stood in the doorway and gestured *after you.* I proceeded through. When he shut the door behind us, it evaporated.

"Getting to the specific example you brought up," God continued, hands in his pockets, "based on what the Semi-Saints have learned, Henry and Naomi didn't need to simply meet. They needed to meet in an impactful way. You meet random people all the time in life—at the market, the gym, the library. This introduction needed to stick. Also, it was vital that Naomi would feel some sort of debt to Henry afterward, which will become relevant later in their lives."

God sighed, almost sadly, which made me uncomfortable.

"I did know that earthquake was coming. Natural disasters aren't my doing; they're a product of our flame-resistant rivals downstairs. However, the codes of conduct between our realms say I have to be notified when one is coming. By pulling some threads, I created a situation where your school and Naomi's law firm ended up in the same place. Then I sent you four to that elevator to achieve what needed to be done, accepting the risks involved. It may seem dangerous, or even cruel, but my Semi-Saints felt strongly that Henry would help Naomi—instilling her with gratitude—Solange would damage your elevator and almost kill you—instilling Naomi with guilt—*and most of all* that you, Grace, were capable of getting out of it. I had faith you would win the day." He looked at me seriously. "I had faith in you since the moment you arrived in the afterlife."

It was a lot to digest. I wasn't sure there was anything a person could do to prepare for God declaring his faith *in you*. That was a bit of flattery mixed with a *ton* of responsibility.

God checked his watch. "Two minutes left. Do you want to get in that third question or would you like to use the remaining time to share a churro or turkey leg?"

Two snack carts magically appeared beside us.

"They're the good kind from Disneyland," my host said. He winked at me. "Even God has a weakness."

I smiled, the humor and smell of snacks bringing me back from my deep reflection. "Tempting, but my third question is necessary."

Between reviewing Memory Prime and the experiences I'd lived through in the last five months, I'd come to appreciate why I was chosen as a Guardian Angel. But I still shied away from the attention my Ninety-Eight status got me because I didn't understand it. I looked to God with desperation, hope, and humility, and spoke the ultimate question.

"What makes me 98% pure good?" I shivered a bit—involuntarily and awkwardly. "Sorry, just saying that out loud makes me feel uncomfortable, and like a full-of-myself fraud."

God studied me. Then he walked over to me. Then he put a hand on my shoulder.

My eyes widened.

God is touching my shoulder. God is touching my shoulder! Ahh.

"What do you think it means to be pure, Grace?" he asked.

"I . . . I don't know. That I make no mistakes, that everyone loves me, that I can have tea and cookies with Mother Teresa?"

He smiled kindly. "Grace, being pure of soul doesn't mean any of those things. Purity and goodness aren't about being flawless or beloved; they're about acting in the name of virtue even if it isn't easy or popular. Sometimes, that even means looking like the bad guy or putting yourself in harm's way." God removed his hand but kept his eye contact.

"Part of your inherent call to action—your desire to fight for others and fight against the wicked—means you are willing to tell the difference between an innocent person and one that doesn't deserve your kindness. Ultimately, Grace, you are mature enough to realize that situations and human beings need to be looked at with understanding on an individual, case-by-case basis. That's a very rare combination of traits in a person, and that's what makes your soul so pure. You don't hold any finite, self-righteous, preconceived notions about anyone or anything. You're a perpetual blank slate in terms of fixed judgment, and that makes you think clearer, feel deeper, and treat everyone and everything fairly. Your Ninety-Eight status just means you have the ability to do this more than anyone who has ever been."

The first double doors I'd come through reappeared.

"Time to go," God said kindly. He walked with me to the doors. I kept up with him, but my mind was in a daze—processing so much revelation and gratitude and wonder in a matter of steps. Was it really time to say goodbye?

"Quick bonus question?" I asked, halting abruptly.

He nodded.

"If I have more things to ask you in the future, will I get to talk to you again or was this a one-time thing?"

"Grace, all people can talk to me at any time. Just because I don't send a direct response doesn't mean I'm not listening. Most answers can be sought and found on your own, but if I ever don't think you can answer a question for yourself, or if you need a little help, I'll send you a message. One way or another."

He pushed open one of the doors for me, revealing the gallery of humankind. I started to step through, then glanced back at God quickly. "*Bonus* bonus question?"

My host raised an eyebrow. "*Yes* . . ."

I pointed behind him. "Can I take a turkey leg for the road?"

He smirked. In a flash, a hot drumstick wrapped in a napkin materialized in my hand. I raised it slightly like I was toasting him.

"Thanks," I said, stepping out of God's office. "It was nice meeting you."

"It was nice meeting you too, Grace," he responded. "Tell your mother I say hi. And tell her congratulations."

I looked at him curiously. "Congratulations on what?"

Now he looked at me curiously. "You don't know yet? Perhaps she is waiting to tell you in person. I won't ruin the surprise." He winked at me again, closed the door, and the entrance to his office disappeared.

I thanked the receptionist and made my way back out onto the balcony. I wondered what had happened to my mom that earned her a congratulations from God. We'd talked via Soul Pulse a couple times this week, but with tonight being the prom we'd skipped our normal Saturday meet-up. Perhaps God was right and she was waiting to tell me this mysterious news in person.

Wings.

My lustrous feathers returned. I prepared to take off, but as I stood on top of the world I paused, taking in the serenity. I leaned against the railing and unwrapped my succulent turkey leg.

The only thing better than a view from the top was eating a snack at the top.

35

UPGRADE

"There's my favorite earthquake disaster buddy."

I turned my head and saw Leo approaching from behind me. I'd arrived early for training and had decided to sit out on the balcony of the GA department, dangling my feet over the thousand-foot drop—wings sprouted but resting in a relaxed position. I liked perching in precarious places knowing that it'd be okay even I fell—that I could take it, and take care of myself.

"Sorry I didn't answer your calls last night and could only text a vague 'I'm okay and Naomi is okay' response," Leo said, joining me at the balcony. "I had a busy night ensuring she was all right, and then debriefing Ana."

"It's fine," I said. "I went through the same thing with Akari and didn't get home until nearly dawn. We can go into a detailed recap with the whole team during training. Monkonjae is going to flip."

"And be jealous," Leo said, pointing at my wings. "We all heard the news about those beauties this morning."

My brow raised. "From who?"

"Celestial TV stations get updates about major angel news, like GA achievements. Your wings were highlights on today's segment of *Heaven't You Heard?*"

I huffed with amusement this time, not exasperation. "Of course they were. That would explain the dozen new messages I've received today from the show's producers. You know, I've gotten daily calls with requests for an interview since I arrived in the afterlife, but I always delete them."

"People want to tell your story and help you shine. That's not a bad thing. Maybe someday you should call them back."

I looked out at the sunny day making the city glisten a little extra. I nodded, thinking aloud. "Maybe I'm finally ready to. Dance like everybody's watching, right?"

Leo smirked. "Yeah. Sure." He hopped onto the balcony railing, sitting with his back to the sky and facing me.

"Leo, be careful," I warned.

"Relax. What could happen?"

"You could fall and become an angelic pancake."

"Oh, posh." He waved his hand haughtily. "That's ridiculous. My balance is legendary. I'm not going to—*whoa!*"

My friend fell backward. I leapt off the railing to the balcony floor, turned, and was about to dive after him, when all of a sudden he rose to eye level. He was grinning. Because he had wings too.

"You earned your wings!" I exclaimed.

He nodded. "It happened last night. I wanted to surprise you. I was super confused about the specifics of why they showed up, but God called me into her office to explain."

I raised an eyebrow. "Your God was a woman. What did she look like?"

"Like a blonde Emily Blunt."

I smiled. "This is why we are friends."

Leo flapped and alighted onto the balcony beside me. He stowed his wings and I did too.

"So what was the verdict?" I asked. "If your purpose is helping others live life to the fullest, what lesson led to you becoming fully realized?"

"It was a lesson that finally calmed my greatest insecurity. I told you I've always felt kind of undeserving of my full-time Heaven afterlife because my illness limited me from doing any really cool, important, impressive things that you'd think a person would need to accomplish to earn a place here. I questioned how I could be worthy, as a person and as a Guardian Angel. But through my own challenges and choices, I've now accepted the truth of the matter. God summed it up pretty perfectly."

His face was a study in pure peace. "Life isn't something you're born with, it's something you make happen."

I beamed at him. "I love that journey for you. And I love that in general. It's a shame it takes death to make most people realize it."

Leo shrugged. "It's never too late to embrace the concept and self-actualize, regardless of what phase of reality you're in."

Suddenly his serene expression jolted with enthusiasm. "Oh! Changing the subject, I seriously wanted to prank you with the balcony drop, but now with that done I need your honest opinion." His Soul Pulse flashed and a pair of thick-framed glasses, kind of old-man style, appeared on his face. "Am I pulling these off? Do they say more nerd, Clark Kent, or old guy from *Up*?"

"Uh . . . all three I guess," I replied, taken off guard.

"Excellent," he said. "That's what I was hoping for."

He pushed the connecting part of the frame up on the bridge of his nose and my jaw dropped. His nervous tick. I finally put it together. "Leo, *did you have glasses on Earth?*"

He nodded. "Heaven fixed my eyesight, like it fixes all health problems, so I didn't need them anymore. I was kind of embarrassed to admit that I missed them, and have been going without, but I figure if I'm some epically enlightened Guardian Angel, why freak out over some dumb little insecurity. This is me. I like me. I'm owning it."

I smiled. "This is also why we're friends."

Leo patted me on the shoulder. "Come on, *bubbeleh*." He offered me his arm and I linked mine through. "Let's go fly circles around the training center and do our mentors proud."

"As long we're making ourselves proud I'm having a good day."

We headed inside together. As we strode across the bustling department, my friend turned to me. "Team dinner tonight? Since we earned our wings, I say Monkonjae's buying."

"Leo, everything is free in Heaven. You only pay with compliments."

He tilted his head side to side. "Well, maybe he can carry our backpacks or something."

My grin turned subtler and more mysterious. "Actually, instead of a team dinner, I was going to invite you all to another event I have planned . . ."

"HA!" I laughed to myself, gazing around at the scene. I couldn't believe that I was doing this. It was so mad it was hilarious.

What happened to me?

In a privately rented celestial movie theater I had assembled my entire blood-related family in Heaven, my GA classmates and mentors, and various other afterlife friends I'd made like Ellis, Pearlie, Gentry, and Sheera—the owner of my favorite cake shop.

"Nugget!" My Nana Robin rushed over and gave me a huge side hug. She held a large stick of chicken satay in her other hand. "I am so excited about this screening. Your Grandpa Jim and I have never seen you dance before. We didn't even know you danced. Very sweet and thoughtful of you to host a viewing party of your recent recital. And my compliments to the exceptionally well-curated snack table." She pointed with her satay at the corner where Leo and Ana were helping themselves to sushi and guacamole simultaneously.

At that moment my mother wandered up the aisle carrying a small plate of charcuterie. She paused when she noticed Nana Robin, but as we'd already seen her, she continued over to us.

"Darla."

"Mother."

The women stared at each other. Then my mom gulped and summoned her strength.

"So . . ." She cleared her throat. "Grace and I have been getting together on Saturdays to reconnect. It's something new and I'm quite enjoying it." My mom rapped a finger against her plate anxiously. "Would *you* like to have tea next weekend? With me. Maybe Sunday morning. We could . . . try to catch up?"

Nana Robin's eyes were wide and blinking like someone who'd just lost a staring match with the sun. "Darla, *I would love that.*"

"Robin!" Grandpa Jim waved to us from across the theater. "We didn't see the tostadas! Come quick! Bring your purse."

Nana Robin patted my head and ventured to squeeze my mother's wrist. My mother gulped again but didn't withdraw, and exchanged the smallest, moderately forced smile with her.

"We'll pick a time later, okay?" Nana Robin said. "Come find me after the show?"

My mother nodded. "Will do."

When Nana Robin was out of earshot, I turned to my mother. "Is it weird for a child to say 'I'm proud of you' to a parent?"

"Hush, Grace. Don't be silly. I am simply following your astute advice. That may blow up in all our faces, but we shall cross that bridge if it happens."

"That's the spirit." I reached over and took a slice of salami from my mother's plate.

"Dear, use a napkin!" my mother said, aghast, reaching for her purse.

I chewed and swallowed the salami. "Too late."

She shook her head. "Given that it is a big night for you, I'm going to let that pass. I am terribly proud of you, Grace. And very impressed. You used to be hesitant of letting even one person see you dance. Now you've invited everyone you know. What changed?"

I shrugged. "I did." Then I put my hand through my mom's arm and hung on kind of like a koala. "Now if it's okay, I'd like to change the subject. I hear you have some news that's worthy of congratulations."

My mother's face warmed with joy. "I do. I wanted to tell you in person because you have everything to do with it."

I tilted my head. "How so?"

"Grace, afterlife timeshares can be reassessed if anything about a person's soul and situation alters." She put the charcuterie plate on a table then motioned for me to sit with her in the theater seats. Once we sat, she brushed a wrinkle out of her skirt and straightened, angling to face me.

"Dear, do you know why people get stuck in Hell?"

"For . . . doing bad things?"

"For hurting people," she responded. "The more people you

hurt and the worse you hurt them, the more time sentenced to Hell and the worse the torture. Although timeshares can be reevaluated based on good behavior and positive contribution to the afterlife, it is very rare that people with Hell on their dockets escape that because *they* are not the ones responsible for imprisoning themselves there. Bad deeds send you to Hell; *the people you hurt* keep you there. And so long as those hurt people—whether in life or afterlife—still feel the pain inflicted upon them by the sinner, that condemned person will remain in Hell to be tortured as punishment."

My mother sighed. "I am not perfect. I have made mistakes. I can be controlling and critical. I've belittled inferiors at work. I've cut off people in traffic. And, truth be told, I once cheated on a high school history exam. However, these small bad things are not enough to make me deserving of Hell. What earned me my spot there . . ." Her eyes fell to the floor a moment. "Is how I treated *you*."

She looked up at me. "In my quest to protect you from becoming my mother and protect myself from watching my daughter live a life full of bad decisions and worse consequences, I tortured you in my own way. It was unintentional, and I only had good objectives, but it's the truth. Our relationship caused you immense pain and, based on how far you've come now, I would say stifled your growth as well."

My mother shook her head dejectedly. "As you recall, months ago I cruelly asserted that the good inside you that allowed you to become an angel was because of my influence. But what *you* said a few weeks ago when we reconnected was correct. You are here because of you. More accurately, you are here *in spite of me*. And I was meant to be served a slice of Hell once a week every week for eternity because you still carried that torch of pain I gave you, even in the afterlife. I probably even made it worse for a while. But now that has changed."

She reached out and squeezed my hand. "Against all odds, you extended an understanding to me that I never gave you. You were strong enough to put love and acceptance before resentment and bad blood. And as a result, you forgave me. You no longer carry the pain I inflicted upon you. And you don't feel anger or bitterness toward me anymore—do you?"

I paused and reflected on the weighty question. After doing an emotional systems check, I shook my head. "No. No, I don't."

"That's what my caseworker told me," my mother said. "And because hurting you was the factor that tipped my soul's scale and made me worthy of Hell, now that the hurt is gone, there is no longer a reason for me to be there."

I blinked and stared at her. "You mean . . ."

"We create our own Hell, Grace. The pain we cause others ensures it. And only the true forgiveness of others—the letting go of that pain—can set us free. You've done that for me. You—my wonderful, audacious, kindhearted daughter—have set me free." She smiled and touched my cheek. "Since you've let your pain go, Hell is letting me go. It has been removed from my timeshare completely and I will only be spending time in Middleground and Heaven from now on."

"Mom! That's fantastic!" I lunged over and gave her a huge hug. She leaned into the embrace and patted my hair. When she pulled away, she held my shoulders at arm's length and stared at me thoughtfully.

"You okay?" I asked.

"I just can't believe I was too foolish to see it before," my mother marveled.

"What?"

"When you open your heart and make people feel safe enough to open theirs, any place can feel like Heaven."

Onscreen, the curtains to the stage where my dance group performed closed with flourish. As the filmed audience began to clap, so did my own in real time. Our theater lights came on and I reveled in the rush of hugs and congratulations and bouquets of flowers that my Heaven family had brought me.

When the crowds dissipated, I spotted Akari chatting with Pearlie and Gentry. Seeing I was free, she strode over and gave me a hug too.

"Well done," she said affectionately. "Between completing Henry's first Plot Points, earning your wings, and facing your personal fears, I honestly couldn't be more proud of you."

"Thanks." I raised a brow at her. "Is this where you say I have graduated angel training with flying colors and you have nothing left to teach me?"

"Oh no. I still have a million things to teach you."

"Of course."

We exchanged a smirk.

"Speaking of graduation," Akari continued. "Since your high school graduation is this week, I thought I'd cancel training for a spell and give you a touch of much needed summer vacation. We can start fresh in a few weeks."

"I like the sound of that," I said. "I could use a break—maybe hit the pool or the spa. Can angels get tan?"

"Always with the questions," Akari mused.

"It's grown on you," I replied sassily. I released a cleansing exhale. "In all seriousness, I'm excited about what comes next. As an added bonus, with Earth school out, it'll be harder for Solange to spend time around Henry."

"And as a *bonus* bonus, you won't have to deal with her for a little while at all. As you noticed when she turned to smoke in the hotel, demons are affected differently by death in their human forms. Whereas we can return instantly after passing through the Soul Sewer, they need the full week to reform in Hell, which means she'll miss your graduation."

"I remember. Such a shame—I was so looking forward to writing 'You Suck' in her yearbook." I sarcastically pouted.

"Congrats again, Grace," Gentry said suddenly, claiming my attention as he and Pearlie joined us. "You sure can twirl like a champ." He turned to Akari. "You ready?"

I looked to my mentor. "You have plans?"

She nodded and we began to walk toward the theater lobby. "I may still have a lot left to teach, but you've taught me some things too, Grace. And helped me realize others."

We made it to the sidewalk outside. I smirk-shrugged. "I'm glad I could—"

Suddenly that glowing ethereal hiccup passed through our plane of existence, rippling through The First City and inspiring my heart with a sense of wonder and warmth that I still didn't understand.

"Okay," I said firmly, pivoting to the trio. "Can someone *please* tell me what that is?"

Pearlie stared at me. "You don't know?"

"I forgot to ask."

Akari gave me a look. "*You* forgot to ask?"

I huffed. "I've had a lot going on. Now please, someone spill the tea."

"It's what happens when Earth's well of pure joy fills to the top," Pearlie explained.

"Pardon?

"Grace," Akari said kindly. "Surely you've had times in life when—even for just a moment—you are so happy and fulfilled that it feels like your heart is glowing. The light you just saw is a reflection of that. It's called the Heart Light. Every time someone on Earth experiences a moment of *pure* joy or love—marrying a soulmate, getting a dream job, having a child, and so on—that is like a drop in the universe's bucket of warm fuzzies. And when that bucket reaches its capacity every ten thousand drops, it overflows and its contents flood through here for all of us to appreciate in the form of *that light*."

Akari released a contented sigh and crossed her arms. "Given the good you've created for others and yourself recently, I would reckon this latest flood is in part contributed to you."

I gazed at the city beside me. The Heart Light occurred fairly frequently. Grasping that made me smile. Akari was right, wasn't she? People on Earth gave evil too much credit. There was so much good in the world, so much wonder all around us. Sometimes all you had to do was look. And if you wanted, you could create some yourself too.

A backtrack thought occurred to me then, and I glanced at Akari with a new question. "Did you just say there are soul-mates?"

"Good night, Grace," Akari said, patting me on the shoulder.

"We'll explore that topic another day." My mentor and I exchanged a smile. Then she glowed.

As Akari was the only one of her friends with inherent wings, she held Pearlie and Gentry by the hand to support their flight. They took off together and I waved to them as they soared into the sky.

When I turned my gaze back to ground level, I spotted Monkonjae talking with Deckland on the curb. They exchanged one of those high-five bro hugs before Deckland's wings formed and he flew off too.

Monkonjae stood there a moment, staring out at the city fading into twilight. The skies were blushing, like I probably did every time I looked at him for too long.

My heart sped faster. I clenched my fists.

No more running and hiding, right?

I stomped over to Monkonjae and tapped him on the broad shoulder. He turned around and smiled. "Hey, Grace. Congrats again. That was very cool of you to share such a personal Earth experience with us. The recital was great."

"Do you want to go out with me?"

He blinked twice. "You mean for a team dinner?"

"No, I mean like a date. Dinner can be involved. Food actually should definitely be involved. But I'm talking about you plus me on a romantic rendezvous. Thoughts?"

Monkonjae's mouth hung agape. "I . . ."

"Look," I said. "I think you are kind, polite, brave, and crazy handsome. And me, well," I waved at my general person, "I'm clearly the total package. I say we give this a shot. I've seen enough movies and TV shows to know that the drama of will they, won't they only delays the inevitable. You and me—that could be inevitable."

I took a breath. That was a lot of babbling and embarrassing honesty, but this time I was not apologizing for it. I stood by those words and I stood by me—the awkward, the blunt, the quirky, and all.

Finally Monkonjae laughed. Not exactly the reaction I was hoping for, but his words a second later made up for it. "Grace

Cariño Reyes Cardiff, I would be absolutely honored to take you on a proper date."

I beamed from ear to ear and my whole body warmed up like a teakettle. I swatted him on the arm. "If I may offer some advice, the next time a girl asks you out, *don't laugh*. Especially if you're into it."

"Sorry." He smiled. "It was just unexpectedly aggressive in the best possible way."

"Well, that's me now." I crossed my arms proudly. "Unexpectedly aggressive in the best possible way."

He shrugged with a grin. "I'm into it."

"Good," I said. "Because so am I."

36

MY NEW ROOMMATE

"Mr. Corrin?" I knocked on my teacher's open door. While I wore a royal blue cap and gown and multiple golden cords around my neck, my tall teacher had on a black robe and matching floppy laureate hat.

He turned from his desk where he'd been rummaging. "Miss Cabrera, I see you are being honored as one of the top students in your class." He gestured at the cords. "Congratulations. One cord per honors class means you had a full load this year and exceeded all expectations."

I smirked and entered the physics classroom. "In more ways than one." I strode over to his desk and held out a folded piece of paper with a bow on it.

"What's this?" he asked.

"The answer. Well, my answer. To the Spider-Man physics riddle you posed all those months ago. No one could figure it out at the time, and I didn't like that. Despite the odds, I knew the hero could succeed and I wanted to prove that. I never gave up on the puzzle and after a lot of work, finally solved it. Every problem has a solution, right?"

Mr. Corrin grinned. He took the paper from me and read its contents. One brow rose up. Then he looked at me. "Creative and surprising."

I shrugged. "The best solutions are."

He alluded to the paper. "Can I keep this? You're the first student to stick with this challenge until you worked your way through?"

"Of course. Here's also a little graduation gift for being my favorite teacher," I said, offering him a gift card. "I don't get it, but Henry and Razel say everyone else likes boba. Anyway, thank you. You made this semester really interesting."

"Glad to hear it. I hope you learned a lot."

"Oh, believe me, I did."

With final waves and well wishes, I departed the classroom and made my way across campus, passing plenty of my fellow graduates, their families, and teachers. They all had some hustle in their step. The seniors and I would have to line up in the halls for commencement soon.

I caught up with my friends by our old history classroom, surrounded by a sea of our chatting classmates. They all sported the same cap and gown I did, but Justin was on crutches.

"You sure you're going to be okay climbing the stage steps like that?" I asked Justin as I approached.

He huffed in amusement. "Please. This is hardly the first bone I've broken. I'm the youngest of five brothers."

"I still can't believe this happened," Razel said, fingers to her temple. "First Henry breaks a toe trying to get his license and now you break your foot at our prom. And right before summer break too. Our group must be cursed by an evil podiatrist."

"Raz, I know it's in your nature, but stop being so dramatic," Justin said. "I feel like frickin' Dwayne Johnson, surviving a crazy earthquake disaster and rising from the ashes like a phoenix."

"Now who's being dramatic?" Razel rolled her eyes.

"*Anyway,*" Justin continued. "It's not ideal, but I'll be healed up before baseball training starts in August. In the meantime, I can get pretty girls to sign my cast. Girls love to take care of injured guys. It's called the Florence Nightingale Effect. Look it up."

Henry laughed and patted Justin on the back.

After prom, I'd told Henry what I could about what had happened. He was shook at first, but true to form, he soon digested, accepted, and leaned into the craziness without much fuss.

Thank God I got such an easy-going, fantasy-loving kid as my assignment.

I still hadn't revealed my wings yet; I was waiting for the right time. And obviously I couldn't say anything about Solange. The official story Hell had sent up the pipeline to our school was that she had a sick relative in France and her family had flown home immediately. Everyone here bought it, and I was enjoying a week of peace.

"Okay, kids!" Mr. Corrin beckoned through a megaphone at the hallway of seniors. He was one of the faculty members presenting diplomas. "I want to see two single file lines in alphabetical order. Keep them straight! Keep them tight!"

Our senior class did as instructed, and graduation proceeded. I got a little misty-eyed during the speeches. They were nice, but I was moved by the simple fact that I was here. Even though I'd died, I'd still gotten the opportunity to live so much life. It was a miracle, a blessing, and a triumph. I wished Gaby and my father knew that I was okay. I guess they would just have to have faith. That's what we all needed to have in the face of pain or loss or struggle . . . faith that things would be okay.

At the end of the ceremony, we all threw our caps into the air in celebration. I imagined the Heart Light glowing in Heaven as Earth's well of pure joy overflowed with the pride, happiness, and hope for the future that beamed from this campus. Hundreds of souls who all had potential.

For the next hour, kids milled around with their families, took pictures, shook hands, and generally celebrated. When I told my friends earlier in the week that my guardian couldn't make it to graduation, Henry and his family had invited me to join them for dinner after the ceremony. At a quarter to six, I'd finished changing and returned my cap and gown. The campus was mostly abandoned by then, and I strode across the deserted halls hearing the clicks of my short heels echoing around me.

I spotted Henry by his locker, straightening his tie.

"Hey," I said.

He turned and closed his locker for the final time. "Hey yourself," he replied. He looked at my fluffy lace dress. "I know you're a fan of jeans and tees, but after seeing you at prom and today, I have to say, fancy looks good on you."

I smirk-shrugged. "Well, good *is* my business."

"You should put that on a bumper sticker for your ridiculous car."

We stood in contented silence.

"I guess you and I are moving on to a new phase in our journey together," Henry said with a wistful smile. "I know I'll probably almost die a bunch more times, but is it weird to say I'm looking forward to it?"

"No. But then, I'm only here for the company." I gestured at him. Then my lips curved into a more mischievous smile. "And the food. When we move to San Diego, we're going to need to go by that lobster roll place at least once a week."

"I love it and I am in."

"I have something else you'll love. A surprise . . ." I checked to make sure the coast was clear then took several strides back and summoned my halo.

"Did you ever hear that saying about what happens when a bell rings?" I snatched the halo from my head and with a controlled flick, so it would only smack not destroy, flung it at the nearest school bell built into the wall. The halo bopped the bell, causing it to sound off briefly. When it did, I caught my halo then produced my outstanding feathers.

Henry's face exploded with excitement. "You earned your wings!"

I nodded. Then I checked my watch. "We have about ten minutes before we said we'd meet your family in the parking lot. How about that victory lap?"

He nodded and came toward me in a daze like a kid who'd just been offered the keys to a candy store. I took his hand in mine, my glow spread over him, and I smiled.

"Hang on."

I looked toward the sky and together, we took off.

"Thank you again for being with us, Ninety-Eight," the famous host of *Heaven't You Heard?* said to me as the show came to a close.

For once, I didn't flinch at the nickname. "You're very

welcome, Mr. Cronkite. It was a pleasure to share my story. I'm sorry it took me so long to get here."

I meant that in all senses. It took me some time to realize, but I'd let fear of vulnerability and embarrassment make me a creature of the shadows. And that was just not me. I was a being of light. Halo or no halo. I wanted to run and bask in all the opportunities that were out there without fear of letting people— *all people*—see me.

Going forward, I would never again allow myself to shy away from things I loved like dance, possibilities with promise like budding relationships, and chances to have new experiences like being on this silly show.

Life was for living. Existence was for relishing. And souls were meant to shine.

Put that on a throw pillow.

"Grace Cariño Reyes Cardiff, everyone—98% pure Guardian Angel, scholar student, and cake connoisseur. And that's the way it is."

The cameras stopped rolling and I shook some hands before departing the studio. It would've been much faster to teleport home but flying just felt *so amazing*. Everything felt amazing right now actually. Becoming fully realized. The dance recital viewing party last weekend. Our lovely graduation yesterday. Summer vacation sparkling ahead.

I alighted on my lawn and entered my cottage with a smile on my face.

"Grace?"

My smile fell to the floor at the sound of that familiar voice as I was closing the door.

"Oliver!"

My heart pounded in surprise. I must've blinked at least ten times in two seconds as I tried to adjust to the very possibility that I could be seeing him in my house.

"What did . . . How did . . ." I took a breath. "Why are you here?"

"I'm on the run."

"I'm sorry, what?"

"As long as demons aren't around, God can see pretty much everything that happens on Earth with his Guardian Angels. Our superior in Hell doesn't have that kind of access, so when I went to help you at the hotel, I thought I could get away with it. All that will go out the window when Solange finishes reforming tomorrow. The second she's back to her demon self, she'll rat me out and I am worse than dead. I had to get out of Hell while I had the chance."

"But won't they know where you—" Oliver's wrist was bare. "Where is your Soul Pulse?"

"I cut it off. Like I did that day in Heaven when we went searching for my mom."

"How the heck did you do that?"

He grimaced. Then he reached into the pocket of his leather jacket and pulled out a sharp piece of metal like a small knife without the hilt. "It's Divine Iron," he said. "Without going into details . . . I found it. And it's capable of slicing off Soul Pulses. All I had to do was cut mine off for the field trip and then put it on again. The band automatically fused back together, so no one ever suspected."

My mouth stayed wide open as I tried to process everything he was saying. I think my brain had a short circuit.

"Okay, that's one part of the puzzle," I finally said. I felt hot. Was I sweating? "But to get to Heaven, you need the Hellevator. And to work the Hellevator, you need—"

"I'm sorry," he said remorsefully. "Remember when we were in Hell and you thought something sharp cut you? I took a sample of your blood with this Divine Iron blade. I used my miraging powers so you wouldn't see it, the cut, or any residue drops of blood. I needed the sample to work the Hellevator in case I ever wanted to try breaking into Heaven to see my mom again."

"You what?!"

"I'm sorry, I'm sorry!" he said, eyes full of fear. "I didn't know you were going to help me with my mom at the time."

"So that makes it okay?" I was filled with fury and dismay, but still mainly shock. I paced the living room, holding my head in

my hands. Droopy looked up curiously from his basket. He was the worst guard dog ever; a demon had literally come into my home and the lazy creature hadn't let it disturb his nap.

"Grace . . ." Oliver tried, coming closer to me. "I can't go back. They'll destroy me for helping you. They could find me on Earth, but they won't be able to find me here. *Please*."

I turned and saw the desperation in his eyes. Droopy tromped over and sat between us. I sighed. "What exactly do you expect from me, Oliver?"

He grimaced and shrugged awkwardly. "I was hoping I could stay here? With you."

Droopy glanced at me, then at Oliver, then he tilted his head up.

"*AAWWWHOO!*"